PEYTON PLACE
and
RETURN TO
PEYTON PLACE

PEYTON PLACE

and

RETURN TO PEYTON PLACE

Grace Metalious

GRAMERCY BOOKS

NEW YORK

This 1999 edition is published by Gramercy Books™, an imprint of Random House
Value Publishing, Inc., 201 East 50th Street, New York, NY 10022, by arrangement with
the heirs of Grace Metalious.

Gramercy Books™ and design are trademarks of Random House Value Publishing, Inc.

Printed in the United States of America

Random House
New York • Toronto • London • Sydney • Auckland
http://www.randomhouse.com/

Library of Congress Cataloging–in–Publication Data

Metalious, Grace.
  [Peyton Place]
  Peyton Place ; & Return to Peyton Place / Grace Metalious
    p.   cm.
  ISBN 0-517-20477-0
  1. City and town life—United States–Fiction. I. Metalious,
Grace. Return to Peyton Place.   II. Title. III. Title: Peyton
Place ; & Return to Peyton Place.   IV. Title: Peyton Place ; and,
Return to Peyton Place.   V. Title: Return to Peyton Place.
PS3525.E77P4   1999b
813'.54—dc21

                                                      99-20443
                                                      CIP

8 7 6 5 4 3 2 1

CONTENTS

PEYTON PLACE

TO GEORGE—
    For All The Reasons he knows so well.

BOOK ONE

◆ I ◆

Indian summer is like a woman. Ripe, hotly passionate, but fickle, she comes and goes as she pleases so that one is never sure whether she will come at all, nor for how long she will stay. In northern New England, Indian summer puts up a scarlet-tipped hand to hold winter back for a little while. She brings with her the time of the last warm spell, an unchartered season which lives until Winter moves in with its backbone of ice and accoutrements of leafless trees and hard frozen ground. Those grown old, who have had the youth bled from them by the jagged edged winds of winter, know sorrowfully that Indian summer is a sham to be met with hard-eyed cynicism. But the young wait anxiously, scanning the chill autumn skies for a sign of her coming. And sometimes the old, against all the warnings of better judgment, wait with the young and hopeful, their tired, winter eyes turned heavenward to seek the first traces of a false softening.

One year, early in October, Indian summer came to a town called Peyton Place. Like a laughing, lovely woman Indian summer came and spread herself over the countryside and made everything hurtfully beautiful to the eye.

The sky was low, of a solidly unbroken blue. The maples and oaks and ashes, all dark red and brown and yellow, preened themselves in the unseasonably hot light, under the Indian summer sun. The conifers stood like disapproving old men on all the hills around Peyton Place and gave off a greenish yellow light. On the roads and sidewalks of the town there were fallen leaves which made such a gay crackling when stepped upon and sent up such a sweet scent when crushed that it was only the very old who walked over them and thought of death and decay.

The town lay still in the Indian summer sun. On Elm Street, the main thoroughfare, nothing moved. The shopkeepers, who had rolled protective canvas awnings down over their front windows, took the lack of trade philosophically and retired to the back rooms

1

of their stores where they alternately dozed, glanced at the *Peyton Place Times* and listened to the broadcast of a baseball game.

To the east on Elm Street, beyond the six blocks occupied by the business section of the town, rose the steeple of the Congregational church. The pointed structure pierced through the leaves of the surrounding trees and shone, dazzlingly white, against the blue sky. At the opposite end of the business district stood another steepled structure. This was St. Joseph's Catholic Church, and its spire far outshone that of the Congregationalists, for it was topped with a cross of gold.

Seth Buswell, the owner and editor of the *Peyton Place Times*, had once written, rather poetically, that the two churches bracketed and held the town like a pair of gigantic book ends, an observation which had set off a series of minor explosions in Peyton Place. There were few Catholics in town who cared to be associated in any partnership with the Protestants, while the Congregationalists had as little desire to be paired off with the Papists. If imaginary book ends were to exist in Peyton Place they would both have to be of the same religious denomination.

Seth had laughed at the arguments heard all over town that week, and in his next edition he reclassified the two churches as tall, protective mountains guarding the peaceful business valley. Both Catholics and Protestants scanned this second article carefully for a trace of sarcasm or facetiousness, but in the end everyone had taken the story at its face value and Seth laughed harder than before.

Dr. Matthew Swain, Seth's best friend and oldest crony, grunted, "Mountains, eh? More like a pair of goddamned volcanoes."

"Both of 'em breathin' brimstone and fire," Seth added, still laughing as he poured two more drinks.

But the doctor would not laugh with his friend. There were three things which he hated in this world, he said often and angrily: death, venereal disease and organized religion.

"In that order," the doctor always amended. "And the story, clean or otherwise, that can make me laugh at one of these has never been thought up."

But on this hot October afternoon Seth was not thinking of opposing religious factions or, for that matter, of anything in particular. He sat at his desk behind the plate glass window of his street floor office, sipping at a cold drink and listened desultorily to the baseball game.

In front of the courthouse, a large white stone building with a

2

verdigris-colored dome, a few old men lounged on the wooden benches which seem to be part of every municipal building in America's small towns. The men leaned back against the warm sides of the courthouse, their tired eyes shaded by battered felt hats, and let the Indian summer sun warm their cold, old bones. They were as still as the trees for which the main street had been named.

Under the elms the black tarred sidewalks, ruffled in many places by the pushing roots of the giant trees, were empty. The chime clock set into the red brick front of the Citizens' National Bank, across the street from the courthouse, struck once. It was two-thirty on a Friday afternoon.

◆ 2 ◆

Maple Street, which bisected Elm at a point halfway through the business section, was a wide, tree-shaded avenue which ran north and south from one end of town to the other. At the extreme southern end of the street, where the paving ended and gave way to an empty field, stood the Peyton Place schools. It was toward these buildings that Kenny Stearns, the town handyman, walked. The men in front of the courthouse opened drowsy eyes to watch him.

"There goes Kenny Stearns," said one man unnecessarily, for everyone had seen—and knew—Kenny.

"Sober as a judge, right now."

"That won't last long."

The men laughed.

"Good at his work though, Kenny is," said one old man named Clayton Frazier, who made a point of disagreeing with everybody, no matter what the issue.

"When he ain't too drunk to work."

"Never knew Kenny to lose a day's work on account of liquor," said Clayton Frazier. "Ain't nobody in Peyton Place can make things grow like Kenny. He's got one of them whatcha call green thumbs."

One man snickered. "Too bad Kenny don't have the same good luck with his wife as he has with plants. Mebbe Kenny'd be better off with a green pecker."

3

This observation was acknowledged with appreciative smiles and chuckles.

"Ginny Stearns is a tramp and a trollop," said Clayton Frazier, unsmilingly. "There ain't much a feller can do when he's married to a born whore."

"'Cept drink," said the man who had first spoken.

The subject of Kenny Stearns seemed to be exhausted, and for a moment no one spoke.

"Hotter'n July today," said one old man. "Damned if my back ain't itchin' with sweat."

"'Twon't last," said Clayton Frazier, tipping his hat back to look up at the sky. "I've seen it turn off cold and start in snowin' less than twelve hours after the sun had gone down on a day just like this one. This won't last."

"Ain't healthy either. A day like this is enough to make a man start thinkin' about summer underwear again."

"Healthy or not, you'd hear no complaints from me if the weather stayed just like this clear 'til next June."

"'Twon't last," said Clayton Frazier, and for once his words did not provoke a discussion.

"No," the men agreed. "'Twon't last."

They watched Kenny Stearns turn into Maple Street and walk out of sight.

The Peyton Place schools faced each other from opposite sides of the street. The grade school was a large wooden building, old, ugly and dangerous, but the high school was the pride of the town. It was made of brick, with windows so large that each one made up almost an entire wall, and it had a clinical, no-nonsense air of efficiency that gave it the look more of a small, well-run hospital than that of a school. The elementary school was Victorian architecture at its worst, made even more hideous by the iron fire escapes which zigzagged down both sides of the building, and by the pointed, open belfry which topped the structure. The grade school bell was rung by means of a thick, yellow rope which led down from the belfry and was threaded through the ceiling and floor of the building's second story. The rope came to an end and hung, a constant temptation to small hands, in the corner of the first floor hall. The school bell was Kenny Stearns' secret love. He kept it polished so that it gleamed like antique pewter in the October sun. As he approached the school buildings now, Kenny looked up at the belfry and nodded in satisfaction.

4

"The bells of heaven ain't got tongues no sweeter than yours," he said aloud.

Kenny often spoke aloud to his bell. He also talked to the school buildings and to the various plants and lawns in town for which he cared.

From the windows of both schools, open now to the warm afternoon, there came a soft murmuring and the smell of pencil shavings.

"Hadn't oughta keep school on a day like this," said Kenny. He stood by the low hedge which separated the grade school from the first house on Maple Street. A warm, green smell, composed of the grass and hedges which he had cut that morning rose around him.

"This ain't no kind of a day for schoolin'," said Kenny and shrugged impatiently, not at his inarticulateness but in puzzlement at a rare emotion in himself.

He wanted to throw himself face down on the ground and press his face and body against something green.

"*That's* the kind of day it is," he told the quiet buildings truculently. "No kind of a day for schoolin'."

He noticed that a small twig in the hedge had raised itself, growing above the others and marring the evenness of the uniformly flat hedge tops. He bent to snip off this precocious bit of green with his fingers, a sharp tenderness taking form within him. But suddenly a wildness came over him, and he grabbed a handful of the small, green leaves, crushing them until he felt their yielding wetness against his skin while passion tightened itself within him and his breath shook. A long time ago, before he had taught himself not to care, he had felt this same way toward his wife Ginny. There had been the same tenderness which would suddenly be overwhelmed by a longing to crush and conquer, to possess by sheer strength and force. Abruptly Kenny released the handful of broken leaves and wiped his hand against the side of his rough overall.

"Wish to Christ I had a drink," he said fervently and moved toward the double front doors of the grade school.

It was five minutes to three and time for him to take up his position by the bell rope.

"Wish to Christ I had a drink, and that's for sure," said Kenny and mounted the wooden front steps of the school.

Kenny's words, since they had been addressed to his bell and therefore uttered in loud, carrying tones, drifted easily through

5

the windows of the classroom where Miss Elsie Thornton presided over the eighth grade. Several boys laughed out loud and a few girls grinned, but this amusement was short lived. Miss Thornton was a firm believer in the theory that if a child were given the inch, he would rapidly take the proverbial mile, so, although it was Friday afternoon and she was very tired, she restored quick order to her room.

"Is there anyone here who would like to spend the thirty minutes after dismissal with me?" she asked.

The boys and girls, ranging in age from twelve to fourteen, fell silent, but as soon as the first note sounded from Kenny's bell, they began to scrape and shuffle their feet. Miss Thornton rapped sharply on her desk with a ruler.

"You will be quiet until I dismiss you," she ordered. "Now. Are your desks cleared?"

"Yes, Miss Thornton." The answer came in a discordant chorus. "You may stand."

Forty-two pairs of feet clomped into position in the aisles between the desks. Miss Thornton waited until all backs were straight, all heads turned to the front and all feet quiet.

"Dismissed," she said, and as always, as soon as that word was out of her mouth, had the ridiculous feeling that she should duck and protect her head with her arms.

Within five seconds the classroom was empty and Miss Thornton relaxed with a sigh. Kenny's bell still sang joyously and the teacher reflected with humor that Kenny always rang the three o'clock dismissal bell with a special fervor, while at eight-thirty in the morning he made the same bell toll mournfully.

If I thought it would solve anything, said Miss Thornton to herself, making a determined effort to relax the area between her shoulder blades, I, too, would wish to Christ that I had a drink.

Smiling a little, she stood and moved to one of the windows to watch the children leave the schoolyard. Outside, the crowd had begun to separate into smaller groups and pairs, and Miss Thornton noticed only one child who walked alone. This was Allison MacKenzie, who broke away from the throng as soon as she reached the pavement and hurried down Maple Street by herself.

A peculiar child, mused Miss Thornton, looking at Allison's disappearing back. One given to moods of depression which seemed particularly odd in one so young. It was odd, too, that Allison hadn't one friend in the entire school, except for Selena

6

Cross. They made a peculiar pair, those two, Selena with her dark, gypsyish beauty, her thirteen-year-old eyes as old as time, and Allison MacKenzie, still plump with residual babyhood, her eyes wide open, guileless and questioning, above that painfully sensitive mouth. Get yourself a shell, Allison, my dear, thought Miss Thornton. Find one without cracks or weaknesses so that you will be able to survive the slings and arrows of outrageous fortune. Good Lord, I *am* tired!

Rodney Harrington came barreling out of the school, not slowing his pace when he saw little Norman Page standing directly in his path.

Damned little bully, thought Miss Thornton savagely.

She despised Rodney Harrington, and it was a credit to her character and to her teaching that no one, least of all Rodney himself, suspected this fact. Rodney was an oversized fourteen-year-old with a mass of black, curly hair and a heavy-lipped mouth. Miss Thornton had heard a few of her more aware eighth grade girls refer to Rodney as "adorable," a sentiment with which she was not in accord. She would have gotten a great deal of pleasure out of giving him a sound thrashing. In Miss Thornton's vast mental file of school children, Rodney was classified as A Troublemaker.

He's too big for his age, she thought, and too sure of himself and of his father's money and position behind him. He'll get his comeuppance someday.

Miss Thornton bit the inside of her lip and spoke severely to herself. He is only a child. He may turn out all right.

But she knew Leslie Harrington, Rodney's father, and doubted her own words.

Little Norman Page was felled by the oncoming Rodney. He went flat on the ground and began to cry, remaining prone until Ted Carter came along to help him up.

Little Norman Page. Funny, thought Miss Thornton, but I've never heard an adult refer to Norman without that prefix. It has almost become part of his name.

Norman, the schoolteacher observed, seemed to be constructed entirely of angles. His cheekbones were prominent in his little face, and as he wiped at his wet eyes, his elbows stuck out in sharp, bony points.

Ted Carter was brushing at Norman's trousers. "You're O.K., Norman," his voice came through the schoolroom window. "Come on, you're O.K. Stop crying now and g'wan home. You're O.K."

7

Ted was thirteen years old, tall and broad for his age, with the stamp of adulthood already on his features. Of all the boys in Miss Thornton's eighth grade, Ted's voice was the only one which had "changed" completely so that when he spoke it was in a rich baritone that never cracked or went high unexpectedly.

"Why don't you pick on someone your own size?" Ted asked, turning toward Rodney Harrington.

"Ha, ha," said Rodney sulkily. "You, f'rinstance?"

Ted moved another step closer to Rodney. "Yeah, me," he said.

"Oh, beat it," said Rodney. "I wouldn't waste my time."

But, Miss Thornton noticed with satisfaction, it was Rodney who "beat it." He strolled cockily out of the schoolyard with an over-developed seventh grade girl named Betty Anderson at his heels.

"Why don'cha mind your own business," yelled Betty over her shoulder to Ted.

Little Norman Page snuffled. He took a clean white handkerchief from his back trouser pocket and blew his nose gently.

"Thank you, Ted," he said shyly. "Thank you very much."

"Oh, scram," said Ted Carter. "G'wan home before your old lady comes looking for you."

Norman's chin quivered anew. "Could I walk with you, Ted?" he asked. "Just until Rodney's out of sight? Please?"

"Rodney's got other things on his mind besides you right now," said Ted brutally. "He's forgotten that you're even alive."

Scooping his books up off the ground, Ted ran to catch up with Selena Cross, who was now halfway up Maple Street. He did not look around for Norman, who picked up his own books and moved slowly out of the schoolyard.

Miss Thornton felt suddenly too tired to move. She leaned her head against the window frame and stared absently at the empty yard outside. She knew the families of her school children, the kind of homes they lived in and the environments in which they were raised.

Why do I try? she wondered. What chance have any of these children to break out of the pattern in which they were born?

At times like this, when Miss Thornton was very tired, she felt that she fought a losing battle with ignorance and was overcome with a sense of futility and helplessness. What sense was there in nagging a boy into memorizing the dates of the rise and fall of the Roman Empire when the boy, grown, would milk cows for a living, as had his father and grandfather before him. What logic was there in pounding decimal fractions into the head of a

8

girl who would eventually need to count only to number the months of each pregnancy?

Years before, when Miss Thornton had been graduated from Smith College, she had decided to remain in her native New England to teach.

"You won't have much opportunity to be radical up there," the dean had told her.

Elsie Thornton had smiled. "They are my people and I understand them. I'll know what to do."

The dean had smiled, too, from her heights of superior knowledge. "When you discover how to break the bone of the shell-backed New Englander, Elsie, you will become world famous. Anyone who does something for the first time in history becomes famous."

"I've lived in New England all my life," said Elsie Thornton, "and I have never heard anyone actually say, 'What was good enough for my father is good enough for me.' That is a decadent attitude and a terrible cliché, both of which have been unfairly saddled on the New Englander."

"Good luck, Elsie," said the dean sadly.

Kenny Stearns crossed Miss Thornton's line of vision, and abruptly her chain of thought broke.

Nonsense, she told herself briskly. I have a roomful of fine, intelligent children who come from families no different from other families. I'll feel better on Monday.

She went to the closet and took out her hat which was seeing service for the seventh autumn in a row. Looking at the worn brown felt in her hand, she was reminded of Dr. Matthew Swain.

"I'd be able to tell a schoolteacher anywhere," he had told her.

"Really, Matt?" she had laughed at him. "Do we all, then, have the same look of frustration?"

"No," he had replied, "but all of you do look overworked, underpaid, poorly dressed and underfed. Why do you do it, Elsie? Why don't you go down to Boston or somewhere like that? With your intelligence and education you could get a good-paying job in business."

Miss Thornton had shrugged. "Oh, I don't know, Matt. I just love teaching, I guess."

But in her mind then, as now, was the hope which kept her at her job, just as it has kept teachers working for hundreds of years.

If I can teach something to one child, if I can awaken in only

9

one child a sense of beauty, a joy in truth, an admission of ignorance and a thirst for knowledge, then I am fulfilled.

One child, thought Miss Thornton, adjusting her old brown felt, and her mind fastened with love on Allison MacKenzie.

♦ 3 ♦

Allison MacKenzie left the schoolyard quickly, not stopping to talk with anyone. She made her way up Maple Street and walked east on Elm, avoiding the Thrifty Corner Apparel Shoppe which her mother owned and operated. Allison walked rapidly until she had left the stores and houses of Peyton Place behind her. She climbed the long, gently sloping hill behind Memorial Park and came, eventually, to a place where the paved road ended. Beyond the pavement, the land fell away in a sharp decline and was covered with rocks and bushes. The drop off was barred with a wide wooden board which rested at either end on a base resembling an outsized sawhorse. The crosspiece had red letters printed on it. ROAD'S END. These words had always satisfied something in Allison. She reflected that the board could have read, PAVEMENT ENDS or CAUTION—DROP OFF, and she was glad that someone had thought to label this place ROAD'S END.

Allison luxuriated in the fact that she had two whole days, plus what was left of this beautiful afternoon, in which to be free from the hatefulness that was school. In the time of this short vacation she would be free to walk up here to the end of the road, to be by herself and to think her own thoughts. For a little while she could find pleasure here and forget that her pleasures would be considered babyish and silly by older, more mature twelve-year-old girls.

The afternoon was beautiful with the lazy, blue beauty of Indian summer. Allison said the words "October afternoon" over and over to herself. They were like a narcotic, soothing her, filling her with peace. "October afternoon," she said, sighing, and sat down on the board that had ROAD'S END lettered on its side.

Now that she was quiet and unafraid, she could pretend that she was a child again, and not a twelve-year-old who would be enter-

10

ing high school in less than another year, and who should be interested now in clothes and boys and pale rose lipstick. The delights of childhood were all around her, and here on the hill she did not feel that she was peculiar and different from her contemporaries. But away from this place she was awkward, loveless, pitifully aware that she lacked the attraction and poise which she believed that every other girl her age possessed.

Very rarely, she felt a shred of this same secret, lonely happiness at school, when the class was reading a book or a story which pleased her. Then she would look up quickly from the printed page to find Miss Thornton looking at her, and their eyes would meet and hold and smile. She was careful not to let this happiness show, for she knew that the other girls in her class would laugh to let her know that this kind of joy was wrong, and that they would tag it with their favorite word of condemnation—babyish.

There would not be many more days of contentment for Allison, for now she was twelve and soon would have to begin spending her life with people like the girls at school. She would be surrounded by them, and have to try hard to be one of them. She was sure that they would never accept her. They would laugh at her, ridicule her, and she would find herself living in a world where she was the only odd and different member of the population.

If Allison MacKenzie had been asked to define the vague "they" to whom she referred in her mind, she would have answered, "Everybody except Miss Thornton and Selena Cross, and sometimes even Selena." For Selena was beautiful while Allison believed herself an unattractive girl, plump in the wrong places, flat in the wrong spots, too long in the legs and too round in the face. She knew that she was shy and all thumbs and had a headful of silly dreams. That was the way everybody saw her, except Miss Thornton, and that was only because Miss Thornton was so ugly and plain herself. Selena would smile and try to dismiss Allison's inadequacies with a wave of her hand. "You're O.K., kid," Selena would say, but Allison could not always believe her friend. Somewhere along the path of approaching maturity she had lost her sense of being loved and of belonging to a particular niche in the world. The measure of her misery was in the fact that she thought these things had never been hers to lose.

Allison looked across the emptiness beyond Road's End. From up here, she could see the town, spread out below her. She could see the belfry of the grade school, the church spires and the wind-

11

ing, blue road of the Connecticut River with the red brick mills, like growths, attached to one of its sides. She could see the gray stone pile of Samuel Peyton's castle, and she stared hard at the place for which the town had been named. Thinking of the story connected with the Peyton place, she shivered a little in the warm sun, deliberately turning her eyes away. She tried to locate the white and green cottage where she lived with her mother, but she could not distinguish her home from all the others in her neighborhood. From where Allison was sitting, her house was two miles away.

The houses in Allison's neighborhood were simple, well constructed, one-family dwellings, most of them modeled on Cape Cod lines and painted white with green trim. Once Allison had looked up the meaning of the word "neighbor" in a book which, although she now knew better, she still thought of as belonging to one man in very peculiar circumstances: Webster's *On A Bridge*. A neighbor, said the book, was one who dwelt in the same vicinity with one, and for a short time Allison had been comforted. Webster's *On A Bridge* apparently found nothing odd in the fact that a neighbor was not a friend. There were, however, no dictionary definitions to explain why the MacKenzies had no friends anywhere in the town of Peyton Place. Allison was sure that the reason for this friendlessness was the fact that the MacKenzies were a different kind of family from most, and that therefore other people did not care to become involved with them.

From Road's End Allison pictured the home she could not see as full of busy, popular people whose telephone rang constantly. From here, she could imagine her house as being no different from any other house—not queer in its emptiness and not all wrong, just as having no father was all wrong, and her life and herself. Only here, alone on the hill, could Allison be sure of herself— and contented.

She hopped down from where she had been sitting and bent to pick up a small branch broken from a maple tree by the cold wind and rain of a few days before. Carefully, she broke all the twigs from the branch so that it became an almost straight stick, and as she walked, she peeled the bark from the wood until it was stripped clean. When this was done, she paused and put her nose against the wood's bare, green-whiteness, sniffing its fresh, wet smell, running her finger tips over its unprotected surface until she felt the dampness of sap on her hands. She walked on again, pressing the stick into the ground with each step, and pretended

12

that she was carrying an alpenstock the way people did in pictures taken in the Swiss Alps.

The woods on either side of Road's End were old. They were one of the few remaining stands of lumber in northern New England which had never been cut, for the town ended below Memorial Park and the terrain above had always been considered too rocky and uneven for development. Allison imagined that the paths on which she walked through these woods were the same trails that the Indians had followed before the white man had come to settle. She believed that she was the only person who ever came here, and she felt a deep sense of ownership toward the woods. She loved them and she had learned them well through every season of the year. She knew where the first arbutus trailed in the spring, when there were still large patches of snow on the ground, and she knew the quiet, shady places where the violets made purple clusters after the snows had disappeared. She knew where to find lady's-slipper, and where there was an open field, hidden in the middle of the woods, and covered in summer with buttercups and brown-eyed Susans. In a secret place, she had a rock where she could sit and watch a family of robins, and she could tell just by glancing at the trees when the time of the first killing frost had come. She could move quietly through the woods with a gracefulness that she never possessed away from them, and she imagined that other girls in the world outside felt always as she felt here, safe and sure, knowing the surroundings and belonging in them.

Allison walked through the woods and came to the open field. The summer flowers were gone now, and tall, tough stalks of goldenrod had taken their place. The clearing was yellow with them, and as she walked through them they encircled her on all sides so that she seemed to be wading, waist deep, in goldenness. She stood still for a moment and then suddenly, with a feeling of pure ecstasy, reached out both her arms to the world around her. She looked up at the sky with its deep blueness peculiar to Indian summer and it seemed like a vast cup inverted over her alone. The maples in the woods around the field were loud with red and yellow, and a warm, gentle wind moved through their leaves. She fancied that the trees were saying, "Hello, Allison. Hello, Allison," and she smiled. In one moment of time, precious with a lack of self consciousness, she held her arms wide and called, "Hello! Oh, hello, everything beautiful!"

She ran to the edge of the field and sat down, resting her back against a wide-trunked tree, and then looked back on the field

13

of goldenrod. Slowly, a wonderful feeling of being the only living person in the whole world filled her. Everything was hers, and there was no one to spoil it for her, no one to make anything less peaceful and true and beautiful than it was right at this moment. She sat for a long time not moving, letting the feeling of happiness settle into a comforting warmth in the pit of her stomach, and when she stood up and began to walk through the woods again, she touched the trees and bushes in her passing as if caressing the hands of old friends. At last she came back to the pavement and the wooden board that said Road's End. She looked down at the town, the feeling of joy beginning to dissolve within her. She whirled around, away from the town, to face the trees again, trying to recapture the sensation that was so warm, so lovely, but it would not come back. She felt heavy, as if she suddenly weighed two hundred pounds, and as tired as if she had been running for hours. She turned and started down the hill toward Peyton Place. When she was halfway down, she lifted the stick that she had been carrying and hurled it far into the woods at the side of the road.

Allison walked rapidly now, hardly aware of distance, until she was below the park and into the town. A group of boys came toward her, four or five of them, laughing and shoving good-naturedly at one another, and the last wisps of Allison's happiness melted away. She knew these boys; they went to the same school as she did. They walked toward her, clad in bright sweaters, munching on apples and letting the juice run down their chins, and their voices were loud and rough in the October afternoon. Allison crossed the street in the hope of avoiding them, but she saw that they had noticed her and she was once more tense, aware and frightened of the world around her.

"Hi, Allison," called one of the boys.

When she did not answer but continued to walk, he began to mimic her, holding himself stiffly and putting his nose in the air.

"Oh, Allison," called another boy in a high falsetto, dragging out the syllables of her name so that it sounded as if he were saying, "Oh, Aa-hal-lissonnn!"

She made herself go on, not speaking, her hands clenched in the pockets of her light jacket.

"Aa-hal-lissonnn! Aa-hal-lissonnn!"

She looked ahead blindly, knowing by instinct that the next street was hers, and that soon she could turn the corner and be out of sight.

14

"Allison, Bumballison, teelialigo Allison. Teelegged, toelegged, bowlegged Allison!"

"Hey, Fat-stuff!"

Allison turned into Beech Street and ran all the way up the block to her house.

◆ 4 ◆

Allison MacKenzie's father, for whom the child had been named, died when she was three years old. She had no conscious memory of him. Ever since she could remember, she had lived with Constance, her mother, in the house in Peyton Place which had once belonged to her grandmother. Constance and Allison had little in common with one another; the mother was of too cold and practical a mind to understand the sensitive, dreaming child, and Allison, too young and full of hopes and fancies to sympathize with her mother.

Constance was a beautiful woman who had always prided herself on being hardheaded. At the age of nineteen, she had seen the limitations of Peyton Place, and over the protests of her widowed mother she had gone to New York with the idea of meeting, going to work for and finally marrying a man of wealth and position. She became secretary to Allison MacKenzie, a handsome, good-natured Scot who owned a highly successful shop where he sold imported fabrics. Within three weeks he and Constance became lovers and during the next year a child was born to them whom Constance immediately named for its father. Allison MacKenzie and Constance Standish were never married, for he already had a wife and two children "up in Scarsdale," as he always put it. He said these words as if he were saying, "up at the North Pole," but Constance never forgot that Allison's first family was painfully, frighteningly near.

"What do you intend to do about us?" she asked him.

"Keep on as we are, I suppose," he said. "There doesn't seem to be much of anything else we can do, without causing an unearthly stink."

Constance, remembering her small-town upbringing, knew well the discomfort of getting oneself talked about.

"I suppose not," she said agreeably.

15

But from that moment she began to plan for herself and her unborn child. Through her mother she spread a respectable fiction about herself in Peyton Place. Elizabeth Standish went to New York to attend the small, family wedding of her daughter Constance, as far as the town knew. In reality, she went to New York to be with Constance when her daughter returned from the hospital with the baby who had been named for Allison MacKenzie. A few years later it was a simple thing for Constance to use a little ink eradicator and to substitute a different number for the last digit in her daughter's year of birth as shown on her birth certificate. Slowly, by not answering letters hinting broadly for invitations to visit the MacKenzies, Constance Standish cut herself off from the friends of her girlhood. Soon she was forgotten by Peyton Place, remembered by her old friends only when they met Elizabeth Standish on the streets of the town.

"How's Connie?" they would ask, "And the baby?"

"Just fine. Everything is just fine," poor Mrs. Standish would say, in a terror lest she give a hint that everything was not fine.

From the day Allison was born, Elizabeth Standish lived with fear. She was afraid that she had not played her part well enough, that sooner or later someone would find out about the birth certificate that had been tampered with, or that some sharp-eyed individual would spot the fact that her granddaughter Allison was a year older than Constance said she was. But most of all, she was afraid for herself. In her worst nightmares she heard the voices of Peyton Place.

"There goes Elizabeth Standish. Her daughter got into trouble with some feller down to New York."

"It's all in the way you bring up a child, what they do when they're grown."

"Constance had a little girl."

"Poor little bastard."

"Bastard."

"That whore Constance Standish, and her dirty little bastard."

When Elizabeth Standish died, Constance allowed the cottage on Beech Street to stand vacant but in readiness for the day when Allison MacKenzie should tire of her, and she should have to return to Peyton Place. But Allison did not abandon Constance and her child. He was a good man, in his fashion, with a strict sense of responsibility. He provided for his two families until the day of his death, and even beyond that. Constance neither knew nor cared about the circumstances in which Allison's wife

16

found herself. It was enough for Constance that her lover had left a substantial amount of money for her in the hands of a discreet lawyer. With this, and what she had managed to save during Allison MacKenzie's lifetime, she returned to Peyton Place and established herself in the Standish house. She did not weep for her dead lover, for she had not loved him.

Soon after her return to Peyton Place, she opened a small apparel shop on Elm Street and settled down to the business of making a living for herself and her baby daughter. No one ever questioned the fact that Constance was the widow of a man named Allison MacKenzie. She kept a large, framed photograph of him on the mantelpiece in her living room, and the town sympathized with her.

"It's a shame," said Peyton Place. "And him so young."

"It's hard for a woman alone, especially trying to raise a child."

"She's a hard worker, Connie MacKenzie is. Stays in that shop of hers 'til six o'clock every night."

At thirty-three, Constance was still beautiful. Her hair still gleamed, sleek and blond, and her face had not yet begun to show the lines of time.

"Good-lookin' woman like that," said the men of the town, "you'd think she'd look to get married again."

"Perhaps she's still grieving for her husband," said the women. "Some widows grieve their whole lives long."

The truth of the matter was that Constance enjoyed her life alone. She told herself that she had never been highly sexed to begin with, that her affair with Allison had been a thing born of loneliness. She repeated silently, over and over, that life with her daughter Allison was entirely satisfactory and all she wanted. Men were not necessary, for they were unreliable at best, and nothing but creators of trouble. As for love, she knew well the tragic results of not loving a man. What more terrible consequence might come from allowing herself to love another? No, Constance often told herself, she was better off as she was, doing the best she knew how, and waiting for Allison to grow up. If at times she felt a vague restlessness within herself, she told herself sharply that this was *not* sex, but perhaps a touch of indigestion.

The Thrifty Corner Apparel Shoppe prospered. Perhaps because it was the only store of its kind in Peyton Place, or perhaps because Constance had a certain flair for style. Whichever it was, the women of the town bought almost exclusively from her. It was the consensus of town opinion that Connie MacKenzie's things were

17

every bit as nice as those in the stores down to Manchester or over to White River, and since they were no more expensive, it was better to trade with somebody local than to take town money elsewhere.

At six-fifteen in the evening, Constance walked up Beech Street toward her house. She wore a smart black suit, the product of a rather expensive Boston shop, and a small black hat. She looked like a fashion illustration, a fact which always made her daughter Allison vaguely uncomfortable, but was, as Constance frequently pointed out to her, very good for business. As she walked toward home, Constance was thinking of Allison's father, a thing she seldom did, for the thought was an uncomfortable one. She knew that someday she would have to tell the child the truth about her birth. Many times she had wondered why this was so, but she had never found a reasonable answer to her question.

It is better that she find it out from me than to hear it from a stranger, she often thought.

But this was not the answer, for no one had ever discovered the truth, and the chances that someone would in the future were very slight.

All the same, thought Constance, someday Allison will have to be told.

She pushed open the front door of her house and went into the living room where her daughter waited.

"Hello, darling," said Constance.

"Hello, Mother."

Allison was sitting in an overstuffed chair, her legs swung over the wide arm, reading a book.

"What are you reading now?" asked Constance, standing in front of a mirror and carefully removing her hat.

"Just a babyish fairy tale," said Allison defensively. "I like to read them over once in a while. This one is The Sleeping Beauty."

"That's nice, dear," said Constance vaguely. She could not understand a twelve-year-old girl keeping her nose in a book. Other girls her age would have been continually in the shop, examining and exclaiming over the boxes of pretty dresses and underwear which arrived there almost daily.

"I suppose that we should think of something to eat," said Constance.

"I put two potatoes in the oven half an hour ago," said Allison, putting her book away.

Together, the two went into the kitchen to prepare what Con-

18

stance referred to as "dinner." She was, Allison realized, the only woman in Peyton Place who did this. Outside, Allison was very careful about saying "supper." To others, she also spoke of "going to church," never to "services," and of a dress being "pretty," but never "smart." Little things, such as different terminology, had the power to embarrass Allison to a point where, thinking about them in bed at night, she writhed with shame, her face scarlet in the darkness, and hated her mother for her differentness, for making her different.

"*Please*, Mother," she would say, in tears, whenever her mother's conversation irritated her to the exploding point.

And Constance, the idioms of her people buried under the patina of New York, would say, "But, darling, it *is* a smart little dress!" or, "But, Allison, the main meal of the day is *always* called dinner!"

At nine o'clock that night Allison, clad in pajamas and robe and ready for bed, set her books down on the mantelpiece in the living room. Her eyes fell on the photograph of her father, and she stood still for a moment, studying the dark face that smiled into hers. Her father's hair, she noticed, had grown into a pronounced peak on his forehead, giving him a rather devilish air, and his eyes had been large and dark and deep.

"He was handsome, wasn't he?" she asked softly.

"Who, dear?" asked Constance, looking up from the account book in front of her.

"My father," said Allison.

"Oh," said Constance. "Yes, dear. Yes, he was."

Allison was still looking at the photograph. "He looks just like a prince," she said.

"What did you say, dear?"

"Nothing, Mother. Good night."

"Good night, dear."

Allison lay in her wide, four-poster bed and stared up at the ceiling where the street light outside made weird shadow figures with the room's darkness.

Just like a prince, she thought, and felt a sudden tightness in her throat.

For a moment she wondered what her life might have been like if it had been her mother who had died and her father who had lived. At once, she sank her teeth into the edge of the bed sheet in shame at this disloyal thought.

"Father. Father." She said the strange word over and over to herself, but the sound of it in her mind meant nothing.

19

She thought of the photograph on the mantelpiece downstairs. My prince, she said to herself, and immediately the image in her mind seemed to take on life, to breathe, and to smile kindly at her.

Allison fell asleep.

♦ 5 ♦

Chestnut Street, which ran parallel to Elm Street, one block to the south of the main thoroughfare, was considered to be the "best" street in Peyton Place. On this street were located the homes of the town's *élite*.

At the extreme western end of Chestnut Street stood the imposing red brick house of Leslie Harrington. Harrington, who was the owner of the Cumberland Mills and a very rich man, was also on the board of trustees for the Citizens' National Bank, and the chairman of the Peyton Place school board. The Harrington house, screened from the street by tall trees and wide lawns, was the largest in town.

On the opposite side of the street was the home of Dr. Matthew Swain. His was a white house, fronted with tall, slim pillars. Most of the townspeople defined it as "southern looking." The doctor's wife had been dead for many years, and the town often wondered why The Doc, as he was informally known, insisted on keeping his big house.

"Too big for a man alone," said Peyton Place. "I'll bet The Doc rattles around in there like a marble in a tin cup."

"The Doc's place ain't as big as Leslie Harrington's."

"No, but it's different with Harrington. He's got a boy that's going to get married someday. That's why he keeps that big house since his wife died. It's for the boy."

"I guess that's so. Too bad The Doc never had kids. Must be lonely for a man with no kids, after his wife goes."

Below Dr. Swain, on the same side of the street, lived Charles Partridge, the town's leading attorney. Old Charlie, as the town called him, had a solid, Victorian house which was painted a dark red and trimmed with white, and where he lived with his wife Marion. The Partridges had no children.

"Seems funny, don't it?" said the townspeople, some of whom

20

lived, with many children, in cramped quarters, "that the biggest houses on Chestnut Street are the emptiest in town."

"Well, you know what they say. The rich get richer, and the poor get children."

"Reckon that's right enough."

Also on Chestnut Street lived Dexter Humphrey, the president of the Citizens' National Bank; Leighton Philbrook, who owned a sawmill and vast tracts of hardwood forest; Jared Clarke, the owner of a chain of feed and grain stores throughout the northern section of the state, who was also chairman of the board of selectmen; and Seth Buswell, the owner of the *Peyton Place Times*.

"Seth's the only man on Chestnut Street who don't have to work for a living," said the town. "He can just set and scribble to his heart's content and never worry about the bills."

This was true. Seth was the only son of the late George Buswell, a shrewd landowner who had eventually become governor of the state. When he died, George Buswell left a healthy fortune to his son, Seth.

"Hard as nails, old George Buswell was," said the townspeople who remembered him.

"Yep. Hard as nails and crooked as a corkscrew."

The residents of Chestnut Street regarded themselves as the backbone of Peyton Place. They were of the old families, people whose ancestors remembered when the town had been nothing but wilderness, with Samuel Peyton's castle the only building for miles around. Between them, the men who lived on Chestnut Street provided jobs for Peyton Place. They took care of its aches and pains, straightened out its legal affairs, formed its thinking and spent its money. Between themselves, these men knew more about the town and its people than anyone else.

"More power on Chestnut Street than in the big Connecticut River," said Peter Drake, who practiced law in town under a double handicap. He was young, and he had not been born in Peyton Place.

♦ 6 ♦

On Friday nights the men of Chestnut Street met together at Seth Buswell's house to play poker. Usually, all the men came, but on this particular Friday evening there were only four of them sitting around Seth's kitchen table: Charles Partridge, Leslie Harrington, Matthew Swain and Seth.

"Small gang tonight," commented Harrington, who was thinking that a small group precluded a large pot.

"Yep," said Seth. "Dexter's got his in-laws visitin' and Jared had to go over to White River. Leighton called me up and said that he had business down to Manchester."

"Alley cat business, I'll bet," said Dr. Swain. "How old Philbrook has managed to avoid the clap this long, I'm sure I don't know."

Partridge laughed. "Probably looks after himself like you taught him, Doc," he said.

"Well, let's play," said Harrington impatiently, riffling the cards with his white hands.

"Can't wait to take our money, eh, Leslie?" asked Seth who disliked Harrington intensely.

"That's right," agreed Harrington, who knew very well how Seth felt and smiled, now, into the face of his enemy.

It excited Leslie Harrington to know that people who hated him nevertheless felt impelled to tolerate him. To Harrington, this was the proof of his success and it renewed in him, every time it happened, a rich sense of the power he wielded. It was no secret in Peyton Place that there was not a single issue that could come to a town vote with any assurance of success unless Harrington was first in favor of it. He was not in the least ashamed of the fact that on various occasions he called his millworkers together and said, "Well, fellers, I'd feel pretty damned good if we didn't vote to put up a new grade school this year. I'd feel so goddamned good that I'd feel inclined to give everybody in this shop a five per cent bonus the week after next." Seth Buswell, in whose veins flowed the blood of a crusader, was as helpless before Harrington as was a farmer who had fallen behind in his mortgage payments.

"Cut for the deal," said Partridge, and the poker game began. The men played quietly for an hour, Seth rising from his chair only when there was a need to refill glasses. The newspaper editor played badly, for instead of keeping his mind on the cards, he had been busily thinking up, and discarding, ways to broach a sensitive subject to his guests. At last he decided that tact and diplomacy would be futile in this case, and when the next hand had been won, he spoke.

"I've been thinkin' lately," he said, "about all the tar paper shacks that this town has got spread around. Seems to me like we ought to think about gettin' zonin' laws into effect."

22

For a moment no one spoke. Then Partridge, to whom this was an old topic of conversation, took a sip of his drink and sighed audibly.

"Again, Seth?" asked the lawyer.

"Yes, again," said Seth. "I've been tryin' to talk some sense into you guys for years, and now I'm tellin' you that it's time to get somethin' done. I'm goin' to start runnin' a series of articles, with pictures, in the paper next week."

"Now, now, Seth," said Harrington soothingly, "I wouldn't be too hasty about this. After all, the folks who own those shacks you're talking about pay taxes the same as the rest of us. This town can't afford to lose any taxpayers."

"For Christ's sake, Leslie," said Dr. Swain. "You must bo going soft in the head in your old age to run off at the mouth like that. Sure the shackowners pay taxes, and their property is evaluated so low that what they pay the town is peanuts. Yet they live in their shacks and produce kids by the dozen. We're the ones who are paying to educate their kids, to keep the roads paved and to buy a new piece of fire-fighting equipment once in a while. The taxes a shackowner pays in ten years wouldn't pay to send his kids to school for one year.

"You know damned well that Doc's right, Leslie," said Seth.

"Without the shacks," said Harrington, "the land that they stand on now would be idle. How many tax dollars would you collect then? Not only that, but you can't raise taxes on the shacks unless you raise everybody's taxes. Rezone the shack areas, and you've got to rezone the whole damned town and everybody'll be madder than hell. No, fellers, I don't like paying to educate a woodchopper's kids any better than you do, but I still say, leave the shacks alone."

"For Christ's sake!" shouted Dr. Swain, forgetting himself and losing his temper in a way that he and Seth had agreed privately beforehand not to do. "It's not only a matter of taxes and the fact that those places are eyesores. They're cesspools, as filthy as sewers and as unhealthy as an African swamp. I was out to another shack just last week. No toilet, no septic tank, no running water, eight people in one room and no refrigeration. It's a wonder that any of those kids ever live long enough to go to school."

"So that's the boil on your ass, is it?" laughed Harrington. "You're damned right it's not the taxes that are bothering you and Seth. It's the idea that some squalid little urchin might catch cold running to the outhouse in his bare feet."

"You're a fool, Leslie," said Dr. Swain. "I'm not thinking of colds.

I'm thinking of typhoid and polio. Let one of those get a toehold around the shacks and it wouldn't be long before the whole town was in danger."

"What are you talking about?" asked Harrington. "We've never had anything like that around here before. You're an old woman, Doc, and so is Seth."

Seth's face colored angrily, but before he could say anything, Partridge intervened quickly and quietly.

"How in hell did you plan to get the owners out of their shacks if they refused to abide by these zoning laws of yours, Seth?" asked the lawyer.

"I don't think that many of them would choose to leave," said Seth. "Most of them can well afford to make improvements on their property. They could use some of the money they drink up to install toilets and tanks and water."

"What are you trying to do, Seth?" asked Harrington, laughing. "Make Peyton Place into a police state?"

"I agree with Doc," said Seth. "You *are* a fool, Leslie."

Harrington's face darkened. "Maybe so," he said, "but I say that when you start telling a man he's got to do this, that or the other thing, you're coming pretty damned close to infringing on a citizen's rights."

"Oh, God," moaned Seth.

"Go ahead and accuse me of being a fool if you want," said Harrington righteously, "but you'll never get me to vote for passing a law that dictates what kind of home a man must have."

Seth and Dr. Swain regarded Harrington with utter disbelief when he spoke this sanctimonious sentence, but before they could speak, Partridge, who was a born pacifist, picked up the deck of cards and began to shuffle them.

"We came here to play poker," he said. "Let's play."

The subject of the tar paper shacks of Peyton Place was not mentioned again, and at eleven-thirty when one of the men suggested playing a last hand, Dr. Swain picked up the cards to deal.

"I'll open," said Harrington, holding his cards close to his chest and peering at them frowningly.

"I'll raise," said Seth, who held his cards one on top of the other in one hand.

Partridge and Dr. Swain dropped out and Harrington raised Seth.

"Again," said the newspaper editor pushing more money into the center of the table.

"All right," said Harrington irritably. "And raise again."

Dr. Swain noticed with distaste that Harrington had begun to sweat.

Greedy bastard, thought the doctor. With his dough, he's worried over a measly hand of five-and-ten poker.

"Again," said Seth coldly.

"Goddamn you," said Harrington. "O.K. There you are. Call."

"All pink," said Seth softly, fanning out his diamond flush on the table.

Harrington, who had held a king high straight, purpled.

"Goddamn it," he said. "The one hand I hold all night and it's no good. You win, Buswell."

"Yes," said Seth and looked at the millowner, "I generally do, in the end."

Harrington looked Seth straight in the eyes. "If there's one thing I hate more than a poor loser," he said, "it's a poor winner."

"Hold up a mirror and you're bound to see your own reflection, as I always say." Seth grinned at Harrington. "What do you always say, Leslie?"

Charles Partridge stood up and stretched. "Well, boys, morning comes early. Guess I'll be on my way."

Harrington ignored the lawyer. "It's the man who holds the best cards who wins, Seth. That's what I always say. Wait a minute, Charlie. I'll walk home with you."

When Partridge and Harrington had left, Dr. Swain put a sympathetic hand on Seth's arm.

"Too bad, feller," he said. "But I think you'd better wait a while and talk to Jared and Leighton before you start anything about those shacks in your paper."

"Wait for what?" demanded Seth angrily. "I've been waiting for years. What'll we wait for this time, Doc? Typhoid? Polio? Pay your money and take your choice."

"I know. I know," said Dr. Swain. "All the same, you'd best wait a while. You've got to educate people to new ways of thinking, and that's a long, slow process sometimes. If you go off half cocked, they'll turn on you the same as Leslie did tonight and tell you how those shacks have been around town for years, and we've never had an epidemic of any kind yet."

"Hell, Doc, I don't know. Maybe a good epidemic would solve everything. Perhaps the town would be better off without the characters who live in those places."

"There is nothing dearer than life, Seth," said Dr Swain gruffly. "Even the lives being lived in our shacks."

"Please," said Seth, his good humor restored. "You could at least refer to them as 'camps' or 'summer dwellings'!"

"The suburbs!" exclaimed Dr. Swain. "That's it, by God! Question: 'Where do you live, Mr. Shackowner?' Answer: 'I live in the suburbs and commute to Peyton Place.'"

Both men laughed. "Have another drink before you go," said Seth.

"Yes, sir, Suburbia," said Dr. Swain. "We could even name these estates. How about Pine Crest, or Sunny Hill, or Bide-A-Wee?"

"You left out Maple Knoll and Elm Ridge," said Seth.

It wasn't funny, though, reflected Dr. Swain half an hour later after he had left Seth and was taking his usual nightly walk before going home.

He walked south, after leaving Chestnut Street, and was no more than half a mile out of town when he passed the first shack. A light shone dimly through one small window, and a curl of smoke rose thinly from the tin chimney. Dr. Swain stopped in the middle of the dirt road and looked at the tiny, black tar-papered building which housed Lucas Cross, his wife Nellie and their three children. Dr. Swain had been inside the shack once, and knew that the interior consisted of one room where the family ate, slept and lived.

Must be colder than hell in the winter, thought the doctor, and felt that he had said the kindest thing possible about the home of the Cross family.

As he was turning to walk back to town, a sudden shrill scream echoed in the night.

"Christ!" said Dr. Swain aloud, and began to run toward the shack, picturing all kinds of accidents and cursing himself for not carrying his doctor's bag at all times. He was at the door when he heard Lucas Cross's voice.

"Goddamn sonofabitch," yelled Lucas drunkenly. "Where'd you put it?"

There was a loud crash, as if someone had fallen, or been pushed, over a chair.

"I told you and told you," came Nellie's whine. "There ain't no more. You drunk it all up."

"Goddamn lyin' bitch," shouted Lucas. "You hid it. Tell me where it is or I'll beat your goddamn lousy hide right off you."

Nellie screamed again, sharp and shrill, and Dr. Swain turned away from the shack door feeling slightly nauseated.

26

I suppose, he thought, that the unwritten law about a man minding his own business is a good one. But sometimes I just don't believe it.

He walked toward the road, but before he had gone more than a few steps, he tripped and almost fell over a small figure crouched on the ground.

"For Christ's sake," he said softly, reaching down and gripping a girl's arm. "What are you doing out here in the dark?"

The girl broke away from him. "What are you doing here yourself, Doc?" she asked sullenly. "Nobody sent for you."

In the meager light that came through the shack windows, the doctor could barely discern the girl's features.

"Oh," he said. "It's Selena. I've seen you around town with the little MacKenzie girl, haven't I?"

"Yes," said Selena. "Allison is my best friend. Listen, Doc. Don't ever say anything to Allison about this ringdangdo here tonight, will you? She wouldn't understand about such things."

"No," said Dr. Swain, "I won't say a word to anyone. You're the oldest of the children here, aren't you?"

"No. My brother Paul is older than me. He's the oldest."

"Where is Paul now?" demanded the doctor. "Why isn't he putting a stop to the goings on inside?"

"He's gone to see his girl in town," said Selena. "And what are you talking about anyway? There's nobody can stop Pa when he gets drunk and starts fighting."

She stopped talking and whistled softly, and a little boy came running from behind a tree.

"I always come outside when Pa starts," said Selena. "I keep Joey out here, too, so Pa won't get after him."

Joey was small and thin, and not more than seven years old. He stood behind his sister and peered timidly at the doctor from around her skirt. A fierce anger filled the old man.

"I'll put a stop to this," he said, and started once more toward the door of the shack.

Immediately, Selena ran in front of him and put her hands against his chest.

"You want to get killed?" she whispered frantically. "Nobody sent for you, Doc. You better get back to Chestnut Street."

A continuous wailing came from the shack now, but the screaming had stopped and Lucas' voice was still.

"It's all over with anyhow," said Selena. "If you went in now, it would just get Pa all worked up again. You better go, Doc."

For a moment the doctor hesitated, then tipped his hat to the girl.

"All right, Selena," he said. "I'll go. Good night."

"Good night, Doc."

He was back on the road when the girl ran and caught up to him. She put her hand on his sleeve.

"Doc," she said, "me and Joey want to thank you anyway. It was nice of you to stop by."

Like a lady bidding her guests farewell after the tea party, thought the doctor. It was nice of you to stop by.

"That's all right, Selena," said Dr. Swain. "Any time you'd like to have me come, just let me know."

He noticed that although Joey was directly behind Selena, the little boy never spoke a word.

♦ 7 ♦

Lucas Cross had lived in Peyton Place all his life, as had his father and grandfather before him. Lucas did not know where his ancestors had come from originally, and this fact did not bother him at all, for he never thought of it. If he had been asked, he would have been dumfounded by the stupidity of such a question and, shrugging, would have replied, "We always lived right around here."

Lucas was a woodsman of a now-and-then variety common to northern New England. Professional lumbermen regarded the forests with respect, knowing that the generations before them had abused the woods, felling them flat without a thought toward conservation and replanting, and approached them now with patience and precision. Men like Lucas looked on them as a precarious kind of security, a sort of padding to fall back on when one was given a shove by life. When all else failed and cash money was needed in a hurry, the task of "workin' the woods" was always available. The lumbermen had nothing but contempt for men like Lucas, and assigned to him the secondary jobs of the lumbering trade: the stacking of logs on trucks, the fastening of chains and the unloading at the sawmills. In northern New England, Lucas was referred to as a woodsman, but had he lived in another section of America, he might have been called an Okie, or a hillbilly, or poor white trash. He was one of a vast brotherhood who worked at no particular trade, propagated many children with a slatternly wife, and installed his oversized family in a variety of tumble-down, lean-to, makeshift dwellings.

In an era of free education, the woodsman of northern New England had little or no schooling, and in many cases his employer was forced to pay him in cash, for the employee could not sign his own name to a check. What the woodsman knew, he knew by instinct, from listening to conversation or, rarely, from observation, and much of the time he was drunk on cheap wine or rotgut whisky. He lived in rickety wooden buildings which were covered on the outside with tar paper instead of clapboards, and his house was without water or sewerage. He drank, beat his wife and abused his children, and he had one virtue which he believed outweighed all his faults. He paid his bills. To be in debt was the one—and only—cardinal sin to men like Lucas Cross, and it was behind this fact that the small-town northern New Englander, of more settled ways and habits, hid when confronted with the reality of the shack dwellers in his vicinity.

"They're all right," the New Englander was apt to say, especially to a tourist from the city. "They pay their bills and taxes and they mind their own business. They don't do any harm."

This attitude was visible, too, in well-meaning social workers who turned away from the misery of the woodsman's family. If a child died of cold or malnutrition, it was considered unfortunate, but certainly nothing to stir up a hornet's nest about. The state was content to let things lie, for it never had been called upon to extend aid of a material nature to the residents of the shacks which sat, like running sores, on the body of northern New England.

Lucas Cross was different from many woodsmen in that he had a trade which he practiced when coaxed with liquor or bribed with outrageous sums of money. He was a skilled carpenter and cabinetmaker.

"Never saw anything like it in my life," Charles Partridge had said, soon after Lucas had been persuaded to make some kitchen cabinets for Mrs. Partridge. "In came Lucas, not drunk, mind you, but he'd had a few. He had this folding yardstick that looked about as accurate to me as a two-dollar watch. Well, he sat and looked at our kitchen walls for a while, then he started in measuring and cussing under his breath, and after a time he began sawing and planing. The next thing I knew, he was done, and if I do say

29

so myself, there are no finer-looking cabinets in any kitchen in Peyton Place. Look."

The cabinets were made of knotty pine and they fitted perfectly in the spaces between the Partridges' kitchen windows. They gleamed like satin.

Over a period of years, Lucas had done much of the interior "finish" work in the houses on Chestnut Street, and most of what he had not done had been done by his father.

"Good cabinetmakers, the Crosses," said the people of the town.

"When they're sober," they amended.

"My wife wants Lucas to make her a buffet for the dining room when he gets through working the woods next."

"She'll have to sober him up first. Whatever money he makes in the woods, he'll spend on one helluva drunk before he starts looking around for work again."

"They're all alike, those shackowners. Work for a while, drunk for a longer while, work and then drunk again."

"They're all right, though. Don't do any harm that I can see. They pay their bills."

Seth Buswell, in a rare philosophical mood, said, "I wonder why our woodsman drinks? One would surmise that he hasn't the imagination to invent phantoms for himself from which he must escape. I wonder what he thinks about. Doubtless he has his hopes and dreams the same as all of us, yet it appears that all he ever dwells upon is liquor, sex and food, in that order."

"Watch that kind of talk, old feller," said Dr. Swain. "When you talk like that, the old Dartmouth education shows through."

"Sorry," said Seth elaborately and reverted to the patois of his people, the one hypocrisy which he consciously practiced. It might not be honest, this omitting of r's and dropping of final g's, but his father had made a barrel of money in spite of it, and had gained many votes because of it.

"Mebbe they're a harmless crew at that, our woodsmen," said Seth. "Sort of like tame animals."

"Except Lucas Cross," said Dr. Swain. "He's a mean one. There's something about him, something around the eyes, that rubs me the wrong way. He has the look of a jackal."

"Lucas is all right, Doc," said Seth comfortably. "You're seein' things."

"I hope so," said the doctor. "But I'm afraid not."

◆ 8 ◆

Selena Cross lay on the folding cot that served as her bed and which was pushed against the wall on the kitchen side of the one-room Cross shack. She was thirteen years old and well developed for her age, with the curves of hips and breasts already discernible under the too short and often threadbare clothes that she wore. Much of the girl's clothing had been inherited from the more fortunate children of Peyton Place and passed down to Selena through the charity-loving hands of the ladies from the Congregational church. Selena had long dark hair that curled of its own accord in a softly beautiful fashion. Her eyes, too, were dark and slightly slanted, and she had a naturally red, full-lipped mouth over well-shaped, startlingly white teeth. Her skin was clear and of a honey-tan shade which looked as if it had been acquired under the sun but which, on Selena, never faded to sallowness in the long months of the harsh New England winter.

"Put a pair of gold hoops in her ears," said Miss Thornton, "and she'd look like everybody's idea of a perfect gypsy."

Selena was wise with the wisdom learned of poverty and wretchedness. At thirteen, she saw hopelessness as an old enemy, as persistent and inevitable as death.

Sometimes, when she looked at Nellie, her mother, she thought, I'll get out. I'll never be like her.

Nellie Cross was short and flabby with the unhealthy fat that comes from too many potatoes and too much bread. Her hair was thin and tied in a sloppy knot at the back of her not too clean neck, and her hands, perpetually grimy, were rough and knobby knuckled, with broken, dirty fingernails.

I'll get out, thought Selena. I'll never let myself look like that.

But hopelessness was always at her elbow, ready to nudge her and say, "Oh, yeah? *How* will you get out? Where could you go, and who would have you after you got there?"

If Lucas was away, or at home but sober, Selena would think, optimistically, Oh, I'll manage. One way or another, I'll get out.

But for the most part it was like tonight. Selena lay in her cot and listened to her older brother Paul snoring in his bed against the opposite wall, and to the adenoidal breathing of her little brother Joey, who slept in a cot like her own. But these sounds could not cover the louder ones which came from the double bed at the other end of the shack. Selena lay still and listened to Lucas and Nellie perform the act of love. Lucas did not speak while thus engaged. He grunted, Selena thought, like a rooting pig, and he breathed like a steam engine puffing its way across the wide Connecticut River, while from Nellie there was no sound at all. Selena listened and chewed at her bottom lip and thought, Hurry up, for Christ's sake. Lucas grunted harder and puffed louder, and the old spring on the double bed creaked alarmingly, faster and faster. At last, Lucas squealed like a calf in the hands of a butcher and it was over. Selena turned her face into her moldy-smelling pillow which was bare of any sort of pillowcase, and wept soundlessly.

I'll get out, she thought furiously. I'll get out of this filthy mess.

Her old enemy, hopelessness, did not even bother to answer. He was just there.

♦ 9 ♦

Allison MacKenzie had never actually visited at Selena's house. She was in the habit of walking down the dirt road to where the Cross shack stood, and of waiting in front of the clearing until her friend came out to her. Many times Allison had wondered why none of the Crosses ever invited her into the house, but she had never quite dared to ask Selena. Once she had asked her mother, but Constance had persisted in saying that the reason was that Selena was ashamed of her home, so Allison had never discussed it with her again. Constance could not seem to understand that Selena was perfect and sure of herself, and that it was only she, Allison, who ever had feelings of shame. But still, it was odd the way no one had ever invited her into the house. Most of the time Selena came right out the shack door as soon as she saw Allison, but once in a while she emerged from the enclosed pen that was attached to the side of the house in which Lucas kept a few sheep. Whenever she had been in the sheep pen, Selena always yelled, "Wait a minute, Allison. I got to wash my feet," but she never asked Allison to come in while she did so. Usually Selena's little brother Joey tagged along behind his sister, but this Saturday afternoon Selena came out of the house alone.

32

"Hi, Selena," called Allison warmly, her antisocial mood of the previous afternoon forgotten.

"Hi, kid," said Selena in the oddly deep voice which Allison found so intriguing. "What'll we do today?"

The question was rhetorical. On Saturday afternoons the girls always sauntered slowly down the streets of the town, looking into shop windows and pretending that they were grown up and married to famous men. They studied every piece of merchandise in the Peyton Place stores, carefully picking and choosing what they would buy for themselves, for their houses and for their children. •

"That suit would be adorable on little Clark, Mrs. Gable," they said to one another.

And, nonchalantly, "Since I divorced Mr. Powell, I just can't seem to work up much interest in clothes any more."

Together, they spent every cent Allison could beg from her mother on junk jewelry, motion picture magazines and ice-cream sundaes. Sometimes Selena had a little money which she had earned by doing some odd job for a local housewife, and then she and Allison would go to a movie at the Ioka Theater. Later, they would sit at the soda fountain in Prescott's Drugstore and eat toasted tomato and lettuce sandwiches and drink Coca-Cola. Then, instead of pretending that they were married to motion picture stars, they would play at being well-to-do local housewives out for an afternoon stroll and stopping for tea while their infants slept peacefully in perambulators parked outside Prescott's front door. Allison held a drinking straw, ripped in half as if it were a cigarette, and carried on what she considered a grown-up conversation.

"When Mr. Beane decided to start up the movie theater," she said, "he didn't have enough money, so he borrowed from an Irishman named Kelley. That's why the theater is named the Ioka. It stands for I Owe Kelley All."

She drew a great deal of satisfaction out of knowing these little town anecdotes and from repeating them, with her own embellishments, while she picked imaginary shreds of tobacco daintily off her tongue. Selena was always an appreciative audience, never mean or stinting with her "Oh's" or "My goodnesses," or her breathlessly disbelieving "No's!"

"Oh, my goodness. Did Mr. Beane ever pay Mr. Kelley back?" asked Selena.

"Oh, sure," said Allison. And then, after a moment's pause in

33

which a better answer occurred to her, "No, wait a minute. He didn't. No, he never paid Mr. Kelley back. He ascended with the funds."

Selena slipped out of her grown-up character long enough to ask, indignantly, "What do you mean, ascended?" She always considered it as hitting below the belt when Allison used words which Selena had never heard of, and oftentimes she thought that Allison made up her own words as she went along.

"Oh, you know," said Allison. "Ascended. Ran away. Yes, Mr. Beane ascended with all the funds, and Mr. Kelley never got any of his money back."

"Allison MacKenzie, you're making that up!" protested Selena, the grown-up conversational game now completely forgotten. "Why, I saw Amos Beane right on Elm Street just yesterday. You're making the whole thing up!"

"Yes," said Allison, laughing, "I am."

"*Absconded*," said Mrs. Prescott severely from behind the soda fountain. "And he never did. That's how gossip gets started, young lady. Outrageous lies, multiplied and divided and multiplied again."

"Yes, ma'am," said Allison meekly.

"Gossip's just like amoebas," said Mrs. Prescott. "Multiply, divide and multiply."

Allison and Selena, struck with a sudden fit of giggles, ran outdoors, leaving their half-finished sandwiches. They clung together on the sidewalk, laughing hysterically, while Mrs. Prescott looked on disapprovingly from behind the plate glass window.

When these long Saturday afternoons were over, the two girls went to Allison's house where they spent many enchanted hours making up each other's faces with minute quantities of cosmetics which they had obtained by sending magazine coupons to companies who offered free samples.

"I think this 'Blue Plum' is just the right shade of lipstick for you, Selena."

And Selena, with lips that looked like swollen Concord grapes, would say, "This 'Oriental #2' is swell on you, kid. Gives you a swell color."

Allison, studying the reflection that looked back at her and which now looked rather like that of a pallid Indian, would say, "Do you really think so? You're not just *saying* that?"

"No, really. It brings out your eyes."

This game had to be over before Constance arrived home. She

34

had a withering way of saying that make-up looked cheap on young girls so that Allison, listening to her, would feel the shine of pleasure rub off her lovely Saturday afternoon, and would be depressed for the rest of the evening.

Selena always stayed to supper on Saturdays, when Constance usually made something simple, like waffles or scrambled eggs with little sausages. To Selena, these were foods of unheard of luxury, just as everything about the MacKenzie house seemed luxurious—and beautiful, something to dream about. She loved the combination of rock maple and flowered chintz in the MacKenzie living room, and she often wondered, sometimes angrily, what in the world ailed Allison that she could be unhappy in surroundings like these, with a wonderful blonde mother, and a pink and white bedroom of her own.

This was the way the two friends had always spent their Saturday afternoons, but today some restlessness, some urge to contrariness, made Allison hesitant to answer Selena's, "What'll we do today?" with the stock answer.

Allison said, "Oh, I don't know. Let's just walk."

"Where to?" demanded Selena practically. "Can't just walk and walk and not go anywhere. Let's go down to your mother's store."

Selena loved to go to the Thrifty Corner. Sometimes Constance allowed her to look at the dresses which hung, shimmering gorgeously, from padded white hangers.

"No," said Allison decisively, wanting to go anywhere but to her mother's store. "You always want to do the same old thing. Let's go somewhere else."

"Well, *where*, then?" asked Selena petulantly.

"I know a place," said Allison quickly. "I know the most wonderful place in the world to go. It's a secret place, though, so you mustn't ever tell anyone that I took you there. Promise?"

Selena laughed. "Where's this?" she asked. "Are you going to take me up to Samuel Peyton's castle?"

"Oh, *no!* I'd *never* go up there. I'd be scared. Wouldn't you?"

"No," said Selena flatly, "I wouldn't. Dead folks can't hurt you none. It's the ones that are alive, you have to watch out for."

"Well, anyway, it's not the castle I'm talking about. Come on. I'll show you."

"All right," said Selena. "But if it's somewhere silly, I'll turn right around and go downtown. I've got a dollar and a quarter from doing Mrs. Partridge's ironing, and the new *Photoplays* and *Silver Screens* are in down at Prescott's."

35

"Oh, come on," said Allison impatiently.

Arm in arm, the two girls walked, Allison leading the way through town and into Memorial Park. She felt excited, the way she often did just before Christmas, when she had a special gift to give to someone, and she felt, too, the particular happiness that comes from sharing something precious with a dear friend.

"Here comes Ted Carter," said Allison in a whisper, although the boy was at the opposite end of the park walk and could not possibly have heard her. "Pretend you don't see him."

"Why?" asked Selena aloud. "Ted's a good kid. Why should I make out not to see him?"

"He's *after* you, that's why," hissed Allison.

"You're nuts."

"I am not. You don't want anything to do with Ted Carter, Selena. He comes from a *terrible* family. I heard my mother talking to Mrs. Page once, about Ted's mother and father. Mrs. Page said that Mrs. Carter is no better than a *hoor!*"

"D'you mean whore?" asked Selena.

"Sh-h," Allison whispered. "He'll hear you. I don't know what Mrs. Page meant, but Mother's face got all red when she heard it, so it must be something terrible, like a thief, or a murderer!"

"Well, maybe it is, in a way," drawled Selena and burst out laughing. "Hi, Ted," she said to the boy who was now almost abreast of the two girls. "What're you doing here?"

"Same thing you are," said Ted and grinned. "Just walking."

"Well, then, walk with us," said Selena, ignoring Allison's elbow in her ribs.

"I can't," said Ted. "I gotta get back and get groceries for my mother."

"Well, if you can't, you can't," said Selena.

"Come *on*," said Allison.

"'Bye, Ted," said Selena.

"'Bye," said Ted. "'Bye, Allison."

The girls walked on through the park and Ted continued on his way toward town. When he reached the end of the walk where it emerged into the street, Ted turned to look back.

"Hey, Selena," he yelled.

The girls turned to look at him and Ted waved his hand.

"I'll be seeing you, Selena," called Ted.

"Sure!" Selena called back, and waved.

Ted turned out of the park into the street and was out of sight.

"*See!*" said Allison furiously. "You *see!* I told you so. He's *after* you."

Selena stopped walking to look at her friend. She looked at her long and hard.

"So what?" she asked finally.

The afternoon was not a success. For the first time during their long friendship, the two girls did not see eye to eye.

What's wrong, wondered Allison, not able to understand a person who remained unmoved by the beauty of the land.

I wonder what ails her, thought Selena, unable to imagine anyone for whom "going downtown" was not a thrilling experience, gaining in new joys with every trip. But then, Allison had a lot of queer ideas, thought Selena. Like when she wanted to be all by herself, or when she got to mooning over her dead father.

After all, Selena reasoned, her own father was just as dead as Allison's father, but no one ever caught her mooning around over some dumb picture the way Allison did. Selena had no idea at all of how her father had looked. He had been killed in a lumbering accident two months before she was born and Nellie had had no framed photographs to show her daughter. Lucas Cross was the only father Selena knew. He had been a widower with one son by a wife who had died in childbirth, and he had married Nellie when Selena was six weeks old. Paul was not Selena's own brother any more than Joey was but, thought Selena, she didn't bother to think of that much. If Allison were in my shoes, mused Selena, I bet she'd always be talking about half brothers and stepfathers and that kind of stuff. I wonder what ails her all the time.

Allison wondered incredulously if Selena could possibly be approaching the stage which Constance described as "being boy crazy." She was certainly in an awful hurry to get downtown. Maybe she hoped that she'd see Ted Carter in one of the stores. Allison frowned at this thought, as she began to climb the long, sloping hill behind the park, Selena at her heels.

Selena did not like one single feature of Road's End and said so in no uncertain terms when she and Allison had reached the top of the hill.

"It's just an old drop-off," said Selena when Allison pointed out the wooden board with the lettering on its side. "Why shouldn't there be a sign there. People might get killed if there wasn't."

Allison was ready to cry. She felt as if she had been unjustly slapped in the face. It was like giving someone a mink coat, or a diamond bracelet, or something just as special as that, and having the person say, "Oh, I have more of those than I can use."

"They're just woods," commented Selena a few minutes later, and flatly refused to walk through them with Allison. "What do I want to walk in any old woods for? There's plenty of woods right around our shack. I get a bellyful of woods every day in the week."

"You're mean, Selena," cried Allison. "You're just plain mean and hateful! This is a special, secret place. No one ever comes here but me, and I brought you up because I thought you were my special friend."

"Oh, don't be such a baby," said Selena crossly. "And what do you mean, no one comes here but you? Boys have been bringing girls up here ever since I can remember, at night, in cars."

"You're a liar!" shouted Allison.

"I am not," said Selena indignantly. "Ask anybody. They'll tell you."

"Well, it's just not true," said Allison. "What would anyone want to come up here at night for? You can't walk in the woods at night."

Selena shrugged. "Forget it, kid," she said, not unkindly. "Don't be mad at me. Come on, let's go downtown."

"That makes the hundredth time you've said that," said Allison angrily. "All *right*. We'll go downtown."

Constance MacKenzie did not wholly approve of Allison's friendship with the stepdaughter of Lucas Cross. Once or twice she had tried, halfheartedly, to put a stop to it, but after a few days of returning home from work to find Allison in tears, vowing that she was totally friendless now that Selena was being kept from her, Constance had relented. She had never been able to answer Allison's questions about Selena satisfactorily.

"I never said that I didn't like Selena," she would tell Allison defensively. "It's just—" and here she would always stop to search for just the right words.

"Just what, Mother?" Allison would prompt her.

Constance would have to shrug, unable to put her finger on what it was in Selena that disturbed her.

"With all the *nice* children in this town," she had said once, but was stopped by Allison's look, and her question.

"Why don't you think Selena is nice?"

"I didn't say that," said Constance, and then she had hunched her shoulders helplessly. "Never mind."

So the friendship between Allison and Selena had continued, full and satisfying, until this Saturday afternoon when each girl had

38

wanted a different something, and neither had been able to understand the other's need.

Together, they walked up one side of Elm Street and down the other, looking into the shop windows, but unable to play the game that had always amused them.

"Let's go to your mother's store," said Selena.

But Allison refused, feeling cheated at spending the lovely afternoon away from her favorite place.

"Go in yourself, if you want to go that bad," said Allison, knowing that Selena would not go into the Thrifty Corner without her.

In the end, they walked around all the counters in the five-and ten-cent store, fingering strands of false pearls, gazing longingly at the rows upon rows of cosmetics, and listening to the popular tunes that came from the music counter. They sat at the store's soda fountain and each ate a huge, gummy banana split, and Allison felt her good humor beginning to return.

"We'll go over to Mother's now, if you want," she offered.

"No, never mind. Let's walk to your house."

"No, really. I know you want to go to the shop. I don't mind. Truly, I don't."

"You don't have to go, just on account of me."

"But I *want* to, Selena. Really."

"All right, if you really want to go."

They wadded their paper napkins into small, round balls and dropped them into the empty sundae dishes, and things were suddenly all right between them again.

Constance MacKenzie waved to them from behind the hosiery counter as they came into the shop.

"There are some new party dresses," she called. "Over there on the second rack."

Selena looked, and as if in a trance, moved toward the shining garments that hung displayed on a movable rack. There seemed to be hundreds of dresses, each one prettier than the last. Selena stared, her fingers aching to touch the lovely fabrics.

Allison stood in front of the shop window and looked out at the traffic on Elm Street. It was always this way. She had to stand around for what seemed hours while Selena looked at every single article in the Thrifty Corner.

Constance finished with a customer and walked toward Selena with the intention of holding up one of the new dresses to show to Allison, but she was stopped short by the glazed expression on Selena's face. The child's parted lips and half-closed, dreaming

39

eyes wrung a sharp pity in Constance. She could understand a girl looking that way at the sight of a beautiful dress. The only time that Allison ever wore this expression was when she was reading.

"Here," said Constance to Selena loudly and suddenly, surprising herself. "This one is your size. Try it on if you like."

She held out a white, stiff-skirted dress, and her eyes began to fill foolishly at the look of gratitude on Selena's face.

"Do you *mean* it, Mrs. MacKenzie?" whispered Selena. "Can I really *touch* it?"

"Well, I hardly see how you can try it on without touching it," said Constance shortly, and hoped that she had managed to cover the shaking of her voice.

A few minutes later, when Selena emerged from the dressing room resplendent in the white dress, even Allison caught her breath.

"Oh, Selena!" she cried. "You look perfectly beautiful. You look just like a fairy princess!"

No, she doesn't, thought Constance, knowing suddenly what it was that bothered her about Selena Cross.

She looks like a woman, thought Constance. At thirteen, she has the look of a beautifully sensual, expensively kept woman.

Later that evening, Selena walked down the dirt road toward her home. She was still warm with the memory of Constance's pancakes which had dripped with butter and maple syrup, and of the coffee which had been served with real cream. She could still see, in her mind, the beautiful MacKenzie living room, with its big chairs and its wrought-iron magazine rack filled with copies of *The American Home* and *The Ladies' Home Journal*. In disgust, Selena thought of her friend Allison, who mooned over a photograph and whispered, "Isn't he handsome? That's my father."

"He's dead—and you're better off, kid," Selena had wanted to say. But she hadn't, because Mrs. MacKenzie might not like it, and Selena never wanted to do anything in the world to offend Allison's mother.

I'll get out, thought Selena as she stepped into the clearing in front of the Cross shack. Someday, I'll get out, and when I do, I'll always wear beautiful clothes and talk in a soft voice, just like Mrs. MacKenzie.

As Selena fell asleep, she was thinking of the way the fire in the MacKenzie fireplace had made shining, shimmering lights in Constance's hair. For Ted Carter, she had not a single thought

to spare, although in his bed Ted was picturing Selena's face
and the way she smiled at him when she said, "Well, then, walk
with us."

Darned if I wouldn't, thought Ted, turning over on his side,
if Miss Prissy Allison hadn't been with her. Ma's groceries could
have waited.

"Selena," he whispered her name aloud in his darkened room.
"Selena," he said, tasting the word on his tongue.

His heart lurched within him in an odd way that caused him to
feel a peculiar mixture of fear and anticipation, and something
else that was almost pain.

◆ 10 ◆

Dr. Matthew Swain was a tall, big-boned man with a head of
thick and wavy silver hair. The doctor's hair was his best feature,
and he was proud of it in an unobtrusive way. He kept it carefully brushed, and every morning he examined it closely to make
sure that it held no yellow streaks.

"A man's entitled to one vanity," he excused himself, and Isobel
Crosby, who kept house for the doctor, said that it was a good
thing that the old man was vain about something. He certainly
didn't care what the rest of himself looked like. His suits always
needed pressing, and he had a terrible habit of eating in the living
room. The doctor's coffee cups, strewn all over the house, were
Isobel's cross.

"It ain't a backbreakin' job to carry a half-empty cup into the
kitchen," she often complained. "It ain't gonna rupture you to lift
one little cup."

"If I never do anything worse than leave a coffee cup hanging
around, Isobel, you can count yourself lucky," replied the doctor.

"It ain't just the cups," said Isobel. "You let your clothes lay.
wherever they drop, you sprinkle the house with cigar ashes, and
your shoes always look like you just came from a long session in
somebody's barn."

"Count your blessings, Isobel," said the doctor. "Would you
rather keep house for some lecherous old devil? At least I haven't
always got a hand up your skirt. Maybe that's what ails you."

"And on top of it all," said Isobel, who had known the doctor for too many years to be shocked at anything he said, "you've got a dirty tongue and an evil mind."

"Oh, go starch some antimacassars," said the doctor crossly.

Everyone in Peyton Place liked Doc Swain. He had warm, blue eyes of the type which, to his eternal disgust, were termed "twinkling," and his kindness was legend in the town. Matthew Swain was one of a rapidly disappearing species, the small-town general practitioner. The word "specialist" was anathema to him.

"Yes, I'm a specialist," he had once roared at a famous ear, eye, nose and throat man. "I specialize in sick people. What do you do?"

At sixty, tho doctor still went out on calls day or night, summer and winter, and it was his habit to send birthday cards to every child he had ever delivered.

"You're nothing but a soggy sentimentalist at heart," Seth Buswell often teased. "Birthday cards, indeed!"

"Sentimental, hell," replied the doctor good-naturedly. "It just gives me a continuous feeling of accomplishment to stop every day and realize all the work I've done."

"Work, work, work," said Seth. "That's your favorite word. I think you hope to give me an inferiority complex by impressing my laziness on me all the time, You'll drop dead of a heart attack one of these days, from your goddamned work, work, work. Just like one of those handsome, silver-haired doctors in the movies."

"Crap," said the doctor. "Heart attacks are so commonplace. Give me a nice troublesome ulcer any day."

"On second thought," said Seth, "you'll die of a bashed in skull administered by one of those nurses you're always tickling over at your hospital."

The Peyton Place hospital was small, well equipped and Dr. Swain's pride and joy. He ran it efficiently and admired it with all the tenderness of a young lover, and the fact that it was often used by citizens of the surrounding towns in preference to other, larger hospitals was a source of unending satisfaction to him. The hospital belonged to the town, but everybody in Peyton Place referred to it as "Doc Swain's hospital," and the girls who used its small but excellent training school for nurses referred to themselves as "The Doc's girls."

Matthew Swain was a good and upright man, and a lover of life and humanity. If he had a fault, it was his careless, sometimes vitriolic tongue, but the town forgave him this for Matthew Swain was a good doctor, and if he spoke gruffly at times, he also always

42

spoke the truth. He had a sense of humor which was sometimes loud, oftentimes lewd, but never deliberately unkind, and for this, too, the town forgave him, for The Doc could laugh longest and loudest at himself. Everyone loved Dr. Swain, with the possible exception of Charles Partridge's wife Marion, and her only reason for disliking him was that the doctor refused to be impressed with the picture she had created of herself.

"It don't pay to puff yourself up in front of The Doc," said the town. "Surer than hell he'll have a pin to stick into you if you do!"

But Marion Partridge could not and would not believe this. She tried continually to make Matthew Swain see her as she was sure the rest of the town saw her, and because he would not, she often referred to him as "that impossible man."

Marion was a medium-sized woman. Seth Buswell, whenever he looked at her, reflected that everything about Marion Partridge was medium.

"*Rien de trop*," said Seth to himself and felt that these words described Marion perfectly, from her medium-brown hair and average figure to her mediocre mind.

She had been born Marion Saltmarsh, the daughter of an impecunious Baptist minister and his tired wife. She had one brother, John, who had decided early in life to follow in his father's religious footsteps and at the age of twenty one had been ordained as a minister. It was John's ambition to carry religion to "the savage peoples of the earth" and immediately after his ordination, he left America as a missionary. Marion, meanwhile, finished her schooling, graduating with average grades, and settled down to live in the parsonage with her parents, ready with them to offer succor to the poor and troubled, and happily rolling bandages for a local hospital every Wednesday afternoon.

In later years, Charles Partridge admitted to himself that he had met Marion by accident and married her in a moment of weakness. After passing his bar examinations, he had been taking a long summer vacation in the seaside town where the Reverend Saltmarsh lived with his family. Charles Partridge was a Congregationalist and had attended a Sunday service at the Reverend Saltmarsh's Baptist church more out of curiosity than from a desire for religious comfort, and there he had seen Marion singing in the choir. The girl had been standing in the front row of the group of singers, her face uplifted and shining with a look of ecstasy. Charles Partridge had caught his breath and believed that the girl looked like an angel. In this he was mistaken. It was neither rapture

43

nor exultation which shone from Marion. She had much of this same look whenever she lay in a tub of hot water, or whenever she ate something she particularly liked. Music affected Marion only sensually, lighting her medium face with a sudden pleasure and making it, for a few moments, extraordinary.

Charles Partridge, young and impressionable, and perhaps with his resistance lowered by the long years of study now behind him, began to court Marion Saltmarsh. In August, five weeks after he had seen her singing in the choir for the first time, they were married, and on the first of September the young couple returned to Charles's home in Peyton Place where he was to begin his career.

As he grew older, Partridge sometimes wondered if he would have married in such haste had he been able, during his years as a student, to afford to patronize the houses of ill repute so enthusiastically acclaimed by his classmates. He thought not.

Success had come easily to Charles Partridge, and as the years passed, he accumulated money and a house on Chestnut Street, and Marion became active in club and charity work. She liked her comfortable life, uncomplicated as it was either by children or lack of money. Guiltily, she often realized that she gloated whenever she compared her circumstances now against what they had been during her childhood, but her guilt was short lived and easily forgotten.

Marion liked things. She surrounded herself with all sorts of small bric-a-brac and odd pieces of furniture. It gave her a thrill of pleasure to open her linen closet and see the piles of extra sheets and towels stored there. The size, purpose or quality of an object was secondary to Marion, coming after her desire to acquire and possess.

Immediately after her marriage, Marion deserted the Baptists and joined the Congregational church, for the latter was considered to be the "best" church in Peyton Place. Marion would have very much liked to instigate some sort of committee, with herself as president, to pass on memberships for her church. She hated to belong to an organization, even a religious one, which allowed "undesirables" to become members, and she had many dark thoughts about persons whom she considered "inferior."

"That MacKenzie woman," she said to her husband. "Don't tell me a young widow like that is any better than she should be. Don't tell me she doesn't do a lot of running around that no one has heard about. Don't tell me she hasn't got her eye on every man in town."

"My dear," said Charles Partridge wearily, "I'd never attempt to tell you anything."

But when Marion said the same things to Matthew Swain the doctor would fix her with a straight look and roar, "What the hell do you mean by that, Marion?"

"Well, after all, Matt, a young widow like that, living alone in a house—"

"Hey, Charlie! Marion feels bad for Connie MacKenzie living all alone. Why don't you pack up and move over there for a while?"

"Oh, that Matt Swain is impossible, Charles. *Impossible.*"

"Now, Marion," replied Charles Partridge. "Matt is a fine man. He doesn't mean any harm. And he's a good doctor."

Shortly after Marion reached the age of forty, she developed symptoms which worried and frightened her, and she called Dr. Swain. He examined her thoroughly and told her she was as healthy as a horse.

"Listen, Marion, this is nothing to worry about. I can give you shots to keep you fairly comfortable, but beyond that I'm helpless. This is menopause, and there isn't much anyone can do."

"Menopause!" cried Marion. "Matt, you're out of your head. I'm a young woman."

"How old are you?"

"Thirty-six."

"You're a liar, Marion. You're over forty."

Marion went home and raged at her husband. She told him that friend or no friend, lifelong or not, Matthew Swain had stepped through her front door for the last time. Thereafter, she went to a doctor in White River who treated her for a delicate stomach condition.

"What the hell, Matt," said Seth Buswell, whenever he saw Marion cut the doctor dead on the street, "you didn't want to be beloved by everyone did you?"

"I wouldn't mind," said the doctor. "Would anyone? Would you?"

"No," replied Seth.

◆ **II** ◆

Indian summer lingered on in Peyton Place for exactly six days and then she was gone as suddenly as she had come. The bright leaves on the trees, beaten loose by cold wind and rain,

45

fell to the ground like tears wept for a remembered past. They lost their colors quickly on the sidewalks and roads. They lay wet and brown and dead, a depressing reminder that winter had come to stay.

Less and less frequently now, Allison walked up to Road's End. Whenever she did she wrapped her raincoat tightly about her and stood, shivering, unable now to see the town clearly from the end of the road. Everything was blurred by a thin, gray mist and the hills, no longer a hot, beautiful purple, loomed black against the horizon. The trees in her woods no longer lifted their arms to shout, "Hello, Allison. Hello!" They hung their tired heads and sighed, "Go home, Allison. Go home."

It was a sad time, thought Allison, a time of death and decay with everything waiting sorrowfully and subdued for the snows that would come to cover the exposed bones of a dead summer.

But it was not the season which weighed heaviest on Allison. She did not know what it was. She seemed to be filled with a restlessness, a vague unrest, which nothing was able to ease. She began to spend the hours after school in sitting before the fire in the living room, an open book in her hands, but sometimes she forgot to read the page before her eyes and sat idly gazing into the flames on the hearth. At other times, she devoured every word she read and was filled with an insatiable longing for more. She discovered a box of old books in the attic, among them two thin volumes of short stories by Guy de Maupassant. These she read over and over again, unable to understand many of them and weeping at others. She had no sympathy for "Miss Harriet," but her heart broke for the two old people who worked so long and so hard to buy another "Diamond Necklace." Allison's reading had no pattern, and she went from De Maupassant to James Hilton without a quiver. She read *Goodbye, Mr. Chips,* and wept in the darkness of her room for an hour while the last line of the story lingered in her mind: "I said goodbye to Chips the night before he died." Allison began to wonder about God and death.

Why was it that good people like Mr. Chips and the Little Match Girl and Allison's father died as indiscriminately as bad people? Was God really the way Reverend Fitzgerald pictured him for her every Sunday from the pulpit of the Congregational church? Was he really all good, all compassionate, loving everyone and truly listening to prayer?

"God hears every word," said the Reverend Fitzgerald. "Every prayer sent heavenward is heard."

46

But, wondered Allison, if God was so good and powerful, why was it that He sometimes seemed not to hear?

For this question, too, the Reverend Fitzgerald had an answer, and like all his answers it held the ring of truth at first, but as soon as Allison paused to think, another question would occur to her, and sometimes the minister's answers made no sense at all, but seemed empty and contradictory.

"He hears every single word," assured the Reverend Fitzgerald, but Allison asked silently, If He really hears, why is it that He often does not answer?

"Sometimes," said the minister, "The Almighty Father must refuse us. Like a loving father on earth, refusing a child for his own good, so must our Heavenly Father sometimes refuse us. But He always acts in our best interests."

Well, then, thought Allison, why pray at all? If God was going to do what He thought was best anyway, why bother to ask for anything one wanted? If you prayed, and God thought that what you asked should be granted, He would grant it. If you did not pray, and it was true that God always acted in one's best interests, you would receive whatever He wanted you to receive anyway. Prayer, thought Allison, was a dreadfully unfair, rather unsportsmanlike affair, with all the advantages on one side.

When she had been younger, she had prayed and prayed that her father might be returned to her, but nothing had come of that. It had seemed unreasonable to her then that a loving God who could perform miracles any time the urge struck Him should want to see a little girl go without a father. Now that she was twelve, this still seemed unreasonable, and unfair as well.

Allison looked up at the gray skies of October and wondered if it was possible that there was no God at all, just as there were no real fairy princesses, no magic elves.

She roamed the streets of the town with an air of searching, and it left her with a hollow feeling of loss when she pulled herself up short and asked herself what she was looking for. She dreamed vague, half-formed dreams that were easily broken, and every day she waited impatiently for tomorrow.

"I wish it would hurry and be June," she told her mother. "Then I'd be ready to graduate from grade school."

"Don't wish time away, Allison," said Constance. "It goes much too quickly as it is. In a little while, you'll look back on these times as the best years of your life."

But Allison did not believe her.

47

"No, don't hurry time, Allison," repeated Constance, and peered into the mirror on the living room wall, searching the corners of her eyes for small lines. "You'll be thirteen next month," she said, and wondered, Can it be possible? Thirteen? So soon? Fourteen, actually. I'd almost forgotten. "We'll have a nice little party for you," she said.

"Oh, *please*, Mother," protested Allison, "birthday parties are so *childish!*"

A few days later Allison said, "Perhaps a party *would* be nice after all," and Constance rolled her eyes heavenward, wondering if she had ever gone through this phase of never knowing what she wanted.

If I did, she thought sourly, it's no wonder that my poor mother died young!

To Allison, she said, "All right, dear. You go ahead and invite your little friends and I'll take care of everything else."

Allison almost screamed that she did not want a party after all, if her mother was going to refer to her classmates as "her little friends." Her mother did not seem to realize that Allison would be thirteen in two more weeks, and on the verge of entering something described in magazine articles as "adolescence." Allison pronounced this word, which she had read but never heard spoken, as "a-*dole*-icents," and to her it had all the mysterious connotations of hearing someone speak of "entering a nunnery."

Allison was not unaware of the physical changes in herself, nor did she fail to notice many of these same changes in others. Size, she had decided, was something that one was stuck with, no more alterable than the slant of one's cheekbones. Selena, she realized, had been different from younger girls for quite a while now, for she already wore a brassière all the time, while Allison was sure that she herself would have no need for such a garment for a long time. She locked herself in the bathroom and examined her figure critically. Her waist seemed slimmer, and she was definitely beginning to develop breasts in an unobtrusive way, but her legs were as long and skinny as ever.

Like a spider, she thought resentfully, and hurriedly put on her bathrobe.

Boys were different now, too, she had noticed. Rodney Harrington had a slight shadow above his upper lip and boasted that soon he would have to go to Clement's Barbershop every day to be shaved, just like his father. Allison shivered. She hated the idea of hair growing anywhere on her body. Selena already had hair under her arms which she shaved off once a month.

"I get it over with all at once," said Selena. "My period and my shave."

Allison nodded approvingly. "Good idea," she said sagely.

But as far as she was concerned, "periods" were something that happened to other girls. She decided that she would never tolerate such things in herself.

When Selena heard that, she laughed. "There's not going to be much you can do about it," she said. "You'll get it the same as everyone else."

But Allison did not believe her friend. She sent away to a company which advertised a free booklet entitled, *How to Tell Your Daughter*, offering to send it in a plain wrapper, and she read this carefully.

Phooey, she thought disdainfully when she had finished studying the pamphlet. I'll be the only woman in the whole world who won't, and I'll be written up in all the medical books.

She thought of "It" as a large black bat, with wings outspread, and when she woke up on the morning of her thirteenth birthday to discover that "It" was nothing of the kind, she was disappointed, disgusted and more than a little frightened.

But the reason she wept was that she was not, after all, going to be as unique as she had wanted to be.

◆ 12 ◆

Constance MacKenzie provided ice cream, cake, fruit punch and assorted hard candies for Allison's birthday party, and then retired to her room before an onslaught of thirty youngsters who entered her house at seven-thirty in the evening.

My God! she thought in horror, listening to thirty voices apparently all raised at once, and to the racket made by thirty pairs of feet all jouncing in unison on her living room floor to the accompaniment of something called "In the Mood" being played on a record by a man to whom Allison referred reverently as Glenn Miller.

My God! thought Constance, and there are still apparently sane people in this world who take up schoolteaching by choice!

She sent up a silent message of sympathy to Miss Elsie Thornton and all others like her who had to put up with many more than thirty children every day, five days a week.

My God! thought Constance, who seemed unable to stop calling on her Maker.

She picked up a book and tried determinedly to shut her mind to the noise that came from the living room. But at nine-thirty things became so quiet that Mr. Glenn Miller's music was clearly audible, and Constance began to wonder what the children were doing. She turned out her bedroom light and moved softly into the hall toward the living room.

Allison's guests were playing post office. For a moment, Constance felt her face stiffen with surprise.

At *this* age? she wondered. So *young*? I'd best go in and put a stop to this right now. I'll have every mother in town down on my neck if this ever gets out.

But she hesitated, with her hand on the door jamb and one foot on the threshold. Perhaps this was the regulation party game these days for thirteen- and fourteen-year-olds, and if she burst into the living room mightn't Allison, to quote her daughter, "Simply die of embarrassment"?

Constance stood outside the darkened living room and tried to remember at what age she had begun to participate in kissing games. She concluded that she had been at least sixteen. Could her shy, withdrawn little Allison actually be playing such games at thirteen?

For the first time since Allison's birth, Constance felt the finger of fear which is always ready to prod at the minds of women who have made what they considered to be "A Mistake."

A quick picture of her daughter Allison, lying in bed with a man, flashed through her mind, and Constance put a shaking hand against the wall to steady herself.

Oh, she'll get hurt! was the first thought that filled her.

Then: Oh, she'll get in trouble!

And finally, worst of all: SHE'LL GET HERSELF TALKED ABOUT!

After all I've done for her! thought Constance in a flush of angry self-pity. After all I've done for her, she acts like a little tramp right under my nose, letting some pimply-faced boy paw her and mush her. After the way I've slaved to give her a decent bringing up!

A frightened anger, which she did not realize was for a dead

50

Allison MacKenzie and a girl named Constance Standish, filled her and was directed at her daughter.

I'll fix her in a hurry, she thought, and took her hand away from the wall.

The voice which came to her then, before she could step over the threshold, filled her with such relief that she began to tremble. Allison was not playing the game; she was on the side lines, calling the numbers.

For a moment Constance could not move, and then, weak with vanishing apprehension, she almost giggled aloud.

The unkissed postmistress, she thought. I should be more careful. I almost made a fool of myself.

When she felt that she could walk, she returned silently to her bedroom. She turned the light back on, stretched out on her chaise and picked up the book she had dropped. Before she had read one sentence on the printed page, the fear came back.

It won't always be like this. Someday Allison won't be content with just calling the numbers. She will want to join in the game. Soon I am going to have to tell her how dangerous it is to be a girl. I'll have to warn her to be careful, now that she is thirteen. No, fourteen. I'll have to tell her that she is a year older than she thinks she is, and I'll have to tell her why, and I'll have to tell her about her father and that she really doesn't have any right to call herself MacKenzie.

These thoughts set up a hammering in her temples, and Constance put a knuckle between her teeth and bit down on it, hard.

Allison was always the postmistress at parties where kissing games were played. This was of her own choosing and, in fact, if she was voted down for this job, she refused to play the game at all, saying that it was time for her to leave anyway, and making her escape before anyone could protest. When Selena said that after all this was Allison's birthday, and it wasn't right for her to be postmistress at her own party, Allison said, "Well, I'm not going to stumble around in the dark letting any old boy kiss *me!* If I can't call the numbers, we won't play at all."

Selena shrugged. She didn't really care who called the numbers as long as she could play herself.

Mr. Glenn Miller's orchestra sobbed a ballad of love and moonlight and Allison said, "A letter for number ten."

Selena felt her way through the dark room and into the foyer. Rodney Harrington groped for her and when he touched her, he wrapped his arms around her and kissed her on the mouth. Then

51

he went back into the living room and Allison said, "A letter for number fifteen." Ted Carter went into the hall. He kissed Selena gently, holding her by the shoulders, but when she realized who her partner was, she pressed herself close to him and whispered, "*Really* kiss me, Ted."

"I did," Ted whispered back.

"No, silly, I mean like *this*," said Selena and pulled his head down.

When she released him, Ted was gasping, and he felt his ears redden in the dark. Selena laughed, deep in her throat, and Ted grabbed her roughly.

"D'you mean like *this?*" he asked, and kissed her so hard that he felt her teeth scrape against his.

"Hey!" yelled Rodney Harrington from the living room. "What's going on out there? Give somebody else a chance."

Everyone laughed when Selena came back into the living room.

"A letter for number four," called Allison, and the game went on.

At ten-thirty, two or three girls said that they had to be home by eleven o'clock, and someone snapped on the lights.

"Nobody gave Allison her thirteen spanks!" cried one girl, and everyone began to laugh and push toward Allison.

"That's right," they agreed. "Thirteen spanks and one to grow on."

"Time to take your medicine, Allison!"

"I'm too big to spank," said Allison. "So don't anybody dare try."

She was laughing with the others, but there was a threat behind her words.

"O.K.," said Rodney Harrington. "So she's too big to spank, kids. Lay off. She's big enough to kiss now."

Before Allison could run or dodge, he pulled her to him and pressed his mouth against hers. He held her so tightly that she could feel the buttons on his coat digging into her. His face was damp and he smelled of lavender soap and sweat, and he pressed her body in a curving arc against his, so that she thought that she could feel the moist heat of his skin through all his clothing.

"Oh!" gasped Allison, when he released her, her face scarlet. "Oh, how dare you!"

She rubbed the back of her hand vigorously against her mouth and kicked Rodney as hard as she could in the shins.

Rodney laughed. "Be careful," he warned, "or I'll give you one to grow on!"

"You're hateful, Rodney Harrington," said Allison, and then she burst into tears and ran out of the room.

Everyone smiled a little uncertainly, but they were all too used to Allison's swiftly changing moods to be actually uncomfortable.

"Come on, kids," said Selena. "The party's over."

She led the way to the dining room where Constance had provided a rack and clothes hangers. Everyone took his own coat and then drifted toward the front door.

"Good-by, Allison," they called up the staircase.

" 'Bye, Allison. Happy birthday. It was a swell party."

"Good-by, Allison. Thanks for asking me."

In her room Allison lay in the dark, feeling tears that were almost cool against her hot face.

"Hateful," she whispered. "Hateful, hateful, hateful!"

Her stomach quivered as she remembered Rodney's wet mouth and the heaviness of his soft, full lips.

"Hateful," she said aloud. "Hateful. He spoiled my whole party!"

♦ 13 ♦

On the Saturday afternoon following her birthday, Allison walked to Selena's house to meet her friend. She stood in front of the clearing, kicking disconsolately at the frozen ground, until finally the door of the Cross shack opened. It was Joey who came running toward her.

"Selena's in the house," said Joey. "She'll be out in just a minute. Come on in the sheep pen. We got new baby lambs."

Joey was a thin, wild-haired child dressed in faded dungarees and a ragged, short-sleeved shirt. His feet were bare on the cold November ground and, as usual, his nose was running. Joey was used to this affliction. He sniffed continually, and from time to time he wiped his dripping nose on his upper arm with the result that his nose was always red and chapped. It made Allison cold just to look at Joey. As she followed him into the sheep pen, she noticed that his bare heels were gray with a crust of dirt.

"Oh-h-h." The sound came from Allison in a whisper of joy as she bent to look at the small furry creatures which Joey displayed with pride. "Oh, how lovely they are, Joey. Are they yours?"

"Naw," said Joey. "They're Pa's, same as the big ones."

53

"Will he let you keep these for pets?"

"Naw. He's gonna raise 'em big like the others, then he can slaughter 'em and sell 'em for chops and legs of lamb and like that."

Allison's face went white. "Oh, that's terrible!" she said. "Don't you think that he'd let you keep these little ones if you asked him? Maybe you could raise them yourself and later you could sell the wool from them."

"Are you nuts?" asked Joey, not facetiously but in a serious tone, as if he really wanted to know. "Folks around here don't raise sheep for wool, they raise 'em for meat. Where do you suppose your Ma gets lamb chops, if it ain't from animals?"

Allison swallowed. She thought of the tender chops which Constance sometimes cooked and served from a platter decorated with parsley.

"Aren't you freezing, Joey?" she asked, to change the subject. She huddled herself down in her warm coat and dug her fingers into the soft lamb's wool.

"Naw. I'm used to it," said Joey, wiping his nose. "My feet's tough."

But just the same, he shivered and Allison saw the duck bumps on his thin arms. She had a sudden, embarrassing urge to take Joey and pull him close to her, to hide him under her coat and warm him with her body.

"What's Selena doing?" she asked, not looking at Joey.

"Making a pot of coffee for Pa, I guess. He just came in from the woods before you got here."

"Oh? Isn't your mother home?"

"Naw. Today's Saturday. She goes down to Harrington's to wax the floors on Saturday."

"Oh, yes. I'd forgotten," said Allison. "Well, I guess I'll go out front to wait for Selena."

"Come on out back," said Joey. "I'll show you my lizard."

"All right."

They walked out of the sheep pen and Joey led the way toward the rear of the house.

"I keep him in a box up on the window ledge," said Joey. "Here, stand up on this crate and you can see right into the box. I got holes punched in it so's he can breathe."

Allison stood up on the wooden crate which Joey upended and peered into the box that had holes punched in it. When she raised her eyes for a moment, she looked right into the Cross kitchen.

So *this* is what the inside of a shack looks like, thought Allison, fascinated. Her eyes took in the unmade cots and the sagging double bed and the dirty dishes which seemed to be strewn from one end of the room to the other. She saw a garbage can in one corner which had not been emptied for a long time, and on the floor next to it was an empty can that had once held tomatoes and one that had contained beans. Lucas was sitting at a table that was covered with a streaked oil cloth so old and filthy that the pattern in it was no longer discernible, and Selena was filling a coffeepot from a pail of water, with a long-handled dipper. Allison thought of the houses in town that Nellie Cross kept spotless, and she remembered the food she had eaten in various homes that had been cooked by Selena's mother.

"Reckon you're gettin' to be quite a gal, makin' coffee for your old pa," said Lucas.

Allison could hear every word through the thin walls as clearly as if she had been in the same room. She knew that she should get down from the packing crate and stop eavesdropping, but she was held still by something in Lucas' face, a sly and evil something that held her motionless, just as a horror movie holds a frightened child to his theater seat in spite of his fear.

Lucas Cross was a big man with a chest like a barrel and a disconcertingly square-shaped head. His lank hair lay in strings on his broad skull, and when he smiled his whole forehead moved grotesquely.

"Yep," said Lucas. "Quite a gal. How old're you now?"

"Fourteen, Pa," said Selena.

"Yep. Quite a gal."

"That's sure some lizard, ain't it?" asked Joey, happy that Allison was so fascinated with his pet.

"Yes," said Allison, and Joey smiled and bent to pick up a stone. He threw it toward the pine trees beyond the clearing, then bent to pick up another.

Lucas got up from the table and went to a shelf over the sink. Allison wondered what in the world the Crosses had a sink for, when they had neither running water nor sewerage. Lucas took a bottle from the shelf and held it to his lips while Allison watched. The brown liquid flowed in an unbroken stream down Lucas' throat, and he did not stop swallowing until the bottle was empty. Then he wiped his mouth with the back of his hand and tossed the bottle over his shoulder into a far corner of the shack.

"We got a trash can, Pa," said Selena disapprovingly. "There's no need to go throwing stuff all over the place."

"Well, well, well," said Lucas. "Miss High and Mighty herself! You gettin' fancy ideas from your little prune-faced friend Allison MacKenzie?"

"No, Pa," said Selena. "I just don't see that there's any call for throwing things on the floor when there's a trash can right beside you. It wouldn't do any harm to take that garbage out and bury it, either."

Lucas grabbed Selena's arm. "Listen, you," he snarled. "Don't you be tryin' to tell your pa what to do."

Selena stood very still and looked down at the hand on her arm. Her dark, gypsy eyes seemed to grow darker and to narrow slightly.

"Take your hand off me, Pa," she said at last, so softly that Allison could barely hear the words.

Lucas Cross slapped his stepdaughter a stunning blow on the side of the head. Selena staggered halfway across the room and fell heavily to the floor, while outside, Allison grabbed onto the window ledge to keep from falling off the crate on which she stood.

"Oh, Joey," she whispered frantically. "What shall we do?"

But Joey had run to the edge of the trees and was busily tossing pine cones at a squirrel.

Allison knew she should stop looking in the window, but she literally could not move. She had never seen a man strike anyone in her life, and she was held now by a terrible fear.

Selena got up from the floor, and the coffeepot which she had not dropped when she fell now flew across the room in a direct line with Lucas' head.

"Oh, no, no, Selena," whispered Allison. "He'll kill you," and she was puzzled that Selena did not look up at the window, for Allison thought she had screamed her words.

The coffeepot sailed past Lucas' head and crashed against the wall behind him.

"You little bitch," he shouted. "You goddamn little bitch. I'll teach you!"

He held Selena with one hand and slapped her face. Back and forth, back and forth went his big hand. Selena fought with all her strength. She kicked and tried to get close enough to Lucas to sink her teeth into him.

"You bastard!" she yelled.

"Reg'lar dirty-mouthed little bitch," said Lucas. "Just like your old lady. I'll teach you, same's I taught her! Don't do no good to be decent to you. If it wasn't for me you'da starved to death,

56

just like your old lady. I been decent to you just as if you was my own. Kept a roof over your head and food in your belly."

Back and forth, back and forth went his enormous hand, striking another blow with every word he spoke.

At last Selena managed to tear herself away from him. She drew back her fist and slammed it into Lucas' mouth as hard as she could, and the man yelped with rage. He wiped the trickle of blood from his chin and looked stupidly at the red stain on his fingers. He cursed unintelligibly, and his face was a terrible, congested purple. Allison waited hysterically for his next move.

"You goddamn' sonofabitch," roared Lucas, beside himself. "You goddamn whorin' little slut!"

He grabbed at Selena and when she wrenched away from his grasp, he was left holding the entire front of the girl's blouse. Selena backed away from Lucas, her breasts naked and heaving in the light of the room's unshaded electric bulb, her shoulders still covered ridiculously by the sleeves of the faded cotton blouse.

Why the ends of hers are *brown*, thought Allison foolishly. And she does not wear a brassière all the time, like she told me!

Lucas dropped his hands and stared at Selena. Slowly, he began to walk toward her while she, just as slowly, began to move backward. She kept moving until her buttocks hit the black sink, and she never took her eyes from Lucas' face.

"Yep," said Lucas, "you're gettin' to be quite a gal, honey."

Slowly, he raised his two grimy hands, and his forehead moved when he smiled his grotesque smile.

Selena's scream ripped the stillness with a sound like tearing fabric, and from behind Allison there came another scream. It was Joey, running frantically toward the door of the shack. He almost fell through the door, and still he screamed.

"Don't you dare put your hands on Selena! I'll kill you if you put your hands on Selena."

The little boy stood in front of his sister, and like a horse swishing his tail, Lucas Cross swept him away. The child lay still on the floor of the shack, and Lucas said, "Yep. Gettin' to be quite a gal, ain't you, honey."

Allison fell off the packing crate and lay on the cold ground. Her whole body was wet with perspiration and the world seemed to undulate over her and around her. She panted with the effort to fight off the blackness that threatened her from every side, but she had to give way to the nausea that fought its way out of her throat.

◆ 14 ◆

Now it was winter and the town lay frozen under a low, gray sky that held no visible sun. The children, clad in bright snow suits although there was still no snow, hurried on their way to school, eager now to reach the comfortable, steam-heated buildings that awaited them at the end of Maple Street. The wooden benches in front of the courthouse were deserted; the old men who had kept them filled all summer had long since moved into the chairs around the stove in Tuttle's Grocery Store. Everyone waited for the snows which had been threatening to arrive since before Thanksgiving, but the ground was still bare in this first week of January.

"The cold'd snap if we got some snow," said one of the old men in Tuttle's.

"Sure looks like we'd get some today."

"Nope. It's too cold to snow."

"That's foolishness," said Clayton Frazier. He lit his pipe and stared into the bowl until he was satisfied with its glow. "Snow's in Siberia all the time, and the thermometer falls to sixty below over there. 'Tain't never too cold to snow."

"That don't make no difference. This ain't Siberia. It's too cold to snow in Peyton Place."

"No, 'tain't," said Clayton Frazier.

"Them fellers still down in the cellar?" asked the man who was so sure that it would not snow that he declined to discuss the matter further with Clayton Frazier.

This was the big topic of conversation in Peyton Place and had been since before Christmas. It had become so familiar that there was no longer any need for anyone to ask, "What fellers?" or "What cellar?"

On the first of December, Kenny Stearns, Lucas Cross and five other men had disappeared into Kenny's cellar where Kenny stored the twelve barrels of cider which he had made early in the fall. They had been armed with several cases of beer and as many bottles of liquor as they could carry, and they had remained in the cellar ever since. The men had fastened a strong, double bolt attachment to the inside of the door and so far the efforts of any outsider to penetrate this barricade had been futile.

"I seen one of the school kids headed over that way yesterday with a bagful of groceries," said one of the old men, putting his feet up on the warm stove in Tuttle's. "Ast 'im what he was doin', and he told me Kenny'd sent 'im for food."

"How'd the kid get into the cellar?"

"Didn't. Told me Kenny handed the money out through the cellar window and took in the groceries the same way."

"The kid see anything?"

"Nope. Said Kenny's got this black curtain fastened to the inside of the window so's nobody can see in, and he said Kenny no more than opened the window a slit to pass out the money and take in the stuff."

"What do you suppose made them fellers go down there and stay all this time?"

"Dunno. There's some say that Kenny promised the next time he caught Ginny runnin' out he was gonna go on a drunk like nobody ever seen. Reckon this is it."

"Reckon so. Them fellers been down in that cellar goin' on six weeks now."

"Wonder if they run out of booze yet. Twelve barrels of hard cider don't go too damn far. Not with seven of 'em drinkin'."

"Dunno. Somebody said they seen Lucas over to White River one night, late. Drunk as a lord he was, with a beard a foot long. Mebbe he sneaks out at night and goes over to White River to get more drink."

"Six weeks. Jesus! I'll bet a nickel they don't even have any beer left, let alone hard stuff."

"Can't understand why Buck McCracken don't put a stop to it, though."

"Reckon the sheriff's ashamed, that's why. His own brother is down in the cellar with Kenny and them."

"Wish I could be a fly on the wall down there, by God. Must be goin's on in that cellar that'd make a man's blood run cold."

"You'd think the cold would freeze 'em out."

"Naw. Ginny told me Kenny's got an old Franklin stove down there, and he'd got in his cord wood long before him and the fellers went down to stay. Ginny said she had to move out because she couldn't get down to get wood for the stoves up in the house."

The men laughed. "Reckon Ginny don't need no wood fire to keep *her* warm!"

"Wonder what Ginny's doin' for company these cold nights. With all her boy friends down in that cellar, she must be gettin' a trifle lonesome."

"Not Ginny Stearns," said Clayton Frazier. "Not by a long shot."

Several men snickered. "How do you know, Clayton? You been takin' up where the others left off?"

Before Clayton could answer, a group of school children came trooping into the store and the men ceased talking. The youngsters crowded around Tuttle's penny candy counter, and the men around the stove smoked silently, waiting. When the children had spent their pennies and one lone boy had bought a loaf of bread, the men rustled themselves and prepared to talk again.

"Wa'nt that the Page kid? The one that bought the bread?"

"Yep. Never seen a kid with such a pinched-lookin' face. Don't know what it is exactly. He's better dressed than most kids and his mother's comfortably fixed. Yet, that kid has the look of a starvin' orphan."

"It's his age," said Clayton Frazier. "Growin' pains."

"Mebbe. He's growed fast in the last year. Could be that's what makes him so pale lookin'."

"Nope," disagreed Clayton, "that ain't it. He's just got one of them dead fish skins, like his mother. His father wa'nt ever too ruddy himself."

"Poor old Oakleigh Page. Reckon he's better off in his grave than he was alive with all them wimmin fightin' over him all the time."

"Yep," the men agreed. " 'Twa'nt no life for a man."

"Oh, I dunno," said Clayton Frazier. "Seems to me like Oakleigh Page ast for all his troubles."

"Ain't nobody asks for trouble."

"Oakleigh did," said Clayton.

The argument began. Oakleigh Page was forgotten once his name had served to start the words flying. The men in Tuttle's began to enumerate the people in town who had—or had not— asked for their troubles. Clayton Frazier's old eyes gleamed. This was the part of each day that he lived for; when his disagreeableness finally provoked a lively discussion. The old man tilted his chair back and balanced himself on its two rear legs. He relit his pipe and wished fleetingly that Doc Swain had more time to hang around. A man didn't have to work hardly at all to get The Doc going, while it sometimes took a considerable while to get the men in Tuttle's riled up.

60

"Don't make no difference what none of you say," said Clayton. "There's folks that just plain beg for trouble. Like Oakleigh Page."

◆ 15 ◆

Little Norman Page hurried down Elm Street and turned into Depot Street. When he passed the house on the corner of Depot and Elm, he kept his eyes on the ground. In that house lived his two half sisters Caroline and Charlotte Page, and Norman's mother had told him that these two women were evil, and to be avoided like mad dogs. It had always puzzled Norman that he should have two such old ladies for sisters, even half sisters. They were really old, as old as his mother.

The Page Girls, as the town called them, were well over forty, both big boned with thick, white skins and white hair and both unmarried. As Norman walked past the house, a curtain in the front room window quivered, but neither a hand nor a figure was to be seen.

"There goes Evelyn's boy," said Caroline Page to her sister.

Charlotte came to the window and saw Norman hurrying down the street.

"Little bastard," she said viciously.

"No," sighed Caroline. "And that's the pity of it all. Better if he were a bastard than what he is."

"He'll always be a bastard as far as I'm concerned," said Charlotte. "The bastard son of a whoring woman."

The two sisters bit off these words as crisply as if they had been chewing celery, and the fact that these same words in print would have been an occasion for book banning and of shocked consultation with the church did not bother them at all, for they had the excuse of righteous indignation on their side.

Caroline dropped the curtain as Norman moved out of sight.

"You'd think that Evelyn would have had the decency to move out of town after Father left her," she said.

"Humph," said Charlotte. "Show me the whore who knows what decency means."

Little Norman Page did not slow his steps or sigh with relief when he had passed the house of his two half sisters. He still had to go by the house of Miss Hester Goodale before he could reach the sanctuary of his own home, and he dreaded Miss Hester every bit as much as he feared the Page girls. Whenever he encountered his half sisters on the street, they merely fixed him with dead looks, as if he were not there at all, but Miss Hester's coal-black eyes seemed to bore right through him, looking right down into his soul and seeing all the sins hidden there. Norman hurried now because it was Friday afternoon and almost four o'clock, and at exactly four on Fridays Miss Hester came out of her house and walked toward town. Although Norman was on the opposite side of the street from the one on which Miss Hester would walk, he was nonetheless afraid, for Miss Hester's eyes, he knew, could see for miles, around corners and everything. She could look right into him as clearly from across the street as she could have if he stood directly in front of her. Norman would have run except that if he arrived home flushed and panting his mother would think he was sick again and put him to bed. She might even give him an enema, and while Norman always got a bittersweet sort of pleasure from that, he had to stay in bed afterward. Today he decided that getting the enema was not worth the hours alone that were sure to follow, so he forced himself to walk. Suddenly he saw a figure ahead of him, and recognizing it as Allison Mac-Kenzie he began to shout.

"Allison! Hey, Allison. Wait for me!"

Allison turned and waited.

"Hi, Norman," she said when he reached her side. "Are you on your way home?"

"Yes," said Norman. "But what are you doing over here? This isn't the way to your house."

"I was just taking a walk," said Allison.

"Well, let me walk with you," said Norman. "I hate to walk alone."

"Why?" asked Allison. "There's nothing to be afraid of." She looked hard at the boy beside her. "You're always afraid of something, Norman," she said jeeringly.

Norman was a slight child, built on delicate lines. He had a finely chiseled mouth which trembled easily, and enormous brown eyes which were filled with tears more often than not. Norman's eyes were fringed with long, dark lashes. Just like a girl's, thought Allison. She could see the lines of blue veins plainly beneath the thin skin on his temples. Norman was very good looking, thought Allison, but not in the way that people thought of as handsome.

He was pretty the way a girl is pretty, and his voice, too, was like a girl's, soft and high. The boys at school called Norman "sissy," a name with which the boy found no quarrel. He was timid and admitted it, easily frightened and knew it, and he wept at nothing and never tried to stop himself.

"I'll bet he still pees the bed," Rodney Harrington had been heard to say. "That is, if he's got a dink to pee with."

"There is too something to be afraid of," said Norman to Allison. "There's Miss Hester Goodale to be afraid of, that's what."

Allison laughed. "Miss Hester won't hurt you."

"She might," quivered Norman. "She's loony, you know. I've heard plenty of folks say so. You never can tell what a loony person will do."

The two of them were now standing directly opposite the Goodale house.

"It *is* sort of sinister looking," said Allison musingly, letting her imagination take hold.

Norman, who had never been afraid of the Goodale house before, now felt his fear spark on the edge of Allison's words. He was no longer looking at a rather small and run down Cape Cod, but at a closed-looking house whose windows stared back at him like half-lidded eyes. Norman began to tremble.

"Yes," repeated Allison, "it has a *definite* sinister look."

"Let's run," suggested Norman, forgetting his mother, the enema, everything, for Miss Hester's house looked suddenly to him as if it were about to sprout arms, ready to engulf children and sweep them through the front door of the brown shingled cottage.

Allison pretended not to hear him. "What does she do in there all day, all by herself?"

"How do I know?" asked Norman. "Cleans house and cooks and takes care of her cat, I suppose. Let's run, Allison."

"Not if she's loony," said Allison. "She wouldn't be doing plain, everyday things like that if she's loony. Maybe she stands over her stove cutting up snakes and frogs into a big black kettle."

"What for?" asked Norman in a shaking voice.

"To make witch's brew, silly," said Allison crossly. "Witch's brew," she repeated in a weird tone, "to put curses and enchantments on people."

"That's foolish," said Norman, striving to control his voice.

"How do you know?" demanded Allison. "Did you ever ask anybody?"

"Of course not. What a question to ask!"

63

"Don't you visit Mr. and Mrs. Card next door to Miss Hester's a lot? I thought you said Mrs. Card was going to give you a kitten when her cat has some."

"I do and she is," said Norman. "But I'd certainly never ask Mrs. Card what Miss Hester does. Mrs. Card's not nosy like some people I know. Besides, how would she be able to see anything? That big hedge between the two houses would keep everybody from seeing into Miss Hester's house."

"Maybe she *hears* things," said Allison in a whisper. "Witches chant something when they stir up a brew. Let's go visit Mrs. Card and ask her if she ever hears anything spooky coming from Miss Hester's."

"Here she comes!" exclaimed Norman and tried to hide himself behind Allison.

Miss Hester Goodale came out of her front door, turned carefully to make sure that it was locked behind her, and walked out her front gate. She wore a black coat and hat of a style fashionable fifty years earlier, and she led a huge tomcat along on a rope leash. The cat walked sedately, neither twisting nor turning in any effort to escape the length of clothesline which was tied on one end to a collar around his neck, and wound several times around Miss Hester's hand at the other end.

"What's the matter with you, Norman?" asked Allison impatiently as soon as Miss Hester was out of sight. "She's just a harmless old woman."

"She's not either. She's loony. I even heard Jared Clarke say so. He told my mother."

"Phooey," said Allison disdainfully. "If I lived on this street like you, I'd sneak around and find out what Miss Hester does when she's alone. That's the real way to find out if people are loony, or witches, or something like that."

"I'd be scared," admitted Norman without hesitation. "I'd be scareder to do that than I would be to go up to Samuel Peyton's castle."

"Well, I wouldn't. There's nothing spooky about Miss Hester Goodale. The castle's full of spooks, though. It's haunted."

"At least there's nobody loony living in the castle."

"Not any more," said Allison.

They had arrived at Norman's house and were standing on the sidewalk in front of it when Evelyn Page came to the front door.

"For Heaven's sake, Norman," called Mrs. Page. "Don't stand out there in the cold. Do you want to get sick? Come in the house this minute! Oh, hello Allison, dear. Would you like to come in and have a hot chocolate with Norman?"

"No, thank you, Mrs. Page. I have to get home."

Allison walked toward the front door of the house with Norman. "Mrs. Page, is Miss Hester Goodale really crazy?" she asked.

Evelyn Page folded her lips together. "There's some who say so," she said. "Come in the house, Norman."

Allison walked down Depot Street the same way she and Norman had come. Now that she was alone, she walked on the same side of the street as the Goodale house, and she stopped directly in front of the gate to look at the small place.

Yes, she thought, it does have a *definite* sinister look. If Mr. Edgar Allan Poe were alive, I'll bet he could make up a swell story about Miss Hester and her house.

She began to walk again, but she had not moved more than a few steps when a brilliant daring thought stopped her in the middle of the sidewalk.

I could, she thought exultantly. *I could write a story about Miss Hester and her house!*

The idea sent cold shivers of excitement crawling up and down her back, and in the next second she felt hot all over.

I could. I'll bet I could write a story every bit as good as Mr. Edgar Allan Poe ever did. I could make up a real spooky story just like "The Fall of the House of Usher." I could have Miss Hester be a witch!

Allison ran all the way home and by the time she reached there the first lines of her story were already framed in her mind.

"There is this house on Depot Street in Peyton Place," she would write. "It is a brown shingled Cape Cod house, and it looks out of place on that street because it sits right next to a lovely little white and green Cape Cod owned by some people named Mr. and Mrs. Card. Mr. Card is big and handsome and does not come from around here, but from Boston or somewhere like that. Now he owns the print shop downtown. Miss Hester lives all alone in her brown house with her cat, Tom, and she is as loony as they come."

Allison wrote these words that same night. She locked herself in her bedroom and set them down in a notebook on white, blue-lined paper, and when they were written she sat and gazed at them for a long time. She could not think of anything else to say. A new respect for Mr. Edgar Allan Poe and for everyone else who had ever written began to take form within her.

Maybe being a writer isn't so easy after all, she thought. Perhaps I shall have to work very hard at it.

She picked up her pencil and made big, impatient x's through the words she had written, then she turned to a fresh page in her notebook. The blank white sheet stared back at her, and Allison began to chew at her left thumbnail.

I can't write about Miss Hester because I don't know her, thought Allison. I'll have to make up a story about somebody I know about.

She did not know it then, but she had just taken the first step in her career.

♦ 16 ♦

Jared Clarke could have told Allison all about Miss Hester Goodale for he had cause to remember her well. Miss Hester had been living in Peyton Place when Jared was born, but it was not until he was grown, prosperous and on the board of selectmen that he had encountered her face to face. Miss Hester represented Jared's first big failure, and he resented her bitterly. When the subject of Miss Hester arose, Jared always told the story of his one visit to her home, and he told it, of course, to his own advantage, but he never could rid himself of the feeling that when people laughed they laughed at him, not with him.

He had gone to Miss Hester's house with Ben Davis and George Caswell, his fellow selectmen, to speak to her about town sewerage. He had knocked at her front door and then stepped back to wait nervously, twisting his doffed hat in his hand until she came to the door.

"We came to talk about the pipes," said Jared to Miss Hester after the preliminary greetings had been exchanged.

"Come in, gentlemen," she said.

It had really given Jared quite a turn, he said later, to walk into Miss Hester's front parlor. The place was as neat as a pin with its horsehair furniture and unfaded rug. There was an air of waiting about the room, as if a welcome guest were expected at any moment, and Jared found himself remembering that once Miss Hester had had a lover.

Of course, he had been only a little shaver back then, but he could remember folks talking about it. Miss Hester's young man used to drive up to the Goodales' front door in a shiny victoria on Sunday afternoons.

"A nice young man," Jared's mother had said. "It's time Hester thought about getting married. She's not getting any younger."

"Young or not," said Jared's father, "She's still a damned fine-looking woman."

"She's the kind that thins out to gauntness after a while," said Jared's mother, ignoring her husband. "She'll have to watch herself before too many more years."

The whole town had waited for Hester Goodale to marry. When her young man had been calling on her for over six months Jared's father said he could not understand what was holding him up.

"He's comfortable," said Jared's father, using the town idiom which described anyone who had a steady job and was free of debt. "And Hester is out of mourning. It's been a year and a half since her mother died."

"Oh, she's probably waiting to make sure," said Jared's mother. "After all, he may be a nice young man, but he doesn't come from around here, and one can never be too careful where marriage is concerned. I'll bet she marries him before June."

But one Sunday afternoon it was Mr. Goodale, Hester's father, who answered the young man's knock at the door. They exchanged only a few words and no one had ever found out what was said, and then Mr. Goodale had closed the door in the young man's face. Hester's friend climbed into his victoria and drove away. The next day he quit his job in Jared's father's feed and grain store and left Peyton Place. No one ever saw him again.

A few months later, Mr. Goodale died and Miss Hester was left alone in the cottage on Depot Street. After that the town never saw much of her. She kept to herself, living carefully on the small amount of money her father had left. Eventually she got herself a cat, and in a few years she was well on her way to becoming a town legend.

"Miss Hester has a broken heart," said the town. "She is only waiting to die."

The prediction that Jared's mother had made came true. Miss Hester's slenderness thinned to gauntness. Her skin seemed hardly to cover her angular bones, and her eyes gleamed like coal set into a sheet of white paper. Her hands were no longer slim fingered, but clawlike, and even her hair thinned to a sparseness that barely covered her bony skull.

Jared Clarke had looked around Miss Hester's front parlor and then he looked at Miss Hester, and he wondered if it could be possible that there had been a time when a man had loved this woman. He shifted his feet awkwardly and cleared his throat. Miss Hester did not ask her callers to sit down.

"Well, Jared?" she asked.

"It's about the pipes, Miss Hester," said Jared. "You must know that it has been quite a fight to get everyone to agree on town sewerage. But that's all over now. We voted in the pipes at the last town meeting."

"What has all this to do with me?" asked Miss Hester.

"Well, we are going to run the mains under the streets," said Jared, "and the town's going to pay for that while everybody has agreed to pay for the sections of pipe used in front of his own house."

"Did you not," said Miss Hester, "just finish saying that the town was going to pay?"

Jared smiled patiently. "The town is going to pay for *laying* the pipe. Labor costs."

"Am I to understand, Jared," asked Miss Hester, "that you are asking me to pay for pipes to be laid under a public street?"

Jared searched his mind for a tactful answer. He had begun to sweat and was actively hating this woman for making his job more difficult than it was.

"It would benefit you as well as the rest of the town, Miss Hester," he said. "From the street lines, you would be able to run pipes into your house."

"What do I want with pipes in this house?" demanded Miss Hester.

Jared Clarke's face flushed with the effort of attempting to find a gentlemanly way to tell Miss Hester that it simply would not do for her to have the only outside privy on Depot Street.

"But Miss Hester—" he began and stopped, unable to go on.

"Yes, Jared?" Miss Hester's voice asked the question, but her tone gave him no encouragement.

"Well, it's this way—" began Jared again. "I mean to say— Well, it's like this—"

George Caswell, who was not hindered by feelings of delicacy, finished Jared's sentence for him.

"It's like this, Hester," said Caswell. "We don't want no more outhouses in town. They're all right for the folks in the shacks, but outhouses just don't look right in the middle of town."

68

There was an embarrassing moment when no one spoke, and then Miss Hester said, "Good day, gentlemen," and led the way to her front door.

"But Miss Hester," said Jared, and got no further.

"Good afternoon, Jared," said Miss Hester and closed the door firmly.

"Great closers of doors in folk's faces, the Goodales," said Ben Davis, and he and George Caswell began to laugh.

But Jared Clarke did not laugh. He was furious. Later, he had been forced to stand up at a meeting of the newly formed Sanitation Committee and admit that he had failed to convince Miss Hester of the advisability of helping to pay for the town's new sewerage system.

"Well, she don't rightly have to anyway," said one of the committee members. "We ain't got no zonin' laws that say anybody's got to do anythin'."

"Maybe she don't have the money," volunteered another member.

"She's got the money all right," said Dexter Humphrey, who was president of the bank.

"She's loony," cried Jared angrily. "That's all there is to it. Looney as hell!"

"Reckon property values will go down on Depot Street now," said Humphrey sadly. "What with Miss Hester's outhouse sittin' right there in her back yard as plain as the nose on your face. Too bad you couldn't talk her into doin' different, Jared."

"I did all I could," shouted Jared. "She's just plain crazy. Crazy as a loon."

"The house next door to Hester's is for sale," said Humphrey. "Nobody'll ever buy it now."

"Too bad," said one of the committee members. "You should have talked louder, Jared."

"Oh, for Christ's sake," said Jared bitterly.

The new sewerage pipes were laid on Depot Street, the town absorbing the cost of those passing in front of the Goodale house, and eventually someone did buy the house next door to Miss Hester.

When the man who had been the town printer died, his family sold his business to a young man named Albert Card, a printer from Boston, and Mr. and Mrs. Card bought the house on Depot Street next door to Hester Goodale's.

"Nice young couple," said Peyton Place about the Cards.

"Yep. A real go-getter, that young feller."

The young Cards joined the Congregational church and the Pine Hill Grange.

"Real nice young man, Card," said Jared Clarke. "Takes an interest. He and his wife are just pitching right in. We need more like them in this town. Real assets to the community."

"Say, listen," said Albert Card one day shortly after he had bought his house. "Who's the old crone lives next door to me?"

"That," said Jared Clarke, pursing his lips, "is Miss Hester Goodale. She's loony as they come."

"Are you telling me? I don't see much of her, that hedge between her place and ours screens the property pretty well, but I hear her roaming around in her back yard. Well, not her exactly, but I hear that goddamn cat of hers. I can hear him meowing over there fit to raise the dead sometimes. She's loony all right."

"No doubt you also hear Miss Hester herself," said Jared sourly, "as she goes back and forth to her outhouse."

"Well, I hear her cat anyway."

"Well, that tom is never anywhere that Miss Hester isn't. Oh, she's loony all right. Never goes out of that house except to go downtown for groceries once a week, and nobody ever goes to visit her, either. I'll bet no one's been inside her house since the time I went there with Ben and George to tell her about the pipes. Now there's a story for you. It was quite a while back, before we had town sewerage, and I was elected to go see Miss Hester about paying for the pipes to run in front of her house. Well I walked up on her front porch, bold as brass, and knocked on her door. 'Look here, Hester,' I said, 'there's no two ways about it, but you're going to have to pay for your share of the pipes. Come on now, let's have no nonsense. Just write me out a check and I'll be on my way.' Well, she began to cry and scream and carry on something terrible, so I told Ben and George right then that she was crazy, and the best thing for us to do was to just leave the poor old soul alone."

Later, after Albert Card had told this story to his wife Mary, she said, "This certainly must be quite a town for characters, what with the story about Samuel Peyton and now this one about Miss Hester Goodale."

Norman Page sat at the kitchen table while his mother poured out hot chocolate for him.

"Did you have a good day, dear?" she asked.

"Sure," said Norman absently. He was thinking of Allison and Miss Hester.

"Tell me about it, dear."

"Nothing to tell. It was just like any other day. We're learning a little bit about algebra now. Miss Thornton says we'll need it when we get to high school."

"Oh? Do you enjoy Miss Thornton, dear?"

"She's all right. She's not crabby like some teachers."

"How come you were walking with Allison MacKenzie, Norman?"

"She just happened to be on this street and she walked along with me."

"But what was she doing on Depot Street? She lives on Beech."

This was the part of every day that Norman hated. Every afternoon he had to sit and drink hot chocolate, or milk, or fruit juice, which he did not want most of the time, while his mother quizzed him about the children with whom he had associated that day.

"I don't know what Allison was doing here," he said crossly. "She just happened to be on Depot Street when I came along."

"Do you like Allison, dear?" asked Mrs. Page.

"She's all right."

"Then you *do* like her!"

"I didn't say that."

"Yes, you did."

"I did not. I just said I thought she was all right."

"It's the same thing. Do you like her as much as you like Miss Thornton?"

"I never said I like Miss Thornton, either!"

"Oh, *Norman!* Your *voice!*"

Mrs. Page sank down into her rocking chair and began to cry, and Norman, stricken with shame and guilt, ran to her.

"Oh, Mother. I didn't mean it. Truly, I didn't. I'm so sorry."

"It's all right, dear. You can't help it. It is your father's blood in your veins."

"It is not! It is not, either!"

"Yes, dear. Yes, it is. You are a great deal like your father and like Caroline and Charlotte."

"I am not."

Norman's eyes filled with tears, and he could not control his throat muscles enough to keep himself from sobbing.

"I am not like them," he cried.

"Yes you are, dear. Yes, you are. Ah, well, maybe you'll be happier when I'm dead and you can go to live with your half sisters."

"Don't talk like that, Mother. You're not going to die!"

"Yes, I am, Norman. Someday soon I'll be dead, and you'll have to go to live with Caroline and Charlotte. Oh, my darling son, even in Heaven I shall weep to see you in the clutches of those two dreadfully evil, wicked women."

"No! Oh, no, no, no!"

"Oh, yes, dear. I'll be dead soon, and perhaps you'll be better off."

"You're *not* going to die. You are not. What would I do if you did?"

"Oh, you'd have Caroline and Charlotte, and Miss Thornton and little Allison MacKenzie. You'd get along without your mother."

Norman collapsed on the floor at his mother's feet. He sobbed hysterically and tugged at her skirt with both his hands, but she would not look down at him.

"No, I wouldn't get along! I'd die myself. I love only you, Mother. I don't love anybody else."

"Are you sure, Norman? There's nobody else you love?"

"No, no, no. There is no one else, Mother. Just you."

"Don't you like Miss Thornton and little Allison, dear?"

"No. No, I hate them! I hate everybody in the whole world except you."

"Do you love Mother, Norman?"

Norman's sobs were dry and painful now, and he hiccuped wretchedly.

"Oh, yes, Mother. I love only you. I love you better than God, even. Say you're not going to leave me."

For a long time Mrs. Page stroked her son's bowed head which rested now on her knees.

"I'll never leave you, Norman," she said at last. "Never. Of course I am not going to die."

◆ 18 ◆

Kenny Stearns raised his head and looked carefully around him. From where he was lying on his cellar floor, he could vaguely discern other shapes lying on the same floor, and he wondered who these people could be.

"Seems to be a slew of 'em clutterin' up this cellar," said Kenny aloud.

"Who're you?" he asked and prodded at one sleeping body with an inaccurately aimed toe. "Who're you?"

Lucas Cross mumbled and turned over on his side. "Go to hell," he said.

"Whadya mean, tellin' me to go to hell in my own cellar?" demanded Kenny. "It is my cellar, ain't it?"

"Go to hell," said Lucas.

Kenny Stearns raised himself to his feet by sliding his back up against the cement wall behind him. At last he was standing, propped against the cold stone.

"Ain't no man tells Kenny Stearns to go to hell in his own cellar," he said truculently.

Two other bodies stirred on the cellar floor and Kenny regarded them calmly.

"More sonsofbitches to tell a man to go to hell in his own cellar," he said.

He made a motion in the direction of one of the men who had just moved.

"Here, you," shouted Kenny. "What're you doin' in my cellar?"

Henry McCracken almost jumped to his feet, so startled was he by Kenny's official-sounding voice. Henry had been dreaming, and in his dream he had heard the voice of the sheriff, his brother Buck, who stood over him ready, as usual, to yell at him about something. Henry focused his gaze on Kenny.

"Jeez, you just give me a helluva turn, Kenny," he said reproachfully. "Thought for a minute you was old Buck standin' there."

Kenny sneered. "Well, I guess not!" he said indignantly. "There ain't no sheriff that's gonna be tellin' my friends what to do in my cellar."

73

"Atta boy, Kenny," said Henry yawning. "Let's you and me get us a little drink and then go back to sleep."

"You're my friend, Henry McCracken," said Kenny, "my one and only true friend."

He looked around him sadly. "I ain't got one other friend in this whole cellar, you know that, Henry? Not one."

Kenny indicated the sleeping Lucas with a jerk of his thumb.

"See him?" he asked. "See that drunken bum? Told me to go to hell not two minutes ago, right here in my own cellar. How do you like that?"

"Terrible," replied Henry, nodding his head in woeful agreement. "Well, that's the way things are in this world. You get the idea that you got a friend, and then he tells you to go to hell. Awful. Wonder if Lucas ever got rid of all them bugs that was botherin' him."

"Dunno," said Kenny. "Seems we'd see some, if they was still here. Gray, they was, and green, and crawlin' all over the walls, so Lucas said."

"He musta got rid of 'em," said Henry, looking fearfully at the cement walls. "Don't see none now."

"Good thing," said Kenny sanctimoniously. "I don't hold with insects. Never did. I don't want no goddamn insects crawlin' around in my cellar."

"I thought you was gonna get a bottle," said Henry.

"Yep. I'll find one. Must be one around here somewheres."

Kenny began to gaze around the cellar floor. His eyes shifted slowly from one spot to another, but they did not fall upon anything that could be mistaken for a full bottle of liquor. At last, with a supreme effort, he swayed away from the wall which had been holding him up and began to shuffle groggily around the cellar. He picked up one bottle after another and stared mournfully into the empty depths of each one.

"Them bastards drunk it all up," he told Henry. "That's what they done."

He moved slowly to the Franklin stove and peered down into its blackness, and then, sighing mightily, he reached down into it and rummaged around thoroughly.

"'Tain't no use, Henry," he said, almost in tears. "Them bastards drunk it all up."

Suddenly Henry gave a glad cry. "Kenny! Look at all them barrels! Look at 'em, lined up against that wall over there, just as pretty as a line of girls at a county fair."

Kenny turned to look at his twelve cider barrels. A remembered perfume came to him, of apples and wood smoke, and he could see again the streams of juice pouring into his barrels.

"Christ, yes," he said, moving almost quickly toward the cider barrels. "I worked like a nigger fillin' the goddamn things. How the hell could I forget a thing like that?"

He leaned his hand against the first spigot, while Henry crawled over to him on his hands and knees.

"Jeez, Kenny, put something under that faucet! Don't let the stuff run all over the floor."

Kenny picked up an empty whisky bottle and held it under the spigot. Nothing happened.

"How do you like that?" he demanded of Henry. "Those bastards went and drained a whole goddamn barrel of my cider."

"Try the next one."

"All right. Hold this bottle under the spigot."

Kenny pressed every spigot on every barrel while Henry held the bottle hopefully each time, and when they had finished there was not a single drop of cider in the empty whisky bottle.

"Well, I'll be a dirty pile of horseshit, if those bastards ain't drained every drop!" yelped Kenny, enraged beyond endurance.

He began tipping the barrels so that they fell onto their sides and rolled creakingly on the cement floor. He kicked at each one hard and viciously and cursed until he was exhausted and Henry began to cry.

" 'Tain't no use, Kenny," wept Henry. "There just ain't no more cider. 'Tain't no use at all." He wiped his eyes and blew his nose on the sleeve of his shirt. "Come on, Kenny, 'tain't no use carryin' on like that. Let's make Lucas wake up. It's the only way. Time for Lucas to make another trip to White River."

Henry dragged himself toward Lucas, and when he reached the sleeping man's side, he began to kick him with both heels.

"Wake up, you pig," commanded Henry. "Wake up and move your ass. Time you went to White River. Wake up, I say!"

Lucas moved protestingly against the sharp heels which dug into his back and buttocks.

"Go to hell," he mumbled.

Henry went on kicking and Kenny came to help him.

"Wake up, you drunken bum," yelled Henry. "Wake up, you cider-drinkin' pig!"

"Go to hell," murmured Lucas.

75

"Hear that?" demanded Kenny shrilly. "What'd I tell you? Tellin' a man to go to hell, right in his own cellar."

"It's insultin', that's what it is," sympathized Henry. "Kick him harder, Kenny."

At last Lucas groaned, turned over on his back and attempted to focus his eyes on the wooden beams of the cellar ceiling.

"What got into you fellers," whined Lucas, "kickin' at a feller fit to rupture his guts?"

"We're out of booze," said Henry. "Time for you to take another trip to White River."

"Like hell," said Lucas. "Just shut up and gimme another drink."

"There ain't any," yelled Henry, in a rage. "Didn't you hear what I said? It's time for you to go over to White River. There ain't nothin' left to drink. Get up."

"All right," sighed Lucas and tried to raise himself to a sitting position. "Oh, Christ."

His last two words were a groan, uttered more as a prayer than a curse, and he collapsed flat on his back.

"Oh, Christ," he moaned. "They're back."

He began to cry and covered his eyes with gray, crusty hands.

"Where?" asked Kenny. "Where they at now, Lucas?"

Lucas kept his eyes covered with one hand, and with the forefinger of the other he pointed to the opposite wall.

"Right there next to you. Behind you. All over the place. Oh, Christ!"

Kenny fixed his eyes on the cellar wall. "I don't see nothin'," he quavered. "I don't see nothin' at all."

"They're there," sobbed Lucas. "All gray and green. Millions of 'em, crawlin' all over!"

He spread two of his fingers apart and stared out through this small slit.

"Watch out!" he screamed and began to slap at his thighs. "Watch out! They're comin' right at us!"

"I don't see nothin'," cried Kenny.

"You crazy bastard," yelled Lucas. "You're drunk, blind drunk, that's why you can't see nothin'. You're drunker than hell. Watch out!"

Lucas turned over on to his stomach and covered his head with his arms, but almost immediately he jumped to his feet and ran to a corner of the cellar where he crouched, panting.

"They was under me," he wept, terror stricken. "Right under me, waitin' for me to lay down so's they could start feastin'."

76

Kenny and Henry bent to examine the spot where Lucas had been lying.

"There's nothin' there," they agreed. "Nothin' at all."

"Drunken bums!" screamed Lucas. "Blind drunk, both of you!"

Two of the other four sleeping men were aroused by Lucas' screams. They looked about with dull, uncomprehending eyes.

"Where's the bottle?" asked one man.

"Watch out!" cried Lucas. "Put your head down!"

"Where's the goddamned bottle?"

"There ain't none," shouted Henry, exasperated with all the sudden confusion.

"I don't see nothin'," said Kenny. "Not a bloomin' thing."

"Where's the friggin' bottle?"

"Ain't none."

"Not a bloomin' thing."

"They're covered with slime. Green slime."

"I'll go after some," said Henry. "I'll go myself, and to hell with Lucas. Gimme some money."

Henry began to feel through his pockets. His fingers searched every possible hiding place in his clothing, but he found nothing.

"I ain't got no more money," he told Kenny.

"I got some, Henry," said Kenny, rummaging through his pockets. "Always got money for my friend Henry McCracken." But after a few more minutes of searching, he said, "Reckon I'm as bad off as you, Henry. Not a cent on me."

"Maybe he's got some," said Henry, indicating the gibbering Lucas.

Together, Henry and Kenny approached Lucas and began to search him, but his pockets, too, were empty. The men who had awakened began to search themselves, but finding nothing they began to feel in the pockets of the two men who still slept.

"Gotta get somethin' to drink," said Kenny. "Come on, empty your pockets, boys. Wake up. There ain't a goddamn thing to drink."

When the men had searched themselves thoroughly, they began to search one another.

"You got some," each accused the other. "You're keepin' it hid. Come on, now, dig it out. All for one and one for all. Put up your money."

In the end, they collected six cents.

"There, by God," said Henry McCracken. "I'll go over to White River myself. To hell with Lucas, I'll go myself."

He stood up and lurched against the wall. "Yep, you can count on me, boys. I'll go right now."

Carefully, he put the six cents into one of his pockets.

"I'll get whisky and a coupla cases of beer," he said to Kenny. "That should hold us until tomorrow."

"Watch out!" screamed Lucas. "Oh, Christ!"

"Where's the friggin' bottle?"

"Come on, Henry. I'll give you a boost out the window."

"I'll get three cases of beer. That'll be better."

"Better get one apiece," advised Kenny.

"Chase 'em out the window," ordered Lucas. "Quick!"

When Henry had gone, all the men except Lucas sat down to await his return. Lucas still crouched in the corner, whimpering, and peeking out from behind his fingers once in a while. Every time he uncovered his eyes he screamed, "Watch out!" then hastily covered them again.

"Takin' Henry one godawful while," said one man.

"Prob'ly gonna stay in White River and get drunk," said another.

"If there's one thing I hate, it's a sonofabitch who won't share."

One man, sitting a little apart from the others, began to move carefully toward the end of the cellar. This was Angus Bromley, and he vaguely remembered having hidden a bottle on top of one of the low rafters. He made his way slowly further away from the others, and they did not notice his movement. They still discussed the fickleness of Henry McCracken who had been gone, now, perhaps eight minutes.

"Greedy sonofabitch, that Henry."

"Prob'ly havin' a big time over to White River."

"Met some whore, that's what he done, and he's showin' her a big time. On our money."

"Oh, Christ!" moaned Lucas. "Oh, Christ, help me!"

"That sonofabitch McCracken. Gone out to get drunk."

"His whole goddamn family drinks. Every last one of the Mc-Crackens is a drunk."

"On our money."

Angus Bromley managed to reach a spot under a beam, and now contemplated the wide rafter over his head. Slowly, he raised himself up on his toes, his hands sliding carefully over the top of the beam over his head, and at last his fingers wrapped themselves around the neck of a quart bottle. He lowered this treasure painstakingly and held it before his eyes.

"Beautiful," he murmured, caressing the shoulders of the bottle

78

as if they had been those of a perfumed woman. "Beautiful, beautiful."

He sat down abruptly on the floor and hastily broke the seal on the top of the bottle. The cap rolled, unheeded, across the floor while Angus raised the mouth of the bottle to his lips.

Kenny Stearns turned his head sharply at the sound of a bottle cap dropping on cement, and he saw Angus—drinking.

"Look!" cried Kenny to the other men. "Angus has got a bottle!"

The men turned toward Angus, who wiped his mouth and quickly hid the bottle under his shirt.

"You're crazy, Kenny," he said and smiled ingratiatingly. "You're drunk, Kenny. Drunk and seein' things. I ain't got no bottle."

"Bastard!" shouted Kenny.

He rushed toward Angus, who had not had time to prepare for an onslaught. He was felled and lay on the floor. Kenny managed to rescue the bottle just in time. He held it in his hands and kicked viciously at Angus' head, and Angus groaned and did not move again. In a few minutes, he began to snore.

"Greedy bastard," mumbled Kenny and turned to face the others. "Who wants a drink?" he yelled.

All the men began to struggle to their feet, and even Lucas lowered one of his hands to look at Kenny.

"Anybody here that can take it away from me gets it," said Kenny, and without another word raised the bottle to his mouth.

The men, like starving animals, snarling and crafty eyed, approached Kenny slowly, circling him, watching for an opening.

Kenny laughed. "Anybody who's man enough to take it away from me gets it," he said, and then raised his foot unsteadily to push at the first man who rushed him.

Kenny had the advantage of a leaning place, for his back was against the broad cellar chimney, but the others had nothing to balance them but their equilibrium which was, at the moment, nonexistent. In ten minutes it was over. The sound of four snoring men filled the cellar and covered the noise of Lucas' whimpering.

"Bastards," gloated Kenny. "Tellin' a man to go to hell right in his own cellar. I guess I showed 'em. To hell with them." He approached Lucas. "You're the only friend I got, Lucas," he said. "The only real, true friend in the whole world. Have a drink."

He did not relinquish the bottle, but held it to Lucas' lips while Lucas swallowed thirstily.

"That's enough," said Kenny, withdrawing the bottle, and Lucas,

79

already saturated with alcohol from the long weeks of drinking, fell unconscious to the floor.

Kenny sat down, leaning against a wall, and took a long pull from the bottle. At once everything began to swing dizzily in front of his eyes, and he was transported back to a wonderful time when he had taken Ginny to a county fair and they had gone for a ride on the Ferris wheel. He half closed his eyes and saw the bright lights of the fairgrounds and heard the thin music of the calliope.

"Once more," he said, and obediently the Ferris wheel began to turn.

Kenny took another drink. After six weeks of the most prolonged spree in town history, Kenny's cellar floor was covered with vomit and feces. The stench had floated up through the floor boards of the story above and Ginny Stearns had long since moved in with a friend of hers who lived down by the river. But to Kenny now, his cellar was a beautiful place of carnival and pleasure.

"Once more," he cried, wanting to stay on the Ferris wheel forever. "Hold my hand, Ginny. Don't be scared."

Kenny looked in the direction of his sleeping friends and saw Ginny's smile.

"Here we go!" he shouted, and reached for her hand.

But abruptly she was gone and Kenny was alone in the Ferris wheel.

"Stop!" he yelled. "Stop! Stop! She fell out! Stop this goddamned thing!"

But the wheel turned faster and faster, and the music of the fair was suddenly sinister, a gay tune gone wrong and played in a minor key.

"Ginny!" he cried. "Ginny! Where'd you go to?"

He staggered to his feet and looked around wildly while the lights of the fair swung crazily all around him, dipping, swaying, hurting his eyes.

"Ginny!" he screamed from the top of the Ferris wheel.

And then he saw her. She was walking arm in arm with a smiling, oily-looking man. The stranger was dressed in city clothes, and he looked up at Kenny, trapped in the wheel, and laughed out loud.

"You bastard!" shouted Kenny. "Come back here. Come on back here with my Ginny!"

But Ginny was laughing, too. She turned her head and looked up at Kenny, her red lips parted so that her teeth showed, square and white, and she laughed and laughed.

"You bitch!" cried Kenny. "You dirty, whorin' bitch!"

Ginny laughed harder than ever and shrugged her shoulders and looked up at the city-dressed stranger. Kenny could see her painted nails resting against the man's dark sleeve, and he could feel her breasts and thighs straining through her dress to rest against the stranger's side.

"I'll kill you," he screamed, standing up in the Ferris wheel. "I'll kill you both!"

But Ginny and the stranger began to walk away, still laughing, as if they had not heard Kenny's threat. They walked slowly, and Ginny reached up and put her finger tips against the stranger's cheek. Kenny dropped the bottle he held and tried to get off the Ferris wheel. He dashed crookedly toward the stairs in his cellar, and when he reached the top, he fell heavily against the door. It would not budge.

"I'm locked in," he shouted, his fingers moving senselessly against the wooden panels. "I'm locked in this goddamned Ferris wheel!" His fingers touched the door's strong double bolt without recognizing it. "Let me out!" he called to the man who was operating the Ferris wheel. "Let me out, you sonofabitch!"

But the man kept the wheel going, smiling up at Kenny, his head like a skull and his yellow teeth gleaming dully in the dark.

Kenny ran down the cellar stairs and grasped the ax that he had put down next to his woodpile weeks before. He turned toward the grinning Ferris wheel operator.

"I'll chop my way out, you bastard!" he shouted.

He ran up the cellar stairs and when he reached the top he began to chop at the panels of the door in front of him.

"I'll kill you both," he yelled at Ginny and the stranger, who had stopped their walking now, to stand and stare at him. Ginny's smile was gone, replaced by a fear that contorted her face and made her mouth droop, and Kenny's heart exulted.

"I'll get you first, you rotten bitch," he called. "I'll get you and hack your pretty face all to pieces."

The ax bit into the wooden door panels once again, and this time Kenny had to struggle to loosen it for another swing. At last he freed it from the wood and raised it above his head. He aimed for the bottom of the Ferris wheel car and swung the ax in a tremendous arc.

Suddenly his foot was bleeding. While he stood and stared stupidly, blood was gushing in a fountain through the sliced leather of his shoe. It poured out redly, all around him, so that he was lost

81

in it, drowning. Kenny Stearns fell forward, out of the Ferris wheel into the crowds below, while Ginny's laughter rang in his ears.

♦ 19 ♦

It was Dr. Matthew Swain who found Henry McCracken. The doctor was on his way home from a call in the country when he saw something in the ditch at the side of the road. Immediately, he braked his car to a stop and got out to investigate, and in the gleam of his car's headlights, he saw a still figure, lying face down, in the dirt. It was Henry, unconscious, unbelievably dirty and bleeding from a nasty gash on his forehead but, as the doctor said later, it was Henry, still breathing and stinking to high heaven. Dr. Swain looked at him once and then picked him up, slung him over his shoulder and carried him to the car where he bundled him into the back seat. He drove straight to the Peyton Place hospital where Henry was entrusted to two nurses who stripped him, washed him and moaned their fate over every inch of Henry's filthy body.

"Cheer up, girls," said Dr. Swain, after he had stitched Henry's head. "Give this boy a few hours' sleep, and you'll be falling all over yourselves trying to get a chance to wait on him."

The two nurses gazed at Henry's drooling mouth and still unshaven face, with its neat forehead bandage giving him a slightly rakish look, and shook their heads at one another.

"You're the limit, Doc," said Nurse Mary Kelley, who was not noted for the originality of her remarks.

"No, I'm not," said the doctor. "*He* is."

Mary made a face at the doctor's retreating back.

"Go home and go to bed, Doc," she called after him. "And don't stop to pick up any more like this one on your way."

"Don't kid me, Mary," said the doctor. "You love 'em all with a wicked lust. Good night!"

Mary Kelley shook her head. "That Doc," she said to Nurse Lucy Ellsworth. "He never minds what he says. I've known him all my life, but I'm still not used to him. When I was in training here I almost got discouraged and quit before The Doc had got done with his teasing."

"Was he teasing you about this same fellow?" asked Lucy Ellsworth.

82

Lucy was comparatively new to Peyton Place and had not yet had a chance to become acquainted with its legends and anecdotes. She had come to town only six months before when her husband had obtained a job in the Cumberland Mills. John Ellsworth was a job shifter, perpetually discontented with his lot and forever looking for a plot of greener grass. Lucy had been a registered nurse when she married John, and she always said that it was a good thing she was, for she had had to work ever since to support the two of them, and later, the daughter who was born to them. Very often, Lucy Ellsworth said that she would leave John if it weren't for Kathy. But after all, a child needed her father, and John might have his faults but he was good to the little girl, and a woman couldn't ask for much more than that now, could she? Kathy was thirteen and in the eighth grade, and sometimes Lucy said that when the child was older, old enough to realize what was happening, then the two of them would leave John and his restlessness.

"Doc teases everybody about everything," said Mary Kelley. "He takes it easy with you because you're new here, but just wait until he gets used to seeing you around, then you'll see what I mean."

"What happened to almost make you quit when you were in training?" asked Lucy.

"Oh, it had nothing to do with Henry, here," said Mary, mournfully smoothing the sheet over Henry's thin legs. "It was over this big, black Negro we had in here once. The man was in a terrible automobile accident, and they brought him here because it was the nearest place. He was the first nigger I ever saw, close to. Well, The Doc worked most all night patching that man up, and then we put him in the ward with the rest of the patients, except of course the others were all white people. Well, every morning The Doc would come out of the ward and whisper to me, 'Mary, you watch that black feller,' and every day I'd ask him why. I took my work very seriously then, and I was trying to learn everything at once. 'Never mind,' The Doc would say, 'you just keep your eyes peeled. That feller there is different from any other man you ever saw.' The Doc is a man who loves everybody. Black, white, green even, if there is such a thing, it doesn't matter to him. 'What do you mean, different?' I asked the Doc. 'Because his skin's so black?' 'No,' The Doc said, and I should have known right then that he was up to some devilment, but I'd just started in training and I had the idea that a hospital was no place for fooling around, besides, I never did get used to The Doc's teasing.

83

" 'No, Mary,' The Doc said. 'It's not his skin. I'm surprised at you, a smart girl like you.' Well, I was almost crying I felt that bad to feel that maybe I'd missed something I was supposed to have learned in class. 'What do you mean?' I asked him, and The Doc leaned down and whispered in my ear. 'Mary,' he said, 'don't you know that niggers fart black?' Well, I can tell you, I was fit to be tied. 'That's nice talk,' I said, 'from the man who brought me into the world.' Oh, I knew that I was supposed to talk respectfully to all doctors at all times, even to The Doc, but I was so mad I just didn't care. The Doc never cracked a smile, but just looked at me, surprised. 'No kidding, Mary,' he said. 'I wouldn't spoof you, not a nice girl like you. I just wanted to put you wise, in case you ever have to take care of a black man again.' Well, fool that I was, I believed him. That's a trick of The Doc's. He can tell out-and-out lies with the straightest face in the world, and he can make anybody believe anything. I can tell you, I watched that black man. He couldn't even burp, much less anything else, without me right there by his side to see what I could see. I watched him for days, and finally one morning The Doc came out of the ward and walked up to me in the corridor. 'There,' he said, 'what did I tell you?' 'What're you talking about?' I asked him, and he looked at me, surprised. 'Why, Mary, didn't you see it?' 'See what?' I asked him. 'Come on, quick,' he said, and led me over to the ward by the hand. Of course, there was nothing there, and The Doc looked around, all innocent and puzzled, and he said, 'Hm, that's funny, it must have all gone out the window.' 'What?' I asked him, all excited by this time. 'The soot,' he said, and right away I got mad, thinking he was making remarks about the way we kids in training kept the room. 'What soot?' I asked him. 'From that black feller,' he said. 'So help me, I was in here a minute ago and that black feller farted and this whole room was black with soot!' "

Lucy Ellsworth laughed so loud that Henry stirred in his sleep, and Mary put a warning finger to her lips.

"Sh-h," she said. "I don't see anything so funny in that story anyway. I think it was a cruel thing to do to a young girl."

She sighed impatiently and put out the light in Henry's room when Lucy dashed for the hall, a handkerchief over her mouth to smother her laughter.

• 20 •

Dr. Matthew Swain drove slowly past Kenny Stearns's house to see if, as he put it to himself, any more bodies had fallen up out of the cellar. He saw Kenny's open cellar window with its black curtain flapping in the cold winter wind, and he pulled his car over to the curb and stopped.

For Christ's sake, he thought, if any of them have gone to sleep with that window open, Mary will have a hospital full of sick drunks on her hands.

He got out of his car and moved slowly toward the cellar window with the idea of glancing in to make sure that everything was well, and of slamming the window shut if none of the drunks were awake to do it for themselves.

That sounds like a noble gesture, he admitted to himself, when the truth of the matter is that I've been panting for a chance to take a look into that cellar. I wonder how they passed the time. He bent to look in the window. And I wonder, he asked himself, how in hell they lived with this stink for six weeks?

"Good God Almighty!" said the doctor aloud.

Kenny Stearns was lying at the foot of the cellar stairs, unconscious and covered with blood.

"He's dead, surer than hell," said the doctor. "If I ever saw a man who had bled to death, it's Kenny Stearns at this minute."

He straightened up quickly and went to the house next door to telephone for an ambulance.

Within minutes, the street in front of Kenny's house began to fill with people so that when the hospital ambulance arrived, the driver and his assistant had to fight a path clear to reach the cellar. Telephones rang all through the town, and people who had been in bed, or reading by their firesides, hurried out into the cold to join the crowds who had gathered to watch The Doc "drag the drunks out of Kenny's cellar."

"It works the same way in prisons," said Dr. Swain to Seth Buswell a few minutes later. "Some call it a grapevine, but it has always seemed like a pair of giant antennae to me. Nobody admits to having said a word, but the minute anything happens everyone seems to know about it."

He turned to the group of old men who usually wandered out

85

into the cold only to make their way to and from Tuttle's Grocery Store.

"For Christ's sake," roared the doctor, "get the hell out of the way!"

The two men who carried the stretcher lifted it gently to the rear of the ambulance, and the crowd began to buzz.

"Poor Kenny."

"Is he dead?"

"Jesus! Look at the blood!"

"Tried to slash his throat with a razor, I heard."

"Cut his wrists with a broken bottle."

"They all got into a fight and went at each other with knives. All of 'em drunk, of course."

The ambulance made four trips in all, taking Kenny on the first trip and Lucas Cross on the last.

Selena Cross stood on the fringe of the crowd, holding tightly to her little brother Joey's hand. When Lucas was dragged from the cellar, screaming, cursing and fighting off imaginary insects, she felt Joey squirm against her, trying to bury his head in the skirt of her dress. The ambulance driver and his assistant had Lucas by the scruff of the neck and the arms, pulling him across Kenny's front lawn.

"There's Lucas Cross!" shouted someone in the crowd.

"Lookit him! Drunk as a lord!"

"He's got the d.t.'s!"

Lucas screamed, "Let me go! Watch out!"

The crowd laughed at the ridiculous picture he made. He dug his heels into the ground and stiffened his body in protest against the men who dragged him.

"Watch out!" cried Lucas, and tried to hide his face in the white coats of the ambulance attendants.

"It's all right, Lucas," said Dr. Swain soothingly. "You're going to be all right. Now go with these boys and you'll be all right."

Lucas looked at the doctor as if he had never seen him before. "Watch out! Don't let them get me! They'll eat me alive!"

Joey Cross began to cry, but Selena did not cry. She watched Lucas with eyes ugly with hate.

Miserable slob, she thought. Crumby bastard. Drunken bum. I hope to hell you die.

"Be careful!" shouted someone in the crowd. "He's getting away!"

Lucas had managed to break away from one of his captors, and

86

now struggled insanely against the other. He kicked at the crotch of the man who still held him, and when the attendant let him go, Lucas began to run drunkenly in wide circles, slapping at his arms and thighs and trying to cover his face at the same time.

"Watch out!" he called to the crowd. "They're all covered with slime!"

The crowd roared and Selena hissed silently between her teeth.

"I hope you die. I wish you'd fall down dead, you rotten sonofabitch."

Joey hid his face and wept.

Charles Partridge waited until Lucas ran directly in front of him and then grabbed the frightened man in a grotesque bear hug.

"Come on, Lucas," said Dr. Swain gently. "Come with me. You'll be all right."

At last they managed to put Lucas into the ambulance and slam the door behind him, but even from inside the long car Lucas' voice was audible to the crowd outside.

"Watch out! Watch out!"

The ambulance moved away and Selena shook Joey. "Come on, honey. Let's go tell Ma that we finally saw him."

The two started away from the crowd, and many faces turned to watch them as they walked.

"There go the Cross kids."

"It's a shame, a man with a family."

"Don't know how his wife stands it."

"It's the children I feel sorry for."

"Well, that's the shackowners for you."

Shut up, Selena wanted to scream. Shut up. I don't need your stinking pity. Just shut up.

She held her head up, as if she were walking alone, and looked neither left nor right. She made her way toward Elm Street, leading her little brother Joey by the hand.

"I'll walk with you," said a voice behind her.

Selena whirled. "I don't need you, Ted Carter," she said viciously, taking out her hurt and anger at the crowd on him. "Beat it back to the right side of the tracks. Your people worked hard enough to get there. Don't leave now to come down by the shacks."

Ted took her arm and it was stiff and unyielding beneath his fingers.

Selena jerked away from him. "I don't need you," she said. "I don't need anybody. Keep your lousy pity for someone who wants it. Take it and shove it."

An innate wisdom kept Ted silent now, and moved him to Joey's side. He took the little boy's hand in his, and he and Selena were on opposite sides of the child, each holding one of his hands. Joey felt almost warmed and comforted.

"Come on, Selena," said Joey. "Let's go home."

The three figures moved down the deserted main street of Peyton Place, and their feet struck sharply on the snowless sidewalks. They walked without speaking to the end of the paved street and onto the dirt road, and when they came to the clearing in front of the Cross shack, Joey broke away from them.

"I'm goin' in to tell Ma," he said, and dashed into the house.

Selena and Ted stood together, still not speaking, motionless in the middle of the road. Then Ted put both his arms around Selena and drew her close to him. He did not kiss her or touch her in any way except to hold her, and at last Selena began to cry. She wept silently, without moving her body, her burning, wet face the only sign that she wept.

"I love you, Selena," Ted whispered in her ear.

She wept until her whole body ached and she leaned, a dead weight, against Ted, so that if he had moved she would have crumpled and fallen. He took her hand and led her to the side of the road, and she followed him like an idiot or a sleepwalker, uncaring and somnolent. Ted made her sit down on the cold ground and then sat next to her, holding her, pressing her face into the front of his coat, and he stroked her hair with his cold fingers.

"I love you, Selena."

He opened his heavy overcoat and sat closer to her, so that part of his coat covered her, and his hands went under the ragged thinness of the jacket she wore, trying to warm her.

"I love you, Selena."

"Yes," she muttered, and it was neither a question nor an exclamation of wonder. It was an agreement.

"I want you to be my girl."

"Yes."

"For always."

"Yes."

"We'll get married, after we finish high school. It's only four years and a little bit more."

"Yes."

"I'm going to be a lawyer, just like old Charlie."

"Yes."

"But we'll get married before I have to go away to college."

"Yes."

They sat quietly for a long time. The one small light in the Cross shack went out, and the darkness from the woods reached out to cover them. Selena was limp against Ted, like a rag doll. When he kissed her, her mouth was soft, but neither resistant nor yielding, and her body neither flinched from his touch nor leaned toward it. She was just there, and tractable.

"I love you, Selena."

"Yes."

It was snowing. The cold had snapped soundlessly under the strength of the thick, quiet flakes that fell and soon covered the ground.

♦ 21 ♦

Allison lay still and listened to the sounds of winter. The snow against her small-paned bedroom window made a tiny sound, like sugar sprinkled over the surface of hot coffee, and it piled itself up quietly, beautifully, so that it was hard to look at it and think of danger. The memory of giant tree limbs broken off by the sly snow's weight, or the tale of the hunter, taken in by the false warmth of a white blanket, who froze to death, or the story of someone's small dog, lost in a silvery wonderland, who fell at last into a drift over his depth and was suffocated were like pain, easily forgotten. Allison listened to the soft sift of snow against her window and remembered only loveliness. She tried not to hear the wind which frightened her with its persistence and power. The winter winds did not blow over northern New England in blasts and gusts. They were like living things, breathing unceasingly and mightily, with breaths as cold as death. Allison hid her head under the bedcovers and was afraid that spring would never come again.

In this second week of February winter still had a long time to stay. But Allison had the feeling that when spring came her life would miraculously straighten itself out. She was assailed by a feeling of vague unrest, yet she could not put her finger on the source of her uneasiness.

"Nothing is the way it used to be any more," she would say angrily.

She saw less and less of Selena Cross these days, for Selena was either with Ted Carter, or busy looking for an odd job to do.

"I'm saving my money," said Selena one Saturday afternoon when Allison suggested a movie. "I'm saving up to buy that white dress in your mother's store to wear when we graduate. Ted's already asked me to the spring dance. Are you going?"

"Of course not," said Allison promptly, preferring to give the impression that she did not choose to go rather than have Selena guess that she had not been invited.

"Ted and I are going steady," said Selena.

"Ted, Ted, Ted!" said Allison crossly. "Is that all you can talk about?"

"Yes," said Selena simply.

"Well, I think it's disgusting, that's what I think," said Allison. But she began to pay a little more attention to her clothes, and Constance no longer had to nag her into washing her hair. She made a secretive trip to the five- and ten-cent store where she bought a brassière with full rubber pads in each cup, and when Constance remarked on the fact that her daughter was filling out nicely and quickly, Allison gave her a withering look.

"After all, Mother," she said, "I'm not getting any younger, you know."

"Yes, dear, I know," said Constance, hiding a smile.

Allison shrugged angrily. It seemed to her that her mother grew more stupid every day, and that she had a positive genius for saying the wrong thing at the wrong time.

"How come we never see Selena Cross around here any more?" asked Constance, toward the end of February.

Allison very nearly shouted that Selena hadn't been inside the MacKenzie house for weeks and weeks, and if it had taken Constance all this time to realize that fact, then she must be blind as well as stupid.

"I guess I've just sort of outgrown Selena," she told her mother.

But it had been bad, at first, losing Selena. Allison had thought that she would die of loneliness, and she spent many a long Saturday afternoon weeping in her room, rather than go poking about in the shops by herself. Then she had become friendly with Kathy Ellsworth, a new girl in town, and she no longer missed Selena. Kathy loved to read and walk and she painted pictures. It was this last which had prompted Allison to tell Kathy about the stories she had tried to write.

"I'm sure you'll understand, Kathy," said Allison. "I mean, one artist to another."

Kathy Ellsworth was small and quiet. Allison often had the feeling that if anyone were to strike Kathy, that Kathy's bones would crumble and disintegrate, and she was often so still that Allison could forget that she was there at all.

"Do you like boys?" Allison asked her new friend.

"Yes," said Kathy, and Allison was shocked.

"I mean, do you *really* like them?"

"Yes, I do," said Kathy. "When I grow up, I'm going to get married, and buy a house, and have a dozen children."

"Well, I'm not!" said Allison. "I am going to be a brilliant authoress. Absolutely brilliant. And I shall never marry. I just hate boys!"

Boys were another question that disturbed Allison that winter. Oftentimes, she lay awake in her bed at night and had the most peculiar sensations. She wanted to rub her hands over her body, but when she did, she always remembered her thirteenth birthday and the way Rodney Harrington had kissed her. Then she would either go hot and prickly all over, or else she would feel cold enough to shiver. She tried to imagine other boys kissing her, but the face that swam beneath her closed lids was always that of Rodney, and she almost wished that she could feel his lips again. She pressed her hands flat against her abdomen, then let them slide up to her small breasts. She rubbed her finger tips over her nipples until they were hard, and this caused an odd tightening somewhere between her legs that puzzled her but was, somehow, very pleasant. One night she began to wonder how it would feel if it were Rodney's hands on her breasts, and her face burned.

"I just hate boys," she told her friend Kathy, but she began to practice sultry looks in her mirror, and all day long, at school, she was aware of Rodney in the seat next to hers.

"Did a boy ever kiss you?" she asked Kathy.

"Oh, yes," replied Kathy calmly. "Several of them. I liked it."

"You didn't!" cried Allison.

"Yes, I did," said Kathy, who, Allison had discovered, would not lie, or even be tactful if it occasioned a slight coloring of the truth. "Yes," repeated Kathy, "I liked it very much. A boy even screwed me once."

"Oh, my goodness!" said Allison. "How did he do that?"

"Oh, you know. Put his tongue in my mouth when he kissed me."

"Oh," said Allison.

Kathy and Allison changed their reading habits radically that winter. They began to haunt the library in search of books reputed to be "sexy," and they read them aloud to one another.

"I wish I had breasts like marble," said Kathy sadly, closing a book. "Mine have blue veins in them that show through the skin. I think I'll draw a picture of a girl with marble breasts."

"Kathy is just wonderful," said Allison to Constance. "She's so talented, and imaginative and everything."

Dear God, thought Constance, first the daughter of a shack-owner and now the daughter of an itinerant mill hand. Allison's taste is all in her mouth!

Constance had not much time to spend with her daughter these days. She had bought the vacant store next door to the Thrifty Corner and was now busily engaged in enlarging her shop. She put in a line of men's socks and shirts and another of infants' wear, and by the first of March she had hired Selena Cross to work for her part time, after school. She also hired Nellie Cross to come in three days a week to clean house for her, and it was at this time that Allison noticed Nellie's newly developed habit of talking to herself under her breath.

"Sonsofbitches, all of 'em," she would mumble, attacking the woodwork viciously. "Every last one of 'em."

And Allison would remember the day she had stood on a packing crate and looked into the Cross kitchen.

"Booze and wimmin. Wimmin and booze," muttered Nellie, and Allison shivered, remembering Selena's scream ripping at the cold November afternoon. She had never been able to bring herself to tell that story to anyone, and she had never mentioned to Selena that she had seen, but soon afterward she saw a book with a paper jacket showing a slave girl with her wrists bound over her head, naked from the waist up, while a brutal-looking man beat her with a cruel-looking whip. That, she concluded, was what had been in Lucas Cross's mind on the afternoon that she had stared through his kitchen window. Lucas must have beaten Nellie until the woman's mind was gone.

"Sonsofbitches," said Nellie. "Oh, hello, Allison. Come in here and sit down, and I'll tell you a story."

"No," said Allison quickly. "No, thank you."

"O.K.," said Nellie cheerfully. "You tell me one."

It was a cold snowy afternoon and Nellie was ironing in the MacKenzie kitchen. Allison sat down on the rocking chair beside the stove.

"Once upon a time," said Allison, "in a land far across the sea, there lived a beautiful princess—"

Nellie Cross ironed on, her small eyes shining and her slack mouth half open. After that, whenever Allison was in the house, Nellie would smile and say, "Tell me a story," and each one had to be different, for Nellie would interrupt at once. "Nah. Don't tell that one. You told me that one already."

"Nellie Cross may look like a pig herself," said Constance, "but she certainly keeps this house shining."

One morning in March, Nellie came to the MacKenzies' before Constance had left for work.

"Guess you ain't heard about Mr. Firth, have you?" she asked.

Nellie had a disconcerting habit of cackling, and she cackled now.

"Dropped dead, he did," she told Constance and Allison. "Shovelin' snow in his driveway, and fell down dead. I always knew he'd get his someday. Sonofabitch, he was. Just like all of 'em. Sonsofbitches."

"For Heaven's sake, Nellie!" remonstrated Constance. "Watch your tongue."

Mr. Abner Firth was the principal of the Peyton Place schools, and he had dropped dead of a heart attack, that morning.

"Isn't that a shame," said Constance absent-mindedly.

"Are you sure, Mrs. Cross?" asked Allison.

"You bet I'm sure. One sonofabitch less in this sad world."

At school, Miss Elsie Thornton was white faced but dry eyed. She asked that every boy and girl bring a dime to school the next day for flowers for Mr. Firth.

"We'll have a bitch of a time replacing old Firth at this time of the year," said Leslie Harrington, who was the chairman of the school board. "Christ, why couldn't he have waited until spring to have his goddamned heart attack."

Roberta Carter, Ted's mother, who was also on the school board said, "There is no need to be profane, Leslie."

"Come off it, Bobbie," said Harrington.

Theodore Janowski, a mill hand and the third member of the board, nodded his head impartially to both Leslie and Mrs. Carter. Janowski was supposed to fill out the Peyton Place School Board and make it truly representative of the town's population, but in his two years of service he had never once voted on an issue. Leslie Harrington decided policy, he and Mrs. Carter argued for a while, and then the two of them declared what was to be done. Occasionally they would turn to Janowski and ask, "Don't you agree, Mr. Janowski?"

"Yes," was always Janowski's answer.

"We'll get in touch with one of those teachers' agencies down to Boston," decided Harrington. "They should be able to come up with someone. Now, I suppose, we'd better all dig down and send old Abner a wreath, goddamn his soul."

It was nearly April, with no sign of a break in the cold weather, before the Boston Teachers' Agency came up with the name of a man qualified to be principal of the Peyton Place schools. His name was Tomas Makris and he was a native of the city of New York.

"Makris!" roared Leslie Harrington. "What the hell kind of name is that!"

"Grecian, I think," said Mrs. Carter.

"I dunno, Mr. Harrington," said Janowski.

"His qualifications are excellent," said Mrs. Carter. "Although I imagine that he is a little unstable. Look at what he gives as a reason for leaving his last job. 'To go to work in Pittsburgh steel mill for more money.' Really, Leslie, I don't think we want anyone like that up here."

"A goddamned Greek, for Christ's sake, and a lousy millworker at that. This Boston agency must be run by screwballs."

Theodore Janowski said nothing, but for the first time he felt a powerful urge to slam his fist into Leslie Harrington's mouth.

"What about Elsie Thornton," suggested Mrs. Carter. "Goodness knows she's been teaching long enough to know our schools inside out."

"She's too old," said Harrington. "She's practically ready to retire. Besides, being principal is no job for a woman."

"Well, then," said Mrs. Carter acidly, "it looks like either this Makris person or no one."

"Take your time, for Christ's sake," said Harrington.

The school board procrastinated until the middle of April. Then they received a curt note from the State Department of Education informing them that a school could not be run without an administrator, and that therefore the Peyton Place School Board would please remedy the situation in their town at once. The fact that Abner Firth had also taught three classes of English, a required subject on all levels, and that these classes had not been held since his death made it imperative, in the eyes of the state department, that a replacement be hired immediately. That same evening, Leslie Harrington attempted to telephone Tomas Makris, long-distance collect, at Pittsburgh, Pennsylvania.

"Will you accept a collect call from Mr. Leslie Harrington?" asked the operator.

"Like hell I will," said the full voice of Makris. "Who is Leslie Harrington?"

"One moment, please," sang the operator.

When she put Makris' question to Harrington, Leslie roared back that he was the chairman of the Peyton Place School Board, that was who, and if Makris was interested in a job there, he had damned well better accept a collect call. Unfortunately, the operator left the line open while Harrington was speaking, and before she could relay his message, in more courteous words, Makris began to roar himself.

"To hell with you, Mr. Harrington," he shouted into the telephone. "If you can't afford to pay for a long-distance call, you can't afford to hire me," and he banged the receiver into place.

Two minutes later his telephone rang and the operator informed him that Mr. Harrington was on the line, prepaid from Peyton Place.

"Well?" demanded Makris.

"Now listen here, Mr. Makris," said Leslie Harrington. "Let's discuss this thing sensibly."

"It's your money," said Makris. "Go ahead."

The next day the whole town buzzed with talk that Leslie Harrington had gone and hired a Greek to come be principal of the schools.

"A Greek?" demanded Peyton Place incredulously. "For God's sake, isn't it enough that we've got a whole colony of Polacks and Canucks working in the mills without letting the Greeks in?"

"Good grief!" said Marion Partridge. "I don't know what Roberta Carter could have been thinking of. The next thing you know, we'll have an all-night fruit store on Elm Street!"

"It's a lucky thing for me that he'll be the only one in town," said Corey Hyde, who owned the largest eating place in town. "You know what they say happens when Greek meets Greek? They take one look at each other and open up a restaurant!"

"You put your foot in it that time, Leslie," said Jared Clarke. "Hiring a Greek, for God's sake. What got into you?"

"Nothing got into me," said Harrington angrily. "He was the only man we could get with decent qualifications. He's got a

95

Master's from Columbia and all that sort of thing. He's a good man."

Leslie Harrington did not admit then, or ever, that he had been unable to keep from hiring Tomas Makris. He never told anyone that he had almost begged Makris to come to Peyton Place, and he could not explain to himself why he had done so.

"What'll you pay?" Makris had demanded. And, when Leslie told him, "Are you kidding? Keep your crummy job."

Leslie had upped the offer by four hundred dollars per year, and had offered to pay for transportation to Peyton Place. Makris had demanded a three-room apartment, steam heated, in a decent neighborhood, and an ironclad contract, not for one year but for three.

"That will be entirely satisfactory with the school board, I am sure," Leslie Harrington had said, and when he hung up he had been sweating and feeling ridiculously weak and ineffectual.

I'll fix your wagon, Mr. Independent Greek Makris, thought Harrington. But for the first time in his life he was afraid, and he could not have said why.

"Qualified or not," said Jared Clarke, "you've put your foot in it this time, Leslie."

Jared's opinion was shared by the whole town with the exception of Dr. Matthew Swain and Miss Elsie Thornton.

"Do the kids good to have a young fellow like that in charge," said Dr. Swain. "Shake 'em up a little."

A Master's from Columbia, thought Miss Thornton. A young man, well educated and unafraid. She sent the dean of Smith College a swift thought. I'll show you yet, exulted Miss Thornton. You'll see!

The old men in Tuttle's to whom the schools had never been of the remotest interest, now talked volubly about the new headmaster.

"A New York feller, you say?"

"Yep. A Greek feller from down to New York."

"Well, I'll be damned!"

"Don't seem right, somehow, what with all the teachers who've been here so long to go givin' the best job to some Greek feller from out of town."

"Oh, I don't know," said Clayton Frazier. "Do us good to see some new faces around."

Allison MacKenzie made a special trip to the Thrifty Corner

96

to tell her mother about the new principal who was coming to town.

"Makris?" asked Constance. "What an odd name. Where is he from?"

"New York," said Allison.

Constance's heart began to knock painfully against her side.

"New York City?" she asked.

"That's what the kids were saying."

Constance busied herself with hanging up a new shipment of skirts, and Allison did not notice that her mother seemed suddenly nervous. She was too nervous herself to notice much of anything, because the real reason she had come into the shop was not to pass on the news about the new principal.

"I'd like to have a new dress," she blurted.

"Oh?" asked Constance, surprised. "Did you have anything special in mind?"

"A party dress," said Allison. "I have a date for the spring dance next month."

"A *date!*" said Constance incredulously, and dropped the two skirts she was holding. "With whom?"

"Rodney Harrington," said Allison calmly. "He asked me this afternoon."

She did not feel calm. She was remembering the night of her birthday party when Rodney had kissed her because she was too big to spank.

◆ 22 ◆

A few days later, Tomas Makris stepped off the train in front of the Peyton Place railroad station. No other passenger got off with him. He paused on the empty platform and looked around thoroughly, for it was a habit with him to fix a firm picture of a new place in his mind so that it could never be erased nor forgotten. He stood still, feeling the two heavy suitcases that he carried pulling at his arm muscles, and reflected that there wasn't much to see, nor to hear, for that matter. It was shortly after seven o'clock in the evening, but it might have been midnight or four in the morning, for all the activity going on. Behind him, there was nothing but the two curving railroad tracks and from a distance came the long-drawn-out wail of the train as it made the pull across the wide Connecticut River. And it was cold.

For April, thought Makris, shrugging uncomfortably under his topcoat, it was damned cold.

Straight ahead of him stood the railroad station, a shabby wooden building with a severely pitched roof and several thin, Gothic-looking windows that gave it the air of a broken-down church. Nailed to the front of the building, at the far left of the front door, was a blue and white enameled sign. PEYTON PLACE, it read. POP. 3675.

Thirty-six seventy-five, thought Makris, pushing open the railroad station's narrow door. Sounds like the price of a cheap suit.

The inside of the building was lit by several dim electric light bulbs suspended from fixtures which obviously had once burned gas, and there were rows of benches constructed of the most hideous wood obtainable, golden oak. No one was sitting on them. The brown, roughly plastered walls were trimmed with the same yellow wood and the floor was made of black and white marble. There was an iron-barred cage set into one wall and from behind this a straight, thin man with a pinched-looking nose, steel-rimmed glasses and a string tie stared at Makris.

"Is there a place where I can check these?" asked the new principal, indicating the two bags at his feet.

"Next room," said the man in the cage.

"Thank you," said Makris and made his way through a narrow archway into another, smaller room. It was a replica of the main room, complete with golden oak, marble and converted gas fixtures, but with the addition of two more doors. These were clearly labeled. MEN, said one. WOMEN, said the other. Against one wall there was a row of pale gray metal lockers, and to Makris, these looked almost friendly. They were the only things in the station even faintly resembling anything he had ever seen in his life.

"Ah," he murmured, "shades of Grand Central," and bent to push his suitcases into one of the lockers. He deposited his dime, withdrew his key and noticed that his was the only locker in use.

Busy town, he thought, and walked back to the main room. His footsteps rang disquietingly on the scrubbed marble floor.

Leslie Harrington had instructed Makris to call him at his home as soon as he got off the train, but Makris by-passed the solitary telephone booth in the railroad station. He wanted to look at the town alone first, to see it through no one's eyes but his own. Besides, he had decided the night that Harrington had called long-distance that the chairman of the Peyton Place School Board sounded like a man puffed up with his own importance, and must therefore be a pain in the ass.

"Say, Dad," began Makris, addressing the man in the cage.

"Name's Rhodes," said the old man.

"Mr. Rhodes," began Makris again, "could you tell me how I can get into town from here? I noticed a distressing lack of taxicabs outside."

"Be damned peculiar if I couldn't."

"If you couldn't what?"

"Tell you how to get uptown. Been living here for over sixty years."

"That's interesting."

"You're Mr. Makris, eh?"

"Admitted."

"Ain't you goin' to call up Leslie Harrington?"

"Later. I'd like to get a cup of coffee first. Listen, isn't there a cab to be had anywhere around here?"

"No."

Tomas Makris controlled a laugh. It was beginning to look as if everything he had ever heard about these sullen New Englanders was true. The old man in the cage gave the impression that he had been sucking lemons for years. Certainly, sourness had not been one of the traits in that little Pittsburgh secretary who claimed to be from Boston, but she said herself that she was East Boston Irish, and therefore not reliably representative of New England.

"Do you mind, then, telling me how I can walk into town from here, Mr. Rhodes?" asked Makris.

"Not at all," said the stationmaster, and Makris noticed that he pronounced the three words as one: Notatall. "Just go out this front door, walk around the depot to the street and keep on walking for two blocks. That will bring you to Elm Street."

"Elm Street? Is that the main street?"

"Yes."

"I had the idea that the main streets of all small New England towns were named Main Street."

"Perhaps," said Mr. Rhodes, who prided himself, when annoyed, on enunciating his syllables, "it is true that the main streets of all *other* small towns are named Main Street. Not, however, in Peyton Place. Here the main street is called Elm Street."

Period. Paragraph, thought Makris. Next question. "Peyton Place is an odd name," he said. "How did anyone come to pick that one?"

Mr. Rhodes drew back his hand and started to close the wooden panel that backed the iron bars of his cage.

"I am closing now, Mr. Makris," he said. "And I suggest that you be on your way if you want to obtain a cup of coffee. Hyde's Diner closes in half an hour."

"Thank you," said Makris to the wooden panel which was suddenly between him and Mr. Rhodes.

Friendly bastard, he thought, as he left the station and began to walk up the street labeled Depot.

Tomas Makris was a massively boned man with muscles that seemed to quiver every time he moved. In the steel mills of Pittsburgh he had looked, so one smitten secretary had told him, like a color illustration of a steelworker. His arms, beneath sleeves rolled above the elbow, were knotted powerfully, and the buttons of his work shirts always seemed about to pop off under the strain of trying to cover his chest. He was six feet four inches tall, weighed two hundred and twelve pounds, stripped, and looked like anything but a schoolteacher. In fact, the friendly secretary in Pittsburgh had told him that in his dark blue suit, white shirt and dark tie, he looked like a steelworker disguised as a schoolteacher, a fact which would not inspire trust in the heart of any New Englander.

Tomas Makris was a handsome man, in a dark-skinned, blackhaired, obviously sexual way, and both men and women were apt to credit him more with attractiveness than intellect. This was a mistake, for Makris had a mind as analytical as a mathematician's and as curious as a philosopher's. It was his curiosity which had prompted him to give up teaching for a year to go to work in Pittsburgh. He had learned more about economics, labor and capital in that one year than he had learned in ten years of reading books. He was thirty-six years old and totally lacking in regret over the fact that he had never stayed in one job long enough to "get ahead," as the Pittsburgh secretary put it. He was honest, completely lacking in diplomacy, and the victim of a vicious temper which tended to loosen a tongue that had learned to speak on the lower East Side of New York City.

Makris was halfway through the second block on Depot Street, leading to Elm, when Parker Rhodes, at the wheel of an old sedan, passed him. The stationmaster looked out of the window on the driver's side of his car and looked straight through Peyton Place's new headmaster.

Sonofabitch, thought Makris. Real friendly sonofabitch to offer me a lift in his junk heap of a car.

Then he smiled and wondered why Mr. Rhodes had been so sensitive on the subject of his town's name. He would ask around and see if everyone in this godforsaken place reacted the same way to his question. He had reached the corner of Elm Street and paused to look about him. On the corner stood a white, cupola-topped house with stiff lace curtains at the windows. Silhouetted against the light inside, he could see two women sitting at a table with what was obviously a checkerboard between them. The women were big, saggy bosomed and white haired, and Makris thought that they looked like a pair who had worked too long at the same girls' school.

I wonder who they are? he asked himself, as he looked in at the Page Girls. Maybe they're the town's two Lizzies.

Reluctantly, he turned away from the white house and made his way west on Elm Street. When he had walked three blocks, he came to a small, clean-looking and well-lighted restaurant. "Hyde's Diner" said a polite neon sign, and Makris opened the door and went in. The place was empty except for one old man sitting at the far end of the counter, and another man who came out of the kitchen at the sound of the door opening.

"Good evening, sir," said Corey Hyde.

"Good evening," said Makris. "Coffee, please, and a piece of pie. Any kind."

"Apple, sir?"

"Any kind is O.K."

"Well, we have pumpkin, too."

"Apple is fine."

"I think there's a piece of cherry left, also."

"Apple," said Makris, "will be fine."

"You're Mr. Makris, aren't you?"

"Yes."

"Glad to meet you, Mr. Makris. My name is Hyde. Corey Hyde."

"How do you do?"

"Quite well, as a rule," said Corey Hyde. "I'll keep on doing quite well, as long as no one starts up another restaurant."

"Look, could I have my coffee now?"

"Certainly. Certainly, Mr. Makris."

The old man at the end of the counter sipped his coffee from

101

a spoon and looked surreptitiously at the newcomer to town. Makris wondered if the old man could be the village idiot.

"Here you are, Mr. Makris," said Corey Hyde. "The best apple pie in Peyton Place."

"Thank you."

Makris stirred sugar into his coffee and sampled the pie. It was excellent.

"Peyton Place," he said to Corey Hyde, "is the oddest name for a town I've ever heard. Who is it named for?"

"Oh, I don't know," said Corey, making unnecessary circular motions with a cloth on his immaculate counter. "There's plenty of towns have funny names. Take that Baton Rouge, Louisiana. I had a kid took French over to the high school. Told me Baton Rouge means Red Stick. Now ain't that a helluva name for a town? Red Stick, Louisiana. And what about that Des Moines, Iowa? What a crazy name that is."

"True," said Makris. "But for whom is Peyton Place named, or for what?"

"Some feller that built a castle up here, back before the Civil War. Feller by the name of Samuel Peyton," said Corey reluctantly.

"A castle!" exclaimed Makris.

"Yep. A real, true, honest-to-God castle, transported over here from England, every stick and stone of it."

"Who was this Peyton?" asked Makris. "An exiled duke?"

"Nah," said Corey Hyde. "Just a feller with money to burn. Excuse me, Mr. Makris. I got things to do in the kitchen."

The old man at the end of the counter chuckled. "Fact of the matter, Mr. Makris," said Clayton Frazier in a loud voice, "is that this town was named for a friggin' nigger. That's what ails Corey. He's delicate like, and just don't want to spit it right out."

While Tomas Makris sipped his coffee and enjoyed his pie and conversation with Clayton Frazier, Parker Rhodes arrived at his home on Laurel Street. He parked his ancient sedan and entered the house where, without first removing his coat and hat, he went directly to the telephone.

"Hello," he said, as soon as the party he had called answered. "That you, Leslie? Well, he's here, Leslie. Got off the seven o'clock, checked his suitcases and walked uptown. He's sitting down at Hyde's right now. What's that? No, he can't get his bags out of the depot until morning, you know that. What? Well, goddamn it, he didn't ask me, that's why. He didn't ask for information

102

about when he could get them out. He just wanted to know where he could check his bags, so I told him. What'd you say, Leslie? No, I did not tell him that no one has used those lockers since they were installed five years ago. What? Well, goddamn it, he didn't ask me, that's why. Yes. Yes, he is, Leslie. *Real* dark, and big. Sweet Jesus, he's as big as the side of a barn. Yes. Down at Hyde's. Said he wanted a cup of coffee."

If Tomas Makris had overheard this conversation, he would have noticed again that Rhodes pronounced his last three words as one: Kupakawfee. But at the moment, Makris was looking at the tall, silver-haired man who had just walked through Hyde's front door.

My God! thought Makris, awed. This guy looks like a walking ad for a Planter's Punch. A goddamned Kentucky colonel in this place!

"Evenin', Doc," said Corey Hyde, who had put his head out of the kitchen at the sound of the door, looking, thought Makris, rather like a tired turtle poking his head out of his shell.

"Evenin', Corey," and Makris knew, as soon as the man spoke, that this was no fugitive Kentucky colonel but a native.

"Welcome to Peyton Place, Mr. Makris," said the white haired native. "It's nice to have you with us. My name is Swain. Matthew Swain."

"Evenin', Doc," said Clayton Frazier. "I just been tellin' Mr. Makris here some of our local legends."

"Make you want to jump on the next train out, Mr. Makris?" asked the doctor.

"No, sir," said Makris, thinking that there was, after all, one goddamned face in this godforsaken town that looked human.

"I hope you'll enjoy living here," said the doctor. "Maybe you'll let me show you the town after you get settled a little."

"Thank you, sir. I'd enjoy that," said Makris.

"Here comes Leslie Harrington," said Clayton Frazier.

The figure outside the glass door of the restaurant was clearly visible to those inside. The doctor turned to look.

"It's Leslie, all right," he said. "Come to fetch you home, Mr. Makris."

Harrington strode into the restaurant, a smile like one made of molded ice cream on his face.

"Ah, Mr. Makris," he cried jovially, extending his hand. "It is indeed a pleasure to welcome you to Peyton Place."

He was thinking, Oh, Christ, he's worse and more of it than I'd feared.

"Hello, Mr. Harrington," said Makris, barely touching the extended hand. "Made any long-distance calls lately?"

The smile on Harrington's face threatened to melt and run together, but he rescued it just in time.

"Ha, ha, ha," he laughed. "No, Mr. Makris, I haven't had much time for telephoning these days. I've been too busy looking for a suitable apartment for our new headmaster."

"I trust you were successful," said Makris.

"Yes. Yes, I was, as a matter of fact. Well, come along. I'll take you over in my car."

"As soon as I finish my coffee," said Makris.

"Certainly, certainly," said Harrington. "Oh, hello, Matt. 'Lo, Clayton."

"Coffee, Mr. Harrington?" asked Corey Hyde.

"No, thanks," said Harrington.

When Makris had finished, everyone said good night carefully, all the way around, and he and Harrington left the restaurant. As soon as the door had closed behind them, Dr. Swain began to laugh.

"Goddamn it," he roared, "I'll bet my sweet young arse that Leslie has met his match this time!"

"There's one schoolteacher that Leslie ain't gonna shove around," observed Clayton Frazier.

Corey Hyde, who owed money at the bank where Leslie Harrington was a trustee, smiled uncertainly.

"The textile racket must be pretty good," said Makris, as he opened the door of Leslie Harrington's new Packard.

"Can't complain," said Harrington. "Can't complain," and the millowner shook himself angrily at this sudden tendency to repeat all his words.

Makris stopped in the act of getting into the car. A woman was walking toward them, and as she stepped under the street light on the corner, Makris got a quick glimpse of blond hair and a swirl of dark coat.

"Who's that?" he demanded.

Leslie Harrington peered through the darkness. As the figure drew nearer, he smiled.

"That's Constance MacKenzie," he said. "Maybe you two will have a lot in common. She used to live in New York. Nice woman, good looking, too. Widow."

104

"Introduce me," said Makris, drawing himself up to his full height.

"Certainly. Certainly, be glad to. Oh, Connie!"

"Yes, Leslie?"

The woman's voice was rich and husky, and Makris fought down the urge to straighten the knot in his tie.

"Connie," said Harrington, "I'd like you to meet our new headmaster, Mr. Makris. Mr. Makris, Constance MacKenzie."

Constance extended her hand and while he held it, she gazed at him full in the eyes.

"How do you do?" she said at last, and Tomas Makris was puzzled, for something very much like relief showed through her voice.

"I'm glad to know you, Mrs. MacKenzie," said Makris, and he thought, Very glad to know you, baby. I want to know you a lot better, on a bed, for instance, with that blond hair spread out on a pillow.

◆ **23** ◆

From the evening of the day when Constance MacKenzie was introduced to Tomas Makris, a new tension began to make itself felt in the MacKenzie household. Where Constance had always tried to be patient and, to the limit of her ability, understand her daughter Allison, she was now snappish and stubborn for no reason at all, and this unfortunate new habit did not confine itself to her home but made itself obvious in her shop as well. To her own dismay, Constance discovered that she had a streak of hatefulness that she had never realized she possessed and, even worse, that it gave her a bitter kind of satisfaction to express thoughts that she had kept buried for years.

"You have too much around the hips to get into an eighteen any more," she told Charlotte Page one day toward the end of April. "You'd better start thinking of women's half sizes."

"Why, Constance!" said Charlotte, stunned. "I've worn an eighteen for years, ever since I began buying my clothes from you. I declare, I don't know what's got into you!"

"You have worn an eighteen for years only because I've always torn the size tag out of everything you ever tried on and sub-

105

stituted one that read eighteen," said Constance bluntly. "Here's a size twenty four and a half that may fit, although to tell you the truth for a change, I doubt it."

"Well!" said Charlotte Page, picking up her umbrella and gloves. "Well!"

Constance winced at the emphatic banging of the door behind Charlotte which said, more clearly than words, "Good-by! And I won't be back!" Then she pushed tiredly at her hair and went to the small room in the back of the shop where she kept an electric plate and a refrigerator. She made herself a bicarbonate of soda and drank it down quickly, shuddering.

I don't know what's got into me any more than you do, Charlotte, she thought.

In the beginning, Constance had told herself it was an overwhelming sense of relief that had shaken her when she first met Tomas Makris and knew that she had never seen his face before. How ridiculous she had been!

Eight million people in the city of New York, she had thought, laughing shakily. And I was worried about the one who found his way to Peyton Place!

But after that first meeting, when relief should have calmed her and left her soothed, Constance began to be plagued with restless nights and frequent attacks of indigestion. Twice she had glimpsed Tomas Makris on the street, and both times she had run rather than face him, but afterward she could not think of a reasonable explanation for her action. Perhaps she had been more apprehensive than she had first thought when Allison had told her of the new headmaster who was coming to town from New York, and she was suffering now from the after effects of a terrible anxiety.

It would, she admitted, have been a distressing situation if Tomas Makris had turned out to be someone who had known Allison MacKenzie and his family from Scarsdale. But since he was not, it was hard to explain why the image of the town's new headmaster stayed with her so persistently.

Anyone, she declared to herself, would be impressed with a man that size, with his almost revolting good looks and that smile that belongs in a bedroom.

But nothing she told herself served to make the thought of Tomas Makris fade from her thoughts.

Late one night, Allison was awakened by a vague stirring somewhere in the house. She lay still, in the unreal world between sleep and wakefulness, and heard the sound of water running in the bathroom.

It's only Mother, she thought sleepily.

With the adaptability of the young, she had accepted her mother's new restlessness without question.

Allison turned over and saw the luminous face of her bedside clock shimmering. She opened her eyes wider, and the clock's face no longer wavered. Two o'clock. With the miraculous facility which seems to disappear with childhood, Allison was suddenly thoroughly awake. She sat up in her bed and circled her knees with her arms. It was raining, the way it had been raining for days, and the white curtains at Allison's window turned and twisted in the wind. For a long time she watched them, noticing that the wind caused not one motion that was ungraceful. Her curtains had the same bodilessness that the branches of the trees seemed to have in the face of a high wind. They dipped and swayed and turned, and every motion was liquid.

I wish, thought Allison, that I could dance like something moved by the wind.

Allison got out of bed quietly and turned on the lamp next to her clock; then she went to the closet where her dress for the spring dance hung. She touched the wide tulle skirts and ran her fingers over the slippery softness of the bodice of her first floor-length and therefore grown-up party dress. When she took the dress from its hanger and held it out and away from her, the air moving through her room caught at the pale blue material and made the skirts billow softly.

It dances by itself, she thought, and held the dress against her body. She moved around the room with small, dancing steps, trying to keep her neck relaxed so that her head moved gracefully from side to side, and it was only when she caught a glimpse of herself in the long mirror attached to the inside of her closet door that she stopped. She looked at her sturdy, pajama-clad body and noticed how her hair hung on her shoulders, fine, limp and plain brown.

If I only had more of a shape, she thought sadly, lowering the party dress. If I were very thin and much taller, I could move like a bluebell in the wind, and everyone would say that I was the best dancer in the world. If I were only completely blonde, like Mother, or very dark, like my father. If I just wasn't so awfully *medium!*

Her cotton pajamas were printed colorfully with dancing circus

107

figures, and the top was cut full and straight, with a small round collar. The bottom had wide legs and was banded at the waist with elastic, and Allison looked at herself with disgust.

What a babyish outfit for a thirteen-year-old girl! she thought resentfully. I look like a child!

Her fingers pulled impatiently at the buttons of her pajama coat, fumbling in their eagerness to shed a garment that underlined her childishness. The silk bodice of her new dress was cold against her bare skin, but it was smooth, like rich soap lather, and the blue of the material reflected itself in her eyes. The tulle scratched uncomfortably against her bare legs, and Allison, panicky now, saw that her first grown-up dress did not make her look grown up at all.

What if *he* doesn't think I'm pretty, she thought. What if he looks at me and is sorry that he asked me!

She ran to her bureau and took her rubber-padded brassière from a drawer. She held it in front of her, over the dress, and studied herself in the mirror, almost afraid to slip the top of her dress down and put on the undergarment; for if the brassière failed to make her look grown up, there was nothing left to try. At last, with her back to the mirror, she lowered the dress top, fastened the brassière into place and slipped the top of her dress back on. She whirled quickly, trying to capture in her own reflection the impression she would make on Rodney Harrington when he saw her dressed like this for the first time. Her mirror assured her that it would be a favorable one. The top of her new dress swelled magnificently, the fabric straining tautly against her rubber breasts, so that her waist seemed smaller and her hips more curved.

Allison bent forward, hoping that the front of her dress was loose enough, and cut low enough, that the top curves of her bosom would be visible to anyone who cared to look at her from that angle. She and Kathy Ellsworth had finished reading a book the previous afternoon in which the hero had been reduced to a perspiring jelly by the sight of his true love's breasts over the bodice of her silver lamé gown. Allison sighed. Her dress covered her completely, and even if it had not, her rubber-cupped brassière did.

But, she thought, turning to get a side view of her figure, I look *very* mature from this angle, and you can't have everything.

"For Heaven's sake, Allison, it's almost three o'clock in the morning. Take off that dress and get to bed!"

108

For a moment, Allison was so startled that she felt as if she had been punched in the stomach. She realized, suddenly, that it was cold in the room, and shivered, and without knowing why, she wondered how a canary bird felt when someone poked inquisitive fingers into its cage.

"You might at least knock before you open my door," she said crossly.

Constance, not realizing that she had broken into a private dream, replied in the same tone.

"Don't be fresh, Allison," she said. "Take off that dress."

"Whenever I say anything, it's always fresh," said Allison furiously. "But no matter what you say, it's always courteous."

"And give me that stupid rubber bra," said Constance, ignoring Allison's remark. "You look like an inflated balloon with that thing on."

Allison burst into tears and let her new dress drop to the floor.

"I can never have a moment of privacy," she wept. "Not even in my own room!"

Constance picked up the dress and hung it up. "Give," she ordered, holding out her hand for Allison's brassière.

"You're mean," cried Allison. "You're mean and hateful and cruel! No matter what I want, you always try to spoil it!"

"Shut up and go to sleep," said Constance coldly, turning off the light.

The sound of Allison's sobs followed her down the hall and into her own room. Constance lit a cigarette. She was smoking too much lately, and she was too often unfair to Allison. That business with the brassière had been unfair, for Constance had let the child go for months thinking that her mother was taken in by the fact that Allison could sprout a voluptuous figure whenever the occasion for one arose.

I should have put a stop to it in the beginning, she thought. Even if it was only something she did around the house, I should have let her know that no one would be fooled by falsies for very long.

Constance sighed heavily and puffed at her cigarette.

"It's the goddamned season that makes me so hard to get along with," she said, to her own surprise, for she never talked out loud to herself and seldom swore.

It's all this rain that makes everything so depressing, she amended silently.

It was easy, that year, to blame the season for anything. Spring

109

had come late and was making up for lost time. She invaded Peyton Place like a whirlwind hurrying, hurrying, hurrying, Allison had thought, like the White Rabbit on his way to the Mad Hatter's tea party. Spring came in a deluge and loosed the ice in the wide Connecticut River so that the river roiled and groaned and overflowed in protest. She washed the snows of winter from the fields and trees, and she battered the earth relentlessly until the thick layers of frost gave way before her and melted into muddy submission. Spring was ungentle that year, so that it was hard to think of her as a time of tender leaves and small, delicate flowers. She was a fury, twisting and beating, a force obsessed with the idea of winning the land in a vicious contest with winter. Only after she had won was she smiling and serene, like a naughty child after a temper tantrum. May was half gone before Spring relaxed and sat back, spreading her green skirts smugly, while the farmers planted their gardens and kept one eye on this capricious maiden who might fly into a rage at any moment. Once Spring had calmed down, the days passed slowly, flowing into one another like the movements of a symphony, and it was only Constance MacKenzie who was left disquieted. Even with the turbulent days of April gone, and with her calendar showing her that it was May and a time of sunshine and silent growth, Constance was as unstill as the river in floodtime. She did not recognize the symptoms in herself as akin to the painful restlessness of adolescence, nor did she admit that the dissatisfied yearning within her could be a sexual one. She blamed the externals of her life; her daughter, the heavier responsibilities of an enlarged business, and the constant effort she had to make toward both.

"It's enough to make a Christian Scientist sick!" she declared angrily one day while unpacking merchandise in her shop.

"What did you say, Mrs. MacKenzie?" asked Selena Cross from behind a counter where she was sorting children's underwear.

"Oh, go to hell," said Constance crossly.

Selena kept quiet. It disturbed her to see Mrs. MacKenzie as unhappy as she had been for the last few weeks. Not that her unhappiness always manifested itself in a sharp tongue, but one could never tell in advance when it would, and it made things in the shop difficult. When Selena had a feeling that Mrs. MacKenzie was going to turn ugly, she always tried to get to the customer first, hoping silently that the customer would not demand to see Constance. But the worst of all for Selena, was the way Mrs. MacKenzie acted after one of her outbursts. She was

110

always sorry and tried to make amends, and as she did so she smiled an uncertain, quivering smile. It made Selena want to pat Constance's shoulder to assure her that everything would be all right. When Mrs. MacKenzie was sorry for something, she looked the way Joey did when he made Selena angry and wanted to make up with her. It was bad enough when Joey looked like that, but when Mrs. MacKenzie did it, Selena wanted to cry. This emotion in Selena was the measure of her devotion to Constance MacKenzie, for Selena could have watched anyone but Constance or Joey suffering the tortures of regret without a quiver.

Constance put an invoice down on the counter and turned to Selena.

"I'm sorry, dear," she said, and smiled. "I shouldn't have talked to you like that."

Oh, *don't*, thought Selena. Please don't look like that!

"That's all right, Mrs. MacKenzie," she said. "I guess we all have our off days."

"My stomach is a little upset," said Constance. "But I shouldn't take it out on you."

"That's all right," said Selena. "Why don't you go home and lie down for a while. It's almost time to close anyway, and I could manage alone until six."

"Of course not," said Constance. "I'll straighten out in a few minutes, I—" she broke off at the sound of the front door opening.

Tomas Makris seemed to fill the entire front of the shop. His shoulders, covered now by a trench coat against the temperament of the May afternoon, gave him a look of strength and power that left Constance terror stricken. Foolishly, she was reminded of the simile of the bull in a china shop, but it did not amuse her in that moment. She could imagine only too clearly the smashing havoc of such a situation.

"I'd like some socks," said Makris, who had contrived this prospective purchase as an excuse to see Constance MacKenzie again.

He had at first hoped to meet her on the street, but when he had glimpsed her twice, only to have her either cross the street or enter a building to avoid him, he had decided to face her in a place where she would not be able to avoid talking to him.

"Socks," he repeated, when Constance did not speak. "Solid colors, if you have them. Size twelve and a half."

"Selena!" said Constance sharply. "Selena, wait on this gentleman, please," and, without looking at Makris again, she fled to the small room at the back of the shop.

111

Makris stood still, looking after her, and his dark eyes narrowed in speculation.

"I wonder why she is frightened?" he asked himself. "And she is frightened."

"May I help you, sir?" asked Selena.

Going on the assumption that anything is possible, thought Makris, who had not even heard Selena, perhaps she has an extrasensory perception that lets her know what I'm thinking. Maybe she is the exception to the rule that all women love to know that a man finds them physically attractive. But if that's the case, why isn't she disgusted, repulsed, anything except frightened?

"Was it something in socks, sir?" asked Selena.

"Yes," said Makris absently and walked out of the shop.

Selena went to the front window and watched the tall, broad figure that moved away on Elm Street. She felt a sympathy for Mr. Makris. He wasn't the first man in town who had hoped, at some time or another, to find his way to Constance MacKenzie's bedroom. It seemed to Selena that all men regarded divorcees or widows as fair game, and Constance had had her share of advances made and remarks passed. It had been more noticeable lately, because of the steady stream of new customers that came into the shop since Constance had put in men's wear. Even Leslie Harrington had come in more than once, although everyone in town knew that he bought all his clothes in New York. What had seemed to discourage the men more than anything else was the fact that Constance seemed unaware that a man might be trying to make up to her, and it had amused Selena to see most of the town's male population struggle for an opening gambit with the town's most beautiful woman. Mrs. MacKenzie had never seemed to realize that men were human, mused Selena, but here she was, the first time Mr. Makris looked at her, not only realizing it but letting it frighten her.

"Did he buy anything?" asked Constance.

"No," said Selena, turning to her. "I guess he didn't see anything he wanted."

Now that Allison was no longer friendly with Selena, Constance had developed a deep affection for the stepdaughter of Lucas Cross. She found her intelligent and a good worker, but it was with a feeling of shock that Constance sometimes found herself discussing adult questions with a child who could answer her in kind.

"What do you think of him?" she asked Selena.

"I think he's the handsomest man I ever saw," said Selena. "Handsomer than Doc Swain must have been when he was young, and even handsomer than anyone in the movies."

Do you think he finds me attractive?

For one lightheaded moment the question quivered on the tip of Constance's tongue, and she almost asked it aloud while Selena waited expectantly.

Why should it matter to me whether he does or not? Constance demanded of herself.

"I'm going to get my dress this week," said Selena to cover the awkward pause. "I have the rest of the money saved so that I can get it on Friday, in time for the dance."

"Take it today, if you like," said Constance. "I told you weeks ago, Selena, that you didn't have to wait until you had the money. You could have taken the dress home any time."

"I'd rather not," said Selena. "I wouldn't want to owe money on it, and besides, I don't have a place to keep it at home."

She went to the closet where Constance kept garments on which deposits had been made and looked at the white dress which hung there, carefully marked. "Selena Cross," said the tag. "Balance due: $5.95."

"You'll be the prettiest girl at the dance," said Constance, smiling. "And you'll be the only one there wearing white. All the other girls will be in colors."

"I just hope Ted will think I'm the prettiest girl there," said Selena and laughed. "I've never been to a dance before. It's a nice feeling to have everything new to go somewhere you've never been before. Then everything is brand new, the feeling, and your clothes, and yourself, almost."

"How old do you think he is?" asked Constance.

"Thirty-five," said Selena. "Leslie Harrington told Ted's mother."

◆ 24 ◆

Selena, who had been kneeling on the floor in front of her cot, sat back on her heels. There was a sickness in her stomach that brought perspiration out on her face and turned her weak, and she balanced her body by placing her hands on the floor.

"It's gone," she said.

"What, Selena?" asked her brother. "What's gone?"

Selena waited until the sick feeling subsided a little, then she stood up.

"My money," she said. "It's gone, Joey. Someone took it."

"Naw," protested Joey. "Naw it ain't, Selena. You just didn't look good."

Selena ripped the thin mattress from the cot and threw it halfway across the shack.

"There!" she demanded. "Do you see it anywhere?"

There was not a trace of Selena's white money envelope anywhere in the bed, nor did it fall out of the torn blanket that she and Joey shook out. The envelope had contained ten dollars in single bills and represented ten afternoons of work at the Thrifty Corner.

"It's gone," repeated Selena. "Pa took it."

Although her voice was low, it held such a terrible sound that Joey was afraid of his sister for the first time in his life.

"Pa wouldn't steal," protested Joey. "He might get drunk and fight and hit, but Pa wouldn't steal."

As if she had not heard, Selena said, "And the dance is tomorrow night and I'll have to stay home."

In a box under her cot, carefully packed in tissue paper, were the things she had bought, piecemeal, to wear with the new white dress; a pair of silk stockings, a pair of black suède shoes, and a set of white underwear.

"The only dress I ever wanted," she said, "and Pa took the money. I was going to have my hair washed at Abbie's Beauty Salon with the rest of the money, and buy a bottle of perfume down at Prescott's. And Pa stole my money."

"Stop saying that!" cried Joey. "Pa wouldn't take it. You just hid it somewhere, and now you forgot where. We'll find it. Remember the time Paul was missing money, and he thought Pa took it? He found it the next day where he hid it in his good pants."

For a short moment Selena was cheered, for it was true that her stepbrother Paul had once unjustly accused his father of stealing. There had been a terrible fight that night, and the next day, after Paul had found his money, he had left Peyton Place and gone north to work. The only trouble was that Selena had seen her white envelope on the morning of this same day. She had taken it out from under the mattress, counted the money in it and returned it to its hiding place.

"He took it," said Nellie Cross. "Your Pa took it. I seen him do it."

114

Nellie was sitting on the edge of the sagging double bed, staring at her toes where they came through the holes in the tips of her house slippers. Selena and Joey were startled when Nellie spoke, for in recent months their mother had developed a talent for erasing herself from most situations. She seemed able to blend herself into the background, so that for long periods of time her children and her husband would forget that she was in the same room with them.

"He took it this mornin'," said Nellie. "I seen him. He took it from under Selena's bed. I seen him, the sonofabitch."

Selena's fists clenched in frustration. "Why didn't you stop him?" she demanded, knowing that her question was unreasonable. "You could have told him it was mine."

Nellie spoke as if she had not heard her daughter. "Sonsof-bitches," she said. "All of 'em."

The door of the shack swung open then, and Lucas Cross stood there smiling and swaying a little.

"Who's a sonofabitch?" he asked.

"You are," said Selena without a moment's hesitation. "Not just a plain, ordinary sonofabitch, but a dumb sonofabitch. You didn't learn anything about drinking from being in the hospital and seeing bugs all over the place until everybody in the town thought you were crazy. It didn't mean anything to you to see Kenny Stearns almost bleed to death, so that even Doc Swain was scared he wouldn't live. You still hang around with that dumb Kenny and get drunk all the time, and now you've gone to stealing money. Give me what's left of it, Pa."

Lucas looked down at her outstretched hand.

"What're you talkin' about, honey?" he asked innocently.

"You know what I'm talkin' about, Pa. The envelope you stole from under my bed. I want it back."

"Watch out what you say to your Pa, Selena. Lucas Cross never stole from nobody yet. The last person said that to me was your brother Paul, and I give him a helluva lickin' for it. Be careful."

"Where's the envelope that was under my mattress then? The one with the ten one-dollar bills in it?"

"You mean this one?" asked Lucas. He held up the envelope which was grimy now, and well creased.

The girl snatched at it anxiously, but Lucas laughed and raised it over his head.

"Give it to me," she said.

"Well, now, hold on a minute," said Lucas in a maddening drawl.

115

"Just you hold on a minute, honey. Seems to me a gal oughta start payin' board if she's workin'. 'Tain't right, Selena, for you to hold out on your pa like you been doin'."

"It's mine," said Selena. "I worked for it, and I earned it. Give it to me."

Lucas moved away from the door and sat down on a chair next to the kitchen table.

"Since your brother went, things ain't been too easy for me," said Lucas in an exaggerated whine. "Seems to me you could help your pa out, a big girl like you."

"You had plenty of money after you got done working the woods this last time," said Selena. "You shouldn't have spent it all for drink. You're not going to drink up my money, Pa. I worked every afternoon after school for that money, and I want it back."

"It's a shame to spend good money to get yourself prettied up for Ted Carter," said Lucas. "A waste of money, if you ask me. Them Carters. Trash, they are. Always were. She's no better than a whore, and him, he's been pimpin' for her for twenty years."

"The Carters have nothing to do with my money," cried Selena. She rushed at her father and attempted to tear the white envelope from his hand, but he moved back quickly in his chair, and Selena almost fell. Lucas laughed.

"Seems to me," he said, "that a gal big enough to talk to her pa like that, a gal big enough to go out dancin' with the son of a whore and a pimp, oughta be big enough to take what she wants from her pa, easy as takin' candy from a baby. If she went about it right."

For a long moment Selena looked at her father. Only for a second did her eyes ask for pity; then they held only realization. Lucas smiled his grotesque smile, and when his forehead moved, the girl noticed the shine of sweat on it.

"From what I understand," he said, "you don't mind rasslin' with Ted Carter, when he's tryin' to get what he wants. I just turned the tables on you, honey. Now you gotta rassle me to get what you want."

Without taking her eyes from her father's, Selena spoke to her brother.

"Go on outside, Joey," she said.

The child stared at his sister. "But it's dark out," he protested. "And cold."

"Go on outside, Joey. Go on outside and stay there 'til I call for you."

She did not speak again until the door closed behind her little brother and then she said: "I'm not going anywhere near you, Pa. Just give me my money."

"Come on over here and get it," said Lucas hoarsely. "You just come on over here and try to take it away from me."

Nellie Cross stared at her toes through the holes in her slippers. "Sonsofbitches," she said softly. "Sonsofbitches, all of 'em."

Although Nellie spoke softly, Lucas started as if he had just realized that she was in the room. He looked first at his wife and then at Selena, and Selena's eyes were filled with hatred.

"Here," he said, after another glance at Nellie. "Take your goddamn money."

He tossed the creased envelope toward Selena and it fell on the floor at her feet.

"Sonsofbitches," repeated Nellie. "All of 'em. Booze and wimmin. Wimmin and booze."

◆ 25 ◆

Rodney Harrington, wearing a white jacket and with his curly black hair well slicked down with water, sat on the edge of a chair in the MacKenzie living room. Constance had left him there while she went upstairs to see if Allison was ready, and now Rodney sat and stared morosely at the braided rug on the floor.

What, he asked himself, ever prompted him to ask Allison MacKenzie to the biggest dance of the year? Especially to this dance, the very first that he was being allowed to attend. There was Betty Anderson, all eager and hot after him, just waiting for him to ask her to the dance, and he had gone and asked Allison MacKenzie. Ask a nice girl, his father had ordered, and look where Rodney had wound up. On the edge of a chair in the MacKenzie living room, waiting for skinny Allison. He could have had a good time with Betty, damn it all.

Rodney felt himself reddening and looked surreptitiously around the empty room. He did not like to think of the afternoon that he had spent in the woods at Road's End with Betty Anderson, unless he was sure that he was by himself. When he was alone, he could not keep from thinking of it.

That Betty! thought Rodney, letting memory take him. Boy, she was really something. Nothing kiddish about her or what she had shown him that afternoon. She didn't talk like a kid, either, or look like one. By God, she was something, whether her father was a mill hand or not, she was still something!

Rodney closed his eyes and felt his breath coming fast with the memory of Betty Anderson.

No, he shook himself, not here. I'll wait until tonight when I get home.

He looked around the MacKenzie living room and once again his thoughts began to lacerate him.

He could have had a swell time at the dance with Betty, and here he was, waiting for Allison. And if that wasn't bad enough, Betty was mad at him for not asking her. You couldn't blame Betty for that, after all, when a girl shared a secret with you, she had a right to expect you to ask her to the biggest dance of the year. He just hoped she'd be at the dance. Maybe he'd get a chance to talk to her and find out if she was still mad. Damn it, he could have talked his father out of putting his foot down about Betty if he had really tried. And there was skinny Allison, always making cow eyes at him, and his father had said to ask a nice girl.

Fool! said Rodney Harrington to himself. Damn fool!

He could hear a stirring on the stairs in the hall, now, so he supposed that Allison was finally coming down. He just hoped she looked decent and wouldn't make those cow eyes at him at the dance, where some of the boys might see. He couldn't afford to have Betty overhear anyone teasing him about Allison or any other girl.

"Here's Allison, Rodney," said Constance.

Rodney stood up. "Hi, Allison."

"Hi."

"Well, my father's outside in the car."

"All right."

"You got a coat or something?"

"I have this. It's an evening coat."

"Well, let's go."

"I'm ready."

"Good night, Mrs. MacKenzie."

"Good night, Mother."

"Good night—" Constance caught herself just in time. She had almost said "Children." "Good night, Allison," she said. "Good night, Rodney. Have a nice time."

As soon as they were out the door, Constance sank wearily into a chair. It had been a difficult week, with Allison alternating between moments of unbearable impatience and hours of demoralizing panic. When she awakened on the day of the dance with an angry red pimple on her chin, she wept and demanded that Constance telephone Rodney immediately to tell him that Allison was ill and would not be able to go out that evening. Constance lit a cigarette and looked at the framed photograph on the mantelpiece.

"Well, Allison," she said aloud, "here we are. Alone at last."

Your bastard daughter is all bathed, curled, perfumed, manicured and dressed, and here we are, Allison, you and I alone, waiting for her to return from her first formal engagement.

It frightened Constance when she thought in that fashion, with bitterness and self-pity, and it shocked her to realize that lately her bitterness was not only for the position in which Allison MacKenzie had placed her fourteen years before. In recent weeks she had been actively resenting the idea of being left alone to cope with a growing girl, and in her angry reasoning the blame for this fell entirely on the shoulders of her dead lover. Allison's crime, and in Constance's eyes it was a crime, was that he had claimed to love her. That being the case, his first thoughts should have been for her protection, coming ahead of his desire to lead her to bed but, as Constance put it to herself, he had not thought of protection until too late, and Constance had ended up by allowing Allison MacKenzie to become a habit with her. She knew that she had not loved him, for if she had, the relationship between them could never have been what it was. Love, to Constance, was synonymous with marriage, and marriage was something based on a community of tastes and interests, together with a similarity of background and viewpoint. All these were blended together by an emotion called "love," and sex did not enter into it at all. Therefore, reasoned Constance, she had certainly not loved Allison MacKenzie. Constance's eyes went again to the photograph on the mantelpiece, and she wondered where, eventually, she would find the words to explain the way of things to the daughter of Allison MacKenzie. The ringing of the doorbell cut across her mind, breaking sharply into her thoughts. Constance sighed again, more deeply than before, and rubbed the back of her neck where it ached. Allison, she supposed, had forgotten a handkerchief in her excitement.

Constance opened her front door and saw Tomas Makris standing on the steps. For a moment she was unable to move or speak, overcome not so much by surprise, as by a feeling of unreality.

"Good evening," said Tom into the silence. "Since you always manage to avoid me on the street and even in your store, I thought I'd come to call formally."

When Constance did not answer but continued to stand with one hand on the inside doorknob and the other leaning against the jamb, Tom went on in the same conversational tone.

"I realize," he said, "that it is not the conventional thing to do. I should have waited to call until after you had called on me, but I was afraid that you would never get around to performing your neighborly duty. Mrs. MacKenzie," he went on, pushing gently at the outside of the door, "I have been standing on the street corner for over half an hour waiting for your daughter to be off with her date, and my feet are damned tired. May I come in?"

"Oh, yes. Please do," said Constance at last, and her voice sounded breathy to her own ears. "Yes, do. Please come in."

She stood with her back against the panels of the closed door while Tom walked past her and into the hall.

"Let me take your coat, Mr. Makris," she said.

Tom took off his coat and folded it over his arm, then he walked to where Constance was standing. He stood close enough to her so that she had to raise her head to look up at him, and when she had done so, he smiled down at her gently.

"Don't be afraid," he said. "I'm not going to hurt you. I'm going to be around for a long time. There's no hurry."

◆ 26 ◆

The gymnasium of the Peyton Place High School was decorated with pink and green crepe paper. The paper hung in twisted festoons from the ceiling and walls. It was wrapped carefully around the basketball hoops and backboards in a hopeful effort at disguise. Some imaginative senior, discouraged with the limp look of the basketball nets, had cleverly stuffed them with multicolored spring blossoms and someone else had fastened a balloon to every spot that provided a place to tie a string. On the wall, behind where the orchestra sat, huge letters cut of aluminum foil had been pasted.

PEYTON PLACE HIGH SCHOOL WELCOMES YOU
TO ITS ANNUAL SPRING HOP

The seniors who had been on the decorating committee drew sighs of relief and looked at their work with well-earned satisfaction. The gym, they assured one another, had never looked better for a spring dance than it did this year. The annual spring dance, which had become a custom in Peyton Place since the building of the new high school, was an affair given by the graduating seniors as a premature welcome to the grade school children who would be entering high school in the fall, and it had come to represent a number of things to different people. To most eighth grade girls it meant the time of their first formal and their first real date with a boy, while to most boys it meant the official lifting of the nine o'clock curfew which their parents had imposed on them. To Elsie Thornton, dressed in black silk and acting as a chaperon, it seemed to be a time of new awareness in the youngsters whom she had taught that year. She could discern in them the first stirrings of interest toward one another and knew that this interest was the forerunner of the searching and finding that would come later.

Not, thought Miss Thornton, that a few of them hadn't done their searching and finding already.

She watched Selena Cross and Ted Carter circling the floor slowly, their heads close together, and although she was not a believer in the myth of childhood sweethearts who grew up, married and lived happily ever after, she found herself hoping that it could be so in the case of Selena and Ted. Her feelings when she watched Allison MacKenzie and Rodney Harrington were very different. It had been like a blow to her heart to see Allison come in with Rodney. Miss Thornton had put up an involuntary hand, and lowered it quickly, hoping that no one had noticed.

Oh, be careful, my dear, she had thought. You must be very careful, or you'll get hurt.

Miss Thornton saw Betty Anderson, dressed in a red dress that was much too old for her, watching Allison and Rodney. Betty had come to the dance with a boy who was a senior in the high school and who already had a reputation as a fast driver and a hard drinker. But Betty had not taken her eyes off Rodney all evening. It was ten o'clock before Rodney got up the courage to approach Betty. He walked over to her the moment that Allison left him to go to the rest room, and when Allison returned to the gymnasium he was dancing with Betty. Allison went over to the line of straight chairs where the chaperons were sitting and sat down

121

next to Elsie Thornton, but her eyes were fixed on Rodney and Betty.

Don't you care, darling, Miss Thornton wanted to say. Don't pin your dreams on that boy, for he will only shatter them and you.

"You look lovely, Allison," she said.

"Thank you, Miss Thornton," replied Allison, wondering if it would be proper to say, So do you, Miss Thornton. It would be a lie if she said it, because Miss Thornton had never looked uglier. Black was definitely not her color. And why was Rodney staying so long with Betty?

Allison kept her head up and her smile on, even when one set of dances ended and another began, and Rodney did not come to claim her. She smiled and waved at Selena, and at Kathy Ellsworth who had come with a boy who was in high school and kissed with his mouth open. She felt a small pang of compassion for little Norman Page who stood leaning against the wall, alone, and stared down at his feet. Norman, Allison knew, had been brought to the dance by his mother, who was going to leave him there until eleven o'clock while she attended a meeting of the Ladies' Aid at the Congregational church. Allison smiled at Norman when he raised his head, and wiggled her fingers at him, but her stomach had begun to churn and she did not know how much longer she could keep from being sick. Betty's finger tips rested on the back of Rodney's neck, and he was looking down at her with his eyes half closed.

Why is he doing this to me? she wondered sickly. I look nicer than Betty. She looks cheap in that sleazy red dress, and she's wearing gunk on her eyelashes. She's got awfully big breasts for a girl her age, and Kathy said they were real. I don't believe it. I wish Miss Thornton would stop fidgeting in her chair—and there's only one more dance left in this set and I'd better get ready to stand up because Rodney will be coming for me in a few minutes. I'll bet that dress belonged to Betty's big sister, the one who got in Dutch with that man from White River. Selena looks beautiful in that white dress. She looks so old. She looks twenty at least, and Ted does, too. They're in love, you can tell by looking at them. Everybody's looking at me. I'm the only girl sitting down. Rodney's gone!

Allison's heart began to beat in hot, heavy thuds as her eyes circled the dance floor wildly. She glanced at the door just in time to see a flash of red, and she knew then that Rodney had left her here alone while he went somewhere with Betty.

What if he doesn't come back? she thought. What if I have to go home alone? Everyone knows I came with him. EVERYONE IS LAUGHING AT ME!

Miss Thornton's hand was cold and hurtful on her elbow.

"My goodness, Allison," laughed Miss Thornton. "You *are* off in a dream world. Norman's asked you to dance with him twice, and you haven't even answered him."

Allison's eyes were so full of tears that she could not see Norman, and her face hurt. It was only when she stood up to dance with him that she realized that she was still smiling. Norman held her awkwardly while the orchestra imported from White River for the occasion played a waltz.

If he says one thing—thought Allison desperately. If he says one word I shall be sick right here in front of everyone.

"I saw Rodney go outside with Betty," said Norman, "so I thought I'd ask you to dance. You were sitting next to Miss Thornton for an awfully long time."

Allison was not sick in front of everyone. "Thank you, Norman," she said. "It was nice of you to ask me."

"I don't know what's the matter with Rodney," continued Norman. "You're much prettier than that fat old Betty Anderson."

Oh, God, prayed Allison, make him shut up.

"Betty came with John Pillsbury." Norman pronounced it Pillsbree. "He drinks and takes girls riding in his car. He got stopped by the state police once, for speeding and drunken driving, and the police told his father. Do you like Rodney?"

I love him! screamed Allison silently. I love him and he is breaking my heart!

"No," she said, "not particularly. He was just someone to come with."

Norman whirled her around inexpertly. "Just the same," he said, "it's a dirty trick for him to leave you sitting with Miss Thornton and go off with Betty like that."

Please, God. Please, God, thought Allison.

But the orchestra continued to play, and Norman's hand was sticky in hers, and Allison thought of the girl in the fairy tale about the red shoes, and the electric lights glared down at her until her temples began to pound.

Outside, Betty Anderson was leading Rodney by the hand across the dark field that served as a parking lot for the high school. John Pillsbury's car was parked a short distance away

123

from the others, under a tree, and when Betty and Rodney reached it, she opened the back door and got in.

"Hurry up," she whispered, and Rodney climbed in behind her.

Swiftly, she pressed down the buttons on the four doors that locked them, and then she collapsed into the back seat, laughing.

"Here we are," she said. "Snug as peas in a pod."

"Come on, Betty," whispered Rodney. "Come on."

"No," she said petulantly, "I won't. I'm mad at you."

"Aw, come on, Betty. Don't be like that. Kiss me."

"No," said Betty, tossing her head. "Go get skinny Allison MacKenzie to kiss you. She's the one you brought to the dance."

"Don't be mad, Betty," pleaded Rodney. "I couldn't help it. I didn't want to. My father made me do it."

"Would you rather be with me?" asked Betty in a slightly mollified tone.

"*Would* I?" breathed Rodney, and it was not a question.

Betty leaned her head against his shoulder and ran one finger up and down on his coat lapel.

"Just the same," she said, "I think it was mean of you to ask Allison to the dance."

"Aw, come on, Betty. Don't be like that. Kiss me a little."

Betty lifted her head and Rodney quickly covered her mouth with his. She could kiss, thought Rodney, like no one else in the world. She didn't kiss with just her lips, but with her teeth and her tongue, and all the while she made noises deep in her throat, and her fingernails dug into his shoulders.

"Oh, honey, honey," whispered Rodney, and that was all he could say before Betty's tongue went between his teeth again.

Her whole body twisted and moved when he kissed her, and when his hands found their way to her breasts, she moaned as if she were hurt. She writhed on the seat until she was lying down, with only her legs and feet not touching him, and Rodney fitted his body to her without taking his mouth from hers.

"Is it up, Rod?" she panted, undulating her body under his. "Is it up good and hard?"

"Oh, yes," he whispered, almost unable to speak. "Oh, yes."

Without another word, Betty jacknifed her knees, pushed Rodney away from her, clicked the lock on the door and was outside of the car.

"Now go shove it into Allison MacKenzie," she screamed at him. "Go get the girl you brought to the dance and get rid of it with her!"

Before Rodney could catch his breath to utter one word, she had whirled and was on her way back to the gymnasium. He tried to get out of the car to run after her, but his legs were like sawdust under him, and he could only cling to the open door and curse under his breath.

"Bitch," he said hoarsely, using one of his father's favorite words. "Goddamned bitch!"

He hung onto the open car door and retched helplessly, and the sweat poured down his face.

"Bitch!" he said, but it did not help.

At last, he straightened up and wiped his face with his handkerchief, and fumbled in his pockets for a comb. He still had to go back into the gymnasium to get that goddamned Allison MacKenzie. His father would drive up at eleven-thirty and expect to find him waiting with her.

"Oh, you rotten bitch," he said under his breath to the absent Betty. "Oh, you stinking, rotten, goddamned bitchy sonofabitch!"

He racked his brain to think of new swear words to direct at her, but he could think of nothing. He began to comb his hair, almost in tears.

Over Norman's shoulder, Allison saw Betty Anderson come back into the gymnasium, alone.

Dear God, she thought, maybe he's gone home alone! What shall I do?

"There's Betty," said Norman. "I wonder what happened to Rodney?"

"He's probably in the Men's," said Allison who could not seem to keep her voice steady. "Please, Norman. Couldn't we sit down. My feet hurt."

And my head, she thought. And my stomach. And my arms, and hands, and legs, and the back of my neck.

It was eleven-fifteen when she saw Rodney walk through the door. She was so overwhelmed with relief that she could not be angry. He had saved her face by returning to her and not leaving her to go home alone. He looked sick. His face was red and swollen looking.

"You almost ready to go?" he asked Allison.

"Any time you are," she said nonchalantly.

"My father's outside, so we might as well go."

"We might just as well."

"I'll get your coat."

"All right."

125

"Do you want to dance one more first?"

"No. No, thank you. I've been dancing so much all evening that my feet are ready to fall off."

"Well, I'll get your coat."

And that, thought Miss Elsie Thornton, is that. Valiant is the word for Allison.

"Good night, Miss Thornton. I had a lovely time."

"Good night, dear," said Miss Thornton.

◆ 27 ◆

To Miss Elsie Thornton, the twentieth of June was the most trying day of the year. It was graduation day, and it always left her with an uncomfortable mixture of feelings comprised of happiness, regret and the peculiar weariness that comes with the relaxation of effort. She sat alone in the empty auditorium after the exercises, enjoying these few minutes by herself now that the crowd had gone. In a little while, Kenny Stearns would come in, with his mops and pails, to begin the work of cleaning up, but for these few moments everything was still, and Miss Thornton looked around tiredly.

The hastily constructed wooden benches, built in graduated rows like bleachers at a football stadium, still stood on the empty stage. A short while before, their nakedness had been hidden by the white skirts of thirty-two girls and the dark trousers of forty boys who comprised the graduating classes of the grade and high schools, but all that was left now to show that the youngsters had been there at all was one lost white glove and three crumpled programs. There were tall letters, made of gilt cardboard, pinned to the black velvet curtain behind the benches: ONWARD!— CLASSES OF 1937. Sometime during the evening, the nine in 1937 had been pulled loose so that it hung now at a tipsy angle, giving a comic look to something that had been arranged with utmost seriousness.

Perhaps, thought Miss Thornton defensively, the entire evening's performance would be comical to an outsider. Certainly, the scratchiness of the Peyton Place High School band attempting to play a composition as pretentious as "Pomp and Circumstance" had its comical aspects. And Jared Clarke, while he had not actually remarked that the graduates were "standing with reluctant feet" had most certainly implied it.

Yes, Miss Thornton imagined, there were many people, especially the dean of Smith College, who would find these things laughable. But Miss Thornton had not been amused. When seventy-two children, among them the forty-odd whom she had taught all year, rose in a body to sing, "Hail, Alma Mater fair, our song to thee we raise," Miss Thornton had been filled with emotion which some might have called "sentimentality" and others, of a younger, more tactless generation, perhaps would label as "corny." Graduation, to Miss Thornton, was a time of sadness and a time of joy, but most of all it was a time of change. On graduation night, the change meant more to Miss Thornton than a simple transition from one school to another. She regarded it as the end of an era. Too many of her boys and girls had ceased to be children this night. They had all looked so grown up and different from where she sat in her front-row seat in the auditorium. Many of them had only the summer ahead in which to enjoy the last days of childhood. In the fall they would be "high schoolers," and already they regarded themselves as adults. She had heard Rodney Harrington speak of "going down to New Hampton" as if he were going off to Dartmouth rather than to a prep school, and she had heard several girls complain of parents who would not allow them to go to "coed" summer camps.

It's all too fast, thought Miss Thornton, realizing that she was not thinking a new thought. She seemed to be full of clichés this evening, the way she was after every graduation, and her mind persisted in framing phrases like, The best years of their lives, and, What a pity that youth is wasted on the young.

Kenny Stearns came limping into the auditorium, the two pails he carried clanking together. Miss Thornton sat up and gathered her gloves together.

"Good evening, Kenny," she said.

"Evenin', Miss Thornton. I thought everybody was gone."

"I was just leaving, Kenny. The auditorium looked lovely tonight, didn't it?"

"It sure did. I'm the one built them benches. Held up good, didn't they?"

"They were perfect, Kenny."

"I pinned them letters up for the seniors, too. Had a helluva time gettin' 'em on straight. That nine wa'nt crooked when I got done, like it is now."

"No, it wasn't, Kenny. That happened during the exercises."

"Well, I gotta get started. Those benches gotta come down tonight. I got a coupla kids comin' in to help me later."

Miss Thornton took the hint. "Good night, Kenny," she said.

"'Night, Miss Thornton."

Outside, the night sky was black. There was no moon and Miss Thornton reflected that there would not have been room for one, for all the available sky space was taken up with stars. She looked up and breathed deeply of the faintly scented June air, and suddenly her depression was gone. There would be another group of children in the fall, perhaps one more promising and rewarding than the last.

BOOK TWO

◆ 1 ◆

Two years had passed since that graduation night. They had passed quickly for Allison. The work was much harder in high school and this provided a mental stimulation for her that had been lacking in the grades. Somehow, too, she had come to accept herself and the world around her more calmly, and while she still had periods of fear and resentment, they were fewer and less wretchedly painful than before. She had also developed a new, insatiable curiosity. Two years earlier she had been content to let books answer her questions, but now she tried to learn from people. She asked questions of everyone whom she dared to approach, and the most sympathetic of these was Nellie Cross.

"How did you ever come to marry Lucas, anyway?" she asked Nellie one day. "You're always cussing him and talking as if you hated him. How come you married him at all?"

Nellie looked up from the brass candlestick that she was polishing, and she was quiet for so long that to anyone but Allison it might have seemed that she had not heard or that she was ignoring the question. But Allison knew that neither of these was true. If Nellie was sympathetic to Allison's questions, Allison had learned to be patient with Nellie's inarticulateness.

"I dunno that I ever did come to it, like you say," said Nellie finally. "Marryin' Lucas wa'nt nothin' I ever come to. It was just one of those things that happened."

"Nothing," said Allison positively, "ever just happens. There is a law of cause and effect that applies to everything and everybody."

Nellie smiled and put the candlestick down on the mantelpiece in the MacKenzie living room.

"You talk good, honey," she said. "Mighty good, with them big words and all. It's like music, listenin' to you."

Allison tried not to look pleased, but she felt the way she often did at school when she received an A in composition from Mr. Makris. Nellie's wholehearted and absolute appreciation of Allison was the basis of their friendship, but Allison never admitted that this was so. She said, instead, that she "just loved" Nellie Cross.

"Now that I think of it," said Nellie, "there most likely was a reason why I married Lucas. I had Selena. Tiny, she was then. Just barely six weeks old. My first husband, Curtis Chamberlain he was, got himself killed by a mess of falling logs. Fell off a truck, the logs did, and killed old Curt deader than hell. Well, there I was, out to there carryin' Selena, and right after she was born I met Lucas. He was alone, too. His wife died havin' Paul. It seemed like a good idea at the time, my marryin' Lucas, I mean. He was alone with Paul, and I was alone with Selena. Don't do for a woman to be alone, or a man either. Besides, what could I do? I wa'nt in no shape to work right then, bein' as how I just had a baby, and Lucas was after me."

She began to cackle, and for a moment Allison was afraid that Nellie would begin to get vague and go off on a conversational tangent the way she often did these days, but Nellie stopped her weird laughter and went on talking.

"More fool was I," she said. "I went from the fryin' pan right straight into hell. Lucas always drank, and fought, and chased the wimmin. And I was worse off than before."

"But didn't you love him?" asked Allison. "Just at first?"

"Well, Lucas and me wa'nt married too damned long before I got pregnant the first time. Lost that one. Miscarriage, The Doc said. Lucas went out and got drunker than hell. Said I was still grievin' for Curtis, Lucas did, but that wa'nt true. Anyways, I got in the family way again and then I had Joey, and after that Lucas didn't seem to feel so bad over Curtis no more. There's some say you gotta love a man to get a child by him. I dunno. Maybe this love you're talkin' about is what kept me by Lucas all these years. I coulda left him. I always worked anyway, and he always drunk up most of his pay, so it wouldn't have made no difference."

"But how could you stay with him?" asked Allison. "How come you didn't run away when he beat you, and beat your children?"

"Why, honey, beatin's don't mean nothin'." Nellie cackled again, and this time her eyes did turn vague. "It's everythin' else. The booze and the wimmin. Even the booze ain't so bad, if he'd just leave the wimmin alone. I could tell you some stories, honey—" Nellie folded her arms together, and her voice took on a singsong quality—"I could tell you some stories, honey, that ain't nothin' like the stories you tell me."

"Like what, then?" whispered Allison. "Tell me. Like what?"

"Oh, he'll get his someday," whispered Nellie, matching her voice to Allison's. "He'll get his, the sonofabitch. They all get it, in the end, the sonsofbitches. All of 'em."

Allison sighed and stood up. When Nellie began to croon and curse, it was futile to try to talk sense to her. She would go on for the rest of the day, swearing under her breath, unaware of all questions put to her. It was this trait in Nellie that caused Constance MacKenzie to remark frequently that something would have to be done about her. But somehow Constance never got around to doing anything, for Nellie, eccentric or not, was still the best house worker in Peyton Place. But it was not Nellie's vagueness or her language which bothered Allison. It was the frustrating way in which Nellie threw out veiled insinuations, like a fisherman casting out line, only to withdraw the bait as soon as Allison nibbled. In times past, Allison had attempted to batter against this wall of things left unsaid, but trying to pin Nellie down to words, Allison had discovered, was a hopeless business.

"What could you tell me, Nellie?" she would ask, and Nellie would cradle her arms and cackle.

"Oh, the stories I could tell you, honey—" but she never did, and Allison was still too young to pity the incapability of an individual to share his grief. She merely shrugged and said crossly, "Well, all right, if you don't *want* to tell me—"

"Well, all right, if you don't *want* to tell me," said Allison on this particular day, "I'll go for a walk and leave you by yourself."

"Heh, heh, heh," said Nellie. "The sonsofbitches."

Allison sighed impatiently and left the house.

In two years Peyton Place had not changed at all. The same stores still fronted on Elm Street, and the same people owned and operated them. A stranger, revisiting the town after two years, would have the feeling that he had been here only yesterday. Now that it was July the benches in front of the courthouse were well filled by the old men who regarded them as their private property, and a stranger might look at them and say, "Why, those old men have been sitting there all this time."

Allison walked down Elm Street in the hot summer sun and the old men in front of the courthouse followed her with heavy, summer-lidded eyes.

"There goes Allison MacKenzie."

"Yep. Growed some lately, ain't she?"

"Got some growin' to do, 'fore she catches up with that mother of hers."

131

The men snickered. It was the consensus of town opinion that Constance MacKenzie was built like a brick shithouse, a sentiment that was given voice every time that Constance walked past the courthouse.

"Good-lookin' woman, though, Constance MacKenzie is. Always was."

"Oh, I dunno," said Clayton Frazier. "Kinda fine drawn for my taste. I never was much taken with wimmin whose cheekbones stick out."

"For Christ's sake. Who the hell looks at her cheekbones?"

The men laughed, and Clayton Frazier leaned back against the hot stone of the courthouse wall.

"There's some men," he said, "who occasionally got their minds fixed on other things in a woman besides her tits and her ass."

"That right, Clayton? Name one."

"Tomas Makris," said Clayton Frazier without a second's hesitation.

The men laughed again.

"Jesus, yes!" they said. "That horny Greek never noticed nothin' about Connie MacKenzie 'cept her brains!"

"Them two got nothin' to talk over these hot nights 'cept literchoor and paintin'," they said.

"Why, that big, black Greek never even notices that Connie MacKenzie's a well-built blonde!"

Clayton Frazier tipped his old felt hat down over his eyes.

"Don't make no difference what none of you say," he said. "I'd bet my next six months' pension that Tomas Makris never laid a finger on Connie MacKenzie."

"I'll side with Clayton," said one man with mock sobriety. "I'll bet Tom never laid a finger on Connie MacKenzie, either. But I wouldn't take no bets that he's laid everything else on her!"

The men roared and turned to watch Allison walk out of sight on Elm Street.

Memorial Park was patchy with grass burnt pale brown by the sun that had shone daily for six weeks of drought. The wide-branched trees stood as if paralyzed in the windless air, their leafy tops dusty green and cicada filled, and they waited for rain with the patience of a hundred years. Allison walked listlessly, feeling overclothed in spite of the brief shorts and sleeveless blouse that she wore, and loneliness weighed heavily on her as she climbed the sloping hill behind the park. Hers was not a loneliness to be alleviated by people, for she could have gone swimming at Meadow

Pond with Kathy Ellsworth and had refused. She had thought of a crowd of young people, a splashing, yelling, playful crowd, and the thought had repelled her. She had thought also of sun reflecting itself on motionless water, and had told Kathy no, she did not want to go swimming. Now she was sorry, for the July heat was like a weight on her bare head as she climbed the hill toward Road's End. But for the sizzling of the cicadas and the scrape of her own feet against the rocky ground, there was no sound and Allison had a feeling of being the only inhabitant in a dry, burnt-out world. It was almost a physical shock to see another figure, standing motionless before the board with the red letters printed on its side, as she turned from the path to approach the place called Road's End.

The figure turned as she came near, not disturbed by sound, for Allison made none, but by a sense of no longer being alone.

"Hi, Allison," said Norman Page.

"Hi, Norman."

He was wearing a pair of the khaki pants known as "tennis shorts" and his knees, like his elbows and cheekbones, were sharp and angular. Norman was the only boy in Peyton Place who wore shorts in the summertime. The others wore dungarees and uncovered their legs only when they donned bathing trunks.

"What are you doing up here?" asked Norman vaguely, as if he had just been awakened.

"Same thing you are," replied Allison unpleasantly. "Looking for a place to cool off and be by myself."

"The river looks as if it were made of glass from here."

Allison leaned against the board that barred the drop-off at Road's End.

"It doesn't seem to be moving at all," she said.

"Nothing in the whole town seems to be moving."

"It looks like a toy village, with everything made out of cardboard."

"That's what I was thinking just before you came. I was thinking that everybody else in the world was dead, and I was the only one left."

"Why, so was I!" exclaimed Allison, turning her head to look up at him.

Norman was staring straight ahead, a lock of dark hair curling damply on his forehead; the skin at his temples was almost translucent. His finely made lips were parted slightly, and his lashes, over half-closed eyes, made tiny shadows on his thin, white cheeks.

133

"So was I," repeated Allison, and this time Norman turned his head and looked at her.

"I used to think," he said, "that no one ever thought the same things as I. But that's not always true, is it?"

"No," said Allison, and looked down. Their hands rested close together on the board that had the red letters printed on its side, and there was a companionable sort of intimacy in the sight of them. "No, that isn't always true," said Allison. "I used to think the same thing, and it bothered me. It made me feel queer and different from everyone else."

"I used to think that I was the only kid in town who ever came up here," said Norman. "It was a kind of secret place with me, and I never told anyone."

"I thought that once," said Allison. "I'll never forget the day that someone told me that it wasn't so. I felt mad and sick, as if I'd caught someone looking in my window."

"Outraged is a good word," said Norman. "That's the way I felt. I saw Rodney Harrington and Betty Anderson up here one afternoon, and I ran all the way home, crying."

"There's one place I'll bet no one knows about. Not even you."

"Tell me."

"Come on. I'll show you."

Indian file, with Allison leading, they made their way through the woods at the side of the road. The branches of low bushes scratched at their legs and they paused every few feet to pick some of the blueberries that grew there. Norman took a clean handkerchief from his pocket and knotted the four corners to make a sort of pouch, and together they filled it with fruit. At last they came to the open field, hidden deep in the woods, and the buttercups and brown-eyed Susans were a sea of brown-dotted gold. Allison and Norman stood close together in the cicada-slivered stillness, not speaking, and ate from the handkerchief basket of berries. After a long time, Norman bent and picked a handful of buttercups.

"Hold up your chin, Allison," he laughed. "If the flowers reflect gold on your skin it means that you like butter and are going to get fat."

Allison laughed and tipped her head back. Her pale brown hair, pulled back now and tied into a tail, moved against her back, and the nape of her neck was damp.

"All right, Norman," she said. "You just look and see if I'm going to get fat!"

He put two fingers under her chin and bent to see if the butter-cups he held shed a reflection.

"No," he said, "I guess not, Allison. It doesn't look as if you'll be fat."

They were both laughing, and Norman's fingers were still under her face. For a long moment, with the laughter still thick in their throats, they looked at one another, and Norman moved his fingers so that his whole hand rested gently on the side of her face.

"Your lips are all blue from those berries," he said.

"So are yours," said Allison, not moving away from his touch.

When he kissed her it was softly, without touching her except for raising his other hand to her cheek. The buttercups he still held were like velvet on their faces.

◆ 2 ◆

Dr. Matthew Swain and Seth Buswell sat in Seth's office in the building that housed the *Peyton Place Times*. The doctor fanned himself with his white straw hat and sipped at Seth's special summertime concoction of gin and iced grapefruit juice.

"Like the man said," remarked Seth, "ninety-nine degrees in the shade, and there ain't no shade."

"For Christ's sake, don't talk about the weather," said the doctor. "I was just being thankful that very few have picked this month to be sick."

"Nobody's got the energy to get sick," said Seth. "It's too god-damned hot to think about layin' on a rubber sheet over in your hospital."

"Jesus!" exclaimed the doctor, half rising to his feet as a car raced past on Elm Street. "Don't push my luck talking about it, or we'll be scraping young Harrington off a road somewhere."

"It'll be Leslie's fault if you do. Damned foolishness, buyin' a sixteen-year-old kid three thousand dollars' worth of convertible coupé."

"Especially Rodney Harrington," said the doctor. "That kid's got as much sense as a flea. Maybe it's a good thing he got kicked out of New Hampton. Leslie can have him here in town where he can keep an eye on him, which isn't worth much, I'll grant."

"Didn't you know?" asked Seth. "Leslie's got Proctor to take

135

him. How he worked getting Rodney into that school, I don't know, but the kid is going there in the fall."

"I don't imagine he'll be there too long," said the doctor. "I saw him over to White River last week. He had that convertible piled full of kids, and they were all drinking. Leslie about bit my head off when I told him about it. Told me to mind my own business and let the kid sow a few wild oats. Wild oats at sixteen. As I remember it, I was considerably older when I started planting mine."

"I don't like that kid," said Seth. "I don't like him one bit better than I ever liked Leslie."

Two figures passed in front of the plate glass window in Seth's office. The girl raised her head and glanced in, waving her hand at the two men inside, but the boy was preoccupied in watching the girl, and he did not look up. He carried a handful of buttercups as if he had forgotten that he held them.

"There goes Allison MacKenzie with the Page boy," said the doctor. "I wonder if his mother knows he's out."

"She went to White River this afternoon," said Seth. "I passed her going in just as I was leaving."

"That accounts for Norman walking on the street with a girl then," said the doctor. "I imagine that Evelyn went to White River to consult John Bixby. She hasn't come near me to be treated since I told her there was nothing the matter with her but selfishness and bad temper. Odd," he continued after a pause, "how hatred manifests itself in different ways. Look at the Page Girls, healthy as plow horses, both of 'em, and then look at Evelyn, always suffering with an ache or a pain somewhere."

"But look at what hatred did for Leslie Harrington," said Seth. "He hated the whole world and set out to lick it. And he did."

"I'd like to see the boy get free of her before it's too late," said the doctor, still thinking of Norman Page. "Maybe if he got himself a nice girl, like Allison MacKenzie, it would counteract Evelyn's influence."

"You're worse than an old woman, Matt," said Seth, laughing. "An old woman and a matchmaker to boot. Have another drink."

"Have you no shame?" demanded the doctor, extending his glass. "Sitting around soaking up gin all day?"

"Nope," said Seth unhesitatingly. "None at all. Here's to little Norman Page. A long life and a merry one, providing Evelyn doesn't eat him alive first."

"I don't think that he's strong enough to fight her," said the
136

doctor. "She expects too much from him—love, admiration, eventual financial support, unquestioning loyalty, even sex."

"Oh, come now," said Seth. "The weather's got you. Don't go tellin' me that Evelyn Page is sleepin' with her son."

"The trouble with you, Seth," said the doctor with mock severity, "is that you think of all sex in terms of men sleeping with women. It's not always so. Let me tell you about a case I saw once, a young boy with the worst case of dehydration I ever saw. It came from getting too many enemas that he didn't need. Sex, with a capital S-E-X."

"Jesus, Matt!" exclaimed Seth, making his eyes bulge with exaggerated horror. "Do you think that's what put old Oakleigh in his grave? Enemas?"

"Don't be a conclusion jumper," protested the doctor. "I didn't say that what I was talking about had anything to do with Evelyn Page and Norman. And, no, Oakleigh didn't die of enemas. He was lashed to death, by the tongues of Caroline and Charlotte and Evelyn Page."

"I'm goin' to stop feedin' you gin," said Seth. "It makes you too goddamned morose, and today it's too hot to be morose or anything else."

"Except drunk," said Dr. Swain, standing up, "which I have no intention of getting at four o'clock on a Friday afternoon. I have to go."

"See you tonight?" asked Seth. "The whole gang is comin' tonight, which makes for good poker."

"I'll be there," said the doctor. "And bring your checkbook, Seth. I feel lucky."

♦ 3 ♦

Selena Cross, standing in front of the window in the Thrifty Corner, saw Dr. Matthew Swain go by. At once, her heart began to pump more heavily as fear gripped her and spread itself through her body. She stared in horror at the tall, white-suited figure that had never shown her anything but kindness.

Help me, Doc, she rehearsed silently. You've got to help me.

"Matt Swain is the only man I ever saw who can wear a white suit successfully," said Constance MacKenzie at Selena's elbow. "He may look unpressed, but he never looks sweaty."

137

Selena's fingers clenched around the middle of the curved-in Coke bottle she held.

I'll wait one more day, she thought. One more day, and if nothing happens, I'll go see The Doc. Help me, Doc, I'll say. You've got to help me.

"Selena?"

"Yes, Mrs. MacKenzie?"

"Don't you feel well?"

"Sure, Mrs. MacKenzie, I feel fine. It's just the heat."

"You're so pale looking. It's not like you."

"It's just the heat, Mrs. MacKenzie. I'm fine."

"Things are so slow today. Why don't you take the rest of the afternoon off?"

"Thanks anyway, but Ted's meeting me at six."

"Well, go on out back and sit down for a while, then. Honestly, I never saw you looking so white."

"All right. I'll go sit down. Call me if you need me."

"I will, dear," said Constance MacKenzie, and at the kindness of her tone, Selena almost wept.

If you knew, she thought. If you knew what the matter is, you wouldn't talk so gently to me. You'd tell me to get out of your sight. Oh, Doc, help me. What if Ted found out, or his folks, or anybody?

Selena had never been one to let the opinions of Peyton Place bother her in any way.

"Let 'em talk," she had said. "They'll talk anyway."

But now, with this terrible thing that had happened to her, she was afraid. She knew her town, and its many voices.

"A girl in trouble."

"She got in Dutch."

"She's knocked up."

"The tramp. The dirty little tramp."

"Well, that's the shack dwellers for you."

If it had not been for Ted Carter, Selena would have stuck her chin out at the world and demanded: "So what?" But she loved Ted. At sixteen, Selena had a maturity which some women never achieve. She knew her own mind, and she knew her own heart. She loved Ted Carter and knew that she always would, and to imagine him looking at her with his heart breaking for all to see was more than she could bear. Ted, with a sense of honor that he had inherited from somewhere, with a rigid self-control that he would not let break. Ted, holding her and saying, "I won't, darling. I

138

won't hurt you." Ted, pulling away from her when he did not want to, saying that in addition to love and respect, he had patience. They had laughed about it.

"We girls from the backwoods are all hot blooded," she had said.

"It's not too much longer," Ted had told her. "Two years. We're only sixteen, and we have our whole lives. We'll get married before I go to college."

"I love you. I love you. I never loved anybody in the world except Joey, and I love you more."

"I want you, baby. How I want you! Don't touch me. What if I ever got you in trouble? It happens, you know. No matter how careful people are, it happens. You know what this town is like. You know how they treat a girl that gets in trouble. Remember when it happened to the Anderson girl, Betty's sister? She had to move away. She couldn't even get a job in town."

Oh, Doc, prayed Selena, putting her head down between her knees against the faintness she felt. Oh, Doc, help me.

"Selena?"

"Yes, Mrs. MacKenzie?"

"Telephone."

Selena stood up and ran shaking fingers over her cheeks and hair, then she went to the front of the store.

"Hello?" she said into the receiver.

"Oh, honey," said Ted Carter, "I'm afraid I won't be able to meet you at six o'clock. Mr. Shapiro has three thousand more chickens coming in, and I have to stay and help."

"That's all right, Ted," said Selena. "Mrs. MacKenzie offered me the rest of the afternoon off. As long as you can't get away, I'll take her up on it."

The rest of the afternoon. The rest of the afternoon. I'll go see The Doc during the rest of the afternoon.

Selena hardly heard Ted's plan to meet her later. She hung up on his telephoned kiss, and stood staring down at the whiteness of her hand on the black receiver.

"Mrs. MacKenzie," she said, a few minutes later, "is it all right if I take the rest of the afternoon after all?"

"Of course, dear. Go home and get some rest. You look all tired out."

"Thank you," said Selena. "That's just what I'll do. I'll go home and take a nap."

Constance MacKenzie watched Selena walk out of sight on Elm Street. It was odd, she mused, that Selena refused to confide in her.

139

In the last two years they had become so friendly that there were very few things that they had not discussed. Selena was the only person who knew that Constance was planning to marry Tomas Makris. Constance had told her, in her first flush of joy, over a year ago. Selena understood how it was with Constance. She knew how careful she had to be, because of Allison. Selena had even offered advice.

"The longer you wait, Mrs. MacKenzie, the worse it's going to be," Selena had said. "Allison always had strong feelings about her father. She'll have them next year, and the year after that. I don't see how waiting until she graduates from high school is going to solve anything."

Constance sighed. Tom didn't see how waiting for Allison to graduate from high school was going to solve anything, either. She had a date with him this evening, and she knew that the subject would come up. It always did. If she could only get up enough courage to tell him the way it had been with Allison's father, if she only dared to tell him everything. But she loved him in the only way a woman of thirty-five can love a man when she has never loved before—wholeheartedly, with all her mind and body, but also with fear. Constance regarded Tomas Makris as the embodiment of everything she wanted and had never had, and she was afraid of losing him. What made the situation even more difficult was the fact that he loved her. He loved, she told herself fearfully, the woman she appeared to be: Widow, devoted mother, respected member of the community. How well would he love a woman who had taken a lover and been stupid enough to bear him a bastard child? Constance, who had despised herself for sixteen years, could not believe that any man could love her once he knew the truth. She had many reasons for not marrying Tom without first telling him the facts, and all her reasons had to do with honor and nobility and truth. The fact of the matter was that she was tired of carrying a burden alone and wanted, at all costs, to share its weight with someone. More than anything, she wanted to be with someone with whom she need not forever be painstakingly, frighteningly careful. Constance MacKenzie, almost as unhappy as she had been two years before, went into the small room at the back of her store and made herself a tall glass of iced tea.

Selena Cross hurried in the late afternoon sun. When she reached Chestnut Street, she felt as though every window held a pair of eyes that stared at her and knew her secret at once.

A girl in trouble, said every pair of eyes. A girl in Dutch. Not a

140

nice girl, a bad girl. No kind of girl for young Ted Carter.

Selena hurried up the flagstone walk, wet now with the spray from two lawn sprinklers that were making lazy circles, and ran up the front steps between two of the pillars of the doctor's "Southern-looking" house. Matthew Swain answered her urgent ring.

"For God's sake, Selena," he said, looking only once at her white face, "come in out of that beastly heat."

But inside, in the wide, cool hall, Selena's teeth began to chatter, and the doctor looked at her sharply.

"Come into the office," he said.

A visiting colleague had once said that Matt Swain's office looked less like a doctor's office than any other anywhere. It was true, for the doctor had used part of what had once been a drawing room for his place of business. Half of the drawing room was shut off with folding doors, and on the other side Matthew Swain had his examining rooms. The floors in both the office and the examining rooms were the same hardwood floors that had been put down when the house was built, and next to the doctor's untidiness the floors were Isobel Crosby's greatest source of complaint.

"It's bad enough," Isobel would say, "that The Doc has all kinds of folks trackin' into the house when he could well afford an office downtown, but hardwood floors! Imagine it. Hardwood floors that you can't run over with a wet mop!"

Selena Cross sat down carefully on the straight chair next to the doctor's desk.

"Relax, Selena," said the doctor. "No matter what it is, it's nothing that won't feel a little better for telling me about it."

"I'm pregnant," said Selena, and immediately bit her lip. She had not meant to blurt it out like that.

"What makes you think so?" asked the doctor.

"Two and a half months and no period makes me think so," said Selena, and this time she twisted her hands, for she had not meant to say that, either.

"Come on in the other room," said Dr. Swain. "Let's see what we can see."

His hands were cool against her hot skin, and once again her mind set up its prayerful refrain.

Help me, Doc. You've got to help me.

"Whose is it?" he asked when they had returned to the office.

Now came the worst part, the part she had rehearsed so carefully in her mind so that she could phrase it in a way that would not antagonize the doctor.

141

"I am not at liberty to say," said Selena.

"Nonsense!" roared the doctor, and she knew that she had failed. "What kind of rot is that? You're not the first girl in the world who has to get married, nor in this town, for that matter. Whose is it now, and no more foolishness. Young Carter's?"

"No," said Selena, and when she bent her head forward her dark hair swung softly on either side of her face.

"Don't you lie to me!" shouted Dr. Swain. "I've seen the way that boy looks at you. What gave you the idea he was inhuman? Come on now, don't lie to me, Selena."

"I'm not lying," said the girl, and in the next moment she lost control of herself and began to shout at him. "I'm not lying. If it were Ted's I'd be the happiest girl in the world. But it's *not* his! Doc, help me," her voice went to a whisper. "Doc, once you told me that if I ever needed you, to come and you'd help me. Well, I'm here now, Doc, and I need help. You've got to help me."

"What do you mean by help, Selena?" he asked, his voice almost as soft as her own. "How can I help you?"

"Give me something," she said. "Something to get rid of it."

"There is nothing I can give you to take, Selena, that would help you now. Tell me who is responsible. Maybe I could help you that way. You could get married only until after the baby is born."

Selena's lips went tight. "He's already married," she said.

"Selena," said Dr. Swain as gently as he knew how, "Selena, there is nothing I can give you at this point that will make you miscarry. The only thing now is an abortion, and that's against the law. I've done a lot of things in my time, Selena, but I have never broken the law. Selena," he said, leaning forward and taking both her cold hands in his, "Selena, tell me who this man is, and I will see that he is held responsible. He'll have to take care of you and provide for the baby. I could work it so no one would know. You could go away for a little while, until after the baby comes. Whoever did this thing to you would have to pay for that, and for your hospitalization, and for you to look after yourself until you get back on your feet. Just tell me who it is, Selena, and I'll do everything I can to help you."

"It's my father," said Selena Cross. She raised her head and looked Matthew Swain straight in the eyes. "My stepfather," she said, and tore her hands away from him. She fell forward onto the doctor's hardwood floor and beat her fists against it. "It's Lucas," she screamed. "It's Lucas. It's Lucas."

142

♦ 4 ♦

Early that same evening, Dr. Swain telephoned to Seth Buswell that he would be unable to join with the other men of Chestnut Street to play poker.

"What's the matter, Matt?" asked the newspaper editor. "Did we push your luck too far? Somebody go and get sick?"

"No," said the doctor. "But some things at the hospital need straightening out and I should attend to them this evening."

"Nothing in the accounting department, I hope," said Seth laughing. "I hear that those guys from the state auditor's office are bastards."

"No, Seth. Nothing in the accounting department," said the doctor, and his hearty laugh was strained. "But I'd better watch my step or the Feds'll be on my tail."

"Sure, Matt," laughed Seth. "Well, sorry you can't make the game. See you tomorrow."

"See you, Seth," said Dr. Swain and hung up gently.

Selena Cross had not left the doctor's house. She lay in a darkened upstairs bedroom with a cool cloth on her forehead.

"Stay here," the doctor had told her. "Stay right here on the bed, and when you feel a little better we'll talk over what we can do."

"There's nothing to do," said Selena and retched violently while the doctor held a basin for her.

"Lie quietly," he said. "I have to go downstairs for a while."

In his dining room, Matthew Swain went at once to the sideboard where he poured himself a large drink of Scotch whisky.

Gin, Scotch, young girls in bed upstairs, I'd better watch out, he thought wryly. If I'm not careful, I'll be getting a reputation as a drunken old reprobate who is no longer the doctor he once was.

He carried the second drink into his living room and sat down on a brocaded sofa in front of the empty fireplace.

What are you going to do, Matthew Swain? he asked himself. Here you've been shooting your mouth off for years. What will you do now, when it is time to put your fancy theories to the test? Nothing dearer than life, eh, Matthew? What is this thing you are thinking of doing if it isn't the destruction of what you have always termed so dear?

143

Dr. Swain drank his second drink. He was honest enough to realize that the struggle he fought with himself now would leave its mark on him for the rest of his life, and he knew that no matter what his decision, he would always wonder if he had made the right one. It was true that he had never broken any of the laws of the land before, unless a weekly game of five-and-ten poker with friends in a state that prohibited gambling could be looked upon as breaking the law.

No exceptions now, Matthew, he cautioned himself. Poker at Seth's is against the laws of this state, so you *have* broken the law before.

But not in my work, protested another part of his mind. Never in my work.

No, not in your work. Rules are rules and you have always abided by them. Certainly, you are not going to start breaking them now, at your age, and that's the end of it. Rules are rules.

But what about the exceptions to the rules?

There aren't any exceptions in your business, Doctor. You report syphilis, you tell the police if a man with a bullet wound approaches you, and you isolate the sick over protest. No exceptions, Matthew.

But if this child of Selena's is born, it will ruin the rest of her life.

That's none of your affair, Matthew. Go to the police. See that this man Lucas is brought to justice. But keep your hands off Selena Cross.

She is only sixteen years old. She has the beginnings of a pretty good life mapped out for herself. This would ruin her.

You might kill her.

Nonsense. I'd do it in the hospital with all sterile precautions.

Are you mad? In the hospital? Have you gone stark, raving mad?

I could do it. I could do it so no one would know. I could do it tonight. The hospital is practically empty. People just haven't been sick this month.

In the hospital? Are you mad? Are you really mad?

Yes, goddamn it, I am! Whose hospital is it, anyway? Who built the goddamn place, and nursed it, and made it go if it wasn't me?

What do you mean, *your* hospital? That hospital belongs to the people of this community whom you are solemnly bound to serve to the best of your ability. The state says so, and this country says so, and that oath you stood up and took more years ago than you care to remember says so. *Your* hospital. Humph. You must be mad.

144

Matthew Swain threw his empty whisky glass against the hearth of the empty fireplace. It shattered noisily and crystal slivers flew out in a circle.

"Yes, goddamn it, I'm mad!" said the doctor aloud, and stamped out of his living room and up the stairs that led to the second floor.

But all the while the silent voice pursued him.

You've lost, Matthew Swain, it said. You've lost. Death, venereal disease and organized religion, in that order, eh? Don't you ever let me hear you open your mouth again. You are setting out deliberately this night to inflict death, rather than to protect life as you are sworn to do.

"Feeling better, Selena?" asked the doctor, stepping into the darkened bedroom.

"Oh, Doc," she said, staring at him with violet-circled eyes. "Oh, Doc. I wish I were dead."

"Come on, now," he said cheerfully. "We'll take care of everything and fix you up as good as new."

And to hell with you, he told the silent voice. I *am* protecting life, *this* life, the one already being lived by Selena Cross.

"Listen to me, Selena," said Dr. Swain. "Listen to me carefully. This is what we are going to do."

An hour later, Constance MacKenzie, riding past the Peyton Place hospital with Tomas Makris in the car that he had bought the previous spring, saw the lights showing through the huge square of opaque glass that she knew screened the hospital's operating room.

"Something must have happened," she said. "The operating room lights are on. I wonder who's sick."

"That's one of the things I love about Peyton Place," said Tom, smiling. "A man can't have so much as a gas pain without the whole town wondering who, why, when, where and what he's going to do about it."

Constance made a face at him. "Big-time city slicker," she said.

"Taking advantage of the farmer's daughter," he added, taking her hand and kissing the finger tips.

Constance relaxed against the seat cushions with a contented sigh. She didn't have to open the store in the morning, for Selena Cross had promised to do it for her. Allison was spending the week end with Kathy Ellsworth, and Constance was on her way to dinner in a town eighteen miles away, far from the prying eyes of her neighbors, with the man she loved.

145

"Why the happy sigh?" asked Tom.

"My cup runneth over," said Constance, and leaned her cheek against his shoulder.

"Cigarette?"

"Please."

He lit two, one after the other, and passed one to her. In the quick flare of his lighter, she saw the pointed arch of one eyebrow and the perfect, Grecian line of his nose. His lips, over the narrow tube of his cigarette, were full without being loose, and the line of his chin was pleasantly pronounced.

"Altogether," she said, "a head from an old Greek coin."

"I like it when you talk like a smitten lady," he said.

"That, I am," she conceded.

There was an easiness to being with him that she had never before experienced with a man. It had been a long time in coming, this easiness, but now was it a part of her and she could almost forget that once she had been fearful of him almost to sickness.

"What is it?" he asked with the peculiar way he had of knowing when she was thinking of something that concerned either him or both of them.

"I was thinking," she said, "of the first time you ever came to my house. It was over two years ago, on the night of Allison's spring dance."

Tom laughed and put her hand to his lips again. "Oh, that," he said. "Listen, forget about that. Start thinking of what you want to eat when we get to the restaurant. Today is Friday, so they'll have all kinds of fish. It always takes you forever to make up your mind, and we're nearly there now."

"All right," she said, "I'll concentrate on haddock, clams and lobster and see what happens."

She linked her hand through his arm, and at once the remembrance of another, later, time with him came to her.

It must have been three months after the first time that he had come to her house, for it had been August, and Allison had been away at summer camp down at Lake Winnipesaukee. It was a Saturday night, she remembered, and hot. She was working on her store ledger, and although every window in the house was open no breeze stirred. When the doorbell rang she was so startled that she dropped her pen, and it made an ugly blot on the white ledger page.

"Damn," she muttered, belting her housecoat more tightly around her. "Damn it all."

She pulled open the front door and Tomas Makris said, "Hi. Let's go for a swim."

In the weeks following the spring dance in May, he had come to call on her perhaps half a dozen times, and once during that time she had gone out to dinner with him. He had made her feel uncomfortable in a way she could not explain, and she did not want to see him.

"Well, of all the nerve!" she said angrily. "What do you mean by ringing my doorbell at eleven thirty at night with some such insane suggestion as that!"

"If you're going to give me hell," he said comfortably, "at least ask me in. What will your neighbors think?"

"Heaven only knows what they think already," she said furiously. "The way you're always barging in here, uninvited, any time you feel like it."

"'Always'?" he asked incredulously. "Six times in the last three months. Docs Peyton Place regard that as 'always'?"

She had to laugh. "No, I guess not," she admitted. "It's just that you startled me, and I dropped my pen and it made a blot on the ledger."

"We can't have that," he said. "Blots on the ledger, I mean."

She felt herself stiffening, and he seemed to feel it, too, for he spoke quickly.

"Get your bathing suit," he said, "and we'll go for a swim."

"You're crazy," she told him. "In the first place, there is no place to go around here except Meadow Pond, and that's always full of necking teen-agers."

"Heaven forbid," he said, "that we should go where the neckers go. I have a car outside that I'm thinking of buying, and there is a lake not eight miles away from here. Let's go try out my prospective car."

"Mr. Makris—"

"Tom," he said, patiently.

"Tom," she said, "I have no intention of going anywhere with you at this hour of the night. I have work to do, it's late, it's after eleven-thirty—"

"It's scandalous," interrupted Tom, clucking his tongue and shaking his head. "Listen, you've worked all day. Tomorrow is Sunday, so you don't have to get up early. Your daughter is away at camp, so you needn't stay home for her. You have no other excuse that you can possibly offer except that you hate my guts, and you aren't going to say that. Get your bathing suit and come on."

The surprising thing, thought Constance as she leaned against Tom's shoulder two years later, was not that he had spoken as he had, but that she had obeyed him.

"All right," she had said, exasperated with his persistence. "All right!"

She had put on her bathing suit in her bedroom and only for a moment, when she caught her reflection in the mirror of her dressing table, did she pause.

What am I doing? she had asked herself.

Something I want to do, for a change, she had answered the face in the mirror.

Resolutely, she fastened the straps of her bathing suit into place, slipped on a cotton dress and a pair of sandals, and ran down the stairs to where Tomas Makris stood waiting in the hall.

"Did you lock your door?" he asked when they were outside.

"That's another thing you'll have to learn about small-town living," she told him. "If you take to locking your door in Peyton Place, people will begin to think that you have something to hide."

"I see," he said. "I should have realized. It must be for this same reason that people here never draw the curtains in their living room windows when the lights are on inside. How do you like the car?"

"Not bad," she said. "It's certainly not new though, is it?"

"Chevvies," he said, "like good wines, are supposed to improve with age. Honest. That's what the used car salesman told me."

He drove to the lake he had spoken of, eight miles from town, and whether the fact that the place was deserted was due to the hour or, as Tom said later, to their almost miraculous good luck, Constance did not know. She knew only that when he had turned off the car lights and cut the motor, the darkness and quiet of the place were unearthly.

"How are we supposed to see to get down to the beach?" she whispered.

"What are you whispering about?" he asked in a normal tone, startling her. "I have a flashlight."

"Oh." Constance cleared her throat and wondered if the first few minutes in a dark, parked car were as awkward for everyone as they were for her.

"Come on," he said, and took her hand to lead her.

It was the first time he had ever touched her, and she felt his grip in her hand, in her wrist, through her whole arm. They dropped the clothes they had worn over their bathing suits on the beach and

148

went into the water together. Now that Constance's eyes had become accustomed to the dark, she could see almost plainly, and what she saw was Tomas Makris standing at her side, massive, naked from the waist up, and evil looking. With a silent cry of fright, she dived into the water and swam away from him.

Oh, God, she thought, why did I ever come? How am I going to get home? Why didn't I stay home in the first place?

She swam until she was exhausted. Her body quivered with fear and chill, and when she swam close enough to the shore to stand, she saw that he was already on the beach, waiting for her. He did not move toward her as she came out of the water toward him, nor did he offer her the towel which he held in his hand. Nervously, she took off her bathing cap and shook her head to loosen her hair.

"My," she said, with a strained little laugh. "It was cold, wasn't it?"

"Untie the top of your bathing suit," he said harshly. "I want to feel your breasts against me when I kiss you."

Two years later, sitting in a car at Tomas Makris' side, Constance MacKenzie shivered again as uncontrollably as she had shivered that night.

"Don't think about it," said Tom gently. "That part is all over with now. Now we are us, and we understand one another. Don't, baby," he said, as she shuddered again. "Don't think about it."

She shook her head and gripped his arm, but she could not help but think about it. Not five minutes before, they had passed the place where it had happened, and Constance could recall it in every detail.

She had stood like a statue, one hand on the back of her neck where she had put it to fluff out her hair, when he spoke. He did not speak again, but when she did not move he stepped in front of her and untied the top strap of her bathing suit. With one motion of his hand, she was naked to the waist, and he pulled her against him without even looking at her. He kissed her brutally, torturously, as if he hoped to awaken a response in her with pain that gentleness could not arouse. His hands were in her hair, but his thumbs were under her jawbone, at either side of her face, so that she could not twist her head from side to side. She felt her knees beginning to give under her, and still he kissed her, holding her upright with his hands tangled in her hair. When he lifted his bruising, hurtful mouth at last, he picked her up, carried her to the car and slammed the door behind her. She was still crumpled, half naked, on the front seat, when he drove up in front of her house.

149

Without a word, he carried her out of the car, and she could not utter a sound. He carried her into the living room where the lights still blazed in front of the open, uncurtained windows and dropped her onto the chintz-covered couch.

"The lights," she gasped finally. "Turn off the lights."

When the room was dark he came to her. "Which room is yours?" he asked coldly.

"The one at the end of the hall," she said, through her chattering teeth. "But it doesn't matter, because you'll never see the inside of it. Get out of my house. Get away from me—"

He carried her, struggling, up the dark stairway, and when he reached the second floor, he kicked open the door of her room with his foot.

"I'll have you arrested," she stammered. "I'll have you arrested and put in jail for breaking and entering and rape—"

He stood her on the floor beside the bed and slapped her a stunning blow across the mouth with the back of his hand.

"Don't open your mouth again," he said quietly. "Just keep your mouth shut."

He bent over her and ripped the still wet bathing suit from her body, and in the dark, she heard the sound of his zipper opening as he took off his trunks.

"Now," he said. "Now."

It was like a nightmare from which she could not wake until, at last, when the blackness at her window began to thin to pale gray, she felt the first red gush of shamed pleasure that lifted her, lifted her, lifted her and then dropped her down into unconsciousness.

It depressed Constance MacKenzie to relive this memory, and it shamed her to remember that she had uttered only one desperate question during that whole, long night.

"Did you lock the door?" she had cried.

And Tom, laughing deep in his throat, had replied against her breasts, "Yes. Don't worry. I locked it."

Looking at him now, as he drove quickly along the road that led away from Peyton Place, Constance wondered again at this man whom she had not yet begun to know.

"What?" he inquired, again reading her mind.

"I was thinking," she said, "that after two years, I really don't know you very well."

Tom laughed and turned into the graveled drive in front of the restaurant they had come to visit. As he helped her out of the car he lifted her chin and kissed her gently.

"I love you," he said. "What else is there to know?"

Constance smiled. "Nothing else that really matters," she said.

Much later, as they returned to Peyton Place, she did not even glance at the dimly lit hospital. It was only when Tom parked the car in front of her house and she saw Anita Titus waiting for her that she felt an uneasy foreshadowing of disaster.

"Your phone's been ringing all evening," said Anita, who was Constance's next door neighbor and on the same telephone party line. "The hospital's been trying to reach you."

"Allison!" cried Constance. "Something has happened to Allison!"

She ran from the car and up her front walk, forgetting her gloves and purse, and leaving Tom to cope with Anita. For a long moment he stood and gazed after this woman who hurried into her own house in order to listen in on Constance's telephone call.

Christ, he thought angrily, I haven't met ten people in this god-damned town who don't need to spend the next year douching out their goddamned souls.

When he went into the house, Constance was already in contact with the hospital.

"Oh, thank you, thank you," she was saying relievedly. "Oh, yes. Thank you for calling me."

"What is it?" he asked, lighting two cigarettes.

"Selena Cross," said Constance. "Dr. Swain performed an emergency appendectomy on her this evening. She had the hospital call me to say that she wouldn't be able to open the store in the morning. Imagine her thinking of the store at a time like that."

◆ 5 ◆

Nurse Mary Kelley closed the door on a sleeping Selena Cross and went quietly, on large, white-shod feet that looked incapable of such quietness, to the desk in the first floor hall. She sat down, adjusting her cap nervously, and sighed as she molded her hips to the straight chair. Once her legs were hidden by the kneehole desk, she spread her thighs cautiously. In the summer, when it was very hot, the insides of her thighs were always chafed. Nothing seemed to help her at these times, neither powder, nor dry cornstarch, nor zinc oxide ointment. She just suffered, and her temper grew short. Now, in addition to night duty and the July humidity and the thighs that hurt as if they had been burned by fire every time she took a step, she was being forced to put a code of medical ethics to the test for the first time in her career. Mary Kelley had been a serious student. She knew all about the ethics that were meat for so many novels and motion pictures and bull sessions in student nurses' quarters.

"What would you do," the students had been fond of asking one another in the long hours after the lights had been put out, "if you saw a doctor make a mistake in the O.R.? A mistake that resulted in the death of a patient?"

"I'd never tell," they assured each other. "After all, everyone makes mistakes. If a carpenter or a plumber makes a mistake, no one is going to ruin him for it. A doctor can make mistakes. Why should he be ruined, or disgraced, or sued?"

"Nurses never tell," they said. "And they see mistakes every day. They keep their mouths shut. It's ethics."

Mary Kelley, sitting spread-legged at the first floor desk, stared down at her hands which were large, square and naked looking in the night dimness of the Peyton Place hospital.

It never stopped there, she remembered, the noble-sounding talk about medical ethics.

"But what if it wasn't a mistake?" they asked one another. "What if a doctor was drunk, or did something deliberately?"

"What if it was your own mother and he killed her to put her out of her misery if she was suffering from some incurable disease?"

"Supposing the doctor had a daughter and his daughter had an illegitimate child and he let the baby die during delivery?"

"I'd never tell," they said solemnly. "You just don't tell on doctors. That's ethics."

Mary Kelley stirred in her chair and spread her legs as far apart as the kneehole in the desk would allow. It all sounded so fine in theory, she thought. It had always sounded fine and beautiful during the bull sessions in the nurses' quarters. Talk was cheap. It cost nothing to give voice to what you wanted people to think you believed. Mary wondered if medical ethics could be compared to the question of tolerance. When you talked you said that Negroes were as good as anybody. You said that Negroes should never be discriminated against, and that if you ever fell in love with one, you'd marry him proudly. But all the while you were talking, you wondered what you would *really* do if some big, black, handsome nigger came up and asked you for a date. When you talked you declared that if you fell in love with a Protestant who refused to change his religion for you, that you would marry him anyway and love him for having the courage of his convictions. You would marry him over parental objections and the objections of the Church, and you would cope intelligently with the problem of a mixed marriage. You knew that you were safe in saying these things, for there hadn't been a nigger living in Peyton Place for over a hundred years, and you didn't date boys who were not Catholics. You said that you knew what you would do if confronted with an unethical doctor, but what, wondered Mary Kelley, putting her face in her large, square hands, did you really do when it happened?

For a moment, she pondered the advisability of going straight to Father O'Brien and confessing to him the sin in which she had taken part this night. She pictured the big, blue-jowled face of the priest, and the narrow, black eyes that could pierce like knives. What if she told him and he refused to give her absolution? What if he said, "Deliver this doctor into the hands of the law, for only in this way can I wash the sin from your soul"? Mary Kelley pictured the face of Doc Swain, his good, kind face, and the hands that she had regarded as next to those of Christ in their gentleness. She had, really, not been able to help herself, for The Doc had not offered her a choice.

"Prep her," he had said, indicating Selena Cross. "I've got to yank her appendix."

Mary's thighs were hurting, her temper was short and she had been annoyed, as always, by The Doc's unprofessional language. He never used the more polished, mysterious words of medicine if he could help it. She had been full of protests.

What about an assistant? she had queried. An anesthetist? An extra nurse? She was alone on night duty in the almost empty hospital. What if there were only three patients in bed at the time? It wasn't right to leave those three unattended while she helped The Doc! What if the telephone rang now that it was evening and the daytime secretary gone? What if someone called up and no one answered the phone? It wouldn't look right, she had told The Doc, if there should be an emergency and there was no one on duty at the desk.

"Goddamn it!" roared The Doc. "Stop your jaw-flapping and do as I say!"

Mary didn't mind when The Doc roared. It was just his way, and a good nurse never interfered with a doctor's way any more than she tried to tell him what to do in the O.R. She had tried, though, later, with Selena Cross unconscious on the table.

"Doc," she had whispered. "Doc, what're you doing?"

He had straightened up and looked at her, his eyes blazing, blue and furious, over his mask.

"I'm removing her appendix," he said coldly. "Do you understand that, Mary? I am removing an appendix so diseased that it might easily have ruptured had I waited until tomorrow morning to remove it. Do you understand that, Mary?"

She had lowered her eyes, unable to look at the pain in his which he tried to cover with rage. Later, she supposed that this had been The Doc's way of offering her a choice. She could have said no, she didn't understand, and run out of the O.R. and called Buck McCracken, the sheriff, right then. But she had, of course, done nothing of the kind.

"Yes, Doctor," she had said, "I understand."

"Make sure you never forget it then," he told her. "Make goddamned sure."

"Yes, Doctor," she said, and wondered why she had always thought that it was only Catholics who were against abortion. It couldn't be so, for here was The Doc, a Protestant, with his eyes full of pain as his hands expertly performed an alien task.

At least, thought Mary later, she supposed that The Doc was a Protestant. He followed no religion at all, and Father O'Brien had always led her to believe that it was only Protestants who fell away and wound up with no religion at all. A Catholic, she told herself, would never have performed this shocking, horrifying, repulsive act, and she had been shocked, horrified and repulsed, as any good Catholic girl would have been. But underneath all that, like a poisonous snake slithering through deep jungle grass, ran a thread of sinful pride. The Doc had chosen her. Of all the nurses he might have picked—Lucy Ellsworth, or Geraldine Dunbar, or any of the nurses who came over from White River to help out when the hospital was loaded—he had chosen Mary Kelley. He could have left her on floor duty and called in someone else, but he had chosen her, and, wrong or not, there was an area of dark happiness in her.

The Doc might make her his accomplice in the most serious of all crimes, but he was not a liar, nor did he make one of her. In the end, when he had finished with the other, he had removed Selena Cross's appendix. While it might be the prettiest, healthiest looking appendix that Mary Kelley had ever seen come out of anyone, The Doc *had* removed it.

"Messiest appendectomy I ever performed," he told Mary when he had finished. "Cean it up, Mary. Clean it up real good."

She had, too. While the patients slept peacefully, she had given thanks, like a seasoned criminal, for the phenomenal good luck that the Fates had bestowed upon The Doc and her, and she had cleaned up the O.R. real good as The Doc had told her to do. She had cleaned up real good, like The Doc said, and she had disposed of everything very carefully and conscientiously.

Mary Kelley twisted in her chair and put her hand under her skirt. She pushed the extra material in the skirt of her slip down between her sweaty, chafed thighs and relaxed.

There, she thought, as the fabric absorbed some of the moisture, that was better.

When the telephone rang, she was almost cheerful again.

"Oh, yes, Mrs. MacKenzie," she said into the receiver. "Yes, I've called you a couple of times. Anita told me you'd gone out, so I told her to have you call me. Oh, dear no, Mrs. MacKenzie. It's not Allison. It's Selena Cross. Emergency appendectomy. Oh, yes indeed. It was about to rupture. She's fine now, though. Sleeping like a baby."

It was only after she had hung up that Mary Kelley realized that she had taken the irrevocable step in the question of ethics. She had made her choice with this first handing out of false information. Resolutely, she picked up the detective novel that she had started the night before. She forced her eyes to concentrate on the printed page, hoping that her mind would absorb what her eyes picked up. There would be plenty of times in the future, when she couldn't read, to think of sin and God and Father O'Brien.

♦ 6 ♦

Dr. Matthew Swain parked his car at the side of the dirt road in front of the Cross shack and then went quickly to the door of the house. He pounded against the flimsy door with both fists, as if to find a physical outlet for the rage that was in him.

155

"Come in, for Christ's sake," bawled Lucas from inside. "Don't break the goddam door down."

Matthew Swain stood in the open doorway, tall, white suited, looking larger than he really was. Lucas was sitting at the kitchen table, dressed only in a pair of greasy dungarees. The black mattress of hair on his bare chest looked as if it might be a hiding place for lice, and his skin was shiny with sweat. There was a game of solitaire spread out on the table, and a quart bottle of beer, half empty. Lucas looked up at Dr. Swain and smiled. His forehead and lips moved at the same time, but his eyes remained flat and still with suspicion.

"Lost your way, Doc?" he asked. "Nobody here sent for you."

At these words, the doctor felt the sweat break out on his own body. It wet his shirt through in seconds and trickled down his sides. Nobody sent for you, Doc. The words brought back a picture of Selena, huddled outside in the night, to protect her little brother Joey against the fists of the man whom the doctor faced now.

"I've got Selena in the hospital," he said hoarsely, as soon as he could control his rage.

"Selena?" asked Lucas. He pronounced it S'lena, and the doctor knew that Lucas had been drinking all day. "What you got Selena in the hospital for, Doc?"

"She was pregnant," said the doctor. "She had a miscarriage this afternoon."

For only a moment, Lucas' smile wavered.

"Pregnant?" he asked. "Pregnant?" he repeated, and tried to put outrage into his voice. "Pregnant, eh? The goddamn little tramp. I'll fix her. I'll give her a beatin' she won't forget in a hurry. I told her she'd get in a mess of trouble, always lettin' that Carter feller rassle around with her. I told her, but she wouldn't listen to her pa. Well, I'll fix her, the little tramp. When I get done with her, she'll listen good."

"You miserable bastard," said Dr. Swain in a voice that shook. "You miserable, lying sonofabitch."

"Now, just you hold on a minute, Doc," said Lucas, pushing away from the table and rising to his feet. "There's no man calls Lucas Cross a sonofabitch in his own house. Not even a high mucky muck doctor like you."

Matthew Swain advanced toward Lucas. "You hold on a minute," he said. "You do the holding on, you sonofabitch. That was your child that Selena carried, and we both know it."

156

Lucas sat down abruptly on his chair. "I can prove it, Lucas," continued the doctor, lying and knowing it, and not caring. "I can prove it was your child," he repeated, using his superior knowledge now in a way he had never done before. To intimidate the ignorant. "I have enough proof," he told Lucas, "to put you in jail for the rest of your life."

Sweat dripped from Lucas' face now, and its odor rose from him in hot waves. "You ain't got nothin' on me, Doc," he protested. "I never touched her. Never even laid a hand on her."

"I've got plenty on you, Lucas. More than I can use. And just to be on the safe side, I've got a paper here I want you to sign. I wrote it up before I left the hospital. It's a confession, Lucas, and I want you to write your name on it. If you won't do it for me, maybe Buck McCracken can sweat it out of you in the cellar of the courthouse with a rubber hose."

"I never touched her," insisted Lucas harshly. "And I ain't gonna put my name on nothin' says I did. What you got against me, Doc? I never did nothin' to you. What you want to come in here and bully me for? Did I ever do a wrong thing against you?"

The doctor leaned on the table, towering over the man who sat and stared sullenly at his folded arms. Matthew Swain knew that Selena had carried Lucas' child. He was as sure of it as he had ever been of anything. Just being sure should have been enough, yet some perverseness in him drove him on. He knew that Lucas Cross was guilty of a crime so close to incest that the borderline was invisible. The knowing should have been enough. With the knowing alone, he knew that he could force Lucas to sign a confession, but something made him drive on, made him bully the man until Lucas should admit in his own words that he had fathered the foetus in Selena's womb.

"Maybe I won't go after Buck," he said softly. "No, I won't go after Buck. Instead, I'll raise an alarm all over town. I'll go personally and tell every father in Peyton Place what you did, Lucas. I'll tell them that their daughters aren't safe with you around. The fathers will come after you, Lucas, the same way they'd go after a wild and dangerous animal. But they won't shoot you." He paused and looked at the figure in front of him. "Know how long it's been since we had a lynching in this town, Lucas?"

The eyes of the man in front of him swiveled around frantically, searching for escape from the merciless voice that drummed in his ears.

"It was so long ago, Lucas, that no one remembers, for sure,

157

just when it was. But lynching seems to be something an outraged man always knows how to do. The fathers will know how to do it, Lucas. Not too good, maybe. Not good enough so's you'd die on the first try, maybe. But they'd get the hang of it after a while."

He waited for a moment, but Lucas did not raise his head. He continued to sit, staring at the matted black hair on his forearms, with the smell of sweat rising from skin that was roughened now with the tiny bumps of fear. The doctor turned as if to leave, but Lucas' moan stopped him before he had taken three steps.

"For Christ's sake, Doc," said Lucas. "Hold on a minute."

The doctor turned and looked at him.

"I done it, Doc," he said. "I'll sign your paper. Give it here."

And this should have been enough. Together with the other, with the knowing beforehand, this final admission, oral and written, should have been enough for Matthew Swain. But it was not enough. He wanted to crush, to crush and grind with his heel; to degrade and humiliate and break. He looked at the pile of broken pieces that more than thirty years of honorable medical practice made when it came tumbling down, and he looked at Mary Kelley's good, Irish Catholic face, overlaid now with a certain hardness made by the cynical knowledge of crime committed. He looked at the gelatinous red mass of Selena's unborn child that would probably have been born and lived a normal number of years, and he looked at Lucas Cross. He wanted to inflict pain on this man of such an acute and exquisite caliber that his own pain would dissolve, and all the while he knew that it was futile. Lucas would feel neither pain nor shame nor regret, for in Lucas' lexicon he had not committed a crime of such magnitude that it could not be overlooked and forgotten. Lucas Cross paid his bills and minded his own business. All he asked of other men was that they do the same. Before he spoke, Matthew Swain knew that Lucas would first present excuses and then make a bid for sympathy, but he could not keep from speaking, nor from hoping to twist the knife in a wound that he knew Lucas did not possess.

"When did it start, Lucas?" he asked in a sly voice that was not his. "How many times did you do it, Lucas?"

The man looked at him out of eyes which held nothing now but fear. "Jesus, Doc," he said to this man with the crazy blue eyes whom he had never seen before. "Jesus, Doc," he said. "What do you want from me? I told you I done it, didn't I?"

"How long, Lucas?" the doctor repeated doggedly. "One year? Two years? Five?"

"A couple," said Lucas in a low whisper. "I was drunk, Doc. I didn't know what I was doin'."

Automatically the doctor's mind registered the first of Lucas' excuses. I was drunk. I didn't know what I was doing. It was a standard with men like Lucas, for everything from fighting and stealing to, apparently, the raping of children.

"She was a virgin when you started, wasn't she, Lucas?" asked the doctor in the same sly voice. "You busted your daughter's cherry for her, didn't you, Lucas, you big, brave, virile wood-chopper?"

"I was drunk," repeated Lucas. "Honest, Doc. I was drunk. I didn't know what I was doin'. Besides, it ain't like she was my own. She wa'nt mine. She's Nellie's kid."

Dr. Swain grabbed a handful of Lucas' hair and twisted with his strong fingers until Lucas' head went back with a snap.

"Listen, you sonofabitch," he said, enraged. "This is no job in the woods that you've messed up. This is nothing that I'm going to listen to your weak excuses about being drunk. You knew what you were doing every minute. Stop being a pig for the one and only minute of your stinking, perverted life and admit that you knew."

Lucas gasped as the doctor's fingers twisted in his hair. "Yes," he said. "I knew. I seen her one day, and I seen she was almost grown. I don't know what got into me."

When the doctor released Lucas' hair, he took out a clean hand-kerchief and wiped his hand carefully. The second standard excuse had now been presented. I don't know what got into me. It was as if men like Lucas expected men like Matthew Swain to believe in the existence of strange devils who lurked, ready and eager to invade the minds and bodies of men like Lucas. The second excuse for misbehavior was always tendered in a wistful, half-apologetic tone, as if the speaker expected the listener to join with him in wonder at this thing which had got into him. I don't know what got into me, but whatever it was, it was none of my doing. Some-thing just got into me, and there was nothing I could do.

Oh, Christ, prayed Matthew Swain. Oh, Christ, keep me from killing him.

"I dunno how many times it was," said Lucas thickly. "A couple —maybe three—when I was half drunk and didn't give a shit." His eyes went blank with remembered lust. "She's a wildcat, Selena is. Always was. I used to hit her 'til she didn't fight no more."

Dr. Swain felt the greenness of nausea in his mouth as he lis-tened to Lucas and watched him lick his dry lips.

This is not true, he thought. It is not true that a man can rape a child time after time and then remember these occasions as if they were the loveliest of dreams. It is simply not true. I can no more believe this than I can believe that the Crucifixion was a publicity stunt or that the object of life is death. It is not true.

"She's pretty, Selena is," Lucas continued dreamily. "She's got the prettiest pair of tits I ever seen, and the little ends was always all brown and puckered up. I tied her up the first time, but I didn't have to, 'cause she wa'nt awake anyhow. She was a virgin all right. Christ, that cherry of hers was in there so solid I was sore for two weeks after. Couldn't hardly work I was so sore."

The excuses which would not satisfy Matthew Swain had been exhausted, and now Lucas had begun his bid for sympathy. Couldn't hardly work I was so sore. Lucas uttered these words in a sick whine, as if he expected the doctor to commiserate with him. What a shame, Dr. Swain was expected to say. What a helluva shame, Lucas, that you could hardly work for two weeks after the first time you raped your virgin stepdaughter.

Oh, Christ, thought the doctor, clenching his fists and feeling the sour sweat on himself again. Oh, Christ, keep me from killing him.

"Pretty, Selena is," said Lucas.

Matthew Swain could hear his own breath, rising and falling, when Lucas finished speaking. It was quiet for a long time in the Cross shack while the doctor fought down his desire to put his hands around Lucas' neck and choke him. It took a long time for the sickness and the rage that come to a man when he realizes how thin the layers of civilization on another man can be, to abate in Dr. Swain.

When he could speak, he said, "Lucas, I'll give you until tomorrow noon to clear out of here. Get out of town. I don't want to see you around tomorrow."

"Whaddya mean, get out of town, Doc?" cried Lucas, horror stricken at the vindictiveness of this man to whom he had never done a wrong thing. "Whaddya mean, get out of town? I ain't got nowheres to go, Doc. This is my home. Always was. Where am I gonna go, Doc?"

"Straight to hell," said the doctor. "But failing that, anywhere you've a mind to go. Just get out of Peyton Place."

"But I ain't of a mind to go nowheres, Doc," whined Lucas. "There ain't nowheres for me to go."

"If I see you around tomorrow, Lucas, I'll have the whole town on your tail. Get out and stay out, and don't try to come back. Not

160

next week nor next year. Not even after I'm dead, Lucas, because I'm going to leave that proof I was talking about in a good safe place. Folks in town will know what to do if you ever come back."

Lucas Cross began to cry. He put his head down on his arms and sobbed at the injustice of this persecution.

"What did I ever do to you, Doc?" he cried. "I never done nothin' to you. How'm I gonna get out of town when I ain't got nowheres to go?"

"Selena had nowhere to go to get away from you," said the doctor. "That made you happy enough. Now the shoe is on the other foot, and if it pinches, that's too bad. I mean it, Lucas. Don't let the noon sun shine on your head tomorrow."

Matthew Swain felt old, as old as time and as weary, as he walked, stoop shouldered now, toward the door of the Cross shack. Lucas' confession weighed heavy in his suit coat pocket, and the words of Lucas were a sore on his soul. There was a tiredness in him such as he had never known and his mouth was filled with the taste of tarnished silver.

If I can make it home, he thought. If I can just get home and into a hot, hot bath. If I can just scrub this filth off myself and get to my dining room sideboard and pour myself a drink. If I could go to sleep tonight and wake up in the morning to find Peyton Place as clean and beautiful as it was yesterday. If I can just make it home.

He had the shack door half open before a high, keening wail behind him stopped him with his hand still on the knob. He turned, horror struck, knowing before he turned that he had committed another act of destruction. His eyes searched the gloom beyond the circle of light shed by the shack's one electric light bulb, and found the sagging double bed against the rear wall of the room. Nellie Cross was lying on it, wailing a high sustained wail, and her body writhed and twisted as if she were in the agonized labor of childbirth.

◆ 7 ◆

Ted Carter put the end of his tongue between his teeth. Painstakingly, he tried again to fold the ends of a sheet of white tissue paper smoothly around the corners of a candy box which he wanted to wrap. No matter how many times he started over, the corners always seemed to bunch up so that the package looked clumsy, and as if it had been wrapped by a child. Ted's mother had glanced over at him several times, but she did not offer to help. She went on washing dishes and staring, when she was not looking at her son, out the small window over the kitchen sink. Ted's father sat in the living room and shook out the pages of his newspaper at frequent intervals, but he, also, kept silent.

Since Ted had started dating Selena Cross, over two years before, there had been an unfriendly tension in the Carter house, and it did not lessen with time. Roberta and Harmon Carter, Ted's parents, had not met the problem of Selena with the smiling tolerance which most parents employ when confronted with an off-spring who is sure he is in love. "Puppy love," with its connotations of childishness, was not a term easily applied to Ted Carter's emotion for Selena Cross.

Roberta Carter swished her hands around in the soapy dishwater and reflected that nothing about Ted had ever been childish. Once, this fact had pleased her. It had made her happy when Ted talked and walked earlier and better than other babies. It had pleased her when his teachers commented on how smart he was, how easily he learned, how mature he was for his age. She had been filled with pride when he could swim at six, ski at seven and hit a baseball at eight. She had looked upon her big, strapping son with wonder, for both she and Harmon were thin, small people, and she had had the satisfaction of a job well done. And she had done a good job with Ted, she knew. He was not only tall and solidly built, but healthy. His teeth were innocent of fillings, his skin never broke out, and he was blessed with twenty-twenty vision. He was kind, considerate and courteous, never raised his voice and seldom lost his temper, and he went at any task with an energy and a conscientiousness seldom seen in sixteen-year-old boys. Even Mr. Shapiro, who owned the huge chicken farm where Ted worked summers and had a reputation of being hard to please, had commented on Ted's steadfastness and industry.

"Nice boy, Teddy," he had told Roberta. "A good boy. He works like a man already, at his age."

It had pleased her to hear that, until she remembered that with Ted's lack of childishness went her comfort in thinking that the boy's love for Selena Cross was a passing, childish love.

When Roberta and Harmon Carter realized that the question of Selena was no longer a question but an established fact, they had been unable to face it with resignation. Had they been able to do so, there might have been a relaxation of the tension in their home and a semblance of friendliness in their lives. They wanted him to be the child he had never been, with a child's swiftly changing moods and easily broken attachments. They regarded as a failure a son who could allow himself to become involved with a girl from the shacks. The stepdaughter of a drunken woodchopping father and the flesh and blood of a slatternly, half-crazy mother.

"What are you doing, Ted?" Roberta asked her son, although she and Harmon both knew very well what he was doing.

"Trying to wrap a box of candy for Selena," he replied.

"Oh?" Roberta spoke only the one word, on a rising inflection, yet she managed to convey biting sarcasm and mocking laughter in that one syllable.

"Oh?" she repeated, but Ted would not enlarge on his original remark, and Roberta felt anger mount in her and redden her throat.

"She is still in the hospital, I presume," she said, managing to make known her low opinion of people who remained in the hospital longer than a week for an operation as simple as an appendectomy.

"Yes," said Ted.

In the living room, Harmon Carter shook out his newspaper.

"Well," said Roberta, "how long is she planning to stay there, taking up a bed which could be used for a really sick person?"

"Until Doc Swain says she can leave, I imagine," replied Ted shortly.

"Theodore!"

"Yes, Dad?"

"Keep a civil tongue in your head when you speak to your mother."

"I wasn't uncivil," said Ted. "I answered her question."

"It's your tone, Ted," said his mother. "I don't think I particularly care for your tone."

"Foolishness," said Harmon from the living room. "Running out every night to go see that little chippy."

"Selena's no chippy," said Ted calmly, "and you know it."

It was true that Harmon knew it, but it enraged him to have Ted tell him that he knew it.

"Goddamn it," he shouted, coming to stand in the doorway between the kitchen and the living room. "I told you to keep

163

a civil tongue in your head. Go to your room until you learn to control your remarks."

Ted finished wrapping his package and did not answer his father.

"Didn't you hear your father, Ted?" asked Roberta. "He told you to go to your room. Your little friend will have to survive without seeing you tonight."

Ted stood up, unzipped his trousers, and stuffed his shirt down into them. He did not speak.

"Did you hear me?" shouted Harmon.

"Yes, Dad," said Ted, picking up the wrapped candy box. "I heard you."

"Well?" Harmon uttered this word in a heavily underlined, threatening tone. "Well?" he demanded, dragging the word out.

Ted opened the door that led out into the back yard. "Good night, Dad," he said. " 'Night, Mother."

For a moment after the door had closed softly behind their son, Roberta and Harmon merely stood and looked at one another. Then Roberta took her hands out of the dishwater and, without drying them, sat down on a kitchen chair and began to cry. Harmon threw his newspaper down on the floor and pounded the fist of one hand into the palm of the other.

"Insolent," he said. "That's what he is. Insolent."

"After all we've done for him," cried Roberta, echoing the remark of untold millions of mothers. "After all we've given him. Everything. A good, decent bringing up and a nice home and everything."

"A prospective college education," said Harmon, taking up the litany. "A chance any boy would jump at."

Harmon Carter had graduated from the eighth grade and had attended high school for two years before quitting to go to work at the Cumberland Mills. To him, a chance at a college education was on a par with a chance at the True Cross.

"I'm not going to sweat blood at the mill to send him to college if this is the way he is going to behave," said Harmon.

Harmon Carter did not sweat blood at the Cumberland Mills. He was a bookkeeper in the office, and the only time he ever broke out in a mild perspiration was when one of the young secretaries there bent over his desk to ask him a question. Nor did Harmon have to worry about the money for Ted's college education. The money had been in the Citizens' National Bank since before Ted was born. It had, in fact, been there since before Harmon married Roberta.

"He's had everything," cried Roberta, wiping her still wet hands on her apron.

This was true, in a way. While the Carters did not live on Chestnut Street, believing that it would be ostentatious for a bookkeeper at the mill to live on the same street as Leslie Harrington, they nevertheless lived in a very good house in a very decent neighborhood. They lived on Maple Street, two blocks away from the schools, a street that was considered as the "second best" in Peyton Place. The Carter house was large, well furnished, well heated in winter, well shaded in summer and well kept. It was given a coat of paint every three years, and Kenny Stearns took good care of the grounds that surrounded it. In addition to the "nice" home which Ted Carter's parents provided for him, he also had the social advantages of good clothes and expensive sports equipment. He had the promise of college and the security of knowing that funds existed to provide against the time when he graduated from college and set up a law office of his own. And in return for all these things, Ted Carter's parents asked nothing of him but his undivided devotion, unquestioning loyalty and immediate obedience.

"I never asked him for a thing," said Roberta, blowing her nose. "I wouldn't even take board money when he worked and practically insisted on giving me part of his wages. I never asked him for a single thing, except to leave Selena Cross alone, and he won't even do that much. After all we've done for him."

All the things that Roberta and Harmon did for Ted had been done for themselves long before Ted was born. For a long time Peyton Place had rocked with the talk of what Roberta and Harmon had done for themselves, and even now, after so many years, there were still those who remembered, and talked.

It had been a long, uphill struggle for Roberta and Harmon to lift themselves out of the ranks of the mill hands. It had taken time and sacrifice to attain a house on Maple Street, a bank account, a good car, a fur coat for Roberta and a solid gold pocket watch for Harmon. Some mill hands worked all their lives to succeed in getting just a few of the things that Roberta and Harmon obtained for themselves before they were thirty.

Roberta Carter had been seventeen years old and her name had been "Bobbie" Welch the year that Harmon Carter, aged eighteen, had conceived his great plan. Harmon was employed at that time as an office boy in the Cumberland Mills, a position he had held since leaving high school at the age of fifteen. Bobbie was em-

165

ployed as a part-time secretary and cleaning woman by Dr. Jerrold Quimby. This was during the same year that young Matt Swain was serving his interneship in the Mary Hitchcock Hospital at Hanover. Young Swain, as he was then called, was supposed to go into Old Doc Quimby's office when he finished at Hanover, for that was the year that Old Doc Quimby was seventy-four years old, and much in need of a younger man to help him.

Bobbie and Harmon were keeping steady company at that time, and it was understood that they would get married as soon as Harmon was promoted from office boy to office clerk at the Cumberland Mills. The two young people either went for walks or sat on the vine-covered Welch porch on their date nights, for Harmon did not have the money for more expensive amusement. They discussed their jobs with one another, and Harmon often laughed at the way Old Doc Quimby depended on Bobbie for everything. One night he did not laugh, for that day he had conceived his great plan. He unfolded it to Bobbie carefully, so as not to startle her with its unorthodox daring. He began by making her dissatisfied with the bleak future that loomed ahead for both of them. He accented, particularly, the constant and continual lack of funds which was sure to plague them as it always had, and as it had plagued their parents and grandparents.

"It takes money to make money," he told her.

And: "The best way to get money is to have a rich relative die and leave you a packet."

And: "Hand to mouth, one payday to the next. That's the life of an office worker's family."

And: "You are so beautiful. You should have everything. Furs and jewels and gorgeous clothes. I can't get things like that for you, and I never will be able to—with my job."

In the end, the seed was planted and began to sprout. Bobbie, who was a fair and buxom creature and had always had a certain cowlike contentment about her, began to see herself as tall and sylphlike, a woman who needed furs and Paris trips to bring out the best in her. Her contentment was replaced by an active dissatisfaction, a feeling of being put-upon by her lot of poverty. Harmon then began to unfold the second step of his great plan.

"Old Doc Quimby's got plenty," he told her.

And: "Old Doc Quimby's got more money than anyone could ever use."

And: "Old Doc Quimby's an old man. A woman smart enough to land him wouldn't have to wait long for his money."

And: "Old Doc Quimby depends on you for everything. He needs you. If you wanted to go ahead and marry him, I'd wait for you."

At first, of course, Bobbie had been shocked. She loved Harmon, she said, and always would, through riches and in poverty, in sickness and in health. Harmon immediately pointed out to her that if she loved him that much, her great love for him would not desert her while she was married to Old Doc Quimby, not even if the Damned Old Fool lived for another five years. "Bobbie" saw the reasonableness of this after a while, and the program of leading Old Doc Quimby to the trough and making him drink was begun. As they often said to each other later, it had been a long, uphill struggle. Old Doc Quimby had been a widower for twenty years, and did not mind it a bit as long as he could hire someone to come in to look after him. There was the hook, and Bobbie, under Harmon's tutelage, sunk it deep. She threatened to quit her job; she refused to cook the old man's meals; she left his dirty clothes where he dropped them; she spread the word around town that he was a vile, old lecher and an impossible man to work for. Old Doc Quimby, unable to find a replacement for Bobbie who would come into his house and look after him, had succumbed wearily. Bobbie married Old Doc Quimby, and Peyton Place rocked with shock and, later, laughter. The town called Old Doc Quimby a senile old man, an old fool of the kind there is no other like, an old fool who did not know enough to see that he was being cuckolded regularly by young Harmon Carter, and into this sorry state of affairs walked Young Doc Swain. Bobbie, still under Harmon's tutelage, refused to let the young doctor into the house. After all, as Harmon pointed out to her, Old Doc Quimby might have plenty, but there was no need to pay any of it out to Matthew Swain. The young doctor turned away angrily from the front door of the big house on Maple Street, where he had expected to have his first office, and went to the home of his parents. He put out his shingle in front of their large, "Southern-looking" house on Chestnut Street and never had cause to regret that he had done so. Peyton Place had laughed harder than ever, when sick people began going to Young Doc Swain. In the end, Peyton Place laughed Old Doc Quimby to death. Two weeks before the date of the first anniversary of his marriage to Bobbie Welch, Old Doc Quimby put his revolver to his head and shot himself.

Small towns are notorious for their long memories and their sharp tongues, and Peyton Place did not spare Bobbie Quimby and Harmon Carter. It was years before the words hurled at them began to soften, and the epithets hurled by Peyton Place ran the gamut from "Whore" and "Pimp" to "Harlot" and "White Slaver." It was many years before the house on Maple Street was forgotten as "The Quimby Place" and called by its now correct name of "The Carter House," and it was as many years before Mrs. Carter succeeded in making Peyton Place call her "Roberta" instead of the frivolous and, to her, harlotish-sounding name of "Bobbie." Even now, when she was over fifty, and had been married to Harmon for more than thirty years, and had a son sixteen years old, there were still those who remembered. It was because of these that Roberta and Harmon Carter were hard pressed for sympathetic listeners whenever they spoke of "all they had done" for their son Ted. It was because of the old-timers, the ones with the long, long memories who had the habit of passing on scandalous stories to their young, that Peyton Place cheered for Ted Carter. When the boy insisted on working part time after school and during the summer vacations, Peyton Place approved.

"Young Carter ain't goin' to live on Old Doc Quimby's money," said the town, "the way his folks always did."

When Peyton Place noticed young Ted Carter walking down Elm Street on a hot July night with a box of candy under his arm, bound for the hospital where his sweetheart lay sick, they approved and cheered him on.

"Nice boy, young Carter is," said the town. "Like to see him make a go of it with Selena Cross. She's a nice enough girl, for a shack girl."

But it was the humiliation to Roberta and Harmon that Peyton Place loved. To see young Carter take up with a shack girl, after his people had worked so hard to escape the same environment that had spawned Selena, had a certain beauty, a poetic justice.

A comeuppance, the town called it. Roberta and Harmon Carter were getting their comeuppance at long last.

◆ **8** ◆

Ted Carter hurried down Elm Street and eventually came to the broad, three-lane highway which was called Route 406 and which was the main road between Peyton Place and White River. It was on this highway, a mile from the center of town, that the Peyton Place hospital was located. Ted walked rapidly, with the wrapped box of candy for Selena under one arm, and his other arm swinging back and forth in rhythm with his stride. In two years, he had fulfilled the promise of size that had been his at fourteen. Now he was only a scant inch under six feet tall, and he weighed close to a hundred and seventy pounds. Although his chest and shoulders were as broad as those of a man much older, he gave the impression of leanness, for years of sports and outdoor work had kept fat to a minimum and made his body hard and muscular.

Ted Carter's was the kind of body that older people look upon with satisfaction. Things can't be so bad, they said, when this country can produce young men like that. In the summer of 1939, when the stage whispers of war in Europe were already audible to the pessimists in America, those who believed that world conflict was inevitable could look at Ted Carter and be comforted. Things won't be so bad, they said, as long as we have big, healthy boys like that to send to war. Because Ted Carter's body had none of the loose-jointedness, the clumsily put together look of many sixteen-year-olds, his was the envy of every adolescent in Peyton Place. Because of it, and also because of his outstanding talent at sports, other, less fortunate, sixteen-year-olds forgave him his good marks in school, his charm, his easy way of making friends, and the good manners which many mothers flung constantly into the faces of sloppy talking, often discourteous sons.

With all his blessings, including everything his parents did for him, Ted Carter should have had the happy, open-faced look of a carefree youngster, but there was none of the child in his face as he walked rapidly toward the Peyton Place hospital. There was a suggestion of shadow on his cheeks and chin, although he had shaved carefully before supper, and there were two diagonal lines in the skin between his eyebrows. He frowned, not because he was upset or angry as he remembered the scene of a short time before with his parents, but because he was perplexed. As he put it to himself, walking along, he just didn't understand his folks. Ever since he could remember, he had been making his own decisions. His folks had said that they were proud of his common sense, and they had never had cause to interfere with him. It was only in the last two years that they had begun to find fault and to criticize. Yet all they ever criticized was his going with Selena, while everything else remained as it always had been. When he had wanted to go to work for Mr. Shapiro, his folks had not interfered. They had told him to go ahead, if he wanted, although the work on a chicken farm was hard and tedious, and Mr. Shapiro was Jewish and hard to work for. They had not tried to influence him when he had started looking around for a used car to buy, and he knew that they would approve his choice if he found one he wanted. Everything he had always wanted to do had always been all right with his folks, so why, he wondered, were they so unyielding, so downright mean and stupid, about Selena? Certainly, since they had always trusted his common sense before, they should do so now. They should be able to realize that he was no dumb kid out for what he could get from a girl. He was planning a career in the law—and his plans included Selena—remaining in his home town to go into practice with Old Charlie, and eventual success in his chosen field. Certainly, his folks should realize that a plan such as his had no room in it for foolishness. He had discussed his hopes in detail and at length with old Charlie Partridge, and the laywer had no fault to find with them.

"It's good to know what you want," Charles Partridge had said. "You go right ahead, boy. When you get done at law school, you come on back here to Peyton Place. I'll need a bright young feller to help me out by then."

"You couldn't do better than Selena Cross," Charles Partridge had said. "Not for looks and not for brains. You go ahead, boy. It's good to know what you want in this world."

Since Ted truly loved Selena Cross and had told his parents so, they should realize that he had enough sense and self-control to keep his hands off her until after they were married. Not that it wasn't difficult, at times, but his folks should realize that Ted's plan had no room in it for foolish mistakes. He had explained all this to Selena long ago, and she had seen the common sense in it. Why, then, couldn't he convince his folks of this, after two years of trying?

The Carters seldom fought between themselves; the swearing and shouting of this evening's scene had been the rare exception rather than the rule. Instead, they argued sensibly, rationally and continually, but it always ended with Ted on one side of the fence and his parents on the other.

It was perplexing, thought Ted, as he walked along the gravel edge of the highway. The only thing he could do was to stick by what he thought was right for him, and hope that his folks would come to see his way of thinking. It would be different, he thought, if they could present one sensible argument against Selena. He was willing, just as he had always been, to listen to reason. But they could say nothing against Selena except that she lived

170

in a shack and that she was the daughter of a drunkard. Ted couldn't see what that had to do with anything. As he pointed out to his folks, both of them had lived in shacks not much better than Selena's when they had been young, and it hadn't harmed them any. As for drinking, old man Welch, Roberta's father, had been one of the most notorious drunkards in town, and that hadn't left any taint on either Ted or his mother. The only other argument his folks had was that people were bound to talk if he kept on with Selena. People were bound to talk anyway, Ted had told them. Look at the way some people still talked about his mother's first husband. People always talked, and they always would. As long as a man worked hard, did not steal or get a girl in trouble, there was nothing that people could say that could harm him much. Ted pointed out carefully, and in detail, the stories he had heard about his mother and father and Old Doc Quimby. He did this to illustrate to them how little talk mattered. Talk, he said, had not harmed his parents, in the long run. They had everything they wanted. His father was head bookkeeper at the mill, and they lived in a nice house in a good neighborhood. They could see, couldn't they, how little talk really amounted to, in the long run?

It was always at this point that an argument between the Carters fell apart. Ted's parents either fell silent altogether so that the tension in their house was almost as palpable as fog, or else they began to talk disjointedly, foolishly. He just didn't know, they said. He was too young. He just did not realize.

Ted Carter walked into the Peyton Place hospital with his head up and a smile on his face. He realized, all right. He realized that he loved Selena Cross so much that the thought of life without her was the same as thinking about being dead.

Selena was sitting up in a chair in the private room to which Dr. Swain had assigned her. She was wearing the bright red robe that Constance MacKenzie had brought her the day after the operation, and her dark hair was brushed out loosely around her shoulders. Ted's heart lifted as he entered the room and looked at her. She looked like herself again. For the first time in the whole, long week since the operation, she looked like the Selena of before, who had never had a sick day in her life. Her lips were red again, and the shine was back in her eyes. Ted bent over her chair and kissed her gently.

"Really kiss me," she said, laughing up at him, and he did.

"I guess you're all better," he said. "Nothing wrong with a girl who can kiss like that."

171

It was wrong, thought Selena, for her to be this happy. But she could not help it. Her room was full of flowers, from friends she did not even know she had, and Mrs. MacKenzie had come to see her every day. Allison had come, too, and Miss Elsie Thornton, carrying a book and a little plant of African violets. There was an enormous, formal bouquet of glads and roses from Mr. and Mrs. Partridge, which had surprised Selena, for she had not been in Marion's house for over two years, since the time when she used to go on Tuesdays to do Mrs. Partridge's ironing. But best of all, creating her happiness and sustaining it, was the news that Dr. Swain had brought her that morning. Lucas was gone. Lucas had left town in the night, a week ago, and he was never coming back. Selena felt as if she had put down a load that she had carried for years. She had actually twitched her shoulders several times during the day, after The Doc had told her the news, and she believed that she could feel a lightness there that she had not known it was possible to feel.

If it was wrong to be this happy, thought Selena, she wanted to be wrong all the rest of her life. When Ted talked, she could close her eyes and see her future stretching out before her as smooth as satin ribbon and as calm as the wide Connecticut River in summer. She had thought carefully about the other, the ugliness of a week ago, and she had expected to feel horror or shame. All she had felt was an overwhelming, grateful sense of relief. Her practical mind decided to forget it, to think no more about it than one would think of a cut suffered long ago, during childhood. It was over and done with, and she would not even be able to find a scar unless she looked hard for it.

"Oh, Ted," she said, shiny eyed. "I can go home tomorrow."

I can go home, she thought, and only Joey and my mother will be there.

"I think I'll buy that Ford I was looking at," said Ted. "I'll buy it tomorrow and come to fetch you home in style."

"How much are they asking for it?" asked Selena.

Ted told her, and they began to discuss the advisability of investing so much capital in a used car. They realized that they sounded like old, married people when they talked this way, and it gave each of them a sense of warmth that nothing else could. They held hands and decided that the Ford wasn't a bad buy, providing that Jinks, the garageowner, guaranteed them a good price if they should want to trade next year.

Ted kissed Selena good night at nine o'clock and walked out

of the Peyton Place hospital with a silent whistle on his lips. When he was halfway to town his happiness would no longer let him be still. He uttered a loud war whoop, without caring if anyone heard and thought him crazy, and ran all the way to Elm Street.

"Evening, sir," he said to the man he met just before he turned the corner into Maple Street.

Reverend Fitzgerald, of the Congregational church, started as if someone had put a gun against his ribs.

"Oh!" he said. "Oh, Ted. You startled me for a minute. How are you?"

"Very well, sir," said Ted, and waited for the minister's next question. It came, as it always did.

"Er, Carter," said Reverend Fitzgerald. "Carter, I didn't see you in church last Sunday. Will we see you this Sunday?"

"Yes, sir," said Ted.

It was odd, thought Ted a few minutes later as he approached his house, that no matter whom Reverend Fitzgerald talked to, he always asked that same question. Every Sunday, the Congregational church was jammed to the doors, but every time Reverend Fitzgerald met a Congregationalist, he always asked the same question. Will we see you next Sunday?

Ted shrugged. It was, he supposed, just one of the eccentricities that people had. The minister asked his question; the old men in front of the courthouse swore and talked dirty; his father hated Jews and shack dwellers. Everyone had an eccentricity of some kind, Ted imagined, and went into his house. His parents were sitting in the living room. Harmon was reading and Roberta was knitting. No one spoke.

◆ 9 ◆

Reverend Fitzgerald glanced up at the second-story windows of the parsonage before he went into the house. The lights upstairs were burning, which meant that Tomas Makris was at home.

Perhaps, Reverend Fitzgerald hoped, he could persuade Tom to come down to sit on the porch and talk for a while.

The Congregationalist minister smiled to himself in the darkened, first-floor hall. Two years ago, he would not have approached Tom with a ten-foot pole, let alone invite him down for a conversation. Reverend Fitzgerald had been furious when Leslie Harrington had asked about renting the apartment over the parsonage. He had refused good-naturedly, and Leslie Harrington had been just as good-naturedly insistent. A second-floor apartment had been installed in the house next to the Congregational church long before the church had bought it for a parsonage. The apartment had been built to accommodate the married son of the man who had first owned the house, and it had stood idle ever since the place had been purchased by the church. Certainly, as Reverend Fitzgerald had pointed out to Leslie Harrington, the millowner could not expect his minister to take kindly to the idea of having someone live up over his head after all his years of privacy. Harrington, though, could not remain good natured for long when he thought that he was being balked. He had a streak of vulgarity in him. He had ended up, over two years ago, by telling the minister that he was lucky to have a roof over his head at all, and that it was people like Leslie Harrington, regular, openhanded churchgoers, who made it possible for Reverend Fitzgerald to be maintained in such style.

"We've been decent to you, Fitzgerald," Harrington had said. "We've seen to it that you had this house, and heat, and a car and a salary. The least you can do is to not make things unpleasant for yourself. I want that upstairs apartment for the new headmaster, and I want it now."

Well, thought Reverend Fitzgerald, that was Leslie Harrington for you. What he could not get by fair means, he obtained by the foul expedient of threats. It was typical of Leslie Harrington to point out bluntly the reality of his regular and generous contributions to the church. And what defense did a dependent minister have against such tactics? How could the minister tell Harrington that he was afraid to have anyone in such close proximity as the upstairs apartment? A minister was supposed to spend his life in close proximity to others. How would it sound if he told Harrington, the Peyton Place Congregational Church's largest supporter, that he, Reverend Fitzgerald, was terrified of having people near him? No, it would not do at all. As the minister put it to himself, his hands were tied and his lips were sealed. He had laughed and clapped Leslie Harrington on the shoulder and told the busy millowner not to worry himself with such petty details. He, Reverend Fitzgerald, would get Nellie Cross to clean the upstairs apartment and get it in shape for Mr. Makris, who was due to arrive in town in three days.

174

When Tom arrived, Reverend Fitzgerald waited until Leslie Harrington was gone to put his foot down.

"See here, Mr. Makris," he said, "I don't want any smoking or drinking or loud radio playing going on upstairs."

Tom laughed. "You stay downstairs, padre," he said, unpleasantly, "and I'll stay upstairs. That way, you won't know if I drink myself senseless every night, and I won't know whether or not you worship idols in secret."

Reverend Fitzgerald gasped. What Tom said was not the truth, but it was a little too close to it for comfort.

"Fitzgerald?" Tom had inquired on that night over two years ago. "Irish, isn't it?"

"Yes."

"Orangeman, eh?"

"No."

That had put an end to that particular conversation, but the Congregationalist minister had spent a few anxious weeks wondering what Tom was thinking.

Francis Joseph Fitzgerald was an Irishman, born and bred a Catholic and raised in a tenement in East Boston. When he was in his late teens, it had pleased him to say that he had remained a Catholic until he was old enough to read. At that time, he used to say, he had discovered too many holes in Catholicism to satisfy an intelligent, intellectual man. He had renounced the Holy Roman Church and become a Protestant. His new religion had so satisfied his questioning that he decided to become a minister. It had not been easy. Protestant theological schools, he had found, were not overly eager to accept former Catholic Irishmen by the name of Fitzgerald. In the end, however, he had succeeded. Not only was he accepted by a good school, he graduated at the head of his class, and when he was ordained and sent out into the field, it had been with many high hopes and good wishes on the part of his teachers.

Thinking it over now, Francis Joseph Fitzgerald could not remember when, exactly, he had begun to wonder about the Catholic faith which he had shed so easily in his youth. He knew that it had been since coming to Peyton Place, twelve years before, but he could not recall the exact moment when Protestantism had begun to be less than enough. If he could recall the moment, he reasoned, he would be able to recall an incident, and if he could do that he would know the reason for his torturing, unending questions. For there must have been an incident, he was sure, some

175

happening so trivial at the time that he had paid it no attention, and it had festered in his mind, producing, at last, the pus-filled, running sore that was his diseased faith. Fitzgerald's mind grew weary with his constant searching, and his tongue ached with the desire to speak, but he could not, of course, discuss his questions with his wife. Margaret Fitzgerald, who had been born Margaret Bunker, the only daughter of a Congregationalist minister from White River, hated Catholicism with a violent, un-Christianlike hatred. Francis Joseph Fitzgerald had discovered that shortly after he married her. He had, in fact, discovered it after they had been married only one week, and while they had still been honeymooning in the White Mountains.

"Peggy Fitzgerald," he had said, laughing in what he later remembered as his one and only attempt at humor with her. "Peggy Fitzgerald," he said, in his easily remembered brogue. "Puts me in mind of me mither, an Irish lass from County Galway."

Margaret Bunker Fitzgerald had not been amused. "You'll never get over it, will you?" she had spit at him furiously. "You'll never get over being an Irishman, a black Irish Catholic from a Boston slum. Don't you ever dare call me Peggy again. My name is Margaret, and don't you forget it!"

He had been shocked. "My mother's name was Margaret," he said defensively, the brogue completely gone now from his speech. "And my father always called her Peggy."

"Your mother," said Margaret, succeeding in making Mrs. Fitzgerald the elder sound like a werewolf. "Your *mother!*"

So, of course, when Reverend Fitzgerald began to wonder, and to be frightened by his thoughts, he could not go to his wife for the comfort that discussion might have brought. He had carried on his work, torturedly asking and trying to find replies to his own questions, until Tomas Makris had come to live in the apartment upstairs over the parsonage.

Reverend Fitzgerald climbed the stairs to the second floor, taking care to avoid every loose board on the way, in the hope of not waking Margaret who slept, snoring softly, in the rear bedroom of the parsonage. Margaret did not like Tom. She said that he was too loud, too brash, too dark, too big and too much lacking in respect for the Congregational church. The real reason that she disliked him was that she could not intimidate him. When she used tactics on him, which would have reduced her husband to an acquiescent lump, Tom merely laughed—at *her.*

The headmaster of the Peyton Place schools was sprawled out

in an easy chair in the living room of his apartment. He was naked except for a pair of athletic shorts, and he held a tall, frosted glass in one hand.

"Join me," he said to Fitzgerald, after the minister had knocked and entered.

"I thought you might like to come down and sit on the porch for a while," said Fitzgerald shyly. Nakedness always made him shy, and he kept his eyes turned away from Tom when he spoke.

"We can't talk down on the porch," said Tom. "We might wake Mrs. Fitzgerald, who has been snoring cozily for the last hour. Sit down and have a drink. It's as cool here as it is outside anyway."

"Thank you," said Fitzgerald, sitting down. "But I don't drink."

"What?" demanded Tom. "An Irishman who doesn't drink? Never heard of one."

Fitzgerald laughed uneasily. Tom did not speak softly, by any means, and Fitzgerald was afraid that Margaret might wake. She hated to have anyone refer to her husband as an Irishman. If she heard Tom she would, undoubtedly, come upstairs and drag Fitzgerald off to bed.

"All right," he said. "I'll have one. Just a little one, though."

Tom went to the small kitchen and returned carrying a glass as tall and as full as his own.

"Here," he said. "This will do you good."

Fitzgerald fascinated Tom. The minister was a perfect study of a man at war with his environment and himself. Often, Tom looked at Fitzgerald and wondered how the older man had survived as long as he had without either running away physically, or taking refuge in a mental breakdown. He had asked Connie MacKenzie about the minister, but she had not agreed with him that something was radically wrong with Fitzgerald. He was all right, she said. Not as gifted as some preachers, maybe, but a good man, conscientious and faithful. But when Tom looked at Fitzgerald, he wondered at the powerful, destructive tendency in humanity which drives a man to painful extremes in order to maintain the picture of himself which he has manufactured for the rest of the world to look upon.

As a very young man, Tom had realized that there were two kinds of people: Those who manufactured and maintained tedious, expensive shells, and those who did not. Those who did, lived in constant terror lest the shells of their own making crack open to display the weakness that was underneath, and those who did not were either crushed or toughened. After much thought, Tom had been able to put the souls of humanity on the simple, uncomplicated plane with bare feet. Some people could walk without shoes with the result that their feet grew tough and calloused, while others could not take a step without the bad luck of stepping on a broken bottle. But the majority, thought Tom with a smile, like Leslie Harrington and Fitzgerald and Connie MacKenzie, would never think of taking off their shoes in the first place. Leslie Harrington played the hardheaded, successful businessman to hide the mediocre mind and fear of impotency that tortured him, while Constance MacKenzie covered the passionate, love-demanding woman that she really was with the respectable garments of the ice maiden. And here was Francis Joseph Fitzgerald, playing the nondrinking Congregational minister when he really longed for the tight white collar and the daily ecclesiastical wine of the Irish priest. Tom longed to put his fist through Harrington's false front, and with Constance he wanted to destroy completely the need for protection, but for Fitzgerald he felt only pity.

Why doesn't the poor bastard chuck what he has, thought Tom, and run as fast as he can to the nearest priest to make his confession?

"We didn't see you at church last Sunday," Fitzgerald was saying. "I'm afraid all my talk has done you no good, Mr. Makris. You are an impossible man to convert."

Fitzgerald prided himself on the fact that he kept his conversations on religion with Tom on a depersonalized, intellectual plane.

"Of course," continued Fitzgerald, "we Protestants are at a disadvantage when it comes to getting the crowds into the churches. We don't have the whip that the Catholics have to hold over our members. If a Catholic misses Mass, he has committed a sin and has hurt only himself, but if a Protestant does not come to church, all we can do is to hope that we see him next Sunday."

"That's one way of looking at it," said Tom. "On the other hand, I don't think much of a religion that holds a whip over anybody for any reason."

Fitzgerald was shocked. "Oh," he said, shaking his head, "I think that your reasoning is faulty, Mr. Makris. I really do. In fact, having a powerful hold over the people is the one point in which I am in complete sympathy with our Catholic friends."

Fitzgerald always claimed that he was in sympathy with only one point of the Catholic philosophy but, Tom knew, before the night was over he would have named a dozen points with which he was in sympathy, and they would run the gamut from birth control to the refusal to bury suicides in consecrated ground.

Just how much, wondered Tom bitterly, was religion, any religion, worth when it could do to a man what it had done to Fitzgerald?

Somewhere, Fitzgerald had lost sight of his larger purpose in life. He had lost it in a welter of man-made contradictions, and now he was fighting with his sanity to find it again. He enumerated for Tom all the rules involved in what he called "serving God." He pointed out carefully the differences between the Catholic rules and the Protestant rules.

"Now I ask you, Mr. Makris, how do the Protestants expect to keep the church strong, if they refuse to outlaw birth control? The Catholics have it on us there, I'm afraid. Watch the number of children who go into St. Joseph's every Sunday. There are twice as many as I get. You have to get plenty of them—and catch them while they are young—for lasting results."

Give me a child until he is seven, thought Tom, and he is forever after mine. When the Fascists say it, they're bums and kidnapers, but when the Church says it, it is known as putting a kid on the right track.

"Listen, Reverend," said Tom when the minister had run down for a moment. "Why do you make such a big thing out of all these differences in ceremony, and this matter of rules? It's ridiculous, isn't it? If I got you and Father O'Brien in here and tried to start up a discussion about the number of angels that can dance on a needle's point, you'd both think I'd gone off my head. Isn't it, then, just as foolish to argue about whether a child will be baptized by total immersion or by a few drops of water sprinkled on the head? Or whether eating meat on Friday constitutes a sin or not?"

Reverend Fitzgerald had gone white. He had heard no more of Tom's sentence after the words Father O'Brien.

They are in league with one another, thought Fitzgerald's sick, tired mind. If they weren't, Makris would never have mentioned his name.

Fitzgerald stood up abruptly, upsetting what was left of his drink. He ran from the room before Tom could look at him with *that* look, Father O'Brien's look. It was a look that recognized a sinner on sight.

You have fallen away, said the look. You have sinned, you have transgressed, you are doomed.

"Is that you, Fran?" Margaret Fitzgerald's voice called.

Tom went to his door to listen for Fitzgerald's answer, but no voice spoke. All he could hear was a panting sound, which came from a figure crouched at the foot of the stairs.

♦ 10 ♦

The next morning, when Tom left his apartment to go out, Reverend Fitzgerald was nowhere to be seen. This was unusual because it was Saturday, and every Saturday morning found the minister hard at work in his small flower garden at the side of the house. Tom stood on the front porch and listened curiously. The town was full of summer morning sounds. Somewhere a lawn mower was being pushed, and from farther away came the scrape of roller skates against cement. Very faintly, from perhaps as far as Depot Street, there came an echo of someone practicing the chromatic scales on the piano, and from behind Tom, coming from Reverend Fitzgerald's quarters, there was the uneven chatter of typewriter keys. All together, thought Tom, a very normal Saturday morning. But where was Fitzgerald? The sound that was missing was the clip of the minister's garden shears, as he cut and snipped and pruned. Tom shrugged and swung down the front steps of the house. It was nothing that concerned him. If the Congregationalist minister was spending the morning in cutting out paper dolls that had the shape of a robed Pope, it was no business of Tom's.

At any other time, in any other place, Tom could and would have gone to someone in a position of authority and said: "Your minister is ill. He is in no condition to lead a flock of searching souls, for he has lost his way. He is ill and needs help," but in Peyton Place, on a sunny Saturday morning in July, Tom shrugged and walked off down Elm Street. He had learned the hard way, the wisdom of minding his own business, at the first town meeting he had attended the year after his arrival in Peyton Place. At that time, he had attempted to state his opinion on town zoning. When he had finished speaking, a man had stood up and looked him up and down.

"You on the voting check list in this town, Mr.—?"

The inquirer had asked his question in a slow drawl, and had let the end of his question peter out, as if he had forgotten Tom's name.

180

Then Tom had understood. He had seen that the privilege of outspoken criticism, the privilege of rectifying a faulty condition, were privileges allowed only to the older residents, and that by "Older Residents," Peyton Place meant people whose grandparents had been born in the town. Tom had laughed at the fact that this was so, but he had not attempted to criticize or correct again. He contented himself with observation, and with the realization that he had made two friends at his first town meeting, Seth Buswell and Matthew Swain.

Now as he passed the building that housed the *Peyton Place Times*, Tom glanced in through the glass window that was between Seth's office and the street. Seth was sitting at his desk and sitting next to Seth, in the visitor's chair, was Allison MacKenzie. She was dressed in a polished, starched cotton dress, and she was wearing a pair of white gloves. Wondering, Tom managed a casual wave of his hand to the two in Seth's office, and continued on his way to the Thrifty Corner.

It would be difficult, he thought, for many people in New York, and quite a few in Pittsburgh, to believe that Tomas Makris was in love at last. Not only in love, but kept dangling impossibly by a widow of thirty-five who had a fifteen-year-old daughter, and who had done him the favor, in over two years, of sleeping with him perhaps a dozen times. A widow, moreover, whom he wanted to marry, but who would not marry him for another two years, if then. Tom smiled. There were men who would wait forever for the woman of their choice, but he had never been one of them. There were also men who preferred to wait to claim their women physically until they were legally married. He had never been one of those, either. Tom admitted cheerfully, in the idiom of Peyton Place, that he was hog-tied and completely swozzled. He would wait for Connie MacKenzie if it took her fifty years to make up her mind.

"That's what I am," he said as he entered the Thrifty Corner.

"What?" laughed Constance MacKenzie, putting down her newspaper and coming to greet him.

"Hog-tied and completely swozzled," said Tom, and bent down to kiss the inside of her wrist.

Constance caressed the back of his head with her free hand.

"Nice goings on in a place of business in broad daylight," she whispered to him.

He could do little things like kissing her finger tips or the inside of her wrist with a complete naturalness and sincerity that kept them from seeming planned or contrived. Once, he had kissed the sole of her bare foot and she had been aroused to the point of powerful and immediate sexual desire. At first, she had been embarrassed by his unorthodox expressions of tenderness, for they had reminded her of love scenes in rather effete novels. They seemed incongruous coming, as they did, from a man of Tom's size and temperament.

"The trouble with you," he had told her, "is that you got all your ideas of virile love-making from paper-backed books and Hollywood."

She had laughed and dismissed herself as a fool for being affected by such gestures as wrist-kissing. She did not laugh now. Her voice grew husky and she trailed her finger tips over the short, tough hairs at the back of his neck.

"So am I," she said.

"What?"

"Hog-tied and completely swozzled," she said.

"Enough," he said, releasing her, "or I'll forget that it is the morning of a business day, and that I am in the women's department of the Thrifty Corner Apparel Shoppe. Shoppe, that is, with two *P*'s and an *E*. Where's the coffee?"

"All made," she said. "I'll get it."

She carried cups and saucers to an empty place on one of the counters, and Tom went to the room at the back of the store for the coffeepot. They leaned against the counter and drank coffee and ate doughnuts.

"I saw Allison in Seth's office," said Tom. "What in the world is she doing there?"

"Don't you remember what you told her months ago?" asked Constance. "You told her that the best place for a writer to get started was on a newspaper. She's gone to ask Seth for a job."

Tom laughed. "Well," he said, "the *Peyton Place Times* wasn't exactly what I had in mind when I spoke with Allison, but it would do nicely for a beginning. She has more imagination than I, to even think of going to Seth. I hope she can talk him into something."

"I don't," said Constance. "Writing social notes for a small-town weekly wasn't what I had in mind for Allison."

"What did you have in mind, then?"

"Oh," said Constance vaguely, "college, then a good job for a while, then marriage to a successful man."

"Maybe Allison doesn't want that," said Tom. "I think she has

182

a talent with words, and I am a firm believer in anyone with a talent working it for all it's worth."

"It doesn't take much talent to write that Mr. and Mrs. So-and-So visited Mr. and Mrs. Somebody-or-Other for the week end. That about covers what Seth puts in his paper."

"It is a beginning," said Tom. "As I said before, Seth's paper wasn't exactly what I had in mind when I suggested newspaper work to Allison. But it will do for now."

"I shan't worry about it," said Constance. "She has two years of high school left. That ought to be enough time for her to get over this foolishness about writing for a living."

Tom smiled, refraining from telling Constance of a few people he knew to whom writing for a living was anything but foolishness. "It's Saturday," he said. "How about driving down to Manchester for dinner tonight?"

"All right," said Constance. "I won't be able to leave until late, though. I'll be glad when Selena is well and can come back to work."

"The pleasures of a teacher's life, also those of a teacher's wife, include a long summer vacation every year. If we were married and you had given up business, you could come down to Mudgett's Hardware with me now and feast your eyes on the fishing equipment. I might even buy you a rod and reel."

"Beat it, laziness," laughed Constance, "before you talk yourself into something you'll be sorry for."

"I'll pick you up here, at six," he said.

"Fine."

She watched him walk down Elm Street, a tall figure in an open-necked sports shirt and tan slacks. She wondered, for the millionth time, what Allison would think about having him for a stepfather, and her mind went from that to the child who was now sixteen, although she still believed herself to be only fifteen, and who should know better, at her age, than to pursue such a flighty course as writing for a living.

In Seth Buswell's office, Allison MacKenzie was feeling far from flighty. She fidgeted nervously with the zipper closing on the brief case she had brought with her. After much soul searching and discussion, she and Kathy Ellsworth had chosen six of what they called, "The Best of Allison MacKenzie," and Allison had taken the six stories from the brief case and handed them to the newspaper editor.

Seth leaned back in his chair and pulled at his lower lip while he read. Allison's stories were thinly disguised portraits of local characters, and Seth pulled at his lip to hide a smile.

Brother! he thought, would these cause a sensation on my front page!

Allison had written up Miss Hester Goodale as a witch who kept the bones of her dead lover hidden in her cellar. She had made the Page Girls into religious fanatics, and turned poor old Clayton Frazier into a lecherous devil. Leslie Harrington was a dictator who came to a bad end, but Matthew Swain was a twinkling, determinedly good-natured creature who devoted his life to Doing Good. Marion Partridge was portrayed as a bosomy club lady with a secret vice. Marion, according to Allison, took snuff on the sly.

Brother! thought Seth Buswell, as he set aside the last of Allison's stories. He cleared his throat and looked at the girl who sat nervously waiting for his decision.

"What did you have in mind, Allison?" he asked. "You know, don't you, that I hire a few out of town correspondents for news in different communities, and that I do all the local stuff myself?"

"I wasn't thinking of writing anything like social items," began Allison, and Seth heaved a silent sigh of relief. "I was thinking that perhaps I could write a little story for you every week. There are a lot of things to write stories about in Peyton Place."

God help my circulation, thought Seth, glancing down at the stories on his desk.

"What kind of stories?" he asked. "Fiction?"

"Oh, no," said Allison. "Fact stories. About points of interest in the community, and things like that."

"Did you ever think about a historical type of column?" asked Seth. "You know, Elm Street as it was fifty years ago, that sort of thing?"

"No, I hadn't thought of it," said Allison, enthusiasm showing in her voice. "But it's a fine idea. We could call it 'Peyton Place Then and Now,' and you could put it in a box on the front page."

Nothing reticent about this kid, thought Seth. A box on the front page, yet!

"We could try it," he said cautiously. "We could run it a few weeks and see how it goes over."

"Oh, Mr. Buswell!" cried Allison jumping up. "When? When could we start?"

That tears it, thought Seth. "Write something up this week," he said. "I'll try it on Friday."

"Oh, thank you. Thank you, Mr. Buswell. I'll start right away. I'll go home and start thinking up things right now."

"Hold on a minute," said Seth. "Aren't you going to ask me what I'll pay?"

"Pay?" cried Allison. "You don't have to pay me. I'll do it for nothing and count it as a privilege."

"That's no way to talk, Allison. If people like your writing, they should be willing to pay for it. I'll give you two dollars for every article of yours that I print."

For a moment, Seth was afraid that the child would either burst into tears or throw up. Her face went white, then pink, then whiter than before.

"Oh, thank you," she said breathlessly. "Thank you, Mr. Buswell."

"And Allison," called Seth after the figure that was making for his office door. "It's going to be too hot to write this week end. Wait 'til Monday. Maybe it will rain before then."

Allison ran out of the building that housed the *Peyton Place Times* and ran straight into the figure of Tomas Makris. She would have fallen if he had not grasped her elbows and steadied her.

"I've got a job," she cried. "I've got a job writing, Mr. Makris. For money. On the paper!"

Over Allison's head, Tom looked through the window into Seth's office. The newspaper editor was bent over the stories that Allison had left behind, and this time he was smiling openly.

"Well," said Tom, looking down into Allison's face that had gone white again, "that calls for a celebration. Everybody's first job calls for a celebration. Come on into Prescott's and I'll buy you a Coke."

He led Allison into the drugstore, and her elbow, still cupped in his hand, trembled. The color was beginning to come back into her face, but she could not stop chattering.

"A historical type thing," she was saying, "and for money. Just like a real writer."

Looking at her, in her trembling excitement, Tom felt suddenly very old.

"I was going to start right away, this afternoon," Allison was saying. "But I'll wait until tomorrow. I promised Norman that I'd go on a picnic with him this afternoon. Isn't that funny, Mr. Makris? I'd forgotten all about the picnic until just this minute. I was so excited about the job. Wait until I tell Norman! He'll just die! Norman writes, too, you know. Poems. I'll have to hurry. I promised
185

Norman that I'd bring the lunch. Isn't that crazy? I just remembered about the picnic!"

Foolishness, eh? thought Tom, remembering Constance's remark. When an adolescent forgets something as romantic as a picnic with another adolescent in the excitement generated by the thought of writing for money, it is difficult to regard it as foolishness any longer.

"Thanks for the Coke, Mr. Makris," said Allison, and she was gone, in a swirl of polished cotton skirts.

Tom put a dime down on Prescott's soda fountain.

Goddamn it, he thought, still feeling old, this waiting has gone on long enough. I'll talk to her again tonight. Two more years to wait is too long. Too much wasted time. We're not getting any younger.

◆ II ◆

Allison ran up the front steps of her house and into the front hall, letting the screen door slam behind her.

"Nellie!" she called. "Nellie, where are you?"

There was no answer, but Allison heard a rattling from the back of the house which meant that Nellie was in the kitchen, doing her regular Saturday morning job of straightening out the cabinets. Allison did not call out again, but ran up the stairs to her room, unbuttoning her dress as she went. She changed into a pair of brief shorts and a sleeveless blouse and, still running, went down to the kitchen.

"Nellie!" she shouted. "Nellie, I've got a job! A job writing. For money!"

Nellie Cross, on her hands and knees in front of a low kitchen cabinet, looked up at her.

"Oh, yeah?" she asked, without interest.

"Oh, Nellie," said Allison. "Is it one of your bad days?"

"Same as any other," said Nellie sullenly. "Ain't nobody feels good when they got nothin' but pus in all their veins."

This was something recent with Nellie, but it disturbed Allison no more than had some of Nellie's previous ideas. It was just different, and Allison accepted it calmly. During the last week, Nellie had gone from cursing Lucas and all other men to believing that she was afflicted with a strange disease.

"It's the clap," she told Allison, nodding her head sagely. "Lucas give it to me, just before he run away."

Lucas Cross, Allison knew, had disappeared from Peyton Place a week before, and his going had caused a flurry of talk in the town for a few days. The consensus of local opinion was that Lucas' going was good riddance to bad rubbish, but, to everyone's surprise, Nellie did not go along with this view. She had gone from cursing Lucas as a sonofabitch to defending him as a man put upon by the forces of society, wronged by bad companions and seduced by diseased women.

"I should think you'd be glad to be rid of him," Allison had said when Nellie told her of Lucas' disappearance. "It would have been better for you if he had gone long ago."

"He wouldna gone now, except he give me the clap and was ascared I'd tell on him. I wouldna told on Lucas, not even if them people from the health department down at Concord was to cut me to pieces. Pus in all my veins, that's what Lucas left me with. He couldn't help it, poor man. He caught it off some hoor, that's what he done. He couldn't help it. He was drunk and forgot himself, is all."

At frequent intervals, the pus in Nellie's veins hardened into lumps which were very painful, and which caused, Allison had learned in the past week, what Nellie referred as as "one of her bad days."

"Yep," she replied to Allison's question, "a real bad day. Them lumps is all through my whole system. I don't know how I'll get through this day."

"I'm so sorry, Nellie," said Allison, eager to get the conversation back to herself. "But aren't you surprised about my job?"

"Nope," said Nellie, spreading fresh paper on the floor of the low cabinet. "I always said you was good at makin' up stories. I ain't surprised. You want to eat?"

"No. I've got to pack a lunch. Norman and I are going on a picnic."

"Humph," said Nellie.

"What?" demanded Allison sharply.

"Humph," repeated Nellie.

"What do you mean by that?" asked Allison, more sharply than before.

"I mean humph, that's what I mean," said Nellie. "Them Pages, humph. That Evelyn Page, always so high and mighty. She married Oakleigh because he was an old man and she thought she'd

187

get his money when he died. Well, he fooled her. Left her, he did, left her flatter than a pancake as soon as them girls of his told him to. Evelyn Page never had nothin' to be high and mighty about. Her husband left her same as mine left me, 'cept that Oakleigh didn't have no excuse for it, and Lucas did."

"You stop talking like that, Nellie Cross!" said Allison. "Mrs. Page is a perfectly fine lady, and it wasn't her fault if Norman's father left her."

"Fine lady my foot!" snorted Nellie. "Tit-fed that son of hers 'til he was four years old. That kid had teeth as solid as the ones in your head right now, and perfectly fine lady Evelyn Page was still nursin' him and lovin' every minute of it! Old Oakleigh never had teeth like Norman had at four years old. No wonder perfectly fine lady Evelyn Page hated to wean that child!"

Allison's face was white and her voice low and furious. "You're a filthy-minded old woman, Nellie Cross," she said. "You don't only have pus in your veins, you have it in your brain. It'll make you crazy, Nellie, that's what it will do. You'll go stark, raving crazy, as crazy as Miss Hester Goodale, and it'll serve you right for talking so mean about people."

"Your mother worked hard to raise you right," cried Nellie. "She didn't raise you to go runnin' out with boys that was tit-fed at four years old. It ain't right, Allison, for you to be runnin' out with that Page boy. All them Pages is trash. Plain, dirty, queer trash. Always was."

"I don't even want to talk to you, you crazy old woman," said Allison. "And I don't want you to say another word about Norman or his family to me!"

She flounced around the kitchen, slamming pans as she put eggs on to boil, and banging the refrigerator repeatedly as she took out food to make sandwiches. When she had finished, she packed everything into a picnic hamper and ran out of the kitchen, leaving a mess behind for Nellie to clean up.

Nellie sighed and stood up, staring down at the vein in the bend of her elbow. It was lumpy. She took one step forward and stopped, putting her hand to her head. Her fingers searched frantically through her stringy hair, and at last they found the lump. It was a big lump, as big as an egg, and it pulsated like a boil.

Crazy. The word burned Nellie's consciousness like hot fat. Crazy. Soon the lump in her head would burst and spread pus all over her brain and she would be crazy, just as Allison had said.

Nellie Cross sat down on the floor in the MacKenzie kitchen and began to whimper.

"Lucas," she whimpered aloud. "Lucas, just you look here and see what you done."

Allison and Norman pushed their bicycles ahead of them, for it was too hot to pedal uphill. The bicycles were heavy because the baskets attached to them were loaded with the picnic hamper, a six-bottle carton of Coca-Cola, a cotton patchwork quilt, two bathing suits, four towels and a thick volume entitled, *Important English Poets*. Allison and Norman pushed and panted, and the July heat rose, shimmering, from the highway that led away from Peyton Place.

"We should have settled for Meadow Pond," said Norman, pushing his sunglasses back into place on his nose.

"We wouldn't be able to get near the water at Meadow," said Allison, raising one hand from her bicycle handle bars to lift the heavy hair that clung to her damp neck. "Every kid in town will be at Meadow this afternoon. I'd rather stay home than go there."

"It can't be much farther," said Norman philosophically. "The bend in the river is exactly one mile beyond the hospital, and we've certainly come almost that by now."

"It's not much farther," agreed Allison. "We passed the mills ages ago."

After what seemed an eternity in the summer afternoon, they came at last to the bend in the Connecticut River. Gratefully, they pushed their bicycles into the shade of the giant trees that grew close to the water's edge, and sank down on the soft, dry pine needles that covered the ground.

"I thought we'd never get here," said Allison, puffing out her bottom lip and blowing at a strand of hair that fell on her forehead.

"Neither did I," said Norman. "It was worth it, though. There isn't another soul around for miles. Listen to the quiet."

When they had rested, he said, "Let's push our bikes into the woods a ways. Then no one will be able to see them from the highway, and no one will know we're here."

"O.K.," said Allison. "There's a place up just a little way. The trees grow farther back from the water, and there's a sort of sandy beach. You can't see it from the road."

When they had arrived at the place which Allison had described, they leaned their bicycles against two trees and began to carry

189

their things down to the beach. They spread the quilt carefully, and placed the hamper, the book and the towels on it.

"Shall we swim or eat first?" asked Allison.

"Let's swim," said Norman. "As soon as I get into my suit, I'll put the Coke underwater to get cold. It's lukewarm now."

"We'll have to change in the woods," commented Allison. "There isn't anywhere else."

"You go first. I'll wait until you're ready."

When they had both changed into bathing suits, they stood at the edge of the water, sliding their feet back and forth slowly in the wet sand. It was dangerous to swim in the river at this point, and they both knew it. The river was full of rapids and the bottom was covered with jagged rocks.

"We'll have to be careful," said Norman.

"You go first."

"Let's go together."

Slowly, cautiously, they let themselves into the water, and suddenly the river did not seem dangerous at all. They began to splash and swim away from the shore.

"It's good and cold. Icy cold."

"Better than Meadow Pond. That's always warm on hot days."

"Can you still touch bottom?"

"Yes. You?"

"Yes. This is far enough."

"I don't believe this place is dangerous, except in the spring, maybe."

"My foot just scraped against a rock."

"Can you float?"

"Yes. I learned how at camp two years ago."

They stayed in the water until they were chilled, and when they stood on the shore again, water clung to them in little rainbow-colored drops. Allison, who swam without a bathing cap, began to towel her hair, and Norman sat down on the quilt to examine his scraped foot. The sun was welcome now, beating down on their cold skins and warming them. Allison sat down next to Norman.

"Do you want to eat?"

"O.K. I'll see if the Coke is cooled off any."

"It should be. That water is like ice."

They munched sandwiches and looked, squinty eyed, across the water where the sun reflected itself as if in a mirror.

"I don't know why it should," said Norman, "but it always gives me a funny feeling to look across the river and think that it's Vermont over there."

"It's like riding in a car and crossing a town line," said Allison. "One minute you're in Peyton Place and the next you're somewhere else. I always say it to myself. Now I'm in Peyton Place—and now I'm not. It always makes me feel funny, just the way sitting here and looking at Vermont does."

"Are there any more egg sandwiches left, or only ham?"

"I brought four of each. You can have one of mine, if you want. I'd just as soon have ham."

"I should have brought some potato chips."

"They're always so greasy in the summertime."

"I know it."

"Have a pickle."

"Do you want to swim again?"

"Not until the sun begins to feel hot."

"Are you going to get married when you're old?" asked Norman.

"No. I'm going to have affairs instead."

"What shall we do with all this waxed paper? We can't just leave it here."

"Put it back in the hamper. I'll throw it away when we get back."

"That's not a very good idea, you know," said Norman. "I read that affairs are very conducive to maladjustment. Besides, people who have affairs don't have children."

"Where did you read that?"

"In a book on sex that I sent away for," he said.

"I never read a book that was exclusively about sex. Where did you send to for it?"

"New York. I saw an ad for it in a magazine. It cost a dollar ninety-eight."

"Did your mother see it?"

"I guess not! I went to the post office every day for the mail for two weeks, waiting for that book to come. My mother'd kill me if she ever thought I was interested in such stuff."

"What else did it say?" asked Allison.

"Oh, it was all about how a man has to have a technique when he makes love to a woman. That's so she'll like it and not be frigid."

"What's frigid?"

"Women who don't like to make love. A lot of women are like that, this book says. It makes for maladjustment in marriage."

"Does it tell what to do?" she asked.

191

"Oh, sure."

"Shall we read for a while?"

"Okay. Shall I, or do you want to?"

"You go ahead. Pick something by Swinburne. I like him the best."

As Norman read aloud from the book, *Important English Poets,* Allison picked up the sandwich scraps and repacked the hamper. Then she turned over on her stomach and lay stretched out on the quilt. Norman propped himself up on his elbows, put on his sunglasses and continued to read for a while longer. Soon, they both slept.

When they awoke, some of the heat had left the sun and it was four o'clock. Their bodies were damp with sweat, and they yawned and decided to swim again. When they had cooled off in the water, they lay side by side on the cotton quilt.

"I feel good," said Allison, looking at Norman through half-closed eyes.

"So do I."

They rested their sun-warmed, water-cooled, relaxed and well-fed bodies on the cotton quilt and squinted up at the cloud patterns in the blue, July sky.

"Someday," said Allison, "I'll write a very famous book. As famous as *Anthony Adverse,* and then I'll be a celebrity."

"Not me. I'm going to write thin, slim volumes of poetry. Not many people will know me, but the few who will will say that I am a young genius."

"I'm going to write about the castle for my first article in the paper."

"How can you write about the castle? You've never been up there."

"I'll make something up."

"You can't make up things to go into a historical article. It has to be fact, all pure, true fact," said Norman.

"Baloney. *Anthony Adverse* is a historical novel, and I suppose you think that isn't made up."

"It's different with a novel. Novels are always made-up stories."

"So are poems."

"Is that when you'll start having affairs? After you write a famous book and become a celebrity?" asked Norman.

"Yes. I'll have a new affair every week."

"You'll be maladjusted if you do."

"I don't care. Men will be dying for my favors, but I'll be very, very particular."

"Aren't you ever going to have any children?"

"No. I won't have time," replied Allison.

"That book I was telling you about said that the natural function of the female body is the bearing of children," said Norman.

"What else did it say?"

"Well, it showed pictures about how women are made. It showed how a woman has breasts to hold milk, and how she is put together inside to hold a baby for nine months."

"I wouldn't spend a dollar ninety-eight just to learn that. I knew all that when I was thirteen. What did it tell about how men are supposed to make love to women?"

Norman put his arms up behind his head and crossed his legs. He began to speak as if he were explaining a troublesome problem in algebra to someone who had no inclination toward mathematics.

"Well," he began, "this book says how all women have certain areas of their bodies which are known as erotic areas."

"Are they the same for all women?" asked Allison, with the exact tone she would have used if she had been the dull math student whom Norman was trying to help.

"Certain ones, yes," said Norman. "But not all. For instance, all women have erotic areas around their breasts and also around their bodily orifices."

"Orifices?"

"Openings."

"Like what?"

Norman half turned onto his side and ran the tip of his little finger around the opening in Allison's ear. Immediately her skin broke out in duck bumps and she sat up with a jerk.

"Like that," said Norman.

"I see," said Allison, rubbing her left arm with her right hand. She lay down again next to Norman.

"The area around the opening of the mouth is, of course, the most highly sensitized of all," said Norman, "except for one other, and that is a woman's vaginal opening. As I understand it—"

Norman's voice went on, but Allison was no longer listening. She wanted him to run his finger around the opening in her ear again, and she wanted him to kiss her the way he had done in the woods at Road's End the previous Saturday. She was getting angrier and angrier as he went on talking in his cool, academic voice.

"—And kissing, of course, is the first, or one of the first, overtures that a good lover makes to a woman."

"Oh, shut up!" cried Allison and jumped to her feet. "Talk, talk, talk. That's all you know how to do!"

Norman looked up at her, shocked, "But, Allison," he said, "you asked me, didn't you?"

"I didn't ask you to quote the whole damned book, word for word, did I?"

"You don't have to swear at me, do you? You asked me and I was telling you. There's no reason in the world for swearing, is there?"

"Oh, shut up," said Allison. "Some boys I know," she lied, "don't have to explain to a girl what wonderful lovers they are. They show her."

"What boys?" demanded Norman, thereby calling her bluff.

"I don't have to tell you anything, Norman Page. Not a single thing."

He reached out and grasped her ankle. "What boys?" he asked.

Allison sat down and Norman sat up. "Oh, forget it," she said. "Nobody you know, anyway."

"Tell me," he said. "I'd like to know who some of these wonderful lovers of yours are."

"I won't tell."

"You can't, that's why. You don't know any. You're a liar."

Allison whirled toward him and slapped him. "Don't you dare call me a liar," she shouted.

He grasped her two wrists and forced her down on the blanket. "You're a liar," he said, looking her straight in the face. "You're a liar, and because you slapped me, I'm not going to let you up until you admit it."

Allison capitulated at once. "I made it up," she said, not looking at him. "You're the only boy who ever kissed me, except for Rodney Harrington, and that was so long ago that it doesn't count. I'm sorry I slapped you."

Norman released her wrists, but continued to lean over her, his hands resting on the quilt on either side of her body.

"Would you like me to kiss you again?" he asked.

Allison felt her face redden. "Yes," she said. "Except that I don't like for you to ask me, Norman. For anything."

He kissed her gently, and Allison wanted to burst into tears of frustration. That wasn't the way she wanted to be kissed at all.

"It's getting late," said Norman. "We ought to be starting back."

194

"I suppose so," replied Allison.

Later, as they were pedaling slowly down the highway toward Peyton Place, a convertible, with the top down, passed them.

"Get a horse!" yelled the voice of Rodney Harrington from the speeding car.

"Smart guy," said Norman.

"I suppose so," said Allison, but she was thinking, resentfully, that at thirteen Rodney had known more about kissing than Norman knew at fifteen.

◆ 12 ◆

Rodney Harrington laughed out loud as he caught a last glimpse of Allison MacKenzie and Norman Page in his rear-vision mirror. The two of them were pedaling for all they were worth, worried, perhaps, about being late for supper. It was too bad that they were riding bikes instead of walking. If they had been on foot Rodney would have offered them a lift in his car. It made him feel good to drive other kids around in his car. None of them ever said anything, but Rodney knew that every last one of them sat in his leather-upholstered seats and wished that they had cars exactly like his. Rodney laughed out loud and wondered what Allison and Norman had been doing so far away from home. Maybe they had stopped off in the woods for a private party. At that thought, Rodney laughed so hard that he almost hit the ditch with his new car.

"I feel good!" he exclaimed to the world at large, and sounded his automobile horn in the classic da-da-da-dada, dum, dum.

Why shouldn't he feel good? he asked himself. He had just been to the mill to hit the old man up for ten bucks, he had a swell car, and he was on his way to meet Betty Anderson. Who the hell wouldn't feel good?

"Don't spend it all in one place," Leslie Harrington had told his son, handing him the ten dollars and giving him a broad wink. "There's not a one of 'em worth over two dollars."

Rodney had laughed with his father. "You're telling me?" he had replied.

His father had clapped him on the back and told him to go on and have fun.

195

Rodney smiled to himself as he drove his car down Elm Street, doing forty in a twenty-five-mile zone. All the crap people dished out about motherless boys was a laugh, as far as he was concerned. He hadn't even a vague memory of his mother. All he knew of her was what he could see in a blurry photograph which his father kept on his bureau. She had been a rather pale and thin-looking character, with a lot of brown hair done up high on her head. Her mouth looked straight and tight, in the picture, and Rodney had never been able to imagine her as married to his father. All he knew about her, and all he cared to know, was that her name had been Elizabeth, and that she had died giving birth to her son at the age of thirty. Rodney had never missed his mother. He and the old man got along swell. They understood each other. They bached it very successfully, in the big house on Chestnut Street, with the help of Mrs. Pratte, who served as cook and general housekeeper. That crap that people put in books, about motherless boys, was just that. Crap. He, for one, was extremely grateful that he had no mother to put up with, always nagging him about something. He had heard too many fellows complain about their own mothers not to be grateful that his own was safely buried. He liked that *status quo*. Him and the old man, and old Pratte handy whenever either of the Harringtons wanted anything.

At sixteen, Rodney Harrington had not changed substantially from the boy he had been at fourteen. He was an inch or so taller, which made him five feet eight now, and he had filled out a bit with the result that he looked more than ever like his father. Other than that, Rodney was unchanged. His hair, which he wore just a trifle too long, was still black and curly, and his heavy mouth still showed a lack of discipline and self-control. There were a few people in Peyton Place who said that it was too late for Rodney Harrington. He would always be just what he had always been—the indulged only child of a rich widowered father. They cited his expulsion from the New Hampton School for Boys as proof of what they said. New Hampton, which had attempted to teach Rodney, had ended by expelling him for laziness and insubordination after two years of trying. New Hampton had a good reputation, and had succeeded in the past, where other schools had failed with other problem youngsters, but it had been unable to leave its mark on Rodney Harrington. Apparently, the only thing that Rodney had learned while away at school was that all boys of good family had had sexual intercourse with girls before reaching prep school age, and those who had not were either fairies

196

or material for the priesthood. Rodney had learned quickly, and by the time he had been at New Hampton for less than a year he could outtalk the best of them. According to Rodney, he had deflowered no less than nine maidens in his own home town before reaching the age of fifteen, and he had almost been shot twice by the irate husband with whose wife he had carried on a passionate affair for six months.

Rodney had the sensual good looks, the money and the glib tongue to make himself believed. He had been considered quite a man among men by the time he was kicked out of New Hampton. Even his own father believed him, although he made his stories much weaker for Leslie, and named fictitious girls from White River as the heroines of his tales. Rodney had told his stories of successful seduction so often, to so many different people, that most of the time he could believe them himself. Actually he had never had a sexual experience in his life, and at times when the truth smote him, he felt as if someone had flung a glass of cold water in his face for no reason. The frightening thought that he would not know how to go about completing the act, if he ever once had the chance to get started, affected him like the sun going behind a cloud on a hot day. It left him chilled, and lent a dreary aspect to his otherwise cheerful world. What horrified him the most about the truth was not the possible personal humiliation to himself, but that the girl with whom he failed might talk. Whenever Rodney thought of what his many friends would say if they ever discovered that he had been spinning fantasies, and that he was, in reality, as inexperienced as a seven-year-old, he turned cold with horror.

He was thinking along this depressing line now, as he swung his car into Ash Street which was a narrow, tumble-down street in the neighborhood where the mill hands lived. He pulled up smartly in front of the Anderson house and sounded his horn with a bravado he was far from feeling. Determinedly, he made the effort to shrug off his fears, and for Rodney Harrington the shaking off of depression or fear had never been a difficulty.

What the hell? he thought, and the sun came back out from behind its dark cloud. What the hell? He had money to spend, a car to get around in, and a pint of rye whisky in the glove compartment. What the hell? He'd know what to do if he ever got old Betty to take her pants off. He'd heard it described enough times, hadn't he? He'd described it enough times himself, hadn't he? What the hell? He had not only talked and heard about it, he had
197

read books about it and seen pictures of it. What the hell was he worried about?

Betty strolled down the short walk in front of her house, undulating her hips fully, as she had seen a musical comedy queen do in a movie the week before. She moved slowly toward Rodney's car.

"Hi, kid," she said.

She was exactly one year and fourteen days younger than he, but she unfailingly called him kid. Tonight she wore a pair of tight green shorts and a small yellow halter. As always, whenever he looked at her, Rodney felt his speech thicken in his throat. The only way he could explain his reaction to Betty was to say that it was just like the way it had been when he was small and old Pratte had let him watch her make pudding. One minute, there was the liquid in the pan, so thin and runny that you thought it would never be any other way, and in the very next minute the stuff turned thick and syrupy, so that old Pratte really had to work to get a spoon through the mess. That was the way he was about Betty. Like pudding. Until he saw her, his mind was clear and cool and liquid, but the minute she leaned over the car door and said, "Hi, kid," his speech thickened, his eyes grew heavy lidded, and he struggled to pull breath through the syrupy mass in his chest.

"Hi," he said.

"It's too hot to get all dressed up to go somewhere," said Betty. "I just want to go for a ride and stop at a drive-in to eat."

Rodney was wearing a shirt and sports jacket because he had planned to take her to a restaurant and then somewhere to dance, but he capitulated without a murmur.

"Sure," he said.

Without another word, Betty opened the car door and flopped into the seat next to him.

"Why don't you take off that coat?" she demanded crossly. "It makes me hot and itchy all over just to look at you."

Rodney immediately took off his coat and put it on the back seat. From the Anderson house, two sullen, tired faces watched him as he put the convertible into gear and roared off down Ash Street. As soon as Rodney had turned the corner, Betty wiggled her fingers at him and he passed her his cigarettes.

"How come you couldn't go out with me last night?" he asked.

"I had other things to do," replied Betty coolly. "Why?"

"I just wondered. Seems funny to me that you have time for me only a couple of times a week, that's all."

"Listen, kid," she said. "I don't have to account to you or anybody like you for my time. Get it?"

"Don't get sore. I was just wondering."

"If it'll make you feel any better, I went dancing last night. Marty Janowski took me over to White River and we went to the China Dragon to eat and dance. Any more questions?"

Rodney knew that he should keep quiet, but he could not let it go at that. "What did you do after?" he asked.

"Went parking over at Silver Lake," replied Betty without hesitation. "Why?"

"I just wondered. Have fun?"

"As a matter of fact, I did. Marty's a swell dancer."

"That's not what I meant."

"What did you mean?"

"I mean after. Parking."

"Yes I did, if it's any of your business."

"What did you do?" asked Rodney, not wanting to hear but unable to keep himself from asking.

"Oh, for Christ's sake," said Betty disgustedly. "Find a drive-in, will you? I'm starved. We mill hands are used to getting our supper at five-thirty. We're not like high mucky muck mill owners who have servants to give them dinner at eight."

"I'll stop at the next one," said Rodney. "Listen, Betty. I don't think it's right for you to go parking with Marty Janowski."

"What!" The word was not so much a question as an exclamation of rage.

"I don't think it's right for you to go parking with Marty Janowski. Not after I've asked you a thousand times to be my girl."

"Turn this car around and take me home," demanded Betty. "At once."

Rodney stepped on the gas and kept going. "I won't let you out until you promise not to fool around with Marty any more," he said doggedly.

"I didn't tell you to let me out," said Betty furiously. "I told you to turn around and take me home."

"If you don't want to go for a ride with me," said Rodney, hating himself for not keeping his mouth shut, "I'll stop the car right here and you can walk back."

"All *right*," said Betty. "You just stop and let me out. I won't have to walk far, I'll guarantee you that. The first car that comes along with a good-looking fellow in it is the car I'll stick out my thumb for. I don't come from a mill-owning family. I don't mind hitch-hiking one damned bit. Now let me out."

"Aw, come on, Betty," pleaded Rodney. "Don't be mad. I wouldn't let you out on the highway like that. Come on, don't be mad."

"I am mad. Damned good and mad. Who do you think you are, telling me who I can go out with, and who I can't?"

"I didn't mean anything. I just got jealous for a minute, that's all. I have asked you, thousands of times, to be my girl. It makes me jealous to think of you with another fellow, that's all."

"Well keep it to yourself from now on," ordered Betty. "I don't take orders from anybody. Besides, why should I be your girl and go steady with you? When you go away to school next fall, I'd be left high and dry. It's hard for a girl to get back in circulation after she's gone steady for a while."

"I thought that maybe you liked me better than anyone else," said Rodney. "I like you better than any other girl. That's why I want to go steady with you."

Betty's expression softened a trifle. "I like you all right, kid," she said. "You're O.K."

"Well, then?"

"I'll think it over."

Rodney turned into a drive-in and a spurt of gravel flew up from behind one of his rear wheels.

"Would you go parking at Silver Lake with me?" he asked.

"I might," she said, "if you'd hurry up and feed me. I want a couple of cheeseburgers and a chocolate shake and a side of French fries."

Rodney got out of the car. "Will you?" he asked.

"I said I might, didn't I?" said Betty impatiently. "What more do you want, a written agreement?"

Much later, after they had eaten and the night had turned thoroughly dark, Rodney drove around Silver Lake. It was Betty who showed him one of the good parking places. When he had cut the motor and turned off the lights, the humid night closed in on them like a soggy black blanket.

"God, it's hot," complained Betty.

"There's a bottle in the glove compartment," said Rodney, "and I bought some ginger ale at the drive-in. A good drink will cool you off."

He mixed two drinks quickly and expertly, by the dashboard

200

light. They were warm and tasted vaguely of the paper cups which contained them.

"Whew!" said Betty, and spit a mouthful of the warm, strong drink over the low car door. "Jeez! What swill!"

"It takes getting used to," commented Rodney, suddenly feeling very man-of-the-world. If there was one thing he knew, it was good liquor and the drinking of it. "Take another sip," he suggested. "It grows on you."

"To hell with that," said Betty. "I'm going in for a swim."

"Did you bring a suit?"

"What's the matter with you, anyway? Haven't you ever been swimming in the raw with a girl?"

"Sure, I have," lied Rodney. "Dozens of times. I was just asking if you'd brought a suit is all."

"No, I didn't bring a suit," mimicked Betty. "Are you coming?"

"Of course," said Rodney, hurriedly finishing his drink.

Before he could get his shirt unbuttoned, Betty had shed her shorts and halter and was running, naked, down the beach toward the water. When Rodney reached the water's edge, feeling very naked and more than a little foolish, Betty was nowhere to be seen. He inched himself slowly into the water, and when he had waded in as far as his waist, she was suddenly beside him. Her head emerged silently from the water, and she spit a stream straight into the middle of his back. He fell forward and when he came up, Betty was standing up and laughing at him. He tried to catch her, but she swam away from him, laughing, taunting, calling him names.

"Wait 'til I get you," he called to her. "You've got to come out sooner or later, and I'll be right here waiting."

"Don't let your teeth chatter," she yelled, "or I'll be able to find you in the dark."

As it turned out, he did not catch her. A few minutes later the blatant sound of his horn rang out in the dark, and he started violently.

"I've had enough," shouted Betty from the car.

Goddamn it. Rodney cursed savagely. He had planned to catch her and throw her down in the sand and roll her around good, feeling her, touching her. He had never been close to her when she was completely undressed before, and now, goddamn it, she had gone and beat him to the car. She must have eyes like a cat to find her way around in this moonless dark. He stumbled several times before he finally discerned the bulk of his automobile up ahead of him.

Betty waited while he stumbled again and nearly fell. She waited until he was directly in front of the car, and then she turned on the head lights. Her hoot of laughter filled the night, and Rodney was only too painfully aware of the ridiculous picture he must make as he stood and stared like a startled animal and tried to cover himself with his hands.

"You bitch!" he shouted, but she was laughing so hard that she did not hear him.

He made his way to the car and grabbed for his trousers, cursing her silently while she laughed.

"Oh, Rod!" she cried, and went off into another spasm of laughter. "Oh, Rod! What a picture to put on a postcard and send home to Mother!"

Rodney got into the car, clad only in his trousers, and immediately pressed the starter. The car's powerful motor roared to life, and Betty reached over and turned off the ignition.

"What's the matter, honey," she asked softly, running her finger tips over his bare chest. "You mad, honey?"

Rodney exhaled his breath sharply. "No," he said, "I guess not."

"Kiss me, then," she said, prettily petulant. "Kiss me to show me you aren't mad."

With something that was almost a sob, Rodney turned to her. This was the thing he could never understand about Betty. For hours, she could act as if the last thing she wanted was for him to touch her. She could make him feel as if she did not even like him particularly, but the minute he kissed her she began to make small sounds in her throat and her body twisted and turned against him as if she could not get enough of his kisses. This was the moment he waited for every time he saw her. It made everything else bearable, from the way she taunted him with her other boy friends to the way she teased him by pretending not to like him.

"Quick!" she said. "Down on the beach. Not here."

She ran ahead of him, and he followed, carrying the car robe. Before he could get the blanket smooth on the soft sand, she was lying down, holding her arms out to him.

"Oh, baby, baby," he said. "I love you. I love you so."

She nibbled hungrily at his lower lip. "Come on, honey," she said, and her body moved ceaselessly. "Come on, honey. Love me a little."

His fingers found the tie of her halter, and in less than half a minute the garment lay on the sand next to the blanket. Betty's back arched against his arm as she thrust her breasts up to him. This was not new to Rodney. She let him do this often, but it never failed to arouse him to near frenzy. Her nipples were always rigid and exciting and the full, firm flesh around them always hot and throbbing.

"Come on, honey," she whimpered. "Come on, honey," and his mouth and hands covered her. "Hard," she whispered. "Do it hard, honey. Bite me a little. Hurt me a little."

"Please," murmured Rodney against her skin. "Please. Please." His hand found the V of her crotch and pressed against it.

"Please," he said. "Please."

It was at this point that Betty usually stopped him. She would put both her hands in his hair and yank him away from her, but she did not stop him now. Her tight shorts slipped off as easily as if they had been several sizes too large, and her body did not stop its wild twisting while Rodney took off his trousers.

"Hurry," she moaned. "Hurry. Hurry."

For only a moment, Rodney was panicky, and after that he did not care, not even when she had to help him. For less than a moment he wondered if all the stories he had read and heard and told about virgins could be wrong. Betty did not scream in pain or beg him to stop hurting her. She led him without a fumble, and her hips moved quickly, expertly. She did not cry out at all. She moaned deep in her throat the way she did when he kissed her, and the only word she uttered was, "Hurry. Hurry. Hurry."

After that, Rodney did not notice what she did or said. He was lost in her, drowning in her, and he did not think at all. In a very few minutes he lay shivering on the blanket next to her, and her voice seemed to be coming from very far away.

"Smart guy," she was hissing at him. "Smart guy who knew all about it. So smart he doesn't even know enough to wear a safe. Get me home, you dumb jackass. Quick!"

But, unfortunately, Rodney did not get her home quickly enough, or her douche was not strong enough, or, as Rodney was inclined to believe, the Fates were out to foul him up good. It was five weeks later, during the third week of August, when Betty faced him with the worst.

"I'm a month overdue."

"What does that mean?"

"It means I'm pregnant, smart guy."

"But how can you tell so soon?" stammered Rodney.

"I was supposed to come around the week after we were at the lake. That was five weeks ago," said Betty tonelessly.

"What are we going to do?"

"We're going to get married, that's what. Nobody's sticking me with a kid and then running out on me, like that bastard from White River did to my sister."

"Married! But what will my father say?"

"That's for you to find out, smart guy. Ask him."

♦ 13 ♦

Leslie Harrington was not a worrier, for he had discovered as a young man that worry is profitless. Early in life, Leslie had learned the best way of beating any problem. Whenever one presented itself, instead of spending hours in futile, squirrel-in-a-cage worry, he would sit down and list on paper all the possible solutions to the problem at hand. When his list was as complete as he could make it, he was able to choose a good, sensible solution which was, more often than not, advantageous to him. This system had never failed him. If it had, he would have discarded it at once and searched for another, for Leslie Harrington could not stand to be bested by anyone or anything. He had never been curious enough to wonder why this was so. It was simply a facet of his personality and he took it as much for granted as he did the shape of his skull. He could not bear to lose, and that was the end of it. On the few occasions when he had lost, he had been physically ill for days and mentally depressed for weeks, but even these bad times served a purpose. In the painful wake which followed a loss, he had time to figure out the reasons why he had not won, and to strengthen the weaknesses which had caused him to lose. At fifty, Leslie Harrington could, and often did, say with pride that he had never suffered the same loss twice.

As a small child, Leslie had thrown himself to the floor in screaming tantrums of rage on the few occasions when his mother or father beat him at a game of lotto or old maid. His parents had adjusted quickly to this twist in their son, and as soon as they had, Leslie never lost another game of any kind when he played with them. Later, he had discovered that it was possible to win at practically anything if one could cheat successfully and well. He had become the star of his basketball team at school as soon as he had learned to knee and elbow so well that the referees could not catch him, and he had graduated as valedictorian of his class after four years of carrying notes on his shirt cuffs and thin tubes of paper in the hollow half of his fountain pen. Leslie Harrington was voted most likely to succeed by his classmates, and this was not the mockery it might have been. It was extremely likely that Leslie would succeed, for he felt he must where others would merely have liked to enjoy the rewards of success. To Leslie Harrington, success was not the vague word of many meanings which it was to a majority of his intellectual classmates. In his mind the word was crisp, sharp and clearly defined. It meant money, the biggest house in town and the best car. But most of all it meant what Leslie termed "being the boss." That he would "be boss" at the Cumberland Mills was a foregone conclusion. The mills had been started by his grandfather and enlarged by his father, and the "boss" chair in the factory offices was cut to fit Leslie, the third generation owner. It was, of course, not enough. What Leslie really wanted was to be boss of the world, and while he wisely limited himself to his mills, his home and his town, he never lost sight of his larger desire.

At the age of twenty-five, Leslie decided to marry Elizabeth Fuller, a tall, slim girl who had the aristocratic look which sometimes comes after generations of inbreeding. At the time when Leslie set out to marry her, Elizabeth had been engaged to Seth Buswell for over a year. The obstacles between Leslie and Elizabeth were of a number and caliber to excite any man who loved a contest which he was sure of winning, and Leslie knew that he would win. He had only to look at Elizabeth, sweet, young and as pliant as a green willow branch, and he knew. The obstacles in his path consisted of her family, Seth and Seth's family and the Harrington family, and there was not a soul among them who thought that marrying Elizabeth was the wise thing for Leslie to do. He had beaten them all and he had won Elizabeth, and in less than ten years he had killed her. In eight years, Elizabeth Harrington miscarried eight times in the third month of each pregnancy, and after every time Dr. Matthew Swain and several Boston specialists to whom Leslie dragged his frail, tired wife, told him that she could not survive another. It was impossible, they said, for Elizabeth to carry a child full term, and none of them realized that with that word, "impossible," they had changed what had been a desire for a son and heir in Leslie to an obsession. When Elizabeth became pregnant in the ninth year of her marriage, Leslie hired a doctor and two nurses from White River. The three of them moved into the Harrington house, put Elizabeth to bed and kept her there for nine months. When she was delivered of a black-haired, red-faced, nine-and-one-half-pound son, Elizabeth lived long enough to hear him cry once. She died several minutes before one of the nurses from White River had had time to clean the baby and put him at his mother's side. When Leslie held his son for the first time, his triumph had been greater than any he had ever known, and it did not horrify him that this time the obstacle in the path of his desire had been his wife.

As the years passed, Leslie continued to "boss" his mills and his town, but he did not "boss" his son. This, too, was of his own choosing. It pleased him when he saw reflected in Rodney the traits which were his.

"Got gumption, that kid has," Leslie often said. "There's not a trace of the weak-kneed Fullers in him."

In this, Leslie Harrington was badly mistaken, for Rodney was weak in the terrible, final way in which only those who are protected and surrounded by powerful externals are weak. Rodney never had to be strong, for strength was all around him, ready-made to protect and shield him. Nor was Rodney driven by a compulsion to succeed as was his father. True, he liked to win well enough, but not to the extent that he would fight and struggle to win, especially if his opponents happened to be his physical match. Before he was ten years old, Rodney knew that there was nothing worth winning that involved effort, for without effort he could win anything he wanted from his father. He had merely to ask or, later, to hold out his hand, and whatever he wanted was his. Yet Rodney was not a fool. He knew that it was politic for him to please his father whenever he could, especially when it involved no sacrifice on his part. Thus, when he had been younger and his father had wanted him to associate with "nice" children, Rodney had done so. It made no difference to him. He could be King anywhere. And later, when his father had wanted him to go to New Hampton, Rodney had gone willingly. He hated school anyway, so it did not matter to him where he went. When he was expelled, he had not been afraid to come home and face his father.

"I got bounced, Dad," he said.

"What the hell for?"

"Too much drinking and girling, I guess."

"Well, for Christ's sake!"

Leslie had gone at once to the headmaster at New Hampton and told him what he thought of a school that tried to prevent a youngster from sowing a few wild oats.

"I'm paying you to teach him a few academic courses," Leslie had shouted, "not to worry about what he does with his free time. I'll worry about that."

But Leslie Harrington had never been a worrier. It was stupid and profitless. He certainly did not worry about his son, for there was no scrape that Rodney could possibly get into that his father could not fix. It was natural for a healthy, red-blooded boy to get into a few scrapes. Leslie said often that he wouldn't give a nickel for a boy who didn't get into a fix now and then. He had a fine relationship with his son, who was a normal, healthy, good-looking boy. He and his son were pals, chums, and while they respected one another in the way good friends would, there were no binding father-and-son strings attached to their relationship.

"Apron strings are for women," Leslie told Rodney often, so that when he was still very young, Rodney learned to love his life in the womanless house on Chestnut Street.

For all these reasons, Rodney, at sixteen, was not in the least afraid of his father. When he asked Betty Anderson what she thought his father would say about the trouble she was in, it was not fear which prompted him but, rather, a curious desire to know.

When Rodney left Betty Anderson on the night she told him she was pregnant, he went at once to his father. Leslie was sitting in the house on Chestnut Street in the room designated as "The Study." The walls of this room were covered from floor to ceiling with shelves containing books in handsome, leather-bound sets, none of which had ever been read. The books had been bought by Leslie's father for decorative purposes and Leslie had inherited them along with the rest of the house. Twice a week, old Pratte dusted the book spines with an attachment which she hooked up to the vacuum cleaner. Leslie was seated at a table in front of a book-lined wall, doing a jigsaw puzzle.

"Hi, Dad," said Rodney.

"Hello, Rod," said Leslie.

The conversation which ensued after this exchange might have shocked and surprised an outsider, but it held neither of these elements for the two participants. Rodney flopped down into a leather-upholstered chair and flung his legs over the wide arm, while Leslie continued to work on the jigsaw puzzle.

"There's this girl down on Ash Street who claims I knocked her up."

"Who's that?"

"Betty Anderson."

"John Anderson's girl?"

"Yes. The youngest one."

"How far gone is she?"

"She says a month, although I don't see how she can know for sure so soon."

"There are ways."

"She wants me to marry her."

"What do you want?"

"I don't want to."

"O.K. I'll take care of it. You want a drink?"

"O.K."

The two Harringtons sipped whisky and soda, the father's drink only slightly stronger than the son's, and talked about baseball until eleven o'clock when Rodney said that he guessed he'd take a shower and go to bed.

On the following Monday morning, Leslie Harrington sent for John Anderson who worked as a loom fixer in the Cumberland Mills. Anderson entered Leslie's pine-paneled, wall-to-wall carpeted office with his cap in his hand and stood in front of Leslie's desk shuffling his feet.

"You got a daughter named Betty, John?"

"Yes, sir."

"She's pregnant."

John Anderson sat down on a leather chair without being asked. His cap fell on the floor.

"She's going around saying my son did it, John."

"Yes, sir."

"I don't like that kind of talk, John."

"No, sir."

"You've worked for me a long time, John, and if you're having trouble at home I'd like to help you."

"Thank you, sir."

"Here's a check, John. It's for five hundred dollars. There's a note attached to it on which I've written the name of a close-mouthed doctor from White River, so that your daughter can get rid of her package. Five hundred will be more than enough, with a little bonus for you in the bargain, John."

John Anderson stood up and retrieved his cap. "Thank you, sir," he said.

"Do you like working for me, John?"

"Yes, sir."

"That's all, John. You can go back to work now."

"Thank you, sir."

When John Anderson had left, Leslie sat down at his desk and lit a cigar. He buzzed his secretary to find out if his coffee was ready.

That same afternoon, Betty Anderson who had not only the morals but the claws of an alley cat, stormed her way past Leslie's secretary and into Leslie's office. Her face bore the marks of her father's rage, and her mouth was still twisted with the filthy names she had called Rodney. She flung Leslie's check down on his desk.

"You're not buying me off that cheap, Mr. Harrington," she screamed. "It's Rodney's kid I'm carrying, and Rodney's going to marry me."

Leslie Harrington picked up the check the girl had flung. He did not speak.

"Rodney's going to marry me or I'll go to the police. They give a guy twenty years for bastardy in this state, and I'll see to it that he serves every single day of it unless he marries me."

Leslie buzzed for his secretary. "Bring my checkbook, Esther," he said, and Betty flounced to a chair, a smile of satisfaction on her bruised lips.

When the secretary had come and gone, Leslie sat down at his desk and began to write.

"You know, Betty," he said, as he wrote, "I don't think you really want to bring Rodney to court. If you did that, I'd have to call in a few boys as witnesses against you. Do you know how many witnesses it takes to testify against a girl and have her declared a prostitute in this state? Only six, Betty, and I employ a great many more than six men in the mills." Leslie tore the new check from his book with a crisp rip. He looked at Betty and smiled, extending the check. "I don't think you want to take Rodney to court, do you, Betty?"

Beneath the red bruises, Betty's face was white and still.

"No, sir," she said, and took the check from Leslie's hand.

With her back to him, on her way to the door, she glanced down at the paper in her hand. It was a check made out to her father for two hundred and fifty dollars. She whirled and looked at Leslie Harrington, who still smiled and who looked right back at her.

"Half of two fifty is one twenty-five," he said quietly. "That's what it'll cost you to come back again, Betty."

That night, Leslie and Rodney Harrington ate an early dinner

209

so that they could make the first show at the movie theater at White River. They went in Rodney's convertible, with the top down, because it gave the kid a big kick to drive people around in his car.

◆ 14 ◆

The gossip about Betty Anderson was like a candy bar in the hands of children. That is, it was not allowed to linger overlong at any one pair of lips before it was passed on quickly to another. The talk was started on its way by Walter Barry, a hollow-chested young man who worked as a teller at the Citizens' National Bank. It was to Walter that John Anderson presented his check from Leslie Harrington. Walter looked at the check curiously and immediately decided that something was up. Something being up was Walter's favorite phrase. It had connotations of mystery and intrigue otherwise missing in the circumspect Irish Catholic life which he shared with his aged mother and his brother Frank. Walter decided that something was up because his brother Frank worked as a foreman at the mills, and Frank had mentioned nothing at home about John Anderson receiving a bonus in the huge amount of two hundred and fifty dollars. At first, Walter, who was a reader of murder mysteries, was struck by the thought that John Anderson was blackmailing Leslie Harrington for some dark, mysterious reason, but no sooner was this thought formed than his face reddened. The idea of anyone blackmailing Harrington was ridiculous. Walter smiled nervously as he counted out two hundred and fifty dollars in bills for John Anderson.

"That's a lot of money, John," said Walter as casually as he could. "You planning to take a little vacation?"

John Anderson had a favorite phrase, too. His was that he, John Anderson, was nobody's fool, not by a damsight. He had expected questions at the bank, friendly, probing questions, but questions, nevertheless, which would demand answers. John Anderson had come prepared. It was not his fault that he had been born in Stockholm, a large, cosmopolitan city, and that in thirty years he had not learned the devious art of living in a small town in America.

"No vacation for me," said John Anderson. "The money's for my daughter Betty. She goes for a while to make a visit with

210

her aunt in Vermont." John had lived in northern New England for thirty years. He pronounced it ahnt. "This aunt is sister to my wife. Old sister, and sick now. Betty goes to take care of her for a while. Mr. Harrington fine man. He loans Anderson money to send Betty to take care of sick aunt."

"Oh," said Walter Barry. "That's a shame, John. Will Betty be gone long?"

"No," said poor John Anderson who was nobody's fool, "not very long."

"I see," said Walter pleasantly. "Well, here you are, John. Two hundred and fifty dollars."

"Thank you," said John and walked out of the bank, secure in the knowledge that he had done very well with the inspired story of Betty and her maiden aunt in Vermont. He had even had the name of a specific place in Vermont picked out, in case anyone should ask. Rutland, he would say. That was far enough away to be safe. John Anderson did not know anyone in Peyton Place who had ever been as far away from home as Rutland, Vermont.

Walter Barry waited until the revolving door into which John Anderson had stepped was empty. Then he went immediately to Miss Soames who worked two cages to the left of Walter's.

"Did you hear about Betty Anderson?" he asked. "Gone to visit a maiden aunt in Vermont."

The lenses of Miss Soames's gold-rimmed glasses gleamed. "You don't say!" she exclaimed.

All this took place between twelve and one o'clock in the afternoon, for John Anderson had come into the bank on his lunch hour. By five o'clock of this same afternoon, the word had fallen on the ears of people who remembered Betty's bruised face of the day before. It fell on the ears of Pauline Bryant, who was the sister of Esther Bryant who was secretary to Leslie Harrington. Pauline, who worked as a clerk in Mudgett's Hardware Store, telephoned to Esther, and Esther, proud of being the only one who was really in the know, as she put it, gladly related the true story about Betty Anderson. That evening, the true story about Betty Anderson was served, along with the meat and potatoes, at every supper table in Peyton Place. Allison MacKenzie heard it from her mother, who used it as a sort of hammer with which to drive home her reasons for chastity in young girls.

"You see what happens," said Constance MacKenzie, "when a girl lets some fellow paw her. The result is what happened to Betty Anderson. That is the way cheap behavior pays off. In trouble."

211

A few hours later, Allison and Kathy Ellsworth sat, tailor fashion, on Allison's bed.

"Did you hear about Betty Anderson?" asked Allison.

"Yes," replied Kathy, who was dreamily brushing her hair. "My father told us at supper."

"Don't you think it's just awful?"

"Oh, I don't know. I think it would be sort of exciting to have a child by one's lover."

Allison rubbed cold cream into her throat with firm, upward motions as she had learned to do from an illustrated article in a women's magazine. "Well, I certainly wouldn't want to be shipped off to Vermont to live with a maiden aunt while my baby was being born."

"Neither would I," agreed Kathy. "Do you suppose Rodney was a good lover?"

"I suppose so. He's had enough experience. Norman was telling me about this book he read. It said in this book that knowledge alone would not make a good lover. It takes experience as well."

"Rodney had that all right. I think he should have married Betty, don't you?"

"No. Why should he? People who have affairs should be intelligent enough to cope with them. Marriage is for clods, and if you go and get married the way you plan, Kathy, that will be the end of your artistic career. Marriage is stultifying."

"What's 'stultifying'?"

"Oh, confining, or binding, or something like that," said Allison impatiently. She always became impatient when asked to define a word of whose definition she was not sure.

"Do you think your mother and Mr. Makris will get married?"

Allison lowered her cream-covered hands and wiped them carefully on a towel. This was a question to which she had given much thought. She knew it was perfectly acceptable for a widow to remarry. Her common sense told her it was entirely possible that her mother might consider marriage to Tomas Makris, but her emotions would not let her believe it. Her mother had been married to Allison MacKenzie, and in the mind of the daughter of Allison MacKenzie it was inconceivable that a woman who had been married to him could ever think seriously of doing anything other than mourn his loss for the rest of her life.

"No, I don't think so," said Allison to Kathy.

"Wouldn't you like it if they did?" asked Kathy. "I think they'd make an adorable couple. He's so dark and she's so fair."

Allison's stomach began to quiver. "No," she said sharply. "I wouldn't like it a bit."

"Why not? Don't you like Mr. Makris? When he first came here, you said you thought he was the handsomest man you ever saw."

"I never said such a thing. I said that next to my father, he was the handsomest man I ever saw."

"I think Mr. Makris is much better looking than your father ever was, if your father looked anything like that picture downstairs."

"Well, he isn't," declared Allison. "Besides, my father was good and kind and sweet and considerate and generous. Looks aren't everything, you know."

"What makes you think Mr. Makris isn't?" asked Kathy.

"Please," said Allison. "I don't want to discuss it any more. My mother won't marry him. I'll run away from home if she does."

"You'd really run away?" asked Kathy, shocked. "You'd quit school, and your job on the paper and everything?"

Allison thought about her job. In the past few weeks she had done articles on Elm Street as it was a hundred years ago, the Peyton Place railroad station as it was fifty years ago, and several other pieces in the same vein. Her job was not at all what she had expected working on a newspaper would be. It was, to use Allison's currently favorite but inappropriate word, "stultifying."

"Yes, I would," said Allison decisively.

"You'd leave your home and your friends and everything?"

"Yes," said Allison with a tragic sigh, for her friends included Norman Page with whom she fancied herself in love. "Yes, I'd leave everyone and everything."

"But where would you go?" asked Kathy, who could sometimes be of a disagreeably practical mind.

"How should I know?" said Allison crossly. "New York, I suppose. That's where all writers go to get famous."

"That's where artists go, too," said Kathy. "Maybe we could go together and be bachelor girls in an apartment in Greenwich Village, like those two girls in that book we read. Of course, I don't know what I'd ever tell Lew."

"Oh, Lew," said Allison, dismissing with a wave of her hand the current love of Kathy's life.

"That's all right for you to say," said Kathy in an injured tone. "Lew isn't in love with you. Maybe Norman doesn't excite you and thrill you the way Lew does me, but that's no reason for you to be jealous."

"Jealous!" exclaimed Allison. "Jealous! Why on earth should I be jealous? Norman is every bit as exciting as Lew. Just because he's quiet and isn't always giving me sexy looks the way Lew does you, is no reason for thinking he can't be very exciting and thrilling, because he can. Norman's an intellectual. He even goes about making love intellectually."

"I never heard of intellectual love," said Kathy. "Tell me what it's like. The only kind of love I know about is Lew's kind, and I like it fine. What's this other kind?"

Allison turned off the light and the two girls got into bed. Allison began to make up a story of intellectual love. Intellectual love differed from physical love, according to her, in that instead of merely kissing a girl, an intellectual first told her that her lips were like ruby velvet. Intellectual love was, in fact, full of similitudes such as, eyes like deep pools, teeth like pearls and skin like alabaster.

"If he talks that much," said Kathy sleepily, "when does he have time to do anything else?"

Allison went to sleep after deciding that the next time she was alone with Norman, she would see if she could make him stop being an intellectual for a while.

At approximately this same time, Constance MacKenzie and Tomas Makris were sitting in the cocktail lounge of the Hotel Jackson at White River. She and Tom, Constance realized, spent quite a lot of time in restaurants and cocktail lounges. There was nowhere else for them to go. Constance would not go to Tom's apartment in the parsonage, and she did not like to have him at her house when Allison was at home. Nevertheless, as she lifted her second drink, Constance decided that she was rapidly growing sick and tired of cocktail lounges and restaurants.

"If we were married," said Tom suddenly, "we could go out for a drink and dinner only when we wanted to. On our wedding anniversary, for instance."

"I was thinking the same thing," Constance admitted. "I'm beginning to feel like a traveling salesman with the nearest bar for my natural habitat."

"And that," said Tom, "is the best opening gambit I've been offered for over two years. My next natural line is to say, 'Well, then?' so I'll say it. Well, then? Or do you want this stylized? Such as, 'Well, then, darling be mine. Two can live as cheaply as one.'"

"Three," said Constance.

"Three can live as cheaply as two. With your Cape Cod and my salary."

"Oh, stop it," said Constance wearily.

Tom looked down into his glass. "I mean it, Connie," he said. "What are we waiting for?"

"For Allison to grow up."

"We've had this same conversation so many times," said Tom, "that we ought to be able to prompt each other with our lines."

"Tom," she said, covering his hand with hers, "I'll begin to mention us to Allison soon. I'll have to step softly. She has no idea that I'd ever consider marriage. But I'll mention it soon, Tom. Just to see how she takes to the idea."

"I hate to sound insistent," he said, "but how soon?"

Constance thought for a moment. "Tomorrow evening," she said. "Come for dinner."

"Moral support, eh?"

Constance laughed. "Yes," she said. "Besides, if you're right there where she can see you, I don't see how she will be able to resist the idea of such a handsome stepfather."

"I hear it, but I don't believe it," said Tom, raising two fingers in the direction of the waiter. "However, I'm a great one for premature celebration."

"I'll simply say, 'Allison, I'm not getting any younger. Soon you will be grown and will leave me. It's time I thought of someone to spend my old age with.'"

"Put it off much longer, and we won't even have much of that left."

"What?"

"Old age."

They held hands and smiled into one another's eyes. "We're worse than a couple of kids," he said, "sitting around holding hands and mooning."

"Speaking of kids," said Constance, "isn't it awful about Betty Anderson?"

"All depends on what you mean by 'awful,'" said Tom, releasing her hand as the waiter put down their drinks. "Awful that she is left with the short end of the stick, yes. Awful that the Harrington boy is getting away with it, yes. Especially awful that Leslie Harrington did what he did, yes. But otherwise, not so awful. Nor unexpected, for that matter."

"For heaven's sake, Tom," said Constance. "You can't mean that you don't think it's awful when fifteen- and sixteen-year-old kids go around—" she paused, searching for the right phrase. "Go around doing things," she finished.

Tom grinned. "That's exactly what I mean," he said.

"Do you actually mean to sit there and tell me that if we got married and Allison did anything, got into trouble, or even if she was lucky and didn't get caught—" she stopped, unable to find words to conclude her thought.

"If Allison, or any kid for that matter, goes around, quote doing things unquote, I cannot say that I think it is something as terrible as you want me to say it is," said Tom and folded his arms and leaned back in his chair.

"For heaven's sake, Tom. It's abnormal in a child that age. There's something wrong with a kid who thinks overmuch of sex."

"What do you mean by overmuch?"

One of the few things about Tom which annoyed Constance was his habit of questioning every questionable word in her arguments. More often than not, she had discovered, he could render her opinions utterly senseless and baseless by making her say exactly what she meant, word for word.

"By overmuch," she said crossly, "I mean just what I say. It is thinking overmuch of sex when a fifteen-year-old girl lets some boy like Harrington take her out and do whatever he wants with her. If Betty hadn't been thinking too much about sex for years, she wouldn't even know enough to realize that a boy wanted to take her out for what he could get. The idea would never enter her head."

"Wow," said Tom, lighting a cigarette. "Are you confused!"

"I am not! It's abnormal for a girl of fifteen to be as wise as Betty is. Well, she wasn't quite wise enough, apparently."

"I'd be inclined to think that if Betty, at fifteen, didn't think about sex she was abnormal. Much more so than because she obviously has thought about it. I think that any normal kid," he said, pointing his cigarette at her—" 'normal' being your word, not mine—has thought plenty about sex."

"All right!" conceded Constance unwillingly. "But thinking and doing are two different things. And nothing you can say is going to make me believe that it's perfectly all right for kids like Betty Anderson and Rodney Harrington to go around having—things to do with each other."

Tom raised an eyebrow. "What the hell have you got against the word intercourse?" he asked. "It's a good, serviceable word. Yet

216

you'd rather rack your brain for fifteen minutes to find a substitute rather than use it."

"Whatever you want to call it, I still don't think it is all right for children."

"In the last few minutes," said Tom, "you've gone from calling what happened between Betty and Rodney 'awful' to 'abnormal' and now to 'not all right.' I'm not going around advocating fornication on every street corner and an illegitimate child in every home, and for those reasons I'll admit that I don't think that it is 'all right.' But since I know that a kid at fifteen or sixteen, and oftentimes younger, is physically ready for sex, I can't agree that I think Betty and Rodney are 'abnormal.' And since I also know that in addition to a child being physically ready for sex at fifteen or sixteen, his mind has been educated and conditioned to sex and he feels a tremendous, basic drive for sex, I cannot agree with you when you say that you think Betty and Rodney are 'awful.' "

"Tremendous, basic drive," scoffed Constance. "Now you're going to go all Freudian on me and tell me that sex is on a par with eating, drinking and defecating."

"In the first place, Freud never said any such thing, but we'll let that pass. And in the second place, I certainly do not put sex on a par with the things you mentioned. I put it next to the urge for self-preservation, where it belongs."

"Oh," said Constance, with an impatient gesture, "you men make me sick. I suppose you were being driven by this tremendous, basic urge at the age of fifteen or sixteen."

"Fourteen," said Tom, and laughed at the look on her face. "Fourteen, I was. She was a kid who lived in a tenement on the same floor as I, and I caught her in the toilet at the end of the hall. I took her standing up, with the stink of potatoes boiled too long in too much water, and filth and urine all around us, and I loved it. I may even say that I wallowed in it, and I couldn't wait to get back for more."

"And that's the second thing about you that annoys me," said Constance. "The first one is the way you always rip my arguments into pieces, and the second one is the way you seem to try to be deliberately crude. You don't care what you say, nor to whom. Sometimes I think that you lie awake nights thinking up things to say for their shock value."

"Faulty reasoning," said Tom. "What am I to do with you?"

"Don't say things like you do," she said. "It's not necessary or even nice."

"God!" exclaimed Tom. "Nice, yet! Some of the things I say may not be particularly 'nice,' but they are true. It was, perhaps, not nice of me to have intercourse with little Sadie, or whatever the hell her name was, in a hallway toilet, but it is true. It happened, and it happened exactly as I told you. Also, my reaction was just what I said it was. What about you? I suppose you never thought of sex at all until you were married, and then you went to your new husband all sweetness and virginity, with never a thought of eagerness."

For a moment Constance hesitated. Here was a perfect opening. She could smile right back at Tom and say: "As a matter of fact, he wasn't my husband." Tonight would be a good time to say it, before she talked to Allison. She glanced up into his waiting face and the moment was gone.

"As a matter of fact," she said, "that's just the way it was. It never changed, either. Sex was always something I allowed him as a sort of favor."

"What a liar you are," said Tom.

She felt her hands grow cold as she waited fearfully for his next words. Now it was coming. Now he would look at her with disgust and say, "He was never your husband. What a liar you are. He was your lover and you bore him a child. Yours was the same situation as Betty and Rodney's, except you were old enough to have known better."

"What a liar you are," said Tom. "Would you have me believe that when you give yourself to me it is as a favor?"

"Not with you," said Constance, and hurriedly finished her drink. "But just the same," she said, laughing a trifle nervously, "you will never make me believe that it is the right thing for children to be doing. Why, if Allison ever did anything like that, I'd kill her."

"There is a shaggy dog story in that vein," said Tom as he stood up and put down a bill on the check the waiter had left. "It has to do with a woman who put a new dress on her little girl. She told the little girl that if the little girl went out and fell into the mud, she'd kill her. So the little girl went out and fell in the mud and her mother killed her."

"This is a joke?" asked Constance, taking his arm as they walked to the car.

"I don't think so," said Tom.

Constance leaned back comfortably in the front seat of the car. "I may have put it a little strongly," she said. "But I mean it when
218

I say that I wouldn't put up with Allison behaving the way Betty Anderson has for years. Luckily, I don't have to worry about putting up with it. Allison isn't like that. I doubt if she ever thinks about it. She always has her nose in a book and her head in the clouds."

"Then you had best watch what she reads," said Tom. "As one fourteen-year-old who developed a crush on me once said, 'After all, Mr. Makris, Juliet was only fourteen.' Watch out that Allison doesn't begin to think of herself in terms of Juliet. Or worse, in terms of Mademoiselle de Maupin."

"What's that?" asked Constance. "That French name?"

"It is the name of a very famous novel by a Frenchman named Gautier," said Tom and burst out laughing.

"Now you are making fun of me because my literary education was sadly neglected. I don't care. I don't have to worry about Allison. At sixteen she still loves to read fairy tales."

"I thought she was only fifteen."

"Well, she will be sixteen in the fall," said Constance and bit her lip against the slip she had made. "And it won't be too long until fall."

"No, it won't," said Tom. "School will be opening in a little over two weeks."

"I'll talk to her tomorrow, about us," said Constance. "Maybe by next summer—"

"Sure," said Tom, and pressed his foot down on the accelerator. The car sped smoothly on the road to Peyton Place.

◆ 15 ◆

The next day was Saturday and it began what Seth Buswell, without his tongue in his cheek for once, later referred to as "the bad time in '39." The drought was still upon Peyton Place. The land lay burnt and fruitless under the August sun, and there was that peculiar, waiting quietness in the air which comes when every man, woman and child watches the hills which encircle his town.

A stranger passed through Peyton Place early on that Saturday morning. He parked his car on Elm Street and made his way into Hyde's Diner. Corey Hyde stood with his fists on his hips and stared out of a window at the back of the diner, and Clayton

Frazier who stood next to Corey, holding a coffee cup, also stared. The stranger craned his neck to look over the heads of Corey and Clayton, but there was nothing to see from the window but a ridge of hills topped with yellowed, unmoving trees.

"Coffee," said the stranger, and for a moment Corey's shoulders tensed before he turned around.

"Yes, sir. Right away," said Corey.

Clayton Frazier shuffled to a seat at the end of the counter but a seat, the stranger noticed, from which the old man could look out the window to the ridge of hills in the distance. Corey put a cup, saucer and spoon down on the counter in front of the stranger.

"Will that be all, sir?" asked Corey.

"Yes," the stranger replied, and Corey left him to take up his post by the window.

This particular stranger was different from the majority of those who pass through northern New England, or from those who come to stay for a while in the summer, in that he was a sensitive man. He was an author's representative on his way to Canada to vacation with his number one client, a prolific but alcoholic writer, and he sensed something of the waiting tension which gripped this town in which he found himself early on a Saturday morning. He slapped his hand down against Corey Hyde's counter.

"What's the matter with everyone around here?" he demanded. "Everyone acts as if he were waiting for doomsday. Not five minutes ago I stopped at a gas station, and the man there was so busy watching and waiting for something that I had a struggle to find out what I owed him. What is everyone waiting for?"

Corey and Clayton, who had started almost fearfully at the sound of the stranger's hand against the counter, were, nevertheless, not so startled that they forgot themselves to the point of answering the stranger with a direct reply.

"Where you headed?" asked Clayton Frazier.

"Canada," replied the stranger, almost mollified now that he had managed to get some response from someone about something in this weary and apprehensive place.

"Drivin'?" asked Clayton, who by now had noticed the gray Cadillac parked outside.

"Yes," said the stranger. "I have two weeks so I thought the drive up would be enjoyably slow and peaceful. I wish now that I had taken a train. It's been wretchedly hot all the way from New York.

"Humph," grunted Clayton. "New York, eh? New York City?"

"Yes," said the stranger.

"Long ways away."

"At least the worst is over now," said the stranger, sipping his coffee. "The Canadian line can't be more than a three-hour drive from here."

"Nope," said Clayton, "it ain't. You should make it easy in three hours. If you go fast, mister, you could make it in less than three hours."

The stranger smiled into the lined, stubbly face of the not-too-clean old man. "Why should I hurry?" he asked pleasantly, and he was thinking what an amusing ancedote this would make to tell his friends when he returned to New York. He would practice that nasal twang, and when he returned home he would tell of the picturesque old native whom he had met and conversed with up in northern New England. "Why should I hurry, old-timer?" he asked jocularly.

Clayton Frazier set his coffee cup down with a little click, and then he looked hard at the stranger for a moment.

"Go fast, mister," he said. "Get over that line of hills as fast as you can go. Mebbe they got rain up to Canada."

The stranger laughed. By God, this was like some story by an impossibly bad writer. Git over that line of hills, stranger, else yore a dead dog.

"What do you mean?" he asked, swallowing his laughter with the rest of his coffee. "What does rain in Canada have to do with my getting there quickly?"

"We ain't got rain here," said Clayton Frazier, turning to look out the window. "Aint had none since June."

"Oh," said the stranger, feeling rather disappointed. "Is that what everyone is waiting for? Rain?"

Clayton Frazier did not look at him again. "Fire," he said. "Everyone's waitin' for the fires to start, mister. If you're smart you'll go fast. You'll get past the hills before the fires start."

A few minutes later, the stranger paused with his hand on the door of his car. He squinted up at the ridge of hills beyond Peyton Place. The hills were topped with trees of a peculiar yellowish color. It was an unhealthy shade, the stranger thought. Ugly. But because he was a sensitive man, he felt a finger of apprehension prod at his mind. He could look at the unmoving, yellow hills and imagine a single, quick-moving, red streak. He could picture the way the red streak would move, eagerly, hungrily, almost gaily, through all the dry, dry quietness that surrounded Peyton Place.

The stranger climbed into his car and drove away, and when he noticed later that his speedometer indicated seventy-five, he laughed at himself, but he did not slow down.

The waiting and watching were everywhere, but other than that, this particular Saturday started off in the way of countless other summer Saturdays gone by.

Allison MacKenzie and Kathy Ellsworth, having spent the night together, breakfasted in the MacKenzie kitchen after Contance had left for her shop. They ate eggs and toast and drank coffee, and there was sunshine all over the yellow tablecloth. Nellie Cross rattled dishes in the sink as a hint for the girls to be finished and gone, but they paid no attention to her.

"I've lived in Peyton Place longer than I've ever lived anywhere," said Kathy, chewing absent-mindedly at a piece of toast. She was looking out the window at the vivid pattern made by hollyhocks against a white picket fence. The MacKenzies' lawn and flowers were the most colorful on Beech Street, kept that way through the weeks of drought by the assiduous hand watering of Joey Cross whom Constance hired for that purpose. "I never want to move away," continued Kathy. "We won't, either. My mother told my father that we wouldn't."

"I'm going to move away," said Allison, "as fast as ever I can after I finish high school. I'm going to go to Barnard College. That's in New York City."

"Not me," said Kathy ungrammatically. "I'm never going away from here. I'm going to marry Lew and live in Peyton Place forever and have a huge family. You know what?"

"No. What?"

"Lew and I are going to *buy* a house after we get married."

"What's so extra about that? All married people buy houses eventually. It's all part of the whole stultifying, stupid pattern."

"We never owned a house. We've lived in nineteen different houses since I was born, and we never owned a one. My mother wants to buy the house that we're renting now, but my father's credit is no good. Mr. Humphrey said so, down at the bank. I guess he'd have let Daddy have the money anyway, but Mr. Harrington wouldn't let him. Mr. Harrington says my father is a poor risk."

"Buy a house like Nellie's shack," said Allison, raising her voice cruelly so that Nellie would be sure to hear. She had not forgiven Nellie for the remarks which Nellie had made about Norman and Evelyn Page.

222

"How much would a house like that cost?" asked Kathy seriously.

Nellie did not answer, nor did she look at Allison. She looked down into the dishwater in the sink and rubbed the vein in her left arm.

"Oh, practically nothing," said Allison in the same unnecessarily loud tone. "My goodness, *anybody* can own a shack. Lew could be a drunken bum and leave you, and you could be a crazy old woman with pus in your veins, but you could still own a shack. *Anybody* can own a shack, even crazy, insane people who have the crazy, insane idea that they're better than other people."

At last, Kathy realized that friction surrounded her. She turned first to look at Nellie, then she turned to Allison.

"You're mean, Allison," she said soberly. "And cruel."

"So are a lot of other people," cried Allison, ashamed at being caught so obviously in an act of unkindness, but unable to back down now. "People who call other people names, for instance, and tell filthy lies about them. I suppose that's not mean and cruel!"

"You are supposed to turn the other cheek," said Kathy virtuously, enjoying this feeling of righteousness at someone else's expense. "I've heard Reverend Fitzgerald say so a thousand times, and so have you."

"Maybe so," cried Allison furiously. "But I've heard about plucking out the eye that offends you. That goes for people whom you consider your friends but who go around sticking up for others."

"If you mean me, Allison MacKenzie, come right out and say so. Don't be such a little sneak."

"Oh!" gasped Allison, outraged. "Now I'm a sneak, am I? Well, I do mean you, Kathy Ellsworth. There. I think that you're silly and stupid with your rented house and your dumb boy friend Lewis Welles, and your eternal talk about getting married and having babies, babies, babies!"

"*Well!*" said Kathy, standing up and maintaining what she was pleased to refer to as "an icy calm," "*Well!* I'm certainly glad that I found out what you think of me before it was too late! Good-by!"

Kathy walked majestically out of the kitchen door, twitching her flat hips indignantly. She did not explain what she meant about finding out what Allison thought of her "before it was too late." Nor did Allison stop to wonder. It was a beautiful exit line, and both girls accepted it as such without question. Kathy walked down Beech Street with her nose in the air, hoping desperately that Allison was watching, and Allison burst into tears.

"Now see what you've done!" she said to Nellie Cross. "If it weren't for you, my best friend wouldn't be mad at me. If it weren't for you, I wouldn't be crying and making my eyes all red. I'm supposed to pack a lunch and meet Norman in an hour. What will he do when he sees me all disheveled and red-eyed? Answer me that."

"Humph," said Nellie. "He'll prob'ly take one look at you and run home to his ma. The minute Evelyn sees him comin', she'll start right in unbuttonin' her dress." To Nellie, also, there were things which were unforgivable. Primarily, she could not forgive Allison for the way the girl seemed to look constantly for opportunities to criticize Lucas who had, since leaving town, become a paragon of virtue in Nellie's eyes. The second reason for Nellie's unwillingness to forgive was because of something Allison had said. She could not rightly remember what it was, but whenever she thought of it, the pus-filled lump in her head began to throb. It was throbbing now, and Nellie turned to Allison and cackled. "You can bet your life on that, honey," she said. "Evelyn don't need to no more than see that snot-nose kid of hers comin' near but what she gets ready to feed him."

"I hate, loathe and despise you, Nellie Cross," cried Allison hysterically. "You're crazy as a loon. Crazier than Miss Hester Goodale, and I'm going to tell my mother not to let you come here to work any more."

Then Nellie remembered the second reason that she was unable to forgive Allison. Allison had said she was crazy. That was it, thought Nellie. She had known it was something wicked like that.

"You're so crazy that you should be locked up in the asylum down at Concord," Allison shouted, her voice high and rough with anger, and hurt, and tears. "I don't blame Lucas for running off and leaving you. He knew that you'd end up in a padded cell down at Concord. And I hope you do. It would serve you just exactly right!"

Allison ran sobbing out of the kitchen and up the stairs to her room. Nellie stood and gazed sightlessly out of the window over the sink.

"That ain't true," she said at last. "Ain't a bit of truth in it. That ain't why Lucas done like he done."

But her head throbbed violently, and the soapsuds in the sink were suddenly thick and slimy, like pus.

Allison stood motionless in the middle of her bedroom floor. Deliberately, she inhaled and exhaled in deep breaths until the pain of anger in her chest and throat was eased, then she went

224

into the bathroom and held a wet washcloth over her eyes. She would not, she decided, allow *anyone* to spoil her day. Back in her bedroom, she powdered her face carefully and applied the small amount of lipstick which Constance permitted, then she went back down to the kitchen. Silently, without even looking at Nellie who still stood in front of the sink, Allison began to make sandwiches. When she had finished packing the picnic hamper, she sat and gazed sullenly out of the window, waiting for Norman. When finally she heard the jangling ring of his bicycle bell, she picked up the hamper and walked out the door without a word. Nellie did not raise her head, not even when Allison took her bicycle off the back porch as noisily as possible, letting the vehicle clatter against each step.

Allison and Norman divided the burdens of picnicking evenly between their two bicycle baskets and pedaled off.

"I hope you didn't get up on the wrong side of the bed," said Allison crossly. "Everyone else seems to have done so."

"Not I," said Norman and grinned. "Who's everybody?"

"Oh, Kathy and Nellie. My mother, too, I suppose. And even if she didn't she'll probably be as cranky as the others by suppertime. It's so hot."

"And dry," added Norman as they pedaled down Elm Street and turned into the highway. "I heard Mr. Frazier say that the state militia has been alerted in case of a forest fire. Look."

He pointed to the hills toward the east, and Allison's eyes followed his direction.

"I know it," she sighed. "Everyone's been waiting for days and days. Maybe it'll rain tomorrow."

The sky was a bright blue, as polished and hard looking as enamel, and it held an enormous sun which was persistent and impossible to look upon because of its hurtful brightness. In all this blue and yellow harshness, no cloud could survive, and not a trace or a wisp of whiteness was to be seen.

"It won't rain," said Norman.

He did not think of it particularly, but his was a statement being spoken all over town that day. The farmers, who long ago had lost all hope of saving their crops, stood with unchanged faces in front of the Citizens' National Bank. Their faces were no different than they had been in the spring, when the men had seeded the earth. But if a deep crease or two in a neck, or carved deep in the skin from nose to mouth, showed gray now, this was understandable. A farmer could not go out for long to stand and gaze at his burnt fields without getting a bit of dust on him somewhere. The farmers stood in front of the bank, waiting for Dexter Humphrey to come in and sit behind his desk in the mortgage loans department, and they looked up at the sky and said, "It won't rain." They said it in the same tone which they would have used had it been raining for a week, and were they expressing their opinion of the next day's weather.

"No, I guess it won't rain," said Allison MacKenzie, pushing her sunglasses back onto the slippery bridge of her nose. "Let's push awhile, Norman. It's too hot to pedal."

They came to the bend in the river at last, and they did much as they had done on previous visits to this place, but there was a subtle difference to this particular day. It was as if each of them sensed vaguely that the Saturday afternoons of youth are few, and precious, and this feeling which neither of them could have defined or described made every moment of this time together too short, too quickly gone, yet clearer and more sharply edged than any other. They swam and ate and read, and Norman brushed Allison's long hair. He put his face against it and told her that it was like silk. Like corn silk in August, when the season had not been dry. For a while, they pretended that they were Robinson Crusoe and Friday, but later they decided that they were both Thoreau, and that the Connecticut River was Walden Pond.

"Let's stay all day," said Allison. "I brought plenty of food to eat."

"Let's stay until dark," said Norman. "We both have lights on our bikes. We can get back easily enough."

"We could see the moon come up," said Allison, enthused.

"Except that we're facing the wrong way," said Norman practically. "The moon doesn't come up over Vermont. It rises from the opposite direction."

"We could pretend," said Allison.

"Yes, we could do that," agreed Norman.

"Oh, what a beautiful day!" exclaimed Allison, stretching her arms wide. "How can anyone be cranky or mean on a day like this!"

"I wasn't," said Norman.

"I was," said Allison, and for a moment the sun seemed less bright. "I was perfectly beastly to Nellie Cross. I'll have to make it up to her on Monday."

The shadow of Allison's shame departed quickly on the feet

226

of her good resolution. The sun returned to its brightness, and Allison grasped Norman's hand.

"Let's run," she cried happily. "I feel so good I could run for an hour without getting tired," and she had no premonition that this was the last day of her childhood.

During the minutes when Allison and Norman were running down the strip of sandy beach on the shore of the Connecticut River, Nellie Cross stepped away from the sink in the MacKenzie kitchen and sat down on the floor. It had seemed only a few minutes that she had been standing as Allison had left her, but she was tired. Her head, she felt, had grown enormous, and she held it carefully on her neck so that it would not fall off and break into pieces on the clean linoleum. She leaned back against a cabinet, and it seemed perfectly natural to her to sit calmly on the kitchen floor on a hot Saturday afternoon, resting her feet which ached from standing too long in one place. She stretched her legs straight out and folded her arms against her chest.

It wa'nt goin' to hurt nothin', she thought, if she just let her mind dwell on Lucas for a minute, and it might make her feel better. Sometimes it did.

But she couldn't seem to think too clearly about Lucas, right this minute. There was so much else going on in her monstrous huge, pus-filled head.

Not that she blamed Lucas for that. It wa'nt his fault that he'd gone and caught the clap off that whore woman, and it was no more than right that he should give the sickness to his wife. Where else could a man leave a thing like that to get rid of it, if he couldn't leave it with his own wife?

But there was something else. Something she should be able to remember. Now what was it? Nellie Cross sat still, first opening her eyes wide and then closing them tightly. Her mouth pursed with the effort to remember, and a line of sweat appeared over her top lip. At last, she shrugged.

Didn't do no good to struggle. Try as she might, her poor head just wouldn't let her think what it was that she should rightly remember. It was somethin' to do with havin' a baby, and she'd be a monkey's uncle if she could recall anythin' else. She could remember layin' on the bed and twistin' and turnin' with the pain of it. Doc Swain was right there, though, same as he always was when you needed him. Stayed all night, he must've, although she couldn't rightly remember havin' seen him when it come daylight.

That was all right, though. She didn't need him no more when it come day. It was all over by then, and she could hear little Joey cryin'. Funny, though, the way little Joey had come in from outside. She could see him plain as anythin', walkin' through the door and bawlin' that his pa was gone. It was after that when she saw the pus for the first time. It was right after Joey'd come in, because that's when she got up and went outside to the privy. That's when she seen it for the first time. Runnin' out of her like a river it was, all yellow and thick. That's when she knew it was no baby she was gettin' the night before. It was the clap she'd been gettin'. Gettin' it off her husband, like any decent woman should. Funny, though. Sometimes she could swear that it was somethin' to do with gettin' a baby. She was sure that she could recollect hearin' The Doc tellin' about a baby. Lucas' baby, The Doc said. She could hear him sayin' it plain as day. Lucas' baby. Now if she could just remember when it had been. Couldn't of been too long ago, because it'd been hot then, just like now, and there hadn't been rain for a long time. The woods was dry, Lucas had told her, dry as gunpowder and just as ready to explode any time. The Doc tellin' about a baby must of been on the same day, because her and Lucas was talkin' while they et, about the woods bein' dry and all. They had waited for Selena for a while, but she hadn't showed up. Off somewheres with that bastard Carter, Lucas had said. Lucas was a good father to his children, and as good to Selena as he was to his own. He didn't hold none with his kids runnin' wild. But Selena didn't come and didn't come, not even after it turned dark. And she couldn't of been with young Carter, because he come lookin' for her. It made Lucas kinda mad when he seen Selena wa'nt with young Carter. Off alley-cattin' with some other bastard, Lucas had said, and in the end Carter and Joey went to look for her. God, how her head hurt! She lifted her arms and spread them as wide as she could, but her hands could not reach the sides of her aching head. It just grew bigger and bigger every second—

Allison was right. Her head was gonna bust wide open and make one helluva mess all over the clean, waxed linoleum. But that wa'nt what Allison had said, was it? She couldn't rightly remember. No. No, that wa'nt it. Allison had said somethin' about Lucas. Somethin' mean, like she was always doin'. And you couldn't tell that little know-it-all nothin'. She was always harpin' about the way Lucas beat Nellie, and no matter how many times Nellie told her that a man didn't go around beatin' a woman he didn't give a damn about, it didn't mean nothin' to Miss Know-It-All Allison. That one always thought she knew it all. And Nellie had told her. When a man didn't give a damn about a woman, he just turned his back on her, but when he thought a lot of her, and wanted to teach her right, he beat her. Well, Allison'd find out different one of these days. So would everybody else. They'd all see that Lucas was a good man who didn't go around givin' the clap to nobody but his own wife. Funny, though, she coulda swore it was somethin' to do with a baby. Lucas' baby. Still, it couldn't of been that, because Lucas'd never go off and leave her when she was havin' a baby. He beat her up plenty, and that showed he cared a lot for her, didn't it? Besides, there was Joey, full grown and cryin', so it couldna had nothin' to do with havin' a baby. Funny, though, the way she could hear The Doc plain as day.

"Nellie."

She looked around the empty kitchen matter of factly.

"That you, Lucas?"

"Yep. I'm upstairs."

With no sense of surprise in her mind, Nellie left the Mac-Kenzie kitchen and mounted the stairs to the second floor. She looked into Allison's empty bedroom.

"You in here, Lucas?" she demanded.

"Over here by the window, Nellie."

She walked to the window and looked down at the empty street below, and then she saw him.

"What're you doin' out there, Lucas?"

"I'm dead, Nellie. I'm an angel now, Nellie. Can't you see the way I'm floatin'?"

"I see you, Lucas. You enjoyin' yourself out there?"

"Well, there's always plenty to drink, and nobody has to work. But a man don't feel right without his woman along."

Nellie giggled coyly. "Was you lookin' for me, Lucas?"

"Been lookin' for you day after day, Nellie. But you don't never stay in one place long enough for me to catch up with you, a pretty girl like you."

"Now go on, Lucas. You was always a big one for the talk."

"Not me, Nellie. I mean every word I'm sayin'. Come on with me, Nellie. I'm lonesome for a pretty girl like you."

"Oh, stop that."

"No foolin', Nellie. You're the prettiest gal I ever seen. Go look in the mirror if you don't believe me."

"Just for that I will, you fancy talker you."

She went to Allison's closet and opened the door. She looked at herself in the long mirror fastened to the inside of the door.

"See, Nellie? What'd I tell you?"

He was right beside her now, blowing on the soft hair at the back of her neck. She could see him behind the reflection of the slim, pretty girl in the mirror.

"A man don't feel right without his woman," whispered Lucas. "Come on, Nellie. It's lonesome as hell without you. My bed gets awful cold."

Nellie smoothed the hair at the nape of her neck with a pretty gesture.

"All right, Lucas," she said. "There's no girl could resist your pretty talk. You go on outside while I get dressed now. It won't take me a minute."

As Nellie spoke, she fingered the strong silk cord of Allison's bathrobe which hung on a hook just inside the closet door, and she was smiling, a moment later, when she dragged a straight chair into the closet. It took two tries before she could get the end of the silk cord over the two-by-four beam which the closet had been constructed to hide.

"You quit that stampin' 'round out there, Lucas," she giggled. "You sound just like a stud horse. I'll be ready in no time. I'm fixin' myself up just like a pitcher I seen in a magazine once."

"Well, damn it, Nellie, a man don't want to wait forever for a girl as pretty as you. Get a move on."

"There was somethin' I wanted to ask you, Lucas," Nellie called. "But I can't rightly remember what it was. It was somethin' to do with a baby."

"That's a helluva thing for a young girl like you to be thinkin' about," Lucas called back. "Come on, now, get a move on."

In the quick second after she had kicked over the chair, and before the strong silk cord of Allison MacKenzie's bathrobe had cut off her life, Nellie Cross remembered.

Selena! she screamed silently. It was Selena havin' Lucas' baby!

◆ 16 ◆

Shortly after six o'clock, Constance MacKenzie entered her house on Beech Street. She had no premonition of tragedy as she surveyed her living room. She was terribly angry. Nothing had been

230

done. The ash trays still held last night's cigarette ends, the sofa pillows had not been straightened, and there were two magazines on the floor, in the exact position in which they had been left the previous day. The rug had not seen a vacuum cleaner since Nellie Cross's last cleaning day, and it should most certainly have been attended to that morning. Constance strode angrily to the kitchen, and she nearly burst into tears at the disorder which she encountered there. There were plates, caked with dried egg yolk, sitting on the table, and dirty dishes in the sink. The garbage had not been taken out, and the glass coffee maker, still half full, sat on one of the burners on the electric stove. "That damned Nellie," muttered Constance angrily, forgetting all the times when she had come home from work to find her house spotless. "She hasn't done a thing all day!"

Constance, who had been looking forward to a cool bath and clean clothes all afternoon, slapped her purse, hat and gloves down on top of the refrigerator. She snatched one of Nellie's tent-like aprons from a hook inside the broom closet door and began to run clean water into the sink.

Steak, French fries and a green salad, she thought. That was what Allison and Tom would get for dinner. There wasn't time for anything else. And as for Allison, where was the child? Constance had told her distinctly to be home in plenty of time to bathe and change, because Mr. Makris was coming to dinner at seven-thirty. Constance glanced at the clock set into the back of the stove. Six-thirty. Well, dinner was going to be late and there was nothing she could do about it. Certainly, no one could expect her to prepare food in a kitchen as messy as this one.

At seven o'clock, when Constance went upstairs to her room, she glanced carelessly through Allison's half-open door. The room was empty, Allison's bed still unmade, and there was a pair of crumpled pajamas on the floor.

Why couldn't that girl do as she was told for once? she wondered angrily. And why hadn't Nellie Cross cleaned the house? Nellie had come in plenty of time this morning. She had come before Constance had left for work. She had had all day to clean. Constance shrugged impatiently. It just went to show, she thought, how little you could depend on anyone. If you wanted anything done to your own satisfaction, it was best to do it yourself.

Constance showered and dressed with the same efficiency with which she did everything. On her way back downstairs, she closed Allison's door. In the event that Tom should want to use the bathroom, she did not want him to glance into her daughter's room and see an unmade bed. When Tom rang the front doorbell at seven twenty-five, Constance met him, looking as if she had done nothing more strenuous all afternoon than buff her fingernails. She carried a frosty cocktail shaker in one hand and a cigarette in the other. In the kitchen, potatoes sizzled in the deep fat fryer, and the salad stood in the refrigerator, waiting to be dressed.

"You didn't, by any chance, see Allison on your way, did you?"

"No," replied Tom, "I did not. Did you tell her the reason for our little dinner party?"

"No. I merely told her that you were coming at seven-thirty, and that I wanted her home early."

"She is probably doing something interesting and has forgotten the time."

"Probably," agreed Constance. "Let's have a drink first. Then I'll call Kathy Ellsworth. Allison must be at her house. What a day," she sighed, after she had poured two drinks. "Hot, no business worth bothering with, and then home to a dirty house. Nellie didn't do a single thing that she was supposed to have done, and Allison can't do me the favor of being home on time. I'd better call Kathy."

It was an evening Tom would never forget.

"Hello, Kathy?" said Constance into the telephone. "Listen, Kathy, will you please tell Allison to come home. She is over an hour late now."

"But Mrs. MacKenzie," protested Kathy, "Allison's not here."

"Not there?" Constance felt a thin jolt of fear. "Well, where is she then?"

"Gone on a picnic with Norman Page," said Kathy, who had shared all of Allison's confidences and did not mind betraying one of them now that she and Allison were no longer on speaking terms. "She went early today, Mrs. MacKenzie," said Kathy.

"Was Nellie Cross still here when you left this morning, Kathy?"

"Yes, she was, Mrs. MacKenzie. Allison was awfully mean to Nellie this morning. She was mean to everyone. She called Nellie a crazy, insane old woman."

"Thank you, Kathy," said Constance, and slammed the receiver into place with a furious crash. Almost at once, she picked it up again and asked the operator to ring Evelyn Page's number.

"Has that son of yours returned home yet?" she demanded as soon as Evelyn Page answered.

"What business is that of yours?" asked Evelyn quickly, angry at once because of Constance's truculent tone.

232

"The fact that he took my daughter off somewhere makes it my business," said Constance. "He took her off on a picnic only God knows where."

"A picnic!" shrilled Evelyn Page, in much the same tone she would have employed if Constance had told her that Allison and Norman were attending a hashish party. "Norman and Allison on a picnic? Alone?"

"I do not suppose for a minute, Mrs. Page," said Constance with heavy sarcasm, "that your son invited a party to go along when he saw his chance to take my daughter off somewhere alone."

"Alone?" repeated Evelyn, unable to get beyond the terrible vision which this word conjured up for her. "Norman alone with Allison?"

Constance hung up viciously.

"Well?" she demanded, turning to Tom who lounged comfortably in an easy chair and blew smoke toward the ceiling. "Well, what do you think of that?"

"I think that we ought to eat," said Tom calmly. "And that we should put Allison's dinner in the oven to keep warm. Then, I think, we should either play checkers or listen to records until she comes home, at which time we should feed her and act as if nothing out of the ordinary had happened."

"She is off in the woods somewhere with Norman Page," cried Constance.

Tom looked at her levelly. "So what?" he asked.

"So what!" Constance shouted. "So what! How does anyone know what they're doing? I didn't slave to bring Allison up so that she could go off into the woods with boys, that's what! I won't have it!" she cried, stamping her foot and flinging her cigarette into the empty fireplace. "I simply will not stand for it!"

Tom did not raise his voice. "You'll have to stand for it until she comes home, at least," he said. "There is nothing to be done about it now, and if you are as smart as I hope you are, you won't act like this when she comes home. As you told me last night, Allison will be sixteen in the fall. She has to try her wings sometime."

"She isn't going to try her wings in the woods alone with some boy!" declared Constance. "Come on. We'll go look for her in your car."

"Oh, cut it out," said Tom disgustedly. "You are making too much ado about nothing. A parent cannot go chasing after a kid without making both himself and the child ridiculous, especially

233

in the eyes of the child. If there has been an accident, you'll hear about it soon enough. But if nothing has happened, as I am sure it has not, Allison will never forgive you for going out to search for her as if she were six instead of almost sixteen. There is nothing to do but wait."

"Nothing!" cried Constance. "Allison isn't your child, so what do you care what she is doing! You keep your fancy theories about children and sex drives to yourself, Tom Makris. I don't want them applied to Allison!"

Tom looked almost shocked. "What makes you so sure that Allison's being late for dinner has anything to do with sex?" he asked.

"Don't be a fool!" said Constance. "What else would she be doing off with some boy in the woods? What else do males ever have on their minds? They're all alike. The first thing that concerns them is their pants!"

Tom did not answer, but he looked at her closely, speculatively, and Constance turned away from him and lit a cigarette with shaking fingers.

"I'm going to look for Allison," she said. "If you won't drive me, I'll walk."

At that moment, Evelyn Page ran into the living room. She had neither knocked nor rung the bell, but simply burst, unannounced, through the unlatched front door. She was disheveled and wild eyed and looked, Makris thought, truly insane.

"Where is he?" she panted, and Constance's face grew mottled with ugly red patches.

"If you kept better tabs on him," said Constance, "you'd not only know where Norman is, but also where he had taken Allison."

"Norman never took Allison anywhere," protested Evelyn. "If there was any taking done, it was Allison who took Norman."

"Don't give me that," scoffed Constance. "He's a male, isn't he? Don't try to tell me who took whom where! He knew what he was doing. Going off into the woods with a boy would never enter Allison's head."

"Don't you dare say a word against Norman!" cried Evelyn hysterically. "He has no interest in girls. He never has had. If Allison has him interested, it is no one's fault but her own. And yours," she concluded with a look in Tom's direction. "Some women never have enough of one man. And daughters often take after their mothers!"

234

"You bitch!" shouted Constance, and if Tom had not stood up, she would have hurled herself at Evelyn.

Good God! thought Tom. "Cut it out!" he demanded sharply, and Constance stopped moving. She and Evelyn looked at one another with murderous, spiteful eyes but the moment for physical violence had passed. Tom almost smiled. It was the first time he had ever heard Constance utter a word such as the one she had used to describe Evelyn Page.

"Listen, girls," he said, and this time he obviously smiled. "Let's dispense with the verbal hair pulling and sit down. There is nothing to get excited about."

"Nothing!" they cried in unison, and while the echo of their combined exclamation still sounded in the room, Allison Mac-Kenzie walked dreamily through the front door.

"Allison!" cried Constance.

"Where is Norman!" demanded Evelyn.

Allison looked around vaguely. "Hello, Mother," she said. "Norman? He was just outside. He went off down the street."

Evelyn ran to the front door. "Norman!" she screamed. "Norman!"

She kept screaming the boy's name until he had returned to the front of the MacKenzie house.

"Come in here!" she ordered in the same screaming voice.

Norman came into the MacKenzie living room. He looked at Allison fearfully, then at Constance, at Tom, and finally at his mother.

"Hello, Mother," he said.

"Hello, Mother. Hello, Mother!" shouted Constance. "Is that all either of you can say? Where the hell have you been?"

Evelyn Page's lips compressed themselves. "There is no need to use vile language in front of Norman," she said.

"Ha!" exclaimed Constance. "I imagine he knows many more vile things than the word hell!"

Allison's face was paper white. She lowered the picnic hamper to the floor. "What's the matter, Mother?" she asked, and her voice trembled.

Tom could not bear it a moment longer. He went to stand beside the girl. "Your mother has been a little worried," he said. "It's dark now, and she didn't know where you were."

"I know where she was all right," said Constance furiously. "Off in the woods with this animal doing God knows what!"

"For God's sake, Constance," protested Tom, turning to her.

235

"Yes, for God's sake indeed!" said Constance. "Well!" She approached Allison. "Well! I'm waiting for an explanation for your incredibly cheap behavior."

"I haven't been behaving cheaply," protested Allison.

"I suppose you were off in the woods doing nothing but reading books!" exclaimed Constance.

"We didn't read today," offered Norman. "Today we pretended that we were at Walden Pond."

"You keep out of this," said Constance, turning on him. "When I want your explanation, I'll ask for it."

"Norman," said Evelyn, grasping his shoulder and shaking him, "what has that evil, wicked girl done to you?"

"Done to me?" asked Norman, bewildered. "Allison hasn't done anything to me."

"What have you done to her?" asked Constance. "That's the important thing."

"He hasn't done anything!" shouted Evelyn.

"So help me God," said Constance, in a low, terrible voice. "I am going to take Allison to see Matt Swain tomorrow. If she isn't the way she should be, I'll have your son arrested for rape."

Norman's face was as white as Allison's. "I didn't do anything," he stammered. "We didn't do anything, did we, Allison?"

"This has gone far enough," said Tom, in a voice choked with outrage. "Take your boy and go home, Mrs. Page."

"I see that you've taken over Mrs. MacKenzie's house along with everything else that you've taken over," said Evelyn spitefully. "Come along, Norman. We don't want to be in the same room with harlots and the men who amuse themselves with them!"

Constance's teeth chattered with an anger such as she had never known. "Get out of my house!" she screamed, and with a sniff, Evelyn took Norman's hand and departed.

It might have ended there, had Allison not chosen that moment to find her voice and make a remark. As soon as Norman and Evelyn were out the front door, Allison turned on her mother.

"I've never," she said, almost spitting the words, "never, never been so embarrassed in my whole life!"

Before Tom could stop her, Constance had swung her arm and slapped Allison across the face. The girl fell backward onto the sofa, and a woman Tom had never seen stood over her. Constance's whole body was stiff with rage, her face distorted with it, spotted red with it, and her voice shaking with it.

236

"You bastard!" shouted Constance at her daughter, and Tom felt sick with the look that washed over Allison's face.

"Stop it!" he said, but Constance did not hear him. She bent over her white-lipped daughter and screamed at her.

"Just like your father! Sex! Sex! Sex! In that way, you're just like him. It is the only thing like him about you! You don't look like him, or talk like him, but you certainly have acted just like him. It is the only thing of his that belongs to you. Not even his name belongs to you. And after the way I've sweated and slaved to bring you up decently, you go off into the woods and act just like a god-damned MacKenzie. The bastard daughter of the biggest bastard of all!"

Her words hung in the quiet room like fog over water. Her breathing was loudly audible, as was Tom's. But Allison did not seem to be breathing at all. The girl sat as if dead, not even her enormous eyes moved. The three figures in the MacKenzie living room were as still, Tom thought, as the stiff figures in a tableau, and when the quietness was smashed, it was Constance who smashed it. She collapsed in a chair and began to sob, realizing too late what she had done. As if on a signal, the other two figures moved at the sounds of Constance's weeping. Tom's mind began to function again, as he realized in this moment what he had tried unsuccessfully to discover for two years. He looked down at Constance's bowed head and fancied that he could see the pieces of her broken shell lying around her feet. But what a cruel way for a woman to emerge from the falseness of her existence. He turned to look at Allison, and as if she had been waiting for his glance, Allison jumped to her feet and ran toward the stairs which led to the second floor. Tom walked slowly toward the front door, and Constance raised her head to look at him.

"I knew that you'd leave me when you knew the truth," she said, and her breath caught on the edge of her tears.

"It is not the truth that is important," he said. "It was your cruel way of putting it to a child that will take some getting used to in my mind."

He winced when he heard Allison's first scream. He thought that the child's reaction to Constance's words was only now beginning to make itself felt. Allison screamed twice again before his numbed brain realized that these were not screams of pain but of terror. He ran up the stairs three at a time. He found Allison, a terrorized, impossibly white Allison who stood and held herself with her back braced against her bedroom wall and stared with eyes gone black

237

with fear at her open closet door. Tom caught her as she fell, and gazed over the limp figure in his arms at the blue-faced, grotesque body of Nellie Cross hanging from the beam in Allison's closet. He carried Allison to the head of the stairs, and when he heard the voice speaking below, he felt as if he were truly living a nightmare.

"This was the only place Ma was s'posed to come today," Joey Cross was saying to Constance. "Selena sent me to look for her. Ma's been awful forgetful this past coupla weeks. Selena thought maybe Ma'd gone and lost her way again."

♦ 17 ♦

"It was as if there was an evil and insatiable spirit loose in our town," said Seth Buswell later. "An insatiable spirit bent on wreaking havoc and destruction."

Seth said these words once when he was very drunk. As a matter of fact, he pronounced the words as "inshayshabul shpirut," but Dr. Matthew Swain, for once as drunk as Seth on this particular occasion, found no quarrel with the words of his friend.

"Precisely," said Dr. Swain precisely. He prided himself on the fact that his own speech never became slurred when he drank.

Others, who had not been directly concerned with Nellie Cross, or with anything that happened later, were inclined to agree with Seth and the doctor nonetheless. It had indeed, everyone agreed, been a bad time back in the late summer of '39.

Clayton Frazier, walking down Elm Street toward his home on Pine Street on the night of the last Saturday in August, 1939, had seen the sheriff Buck McCracken driving quickly in the opposite direction with Doc Swain sitting next to him. The fact that The Doc was sitting next to Buck in the sheriff's car was an oddity, for The Doc always drove his own car. Clayton wondered what The Doc was doing, sitting next to Buck in Peyton Place's official police car, but as he put it to himself, he didn't intend to worry about it none. He was too tired, and whatever the reason for The Doc and Buck ridin' together was, it'd be all over town by mornin', and he'd hear all about it then.

Clayton Frazier turned at his door for a last look around as was his nightly habit, and it was then that he saw it—a red finger, probing toward the sky on the ridge that was called Marsh Hill.

It was an insidious, evil-looking finger, glimpsed for only a fraction of a second before it disappeared, but Clayton knew that he had seen it. He waited only a moment more before it appeared again, and then Clayton waited no longer.

"Fire!" he shouted, running into the street, for he had no telephone in his house. "Marsh Hill's afire!"

A passing motorist stopped to pick up Clayton, and together the two men sped to the firehouse. In the very few minutes that this consumed, the red finger had touched half of Marsh Hill and set it ablaze.

"Fire!" cried Clayton, and the vast machinery which the state and the town maintained for the fighting of forest fires groaned and moved quickly into operation.

It was the local custom for the sheriff and the doctor to go at once to a forest fire area. The sheriff because he was a volunteer fireman, and Dr. Swain because he always anticipated the possibility of injury to the men. On the walk leading to the MacKenzies' front door, both the doctor and sheriff paused and turned as soon as they heard the wail of the town's two fire engines, to search the hills which surrounded Peyton Place. Marsh Hill was completely ablaze now, and the flames had begun their swift climb up the slope of the next ridge which was known as Windmill Hill.

Buck McCracken sighed. "It'll be bad," he said.

"Yes," said the doctor, and the two men continued on their way to the MacKenzies' front door. They had come in response to Tomas Makris' telephone call.

"Come at once, Matt," Tom had said. "And bring Buck with you. Nellie Cross has hanged herself in a bedroom closet at the MacKenzies'."

"And this ain't gonna be no choir rehearsal, either," said Buck as he rang the doorbell a few minutes later.

At first glance, things did not seem to be as bad as Buck had feared they would be. In the MacKenzie living room, everyone was under a sort of tight control and seemed to remain under it by the force of Tomas Makris' will. Allison MacKenzie lay unconscious on the sofa with Constance perched on the edge, next to Allison's feet. Joey Cross, who had run to fetch his sister as Tom had told him to do, sat in an easy chair at one side of the fireplace while Selena sat in a matching chair at the opposite end of the hearth. Only Tom was standing, and he stood still as if afraid that his control over the group would break if he moved. Matthew Swain went at once to Allison.

"She faint?" asked Buck of Tom. Tom nodded. "Prob'ly be just as well if she stays that way 'til we get done—" Buck hesitated and glanced at Selena and Joey. "With what we have to do," he concluded.

At that moment, Allison opened her eyes. She did not cry out or look about in bewilderment. She merely opened her eyes, looked at her surroundings and then closed her eyes again.

"I'll want her in the hospital for a couple of days," said Dr. Swain to Constance. "I'll send for the ambulance."

After the doctor had telephoned, the three men went upstairs to Allison's room. A few minutes later, after the arrival of two more men from Buck's office, the doctor did what he had to do and Buck and his men prepared to take Nellie Cross's body away. Matthew Swain closed his eyes in an effort to shut out the thumping sounds which came from the hall as Buck and his men attempted to move the now stiff corpse that was Nellie down the narrow stairway of the MacKenzie cottage.

Is there no end? he wondered. First Selena's child, then Lucas and now Nellie. Will it never be over? I have destroyed them all. Even with Lucas alive, he is as good as destroyed. I have made him an exile.

The doctor shuffled wearily down the stairs. Selena, dry eyed, her face carved into the features of self-control, was waiting for him in the hall.

"Doc," she said. "Was it because Ma knew? Is that why she killed herself?"

Dr. Swain looked straight into Selena's eyes. "No," he said evenly. "She had cancer, but she wouldn't let me tell anyone."

Selena, also, looked straight into the doctor's eyes. Without knowing how he knew, Matthew Swain knew that she knew that he lied.

"Thanks, Doc," she said, her voice as even as his. She turned to the living room. "Come on, Joey," she said. "It's time we went home."

Dr. Swain watched the two figures move down the walk and turn into Beech Street.

What will she think about, all during this long, long night? he wondered. What will she say to herself as she lies on her back in her bed and looks at the ceiling?

Dr. Swain shrugged and turned to Tom. "Will you give me a lift to my house in your car?" he asked. "I want to get mine so that I can go over to the hospital."

240

A short while later, as the doctor drove toward the hospital with Constance and Tom following close behind him, he turned to look at the ridge of hills where the fire raged. The entire sky line, to the east of Peyton Place, was a mass of flame. For a moment, the doctor entertained the fanciful thought that perhaps the fire was a symbol. The purging of evil by fire, he thought, and laughed at himself.

Scandalous occurrences, of a public nature that is, do not often take place in small towns. Therefore, although the closets of small-town folk are filled with such a number of skeletons that if all the bony remains of small-town shame were to begin rattling at once they would cause a commotion that could be heard on the moon, people are apt to say that nothing much goes on in towns like Peyton Place. While it is true, no doubt, that the closets of city dwellers are in as sad disorder as those of small-town residents, the difference is that the city dweller is not as apt to be on as intimate terms with the contents of his neighbor's closet as is the inhabitant of a smaller community. The difference between a closet skeleton and a scandal, in a small town, is that the former is examined behind barns by small groups who converse over it in whispers, while the latter is looked upon by everyone, on the main street, and discussed in shouts from rooftops.

In Peyton Place there were three sources of scandal: suicide, murder and the impregnation of an unmarried girl. There had not been a suicide in the town since Old Doc Quimby had put his gun to his head and shot himself many years before. By killing herself, Nellie Cross caused more of a sensation in the town than she had ever done in her life. The town buzzed with talk, and when it came out the day after she killed herself that Nellie had been a baptized Catholic, the talk went from a buzz to a roar. Everyone speculated about what Father O'Brien would say and do, but the time of speculation was short, for the Catholic priest did what he had to do and he did it quickly. He refused to bury Nellie in the consecrated ground of the Catholic cemetery. The Catholic members of the local population nodded to each other and said that Father O'Brien was a man of principle, a man with the courage of his convictions. While it was true that the Church had rules to keep priests in line, Father O'Brien had not shilly-shallyed when it came time to do his duty. He had not hemmed and hawed as some men might have done.

"Certainly not," said Father O'Brien to Selena Cross.

The Protestants smirked. What kind of man of God was it, they

241

asked one another loudly enough for the Catholics to hear, who would refuse to bury the dead? Protestants, especially Congregationalists, were certainly more Christian minded in their attitude than that. Reverend Fitzgerald would never refuse a decent burial to anyone, not even a Catholic.

And for the second time in less than twenty-four hours, Peyton Place was rocked to its foundations.

"Certainly not!" said Reverend Fitzgerald, when Selena asked him to bury her mother.

Now it was the Catholics who smirked, and the Congregationalists who fumed with rage. United we stand, declared the Catholics, divided they fall. In a body, several of the more influential Congregationalists, among them Roberta and Harmon Carter, which surprised everyone, the Page Girls, and every member of the Ladies' Aid Society went to call on their minister. Margaret Fitzgerald, who had escaped from her house through the back door, joined her friends on the sidewalk in front of the parsonage.

"I don't know what ails him," she replied to the many questions put her. "I just don't know what got into him to make him act like this."

Margaret uttered these words in a puzzled and martyred tone, but her mind seethed with hate and outrage. To her friends, Margaret proclaimed her husband overworked, tired, weary, exhausted and ill. In her mind she called him the vilest of traitors, a bastard of a black Irishman, a Pope lover and a weakling.

Reverend Fitzgerald met the members of his congregation, who had more the aspect of an angry mob at this point than of a flock come to consult with its leader, at the door and kept them at bay on the porch.

"What do you want?" he demanded truculently.

Roberta Carter, who had appointed herself as spokesman for the task at hand, said: "We came to ask you about burying Nellie Cross."

"Well? What is it you want to know?" asked the minister in the same fists-cocked-and-ready-for-a-fight tone. "I have made my answer directly to the party concerned."

"You can't do that!" said a voice in the crowd, and in seconds several others had taken up the chant.

"You got to bury Nellie if her kin want you to bury her!"

"It's one of your jobs to bury the dead!"

"What are you? A Catholic?"

Reverend Fitzgerald did not speak as long as the crowd continued to rumble. At last, everyone fell quiet, each feeling that his words must have made an impression, for the minister kept silent so long.

"Has everyone had his say?" shouted Reverend Fitzgerald.

The mob was so still that even Seth Buswell, standing with Tomas Makris at the edge of the street, was surprised. The moment when the minister waited for an answer seemed eternally long, but at last he spoke.

"I've had my say, too," shouted Reverend Fitzgerald. "I am not going to bury a Catholic who has committed suicide. Killing is a sin, and whether a human kills another or himself, it is all the same in the eyes of the Church. I cannot and I will not bury a Catholic who has killed herself."

Although the minister did not preface the word Church with the words, Holy Roman, there was not a man, woman or child in the crowd who did not realize at once that Reverend Fitzgerald had meant to imply them. At once, shouts went up, but they rained against the closed door of the parsonage, for the minister had retired to the inside of his house. The cries ranged from "Papist" to "Money-changer," and they were of such violence, and uttered with such hatred, that even Seth Buswell, one of the most tolerant of all men, was sickened.

Seth, who had joked in his newspaper about the opposing religious factions in his town, who had called them book ends and mountains, turned away from the crowd in disgust.

"Christ, Tom," he said to Makris. "I need a drink."

"We'll get in touch with the proper authorities," Roberta Carter was telling the crowd. "We'll have this man dismissed from our church and replace him with someone who knows his place!"

But there was no organization to channel the crowd's anger. By the time the Congregationalists could have agreed on a committee to contact the proper authorities, the remains of Nellie Cross would have begun to putrefy, and there was not a Protestant in the entire mob who did not realize this fact. In the end, it was a man named Oliver Rank who buried Nellie. He was the preacher for a religion so new to Peyton Place that it was still referred to as "A Sect." The denomination of which Mr. Rank was the head was called The Peyton Place Pentecostal Full Gospel Church. It was referred to by those who did not attend its services as "That Bunch of Holy Rollers Down on Mill Street." Oliver Rank went to Selena Cross and relieved her of all the involved details which are part of the ritual called The Burying of the Dead. Two days after she had hanged herself, Nellie was laid to rest on a knoll of land behind the building which Mr. Rank's congregation used as a church. Not much grass grew on this land, for it was too close to the factories. Smoke and soot hovered over it continually and the ground was hard and bare.

The next day, Francis Joseph Fitzgerald was seen emerging from the rectory of the Catholic church where he had gone to make his confession to Father O'Brien. That same afternoon Fitzgerald presented his resignation to the deacons of the Congregational church, and in the parsonage on Elm Street, Margaret Fitzgerald began to pack her belongings for her return to her father and White River. In White River, so Margaret said, everyone knew exactly where he stood on religious matters.

"Well, that's that," said Seth Buswell to Matthew Swain. "Now perhaps things will return to normal in Peyton Place. It was a bad time while it lasted, but now it is over."

Dr. Swain looked beyond the town to where the fires still burned in the hills.

"No," he said. "It's not over."

◆ 18 ◆

Allison MacKenzie remained in the hospital for five days. For the first two days of these five, she was in what Dr. Swain described to Constance as a state of shock. She answered when spoken to and ate when food was placed before her, but afterward she had no conscious memory of her words or actions.

"She is going to be all right," the doctor told Constance. "She's only escaped, for a little while, into a shadow world. It's a fine place, extremely comfortable and provided by Nature for those exhausted by battle, or terror, or grief."

On the third day, Allison emerged from her vague dreaminess. When Matthew Swain arrived at the hospital, he found her lying face down on the bed, her head hidden in the pillow to muffle the sounds of her weeping.

"Now, Allison," he said, placing his hand gently on the back of her neck, "what seems to be the matter?"

He sat down on the edge of the bed, a habit which Nurse Mary Kelley considered highly unprofessional but one from which many patients seemed to derive comfort.

"Tell me what the trouble is, Allison," he said.

She turned on to her back and covered her swollen, red face with her hands.

"I did it!" she sobbed. "I killed Nellie!"

Her words came in a flood, and the doctor listened silently while Allison wept and lacerated herself and gave way to her agony of guilt and shame. When she had finished, he took both her hands in one of his and bent over to wipe her wet face with his hand-kerchief.

"It is indeed a sorry thing," he said, as he daubed at her cheeks, "when we are not given the opportunity to right our wrongs before it is too late. Unfortunately, this is something which happens to most of us, so you must stop thinking, Allison, that you are alone in what you have done. You wronged your friend Nellie when you said the things you said to her, but you must abandon the idea that you killed her. Nellie was ill, horribly, incurably ill, and that is why she did as she did."

"I knew she was sick," said Allison, and sighed with a sobbing breath. "She told me she had pus in all her veins, and that this sickness was something called the clap. Lucas gave it to her, she told me."

"Nellie had cancer," said the doctor, and Allison had not the shrewd eye of Selena to discern his lie. "There was nothing to be done for her, and she knew it. I don't want you to repeat to any-one else what Nellie told you about her illness. It was only an excuse she made. She didn't want anyone to know what the matter with her really was."

"I won't tell," promised Allison, and turned her face away from the doctor. "The way I feel, I don't care if I never talk to anyone again."

Dr. Swain laughed and turned her face back toward himself. "This is not the end of the world, my dear," he said. "In a little while you will begin to forget."

"I'll never be able to forget," said Allison, and began to cry again.

"Yes, you will," he said softly. "There have been many remarks made about time, and life, and most of these have become bro-mides. What writers call clichés. You'll have to avoid them like the plague if you plan to write, Allison. But, do you know some-thing? When people scoff at the triteness of great remarks, I can't help but think that perhaps it was truth which caused repetition until the words of wisdom became overused and trite, and finally

245

came to be called bromides. 'Time heals all wounds' is so trite that I suppose many people would laugh at my use of it. Still, I know that it is true."

His voice had become so soft that it seemed to Allison as if the doctor had forgotten her presence entirely, that he was not talking to her at all. It was as though he were musing out loud, but only for himself. At Allison's age, it still came as a shock to her that there were people other than herself, who thought thoughts worth musing upon.

"Time heals all wounds," repeated the doctor. "And all life is like the seasons of the year. It is set in a pattern, like time, and each life follows its own pattern, from spring through winter, to spring again."

"I never thought of it like that," Allison interrupted. "I have often thought of life in terms of the seasons, but when winter comes, the life, like the year, is over. I don't understand when you say 'to spring again.'"

Matthew Swain shook himself a little and smiled. "I was thinking," he said, "of the second spring which a man's children bring to his life."

"Oh," said Allison, eager not so much to listen, now, as to express ideas of her own. "Sometimes," she said, "I've thought of each life as a tree. First there are the little green leaves, that's when you're little, and then there are the big green leaves. That is when you are older, the way I am now. Then there is the time of Indian summer and fall, when the leaves are bright and beautiful, and that's when you're really grown and can do all the things you've always wanted to do. Then there are no leaves at all, and it's winter. Then you are dead, and it's over."

"But what about the next spring?" asked the doctor. "It comes, you know. Always. I've done some thinking about trees myself," he admitted with a smile. "Whenever I look at a tree and I take the time to stop and think, I'm always reminded of a poem I read once. I can't remember the name of it, or the name of the man who wrote it, but it had to do with a tree. Somewhere in that poem it says, 'I saw the starry Tree Eternity, Put forth the blossom Time.' Maybe that's a bromide, too. But sometimes it comforts me even more than the one about time healing all wounds, in a different way, of course. Sometimes, it makes me feel pretty good to think of all of us living our lives as blossoms of time on a tree called Eternity."

Allison did not speak again. She closed her eyes and thought

246

of Dr. Swain's poem, and suddenly it did not seem to matter so much that Norman Page had not come to visit her in the hospital, and that her mother had said wretched, cruel things to her.

I saw the starry Tree Eternity, Put forth the blossom Time, thought Allison. She was asleep when Matthew Swain closed the door behind him and stepped out into the corridor.

"How's she look to you, Doc?" asked Nurse Mary Kelley.

"Fine," said the doctor. "She can go home before the week is out."

Mary Kelley looked at him sharply. "You ought to go home yourself," she told him. "You look exhausted. Terrible about Nellie Cross, isn't it?"

"Yes," said the doctor.

Mary Kelley sighed. "And the fires are still going strong. It's been an awful week."

As the doctor was leaving the hospital, he caught a glimpse of himself in the plate glass front doors. The reflection of his tired, lined face looked back at him, and Matthew Swain turned away.

Physician, heal thyself, he was thinking as he walked quickly to his car.

Because she did not leave the hospital until the Friday following the Saturday when Nellie had died, Allison was spared the ugliness of Nellie's funeral and the first sight of the consequences it had left behind in Peyton Place. Norman Page was not as fortunate. He had been forced to attend Nellie's bleak funeral with his mother who went more in protest of Reverend Fitzgerald's behavior than from a desire to see Nellie comfortably buried. Then he had had to listen to Evelyn explain her opinion of the Congregationalist minister, often and in detail, for the rest of the week. Norman's mother, it seemed, could not abide folks who were not "morally and spiritually strong." Whatever that meant, thought Norman resentfully as he sat down on the curbstone opposite the house of Miss Hester Goodale on Depot Street. He could remember the time when he had been terrified of Miss Hester, and Allison had laughed at him and tried to frighten him even more by saying that Miss Hester was a witch. Norman poked at a fat beetle with a stick and wished that he could go to see Allison, but her mother would not allow it any more than his own mother would let him go. He had missed Allison. During the short time when they had been "best friends," they had told each other everything about themselves. Norman had even told her about his father and mother, or at least he had told her everything he knew about them, and he

247

had never told that to anyone else. Allison had not laughed.

"I don't believe that it's true when people say my mother married my father because she thought he had money," Norman had told Allison. "I think they were both lonely. My father's first wife had been dead for a long, long time, and my mother had never been married at all. Of course, he was much older, and folks said he should have known better than to marry a woman as young as my mother, but I can't see that being old makes you any less lonely. The Page Girls are my sisters, did you know that? Not really and truly sisters, but half sisters. Their father and my father were the same man. The Page Girls hated my mother. She told me so herself, but she never understood why. I think that it was because they were jealous. My mother was younger than they when she married my father, and of course, she was beautiful. They hated her and tried to get my father to hate her, too. It was awful, my mother said, the things the Page Girls said about her to my father. They wouldn't even have her in the house, so my father bought my mother her own house. It's the one we live in now. It was worse after I came, my mother said. Then the Page Girls tried to make everyone believe that I wasn't my father's son, and that my mother had been with another man, but my mother never said anything. She said that she would not stoop so low as to argue with anyone like the Page Girls, and that she would not fight over a man like a dog over a bone. Maybe that's why my father went back to live with the Page Girls, instead of staying at our house with us. My mother says that my father was morally and spiritually weak, whatever that means. She never spoke to him again, and I don't remember him hardly at all. When he died, the Page Girls came to tell my mother. They did not call him her husband, or my father, or their father. They said, 'Oakleigh Page is dead,' and my mother said, 'God rest his morally and spiritually weak soul,' and closed the door right in their faces. There was an awful fight about my father's money, after he was gone. But there was nothing the Page Girls could do. My father had left a paper to tell how he wanted his money divided up, and my mother got the most. That's why the Page Girls hate her more than ever now, she said. They still try to say that my mother married my father for his money, but my mother said that she married him because she was lonely, and sometimes lonely people make mistakes. She said that she is glad she did it, though, because she got me. I guess I'm all she did get, except maybe the money."

Allison had not laughed. She had cried, and then she had told

248

him about her own father, who was as handsome as a prince and the kindest, most considerate gentleman in the world.

It was going to be awful without Allison, thought Norman disconsolately. He wouldn't have anyone to talk to at all.

Angrily, he crushed the beetle he had been teasing. It wasn't fair! It wasn't as if he and Allison had done anything terrible, although his mother had tried hard enough to make him admit that they had. When he had confessed to kissing Allison a few times, his mother had wept and her face had turned very red, but she had pressed on anyway, trying to get him to say that he had done something else. Norman's face flamed in the hot summer quiet of Depot Street as he remembered some of his mother's questions. In the end, she had whipped him and made him promise never to see Allison again. Norman had not minded being whipped, but he was very sorry now that he had made the promise about not seeing Allison.

"Norman!"

It was Mrs. Card, who lived in the house next door to Miss Hester's. Norman raised his hand and waved to her.

"Come on over and have a lemonade," called Mrs. Card. "It's so hot!"

Norman stood up and crossed the street. "A lemonade would taste good," he said.

Mrs. Card had a wide-lipped mouth, and when she smiled, all her teeth showed. She smiled at Norman now and said, "Let's go out back. It's cooler there."

Norman followed her through the house and out into the back yard. Mrs. Card was pregnant, eight and a half months gone, Norman had heard his mother say to a friend of hers. She certainly was enormous, however far gone she was, thought Norman, and he wondered why Mr. and Mrs. Card had waited so long to have a baby. They had been married for over ten years, and now Mrs. Card was pregnant for the first time.

"It's about time!" Norman had heard several people tease Mr. Card, but Mr. Card did not mind. He had a reputation for being good natured. "Any time's good enough for me!" he had replied to those who teased him.

But Norman felt sorry for Mrs. Card, especially when she groaned as she lowered herself into the long chair in the back yard. It was the kind of chair which Norman thought of as a "chayze lounge," because "chayze" was French for chair and it was certainly a chair made for "lounging."

"Phew!" said Mrs. Card and laughed. "Will you pour, Normie? I'm bushed."

She always called him Normie and treated him as if he were the same age as she which, he knew, was thirty-five. Rather than pleasing him, her attitude always made him vaguely uncomfortable. He knew that his mother would not have approved of some of the things which Mrs. Card discussed with him. She spoke of pregnancy as if it were something that people discussed all the time, like the weather, and she had gone so far as to hold up her female cat, who was due to kitten anytime, and insist that "Normie" touch the animal's swollen body so that he might "feel all the tiny babies closed up inside." It had made him slightly ill. But he had finally persuaded his mother to allow him to have a kitten, so naturally he was interested in "Clothilde" as Mrs. Card called her cat. Mrs. Card had promised him first choice of Clothilde's babies.

Norman filled a glass with lemonade and handed it to Mrs. Card. He noticed that Mrs. Card had not let herself get sloppy just because she was pregnant. Her fingernails were filed into perfect ovals, and the ovals were covered from tip to cuticle with bright red polish.

"Thank you, Normie," she said. "There are some cookies there on the table. Help yourself."

It was as he was reaching for a cookie that Norman heard a faint "Meow."

"Where's Clothilde?" he asked.

"Fast asleep on my bed, the naughty girl," replied Mrs. Card. "But I just don't have the heart to push her off when she climbs up on the furniture. She's due any time now, and I know exactly how she feels."

Mrs. Card laughed, but even over that sound, Norman heard again the faint "Meow" of a cat. Surreptitiously, so as not to make Mrs. Card suspicious, Norman turned and looked at the tall, thick green hedge which separated the Cards' back yard from that of Miss Hester Goodale. It was Miss Hester's cat that he had heard, and he knew very well that the cat was never anywhere that Miss Hester was not. The back of his neck was suddenly cold.

Why, she's watching us! he thought, shocked. Miss Hester's watching us through the hedge! What else would she be doing out in her yard, if she weren't watching?

But there was nothing for Miss Hester or anyone else to see in the Cards' back yard, and for that reason, Norman began to wonder just exactly what it was that Miss Hester watched. He knew that Miss Hester sat and watched something for the mewing of the tom cat was the regular, soft mewing which a cat makes when he rubs against the legs of someone who is still and pays no attention to him. Norman was not an overly curious child. He had never been plagued by the affliction to which he referred as "nosiness," but now he was assailed by a sudden and terrible longing to know *why* Miss Hester watched, and, more important, *what*, and in the next moment it came to him that this was Friday, and always, on Fridays, at four o'clock, Miss Hester left her house and walked toward town. He gulped his lemonade.

"I have to go, Mrs. Card," he said. "My mother wants me home by four o'clock."

He ran out into the street and to a point far enough beyond Miss Hester's so that Mrs. Card would not be able to see him if she should decide to go into her own house and look out the front windows. Then he sat down on the curbstone to wait for four o'clock.

Norman did not, or perhaps he could not, analyze this strange feeling that was in him. It was a frantic need to see and to know, and of such proportions that he knew he would never have a moment's peace until he had seen and until he knew. It was fortunate for Norman that he realized the dimensions of his desire, for after this one time, he was never able to do so again. Years later, when he fell prey to vague longings of an indeterminate nature, he brushed them away as foolishness. He never again realized the enormity of a desire the way he did on this hot Friday afternoon in 1939.

He *had* to know, thought Norman, and his thinking did not go beyond that point. When it was four o'clock, and he saw Miss Hester walk out of her front gate and move down the street, his heart began to pound with anticipation, as if he were on the brink of a world-shaking discovery. He waited until she was out of sight, and before he could think any more about it and grow frightened, he ran across the street and through Miss Hester's front gate. It was the first time he had ever been beyond the walk in front of her house.

The grass around Miss Hester's house was tall and unkempt. It came nearly to Norman's waist as he made his way to the rear of the cottage. When he had reached a point directly in front of the back porch, he paused to study what he saw. The only article of furniture on Miss Hester's porch was a wicker rocking chair, painted green. It was turned to face the hedge which sep-

251

arated her yard from that of the Cards'. Softly, with his heart thumping, Norman made his way to the porch. He sat down in the rocking chair and looked at the hedge. There was a gap in the green, he saw, of perhaps three inches, and through this gap he could see Mrs. Card sitting in her "chayze lounge." Mrs. Card was reading a bright-jacketed book, and smoking. Occasionally, she reached down and scratched at the monstrous lump which was her abdomen. Norman's heart sank with disappointment.

If this was all, Miss Hester must be as loony as folks said she was. Only a really loony person would sit and watch Mrs. Card read and smoke and scratch herself. There *must* be something more. This couldn't be all.

He sat in Miss Hester's rocking chair for a long time, waiting for something to happen, but nothing did. It was hot, a hot, sleepy afternoon. The "sizzle bugs" in the trees never stopped their scraping, and a smell of smoke lay over everywhere. It came from the forest fires which burned almost three miles away, but which were coming closer and closer to town every minute. It was a sleepy, sleepy smell, the smell of smoke. Norman started. Too late, he heard the echo of the clock on the front of the Citizens' National Bank on Elm Street. It had rung five times, and the sound Norman heard now was the latch on Miss Hester's front gate.

Without a thought, except that he must not be caught by Miss Hester, Norman hurled himself off the porch. There was a space between the under part of the porch and the hedge of perhaps a yard in width, and Norman lay there, flat on his stomach. He prayed that Miss Hester would not walk to the edge of her porch and look down, for she would see him at once, and God only knew what she'd do. You could never tell what a loony person would do, and anyone who spent her time in looking through the gap in a hedge when there was nothing to be seen must be really loony. Norman heard the soft snap of Miss Hester's screen door, and the softer squeak of her rocking chair as she sat down. Evidently, she was not going to come to the edge of the porch and look down. He heard her whispering to her tom as she tied him to a rung of her chair, and he wondered how long she would stay out on the porch. Until dark, probably, and then wouldn't he catch it when he got home. He heard a car pull up in the driveway next door. It was Mr. Card, arriving home. Norman turned his head in minute fractions of an inch to look through the gap in the hedge. Sweat made him itch, and the dry blades of grass on which he lay tickled his nose. He had an hysterical desire to sneeze and just as strong an urge to urinate.

"Hi, baby!" It was Mr. Card, coming around the corner of his house and into his back yard.

Mrs. Card dropped her book and held out her arms to him, and Mr. Card came to sit on the edge of the "chayze lounge" next to his wife.

"Poor darling," said Mrs. Card. "You're all hot and sweaty. Have a lemonade."

Mr. Card unbuttoned his shirt and then took it off. His chest and shoulders gleamed as he reached forward to the small table to pour himself a cool drink.

"Hot," he said, "I guess to hell it is. Hotter than the hinges down at the shop." His throat muscles contracted as he drank, and he set his glass down on the table with a little snick.

"Poor darling," said Mrs. Card, and ran her hand over his bare chest.

Mr. Card turned to her, and even from where he lay, Norman could see the difference in him. His shoulders, the back of his neck, his whole body had stiffened, and Mrs. Card was laughing softly. Mr. Card gave a little cry and buried his face in her neck, and up over Norman's head, Miss Hester's tom meowed softly. The rocking chair in which Miss Hester was sitting did not creak at all. If Norman had not known better, he would have sworn that there was no one on the porch but Miss Hester's tom. Norman could not take his eyes off the Cards. Mr. Card had unbuttoned the straight, full jacket of Mrs. Card's dress, and now he was loosening her skirt. In the next instant, Norman could see the huge, blue-veined growth which was Mrs. Card's abdomen, and he thought he would throw up. But Mr. Card was running his hand lovingly over the growth; he caressed it gently and even bent his head and kissed it. He held Mrs. Card in the circle of his dark, black-haired arms, and Mrs. Card's body looked very, very white. Norman dug his fingernails into the dry grass beneath his hands and clenched his eyes tightly shut. The desire to be gone and away from this place was a physical sickness in him. Why didn't Miss Hester get up and go into the house? Would she never go? Mr. Card's big hands were cupping Mrs. Card's breasts now, and Norman saw that these, too, were swollen and blue veined. How was he going to get away? If he jumped up and tried to run, Miss Hester might chase him. Miss Hester was tall, and presumably long legged, and if she tried, she could probably catch him. What would she do with him then? If she was as loony as folks said she was, there was no telling what she might do. You could never tell about a loony person. Nor could Norman try to crash through the hedge and into the Cards' back yard. What would they think of him, after they had befriended him, given him lemonade and promised to give him first choice of Clothilde's kittens, if they ever found out that he had spied on them. Norman glanced through the gap in the hedge. Mr. Card was on his knees on the ground, his face hidden in Mrs. Card's flesh, and Mrs. Card was lying very still, with her legs spread a little, and a smile on her face that showed her teeth.

I've got to get out! thought Norman desperately. Whether old Miss Hester catches me or not, I've got to get out!

He raised himself slowly to a crouch, so that his eyes came just barely to the edge of the porch. Then he knew that he did not have to worry about Miss Hester chasing him. Miss Hester was sitting rigidly in her chair, her fists clenched on the arms, her eyes staring glazedly through the gap in the hedge, and there was a line of sweat over her top lip. The tom, black, fat and sleek, was tied to a rung of the chair, and he rubbed gently against Miss Hester's legs, uttering his gentle, mewing bid for attention. Norman stood up and ran, and Miss Hester never turned her head to look at him.

"What happened to the front of your shirt, Norman?" asked his mother when he went into his house. "It is all grass stained."

Norman had never lied to his mother. True, there were things that he had occasionally omitted telling her, but he had never actually lied to her.

"I fell," he said. "I was running around in the park, and I fell."

"For Heaven's sake, Norman, how many times do I have to tell you that you must not run in this heat?"

Later, after supper, Evelyn Page discovered that she was out of bread, and she sent Norman to Tuttle's for a loaf. It was in the quickly gone period, between dusk and dark, when Norman passed Miss Hester's house on his way home from the store. He was almost abreast of the house, when he heard the most dreadful sound he had ever heard. It was a fierce caterwauling, the screaming of a terrorized animal fighting for freedom that he heard. Carefully, Norman put his mother's loaf of bread down on the sidewalk next to Miss Hester's front gate, and he walked toward the back of Miss Hester's house. He knew, with a dreadful certainty, what he would find there, but he forced his legs forward.

Miss Hester was sitting in her wicker rocking chair. Her position had not changed since Norman had seen her that afternoon, except that there was a new quality to the stiffness which held her now. Norman watched the tom, who struggled insanely with the rope that held him bound to the stiff, dead thing in the chair. The cat twisted, turned, leaped, but he could not get away from Miss Hester, and all the while that he tried, his throat emitted terrible, shrieking sounds of fear.

"Stop it!" whispered Norman from the porch steps. "Stop it!" But the terrorized animal did not even notice him.

"Stop it! Stop it!" Norman's voice had risen until he was almost shouting, but the tom paid him no attention, and when Norman could stand it no longer, he jumped at the cat and fastened his hands around its throat. The tom fought, digging his claws deep into Norman's hand, but to the boy the scratches were no more than red marks made by a feather dipped in paint. He squeezed and squeezed, and even when he knew that the tom was quite dead, he continued to squeeze, and all the while he was sobbing, "Stop it! Stop it! Stop it!"

It was Mr. Card who found Miss Hester. He and Mrs. Card had spent the evening at a movie, and when he opened the back door to let Clothilde out, after they had returned, the cat headed straight for the hedge and Miss Hester's back yard.

"Jesus! What a sight that was!" said Mr. Card later. "There was Miss Hester, sitting straight as a stick in that rocking chair, dead as a doornail. And that tom, with his neck broken, still tied to a rung. What I can't figure is, how come that tom didn't scratch when she choked him? There wasn't a mark on her!"

"Now perhaps it will be over," sighed Seth Buswell as he put a drink together for his tired friend Matthew Swain.

"They say that deaths come in threes," said the doctor, smiling to keep the seriousness from his words.

"Superstitious drivel," declared Seth angrily, angry because he was afraid that his friend was right. "It's been a bad time, but it's over now."

Matthew Swain shrugged, and sipped his drink.

In the Page house, Evelyn was holding Norman's head as he stood over the toilet and vomited.

"I got into a fight," he said, when she asked him about the deep scratches on his arms and hands.

255

"Your little tummy is all upset, dear," she said gently. "I'll give you an enema and put you to bed."

"Yes," gasped Norman. "Yes, please," and in his head everything kept running together. Allison, and the Cards, and Miss Hester and the tom.

On the hills beyond Peyton Place, the fires raged, unchecked and uncontrollable.

◆ 19 ◆

Everything that men know how to do for the fighting of forest fires had been done in Peyton Place by the first week in September. Backfires had been made and had proved useless, for the wooded hills blazed in too many places at once. Weary men, in twenty-four-hour shifts, lined up on the tarred roads which cut through the hills and waited patiently, their backs bent under the filled Indian pumps they carried, for the blaze to reach their particular position. Other, more experienced, men fought on the dirt roads where they were enclosed on both sides by the tall, flaming trees, and everywhere the fight was futile, for the strength was all on one side. The fires which encircled Peyton Place in the late summer of 1939 were uncontrollable for the reasons a forest fire is always uncontrollable. A combination of too much fire in too large an area with too few men and too little equipment, plus just enough wind to fan and spread flame and too little, much too little, water. The only stream of any size which was not completely dried up by the drought of '39 was the Connecticut River.

"When the fire reaches the river—" the men said, and then stopped. If the fire progressed far enough to the west, it would eventually reach the river and be stopped, but there was no river to the east to compare in size and width with the Connecticut.

"If it would rain—" and there was the answer which everyone knew to be the only answer. As the fire crept swiftly to within a mile of Peyton Place, everyone looked up at the cloudless September sky and said, "If it would rain—"

The shops and business of the town were either closed altogether or opened for two hours a day whenever the men could remain away from the fire area for that long. The Cumberland Mills were closed completely, and it was not only the lack of textile production which caused Leslie Harrington to curse senselessly and pace his floor. It was the fact that in northern New England there was a gentlemen's agreement which decreed that an employer would continue to pay his help as if they were working at their regular jobs while they were out fighting a fire. It was the prohibitive cost of the fire which enraged Leslie, plus the fact that there seemed to be nothing he could do to rectify the situation. No matter how he cursed and raged, the fire would not stop. By the end of the first week in September, Leslie was the only able-bodied man in town who had not been out into the hills.

"The fire is costing me plenty," he said. "I've paid a hundred times over for the right to sit back and watch this show."

Also, by the time the Labor Day week end rolled around, he had other things to do. Besides the Cumberland Mills, Leslie Harrington was the owner of a small carnival. There was a rather tired town joke concerning Leslie's carnival. The mill hands said that Leslie kept them working all summer in order to be able to take their money away from them with the penny-pitch and wheel of fortune games which were the high spots of his carnival. Leslie had come into possession of the carnival after having taken over the mortgage on it from the Citizens' National Bank. The bank had been ready to foreclose on the carnival's original owner, a true "carny" by the name of Jesse Witcher, who liked his whisky and his women, as he put it, a helluva lot more than he enjoyed paying his bills. This attitude was not one to arouse sympathy in the hearts of bankers, especially in Peyton Place where everyone remembered the Witchers. Feast or famine, that was the Witchers. They had always been like that. The bank had been on the verge of sending Buck McCracken to serve a foreclosure notice on Jesse Witcher when Leslie Harrington had intervened.

"For God's sake, Leslie, have you gone off your rocker?" Charles Partridge had asked. "A carnival! What for? You'll get stuck with it. Witcher won't pay you any more than he paid the bank."

"I know it," Leslie had admitted.

"Well, then. Leave it alone, Leslie. What in hell would you do with a carnival? It's no kind of investment."

"Don't I have the right to buy something to enjoy myself with, same as anybody else?" Leslie had shouted, angry at having to explain a senseless business venture to his lawyer who had always regarded him as practical and hardheaded. "God damn it, Charlie, I got a right to have something just for the hell of it, don't I? With some men it's electric trains or postage stamps. With me it's carnivals."

Leslie had jutted out his chin at a belligerent angle, daring Partridge to laugh or criticize, but Partridge, a pacifist, did neither. He drew up the papers, and not too much later he instigated the foreclosure proceedings which made Leslie the sole owner of a carnival heretofore known as "The Show of 1000 Laffs." Jesse Witcher was well pleased. He could still run his beloved carnival, as Leslie's manager, without any of the worries which besieged an owner.

The Show, as Leslie liked to refer to it casually, had played Peyton Place on every Labor Day since Leslie had become owner six years before, a fact which had shocked Witcher at first, and shocked him still.

"This ain't no place to play over Labor Day," complained Witcher. "Labor Day's big. A long week end. We oughta be down around Manchester or someplace like that where we'd get a crowd. There ain't enough people around here to make a decent-sized crowd."

"The mills are closed over Labor Day," said Leslie. "So I might just as well be making a few nickels one way as another."

"But you could be making dollars instead of nickels someplace else," protested Witcher.

"I like to see money being made," Leslie said, and Witcher shrugged and set up his rides and games and soft drink stands on a large empty field, also owned by Leslie Harrington, near the mills.

Witcher had not protested again after his first year as manager of The Show, but when he arrived in Peyton Place on the Friday before Labor Day, 1939, and saw the empty streets, the closed shops and the fires, he went at once to Leslie Harrington.

"This time," he said, "it ain't only a question of making a few nickels. It's a question of losing money. There ain't nothing sadder, nor more expensive, in this world than a carnival with no people. And there won't be no people in Peyton Place this week end."

"They'll come," said Leslie. "Set it up."

Witcher rubbed at eyes made sore by the smoke that seemed to be everywhere. It hung suspended over the empty field where Witcher coughed out orders for the unloading of the vans. He looked through the smoky haze to where the fires burned.

"It's like dancing at somebody's funeral," he grumbled.

Surprisingly enough, people did turn out. It might have seemed like dancing at a funeral to Witcher, but to the fire-tired, smoke-weary residents of Peyton Place the carnival seemed like a breather,

258

an oasis of fun in the midst of extremely uncomical surroundings. Allison MacKenzie was there because Dr. Swain had said that she should get out of her room and into a crowd. She was still pale and tired looking, but she was there, flanked by Tomas Makris and Constance. Rodney Harrington was there with a bright-lipped girl from White River who looked up at him as if she thought all the wonderful things that Rodney wanted her to think. Kathy Ellsworth was there with her crew-cut boy friend Lewis Welles. There were some in Peyton Place who did not take to Lewis. He was an open-faced boy who wore a constant grin. It was Lewis' ambition to become the top salesman in the drug concern at White River where he now worked as a stock boy, and there were some who said that Lewis should not have a hard time in realizing his hopes. They referred, of course, to his easy smile, his penchant for practical jokes and his sorry habit of greeting people with a resounding slap across the shoulders. Where others found him insincere and loud, Kathy thought him diplomatic, gay and wonderful.

On the evening of Labor Day, the empty field near the mills was no longer empty. In fact, everybody in town was there except Norman Page. It was a shoving, laughing, raucous crowd, a crowd that made the noises of gaiety in a fiercely determined way which Seth Buswell found peculiarly terrible.

"They're goin' to have a good time or die tryin'," he told Tom grimly.

From the ground, it was impossible to see the top seats on the Ferris wheel. Only the bright lights which decorated the sides of the wheel were visible through the smoky haze, so that it looked as though the people in the seats were disappearing into another world as the wheel spun slowly. For some reason, Allison thought of a play she had read called *Outward Bound*, and she shivered, but the wheel was getting a heavy play.

"Take a ride on the Ferris wheel," barked Witcher. "Get up there and breathe air again. No smoke when you get to the top in this gigantic wheel of pleasure."

The people laughed shrilly and pushed and did not believe him, but they rode the Ferris wheel. Children rubbed red-rimmed eyes and cried for rides on the carousel through dry, itching throats, and older children screamed on the dodgem and on the whip, while grownups were taken, retching, from the loop-the-loop. Allison shivered more violently than before as she absorbed the sights and sounds all around her, and Tom said: "We had better take you home."

259

"Oh, don't!" cried Kathy Ellsworth, who had had a tearful reunion with her friend Allison the week before. Kathy clung to Lewis Welles's hand and said, "Oh, don't take her home! Come with us, Allison. We haven't gone to the fun house yet. Come on!"

"The wind!" yelled someone in the crowd. "The wind's comin' up strong. It's gonna rain!"

The crowd screamed with laughter, and Seth Buswell tipped his head back. Although he could not see the sky, he could feel a new stirring in the air.

"Maybe," he said.

"Come on, Allison. We haven't gone to the fun house yet. Come with Lew and me!"

Someone carrying a fat cone of cotton candy pushed past Allison, and a shred of the fuzzy stuff brushed against her cheek. Once when she was a child playing hide and go seek she had run into a barn and straight into a cobweb. It had stuck to her face stickily, just like cotton candy. Allison felt as if she were in a nightmare and trying to vomit, but unable to because she could not wake.

"Soft drinks right here!"

"Ride the Ferris wheel and breathe air again!"

"Step right up, gentlemen, step right up. Three balls for a quarter."

"Win a beautiful, genuwine French doll for your lady, mister. Try your luck."

"Ice cream. Peanuts. Popcorn. Cotton candy."

"The wheel of fortune goes round and round, and where she stops nobody knows!"

And over it all, the music, playing in the peculiar up-and-down, and-up-and-down-and-around rhythm of the carousel. Allison grabbed at Kathy's free hand as if she were drowning.

"Come with us, Allison. Come with us!"

"Connie, I don't think she feels well."

Allison ran with Kathy and Lewis, and Tom's voice calling her disappeared like a shadow in a thunderstorm.

The fun house of "The Show of 1000 Laffs" was the regulation building of horrors common to all carnivals. Parents who knew from experience that their young would be carried from it, screaming, if allowed to enter, avoided it, but it was doing a big business with the youngsters of high school age and older. The fun house, it was said, was guaranteed to have a fellow's girl clinging to him within seconds, or your money back. Jesse Witcher was justly proud of his fun house. It had helped to bankrupt him. It had everything—evil faces which jumped up in front of the patrons at unexpected moments, distorting mirrors, slanted floors, intricate mazes of dimly lit passages, and a laugh-getting, blush-producing wind machine. Witcher loved the fun house. Usually he presided over it himself, and always he saw to it personally that the machinery to operate his horribly funny effects was well oiled and in perfect running order.

"There's nothing falls flatter," he had told Leslie Harrington, "than a scary effect that happens a second too late, or the bat of an eyelash too soon."

But this Labor Day week end had been a hectic one. The local labor on which Jesse Witcher depended to help with the setting up of the carnival had been nonexistent this year. All the men and boys old enough and strong enough to be of any use were off fighting the fire. Witcher had been everywhere, "like a goddamned mosquito," as he later explained to Leslie, trying to get the carnival going. He had seen to it that the fun house was erected, and the machinery in operation. Then he had entrusted the final details to a performer who threw knives at his mistress in the show, and to a thin-shouldered boy of sixteen from White River, whose ambition it was to be a mechanic with a traveling carnival. Witcher had not regretted hiring the boy. The fun house was drawing a crowd, and from the shrieks that came from the exit, where the wind grate was, the boy must certainly be pushing the right buttons at the right time. At four o'clock, Witcher had set out to take a look at the fun house, to make sure that everything was as it should be. He had not had a chance to check it over all week end, but as he was walking toward it, someone had called to him and he had gone to help fix the wheel of fortune which was Leslie Harrington's favorite, and with which something had gone momentarily wrong. As he later explained, the crowd had begun to come then, and he had not had a chance to check the fun house at all.

It was after nine o'clock in the evening when Allison, dragged along by Kathy and Lewis, passed through the entrance of the fun house. The three made their way, single file, with Lewis leading them through the dim, purple-lighted maze of corridors. Kathy giggled nervously and clung to the back of Lewis' shirt, while Allison, feeling the sweat on her that all small, tight places brought, clung to the back of the waistband on Kathy's skirt. It was crowded and hot in the narrow passages, and when they reached the room full of distorting mirrors, Kathy stretched and jumped happily.

261

"Look at me!" she cried, as she ran from one mirror to the next. "I'm two feet tall and big as a barn!"

"Look at me! I'm a bean pole. Look! I've got a triangle-shaped head!"

"Oh, look! This must be the machinery that run everything. Look at the way all those wheels go round and round. Oh! Look at that huge fan. It must be what makes the wind blow at the exit!"

The machinery was on the ground, under the floor, but visible through a square cut in the floor boards. The square was large enough to allow a man to get down to work on the machinery once the fun house had been erected, and it was in a far corner of the room which housed the distorting mirrors. There was nothing near the square opening, and perhaps Kathy would never have noticed it if she had not been dancing around delightedly in front of the tall, wavy series of distorting mirrors. Afterward, neither Lewis nor Allison could say what it had been that attracted Kathy to the far corner of the room. It could not have been a sound from the machinery, as Jesse Witcher later testified, for the machinery was well oiled, in good condition and fairly silent. Besides, he said, the fun house was made of plywood, certainly not soundproofed, and the noise of the carnival outside would penetrate into the building to the point where the sound of well-oiled machinery would never be heard. In addition to that, the wind had come up and it had begun to thunder, so Kathy could not have been attracted to the square opening by a sound. She was plain nosy and careless, and that was what had caused the accident. Oh, yes, it was true that the square opening should have been covered. It usually was. If one looked, one could see the holes where the hinges that held the cover had been made. But after all, Witcher was only one man, and he couldn't be everywhere at once seeing that everything was as it should be. Now could he? The kid should never have gone near the opening. She had had no business there. She was in a fun house, wasn't she? She should have been busy having fun, and not gone poking her nose in where it didn't belong.

"Oh, look!" cried Kathy. "See how beautifully all the wheels go around together!"

"Oh, look, Lewis! Look, Allison!" said Kathy, and leaned forward for a closer look and fell down into the machinery.

The other young people began to move hastily out of the room, for they had been well taught the danger which could result from being called upon as witnesses. Lewis and Allison began to laugh in the way that people laugh at a drunk who steps happily in front of a moving truck, or at an old man who slips on the ice. Lewis squatted down on his heels and tried to reach Kathy's hand, but Kathy's hand was on the end of an arm no longer attached to her body. Allison laughed and laughed as she made her way out of the fun house. She shrieked with laughter when the wind machine blew her skirts up over her head, and she was still laughing when Tom came running to her. She clenched the front of his shirt and laughed until she cried.

"Kathy fell into the hole in the floor!" she screamed, laughing so hard that she could not get her breath. "Kathy fell and her arm came off, just like a toy doll."

The wind was blowing much harder now. It blew the smoke in gusts and filled Tom's eyes with sand. The skirts of the women who hurried past him, eager to get home before the rain started, ballooned grotesquely in the wind, so that they all looked fat and misshapen.

"Seth!" cried Tom into the wind, and when the newspaper editor did not hear him but continued to move away, Tom cursed the luck which had separated him from Constance in the crowd. He left Allison propped against the side of the fun house, for she was laughing so hard she could scarcely stand, while he went to tell the boy from White River who wanted to be a mechanic to shut off the machinery.

"But I don't know how," protested the boy, and Tom left him standing openmouthed, thinking that here was a big, black drunk, while he ran against the crowd to find Witcher.

Up in the hills, the fire fighters recoiled with forearms against foreheads as the first drops of rain fell. Steam rose around them as they turned and made their way toward Peyton Place.

"It's rainin'," they told one another unnecessarily.

BOOK THREE

◆ I ◆

The nearest that Kenny Stearns could ever come to describing Indian summer in northern New England was to say that it was "a pretty time." It was also, for Kenny, a busy one. There was always a multitude of last-minute chores to be done before winter set in; lawns to be mowed for the last time, mowers to be oiled and stored, leaves to be burned and hedges in need of one last clipping. But to Kenny Stearns, Indian summer offered a bonus other than her beauty and the time of the last warm spell. During this short time of sun and color before winter, Kenny was always aglow with the satisfaction of a season's work well done. As he walked down Elm Street on a Friday afternoon late in October, 1943, Kenny glanced at all the lawns and shrubs which lined the main thoroughfare and for which he had cared during the previous spring and summer. He seemed to notice every blade of grass and every twig and branch, and he spoke to all of them as he might have done to pretty, well-groomed children.

"Hello there, Congregational lawn. You look mighty fine today," said Kenny, smiling fondly.

"Afternoon, little green hedge. Need a haircut, dontcha? I'll see what I can do for you tomorrow mornin'."

The old men who roosted on benches in front of the courthouse, taking advantage of the last warm sunshine of the year, opened drowsy eyes to watch Kenny.

"There goes Kenny Stearns," said one old man, and took a gold watch from his pocket. "Headin' for the schools. Must be gettin' on for three o'clock."

"Lookit 'im, noddin' and grinnin' and talkin' to that hedge. He ain't right in the head. Never was."

"I wouldn't say that," said Clayton Frazier, who was much older and feebler now, but who still loved to argue. "Kenny was always all right 'til his accident. He's still all right. Mebbe drinks a little more, but he ain't the only one that drinks in this town."

"Accident, my arse! That wa'nt no accident when Kenny got his

264

foot cut up. It was the time him and all them fellers went down in his cellar and stayed all winter, and had that brawl and cut each other up with knives. That's how Kenny got that bad foot."

" 'Twa'nt all winter," declared Clayton, imperturbably. " 'Twa'nt more'n five, six weeks that them fellers stayed down there in Kenny's cellar. Anyway, there wa'nt no drunken brawl. Kenny fell down the stairs while he was holdin' his ax and cut himself. That was what happened."

"That's *his* story. I heard different. Don't make no difference what happened anyway. It didn't cure Kenny from drinkin'. I don't guess he's drawed a sober breath in over ten years. No wonder his wife does like she does."

"Ginny was never no good," said Clayton, and tipped his old felt hat down over his eyes. "Never. That's what set Kenny to drinkin' in the first place."

"Mebbe so. But you can't blame her none for not changin' her ways if he won't change his."

"Ginny'd have some changin' to do, I reckon," said Clayton Frazier wanting and getting, as he usually did, the last word. "She was born doin' what she does. Kenny, at least, was born sober."

None of the men could think of a suitable rejoinder for this remark, so they turned silently and watched Kenny Stearns turn into Maple Street and walk out of sight. It did not occur to any of them that they had been watching Kenny Stearns turn into Maple Street and walk out of sight every day for years.

"Hello, double-headed Quimbys," said Kenny to a row of purple asters. "No, that ain't right. Hold on a minute."

Kenny stood for a long moment in front of a large white house on Maple Street which he had helped to paint the previous spring. He scratched at the back of his lined, continually sunburned neck. The window shades in the white house were pulled neatly and evenly to a point halfway between the top and the bottom, and it was this that reminded Kenny. He turned toward the border of asters and bowed formally.

" 'Scuse me," he said. "Hello, double-headed Carters. I beg your pardon." He stood still for a moment and looked down at the flowers, a thoughtful frown on his face. "Don't know but as I'd *rather* be called Quimby, even by mistake," he said at last.

Happy at having made what he considered a gross insult to Roberta and Harmon Carter, Kenny proceeded on his way toward the Peyton Place schools. At the hedge which separated the grade school from the first house on Maple Street, Kenny paused and looked up toward the belfry. There she was! Gleamin' and winkin' at him to beat the band in the October sunlight.

"Hello, beautiful!" called Kenny, addressing his school bell. "I'll be right with you!"

The polished bell gleamed and winked encouragingly as Kenny headed toward the front doors of the grade school. He walked with an eagerness now which he never had when approaching anything other than his bell.

And didn't that bell know it? thought Kenny. She certainly did. Look at the way she'd turned almost coal black from a lack of loving care 'way back when he'd had his accident. But how she had shone when he returned!

"Thought I was dead that time, didn'tcha, beautiful?" called Kenny.

There was lots of folks who'd given him up for dead that time, thought Kenny. Even old Doc Swain. Oh, they all denied it afterward, but Kenny could remember the way they'd talked. He could remember like it was yesterday, the way The Doc'd leaned over him.

"He's a dead one if I ever saw one," The Doc had said, and Kenny had answered, "Like hell I am!" but no one seemed to be listening to him.

They had rolled him onto a sort of bed, carried by a coupla big guys, and lugged him off to the hospital, Kenny remembered. All them nurses thought he was dead, too, but when Kenny hollered different, they didn't listen to him any more than The Doc had. Ginny had thought he was dead, or dying anyway.

"Is he dead, Doc?" Kenny could hear her asking it plain as day.

"No, you bitch!" he had shouted, but she hadn't heard him.

He had told her about it afterward. "Thought I was dead, didn'tcha? Well, I ain't and wa'nt. It takes more than a little ax cut on the foot to kill me!"

"By Jesus, it does!" roared Kenny, addressing his school bell in loud, carrying tones. "Takes more'n a goddamn little cut to kill this feller!"

Kenny's voice carried easily through the open windows of the classroom where Miss Elsie Thornton presided over the eighth grade. Before the echo of Kenny's voice had died, Miss Thornton had rapped sharply on the edge of her desk in an attempt to forestall the disorder which Kenny's remarks always caused.

He is drunk again, thought Miss Thornton wearily. Something will have to be done about Kenny. I should bring it up before the

266

school board. One of these days, he'll fall out of the belfry, or go head first down a flight of stairs, and that will be the end of Kenny. A sorry end for a wasted life.

Later, Miss Thornton was to remember her thought of this particular Friday afternoon, but at the moment she wasted no more time on it. She rapped again on the edge of her desk, and asked her stock question about people who wished to spend the thirty minutes after dismissal with her. Finally, the room quieted, but as each day passed, it was becoming increasingly difficult for Miss Thornton to retain her iron hand over her students. Most of the time, she could blame this state of affairs on the people whom the bright young teachers out of college told her to blame; namely, the parents of the children whom she taught. Misbehavior in class, these bright young teachers told her, was a direct reflection on a child's home environment. In the last four or five years, Miss Thornton had learned to use a word which had never been particularly popular when she had been at Smith College. The word was "complex." Every child had at least one, said the bright young teachers, and it was whichever complex a particular child had which caused him to misbehave in class. Much of the time, Miss Thornton could go along with all these new theories, but sometimes, especially when she was very tired as she always was on Friday afternoons, she remembered the days when complex or no complex, she had been able to force a child to behave while in the confines of her classroom. On afternoons like these, Miss Thornton realized that she was getting old and that she was very, very tired indeed.

"You may read for the rest of the period, Joey," she said, after a glance at her watch had shown her that it was ten minutes before three.

Joey Cross stood up and began to read aloud from *The Adventures of Tom Sawyer*. He read well, enunciating his words clearly, but with that singular lack of expression so often found in boys of grade school age who are called upon to read to a class of their contemporaries. Miss Thornton half closed her eyes, and the only part of her mind which was alert to Joey's voice was the part which tells an experienced teacher when a word has been brutally mispronounced.

Now there, thought Miss Thornton, is a child who should have every complex in the book. A drunken beast for a father, who had run off and abandoned him, a suicide for a mother, and never a morsel of decent food or an adequate amount of shelter or clothing

267

until after he was nine years old. Yet, he seems to be the victim of fewer complexes after making the adjustment to a decent standard of living than most children are who are born knowing nothing different from what Joey has known for only four years. He is the smartest child in the room, and he misbehaves less than most, and fights and swears no more than the others outside. Complexes? Humph. I'm getting old, that's all. I just wish that they were all as smart and as easy to handle as Joey Cross.

Joey did not know it, nor did any of his classmates, but he was Miss Thornton's pet. It was Joey's image which crossed her mind whenever she grew discouraged and dreamed of retirement. *If I can teach one thing to one child.* Whenever she thought her most secret, hopeful thought, it was always Joey whom she saw. It was true that Miss Thornton had a different pet every year. It had not been Joey last year, nor would it be Joey a year hence, but for the short time that he was in the eighth grade, it was on him that Miss Thornton fastened her current hopes of fulfillment.

It had been a bad time for Selena and Joey Cross, back in '39. After Nellie had killed herself, the Cross children had found themselves alone in the world, with Selena barely turned sixteen, and Joey a thin, undernourished boy of nine. No sooner was Nellie decently buried than someone—and there were plenty of people in Peyton Place who said that it was Roberta and Harmon Carter—had notified the state welfare department about Selena and Joey. In due time, a social worker had appeared at the door of the Cross shack. Selena and Joey had been out in the sheep pen at the time, and since long black cars with the state seal emblazoned on the front doors, and trim suited, short-haired women who carried brief cases were a rarity indeed in Peyton Place, Selena had become suspicious at once. As soon as the social worker had stepped through the unlocked front door of the shack, Selena had grabbed Joey by the hand and fled to Constance MacKenzie. Constance, in deadly fear lest she be discovered, had hidden the Cross children in the cellar of her house while she contacted Seth Buswell and Charles Partridge. It had been Seth who had finally located the eldest of Lucas Cross's children, Selena's stepbrother Paul.

Paul Cross had arrived in town driving his own car and accompanied by his wife, whom he had met and married in the northern part of the state. Her name was Gladys, and Gladys had made all the difference in the world. There were plenty of people in Peyton Place ready and eager to criticize Paul's wife, for Gladys was a busty blonde with hair so obviously dyed that even small children noticed and commented upon it. There were some who said that Gladys had been one of the loose women who hung around up at Woodsville, ready to accommodate lumberjacks with money to spend, but all Miss Thornton knew of her was what Joey had told her, and what she had learned from Seth Buswell and Matthew Swain.

Gladys, according to Matt Swain, had entered the Cross shack, taken one look at her surroundings and said: "Christ, what a shit house this is!"

The very next day, the word went around town that Paul Cross was home to stay. He obtained a good job in one of the sawmills almost at once, and within two weeks there was running water at the Cross shack. Within a year, it was no longer a shack but a house, complete with plumbing and a bedroom for everyone. The only remnant of the Cross property as it had been was the old sheep pen which Lucas had built and which now housed the sheep which Joey raised. It was Joey's greatest source of pride that one of his ewes had taken three blue ribbons at three county fairs all within one year.

"Paul's crazy to let his wife put all that money into a place that ain't even his," said a few people in the town. "That house and land still belongs to Lucas Cross."

"Lucas must be dead," said the majority of Peyton Place. "If he weren't, he'd have been back before now."

Paul Cross, whom no one had ever suspected of having such a noble emotion as family love, had confounded the town by returning home to provide for his half brother and stepsister. In December, 1941, on the day after Pearl Harbor, he confounded everyone still further by quitting his job and enlisting in the Army.

"Now, we'll see," said Peyton Place, with both eyes fixed on Gladys. "It won't be long before she runs off and leaves the Cross kids to shift for themselves."

But Gladys, newly tight lipped, but as busty and brassy blond as ever, remained in Peyton Place until after Selena was graduated from high school. Two weeks afterward, when Selena went to work at the Thrifty Corner Apparel Shoppe as the store's manager, Gladys left town and went to Texas to join Paul.

Complexes? Humph, thought Miss Thornton as she looked at Joey who would run home after school to feed his sheep and to start supper for his sister. Show me a boy who is as loyal and devoted to his own mother as my Joey is to his sister.

Above her head, the first joyous note of Kenny's bell sounded, and the classroom began to buzz.

"Quiet!" ordered Miss Thornton. "You may stop reading, Joey. All of you will remain quiet until I dismiss you."

There was a sullen murmuring from the back of the room which she ignored.

"Are your desks cleared?"

"Yes, Miss Thornton."

"You may stand."

"You may stand," mimicked a voice from the rear.

"Dismissed!" said Miss Thornton.

The thunderous exodus began, and all but one boy made it out the door.

"Everett," said Miss Thornton. "Sit down, Everett. You may spend the next thirty minutes with me."

There, she thought, I'm not so old after all, when I can still snap them around like that.

It did not occur to her that a few years ago, no child would have dared to mimic her from the back of the room. But if it had come to her mind, Miss Thornton could have found a place to put the blame.

"The war," she could have said, as people all over the world were saying in the autumn of 1943. "Nothing is the same since the war started."

◆ **2** ◆

Constance Makris closed the oven door of her stove and straightened up with a startled squeak. Her husband had come up quietly behind her and encircled her with his arms. He tightened his hold on her as she started and at once she relaxed against him.

"Don't sneak up on me like that," she said, laughing.

"I can't help it," he said with his lips against the nape of her neck. "When you bend over the way you do when you look into the oven my lust overpowers me. It's the sight of your rear end that does it."

"For an old man of forty-one you have remarkably young ideas," she said, moving her head sensuously as he kissed her neck.

He crossed his arms in front of her and cupped her breasts with his hands. "And you," he said softly, breathing in her ear, "have a remarkably young body for a lady of thirty-nine."

"Stop it," she said. "My cake is going to burn if you don't stop it at once and let me go."

"Cake," he said, in a derogatory whisper. "Who wants cake?"

"No one," she said and turned to face him, pressing close to him and raising her lips.

He kissed her in a way he had, first softly and rather seekingly, then hard, then softly again.

"Four years," he said huskily, "and you still make me feel as if I were about to have you for the first time."

"The cake," she said, "is definitely going to burn. I smell it."

"Do you know that you have the breasts of a virgin?" he asked. "I can't understand it. You should have some of the sexy sag of maturity that the kid stuff never has. Yet here you are, all pointed and tip tilted, as the detective always says just before he seduces the beautiful young suspect in a murder mystery."

"And do you know that you have no tact at all?" she asked. "And no sense of time fitness? Breasts are not a subject to be discussed just before dinner."

Tom grinned and leaned the top part of his body away from her to look down into her face. "What shall we discuss, then?" he asked, moving his hips and thighs slowly against hers.

"Cake," she said with mock severity. "That's what. Also fish, which comes first this evening."

"Fish!" said Tom and lowered his arms.

"Yes, fish. It's good for you," said Constance.

"I'll go make us a drink," he said sorrowfully. "If I have to eat fish I must be well fortified in advance."

"Light me a cigarette while you're at it, will you?" called Constance as he disappeared into the living room. "The new *McCall's* came today. It has a story by Allison in it."

"Where?"

"Right there on the end table."

Tom came back into the kitchen carrying two glasses, two cigarettes and a magazine. He handed Constance her drink and one of the cigarettes and then sat down at the kitchen table, sipping and leafing through the magazine.

"Here it is," he said. "This is some title. 'Watch Out, Girl At Work.' "

"It's all about a girl who works in an advertising agency in New York," explained Constance. "She is a career girl who wants her boss's job. This boss of hers is young and handsome and the girl can't help herself. She falls in love with him. In the end she marries him, after deciding that she loves him more than her career."

"Good God," said Tom and closed the magazine. "I wonder if she has done anything with the novel she was thinking of doing?"

"I don't know. Hand me a pot holder, will you please?" Constance removed a cake from the oven. "Maybe she gave up the idea of writing a novel. The magazines pay very well, you know. And she is still so young. I always thought that novelists had to be middle aged."

"Not if they have as much talent as Allison. On the other hand, I've always understood that authors have to have some experience with life before they can sit down and write about it successfully." Tom chuckled. "I wonder if the editor who bought Allison's first short story is still in the business. Also, I wonder if he has any idea of the ramifications of his act."

Constance laughed. "That was some story. 'Lisa's Cat.' I wonder where Allison ever got the idea for it."

"Straight out of Somerset Maugham," said Tom. "Allison really believed that she had burst into the top literary circles when that story won the prize."

"Well, it certainly finished making up her mind about not going to college anyway."

"Lisa's Cat" had not been a very good short story. Allison had written it at the age of seventeen as an entry in a contest which a slick magazine was running at the time. The magazine had run a full-page illustration of a black cat against a background consisting of a half-open window, draped with red, and a vase of spring flowers resting on the same table on which the cat sat.

"Write a short story of not more than five thousand words to fit this picture," the magazine invited its readers, and offered a first prize of two hundred and fifty dollars.

More important to Allison at the time was the fact that the magazine announced that it would publish the prize-winning story in its next issue. Allison had sat down at once and begun to write a cat story. It had to do with an English gentleman in the Foreign Service who gave his faithless wife Lisa a black cat as an anniversary gift. As the English gentleman returned home from his office unexpectedly one afternoon, the cat's sad cries had aroused his attention and he had discovered his faithless Lisa in the arms of her lover.

Perhaps, Tom had often thought, the editor whose job it was to
272

read the contest entries was weary, or perhaps the sad ending of the story, where the English gentleman went to a place designated by Allison as "up country" and caught the plague and died, pleased his fancy. In any case, Allison was declared the winner, received a check for the amount promised, and in the next issue the story appeared.

"Maybe Allison was too lucky too quickly," Tom said as he sipped his drink. "Perhaps she is too busy working in New York to take time out for experiences."

Constance began to set the table absently, putting the plates and glasses in their proper places through long habit rather than by conscious thought.

"I never really believed she would stay away from home as long as she has," she said. "I thought she'd be back inside of six months and now she has been in New York for more than two years. Do you think that we ever made her feel like the third person who makes up a crowd after we were married?"

"No, I don't," said Tom. "Although Allison and I never came to understand one another as well as I should have liked, I think that she began to think of leaving here right after Nellie Cross killed herself."

There was an unspoken agreement of a sort between Tom and Constance. Whenever they referred to Peyton Place's bad time back in '39, they spoke of their own particular unhappiness in terms of Nellie Cross's suicide. They did not speak of this same time as the period when Allison had learned about her father and of the circumstances of her birth.

"But I think her determination took on form," continued Tom, "after Kathy Ellsworth's accident, during the trial. I don't think that she ever felt the same about Peyton Place after that was over with."

"If that was her main reason for leaving it was rather foolish," declared Constance. "The Ellsworths suing Leslie Harrington had nothing to do with Allison. It was none of her affair."

"It was everyone's affair," said Tom quietly.

Later, as Constance stood at the sink doing the dinner dishes, she reflected that Tom had probably been right when he had said that the Ellsworths suing Leslie Harrington had been everyone's affair. It was a situation which had split Peyton Place apart and for that reason alone it had become of concern to everyone whether they wished to be concerned or not. But still, Constance remembered, it was not the Ellsworth affair alone which had changed

273

Allison. Allison had begun to change before that. She had never been a child again after Constance had brought her home from the hospital following that unfortunate business with Norman Page and the terrible tragedy of Nellie Cross. And the other, too, thought Constance reluctantly. The truth about her father and me. She must mind terribly although she always pretends not to give a damn. I wonder if it's true what they say about bastards usually being successful in their chosen fields because they feel they have to be to make up for not having had fathers. Constance looked down into the soapy dishwater and the suds were suddenly rainbow colored and shimmering through her tears. She had no right to be so happy, not after the way she had failed Allison. She wiped a tear from her cheek by brushing her face against her shoulder, and she listened to the sound of Tom's tuneless whistle which came from the cellar where he worked at his buzz saw.

I have so much, she thought guiltily. But I should have seen to it that Allison came first.

She had certainly not put Allison first back in '39. She remembered only too clearly the hot night of Nellie Cross's suicide, with Allison lying in a state of shock at the hospital. The fear uppermost in Constance's mind that night had been that she had lost Tomas Makris. When everything had been taken care of as well as possible that night, Tom had driven away slowly from the parking lot behind the Peyton Place hospital. He did not speak, Constance remembered, and neither did she as she sat in the front seat of the car next to him. He did not ask her to move closer to him as he usually did, or reach for her hand, and Constance sat still, leaning against the door on her side of the car with her fear making a bad taste in her mouth. Silently, Tom drove to a place called Road's End and when he turned off the car lights the whole town lay spread out below, like a patterned carpet. He sat still for a long time, staring down at the town, and Constance did not dare to speak. At last, he flung his cigarette end out into the dark and turned to her. In the thin moonlight his face seemed more sharply etched than she had ever seen it and she began to tremble.

"Tell me about it," he said, but he did not touch her, not even when she was unable to keep from crying any longer.

"There is nothing to tell," she said. "I have never been married in my life. That's all there is to it. Allison is an illegitimate child and I've tried very hard to keep it a secret ever since she was born. I've worked hard to protect Allison, Tom. When she was born my mother and I fixed her birth certificate so that no one would ever

274

know. She is a whole year older than she thinks she is. I did everything I could think of to protect her, but I can't change the fact that she is a bastard."

"That noble-sounding business about protecting your child is a lot of crap," said Tom brutally. "You finagled around to protect yourself, not her. And as for the fact, did you have to fling it at her the way you did? I have seen cruelty in my time, Constance. Plenty of it. But I have never seen anything to compare with what you did to Allison tonight."

"What the hell did you expect me to do?" cried Constance, knowing that she sounded like a shrew and not caring, unable suddenly to stop the words which bubbled crudely to her lips. "What the hell should I do with her? Let her run wild? Let her go into the woods to screw every boy she meets up with? Is that what I should do, just so that you would have one mother in the world who would agree with your fancy theories about sex for children?"

"But you don't know that Allison was doing anything with Norman of which you might not approve," said Tom coldly.

"Like hell I don't! She is just like her father. The more I look at her, the more I can see Allison MacKenzie in her. Sex. That's all he ever thought of and his bastard daughter is the same way. I don't even have to look very hard to see her father in Allison."

"It is not Allison MacKenzie whom you see in your daughter," said Tom. "It is yourself, and that is what horrifies you. You are afraid that she will turn out to be like you, that she will wind up with an illegitimate child on her hands, as you did. That is what you saw when you looked at Allison and Norman this evening. It never occurred to you that perhaps she is different from the way you were."

"That isn't true!" cried Constance. "I was nothing like Allison at that age. I would never have gone into the woods with a boy to do the things that Allison has done."

"How do you know what Allison has done? You never gave her a chance to tell you before you began to lash out on all sides with your poisonous tongue."

"I just know, I tell you!"

"From experience?" asked Tom.

"Oh, how I hate you!" she said venomously. "How I hate you!"

"No," said Tom, "you don't hate me. You hate the truth, but you don't hate me. The difference between us, Constance, is that I don't mind the truth, no matter how sordid it is. But I do hate a liar."

He started the car and drove swiftly to her house on Beech

Street without speaking another word, and Constance knew that she had lost him.

"How could you ever have said that you loved me?" she said as she stepped out of the car. "How could you have loved me and then speak as you have spoken tonight?"

"I said nothing about loving you less, Constance," said Tom wearily. "I only said that I hate a liar. I've wanted to marry you for two years because I loved you. I still want to marry you because I still love you, but I cannot stand to look at you and know that you lie every time you find the truth too disagreeable to be faced."

"I suppose you've never lied," she said childishly.

"Only rarely," he said, "when the truth would have done more harm than good, and I have seldom gone so far as to lie to myself. Moreover, Constance, I have never lied to you. There can be neither beauty, nor trust, nor security between a man and a woman if there is not truth."

"All *right*," said Constance angrily. "If it's truth you want, come into the house and I'll give you truth. Every last damned word of it. Come on."

He followed her into the house, locking the door behind him, and she led the way into the living room. He drew the drapes together at the windows and closed the door leading into the front hall while she sat stiffly on the couch and watched him.

"Would you like a drink?" she asked timidly, her anger suddenly gone.

"No," he replied from where he stood leaning against the closed door which led into the hall. "And neither do you. Let's get this over with. Start, and start from the beginning and for God's sake try to be honest with the two of us for once."

He had the air of a jailer as he stood waiting for her to speak and his features had a quality of hardness which she had never seen before. Nor did he soften when she began the hesitating recital of facts about herself. Several times he paced away from the door to light a cigarette but he did not offer her one, and several times, in a voice which she did not recognize as his, he picked her up on the loose ends in her stories.

"That's a lie," he said once, and Constance, caught in a web of her own making, began the retelling of a particular incident.

"What are you leaving out?" he demanded, and she put in a fact about herself which she had always considered shameful.

"Go back over that one again," he said. "Let's see if you can tell it the same way twice."

It was a night that Constance never forgot and when it was over Tom leaned against the closed door, white faced and haggard.

"Is that everything?" he asked.

"Yes," she answered, and he believed her.

It was not until much later that Constance realized fully what Tom had done for her. In the weeks which followed it was as if she were a new and different person who walked freely and unafraid for the first time. It was never again necessary for her to take refuge in lies and pretenses, and it was only when she finally realized this that she knew what Tom meant when he had spoken of the dead weight of the shell she had always carried. But that night there was no realization. There was nothing but a terrible need, a hunger that caused her to reach forward for the first time in her life.

"Please," she whispered, and before he could move toward her she ran to him. "Please," she cried. "Please. Please."

And then he was holding her and his lips were against her cheek, at the corners of her eyes, soft against her ear as he murmured, "Darling, darling, darling," while Constance wept. His fingers were firm against her back, rubbing away the tenseness between her shoulder blades, until at last she quieted and then they were gentle and caressing at the nape of her neck. He sat down without releasing her and held her on his lap, his arms cradling her, and she put her head against his shoulder, warming herself in her own desire to give and give and give. Her finger tips traced a pattern down the side of his face, and with her mouth almost against his she whispered, "I didn't know it could be like this, so comforting, with nothing to fear."

"It can be a lot of different things—even fun."

She gave him the soft nibbling kisses of love not in a hurry, and soon their words were almost indistinguishable to themselves and each other.

For the first time in their relationship she undressed herself and let him watch her, and still there was this joy of giving in her. She could not lie still under his hands.

"Anything," she said. "Anything. Anything."

"I love this fire in you. I love it when you have to move."

"Don't stop."

"Here? And here? And here?"

"Yes. Oh, yes. Yes."

"Your nipples are as hard as diamonds."

"Again, darling. Again."

277

"Your legs are absolutely wanton, do you know it?"

"Am I good for you, darling?"

"Good! Christ!"

"Do it to me then."

He raised his head and smiled down into her face. "Do what?" he teased. "Tell me."

"You know."

"No, tell me. What do you want me to do to you?"

She looked up at him appealingly.

"Say it," he said. "Say it."

She whispered the words in his ear and his fingers dug into her shoulders.

"Like this?"

"Please," she said. "Please." And then, "Yes! Yes, yes, yes."

Later she lay with her head on his shoulder and one hand flat against his chest.

"For the first time in my life I'm not ashamed afterward," she said.

"Shall I be revolting and say 'I told you so'?"

"If you like."

"I told you so."

She moved her head a little and bit his shoulder.

"Ouch!"

"Take it back!"

"All right! All right! Turn loose."

"Sure?"

"Yes, for Christ's sake!"

"Promise?"

"You cannibal! Yes."

She put her lips against the spot where her teeth had been. "Love me?"

He raised himself up on one elbow and put a hand gently on her throat so that she could feel her pulse against his finger tips. For a long moment he looked down into her eyes until she could feel desire begin again, thick within her.

"Can't stand the sight of you," he said huskily.

"You just stick around me for sex, do you?"

"I don't know. I'd have to try you out again first."

"That'll be two dollars, please."

"Be good and I may tip you."

"Oh, darling," she said suddenly. "Darling, I'm not afraid any more," and her voice throbbed with happiness and relief.

278

"I know," he said. "I know."

A few weeks after that, when Tom asked her to marry him, she gave him a simple, straightforward "Yes" and went home to tell Allison.

"Tom and I are going to be married, Allison," she said.

"Oh?" said the child who was no longer a child. "When?"

"As soon as possible. Next week end, if we can."

"Why the big rush all of a sudden?"

"I love him and I have waited long enough," said Constance.

Constance Makris finished wiping the silverware and put it away. It was not, she thought, in marrying Tom that she had failed Allison. It had been during the long talk which the two of them had had about Allison's father that Constance had failed. Yet, she had tried faithfully to reply with only the most truthful of answers to her daughter's questions.

"Did you love my father?" Allison had asked.

"I don't think so," Constance had answered frankly. "Not the way I love Tom."

"I see," Allison had said. "Are you sure he was my father?"

She hates me, Constance had thought, and tried to be gentle with her daughter.

"I shan't make excuses for myself," she had said, "but what happened between your father and me could happen to anyone. I was lonely. I needed someone and he was there."

"Was he married?"

"Yes," Constance had replied in a low voice. "He was married and had two children."

"I see," Allison had said and later Constance was sure that this had been the moment when Allison had begun to think of leaving Peyton Place.

The Ellsworth affair, when Allison had been made to feel that there was no one in Peyton Place who was her friend, was secondary.

Constance hung the dish towel on a line out on the back porch and breathed deeply of the October evening air. Allison, she remembered, had always loved October in Peyton Place.

Oh, my dear, thought Constance, try to be a little gentle. Try to forgive me a little, to understand a little. Come home, Allison, where you belong.

Constance went back into the kitchen slowly. She ought to drive down to see Selena Cross. It was terrible the way she had paid absolutely no attention to business since Selena had begun to manage the Thrifty Corner. But Constance didn't have to worry with Selena in charge. The girl could run the place as well as Constance herself had ever done. Constance smiled as she paused to listen to Tom's whistle. She was, of course, making excuses. She would much rather spend the evening at home than at Selena's going over accounts and receipts.

"Hey," she called down the cellar stairs. "Are you going to stay down there all night?"

Tom shut off the buzz saw. "Not if you're free and willing," he said, and Constance laughed.

◆ 3 ◆

On this same Friday in October, at about four o'clock in the afternoon, Seth Buswell met Leslie Harrington on Elm Street. They exchanged greetings for they were, after all, civilized men who had been born on the same street in the same town, and had attended school together as boys.

In fact, reflected Seth wryly, he and Leslie had quite a lot in common if one really stopped to think about it.

"You fellows still playing cards Friday nights?" asked Leslie.

Seth could hardly conceal his surprise, for this was the closest that he had ever come to hearing Leslie make what amounted to a request.

"Yes," Seth replied, and an awkward pause followed the single word. Each man waited for the other to speak, but Seth did not proffer the expected invitation, and Leslie did not ask for it again. The men parted casually, but the same thought was in both their minds. Leslie Harrington had not played poker with the men of Chestnut Street since 1939, and if Seth had his way, he never would again.

For years, there had been an understanding between the Friday night poker players, that if one of them was unable to attend the weekly card game, he would telephone Seth to inform him as soon as possible after supper on the evening of the gathering. One night, four years before, Leslie had telephoned him. It was the evening of the day when the jury had reached a decision in the case of Ellsworth vs. Harrington.

"Seth," Leslie had said, "I'm pooped from being in court all day. Count me out of the game for tonight."

"I'll count you out, Leslie," Seth had said, with his rage of the afternoon still a pain within him. "Tonight and every other Friday night from now on. I don't want you in my house again."

"Now don't go off half-cocked, Seth," Leslie had cautioned. "After all, we've been friends for years."

"Not friends," Seth had replied. "By coincidence, we happen to have been born on the same street in the same town. By an unhappy coincidence, I might add," and with that, he had hung up on Leslie.

Yes, indeed, thought Seth, as he mounted the wide steps in front of his house, Leslie and I really have quite a lot in common. The same town, street and friends. Even the same woman, once. How easy it is, how dangerously easy it is to hate a man for one's own inadequacies.

This last thought caused an uncoiling of self-loathing in Seth to a point where he fancied that he tasted bile, and as soon as he had entered his house he poured himself a drink large enough to kill the most disagreeable of flavors. By the time Matthew Swain arrived, a few minutes before the others, the newspaper owner was quite drunk.

"For Christ's sake!" exclaimed the doctor, stepping over Seth's outstretched legs to reach the table where the bottle stood. "What brought this on?"

"I have been thinking, dear friend," said Seth, drunk enough to pronounce been as bean, a thing he would never have done when sober, "of the ease with which one man blames another for his own inadequacies. And that, old friend," Seth closed one eye and wiggled a forefinger at the doctor, "is a thought of some scope. To use an idiom on your level, I might even say that it is a pregnant thought."

The doctor poured himself a drink and sat down. "I can see that it's not going to be hard to take your money tonight," he said.

"Ah, Matthew, where is your soul that you can talk of cards when I have found the solution to the world's problems."

"Excuse me, Napoleon," said the doctor. "The doorbell is ringing."

"If every man," declared Seth, ignoring the doctor's remark, "ceased to hate and blame every other man for his own failures and shortcomings, we would see the end of every evil in the world, from war to backbiting."

Matthew Swain, who had gone to answer the bell, re-entered the room followed by Charles Partridge, Jared Clarke and Dexter Humphrey.

"All of us in the same leaky boat," said Seth, by way of greeting.

"What's the matter with him?" demanded Jared Clarke unnecessarily.

"He has found the solution to the world's problems," said Dr. Swain.

"Humph," said Dexter Humphrey, who was notoriously lacking in a sense of humor. "He was all right when I saw him this afternoon. Well, I came to play cards. Are we going to play?"

"Help yourselves, gentlemen," said Seth, waving a generous hand. "Make yourselves at home. I, for one, shall sit here and meditate."

"What the hell got into you, Seth, to make you start in so early on the bottle?" asked Partridge.

Seth eyed the lawyer. "Did it ever occur to you, Charlie, that tolerance can reach a point where it is no longer tolerance? When that happens, the noble-sounding attitude on which most of us pride ourselves degenerates into weakness and acquiescence."

"Whew!" exclaimed Partridge, wiping exaggeratedly at his forehead. "You sound like somebody at a fraternity bull session. What're you trying to say?"

"I was referring," said Seth with dignity, "to you and me and all of us, in conjunction with Leslie Harrington."

There was an uncomfortable silence while Seth looked owlishly from one of his friends to the other. At last, Dexter Humphrey coughed.

"Let's play cards," he said, and led the way to Seth's kitchen.

"All of us, every last, damned one of us hating Leslie because of our own inadequacies," said Seth, and slumped back into his chair and drank slowly from his glass.

If Seth Buswell and Leslie Harrington had a trait in common, it was that Seth, like Leslie, was not a worrier. The difference between them, on this point, was that where Leslie had taught himself not to be, Seth had never had to be. George Buswell, Seth's father, had been as wealthy as Leslie Harrington's father, and much more prominent in the state, and he had cast a long shadow. But where Leslie had suffered from a compulsive need for success, Seth had abandoned all hope of making his own mark at an age so young that he could no longer remember when it had been, and this had saved him the worry of failure with which Leslie had had to learn to cope. Seth could not recall a conscious memory of his decision, for over the years it had faded into the vaguest of feelings.

No one will ever be able to say that I do not measure up to my father in spite of my efforts, for I shall never try to measure up to him.

This feeling in young Seth was the beginning of what his father was later to deplore as "Seth's laziness," and his mother to label as "Seth's total lack of ambition."

Whatever its name, the unremembered decision had resulted in Seth's calm drifting. He had drifted through his youth and through four years at Dartmouth in much the same way he had later drifted into the ownership of the *Peyton Place Times*. He had drifted, as if detached, through the death of his parents and the loss of his sweetheart, and soon after that Seth's detachment had become known in Peyton Place as Seth's tolerance.

"If you don't care a damn about anything, it is easy to be tolerant," Seth had once said to his friend young Doc Swain. "Neither side of any picture disturbs you, which enables you to see both sides clearly and sensibly."

Young Doc Swain, who had been married two weeks before to a girl by the name of Emily Gilbert, had said: "I'd rather be dead than not care a damn about anything."

And since it is difficult, if not impossible, for a man to survive without loving something, Seth had turned his love to Peyton Place. His was a tolerant, unbiased love which neither demanded nor expected anything in return, so that to everyone else it seemed more like interest and civic pride than love.

"We ought to have a new high school," Seth had written in an editorial, "but of course, it'll cost us something. Taxes will go up. On the other hand, we're not going to turn out many bright kids with the inadequate facilities which we now have. Looks to me like it's up to you folks with kids, and those of you who ever expect to have kids, to decide whether we'll pay $1.24 more per thousand in property taxes, or whether we'll settle for second-rate education."

The people of northern New England were Seth's people, and he knew them well. His tolerance, his seeming indifference, succeeded with them where force and salesmanship would have failed. Everyone in Peyton Place said that Seth never used the *Times* as a weapon, not even during political campaigns, and this was the truth. Seth published items of interest to the residents of his town and the surrounding towns. Whatever world news he printed came from the wires of the Associated Press, and Seth never commented or enlarged upon it in his editorials. "Social items and town gossip of a watered down nature, that's what you get in the *Times*," other newspaper owners in other parts of the state were apt to say. Yet, during the first few years during which Seth had owned the paper, he had not only succeeded in getting a new high school built in his town, but also in getting Memorial Park built and funds appropriated for its care and maintenance. He had raised much of the money that went into the building of the Peyton Place hospital, and through the pages of the *Times* volunteers were recruited for the building of a new firehouse. For years, Seth, in his tolerant, unforceful fashion, saw to it that his town grew and improved, and then Leslie Harrington's son was born. It was as if Leslie, having succeeded in one field, turned now to new interests. In the year following Rodney's birth, voices were raised against Seth's for the first time at town meeting, and the voices raised were those of the mill hands. Year after year, when items dear to Seth's heart such as a new grade school and town zoning came up to a vote at the meeting, the newspaper owner was defeated by overwhelming numbers. Seth retired behind his tolerant detachment and allowed Leslie Harrington to assume a position in Peyton Place which had the dimensions of dictatorship, and he steadfastly refused to use the *Times* as an extension of his own voice. Seth shrugged and said that the people would soon tire of Leslie's dictatorial methods, but in this he was wrong for Leslie did not dictate, he bargained. When Seth realized this, he shrugged again, and everyone in Peyton Place said that his tolerance was of heroic proportions. Seth had believed it himself until one day in 1939 when Allison MacKenzie had come, white faced and with fists clenched, into his office.

"The Ellsworths are suing Leslie Harrington," Allison had said, "and everyone is saying that they'll never get a dime because the jury will be made up almost entirely of mill hands. What are we going to do?"

Seth had looked at this girl, too tense and fine drawn for a child of sixteen, and had tried to explain to her why they were going to do nothing about the case of Ellsworth *vs.* Harrington.

"I get riled up the same as you," he had said. "In fact, I've often threatened to use the paper as an instrument of exposure. I threaten to do it every year, just before town meeting, when I know that I'm going to get beat on an issue that I don't want to get beat on, like zoning, or a new grade school. But I never do it. Why? Because I believe in tolerance, and one of the requirements of tolerance is not only that you will listen to the other fellow's viewpoint, but also that you won't try to cram yours down his throat. I'll say what I think to anyone who is willing to listen, but I won't force anyone to read about it in the pages of my paper."

"Even when you know that your viewpoint is the right one?" Allison had demanded, her voice rising in angry disbelief.

"That isn't the point, is it? One's viewpoint and a man's right to defend himself against it are two different things. When I print something in the paper, and a man reads it later in his own home, I am not there for him to disagree with if his viewpoint is not in accordance with mine. The only recourse he has then is to sit down and write a 'Letter to the Editor,' and then he is being unfair to me because he is not here for me to argue with if I wanted to do so."

"I don't know," Allison had said in a tightly controlled voice, "how you came to think the way you do, and I don't care. I have something here which I've written. I'm not asking you to print your own words in your paper. Print mine, with my name at the head of it. I'm not afraid to write what I think, and I don't care who reads it or who might disagree with me. I know when I am right."

"Let's see what you've written," Seth had said, extending his hand.

Allison had written a great deal, much of it to do with the Constitution and the Declaration of Independence, and the individual's God-given right to a fair trial by jury. She had written also of the miser's desire to make money to a point where he grossly overlooked the means by which he made it. She charged Leslie Harrington with negligence and carelessness, and said that if he were any kind of man, he would never have waited to be sued. He would have put his money at the disposal of the Ellsworths, and he would carry the marks of what he had done to Kathy on his conscience for the rest of his life. It was time, Allison had written, for men of honor to stand up and be counted. When the time came that an individual in a free American town was forced to fear a prejudiced hearing, it was indeed a time to try men's souls. Altogether, Allison had written seventeen typewritten pages expressing her opinion of Leslie Harrington and the grip in which he held Peyton Place. When Seth had finished reading, he put the manuscript down carefully.

"I cannot print this, Allison," he had said.

"Cannot!" the girl had cried, sweeping up the typewritten pages. "You mean will not!"

"Allison, my dear—"

Angry tears had rushed to the girl's eyes. "And I thought that you were my friend," she said, and had run out of his office.

Seth's cigarette burned his fingers and he sat up with a jerk. For a moment, his mind refused to comprehend his circumstances, but then his eyes fell on a bookcase at the opposite side of the room and he understood that he was sitting in a chair in his own living room.

"Goddamn it," he muttered, and began to search the floor around his chair for the cigarette end which he had dropped. When he found it, he ground it into the carpet with the toe of his shoe, then he settled back and picked up his half-finished drink. From the kitchen, there came a low murmur of men's voices and the whisper of new playing cards.

"Raise you."

"I'll pass."

"Call."

"Full up."

"Christ, and me sitting with three kings."

My friends, thought Seth, swallowing a nausea caused by too much to drink on an empty stomach, and caused, too, by unpleasant remembrances. My good, tried and true blue friends, thought Seth, and like a phantom a voice from the past struck him.

"And I thought that you were my friend!"

Seth finished his stale drink and poured himself another. I was, you know, he thought, addressing an Allison MacKenzie of long ago. If you had listened to me, you would have been spared a lot of hurt. I was trying to teach you not to care too much. That business of caring too much was always obvious in you, my dear. It showed in your writing, and that, my dear, my too young, my sweet, my talented, my beautiful Allison, does not make for clear, coolheaded, analytical prose.

"Straight, queen high and all black, by God! In spades!" came the enthusiastic voice of Charles Partridge.

My friend, thought Seth drunkenly, my good friend Charlie Partridge. What excuses we have made to one another in our time, Charlie. What beautiful, noble, high-sounding excuses!

And suddenly Seth was back in 1939. October, 1939. Indian summer, 1939, and a crowded courtroom, with his friend Charlie Partridge talking softly to his friend Allison MacKenzie.

"Now, my dear, remember that you are sworn to tell the truth.

286

I want you to tell the court exactly what happened on the evening of Labor Day of this year. Do not be afraid, my dear, you are among friends here."

"Friends?" The child's voice was not the voice of a child, not the same voice which had thanked Seth for a chance to write for the paper. For money. "Friends?" Such a tense, tightly controlled voice for a little girl of sixteen. "Kathy Ellsworth is my friend. She is the only friend I have in Peyton Place."

Seth had comforted himself later with the thought that he had only imagined that Allison MacKenzie's eyes had found his in that packed courtroom.

"Now," said the remembered voice of Charles Partridge, Leslie Harrington's attorney, "could it not be that your friend Kathy became dizzy as she looked down into the moving wheels of the machinery in that building at the carnival?"

"Objection, your Honor!" It was the voice of Peter Drake, a young lawyer who had set up an office in Peyton Place, for God only knew what reason. He came from "away from here," as the townspeople put it, and until the case of Ellsworth vs. Harrington, he had handled nothing but deeds and the petty problems of the mill hands. And here he was, daring to object to something that Charlie Partridge, who had been born in town, was saying.

Honorable Anthony Aldridge, who stubbornly refused to live on Chestnut Street, although he was a judge and could afford it, upheld Peter Drake. The court was not interested in what Allison thought, but only in what she had seen. Seth looked surreptitiously at the jury to see what damage Charlie's question had done, for the jury was comprised of people who would surely favor Leslie Harrington. It would have been impossible to find twelve people in Peyton Place who neither worked at the mills nor owed money on mortgaged property at the Citizens' National Bank where Leslie was chairman of the board of trustees, and Leslie had acted quickly, once legal proceedings had been instigated against him. He had fired John Ellsworth, Kathy's father, and had suddenly found a buyer for the house which the Ellsworths rented. No wonder the mill hands fastened so thankfully on a morsel of evidence in favor of Leslie Harrington, thought Seth, as he turned his eyes from the jury to Allison MacKenzie on the stand.

The case continued for three days, and the only person to support Allison MacKenzie was Tomas Makris, who testified that when he had gone to the fun house operator to tell him to shut off the machinery which ran the place, the operator had stated that he did not know how to comply with this request. Lewis Welles's testimony, according to Peyton Place, did not count, for everyone knew that he and Kathy were "going together" and naturally he'd stick up for the girl, especially when it might mean thirty thousand dollars.

Thirty thousand dollars! Peyton Place never grew weary of saying the words.

"Thirty thousand dollars! Imagine it!"

"Imagine suing Leslie Harrington for thirty thousand dollars!"

"At thirty thousand dollars apiece, I'd let both my arms get ripped off!"

"And who the hell does this Ellsworth think he is anyway? Where does he come from? He's behind it. The girl would never have done it on her own without her father pushing her!"

After three days the jury deliberated, according to Seth's watch, exactly forty-two minutes. They assessed Leslie Harrington the sum of twenty-five hundred dollars, the figure for which he had been heard to say that he would settle. Kathy Ellsworth, who did not appear in court, took the news more calmly than anyone else. Her right arm was gone, and that, as she said, was that. Neither thirty thousand, nor twenty-five hundred was going to alter the fact that she would have to learn to use her left hand.

"Listen, baby," said Lewis Welles, in his brisk, salesman's voice to which many people objected, "you don't need a right arm to hold a kid. I've seen lotsa women holding babies with their left arm."

That night, when the men of Chestnut Street, with the exception of Leslie Harrington, gathered at Seth's to play poker, Charles Partridge had been full of excuses.

"Christ," he had said, "I know it wasn't right. What could I do? I'm Leslie's lawyer. He pays me a yearly retainer for which I agree to take care of his affairs to the best of my ability. Thirty thousand dollars is a lot of money. I had to do what I did."

"It wasn't as if the sonofabitch couldn't afford it," said Dexter Humphrey, the president of the bank.

"Leslie has always been a cheap skate," said Jared Clarke. "I don't think he's ever bought a single thing without trying to beat the price down."

"For a while," said Matthew Swain, "I didn't think the girl would live."

"Someday," said Seth, "that bastard will get his. In spades. He'll get his comeuppance so good that he'll never forget it. I just hope I'm around to see it."

All of us, every single, goddamned one of us, hating Leslie Harrington because we haven't the guts to stand up and tell him, and everyone else, where we stand, thought Seth, as he sat and drank in his house, in the fall of 1943. He raised his empty glass and threw it with all his remaining strength against the opposite wall. The glass did not even break. It rolled across the carpet and came to rest against the bookcase.

"My friends!" said Seth thickly. "My good, true blue friends. Screw 'em all!"

"What did you say, Seth?" asked Dr. Swain, coming into the room followed by the poker players who had finished with the cards.

"'Septyou, Matt," muttered Seth. "Screw 'em all, 'sheptyou, Matt," he said, and fell asleep, leaning back in his chair, with his mouth open.

◆ 4 ◆

The snow came early that year. By the middle of November the fields were white with it and before the first week of December had passed, the streets of Peyton Place were lined on either side with peaked, white piles of snow pushed there, out of the way of traffic and pedestrians, by the town's sharp-nosed plow.

Tuttle's Grocery Store was always more crowded during the winter months, for the farmers who were hard pressed for a moment of rest in the summer found themselves with hours of free time to spend. The majority of them spent it in Tuttle's, talking. It was talk which mattered little, solved nothing and which, in the winter of 1943, was concerned mostly with the war. Yet, the war had changed the face of Peyton Place but little, and the group in Tuttle's not at all. There were very few young men left in town, but then, young men had never congregated around the stove in Tuttle's so that the talkers there were the ones who had been there for years. There were fewer products for sale in the store, but the old men around the stove had never had much money to buy things anyway, so the shortage of civilian goods did not affect them particularly. As for the farmers, food was no more of a problem now than it had ever been. War had not made the soil of northern New England less rocky, more yielding, or the weather more predictable. The wresting of life from the land had always been difficult, and the war made no difference one way or another. The old men in Tuttle's talked and talked, and the farmers did not feel cheated in having spent the hard-earned hours of leisure in these conversations. When local talk faded, there was always the fascinating, unending talk of war. Every battle on every front was refought with more finesse, more brilliant strategy, more courage and more daring, by the old men around the red-hot stove in Tuttle's. The men, including those with sons gone to battle, spoke the words of concern assiduously, for they felt this was expected of men whose country was at war. Yet, there was not one among them who believed even remotely in the possibility of an American defeat, although they discussed the possibilities with infinite care. The idea of an alien foot, whether German or Japanese, trodding the acres first settled by the grandfathers of the old men in Tuttle's was one so farfetched, so impossible to visualize, that it was spoken of—and listened to—with the hushed attitude in which the men might have held a discussion on extrasensory perception. It was all right to talk and to listen, but one simply did not believe it. A stranger, coming to Peyton Place for the first time from a place where the war had passed, might well have been dumfounded by the lack of concern in evidence in the town. The largest, single change which had taken place was in the Cumberland Mills, which had gone into war work more than a year before. The mills worked in three shifts now, operating twenty-four hours a day, and the fact that more people had more money to spend was not particularly obvious, for there was nothing to be bought with this newly acquired prosperity. To the old men in Tuttle's, the war was almost like a game, a conversational game, to be played when other subjects were exhausted. A stranger to Peyton Place might easily have mistaken disbelief of danger for courage, or faith for indifference.

Selena Cross was one of the few in town to be emotionally involved with the war. Her stepbrother Paul was with the Army somewhere in the Pacific, while Gladys was working in an aircraft factory at Los Angeles, California. Selena fought a continual feeling of restlessness and a sense of frustration during the winter of 1943.

"I wish I were a man," she had told Tomas Makris. "Nothing would hold me back then. I'd join up in a minute."

Afterward, she was sorry that she had said this, for Tom, she had heard, had tried several times to enlist. None of the branches of the service were eager, it seemed, to accept Tom who was over forty, and who had had both knees fractured in the past.

Restless and frustrated, Selena wrestled also with a sense of guilt. She should, she knew, be grateful that Ted Carter was safe at the state university, studying for his eventual legal career and being kept from active duty by virtue of his good grades and the R.O.T.C. But somehow she was not. She felt that Ted should be fighting side by side with Paul and all others like him, and it irritated her when Ted came home week ends, or wrote enthusiastic letters remarking on his good fortune in "managing to stay in college."

It was fine, Selena admitted, for a man to have his goal firmly fixed in his mind, and Ted, she knew, was not a coward. He was more than ready and willing to go to war, after his schooling was done.

"If I can stay in for just one more year, including summers, I'll have my Bachelor's. That will leave only law school, and who knows? The war may be over before then," Ted had told her.

She had been furiously angry. "I should think that you'd *want* to go. After all, the United States is at war."

"It's not that I don't want to go," he had replied, hurt at her unreasonableness. "It's just that this way, I won't be losing any time and we can be married that much sooner."

"Time!" Selena had scoffed. "Let the Germans or the Japs get over here, and see how valuable your time is then!"

"But Selena, we've had this all planned for years—ever since we were kids. What's the matter?"

"Nothing!"

As a matter of fact, Selena could not have told Ted what the matter was. She knew that her feeling was a childish, unreasonable one, so senseless as to be unexplainable, yet it was there. She could not get over the idea that there was something not quite right in a strong, able-bodied man wanting to stay in a sleepy college town while a war raged over the rest of the world.

Since Nellie's death and the advent of Paul and Gladys with its consequence of tidiness and its measure of security, the Carters had relented somewhat in their attitude toward Selena. After all, said the Carters, it took a real smart girl to manage a business all by herself with no help at all from the owner. Connie had scarcely set foot in the shop from the day she had married that Greek fellow. Selena did it alone, and a girl had to be real smart to be able to do that at the age of eighteen. Now that Selena was alone with

Joey, Roberta sometimes invited the two of them to Sunday dinner, and she always insisted on sharing her letters from Ted with Selena, in the hope that Selena would reciprocate. Selena never did. She did not like Roberta and Harmon, nor could she bring herself to trust them. She accepted Roberta's invitations warily, for she could see no graceful way to avoid them, but she never spent a comfortable Sunday in the Carter house, and whenever one of these Sundays was over, she and Joey acted like a pair of children let out of school. They ran and laughed all the way to their own house, and when they reached it, Selena made hamburgers and Joey did imitations of Roberta's hyperladylike mannerisms while they ate, Selena's food growing cold while she laughed.

I haven't a thing to kick about, thought Selena, as she walked home one cold December evening after closing the Thrifty Corner. If I had an ounce of gratitude in me, I'd know enough to be grateful for all I have.

Just before she opened the door to enter the house, she paused and looked up at the heavy sky. It's going to snow, she thought, and hurried inside to warmth, where Joey had already started supper and where another letter from Ted awaited her. Joey had started a fire in the fireplace, too, for he knew that Selena loved to watch a fire while she ate. The fireplace had been a needless extravagance, installed with much labor and thought by Paul Cross after he had learned from Gladys that, to Selena, no home was complete without one.

"Fireplaces!" Paul had scoffed good-naturedly when Selena had begun to cry the first time she saw the completed hearth. "They're dirty and old fashioned. Where'd you ever pick up such notions?"

"From Connie MacKenzie," Selena had answered. "I used to sit in front of hers, with Allison, and think about the day when I'd have one of my own."

"Well, now you've got it," Paul had said. "Don't you squawk to me when the wood is wet, or the chimney doesn't draw and fills the house with smoke."

Selena had laughed. "I used to wish that I had blond hair so that when I had my fireplace I could sit in front of it and let the fire make highlights in my hair, like it does in Connie's. I would have given anything to look like her, to be that beautiful."

"Nothing could have helped you!" hooted Paul, teasing her. "You've got a shape like a broom handle and a face like a hedgehog. Connie MacKenzie indeed! Not a chance."

Although Selena did not resemble Allison's mother in the least,

292

as she had wished, she was, nevertheless, beautiful. By the time she was twenty, she had fulfilled all the promises of adolescence. Her eyes held a look of unshared secrets, but they no longer seemed old and out of place as they had when she was a child. People turned to look twice and three times at Selena, no matter where she went, for she had an air of experience suffered, of mystery untold, which was far more entrancing than mere beauty. Sometimes, when Joey Cross looked at her, his love so overwhelmed him that he felt compelled to touch her, or, at the very least, to call her name and force her to look at him.

"Selena!"

She raised her eyes from the book she held and turned to look at him. The firelight highlighted her cheekbones so that the hollows beneath the bones seemed deeper than they actually were.

"Yes, Joey?"

He lowered his eyes to the magazine in front of him. "It must be snowin' real hard," he said. "The wind's howlin' like a sick hound."

She stood up and went to a window and pressed her face against the glass, making blinders with her hands at the corners of her eyes.

"I guess it's snowing!" she exclaimed. "Blowing up a real blizzard. Did you close up the sheep pen real well?"

"Yep. I knew it was goin' to blizzard. Clayton Frazier told me. He showed me how he can tell, from lookin' at the clouds no later than four o'clock in the afternoon."

Selena laughed. "What happens if the clouds don't blow over until after four?"

"Then it won't blizzard that night," said Joey positively. "It'll hold off 'til the next day."

"I see," said Selena seriously. "Listen, how about a cup of cocoa and a game of checkers?"

"O.K. with me," said Joey casually, but his heart, and very nearly his eyes, overflowed with love for her.

Selena always made him feel big and important. Like a man, instead of a kid. She depended on him, and liked to have him around. Joey knew boys at school whose older sisters would rather be dead than have their brothers hanging around them. Not Selena, though. Whenever she hadn't seen him for a while, even if it was only a couple of hours, she always acted like he had just come back from a long trip. "Hi, Joey!" she'd say, and her face got all smily and lighted up. She never kissed him or fondled him, the way he had seen some women do to some boys. He'd have died, thought Joey, if she ever did that. But sometimes she gave him a playful poke, or rumpled his hair and told him if he didn't hurry and get a haircut, the barber would soon be chasing him down Elm Street, waving a pair of shears. She rumpled his hair and said that, even when he didn't really need a haircut.

"Come on, poky," said Selena, rumpling his hair. "Get out the board. And when are you going to get that mop cut? If you don't hurry, Clement will chase you right down Elm Street one of these days, waving his shears and yelling for you to wait until he catches up with you."

They drank cocoa and played checkers, and Joey beat Selena three games straight while she sat and groaned, apparently helpless to stop her brilliant opponent. Then they went to bed. It was much later, close to one o'clock in the morning, when the doorbell rang.

Selena sat up in bed with a start. Paul! she thought, scrambling around vainly in the dark, trying to find the button on the lamp next to her bed. Something has happened to Paul, and there is someone outside with a telegram. She knew what to expect. The yellow telegram with the one or two red stars pasted inside the glassine window which was the government's way of preparing people for the shock of learning that their loved ones were either maimed or dead. Almost unconsciously, her mind registered the fact that the wind was blowing fiercely, driving icy pellets of snow against the windows. She struggled with one sleeve of her robe while she put on the living room lights, and when she opened the door at last, the wind yanked it out of her hand, ramming it against the wall behind, and a sharp drift of snow struck her in the face. Lucas Cross stumbled through the open door, while Selena's shocked mind could think only of getting the door closed behind him.

"Christ, you kept me waitin' long enough, out there in the cold," said Lucas, by way of greeting.

Selena's mind began to function again. "Hello, Pa," she said wearily.

"Is that any way to greet me, after I've traveled hundreds of miles just to see you?" demanded Lucas.

His smile had not changed, she noticed. His forehead still moved as if controlled by his lips. Then she realized that he was wearing a navy uniform, with a pea jacket, and a white cap placed firmly on his oddly square head.

"Why, Pa!" she exclaimed. "You're in the Navy."

"Yes, goddamn it. Wish to hell I'd stayed in the woods, I can tell ya. Histin' an ax is a lot easier than the things they can think up for a man to do in the Navy. Listen, I hitchhiked all the way up from Boston. You gonna keep me standin' here all night? I'm froze."

"You're nowhere near frozen," said Selena acidly. "Not with all you've got in you. I see that the Navy hasn't managed to cure you of drinking."

"Cure me?" demanded Lucas, following her into the living room. "Hell, honey, the Navy's taught me tricks I'd never heard of!"

"I can imagine," she said, stirring up the embers in the fireplace and putting on another log.

"Say!" he exclaimed, taking off his jacket and tossing it into a chair. "There's been some changes made around here, ain't they? I didn't notice too good from outside. It's blowin' up one helluva blizzard. But I can see there's been a lot of improvements inside. Christ, it's cold. Feller gave me a ride as far as Elm Street, and I hadda walk from there. Goin' up to Canada, this feller was. Just passin' through. You'd a thought he coulda given me a lift to the house, but no. He didn't like it 'cause I was sippin' at a little insulation on the way up. The bastard."

I knew it, thought Selena. I knew all along that things were too good to last. This is what I get for my ingratitude, for complaining when I had no grounds for complaint.

She turned to look at Lucas, who was drinking from a pint bottle. When he had finished and the bottle was empty, he threw it toward the fireplace, where it smashed against the hearth.

"Listen, Pa," said Selena furiously. "You were right when you said that there had been some changes made around here. Furthermore the changes are going to remain. If you want to throw empty bottles around, you can get out and go do it somewhere else. You can't do it here. Not any more."

A great deal of liquor, plus the quick change from extreme cold to warmth, made Lucas feel much drunker than he believed himself to be, and, as always, drunkenness made him ugly.

"Listen, you," he snarled. "Don't go tellin' me what to do in my own house. I don't give a shit what you've done to the place while I was gone. It's still my place, and don't you forget it."

"Did you come back just to make trouble?" demanded Selena shrilly. "Haven't you done enough? Wasn't it enough what you did to me, and to Ma? You heard about Ma, didn't you? Killed herself. That's what you did to Ma. Isn't that enough for you?"

Lucas made a deprecating gesture with his hand. "Yeah," he

said. "I heard about what Nellie done. A disgrace to the family, that's what it was. There's never been a Cross who killed himself before, 'til Nellie went and done it. She musta been crazy. But I don't give a damn about that," he said, and began to smile. He stood up, swaying a little, and began to move toward Selena. "I never did give a damn about Nellie," he said. "Not after I got to know you real good, honey."

In one terrible flash, the memory of her day with Dr. Swain returned to Selena. She could feel the heat of the July sun on her back, bringing out the sweat, and the doctor's probing hands. She could hear his gentle voice, and she remembered the pain when she had awakened and it had been over with. She remembered Nellie's blue, swollen face, and the doctor lying, telling her that Nellie had had cancer. Selena's hand tightened on the fire tongs which she had not put down after fixing the fire.

"Don't come near me, Pa," she said, and fear and revulsion made her choke on her words.

"Still a little wildcat, ain't ya, honey?" said Lucas softly. "Ain't had a man around since I left who could tame ya. I can see that." He walked closer to her, until he was standing directly in front of her. "Be nice to me, honey," he said in the old whining voice she remembered so well. "Be good to me. It ain't like I was your real pa. There ain't nothin' wrong in you bein' good to me." He put his big hands on her shoulders. "Be nice to me, honey. It's been a long time."

Selena threw back her head and spit square in his face. "You dirty old bastard," she said, her voice furiously low. "Take your crummy hands off me."

Lucas raised one hand and wiped her spittle away. "Little wildcat, ain't ya," he said, smiling his smile. "I'll fix ya. Same's I used to fix you long ago. Comere."

And then Selena realized that she was fighting for her life. In his effort to subdue her, Lucas' hands had fastened about her throat and she began to feel the lightheadedness which comes with the lack of sufficient air.

"Little bitch," he spat as her knee came up to hit him in the groin. "I'll fix ya!"

His face was congested with blood as he reached for her again, and in the quick second before his hands could touch her she brought the fire tongs around with both her hands and smashed them with all her strength against the side of his head. He fell to the floor at once, almost at her feet, and in fear lest he gather his strength and stand up, Selena brought the tongs down again and again on his head. Blood gushed up in a fountain and bathed her face.

He must not stand up! If he stands up he will kill me! I must not allow him to stand up! He must be dead.

But Selena dared not uncover her eyes to look. She felt two thin arms from behind, pulling her, pulling her away from the thing at her feet, and still she dared not uncover her eyes. It was not until she felt a sharp blow against her chin that she lowered her hand and looked straight into the eyes of her little brother Joey. Behind her the fire made a crisp, crackling, friendly sound as the log she had placed across the andirons began to burn.

So quickly, she thought numbly. In just the short time it takes for a log to catch fire and begin to burn.

She raised her left hand and wiped it across her mouth. It came away smeared with blood. She licked her lips and tasted blood.

"I cut my lip," she said stupidly.

Joey shook his head. "It's from *him*," he whispered. "It's all over you. You're all covered with blood."

All Selena wanted to do was to lie down somewhere and go to sleep. She felt as if she had not slept for weeks, and she shook her head now, against the weariness which was on her. I must not go to sleep, she thought sleepily. I must stay awake and think. With an effort, she finally thought of what it was she must do. She walked toward the telephone as if she were wading through mud, and her hand was on the receiver before Joey reached her. He slapped her hand away, viciously.

"What're you doin'?" he demanded. He had wanted to shout, but the words came out in a hoarse whisper.

"Calling Buck McCracken," said Selena, and reached again for the telephone receiver.

"Are you crazy?" whispered Joey, his fingers around her wrist. He coughed. "Are you crazy?" This time the words came out in a normal tone which seemed too loud. "Are you crazy? You can't do that. They'll arrest you, if you call the sheriff."

"What else is there to do?" asked Selena.

"We'll have to get rid of him," said Joey. "I heard you talkin'. Nobody knows he's here. We'll get rid of him, and nobody'll ever know."

"How can we get rid of him?"

"We'll bury him."

297

"We can't. The ground's frozen. We could never dig a hole deep enough."

"The sheep pen," said Joey, and the two of them stood still, thinking of the sheep pen. Neither of them looked at the body in front of the fireplace.

"The ground ain't frozen in the sheep pen," said Joey. "I've had that infra-red lamp goin' for two days in there, on account of the lambs. It'll be soft, the ground will. Just like it is outdoors in the summertime."

"We'll get caught," said Selena. "There's blood all over the place. We'll get caught."

"Listen, we *can't* get caught. If we do, they'll arrest you and put you in jail. They'll put you in jail and then hang you." Joey sat down and began to cry. "Selena!"

"Yes, Joey?"

"Selena, they'll hang you! Just like Ma went and hung herself. They'll hang you by the neck 'til you turn blue and die!"

"Don't cry, Joey."

"Selena! Selena!"

As if Joey's sobs were a stimulant, Selena began to think. She forced herself to look at Lucas, and then she swallowed the vomit which the sight of him raised in her mouth.

"Get a blanket, Joey," she said calmly.

A moment later, after he had handed her a woolen blanket taken from the foot of her bed, she said: "Go let the sheep out of the pen," in the same calm voice.

She wrapped the blanket around the crushed thing that had been her stepfather. Only his body was recognizable. When she and Joey dragged him out of the house, the wind caught at the skirts of her robe and nightgown and wrapped them tightly around her legs. Lucas' blood seeped through the blanket and left a red trail in the drifting snow.

Selena and Joey buried Lucas in a grave three feet deep, and when it was done, Joey let the sheep back into the pen. At once, they began to wander around, as was their fashion, and in minutes the newly dug grave was tamped down and covered with small hoof prints. But the digging and burying was simple in comparison with the work involved in cleaning the living room. It was daylight, with the wind still blowing and pushing the icy flakes of snow, when they finished. They stood together and looked out one of the front windows. The walk from the house to the sheep pen was completely drifted over, so that it looked as if no one had passed that way at all.

◆ 5 ◆

Soon after the first of the new year, Joey Cross contacted a man by the name of Enrico Antonelli who owned a pig farm on the outskirts of town and who also operated as the local butcher. Mr. Antonelli had been born in Keene, New Hampshire, and had come to Peyton Place as a child with his parents. Yet, he was generally referred to by the town as "that Eye tye over on the Pond Road." He had the curly black hair, the bright, dark eyes and the generous belly of a comic opera Italian, and it was a source of continual pride to Mr. Antonelli to know that he spoke better English than most of the townspeople who had been born of ancestors who had been living in America during the 1600's.

"It is a bad time of the year to slaughter, Joey," he said. "How come you are in such a hurry?"

"I'm just sick of sheep is all," replied Joey. "I'm thinkin' of puttin' in chickens in another month or so. I want all the sheep gone before then."

"Even Cornelia?" asked Mr. Antonelli, referring to Joey's three-time blue ribbon winning ewe.

"Yes," said Joey, not without an effort, "even Cornelia."

"Joey, you are making a mistake. Keep the sheep for another couple of months. Fatten them up. Meat will be bringing a much better price by then."

Joey, terrified of creating even the slightest suspicion that all was not as it should be at the Cross house, tried to keep his voice calm and dispassionate. "No, I don't think I'll do that, Mr. Antonelli," he said. "I don't wanna take care of 'em no more."

Mr. Antonelli ran his fingers through his thick, curly, comic opera Italian hair and shrugged eloquently. "Isn't that odd," he said. "I always had the idea that you loved those sheep as if they were your brothers."

"I did," admitted Joey, trying to imitate Mr. Antonelli's shrug, and failing. "But I don't no more."

"Well," sighed Mr. Antonelli, "I'll try to get over to your place in the morning. If Kenny Stearns is sober enough, perhaps I can get him to help me."

"I'll be home," said Joey. "It don't do to count on Kenny to show up for nothin'."

It was just as well that Joey absented himself from school in order to remain at home to help Mr. Antonelli, for Kenny Stearns was certainly in no condition to help the butcher the next morning.

"I told you it didn't do to count on Kenny," remarked Joey as he helped Mr. Antonelli load sheep into the Italian's truck.

Mr. Antonelli shook his head. "I saw him last night," he said, "and he promised me faithfully that he would be at my place at six this morning."

How Kenny Stearns managed to reach the schools in town, let alone being able to find his way to Antonelli's in the outskirts, was a mystery, for he was so drunk at seven o'clock that morning that he could not have read a steam pressure gauge accurately had his life depended on it. He put his hand gingerly against the plump sides of the school furnaces and knocked experimentally on both boilers, then, satisfied that the fires were hot enough and the boilers had enough water, he made his way staggeringly, down Maple Street toward Elm and to his own home. Upon reaching his house, Kenny immediately locked himself in the back woodshed for the rest of the day, and the efforts to rout him out of his retreat by his wife Ginny and the few townspeople for whom Kenny was supposed to work that day were futile.

"He's in the woodshed, drunk as a skunk," said Ginny to those who came to inquire for him. "I can't make him come out but you go ahead and try if you want."

But for Ginny and his employers alike, Kenny had one answer. "Kiss my arse."

Ephraim Tuttle, who owned the grocery store, was the only man in town who managed to get another word out of Kenny that day.

"I would, Kenny," said Ephraim, in reply to Kenny's one remark, "if you'd just come out of that woodshed and down to the store to shovel the walks like you promised."

"Frig you," said Kenny hostilely, and those were the last words anyone heard from him that day.

Ginny, who in addition to being cold due to her inability to get into the shed for wood to keep the house stoves going, grew rapidly bored and left the house early in the afternoon.

"I'm going down to The Lighthouse," she said, referring to Peyton Place's one beer saloon, a horribly misnamed place, for not only was it nowhere near the sea but it was neither light nor a house. It was located on Ash Street, and was a dismal, barnlike

affair from which emanated an odor of sweat, stale beer and sawdust every time the door was opened. "I'm going down to The
Lighthouse," repeated Ginny, "where there's a few that appreciates
me."

Ginny Stearns was a tragic example of blonde prettiness gone
to ruin. At forty-odd years of age, she had faded from pink-and-
white rosiness to a rather pallid flabbiness, but Kenny still believed, with his whole heart, that no man breathed who, after
one look at Ginny, was not ready to fall at her feet like—as he put
it—"a cockroach after one taste of Paris green." In her youth, Ginny
had been a victim of such insecurity that it had been necessary
to her to prove her worth to herself continually, a feat which she
had accomplished, in some measure, by sleeping with any man who
asked her. Ginny, however, did not put it on any such crude basis
as that. In later years, she always said: "I could count on the fingers
of one hand the men in Peyton Place and White River who have
not loved me," and by love, Ginny meant a noble emotion of the
soul rather than a baser one of the sex glands.

"You hear me, Kenny?" she cried, pounding resentfully against
the locked door of the woodshed. "I'm going out."

Kenny did not deign to answer. He sat on a pile of cordwood
in his shed and opened a fresh bottle of whisky.

"Whore," he muttered, as the tap of Ginny's high-heeled shoes
reached him. "Harlot. Slut."

Kenny sighed. He had, he knew, no one to blame but himself
for getting tangled up with Ginny. His own father had warned him
against her.

"Kenneth," his father had said, "no good will come of your mat-
ing with Virginia Uhlenberg. The young of the mill hands are all
alike. No good a-tall."

Kenny knew that his father had been a smart man. He hadn't
been a handy man like Kenny, but a real landscape gardener who
had landscaped the grounds of the state house.

"Pa," Kenny had said, "I love Ginny Uhlenberg. I'm gonna marry
her."

"God rest your soul," said his father, who was given to flowery
phrases and biblical quotations.

Nope, thought Kenny, taking a drink from the newly opened
bottle, ain't got nobody to blame but myself. Pa told me. He told
me that he told me so, right after Ginny started runnin' out. He
told me every year 'til he died, the sonofabitch. I'll bet he never got
over bein' sore that he couldn't have Ginny for himself.

301

Kenny spent the rest of the afternoon and part of the evening in trying to convince himself that Ginny had never cuckolded him with his own father. It was a hopeless task. In the end, the idea became a sharp sword of torture in his mind and he could stand it no longer. He decided to go to The Lighthouse and face Ginny with it.

"Ginny," he would demand in a terrible voice, "did you ever do it with my father?"

Let her try to deny it, the bitch, he thought. Just let her try. He'd beat the lying words right out of her with the jagged end of a broken bottle.

This last was a prospect which propelled him out of his house and into the cold January night. It kept him warm all the way to Mill Street and then deserted him abruptly. He stood on the street corner, shivering under the thin shirt he wore, and his teeth began to chatter. Up ahead of him lights shimmered in the darkness, and Kenny decided to go into the building behind the lights to get warm. He drank the last inch or so of whisky which remained in the bottle that he was going to break into jagged points to beat Ginny with, and tossed it into the street. He did not realize that he walked erratically as he headed for the lighted building ahead. His only thought was that it was taking him a helluva long while to get there. When he finally reached the steps of the building, he fancied that he heard singing, but he did not notice the black, gilt-lettered sign next to the entrance which proclaimed this as The Peyton Place Pentecostal Full Gospel Church. Kenny lurched through the door, and spying a long, wooden bench close to the entrance, he sat down abruptly. No one turned to look at him. Kenny sat for what seemed a long time, letting the comfortable warmth of the building soothe him, and hearing, without listening, the voices which testified to the all-powerful healing ability of God. Occasionally, the whole group burst into song, and when this happened, Kenny raised his heavy lids to look around.

Why don't they, for Christ's sake, shut up, he thought resentfully, for the voices, together with hand-clapping and the reverberant booming of the organ, set up a painful throbbing in his head.

When the minister, Oliver Rank, began to preach in rolling, ringing tones, Kenny regarded this as the last straw. A man, he decided, could stand just so much. Goddamn it, where the hell were his feet? Kenny looked down, trying to locate the legs which would not allow him to stand, and when he did so, his head began to revolve in wide, sickening arcs. At last, he raised himself. He took one step forward into the aisle between the wooden pews, and fell flat on his face with a resounding thud.

Well, I'll be a dirty sonofabitch, thought Kenny, if some bastard didn't push me.

He did not realize it, but his thought formed itself on his lips and left them in a low, indistinguishable whisper.

"Hark!" cried Oliver Rank. "Hark!"

Hark yourself, you sonofabitch, muttered Kenny, but fortunately his words came out in a confused jumble of sound. Any man who would shove another man is a sonofabitch, thought Kenny, beginning to feel sorry for himself.

"Hark!" cried Oliver Rank again, for he was ever one to press any advantage which came his way. "Hark! A stranger speaks in our midst. What says he?"

I say, thought Kenny, that you are a sonofabitch who would screw his own mother and sell his grandmother to a white slaver. Any man who'd push another is a sonofabitch.

Kenny did not try to stand, or to change his position. The main aisle of the church was carpeted with a soft red carpeting, and the building was warm and he was extremely cozy.

"It's Kenny Stearns!" exclaimed one member of the congregation. "He must be drunk."

"Tread easy, brother," intoned Oliver Rank. "Call not thy brother by vile names. What says he?"

"Oh, God!" moaned Kenny aloud, why don't you keep your bloody mouth shut?

The congregation, which had heard only Kenny's fervent, "Oh, God," began to murmur among themselves.

Kenny turned over onto his back and winced as the bright lights of the church struck his eyes. "Oh, sweet Jesus Christ," he groaned, "why don't somebody turn off the friggin' lights," and again, the end of his sentence came out in unrecognizable syllables.

"The unknown tongue!" screamed a hysterical woman. "He speaks the unknown tongue!" and at once, the congregation went into an uproar. The unknown tongue, the minister had told them, was a language of revelation spoken only by the most holy. The ability to speak and interpret this unknown language was a God-given gift, presented only to the prophets.

"Speak, O holy one!" cried Oliver Rank, as excited as any member of his flock, for he, no more than they, had ever seen or heard a prophet who spoke the unknown tongue of the holiest. "Speak! Speak!"

For two hours, Kenny lay on the floor of the church and raved drunkenly in unintelligible words.

"A prophet!" cried those who listened to him.

"A Messiah come to lead us to Jordan!" cried Oliver Rank.

"A holy messenger who brings news of the Second Coming!" screamed the same woman who had first cried out.

One man, completely carried away, ran into the street shouting of the glory which had come to Peyton Place. He ran all the way to The Lighthouse to fetch Ginny Stearns, who first hooted, but then consented to go to the church provided that she could bring her friends with her. The regular churchgoer, followed by Ginny and half a dozen of her cohorts, rushed back to the church where Kenny still held forth. There was Ginny's husband, lying on the floor and raving the same as he always did when he was dead drunk, while a whole churchful of sober and apparently sane people listened as if he were telling them where to find gold.

"Kenny Stearns!" shrilled Ginny, who had been drinking most of the day herself. "Get up off that floor." She prodded him with her toe. "You're drunk."

"Let he who has not sinned cast the first stone!" roared Oliver Rank, seeing that Ginny was intoxicated.

Ginny shrank back as if Mr. Rank had breathed fire on her, and the only part of Kenny's next sentence which was understandable was the word "Whore."

"A revelation!" cried Mr. Rank, pointing an unusually sharp forefinger at Ginny. "The sinners in our midst are uncovered!"

Ginny skittered away from Kenny and hid behind two of her friends.

At the end of two hours, Kenny passed out completely. His eyes rolled back in his head until only the whites were visible, and four members of the congregation carried him tenderly to his home.

In time, Kenny came to believe that it was the sure hand of God which had led him to the church, and that it was the Lord who had put the words of revelation into his mouth. Exactly what words, Kenny was never absolutely sure, but that did not bother him. The members of the Peyton Place Pentecostal Full Gospel Church accepted him as a man of holiness, and before too many years had passed Kenny was baptized and ordained as a minister in the sect. Fortunately, this religious group did not believe it necessary for its ministers to attend a theological school of any

304

kind, for Kenny would have been hard pressed indeed to define his philosophical beliefs.

Peyton Place never recovered from the shock of seeing the ex-town handy man and ex-drunkard walk rapidly down Elm Street clad in a frock coat and carrying a Bible under his arm. The men patrons of The Lighthouse remembered Ginny Stearns wistfully, now that she had reformed and accepted her husband's religion. As for Ginny, whenever Kenny took her in the same uncouth, un-gentle way he had done in years past, she did not mind. She felt as if she were the Virgin Mary and Kenny the angel come to tell her that the Lord had chosen her as the mother of a new world hope. Only very, very rarely did something in Kenny pull him up short and cause him to wonder what he was doing as a minister, and also to wonder what road had led him to the path he now followed. At these times, Kenny would shrug and blame it all on the sure hand of God.

In the early winter of 1944, Peyton Place talked of little else besides Kenny Stearns. It did not even cause much of a stir when two men from the Navy Department came to town, making in-quiries about Lucas Cross who, it seemed, had been in the Navy and was now absent without leave. The men from the Navy De-partment went with Buck McCracken to the house where Selena and Joey Cross lived and asked a few questions, but the Crosses said no, that they had not seen Lucas since he had left Peyton Place back in '39. The Navy men asked a few questions in town, but no one had seen or heard from Lucas, so they went away, and the town went back to talking about Kenny Stearns, who had been the hero in A Miracle.

◆ 6 ◆

Before the sensation caused by Kenny Stearns had begun to abate properly, the town was subjected to further excitement, for little Norman Page came home from the war. He returned to Peyton Place in March of 1944 as a hero, with a chestful of cam-paign ribbons, medals and a stiff leg on which he walked with the help of a crutch. He was helped from the train by his mother, who had gone down to Boston to fetch him home, and he was greeted by the Peyton Place High School Band playing "The Stars and Stripes Forever," and the welcoming cheers of the townspeople.

Jared Clarke made a speech in which he welcomed Norman as "a hunter home from the hill, and a sailor home from the sea," although Norman had served as an infantryman with the Army. The Ladies' Aid Society, in conjunction with the board of selectmen and the school board, declared the twentieth of March as Norman Page Day, and then proceeded to organize a parade and to give a sumptuous banquet, at which everyone in town was welcomed. Norman, at the head table at the banquet, stood up and made a speech, and when he finished there were very few dry eyes in the high school gymnasium, where the feast had taken place. Peyton Place did, in fact, cover its first returning hero with a surfeit of love and sentimentality.

"Poor boy. He's so white," they said, and no one pointed out that Norman had always been a pale child.

"The dear boy. So young to have seen so much."

Seth Buswell photographed Norman as the young hero stood, leaning on his crutch, in front of the monument to the dead of World War I in Memorial Park. There was a lot of unpleasant talk directed toward Seth when this photograph never appeared on the front page of the *Times*. What the town did not know was that on the evening of the day when Seth had taken the picture, Dr. Matthew Swain had approached the newspaper owner. "Don't run that picture, Seth," said the doctor.

"Why not?" demanded Seth. "It's a good photo. Local hero returns home, and all that. Good stuff."

"Somebody from out of town might see it," said the doctor.

"So what?"

"So nothing, except that I'd bet my diploma, my license to practice and my shingle that there's nothing the matter with Norman Page's leg. He's never even been wounded."

Seth was shocked. "But what about all those medals?" he asked. "The kid's got ribbons from his waist to his shoulder, practically."

"Ribbons, yes," said the doctor, "medals, no. Anybody can go into a store near a service base and buy those ribbons by the gross. There's a store like that in Manchester. I noticed it when I was down there last week. I'll bet everything I own that Evelyn went into one of those stores in Boston and bought every single ribbon that Norman has on his tunic."

"But why? There isn't any sense to a thing like that. Plenty of boys don't come home as heroes. Why should she feel that Norman had to."

"I don't know, but I'll sure as hell find out. Fella who went to med school with me is one of the big brass down in Washington now. He should be able to tell me."

The next day, the doctor went to the state house to register his automobile, and while at the state capitol, several miles away from Peyton Place, he telephoned to his friend in Washington.

"Sure, I can find out, Matt," said the friend. "I'll call you tonight at your home."

"No, don't do that," protested the doctor, thinking of Alma Hayes, the town's telephone operator who had a reputation for listening in on everyone's long-distance calls. "Write me a letter," he said. "I'm in no hurry."

A few days later, the letter came and Dr. Swain took it at once to Seth. Norman Page, according to the records, had been given a medical discharge on the grounds that he was mentally unfit to handle the duties of a soldier. While Peyton Place had sympathized with Evelyn Page, whose son, according to her, lay wounded in a hospital in Europe, Norman Page had been recovering from a bad case of battle fatigue in a hospital in the United States. Matthew Swain's friend wrote further, that as far as he could learn, Norman had gone PN under fire in France.

"What's that?" asked Seth, pointing to the letters PN.

"Psychoneurotic," said the doctor, and reached across Seth's desk for the newspaper owner's cigarette lighter. He held the letter over an empty wastebasket and set it afire. "I can see Evelyn's fine hand in this," he said.

"So can I," agreed Seth.

Together, the two men decided that since they had discovered a truth which would only hurt Norman in the town and possibly get him into trouble with the Army authorities if it were known, they would forget the matter entirely. Seth destroyed the photograph of Norman, together with the negative, and let the angry talk of Peyton Place buzz over his head while Matthew Swain had only one more comment to make.

"Somebody," he said, "should teach that boy how to walk properly stiff-legged, and how to handle that crutch a little more realistically."

Evelyn Page, meanwhile, was totally unaware that anyone had seen through her "little subterfuge" as she referred to her hoax when she spoke of it to Norman. She excused herself on the grounds that she had never meant to carry her deception so far, that it was just one of those unfortunate things which had got out of hand. After all, she told herself privately, one had to make the best of it once the fat was in the fire, and no one but a fool ever wept over spilt milk. She never regretted the decision she had made when the government had notified her that Norman was back in the United States suffering from a mental disorder. She had pondered on what to do for several days before going to the hospital where Norman lay ill. In the end, she had notified her friends that Norman had been wounded, that he lay near death in a foreign hospital, with a terrible leg wound. When Evelyn left town to go down to Connecticut to visit her sister, her friends saw her off with many tears and good wishes. After all, the poor soul was stricken with grief and worry; it was understandable that she did not want to remain alone in her house on Depot Street.

A few months later, when she received word of Norman's impending discharge, she passed the word around town that she was going down to Boston to await the ship which would bring "Norman's poor, broken body home to her." For two weeks after Norman was medically discharged, she remained in a Boston hotel with her son, coaching him in the role he must play when the two of them returned home.

"Do you want everyone in town to think of you as crazy?" she cried, when Norman protested. "Crazy the way Hester Goodale was crazy?

"Do you want everyone up home to think of you as a coward who ran under fire?

"Do you want to disgrace the both of us so that we can never hold up our heads again?

"Do you want to give the Page Girls something on us that they can really talk about?

"You do what Mother says, dear. Have I ever steered you a false course?"

Norman, weary to death in mind, body, soul and spirit, finally nodded in acquiescence, and Evelyn telephoned the joyous news to Peyton Place that she was bringing Norman home. After the welcoming ceremonies and the banquet, she congratulated him enthusiastically on the fine tone with which he had delivered his speech, and for days afterward, she propped him up in a chair in the living room, with his "bad leg" extended on a matching ottoman, and smiled tearfully at the friends who came to visit him. Even the Page Girls came, with their fat faces neatly powdered and their bulky bodies encased in black silk. Caroline carried a jar of homemade soup and Charlotte held a bottle of homemade dandelion wine.

"We have come to see Oakleigh's boy," they told Evelyn.

The house was empty at the time, except for Norman, so that Evelyn finally had a chance to taunt her dead husband's daughters.

"Afraid of what Peyton Place would say, weren't you, if you hesitated to come to see your war-wounded brother?"

Since this was the truth, the Page Girls had no ready answer. They withstood another five minutes of Evelyn's tongue-lashing without flinching before she let them into the living room where Norman sat. It was the first time that the girls had ever been in Evelyn's house. Their faces, their attitude, their soft voices, when they spoke to the child they had maligned for years, made every speck of effort involved in Evelyn's "little subterfuge" well worth while.

"You see?" she told Norman triumphantly, when the Page Girls had gone. "What did I tell you? Isn't it better this way than if folks went around thinking that you were crazy?"

As for Norman, he felt as if he moved through an unreal world. He continued to suffer from nightmares, not all of them to do with the war. He still dreamed the old, recurrent dream about Miss Hester Goodale and her tomcat. In his dream, Miss Hester always wore the face of his mother, while the two people whom she watched through the gap in the hedge were no longer Mr. and Mrs. Card, but Allison MacKenzie and Norman. In his dream, when he stroked Allison's abdomen he would feel a tight excitement in his genitals but always, just at the moment of release, Allison's abdomen would burst open and spew forth millions of slimy blue worms. The worms were deadly poisonous, and Norman would begin to run. He would run and run, until he could run no longer, while the worms crawled swiftly after him. Sometimes he woke up at this point, covered with sweat and choking with fear, but most of the time he succeeded in reaching the arms of his mother before he awoke. It was always at that moment, when he reached his mother, that Norman reached a climax in the excitement engendered by Allison. At such times, Norman awoke to warmth and wetness and a sense that his mother had saved him from a terrible danger.

In time, the "stiffness" disappeared from Norman's "bad leg," and he began to look around for something to do. Finally, Seth Buswell offered him a job as a combination bookkeeper and circulation manager on the *Times,* and Norman went to work. He worked faithfully every day and carried his pay check home to his mother, uncashed, at the end of every week.

It was Norman's circumspect behavior which really "showed up" Rodney Harrington in the town's eyes, for Rodney had not gone to war. As soon as the draft had become a reality, Leslie Harrington had found a job for his son in the Cumberland Mills of enough importance so that Rodney was classified as "essential" to the war effort as a civilian. There was a lot of ugly talk in Peyton Place about that. There were some who said that the three men on the local draft board lived in houses with mortgages held by Leslie Harrington, and, furthermore, that the sons of these men worked in jobs also considered as "essential" in the mills.

The position which Leslie Harrington had enjoyed for years, and which had begun to be undermined in 1939, was seriously in danger by the spring of 1944. People who had considered it folly, and worse, for the Ellsworths to sue Leslie back in '39, began to change their minds soon afterward. With quiet courage, Kathy had harmed Leslie far more than she could have done with words. She had married Lewis Welles shortly before his induction into the Army, and she had become pregnant at once. During the war, there were a good many people in town who felt a thick shame whenever they watched Kathy Welles walk down Elm Street, pushing a baby buggy with her one hand. They looked at Kathy, who awaited the return of Lewis with a hope that never faltered, not even during the dark days of Bataan and Corregidor, and they began to wonder about Leslie Harrington, who could well have afforded to make things a little easier for Kathy.

"Twenty-five hundred dollars," said Peyton Place. "Don't seem like much, even if he did take care of her medical bills besides."

"Leslie Harrington would sooner sell his soul than part with a dollar."

"Don't seem right, somehow. Her with her husband gone off to the war, and Leslie with his son right at home."

"Kathy Welles got the short end of that stick, all right. Even thirty thousand dollars wouldn't've put her arm back on, but it would've made things a mite easier. She coulda hired someone to help her around the house, and to take care of her baby. I hear she whips around that house of hers so good and so fast that she don't really need two arms."

"It's a shame though, the way Leslie Harrington got away with it so cheap. His son is a great hand for gettin' away with things, too. Look at the way he's stayed out of the war, and the way he always seems to have plenty of gas to hell around in his car. Gas is rationed to everybody else."

"Rodney was always a great hand for gettin' away with things. Remember Betty Anderson?"

"I hear tell he's got some girl down to Concord now. Goes to see her every night, I hear."

"He'll get his, one of these day. So will Leslie. The Harringtons have been due for their comeuppance for a long time."

Yet, Leslie Harrington was never able to put his finger on the moment when he had begun to lose his grip on Peyton Place. He was inclined to believe that it had been when the AF of L succeeded in unionizing the mills, a thing unheard of, even undreamed of, in Peyton Place. Leslie had roared and threatened to close down the mills and put everyone out of work forever, but he had, unfortunately for him, signed contracts with the government which precluded his doing so, and the mill hands knew it. Everything, according to Leslie, had begun to fall apart with the unionizing of the mills. Business at the bank had fallen off, as people began to transfer their mortgages to a bank in a town ten miles to the south. Once, Leslie would have fired a man for doing this, but with the union in command, he was unable to do as he would have liked. It had been Tomas Makris, or so Leslie had heard, who had informed the mill hands of the bank in another town which was eager for new business, and even against this perfidy, Leslie was helpless. He had been defeated when he had run for the school board that spring, a fact which had left him dazed for weeks, and the school board in control now thought that Tom was the best headmaster Peyton Place had ever had. In the spring of 1944, Leslie Harrington lived with fear, and his only comfort was his son, whom he had managed to save from the war.

"I'll get even," he raved to Rodney. "Just you wait 'til this goddamned war is over with. Wait and see how long the goddamned union lasts in my mills then. I'll fire every sonofabitch who works for me now, and I'll import a whole new population to Peyton Place."

But Peter Drake, the young attorney who had fought Leslie in the case of Ellsworth *vs.* Harrington, took another view.

"The backbone of Chestnut Street is broken," said Drake. "When one vertebra is out of kilter, the whole spine ceases to function efficiently."

Rodney Harrington, however, was not concerned with either the mills, the backbone of Chestnut Street or the changes in Peyton Place. He was, as always, concerned primarily with himself. He had two sets of attitudes, each completely separate and distinct from the other. The first set was comprised of the attitudes which he knew it was politic for him to hold, and the second of those which he actually did hold. It was an attitude of the first set which often prompted him to say, "There is nothing more frustrating than an essential war job. I feel so utterly useless, safe here in America, while our boys are fighting for their lives overseas." He usually said this to some pretty girl who consoled him eagerly by telling him that he was most essential to her.

"Oh, yeah?" Rodney would generally reply. "How essential? Show me, baby!"

There were not many girls, in the man-lean spring of 1944, who refused to comply with this request.

But one particular attitude in Rodney's second set would not be denied. He was, as he admitted privately, damned glad to be out of the war. The thought of filth, lack of good food, cramped quarters, bad clothes and, above all, regimentation, was an abhorrent one to him. Every man, Rodney was sure, who had a grain of honesty in him would agree with this attitude. Nobody *wanted* to go off to war any more than he did. He just happened to be luckier than most, and was damned grateful for the fact.

And what good could a fellow do himself? Rodney wondered. Just supposing that a fellow could overlook all the disadvantages of being in the service, just what was in it for him? Look at that half-assed Norman Page. Back home from the war to a piddling little job on the paper, with nothing to show for his effort but a few tin medals and a gimpy leg. No sir, that wasn't for Rodney Harrington, not by a long shot.

He pressed his foot down on the accelerator of his car, confident of the full gas tank and the four good tires under him as he drove swiftly toward Concord and a date with his best girl.

She was a honey, all right, Helen was, he thought. But if he didn't get to her tonight, he was going to tell her to go blow. There were too many other girls eager to hook up with a good steady civilian, one with plenty of money and a decent car.

With the idea of "getting to Helen" foremost in his mind, Rodney stopped at a liquor store on Concord's Main Street and bought another fifth of rum. Helen "just adored" rum when it was mixed with Coca-Cola. In addition to the rum, he had six pairs of black market nylon hose in the glove compartment of his car as extra persuasion.

"Oh, what're these!" cried Helen a few moments later as she held up the stockings.

Levers to pry your pants off, thought Rodney, but he said: "Pretty nylons for pretty legs," and the inanity of it was lost on Helen, who had a nature as acquisitive as a squirrel's in autumn.

All in all, the two spent a highly pleasant evening. By ten o'clock they were both feeling very rum-warmed and comradely.

"You understand me so well," purred Helen, smoothing the fingers of one of his hands with her own.

"Do I?" he asked, circling her with one arm and resting that hand just under her breast. "Do I?" he whispered, against her cheek.

"Yes," said Helen, snuggling up to him. "You understand about the finer things in life. Books and music, and all that."

Helen's biggest trouble, thought Rodney, was that she had seen too many movies. She tried to talk and act the way she imagined a motion picture actress would, after a hard day on the lot. His kisses left her unmoved if they were not of the expert, no noses bumped variety. Too bad, thought Rodney, that they had not yet begun to make the sexual act a part of every motion picture, for then Helen would have fallen into his hands like an overripe grape. He sighed and thought of the girls he had known, and left, who had not been movie fans. Getting to Helen, he was afraid, was going to be a long, hard process, and he was not at all sure that the game was going to be worth the candle, as someone or other had put it.

"Hm-m," murmured Helen, against him. "We go together like peaches and cream."

"Ham and eggs," he said, beginning to massage her breast with his hand.

"Pie and ice cream," she giggled, moving a little under his touch.

"Hot dogs and football games," said Rodney, putting his other hand on her thigh.

"Speaking of hot dogs," said Helen, jumping up, "I'm hungry. Let's go get something to eat."

And that, thought Rodney savagely, was that. He'd buy her a goddamned hot dog, a dozen if she wanted, but he was goddamned if he was going to bother with her again after tonight.

Helen giggled all the way down the stairs from her apartment to the car, and she giggled nerve rackingly as Rodney drove to a drive-in a short way outside of the city. He did not speak.

"Oh, honey," giggled Helen, chewing at the last of her hot dog. "Is my little old honey mad at poor little me?"

Unaccountably, Rodney thought, he was thinking of Betty An-

313

derson. He could almost hear those same words coming from a contrite Betty on a summer night of long ago.

"I guess not," he said, and again he had the eerie feeling of having spoken those words before.

"Don't you be mad at me, doll," whispered Helen. "I'll be good to you. Just you take me back to the apartment, and I'll show you how good I can be. I'll be the best you ever had, baby, just you wait and see."

Playing at hard to get, in his turn, Rodney looked down at her and smiled. "How do I know?" he asked.

And then Helen did the most exciting thing that Rodney had ever seen in all of his twenty-one years. Right there in the car, with the lights of the drive-in shining all around them and people sitting in cars not six feet away from them on either side, Helen unbuttoned her blouse and showed him one perfect breast.

"Look at that," she said, cupping the breast with her hand, "no bra. I've got the hardest breasts you ever played with."

Rodney raced the car motor violently in his eagerness to be gone from the drive-in's parking lot. Helen did not rebutton her blouse, but leaned back in the seat, leaving her breast exposed. Every few seconds, she inhaled and sat up a little, running her hand sensuously over her bare skin, flicking her nipple with a snap of a fingernail. Rodney could not keep his eyes off her. She was like something that he had read about in what he termed "dirty books." He had never seen a woman so apparently enamored of her own body before, and to him there was something wicked, forbidden, exciting about it.

"Let me," he said, reaching for her as he sped along the highway toward Concord.

She snapped her head away from him quickly. "Look out!"

It was a scream of warning, uttered too late. When Rodney recovered himself enough to look up, the brightly lit trailer truck seemed to be right on top of him.

♦ 7 ♦

Each spring, it was the duty of Dexter Humphrey, as chairman of the Budget Committee, to act as moderator at town meeting. He took this responsibility seriously, reading each item of the town warrant in sonorous tones and preceding each vote with a sepulchrally voiced question.

"You have heard the item as listed in the warrant for this town. What is your wish in this matter?"

The townspeople then either voted immediately or discussed the issue until it was settled.

"The town meeting," said Tomas Makris to the high school students every spring, "is the last example of pure democracy existing in the world today. It is the one function which remains where each man may stand up to express his ideas and opinions on the running of his town."

Of course, thought Tom, remembering his first year in Peyton Place, that does not mean that each will be listened to, but he *is* allowed to speak.

At the town meeting held in the spring of 1944, the old, hot issue of a new grade school had not been included in the warrant because of wartime restrictions on building, but the other, equally controversial question of town zoning was in its regular position. The Budget Committee always listed the question on zoning as the very last item in the warrant, for the arguments on the issue were apt to be long and many.

"We come now," intoned Dexter Humphrey, "to the twenty-first and last question in the warrant." He paused and cleared his throat.

The townspeople, each of whom held a printed copy of the warrant, knew very well what the last question was, yet everyone waited for Dexter Humphrey to read it aloud.

"Whether this assembly will vote to accept Article XIV, in Chapter XXXXIV, of the revised laws of this state," said Dexter.

A stranger might have begun to scramble furiously through the booklet in which the warrant was included, at this point, to try to locate the contents of Article XIV, Chapter XXXXIV of the revised state laws, but the townspeople knew well enough how this law read. Everyone waited for Leslie Harrington to rise to his feet, as he always did, when Dexter had finished reading the question. Never before had Leslie waited for longer than it took Dexter to read the item, and the moderator looked around now in puzzlement.

"You have heard the item as listed in the warrant for this town," said Dexter, staring stupidly at the front row of seats where Leslie sat. "What is your wish in this matter?"

Surely, Leslie would now stand, glance at his gold watch as if he were pressed for time, and say the words he had always said.

"Mr. Moderator, I move that this question be stricken from the warrant."

Then would come: "Second the motion," from whichever of his workers Leslie had picked for this yearly honor.

And then Dexter would say: "A motion to strike this item from the warrant has been made and seconded. What is your wish in this matter? All those in favor?"

The "Ayes" would shake the rafters, while Seth Buswell and a few others would utter the only "Nays."

Dexter Humphrey coughed. "What is your wish in this matter?" he demanded frantically, refusing to put the question to a vote until someone spoke.

Leslie Harrington continued to sit still, staring thoughtfully out of a window in the courthouse meeting room. Dexter's eyes sought the room, trying to locate Seth Buswell. The newspaper owner sat with Matthew Swain and Tomas Makris in a seat toward the rear of the room. Seth studied his fingernails with a deep concentration, but he did not rise to speak.

Fool! thought Dexter Humphrey angrily. Damned fool! He's been shooting his mouth off for years about zoning, and now when he has a chance to see the bloody question come to a vote, he does not rise to press his advantage.

The tension in the room mounted to an almost unbearable degree while Dexter waited. When a farmer finally stood up and cleared his throat preparatory to speaking, the gathering let out its breath as if in one gigantic sigh.

"Does this here zonin' business mean that if I wanna put up a new chicken house, I gotta go and ask somebody?" asked the farmer.

"A pertinent question indeed, Walt," said Dexter, who prided himself on knowing every citizen with his name on the check list. "Jared, would you mind answering Walt's question?"

Jared Clarke stood up. "No, Walt," he said, "it don't. This Article XIV affects only dwellings for human habitation. That is, a place where people arc gonna live. For instance, if you wanted to put up a house here in town, you'd have to get a permit from the board of selectmen. The board, of course, is permitted to restrict the type of dwelling to be erected."

"What you mean to say, Jared," said the farmer named Walt, "is that you and Ben Davis and George Caswell kin tell a man what kind of a house he's gonna build. That right?"

"Not exactly," said Jared carefully, realizing that he was tread-

316

ing on dangerous ground here. "The idea of zoning," he said, turning to face the crowd, "is to protect property values in a town. That is its only purpose."

"Yeah, but that ain't what I asked you, Jared," said Walt. "What I asked was, how come you and Ben and George are gonna have a right to tell a man what kind of a house to build?"

"The type of house," said Jared, feeling warm, "doesn't enter into it at all."

"You mean to say then, that if I wanted to put up a tar paper shack on Elm Street, I could?"

"The way things stand now," said Jared acidly, "you certainly could."

"But I couldn't if we had zoning."

"No," replied Jared flatly. "The minute a shack goes up in a decent neighborhood, the values on all the rest of the property go down. It isn't right, and it isn't sensible. Zoning would be an asset to this community. Perhaps we could do away with chicken houses within a block of Elm Street, if we had zoning."

"What?" It was a scream of outrage from the rear of the room, uttered by a crafty old man who had noticed Jared's contradiction of himself. "What's wrong with a man keepin' a few chickens?" demanded Marvin Potter, who was one of the old men who hung around Tuttle's. "What's wrong with a man tryin' to do a little something to make extra money?" demanded Marvin. "Something like keepin' a few chickens?"

Marvin did not keep a few chickens in the back yard of his house on Laurel Street. He kept a few minks, and in summer the stench from Marvin's few minks wafted gently over Elm Street when the wind was right, so that the townspeople shrugged and rolled their eyes heavenward, while strangers looked around suspiciously.

"Chickens is one thing," said Jared, looking sharply at Marvin, "and minks is something else."

"And I say," roared Marvin, "that being a selectman is one thing, and tryin' to be a dictator is something else again." As was the way with the townspeople, Marvin pronounced "selectman" as if it had been three words: "See-leck-man."

"Mr. Clarke?" It was the poised, low voice of Selena Cross speaking. "Mr. Clarke, since the house where I live with my brother is well within the limits known to all of us as The Village, would zoning mean that I would have to remove my brother's sheep pen from our premises?"

317

Jared hemmed and smiled and coughed, but there was only one answer and he knew it. "Yes," he said.

"Now ain't that a helluva thing," said someone who did not rise to identify himself.

Dexter Humphrey pounded with his gavel to restore order, and Seth Buswell looked narrowly at Selena Cross. As far as he knew, Selena had always been in favor of zoning in years past, and he wondered what had happened to change her mind.

"I move," said Selena Cross, "that this item be stricken from the warrant."

"Second the motion," cried Marvin Potter.

"All those in favor?"

There were perhaps six voices who agreed with Selena's firm "Aye."

Dexter Humphrey wiped his hands with a handkerchief. He picked up his copy of the warrant and read the twenty-first item again. After he had asked his regular question, he put the matter to a vote at once, and for the first time in history, the town of Peyton Place voluntarily gave new powers to its selectmen in the matter of zoning.

When the meeting was over, Peter Drake stood in the lobby of the courthouse and lit a cigarette. Tomas Makris joined him, not by any previous arrangement, but because they both happened to be in the lobby at the same moment. Together, Tom and Drake stood and watched Leslie Harrington leave the courthouse. When the millowner walked out, he was flanked on either side by Seth and Dr. Swain, and Jared Clarke and Dexter Humphrey.

"Isn't it odd," remarked Drake with a little smile, "that while they stood divided against one another, each of them stood strong, while today, when they stood together in silence, one of them fell. I always thought Seth hated Leslie's guts. He'll never have another chance to beat Leslie the way he could have done today."

Tom looked at the tip of his cigarette. "Harrington has lost his son," he said. "That's why none of them spoke but Jared. And Jared would not have spoken, if he had not been asked direct questions."

"Someone's losing a son would never have stopped Harrington in the old days," said Drake viciously. "How come everyone's gone soft on that sonofabitch all of a sudden?"

Tom looked sharply at the lawyer. "Where are you from, Drake?"

318

he asked, and it was a full minute before he realized the suspicious-
ness of the tone he had used.

By Jesus! he thought, I'll have to watch it. I'm beginning to
sound like a true shellback. He threw back his head and began
to laugh.

"From New Jersey," said Drake, eying the laughing Tom. "You?"

"From Peyton Place," said Tom, "via New York, Pittsburgh, and
other points to the south."

Outside, the men of Chestnut Street stepped into Leslie Harrington's car.

"I wonder where Charlie Partridge was today?" asked Drake.

"Home in bed with the grippe," said Tom. "If he weren't, he
would have been here, and he would be riding back to Chestnut
Street with the others right now, in Leslie's car."

"All the same," said Drake, dropping his cigarette and stepping
on it, "the old order changeth. The backbone of Chestnut Street
is broken for fair."

"Maybe," said Tom, and walked out of the courthouse.

♦ 8 ♦

It was one sunny, fresh-scented May morning when Buck Mc-
Cracken first realized the meaning of words to which he had
listened for years.

"It's a small world," people said, but Buck always disagreed
silently and violently.

It was an enormous world, thought Buck, millions of miles tall,
and deep, and wide. Let one of those who always spoke of a small
world set out to walk from Peyton Place to Boston some fine day.
Maybe then they'd quit their gab about a small world and realize
what a damned big place the world really was.

Buck was sitting at the counter in Hyde's Diner on this particular
morning. He always sat in the end seat, if he could, which was
not too often, for this was regarded by practically everyone as
"Clayton Frazier's seat." No matter who was sitting in the end
seat, if Clayton came in, he always stood up and moved somewhere else. Buck liked to sit in the end seat because it was next
to a window which overlooked Elm Street, and from it he could
look out at his black sheriff's car parked at the curb. The red

319

blinker on the car's roof gleamed in the sunlight this morning, and the sharp, pointed antenna of the two-way radio rose like a shaft in the bright morning. Buck was proud of his official car. He kept it washed and polished and looked at it often and fondly. With a contented smile, Buck turned away from the window as a stranger came into the diner.

Salesman. Buck's mind ticketed the stranger at once, although the sheriff pretended not to stare at the stranger. He sipped his coffee and seemed to be lost in thought when the stranger spoke.

"This place looks a lot different than it did the last time I was through here," he said.

Buck looked up disinterestedly. "Oh? Come this way often?"

"No, thank God, although as I say, the place looks pretty good this morning. The last time I was here, it was in the dead of winter. Snowing and blowing like the hounds of hell. That was a night, I'm telling you. I couldn't make it beyond White River, and had to spend the night there. I brought a fellow up with me that night, all the way from Boston. Ask him. He'll tell you what a night it was."

"Feller from here?" asked Buck, trying to remember who had been out of town last winter during the big blizzard.

"Sure," said the salesman. "Navy man. Can't remember his name right now, but he told me what it was. God, how he told me! Drank like a fish, all the way from Boston."

"Navy man, you say?" asked Buck, standing up as Clayton Frazier came into the diner. Clayton sat down in his accustomed seat, and the sheriff moved to the stranger's other side. "I can't remember nobody from here was in the Navy last winter. Can you, Clayton?"

"Nope," said Clayton, picking up the cup of coffee which Corey Hyde had put down in front of him. "You, Corey?"

"Nope. Nobody I know."

"Listen," said the stranger, becoming flustered by all the opposition to his simple statement, "this man came from here all right. He told me so. And he was in the Navy. I picked him up right outside Boston and gave him a lift all the way to here. He said he was coming home to visit his children, and that he hadn't been home since 1939."

Buck, Corey and Clayton looked at one another. Lucas Cross, they thought, as if with one mind, but they would not give the stranger the satisfaction of knowing he had stumped them momentarily.

320

"What'd the feller look like?" asked Buck, fixing the stranger with a suspicious eye.

"Well, I can't remember exactly," said the stranger uncomfortably. "He was big."

"So am I," said Buck. "Was it me?"

"No. No, of course not. This fellow drank quite a lot. I remember that."

"Well, that could make him just about anybody in town," said Corey Hyde. "Is that all you can remember?"

The stranger scratched his cheek thoughtfully. "There was something else," he said. "Something about the way this man smiled. I never saw anybody else smile in quite that way. When this man smiled, his forehead moved. Craziest looking thing I ever saw. I never forgot it. I'd know that smile if I ever saw it again."

"Listen, mister," said Buck softly, "I think you musta been the one drinkin' that night. I've lived in Peyton Place all my life, and I never yet seen a feller who smiled with his forehead. You musta been the one drinkin', and I don't take kindly to fellers drivin' drunk through my town."

"Now listen here," said the stranger, and looked at the faces of Buck, Clayton, and Corey. He did not say anything else. He finished his coffee and walked quickly out of the diner.

For a few minutes, neither of the three men in Hyde's spoke. Then Clayton Frazier set his cup down in his saucer.

"Seems funny," he said, "that Lucas'd come home and nobody'd know about it."

There was another long pause before Buck said: "Selena and Joey didn't see him if he did come. I was over to their place when them Navy men was here lookin' for Lucas. Selena and Joey both said they hadn't seen him."

Corey Hyde refilled the coffee cups. "Selena is no liar," he said. "Neither's the boy."

"Nope, they ain't," agreed Buck and Clayton. "Still, seems funny the way that stranger could describe Lucas so good. I never seen another man smiled like Lucas, either. No more than that salesman ever done."

"Of course," said Buck, quoting as nearly as he could remember from a policeman's manual of long ago, "We have to consider the possibility of foul play."

"Whaddya mean, foul play?" demanded Corey.

"Oh, you know," said Buck. "Somebody hittin' a guy over the head and takin' his money, and like that."

"Who'd hit Lucas over the head?" asked Clayton. "Here in Peyton Place."

"I dunno," said Buck. "I didn't say somebody did. I just said we had to consider the possibility."

"That's one possibility seems highly improbable to me," snorted Clayton. "The idea of one of Lucas' neighbors hittin' him over the head for his money. Lucas never had no money."

"I never said one of his neighbors," said Buck defensively. "It coulda been somebody else, couldn't it? What about that salesman feller. How do we know he didn't do it?"

"Yeah," said Corey disgustedly. "He'd be sure to come right back to Peyton Place and start talkin' about Lucas if he'd hit him over the head."

"Oh, I dunno," said Buck, in a superior tone. "Criminals often return to the scene of the crime."

"Wonder who that salesman worked for?" said Clayton.

"S. S. Pierce, out of Boston," said Buck, in a snappy tone. "I seen it on that brief case he was carryin'."

"Maybe you oughta go after him and ask him if he hit Lucas over the head," said Clayton derisively.

"No, I won't do that," said Buck thoughtfully. "First, I'll get in touch with them Navy fellers and see if Lucas ever went back to his ship in Boston. If he didn't, then I'll begin to do some wonderin'."

"Ain't it a small world," said Corey. "A stranger passin' through town on his way north, stops for coffee in my diner and sits down right next to the sheriff and tells him that he's seen a man nobody in town has seen since '39. Ain't it a small world?"

"Yeah," agreed Buck McCracken thoughtfully, and walked out of the diner to the shiny sheriff's car parked at the curb.

It did not take long for Buck to receive a reply to the inquiries he had made of the Navy Department. Within three days the same two men who had been searching for Lucas Cross during the winter were back in Peyton Place. They contacted the Boston office of the S. S. Pierce Company and located the salesman who had passed through Peyton Place. His name was Gerald Gage, and the Boston office of his company said that he was, at the moment, making business calls on stores in Montpelier, Vermont. Mr. Gage was contacted at Montpelier, and requested to return with all speed to Peyton Place, which he did. He eyed Buck McCracken warily as the two men from the Navy Department questioned him. Yes, he had on the night of, let's see—the twelfth of December, he'd guess, because it was his last trip north until after the holidays, and he was due in Burlington on the thirteenth, picked up a hitch-hiker who wore the uniform of the United States Navy. No, he had not asked the sailor if he was on leave. Why the hell should he? The guy wanted a ride, and he, Gerry Gage, being a good sort, had offered him one. He wished to hell he'd never done it now. But that was his trouble, too goodhearted. He could never pass a fellow up on the road, especially on a night like that one had been last December. Snow? He guessed to hell it was snowing. And windy. Oh, about half-past twelve, he'd guess. He'd noticed the time on account of he was worried about finding a room in Burlington at that hour. As it turned out, he never did make Burlington that night. Got hung up in White River and couldn't drive another yard. That's how hard it had been snowing. Sure, he guessed that he'd recognize the fellow again, all right. Of course, it had been dark when he picked him up, and dark in the car, but they had stopped for coffee down below Nashua someplace, and he'd got a close look at the guy then. Big fellow, and tight as a tick. Drank whisky all the way up from Boston. He'd recognize him again, all right. In his business, it didn't do to forget a face, or a name, either. He'd remembered the name the hitch-hiker had given him a couple of days ago. Lucas Cross, that was the name the guy had given him. Lucas Cross. He was coming home to visit his kids. Said he hadn't been home since '39. And what was all this anyway? What had the sailor done? What did they want with him, Gerry Gage? There was no law against picking up hitch-hikers that he knew of, so how about if they let him go back to work, huh? What? Why, he'd let him off right on Elm Street. What did they want from him? That he take the guy right to his door and see him in? No, the sailor hadn't said where he lived except that it was a long walk on a cold night. Tough, that was what Gerry Gage had told him. He had plenty of liquor inside of him to keep him warm all the way to White River, if need be.

A short while later, on the same day, the two men from the Navy Department went to the Thrifty Corner Apparel Shoppe to see Selena. They told her that a salesman from Boston had positively identified her father from a batch of Navy photographs, as the man whom he had picked up in Boston and set down in Peyton Place.

"I can't understand it," said Selena levelly. "If Pa came home on leave, why didn't he come to the house?"

Less than an hour later, Joey Cross, protected by Miss Elsie

Thornton, was giving the same answer in the office of the grade school.

"It seems odd," said Miss Thornton coldly, "that neither of you two gentlemen have anything better to do with your time than the questioning of little children."

"Yes, ma'am," said the two men, and returned to Buck Mc-Cracken's office in the courthouse.

It was all over town that same afternoon. Everyone buzzed with it.

"Seems funny that Lucas'd come home and nobody'd know it."

"Not even his own kids."

"Who'd ever've thought that Lucas'd join up with the Navy?"

"Seems funny. You'd think *somebody* would've seen him."

"Well, Selena's no liar. Never was. Neither is Joey. Lucas was always the crooked one in that family. Nellie wa'nt never too bright, but she was honest as the day is long."

"Nope. The Cross kids are no liars. If they say Lucas never reached home, he never reached home, and that's the end of it."

Nevertheless, the two men from the Navy Department, together with an embarrassed Buck McCracken, went to call on Selena and Joey that evening. Buck sat in a chair, twisting his doffed hat nervously, and wished that he'd never started any of this. The Navy men asked polite questions, to which Selena and Joey replied with one answer. No. No, they had not seen Lucas. They had not heard from him in years. No. Never. He never wrote home. They had not even known that their father had been in the Navy, until these same two gentlemen had informed them of this fact last winter. In the end, the two men went away, followed by a sullen Buck McCracken who whispered an apology to Selena behind their backs.

"Selena!"

"Don't be afraid, Joey."

"But, Selena, so many questions!"

"Don't be afraid, Joey. They don't know anything. They can't. We were too careful. We buried him, and we scrubbed and cleaned and burned everything that might have given us away. Don't be afraid, Joey."

"Selena, are you afraid?"

"Yes."

Ted Carter came home that week end, and when he learned of the apparent disappearance of Lucas Cross from Peyton Place, he went at once to Selena.

"Didn't your father come here at all?" he asked.

Selena's tautly held nerves quivered. "Listen," she said, "stop making noises like a lawyer around me! I've answered questions until I'm ready to heave, and I've only one answer to make to any question. No. No! No! No! Now leave me alone!"

"But Selena, I only want to help."

"I don't need your help."

He gave her an odd look. "Don't you want Lucas found?" he asked.

"You have known me for years," said Selena wearily. "If you had had to live with him would you want him found?"

"I should at least want to know what had happened to him."

"Well, I don't. I pray to God that no one ever finds him."

The next morning, the child of a pair of shackowners from out on the Meadow Road came into Buck McCracken's office carrying a newspaper-wrapped parcel. The two men from the Navy Department were very interested in the contents of the package, but Buck McCracken, feeling sick, turned away from the articles spread out on his desk. There were the burned remains of a Navy pea jacket, with its round buttons still intact, and the scorched shreds of what had apparently been a woman's bathrobe. Even from where Buck stood, a good six feet away from the desk, he could see the rusty stains of blood on the sprigged, feminine-looking fabric of the robe. The child, a boy of about twelve, who had brought the parcel into town claimed that he had found it just as the men saw it now, in a pile of rubbish at the town dump. The boy's next remark had to do with the question of a possible reward.

"Beat it," Buck McCracken told him savagely, and from the waiting room, outside the office, came the whining voice of a shack woman.

"I tole you, sonny," she whined. "I tole you 'n' your Pa both, that it wa'nt no good at all, gettin' mixed up with what's none of our business."

One of the navy men poked at the burned pea jacket with the tip of a pencil. "Looks as if Lucas Cross must have had a good reason for being A.W.O.L. after all," he said.

A good officer, recited Buck silently, never eliminates the possibility of foul play. "Lucas musta been keepin' a woman that none of us knew about," he said aloud.

"I'll settle for the girl," said one Navy man.

"What girl?" demanded Buck, innocently.

"Selena Cross," replied the second Navy man.

It was still early when Buck and the two Navy men drove up in front of the Cross house. Selena had not left for work, and Joey was still in his pajamas. Selena let the men into the house and led the way to the living room. She acted as if she had not seen the package under the arm of one of the Navy men. The man put the parcel down on the couch, opened it and spread out its contents. Then he straightened up and looked Selena straight in the eye. She neither moved nor spoke, and for all the emotion which showed in her face, she might as easily have been examining a line of dry goods which did not particularly impress her.

"We know you did it," said the man.

Joey Cross hurled himself across the room and stood in front of his sister.

"I did it!" he screamed. "I did it! I killed him and I buried him in the sheep pen, and I did it by myself. I did it alone!"

Selena pressed his head to her side and rumpled his hair for a short moment.

"Go into the other room, Joey," she said. "Go get dressed like a good boy."

When he had gone, she turned to face Buck McCracken.

◆ 9 ◆

It's a small world.

In later years, Buck McCracken used to say that he wished he had a nickel for every time he heard those words spoken during the weeks before Selena Cross came to trial.

Those were the short weeks of long days during the late spring and early summer of 1944. In years past, these had been the weeks of the spring hop, of graduation, of vacation for some and of work in the fields for others, but in 1944, these were weeks of excitement of such pitch that all else paled, including the war.

Peyton Place was overcrowded during the weeks preceding and during the trial. Newspaper reporters walked streets where only Seth Buswell had walked, as a newspaper man, before, and the summer people who usually by-passed Peyton Place in favor of the better known, more highly advertised sections of the state, came to town in streams of expensive cars, all bearing out-of-state license plates. It was unlikely that the case of Selena Cross would

326

ever have drawn much attention if it had not been for a brash young reporter who worked for a Hearst-owned Boston newspaper. The young man, whose name was Thomas Delaney, had a talent for attention-getting headlines. The day after Selena was arrested, the *Daily Record,* for which Delaney worked, bloomed with a headline of three-inch letters. PATRICIDE IN PEYTON PLACE. These words were hastily picked up and flung across front pages by other newspapers throughout northern New England, so that by the time three days were gone, they had appeared and been read by practically everyone in four states. Editors dispatched their best reporters to cover the trial of Selena Cross, and Peyton Place took on the aspects of a large, open-air, lunatic asylum. The town was without either hotel, inn, tavern or rooming house, so that the reporters and tourists who had come to write or stare, each according to his own vocation, were forced to use the inadequate facilities at White River. Every morning these people flowed into Peyton Place, and every evening they left, but they wrought havoc during the hours in between. For the first time since anyone could remember, the old men who peopled the benches in front of the courthouse were forced to flee and scatter against the onslaught of photographers and reporters who insisted on taking pictures of these "picturesque old characters" and on buttonholing them with questions which always began with: "What do *you* think about all this?" The only one of the old men who did not run was Clayton Frazier, who had developed a liking for Thomas Delaney, the Hearst reporter from Boston. This strange alliance had begun on the day when Delaney had arrived in Peyton Place, and had been discovered by Clayton in Hyde's Diner, sitting unconcernedly in the old man's favorite seat at the counter. Clayton had been furious, and everyone else in the diner who was from Peyton Place had watched eagerly to see what the old man would do. Clayton sat down on the stool next to Delaney.

"Newspaper reporter, eh?" asked Clayton.

"Yes."

"Who for?"

"The Boston *Daily Record.*"

"Oh, one of them Hearst papers."

"What's the matter with the Hearst papers?"

"Nothin', if you go for that kinda thing. Read somethin' once by a feller named Arthur J. Pegler. Reckon he's dead by now. He's got one of his relations workin' for Hearst now. Anyhow, this Arthur Pegler told how 'A Hearst newspaper is like a screaming woman running down the street with her throat cut.' Now, I reckon there's nothin' wrong in that, if a body's got the kinda mind that goes for that stuff."

Without an eyelash flicker, Delaney picked up his coffee cup. "I'd be inclined to go a step further than Mr. Pegler," he said. "I should describe it as a *naked* woman running down the street, and so forth."

"Of course," said Clayton, "I'm not sayin' it don't take imagination to work for Hearst. What you don't know, you have to make up, and that must take some imagination."

"Not so much imagination as nerve, Mr. Frazier," said Delaney. "Plain, brassy nerve."

"Who told you my name?" demanded Clayton.

"The same fellow who told me I was sitting in your seat when he saw you approaching this place."

Clayton and Delaney became friends, although to listen to the insults which they hurled at one another, one would never have suspected it. The reporter remained in Peyton Place during the time before Selena's trial. He wrote reams of background on the town and its people with the idea, so he told Clayton, of eventually using this material for the basis of a novel.

"But why Peyton Place?" he asked Clayton Frazier one day. "Crazy damned name. Nobody around here seems overly eager to talk about it, either, except to say that the town was named for a man who built a castle. What about this man and his castle?"

"Come on," said Clayton. "I'll show you the place."

The two men walked along the tracks of the Boston and Maine Railroad line with Clayton leading the way. The sun beat down, hot and bright, on the treeless strips of rocky ground along the tracks. Soon, Delaney removed his suit coat and necktie and carried them slung over his shoulder. At last, where the tracks curved slightly before reaching the bridge which crossed the Connecticut River, Clayton stopped walking and pointed to the highest hill of all. On top of this hill sat the towered and turreted gray pile of stone which was Samuel Peyton's castle.

"Feel like walkin' up that hill?" asked Clayton.

"Yes," said Delaney, making a mental note of the castle's sinister, dark look, sinister and secretive looking even in the hot, open-faced sunlight. "Who was this Samuel Peyton?" he asked as he and Clayton trudged up the steep, bramble-covered hill. "An exiled English duke, or earl, or something?"

"Everybody thinks that," said Clayton, pausing to wipe his face

328

with his sleeve. "Fact is, that castle was built—and this town named —for a friggin' nigger."

"Oh, now listen—" began Delaney, but Clayton refused to speak another word until they had reached the walls of the castle.

The walls were high, so high that standing in front of them one could not see the castle as it was possible to do from a distance, and thick, with the gates which broke them at intervals securely locked and barred. Clayton and Delaney sat down, resting their backs against one gray wall, and Clayton uncorked a bottle of whisky which he had been saving for this moment. It was almost cool, up on the hill, with the trees shading the two men from the sun.

Clayton took a drink and passed the bottle to Delaney. "Fact," he said. "A friggin' nigger."

Delaney drank and returned the bottle to Clayton. "Come on," he said. "Don't make me pull it out of you one word at a time. Tell it from the beginning."

Clayton drank, sighed and adjusted his back against the stone wall. "Well," he began, "quite a spell before the Civil War, there was this nigger down South someplace. He was a slave, and he worked for a plantation owner by the name of Peyton. Now this nigger, whose name was Samuel, musta lived before his time, or out of his element, or whatever you want to call it. Anyhow, he lived a long time before anybody ever heard of a feller called Abraham Lincoln. The reason I say he lived out of his time was that Samuel had funny ideas. He wanted to be free, and this was at a time when most folks looked on niggers as work horses, or mules. Anyhow, Samuel decided to run away. There's some say he done it on gold stolen from his owner, this feller by the name of Peyton. Don't ask me, 'cause I don't know. Nobody knows. No more than they know how he done it. Samuel was a big, strappin' young buck. He had to be, 'cause I don't imagine it was an easy thing for a nigger slave to escape from the South in them days. Anyhow, he escaped and got on a boat goin' to France. Don't ask me how he done it, 'cause I don't know that, either. There's some say the captain of the boat goin' to France was one of them half-breed fellers. Whaddya call 'em?"

"Mulattoes?" offered Delaney.

"Yep," said Clayton, drinking and passing the bottle, "that's it. Mulatto. Well, there's some say that the boat captain was a mulatto. I don't know. Nobody knows for sure. Anyhow, Samuel got to Marseilles, France. It couldn't've been easy, like I said, 'cause

Samuel was big and strappin' and black as the ace of spades. But he got there, and in a few years he had made a fortune out of the shippin' business. Nobody knows how he got started, although there's plenty who say he still had a pile of this Peyton feller's gold when he got over on the other side. Anyhow, he made money, plenty of it and no mistake. But over there in France, he got another one of his crazy ideas. He musta been a great one for crazy ideas, Samuel. He got the idea that since he was free and had plenty of money, he was as good as any white man, and he went and married a white girl. French girl, she was. Her name was Vi'let. Not the way we spell Vi'let, but with two t's and an e on the end. French. There's some say she was pretty—frail lookin' like a piece of china. I don't know. Nobody around here now knows, 'cause this was all such a long time ago. Anyhow, Samuel decided to come back to America. It was durin' the Civil War when he came back. That lady from Massachusetts named Stowe had already wrote that book about the slaves, and there was plenty of people who started lovin' niggers overnight. At least, they loved 'em with their mouths. Well, Samuel and Vi'let got to Boston. Reckon Samuel musta thought that with all his money, and everybody lovin' the niggers, that he was gonna be able to move right onto Beacon Hill and start in entertainin' the Lowells and the Cabots. Well, the up-shot of it was that Samuel couldn't even find any kind of a house anyplace in Boston. If he'd of been in rags with welts all over his back, and if Vi'let had been black and had looked like she was all pooped from bein' chased by bloodhounds, maybe they'd of had an easier time of it. I dunno. I reckon Boston wa'nt too used to seein' a nigger wearin' a starched frill and a hand-embroidered waistcoat, and boots that cost forty dollars a pair. Forty dollars was a heap of money, in them days. Well, with all his money, and his white wife and bein' free and all, Samuel couldn't find a place in Boston. There's some say he went into one of them black rages niggers are supposed to have. I dunno. All I know is he came up here. There's some say he wanted to get far enough away from Boston that he'd never set eyes on a white man again as long as he lived. Anyhow, he came here. There wa'nt no town here, then. Nothin' but the hills and the woods and the Connecticut River. Course, there was towns and cities to the south, but nothin' up here back then. Well, Samuel picked the highest hill of all and decided to build him a castle for him and his white wife named Vi'let. They lived in a cabin, because it took a long time for this place to be built. Gimme the bottle."

Delaney passed the bottle to Clayton, who drank. "See this?" he asked, slapping the flat of his hand against the stone wall behind them. "Imported. Every stick and stone, every doorknob and pane of glass of the castle was imported from England. I dunno, but I'd still be willin' to bet that this here is the only real, true, genuwine castle in New England. All the furniture inside was imported, too, and the hangin's, and the paneling for the walls. When it was done, Samuel and Vi'let moved in and neither one of 'em ever set foot outside these walls again. It wa'nt too long before a feller by the name of Harrington came along and built them mills down alongside the river, and after that there started to be a town here. Pretty soon, the B & M put in the railroad line to White River through here. Folks ridin' on the train used to look up here at Samuel's castle and say, 'What's that?' and the conductors would lean down and look out the windows of the coaches and say, 'Why, that's the Peyton place.' And that's how the town got its name."

"But what happened afterward?" demanded Delaney.

"Whaddya mean 'afterward'?"

"The story can't end there," said the young reporter. "What happened to Samuel and Violette?"

"Oh, they died," said Clayton. "Vi'let went first. Some say she had the consumption, and there's others say she just faded away from bein' cooped up in the castle. I dunno. Samuel buried her out in back of the castle. There's a tall, white stone marks her grave, made outa Vermont marble. When Samuel died, he was buried right next to her. But the stone over Samuel's grave is short and squat, and made out of that black marble that comes from Italy, or one of them foreign countries. It was the state buried Samuel, on account of he left 'em all this land and the castle besides. There's some say this state ain't fussy about takin' presents."

"But what does the state get out of this place?" asked Delaney, looking at one of the barred gates in the wall.

"Nothin' from this place," said Clayton. "But Samuel wa'nt dumb. He owned forest land to the north of here. Lumber is what the state gets, or used to get anyway. Now they got one of these forestry places up there. In return, they got to look after this place 'til it falls apart. Make sure the gates stay locked, keep people outa the place and like that. There wa'nt nothin' in Samuel's will about lookin' after the inside of the place, though. And inside, things has rotted away. The drapes hang all torn and crooked, and rats have et holes in the upholstery of Samuel's imported furniture, and the wooden paneling is cracked and fallen apart. The big

331

chandelier in the front hall got torn loose of the ceilin' back durin' a storm we had once. The glass is still layin' on the floor in Samuel's castle."

Delaney eyed Clayton suspiciously. "From the way you describe the interior of the castle, I'd say that you had been in it at one time or another."

"Sure," admitted Clayton. "There's a way to get in, or at least there was when I was a boy. There was a tree grew around at the other side, and there was a branch of this tree hung right over the wall. You used to be able to climb the tree and go hand over hand along the branch. Then, if you didn't think too much about breakin' a leg, you could drop off the end of the branch right into Samuel's back yard. It was hell gettin' back over the wall, as I remember, but I done it once. You want to try?"

Delaney stood up and looked at the blank-faced wall before him. He thought for a long time. "No," he said at last. "No, I don't think so. Let's start back. It's getting late."

As the two men walked down the hill, the lead for Delaney's next story formed itself in his mind.

"In the tragic shadow of Samuel Peyton's castle," he would write, "another tragedy has taken place. On a cold, blizzard-whipped night in December, Selena Cross—"

Just before they reached Elm Street, Delaney turned to Clayton. "Listen," he said, "you're a fairly tolerant man, for a northern New Englander. How come you always refer to Samuel Peyton as a 'friggin' nigger'?"

"Why?" demanded Clayton. "There's some say—and amongst 'em was my own father—that durin' the Civil War, toward the end of it, Samuel Peyton was runnin' boats out of Portsmouth carryin' arms to the South. If that ain't the act of a sonofabitch, I never hope to hear of one. If Samuel's skin had been of a different color, I'd say he was a 'friggin' rebel.' But Samuel was a nigger."

◆ 10 ◆

There were, of course, those in Peyton Place who remained calm, as does the core of a hurricane, amidst the furor engendered by the coming trial of Selena Cross. Among these was Constance Makris who, after her first shock, started back to work at the Thrifty Corner. To all questions, and there were many, she replied:

"I'm only back temporarily. Selena will be in charge again as soon as this mess is cleared up."

Toward the end of clearing up what she referred to as "the mess Selena is in," Constance had offered to pay for any legal services which the girl might require.

"Although," as she said to Tom, "why the child should need a lawyer is beyond me. If she killed Lucas, and I don't believe for a minute that she did, she had a good reason. Lucas was a brute and a beast. He always was. I can remember Nellie telling of how he used to beat her and the kids. He was a terrible man."

"Maybe so," replied Tom, "but Selena is doing herself more harm than good by keeping quiet at this time. She ought to unbend a little if only to her attorney, but Drake says that she won't say a word."

This was true. Beyond saying that she had killed Lucas with a pair of fire tongs while the two of them were in the Cross living room and that, alone and unaided in spite of what Joey said, she had dragged him into the sheep pen and buried him, Selena refused to comment. She had made this statement on the day she was arrested and the efforts of Peter Drake to make her tell why she had done as she had were futile. Peyton Place talked of little else.

"I don't believe she killed him. She'd tell why, if she had."

"If she didn't do it how come she knew right where he was buried?"

"How come they found blood stains on the floor in the house? All the scrubbin' in the world won't take out blood if someone is really lookin' for it."

"Yep. If she didn't do it, where'd all the blood come from?"

"I thought it was funny the way Joey got rid of all his sheep back in January. January ain't no time to slaughter. I always thought that was mighty peculiar."

"He done that so's nobody'd be tryin' to get into the sheep pen to look around. Kinda foolish though. He'd a done better to leave them sheep right where they was."

"Well, I wouldn't say that. There's always some Jeezless nosy sonofabitch ready to poke around somebody's animals. If it was me buried my old man in a sheep pen it'd make me feel mighty queer to have somebody pokin' around, walkin' right over his grave you might say."

"Remember how Selena tried to squash the zonin' at town meeting? I bet that was because she was scared somebody'd go out to her place and poke around."

"Well, I don't give a goddam what none of you say. I don't believe she done it. She's shieldin' somebody."

"But who? Nobody'd want to kill Lucas."

"No. That's true."

"And how come she won't tell why?"

Why? It was a question on the lips of practically everyone. Ted Carter had gone to Selena, after assuring Drake that she would tell him the real reason for what she had done.

"I did it. What else is there to say?" Selena said sullenly. "I killed him and that's the end of it."

"Listen, Selena," said Ted, a trifle impatiently, "Drake has to know why if he is to defend you. With a good reason he could plead temporary insanity and perhaps get you off the hook."

"I was as sane as I am this minute when I killed him," said Selena. "I knew what I was doing."

"Selena, for God's sake, be sensible. Without a good reason you will be tried for murder in the first degree. Do you know what the penalty for that is in this state?"

"Hanging," said Selena bluntly.

"Yes," said Ted on an indrawn breath, "hanging. Now smarten up and tell me why you did it. Did Lucas threaten to beat you? To put you and Joey out of your home? Why did you do it?"

"I killed him," said Selena in the flat voice which she had cultivated during the past few days. "And that's the end of it."

"But you didn't mean to do it, did you? Perhaps you intended to frighten him and struck harder than you meant to do. Isn't that the way it was?"

For a moment Selena paused and tried to remember the way it had been. *Did I really mean to kill him?* she wondered dully. She tried to recall the moment of striking and the thought which must have been in her mind, but all that came to her was the remembrance of fear.

"I killed him," she said. "When I swung at him I swung with everything I had. I'm not sorry he's dead."

Ted stood up and looked at her coldly. "Listen, you'd better get smart in a hurry and change your tune if you expect to get out of this. Think about it for a while. I'll be back tomorrow."

"No you won't," said Selena as he walked away, but she said it so softly that he did not hear.

That night was one of sleepless indecision for Ted Carter. In less than two weeks he would be graduated from the university and be commissioned as a second lieutenant in the Army. If the war was still on, which seemed highly likely at this point, he would then be sent somewhere for additional training. But Ted's mind did not dwell upon these present realities. He thought of the future, of the day when he would graduate from law school and come home to practice. How far would a man get in the legal profession tied to a wife who was a murderess? he wondered. True, he loved Selena and probably always would, but how much chance did they have together now? Ted spent the long hours of the night going over his plan for the future, but nowhere could he find a loophole in his plan large enough to accommodate a wife with a cloud over her head. Even if Selena were found innocent—and how could that be since she had already confessed to her crime—would there not always be people who wondered? As for the plea of insanity, even temporary insanity, that was no kind of way out. Insanity was looked upon with disfavor and shame by Peyton Place. Selena would fare better in her town as a convicted murderess than she would as a victim of insanity, Ted knew. Justifiable homicide? In the dark of his room Ted shook his head. Lucas might have been a drunkard, a wife and child beater, the most irresponsible of fathers, but he had paid his bills and minded his own business. And the fact that he had not been Selena's own father would hurt her in Peyton Place, Ted knew. Had she been of Lucas' flesh and blood she would fare better. As it was, Ted knew what the town would say. She wasn't even his own, Peyton Place would say. He married Nellie when Selena was just a newborn baby, but he provided for the child just as if she was his own. To the name of murderess would be added the tag of ingrate. Ted Carter bit the knuckle of his forefinger. He could well imagine the looks on the faces of the jury if Drake tried to plead justifiable homicide for Selena. If the lawyer tried that, Selena was as good as hanged right now. Ted sat up in his bed and put both hands to his head. With stiff fingers he tried to massage a scalp suddenly tight and prickly. And if, he thought, by some impossibly lucky chance, by some fluke of luck, Drake managed to get Selena off, what kind of life could the girl have in Peyton Place. Forever after people would remember. There goes the Cross girl. She did in her father. Well, he wasn't really her father. He was more than that. He provided for her all her life, and he didn't have to do it. She wasn't his own. There goes the Cross girl. Married that young lawyer named Carter. Better keep away from him, a feller that'd take up with a murderess.

But Ted's mind was not filled only with thoughts of the future that night; it was plagued also with memories of the past. He remembered kisses, conversations, hopes and dreams shared. He pictured the hill that he and Selena had looked at, the one where they would build a house that was made up almost entirely of windows, and he recalled the arguments about the number of children a house of this type would hold adequately. He remembered all the years when it had been only Selena, when the thought of life without her had been like thinking of being dead.

"You and me and Joey," Selena had said, laughing against him so that he could feel her breath against his cheek. "Just us, with no one else mattering at all."

It was true that Selena had changed a little since the war. She was inclined to be a little sharp at times, a little unreasonable. But war affected many women in that fashion. She sometimes seemed to think ill of him because he was not off in a ditch somewhere, like her stepbrother Paul, fighting for his life. But Ted had not worried overmuch about that. It was a feeling in her which would pass when the war was over. Then she would be as she had been before.

"Theodore H. Carter, Esquire," she had said, her eyes shining the way they always did when she was happy. "Mr. and Mrs. Theodore Carter, both esquires. Oh, Ted, how I love you."

It was dawn when he turned his wet face into his pillow. But my plan, Selena, he thought. What about my plan? What chance would we have in Peyton Place? he asked silently, and all the while he knew the answer and knew what he must do. At last he slept, and he did not go to see Selena the next day. Shortly afterward, when her trial was in session, he wrote his mother that he was unable to get away from the university.

Selena had not waited for him the day after she had seen him for the last time. But still, a tight little smile twisted her lips that night.

I knew he wouldn't come, she thought. I'm not part of his plan any longer. He can't afford the luxury of not giving a damn what people say. By God, I can. If I have nothing else, I have that. I don't give a damn.

She reflected that not too long ago she would not have been able to stand it to think that Ted would desert her in a time of need, but in the early summer of 1944 it did not seem to matter at all. Nothing mattered except her constant, nagging worry over what was going to happen to Joey. That she would be convicted and hanged she had no doubt.

"If you'd just tell me why," Peter Drake said to her, over and over. "Perhaps I could help you. This way, the very least you can hope to get is life. If we're that lucky. Help me to help you."

But what shall I say? thought Selena. Shall I say that I killed Lucas because I was afraid he'd get me in trouble again? She thought of Matthew Swain to whom she had given a solemn promise of silence, and she thought also of the faces of her friends and neighbors if she ever told the truth about herself and Lucas. No one would believe her. Why should they? Why had she kept silent for years and years? Why had she not gone to the police if Lucas was molesting her? Because a shack dweller never goes to the law, thought Selena wryly. A good shack dweller minds his business and binds up his own wounds. She remembered a time when Buck McCracken, the sheriff, had come to the grade school to give a talk on safety.

"Now I want allaya to remember that the policeman is your friend," he had concluded, and Selena recalled the look in the eyes of the shack-dwelling children.

Friend my arse, said the look. *Busybody. Mindin' everybody's business but his own.*

I'll never tell, thought Selena desperately. Not even when they take me out to hang me. They'll never find out why from me. Let them ask. They'll never find out.

In the entire population of Peyton Place, there was one man who did not wonder why. This was Dr. Matthew Swain, who knew very well why. The doctor had not worked since the day of Selena's arrest. He pleaded sickness and directed his patients to Dr. Bixby at White River.

"He must be sick," said Isobel Crosby to anyone who would listen. "He don't even bother to get dressed in the mornin' and he just sets all day long. Just sets and stares and does nothin'."

This was not quite true. Very often during the day, and always during the night, Matthew Swain bestirred himself enough to walk from his dining room sideboard where he kept his liquor and back to whichever chair he happened to be using at the time. He thought thoughts which he phrased in what he termed brilliant rhetoric and all the while he knew what he must do.

And now the destruction has come full circle, he told himself, staring down into his full glass. It began with Lucas and it has ended with Lucas. Almost, but not quite. In the beginning I destroyed life and now I must pay with my own.

At times, when he got really drunk during the night, he took a small photograph of his dead wife Emily from its hiding place.

Help me, Emily, he would plead, gazing into the kind, deep eyes in the picture. Help me.

There had been quite a fuss made about photographs right after Emily had died. He had insisted on having the large, silver-framed one of her which had stood in his office for years removed.

"I should think you'd want that picture to stay right where it is," Isobel Crosby had said piously. "I should think you'd want her right there, so's you could be reminded of her."

"Do you think I need photographs to be reminded?" the doctor had roared, sweeping the picture of Emily from his desk with a vicious swipe of his hand. "Do you think I need anything to be reminded?"

Roaring was an expedient cover up for tears, and the doctor had done a lot of roaring in the days after Emily had died. Isobel, of course, lost no time in spreading the word of his behavior all over town.

"Threw her picture right off his desk," said Isobel. "Threw her picture down so's the glass smashed and the frame bent, and yelled at me. And her not in her grave a week yet, poor thing. You saw how he acted at the funeral, didn't you? Never shed a tear, or tried to throw himself into the open grave or anything. He didn't even kiss her poor dead cheek before the minister closed the coffin. Wait and see. He'll get married again before six months are gone."

The doctor put the last remaining photograph of Emily away carefully. He was, he realized, getting maudlin indeed when he expected help from a faded picture.

First the child, he thought, destroyed because it had no choice, and then Mary Kelley destroyed by a knowledge and a guilt which I had no right to press on her. And then Nellie, destroyed because I could control neither my temper nor my tongue and now Lucas, destroyed by Selena because I had not the courage to destroy him myself. And that's the way the world ends, thought the doctor, drunkenly trying to remember the last part of the quotation. Something about a whimper, or a whine, or something.

The night before the day when Selena was to go to trial, Matthew Swain went through his house picking up empty bottles. He soaked for an hour in a hot tub and followed this with a cold shower. He shaved and shampooed his beautiful white hair and he telephoned to Isobel Crosby.

"Where the hell have you been?" he roared when she answered. "It's summer and my white suit hasn't been pressed and I have to be in court at nine in the morning."

Isobel, who had tried unsuccessfully to get into the doctor's house morning after morning, hung up angrily.

"What do you think of that?" she asked her sister in an injured tone.

◆ **||** ◆

On this same evening Allison MacKenzie returned to Peyton Place. She stepped off the train at eight-thirty and decided to walk home.

"Hello, Mr. Rhodes," she said to the stationmaster as she went into the station.

" 'Lo, Allison," he said in exactly the same tone he would have employed had she been returning from a day of shopping in Manchester. "Get sick of the big city?"

"A little," she admitted and thought, Oh, if you knew how sick, Mr. Rhodes. How sick and tired and fed up and ready to die I am.

"Ain't a bad place to visit, New York ain't," said Rhodes. "You want a ride home? I'm ready to close up."

"I thought I'd walk," said Allison. "It's been a long time since I walked in Peyton Place."

Rhodes glanced at her sharply. "The town'll be here in the mornin'. You better let me ride you home. Look a little tired."

Allison was too tired to argue. "All right," she said. "My bags are outside."

As they drove up Depot Street Allison stared absently out the car window. It doesn't change, she thought wearily. Not a stick or a stone, a tree or a house changes. It stands still.

"Hear about Selena Cross?" asked Rhodes.

"Yes," replied Allison. "That's the main reason I came home. I thought it might make a good story."

"Oh?" asked Rhodes. "You still writin' them stories for the magazines? The wife always reads 'em. Say's they're good, too."

"Yes, I'm still writing for the magazines," said Allison and thought,

Mr. Rhodes doesn't change either. He's still as nosy as ever. She wondered what he would say if she told him of the novel she had worked on for over a year which turned out to be no good. He'd be glad. Mr. Rhodes was always glad when someone failed at something.

"How'd you hear about Selena?" he asked. "Your mother call you up?"

"No. I read it in a newspaper."

Mr. Rhodes stalled his car. "You mean to tell me it made the New York papers? They know all about it down there to New York?"

"No, of course not. There is a man in New York who traffics in homesickness. He runs a newsstand on Broadway where he sells copies of out of town newspapers. I was walking by there one day and I saw the headline on a four-day-old *Concord Monitor*."

Mr. Rhodes chuckled. "Musta give you a turn, seein' somethin' about Peyton Place right in the middle of New York."

No, not really Mr. Rhodes, said Allison silently. I was too busy thinking of something else at the time to be overly concerned with Peyton Place. You see, I had just spent the week end in bed with a man whom I love and it turned out that he was married.

"Yes," she said aloud. "It gave me quite a turn."

"Well, it's sure raised hell here," said Mr. Rhodes. "The streets ain't fit to walk on these days. Full of newspaper reporters and tourists and just plain nosy people from over to White River. The trial's tomorrow. You goin'?"

"I imagine so," said Allison. "Selena will probably need every friend she ever had tomorrow."

Mr. Rhodes chuckled and it occurred to Allison that there was something obscene in the old man's laughter. "Ain't nobody really thinks she done it. Leastways, not by herself. Well, here's your house. Hold a minute and I'll give you a hand with your things."

"Don't bother," said Allison stepping out of the car. "Tom will come out for them."

"Yep. Tom," said Rhodes and chuckled again. "That Greek feller your mother married. How do you like having him for a father?"

Allison looked at him coldly. "My father is dead," she said and walked up the walk in front of her house.

Constance and Tom jumped up in surprise as Allison walked through the front door and into the living room.

"Hello," she said and stood there, pulling off her gloves.

They surrounded her and kissed her and asked her if she had eaten dinner.

"But darling, why didn't you let us know you were coming? Tom would have gone down to the station to pick you up."

"Mr. Rhodes drove me home," said Allison. "I had a sandwich on the train."

"What's wrong?" cried Constance. "You're so white and you look exhausted. Are you ill?"

"Oh, for Heaven's sake, Mother," said Allison impatiently. "I'm just tired. It's a long trip and it was hot on the train."

"Would you like a drink?" asked Tom.

"Yes," said Allison gratefully.

Something is wrong, thought Tom as he mixed a Tom Collins for Allison. Something has happened. She has the same look that she always had whenever she was running away from a disagreeable experience. A man?

"I tried to telephone you about Selena," Constance was saying, "but that girl you share your apartment with said you were visiting someone in Brooklyn. What's the girl's name? I never can remember it."

"Steve Wallace," said Allison, "and I don't share my apartment with her. She shares her apartment with me."

"Steve," said Constance, "that's the name. Didn't you tell me that her actual name is Stephanie?"

"Yes," replied Allison, "but no one ever calls her that. She hates it. Poor Steve. I hope she can find someone else to share her place. I'm not going back."

"Is something wrong?" asked Constance at once.

"I told you, Mother. Nothing is wrong," said Allison and burst into tears. "I'm just tired, and sick of New York. I just want to be left alone!"

"I'll go up and fix your bed," said Constance who had never been able to cope with Allison's moods.

Tom sat down and lit a cigarette. "Can I help?" he asked.

Allison wiped her eyes and blew her nose; then she picked up her drink and gulped half of it down.

"Yes," she said in a tightly controlled voice. "You can help me. You can leave me the hell alone. Both of you. Or is that too much to ask?"

Tom stood up. "No," he said gently, "that's not too much to ask. But try to remember that we love you, and we'd be glad to listen if you wanted to talk."

341

"I'm going to bed," said Allison and ran upstairs before she started to cry again.

But later Constance and Tom could hear her muffled sobs as they lay in bed.

"What's wrong?" asked Constance, frightened. "I should go to her."

"Leave her alone," said Tom putting a hand on his wife's arm.

But Constance could not sleep. Long after Tom slept she went silently to Allison's room.

"What's wrong?" she asked in a whisper. "Are you in trouble, dear?"

"Oh, Mother, don't be so stupid!" said Allison. "I'm not you. I'd never be so stupid as to let a man get me in trouble. Just leave me alone!"

And Constance, who had not meant pregnancy when she spoke of trouble, crept back to her bed and tried to warm herself against Tom's back.

◆ 12 ◆

The trial of Selena Cross began at nine o'clock on a warm June morning. It was held in a courtroom packed with townspeople and farmers, and it was presided over by Judge Anthony Aldridge. A stranger to Peyton Place might have looked around in panic on that particular morning, wondering if he could have miscalculated the day or month of the year, for Elm Street was as closed and deserted looking as it might have been on a Sunday or holiday. All the shops were closed, and the benches in front of the courthouse were empty of the old men who would usually have appeared as if rooted there, now that it was June. Selena's trial opened with what Thomas Delaney, of the Boston *Daily Record,* later described as "a bang."

The "bang" to which Delaney referred came when Selena Cross repudiated her earlier confession and pleaded not guilty.

A girl who called herself Virginia Voorhees leaned toward Thomas Delaney. "Damn it," she whispered hoarsely, "they're going to try to get away with temporary insanity." Her name was not Virginia Voorhees, it was Stella Orbach, but she wrote articles for the Boston *American* Sunday supplement under the name of Virginia Voorhees. Her articles always bore the same title: "Was Justice Done?" She sighed dejectedly as Selena Cross sat down after pleading innocent to first degree murder. "Damn it," she muttered, "there goes a good story."

"Shut up, will you?" requested Delaney in a whisper, but Virginia Voorhees did not hear him above the surprised buzzing which filled the courtroom.

"Not guilty?" whispered Peyton Place.

"But she said she did it!"

"She knew where the body was buried!"

Charles Partridge, in his capacity as county attorney, was speaking against the noise. "It is not the duty of this office," he was saying, "to prosecute the innocent, but to bring the guilty to justice."

The lawyer's voice was soft, and his manner clearly apologetic for his presence in the courtroom at all. His words left no doubts in the minds of anyone that he was on Selena's side and that he hoped to help Peter Drake prove the girl's innocence.

"For Christ's sake," mumbled the girl who called herself Virginia Voorhees, "this is turning into a fiasco. Have you ever heard anything like this?"

Behind Partridge, in a seat two rows from the front, Marion Partridge stirred restively, not listening to her husband's words.

It certainly showed ingratitude on Selena's part, thought Marion, when the girl deliberately set out to make Charles look foolish by changing her plea like that. Charles had worked hard on this case, it was his first murder trial, and he had spent a lot of time on it. Not that he had wanted to be the one to prosecute Selena; he definitely had not. In fact, thought Marion pursing her lips, it looked to her as if Charles had tried harder to find a loophole for Selena than Peter Drake had. But even so, Charles was the county attorney, and there was no excuse for murder, so he had to prosecute. Oh, Marion had tried to tell him. A murder trial which drew the publicity that this one had was bound to be the making of the county attorney. Especially when he had an airtight case. Selena had done it, and Selena had confessed, and the little ingrate needn't think that Charles Partridge was going to be taken in by an about-face at this late hour. It just went to show, thought Marion grimly, that the more you did for shack people, the less they appreciated it. The fact that Selena and Joey no longer lived in a place which could be termed a shack did not matter to Marion. Put people like the Crosses in Buckingham Palace, and they would still be shack

343

people. Just look at that girl! All rigged up as if she were going to a dance.

Marion Partridge sniffed a little, for she had the beginnings of a summer cold, and she hated to keep using her handkerchief. She passed a casual forefinger under her nostrils and stared at Selena.

The girl was wearing a dress of lavender linen, which Marion was willing to bet cost at least twenty-five dollars, and a pair of sheer stockings which Marion immediately classified as black market nylon. Selena's shoes were new, and Marion wondered if the girl had used a wartime ration coupon to buy them, or whether Constance Makris had got them from a friendly salesman.

I always told Charles that Connie MacKenzie was no better than she should be, but he wouldn't listen. I guess he saw what was what when she began to carry on with that Makris fellow. Why, Anita Titus told me that the goings-on in that house were something terrible. I'll bet they had to get married. Connie must of had a miscarriage later. She and Selena were always too friendly to suit me. Well, what can you expect? Birds of a feather. Look at that girl! Earrings in court! Selena is the type who will cross her legs and hoist her skirts when she gets on the stand. The little ingrate, trying to make a fool of Charles. After all, I've been good to Selena. I hired her for odd jobs when she didn't have a cent, and I always tried to keep Nellie busy when Selena and Joey were younger. And look what we paid Lucas, God rest his soul, to build our kitchen cabinets. Outrageous, but we paid what he asked. You'd think that Selena would remember favors like that. Well, Charles will fix her. He'll see to it that she doesn't get away with murder. Charles will see her hanged before he lets her get away with anything like that!

"—To prove that Selena Cross struck down Lucas Cross in self-defense, and that her act, therefore, was one of justifiable homicide."

Marion Partridge sat up straight in her seat as if someone had stuck a pin in her. It was Charles Partridge speaking, talking now of saving the state's money by foregoing a lengthy trial now that new evidence had come to light. Marion was bathed in the sweat of a hot flash.

But this is impossible, she thought frantically. He is throwing away his big chance. There is no new evidence. He would have told me beforehand. He's making it all up to save Selena's neck.

Marion took out her handkerchief and wiped her wet temples, and in that moment it came over her that Charles was in the throes

344

of a violent love affair with his pretty young prisoner. She glanced around surreptitiously, and it seemed to her that people were smiling and casting sly looks in her direction. Feeling sorry for her because Charles had thrown away his chance to be written up in the law books because of his lust for Selena.

I'll kill her myself, thought Marion, and the resolve calmed her. The hot flash passed, and she sat back in her seat, her eyes boring like needles dipped in poison into the back of Selena's neck.

Later, when the trial was over and Thomas Delaney said that there was not a single person in the Peyton Place courthouse who wanted to see Selena found guilty, he did not know about Marion. Delaney thought that he had found a place where there was no one eager to cast stones at the fallen, and he did not see Marion, who could not forgive a deviation from a norm set up by herself. Delaney was city bred, and did not realize that in very small towns malice is more often shown toward an individual than toward a group, a nation or a country. He was not unfamiliar with prejudice and intolerance, having been called a Mick an extraordinary number of times himself, but name calling and viciousness had always seemed, to him, to be directed more at his ancestors than at him as an individual. Clayton Frazier had attempted to explain something of the way of it to him, but Delaney was a realist. He wanted to see Clayton's examples in the flesh, to hear maliciousness with his own ears, and to see the results of it with his own eyes.

"I told you about Samuel Peyton, didn't I?" demanded Clayton Frazier. "Times and folks don't change much. Didn't you ever notice how it's always people who wish they had somethin' or had done somethin' that hate the hardest?"

"I don't know what you mean exactly," Delaney had replied.

"Well, I know what I mean," said Clayton testily. "I can't help it if I can't phrase it fancy. I don't work for Hearst."

Delaney laughed. "Tell me what you mean in unfancy talk, then."

"Didja ever notice what woman it is who has the most fault to find with a young, pretty girl who runs around havin' a swell time for herself? It's the woman who is too old, too fat and ugly, to be doin' the same thing herself. And when somebody kicks over the traces in a big way, who is it that hollers loudest? The one who always wanted to do the same thing but didn't have the nerve. Had a feller lived here, years ago, got fed up with his wife and his job and his debts. Run off, he did. Just upped and beat it, and the only one I ever heard holler about it, for any length of time, was Leslie Harrington. Another time, we had this widder woman got

345

her a house down by the railroad tracks. Nice-lookin' woman. She had just about every man in town keepin' his hands in his pockets. She wa'nt a tramp, like Ginny Stearns used to be. She had class, this widder did. I read in a book once about one of them French courtesans. That's what the widder was like. A courtesan. Grand and proud and beautiful as a satin sheet. None of the women in town liked havin' her around much, but the one hollered the loudest, and finally made poor Buck McCracken run her out of town, was Marion Partridge. Old Charlie's wife."

"I've been working for Hearst too long," said Delaney. "These parables of yours are over my head. What are you trying to tell me?"

Clayton Frazier spat. "That if Selena Cross is found innocent, there's gonna be some that'll squawk about it. It'll be interestin' to see which ones holler the loudest and the longest."

Charles knows better than this, thought Marion Partridge. Honor thy father and thy mother. That's as plain as anything and no argument about it. If he thinks that there is a reason good enough to excuse a girl murdering her father, even a stepfather, he must be tottering on the verge of senility and assume that the rest of us are, too.

Marion acknowledged coldly that she would rather have Charles slobbering at the mouth and wetting the bed than to have him infatuated with Selena. Folks could feel sorry for a woman with a sick husband, but a woman with a husband who ran after young girls automatically became a laughingstock.

"There is no need to clear the court," Charles protested, and Marion raised furious eyes to look at him. "This girl is among her friends and neighbors."

And if her friends and neighbors don't hear every word of the evidence, Seth Buswell was thinking from his front-row seat, there will always be a shadow of doubt in their minds if Selena is found innocent. Smart old Charlie. I wish to hell I knew what he's talking about. When I talked to Drake yesterday, things looked pretty black to him.

Allison MacKenzie, who was sitting halfway back in the courtroom, between her mother and Tomas Makris, put her finger tips to her lips when Charles Partridge uttered the word friends.

Friends! she thought, shocked, and immediately began to try to send warning thought waves in the direction of Selena Cross.

Don't let them fool you, Selena, she thought, concentrating with all her mind. Don't be fooled and taken in by their pretty words.

346

You haven't a friend in this room. Quick! Stand up and tell them so. I know. They tried to tell me that I was among friends, right in this same room, once. But I wasn't. I stood up and told the truth, and those whom I had called my friends laughed and said that I was a liar. Even those who didn't know me well enough to call me a liar to my face did it when they robbed Kathy to save Leslie Harrington. Look at Leslie Harrington now, Selena. He is on the jury that is going to play with your life. He's no friend of yours, no matter how you may think he has changed. He called me a liar, right in this room, and I've known him ever since I can remember. Don't trust Charles Partridge. He called me a liar, and he'll do the same for you. Stand up, Selena! Tell them that you would rather be tried by your enemies than by your friends in Peyton Place.

"Call Matthew Swain," said a voice, and Allison knew that it was too late. Selena had put her trust in her friends, as Allison had once done herself, and her friends would turn on her and tell her she lied. Allison felt the weak tears that came so easily since her return to Peyton Place, and Tom reached out and put a gentle hand on her arm as Matthew Swain was sworn in.

The doctor told his story in a voice familiar to everyone in Peyton Place. He did not attempt to tidy up his English for the benefit of the court.

"Lucas Cross was crazy," began the doctor bluntly. "And he was crazy in the worst way that it's possible for a man to be crazy. There's not one of you here today, except a few out-of-towners, who don't know some of the things Lucas did in his lifetime. He was a drunkard, and a wife beater, and a child abuser. Now, when I say child abuser, I mean that in the worst way any of you can think of. Lucas began to abuse Selena sexually when she was a child of fourteen, and he kept her quiet by threatening to kill her and her little brother if she went to the law. Well, Selena didn't go to Buck McCracken. When it was too late, and she was in trouble, she came to me. I took care of her trouble in the way I thought best. I fixed her so that she wouldn't have Lucas' child."

The courtroom began to buzz. Virginia Voorhees scribbled furiously.

"Abortion!" she whispered to Thomas Delaney. "This doctor has ruined himself!"

But what a magnificent old gentleman, thought Delaney, ignoring his colleague. White suit, white hair and those bright blue eyes. What a gentleman!

"Now, I reckon there's going to be some questions asked as to how I know it was Lucas' baby that Selena carried," said the doctor, and the buzzing courtroom quieted as if everyone had been struck dead but Matthew Swain. "I know it because Lucas admitted it to me. There's no one here who doesn't remember when Lucas left town. Well, he left because I told him he had to go. I told him that the men of this town would lynch him if he stayed In short, I scared the piss out of him and he went. There's no question about how I should have gone to Buck McCracken when I first found out about Lucas. It was a wrong thing that I didn't go, but I didn't and I'm not the one on trial here today. I should be. Had I done what I should have done, Lucas would not be dead today. He would be alive and in jail. He would never have left town with an opportunity to come and go as he pleased, especially with the opportunity to molest a child again. When he did return and attempted to do what he had done with her in years past, she killed him. I don't blame her. Lucas Cross needed killing." The doctor raised his head only a shade over the normally high angle at which he always held it. "If my words need corroboration in the mind of anyone here, I have it." He slipped his hand into the inside pocket of his suit coat and brought forth a folded sheet of paper which he passed to Charles Partridge. "That paper is a signed confession," he said. "I wrote it up the night I took care of Selena, and Lucas signed it. That is all I have to say."

Matthew Swain stepped down from the stand and life returned to the courtroom. In the back row, Miss Elsie Thornton pressed the black-gloved fingers of one hand to her eyes and encircled Joey Cross with her free arm. Joey was quivering, his fatless body as tight as a wound-up toy against Miss Thornton's side.

In the front row, Seth Buswell lowered his head against the shame he was afraid would show in his eyes. Oh, Matt, he thought, I would never have had the courage.

In the second row, Marion Partridge shook with rage. I might have known, she thought. Matt Swain's doing, all of it. A criminal and a murderer himself, and everyone listens to his words as if he were God. He'll pay for this, ruining Charles's big chance. He and the girl were in it together, to make a fool of Charles.

The main reason why Virginia Voorhees later described the trial of Selena Cross as "a fiasco" was that the court looked no farther than Matthew Swain for an excuse for the girl. The confession which the old doctor claimed to have obtained from Selena's stepfather was marked and admitted as evidence. It was passed to the jury for examination but, Virginia noticed, not one man of the twelve looked down at the paper as it went from hand to hand. The judge's words to the jury were words which Virginia had never heard uttered in a court of law.

"There's not one of you on the jury who don't know Matt Swain," said the judge. "I've known him all my life, same as you, and I say that Matt Swain is no liar. Go into the other room and make up your minds."

The jury returned in less than ten minutes. "Not guilty," said Leslie Harrington, who had been acting as foreman, and the trial of Selena Cross was over.

"It may have started off with a bang," said Virginia Voorhees to Thomas Delaney, "but it certainly ended with a sound most generally associated with wet firecrackers!"

Thomas Delaney was watching Dr. Matthew Swain as the old man made his way out of the courtroom. A few minutes later, the reporter noticed that the doctor was being escorted outside by five men. Seth Buswell held loosely to one of his arms, while Charles Partridge walked at the doctor's opposite side. Jared Clarke and Dexter Humphrey walked slightly behind him, and Leslie Harrington walked ahead to open the door of the doctor's car. The six men got into the car and drove away, and Delaney turned to find Cayton Frazier at his side.

"Nice-lookin' bunch of old bastards, ain't they?" said Clayton affectionately, and Delaney realized that this was the greatest compliment Clayton felt that he could pay anyone.

"Yeah," he said, and fought his way through the crowd to the side of Peter Drake.

"Congratulations," he said to Selena's attorney.

"What for?" demanded Drake.

"Why, you've just won a big case," said Delaney.

"Listen," said Drake sharply, "I don't know where you come from, but if you couldn't see that this was Charlie Partridge's big case from beginning to end, you've got a lot to learn about Peyton Place."

"What will happen to the doctor?" asked Delaney.

Drake shrugged. "Nothing much."

"I realize that I have a lot to learn about Peyton Place," said Delaney sarcastically, "but I do think that I know enough about this state to realize that abortion is against the law."

"Who's going to charge Matt Swain with abortion?" asked Drake. "You?"

349

"No one has to. The minute the state hears of this, they'll lift his license to practice."

Drake shrugged again. "Come back in a year," he said, "to see if Matt Swain is still in business. I'll bet you a solid gold key to Peyton Place that he'll still be living on Chestnut Street and going out on night calls."

"What about the girl?" asked Delaney, nodding in the direction where Selena Cross stood, surrounded by a large segment of the town's population. "Has she any plans? Where will she go?"

"Listen," said Drake wearily, "why don't you ask her? I'm going home."

♦ **13** ♦

The summer passed slowly for Allison MacKenzie. She spent much of it in sitting alone in her room and in walking the streets of Peyton Place. She went to bed early and arose late, but the lethargic weariness which weighed heavily on her would not leave her. Sometimes she visited with Kathy Welles, but she could not find comfort on these occasions. It was as if a wall existed between the two friends, and it did not lessen Allison's sense of loss to know that it was a wall, not of unfriendliness or lack of understanding, but a wall made by Kathy's happiness.

A wall of happiness, thought Allison. What a wonderful thing to live behind.

Kathy held her baby with her left arm and rested the child against her hip. The empty right sleeve of her cotton dress was neatly pinned back, and Allison wondered how Kathy dressed herself every morning.

"Happiness," said Kathy, "is in finding a place you love and staying there. That's the big reason why I was never sorry about not getting a lot of money after the accident. If Lew and I had had money, we might have been tempted to travel and look around, but we would never have found a place like this one."

"You always were infatuated with Peyton Place," said Allison. "I don't know why. It is one of the worst examples of small towns that I can think of."

Kathy smiled. "No, it's not," she said.

"Talk, talk, talk," said Allison impatiently. "Peyton Place is famous for its talk. Talk about everybody."

"Crap," said Kathy inelegantly. "Everyone talks all over the world, about everybody else. Even in your precious New York. Walter Winchell is the biggest old gossip of all. He's worse than Clayton Frazier and the Page Girls and Roberta Harmon all put together."

Allison laughed. "It's different with Winchell," she said. "He gets paid to gossip."

"I don't care," said Kathy. "If I ever saw a back fence, I see one when I look at his column. At least, we don't put our dirty wash into the newspapers in Peyton Place."

Allison shrugged. "The papers confine themselves to big names anyway," she said. "In Peyton Place, anybody is fair game."

"Selena Cross is a sort of celebrity up here," said Kathy shrewdly. "And Selena in relation to Peyton Place is what is bothering you, isn't it?"

"Yes," admitted Allison. "I think Selena was a fool to stay here. She could have gone out to Los Angeles with Joey and lived with Gladys, where no one knew about her. She's behaving like an ostrich by staying here, as if nothing had happened. Right or wrong, it happened, and it was only a matter of time before people would start to talk. All the fine friends who didn't want to see her hang for murder are hanging her themselves with their vicious talk."

"And this too shall pass away," quoted Kathy. "It always does, Allison."

"After about a hundred years of being talked about and hashed over," said Allison, and rose to leave. "You'll see. In the end, Selena will have to leave."

"She doesn't act as if she is going to run away," said Kathy. "I was in your mother's store yesterday and Selena was having a very friendly talk with Peter Drake. She won't leave."

"You always were one to see a prospective love match in every casual conversation," said Allison crossly. "Don't worry. Drake isn't about to jeopardize himself by taking up with Selena. Ted Carter didn't do it and neither will Drake. Men are all alike."

"For Heaven's sake," exclaimed Kathy. "What ever happened to you in New York? You never used to have such an attitude as that before you went away."

"I got smart," said Allison.

"Nuts," said Kathy. "What you need to do is to find a nice fellow and get married and settle down."

"No thanks," said Allison. "Love and I don't mix well."

She said this flippantly, but too often, during that long summer and she not only thought about the words but believed them. For love had caused the pain which had not come before she left New York but had waited until she reached Peyton Place to overwhelm her. And when it had finally come to her she had thought she would die of it. It was pain of such power that it left her gasping, and pain of such sharpness that it stripped her nerves bare and left them rawly exposed to more pain.

She relived every childhood experience of rejection and wept in an ecstasy of sorrow for herself: *I lost Rodney Harrington to Betty Anderson, and Norman Page to his mother, and my mother to Tomas Makris. But I thought it would be different in New York. Where did I go wrong? What's the matter with me?*

It had been September, three months to the day after her graduation from high school, when she had arrived in New York. Constance had insisted that she stay in one of those depressing hotels for women, but Allison had wasted no time in asserting her new-found independence and had set about scanning the want ads in the *New York Times* within fifteen minutes of stepping off the train at Grand Central. She had seen one notice which attracted her at once.

GIRL WHO LIKES TO MIND HER OWN BUSINESS INTERESTED IN SHARING STUDIO APARTMENT WITH CONGENIAL FEMALE WHO ENJOYS DOING SAME.

Allison made a careful note of the address and within the hour she had met, decided she liked, and moved in with a girl of twenty who called herself Steve Wallace.

"Don't call me Stephanie," Steve had said. "I don't know why it should, but being called Stephanie always makes me feel like something pale and dull out of Jane Austen."

Steve was wearing a pair of leopard-spotted slacks and a bright yellow shirt. Her hair was a rich auburn-brown and she wore a pair of enormous gold hoops in her ears.

"Are you an actress?" Allison asked.

"Not yet," said Steve in her husky voice. "Not yet. All I do now is run around to the casting offices, but I model to pay the rent and feed myself. What do you do?"

"Write," Allison said, not without fear for she had been laughed at too many times in Peyton Place to say the word now without a quiver.

"But that's wonderful!" cried Steve, and Allison began to be very fond of her in that moment.

But writing stories and selling them were two very different things, as Allison soon discovered. She began to realize that she had been unbelievably lucky to sell her first story at all, and that the road to her next sale was going to be a rocky one indeed.

"Oh, for an editor like the one who bought 'Lisa's Cat,'" she said often and fervently, particularly on the day of every week when she received a generous check from Constance.

Allison had hung the full-page color illustration which the magazine had run with "Lisa's Cat" on the wall of Steve's living room. During that first year in New York she had glanced at the picture often and had even drawn encouragement from it, for there had been times when she was afraid that she would never be able to support herself with her writing. But then she met Bradley Holmes, an author's agent, and new doors began to swing open for her. She would never have begun to be successful without Holmes, but the thought of him as she sat in her bedroom in Peyton Place on this hot summer afternoon was so painful that she turned her face into her pillow and wept.

Oh, I love you, I love you, she wept, and then she remembered the touch of his hands on her and shame added itself to her grief. The more tightly she closed her eyes, the sharper his image became behind her clenched lids.

Bradley Holmes was forty years old, dark haired and powerfully built although he was not much taller than Allison. He had a sharp, discerning eye and a tongue which could be both cruel and kind.

"It's easier to sell directly to a publisher," a friend of Steve's had told Allison, "than it is to sell a good agent on your work."

And after a series of rebuffs from agents' secretaries and agents' receptionists, Allison thought that this was probably true. It was after one particularly crushing experience, when she had almost decided that it was not so much a matter of selling an agent on her work as it was a problem of getting past the desk in his reception room, that Allison had sought refuge in the New York Public Library. The book she chose was a current best seller and the author had dedicated it to his "friend and agent, Bradley Holmes" who, according to the author, was a true friend, a genius with the soul of Christ and the patience of Job in addition to being the finest agent in New York.

Allison went directly to a pay station where she looked up the address of Bradley Holmes in a telephone directory. He had an office on Fifth Avenue and late that same afternoon she sat down at her typewriter and wrote a long hysterical letter to Mr. Bradley Holmes. She wrote that she had been laboring under a misapprehension, for she had always thought that the function of a literary agent was to read manuscripts brought to him by authors. If she was right, how was it that she, a prize-winning writer, was unable to meet an agent face to face? And if she was wrong, what on earth were literary agents for anyway? There were eight pages more, in the same vein, and Allison had mailed them to the Fifth Avenue address without rereading them, for she was afraid that she might change her mind if she paused to think about what she had written.

A few days later, she had received a note from Bradley Holmes. It was typewritten on exquisitely heavy, cream-colored paper, and his name was engraved in black at the top of the sheet. The note was short and invited Miss MacKenzie to his office to meet him and to leave her manuscripts which Mr. Holmes would read.

Bradley Holmes's office was full of light and warmth the morning when Allison went there for the first time, and it smelled of expensive carpeting, and crushed cigarette ends, and of books in leather bindings.

"Sit down, Miss MacKenzie," said Bradley Holmes. "I must confess that I am rather surprised. I hadn't expected someone so young."

Young was a word which Brad used often, in one form or another, in all his conversations with Allison.

"I am so much older," he would say.

Or: "I've lived so much longer."

Or: "You have a surprisingly discerning eye, for one so young."

And many, many times, he said: "Here is a charming young man whom I think you will enjoy."

Allison had spent perhaps fifteen minutes with him, and then he had led her politely to the elevator in the hall.

"I'll read your stories as soon as I can," he told her. "I'll get in touch with you."

"Humph," said Steve Wallace later. "The old casting director's line. Don't call us, we'll call you. Fortunately, I've never run into it in modeling, but the theatrical offices I've been ushered out of with those words! Nothing will come of Mr. Bradley Holmes, though. You'd better try someone else."

Three days later, Bradley Holmes had telephoned Allison.

"There are a few things I'd like to discuss with you," he said. "Could you come down to the office today?"

"You have a great deal of talent with words," he told her, and in that moment, Allison would have died for him. "Also," he said, "you have a clever little knack with the slick type of short story. I think we ought to concentrate on that for the time being. Save the real talent for later, for a novel perhaps. Unfortunately, I don't know of a place where your best short stories would fit. The slick magazines, the only ones which pay enough for you to live on, aren't particularly partial to stories full of old maids, and cats, and sex. Here."

He handed Allison a stack of manuscripts which represented her better stories.

"We'll work on these others," he said.

Within two weeks, Allison had come to regard Bradley Holmes as a genius of the highest order. Within a month he had sold two of her stories and she had begun to think of doing a novel.

"You have plenty of time," he told her. "You are so young. But still, once you begin to make a respectable amount of money with the magazines you may never decide to try a book. Go ahead, if you like, and see what you can do."

"Yes, Brad," Allison had said. If he had told her that it was all right for her to step into a whirling propeller blade she would have said, "Yes, Brad."

They were having dinner together in one of the good restaurants on the East Side which Brad patronized.

"I don't have to travel 'way downtown to meet characters and perverts," he said. "I can see more of those than I care to at a variety of so-called literary teas."

After that, Allison began to shy away from the Village, but it was a long time before Bradley Holmes began to realize the influence he wielded over his youngest client.

"Think for yourself," he told her sharply. "This is not a Trilby–Svengali relationship which we have. Don't go thinking that it is."

But Allison had formed the habit of dependence. She had telephoned him and run to him for advice on a multitude of details which she could easily have resolved for herself.

"Don't start thinking of me as your father," he warned her.

Allison didn't. She thought of him as God.

Then Brad had started introducing Allison to a variety of young men. The most interesting was a tall, thin young man named David

355

Noyes who wrote what she referred to as "Novels of Social Significance."

"I wish that Allison would look at me just once the way she looks at Brad Holmes all the time," David told Steve Wallace. "It is almost embarrassing to watch her look at him. Such love, such worship. I wouldn't be able to stand it. I wonder how he does?"

Allison enjoyed David. He opened a whole new realm of thoughts and ideas to her, and he helped over the bad stages when she began work on her novel. She told him the legend of Samuel Peyton's castle and he listened attentively.

"Sounds good," he told her. "Of course, it may prove a little difficult to handle. You're going to have to work like hell to make Samuel a sympathetic character. If you goof, he turns into a villain."

"Brad thinks it's a wonderful story," Allison said. "He thinks it will be a big best seller."

"Smeller," amended David.

"Well, everyone can't be a boy genius," said Allison.

David was twenty-five and had been hailed as a brilliant new talent by the critics on the publication of his first novel. He wanted to reform the world and he had a difficult time understanding people like Allison who wanted to write for either fame or money. David saw a world free from war, poverty, crime and penal institutions and he was constantly trying to make others see what he saw. Brad Holmes called David a "dedicated young man" so, of course, Allison saw him that way, too.

"Brad is dedicated himself," said David when Allison told him what the agent had said. "He is like the city of New York. Hard, bright and dedicated to the race after the dollar.

"Brad and New York have everything in common, and the criterion of both is cash."

"Oh, what a terrible thing to say!" Allison exclaimed, angry almost to tears. "Why Brad is the sweetest, most gentle man I've ever known."

"Brad is a goddamned good agent," said David, "and I have seldom, if ever, seen money and gentleness go hand in hand."

"Sometimes," said Allison viciously, "in fact, most of the time, you sicken me. Brad is the best friend I ever had."

"Oh?" asked David sarcastically. "What about this Makris fellow whom you told me about? The one who stood by your side when your friend Kathy was hurt. Isn't he your friend? When he stood up with you, he was jeopardizing his job, his hard-won position in

that charming snake pit you call Peyton Place, and just about anything else you can name. What of Makris? He sounds like your
best friend to me."

"Oh, him," said Allison with a shrug. "He's different. He's my
mother's husband."

"Sometimes," said David slowly, "I think that one would have
to put your soul under a powerful microscope before it became
at all obvious that you have one."

"David, let's not argue. Just for one evening, let's not parry
words. Let's just be friends."

David had looked at her for a silent moment. "I don't want to
be your goddamned friend," he said.

"Well, what would you like to be then?" she asked.

"Your lover," he said bluntly. "But I don't have a set of pretty
clichés to let you know this."

They were sitting at a table in a Greenwich Village basement
restaurant. The table was covered with the standard red-checked
cloth and a candle, stuffed into the neck of an empty wine bottle,
burned sulkily at its far side. David had leaned toward Allison
and twined his fingers gently in the ends of her long hair.

"The only pretty thing I can think of to say, when I look at you,
is that you have lovely hair."

"Thank you," said Allison staring down at her hands. A low-
voiced compliment from David was something with which she was
not prepared to cope. "Hadn't we best hurry? I've never been to
the ballet before. I don't want to get there late."

They saw *Les Sylphides* that evening and Allison had looked at
the costumed dancers and thought of Peyton Place and April coming wetly through an open window. She shivered a little and David
reached over and took her hand in the darkened theater. Allison
had felt closer to David after that evening but still, when she
thought of love at all, she thought of Bradley Holmes.

"Allison!" It was Constance's voice calling her from the foot of
the stairs.

"Yes, Mother?"

"Tom is home. Come on down and have a drink with us."

"Thank you. I'll be down in a minute."

She washed her tear-swollen face and brushed her hair. David,
she was thinking. David would have been gentle with me.

Several days later, on an evening during the first week in September, Allison sat on the back porch of her mother's house with

357

Constance and Tom. Allison watched a moth try to battle his way through the porch screening and only half listened to Constance who was talking about Ted Carter.

"I don't believe that he ever loved Selena at all," said Constance.

"I don't agree with that," said Tom, stretching his long legs and sitting on the end of his spine. "It is true that love has different depths but deep or shallow, it is still love." Carefully, he did not look at Allison. "When a man does nothing more than sleep with an available woman, he is still expressing a love of sorts."

Constance snorted. "Next you'll be saying that a man is expressing love when he goes to a whore house."

"Mother! For Heaven's sake," protested Allison.

"Speak to Tom," said Constance comfortably, fishing for an orange slice in the bottom of her glass. "He's the one who taught me to call a spade a spade."

"A spade is one thing," said Allison, "and a bloody shovel is something else again. Anyway, I don't see what all that has to do with Ted and Selena. He led her on for years, pretending that he wanted to marry her, and look at what happened the minute she was in trouble. He left her. For years, we all thought that Ted Carter was so much and in the end he turned out to be a miniature of Roberta and Harmon. Ted and his big plans! The coward couldn't find room in them for Selena."

"But what does that have to do with whether he loved her or not?" asked Tom.

"If he had really loved her, he would have stood by her," said Allison hotly, glad that it was dark enough on the porch so that she did not have to look at Tom.

"Not necessarily," he said. "There is such a thing as love not meeting a test, but that does not mean that it was not a kind of love to begin with. Love is not static. It changes and fluctuates, sometimes growing stronger, sometimes weaker and sometimes disappearing altogether. But still, I think it is difficult not to be grateful for the love one gets."

"It's not worth it," said Allison. "You get too much pain for every little bit and scrap of love."

"The thing to do, Allison, is to remember the loving and not to dwell upon the loss," said Tom gently.

"What do you know about it?" cried Allison, jumping to her feet and starting to cry. "You never lost anything. You got what you wanted." She ran from the porch and up to her room.

"Well!" said Constance, surprised. "What ails her?"

"Growing pains," said Tom.

In her room, Allison lay face down on the bed. Remember? she thought desperately. Remember what?

Her shame when she thought of herself with Bradley Holmes made her wince and clench her fists and pray for forgetfulness. Remember the loving and not the loss, Tom had said. How could one forget altogether?

Oh, God, groaned Allison lying on her bed with her cheek hot against the crisp pillowcase, why did he have to mention love at all?

It had happened on the day when she had finished her novel. It was eight-thirty in the morning and she had been up all night writing and at last she wrote the two beautiful words THE END. She arched her neck and moved her shoulders, feeling the pain of weariness and strain, and then she glanced at the clock and lit a cigarette. It was almost nine o'clock and she could call Bradley Holmes at his office.

"Oh, Brad," she said as soon as she heard his voice. "I'm finished with it."

"Wonderful!" he said. "Why don't you bring it around on Monday?"

"On Monday!" cried Allison. "But Brad, I thought we could have dinner and read it over together later."

"That would be nice," Brad had said, "but I'm leaving early this afternoon to go up to Connecticut."

"Oh?" Allison asked. "Are you going alone?"

"Yes."

"Brad." Allison was silent for what seemed a long moment. "Brad?"

"Yes?"

"Take me with you."

He was silent for a long time in his turn. "All right," he said at last. "I'll pick you up at about four."

"I'll be ready."

"And Allison."

"Yes, Brad?"

"Leave the manuscript at home. We can talk it over if you like, but I've had a helluva hard week. I'd like to rest this week end."

"All right," she said and hung up slowly.

Steve Wallace came out of the bedroom, yawning. It was one of the rare mornings when she had no early appointments and she was enjoying it thoroughly.

"Hi," said Steve, rubbing her scalp with her finger tips. "Coffee ready?"

"I'm going away for the week end with Brad," said Allison.

Steve began to stretch her torso in a rhythmic exercise guaranteed to keep the waist trim. "Well, don't act as if you were about to die and go to heaven."

Allison turned work-weary, red-rimmed eyes to look at her. "I've never been away for the week end with a man."

"In the first place," Steve had emphasized her point with an extended forefinger, "I don't think that what you are thinking will come to pass. Not with Sir Galahad Holmes at the helm. And in the second place," this time she extended two fingers, "it sure as hell won't happen if you don't take a nap and get rid of those bloodshot eyes."

"I've finished the book."

"Eureka!" cried Steve. "Or gazooks! or something." She ran to the bridge table which held Allison's typewriter and looked at the beautiful words typed on the sheet of white paper. "The End," she said. "Thank God! I was afraid you'd have a nervous breakdown before it came to this. Oh, Allison, isn't it wonderful!" She did a few dance steps of joy, in her bare feet. "You're done!" She stood still and looked at her friend. "Oh," she said, "that's why Brad is taking you away for the week end. To read the book."

"No. He just wants me to tell him about it. And he wants to rest."

"Nonsense," said Steve. "If I ever saw a man sunk with love it's Brad Holmes. His problem is that he is over forty which makes him just about twice your age." She was speaking from the kitchen and Allison was sitting in the living room. "Of course, a little thing like that wouldn't bother most men, but most men are not Brad Holmes."

"I don't see what age has to do with love. Do you?"

"No, I don't. Why don't you ask Brad?"

"Maybe I will, later. Right now I'm going to bed."

"I'll call you in plenty of time for you to make yourself gorgeous for the week end."

Allison stood up and moved to the window of her room in Peyton Place.

How clever and cosmopolitan Steve and I thought we were that day, she thought. We were so blasé and nonchalant about my going off for the week end with a man. How daring I felt, and grown up, and unafraid.

"Doesn't it shock you a little that I am going off for the week end alone with a man?" she had asked Steve.

"Not if the man is Brad Holmes," Steve had replied as she packed Allison's shapeless cotton pajamas into a suitcase. "The biggest favor that guy ever did you was to introduce you to David Noyes. He knows it and so should you. I've no doubt that you'll return to the city on Monday as virginal as when you leave."

Allison moved restlessly away from her bedroom window and fumbled for a cigarette among the things on the night table. Her fingers found an empty package and she crumpled it in her hand as she made her way quietly downstairs. Constance and Tom had long since gone to bed and only one small light burned in the living room. Everything was still as Allison opened the front door and looked out into Beech Street; the night had turned off chilly as the September nights so often did in Peyton Place. She closed the door softly and went back into the living room. The hearth was cold and dark looking and Allison built a small pile of kindling wood on the andirons. When the fire was lit she sat down in an armchair and stared at the flames.

I should have run, she thought. I should have run from Brad and back to David. But did I really want to? In that minute when I could have turned away and said no, did I want to? Until now, Allison had made many excuses to herself. *I couldn't help it,* she had thought. *I did not realize. I loved him. It was all his fault. He should have known better.* Allison stared into the fire in the living room of her mother's house and for the first time since she had learned of her mother's defection she wondered about the heart and mind of Constance.

"It could happen to anyone," Constance had said. "I was lonely and he was there."

But I wasn't lonely. I had my work, and Steve, and David. I was not alone.

The fire made sparks as a log began to flame and at once Allison could feel the presence of Bradley Holmes. Strangely, where there had been a hideousness in remembrance before, she could remember now with curiosity.

He had stood in front of the fireplace in the living room of his Connecticut farm and extended a glass toward her.

"It may be contributing to the delinquency of a minor," he had said, "but a little sherry never hurt anyone. Here."

"Here's to *Samuel's Castle,*" he said, "and fifty-two weeks on the

361

lists. If you have written it as well as you have told it tonight, we'll have an immediate best seller."

Smeller, she thought, remembering David Noyes, but she did not say it aloud. She looked at him. "As long as you like it," she said, "I don't care if it's rejected by every publisher in New York."

"Don't talk like that," said Brad, sitting down next to her on the couch. "How do you expect me to pay the office rent without a best seller once in a while?"

There was a long silence during which she sipped at her drink, smoothed the skirt of her dress and lit a cigarette. She sat and gazed into the fire as Brad was doing, and for the first time since she had met him she felt uncomfortable in his presence.

"You needn't, you know," said Brad, and she was so startled that she nearly dropped the glass she held.

"Needn't what?"

"Feel uncomfortable." He stood up and went to stir the fire, keeping his back to her. "I wonder if you knew what you were saying this morning when you asked to come with me, or whether you were leaving it up to me to figure out."

"And what did you decide was the right answer?"

"I decided that a young lady who asks to spend the week end with a man is either after sex or well on the way to making a fool of herself. I am gratified that you showed enough wisdom to choose me as your companion. You must have known that no harm could come to you in the company of a man old enough to be your father."

"David Noyes doesn't regard me as such an infant," said Allison crossly. "He asked me to marry him a short while ago. I wish you'd stop using the words young and old as if they were our first names just for this one evening."

"Well, I can't," said Brad. "Not on this particular evening. If I put us on a basis of equal age this evening it might prove to be a provocative thought."

"Perhaps I'd rather like to provoke you into having a few thoughts. A few thoughts about *me*, as an individual, instead of me in connection with my work."

"Don't allow yourself to become piqued, my dear," he said coolly. "Pique often puts words into the mouth of a woman for which she is heartily sorry afterward."

"Well!" she exclaimed, with heavily underlined surprise. "Ring the bells, hang out the flags, close the schools. Bradley Holmes has come right out and said that Allison MacKenzie is a woman!"

He went to her quickly and raised her to her feet with his hands under her elbows. In the second before he kissed her, she had thought fleetingly that she was glad she had remembered to wear flat-heeled shoes. In flat heels, the top of her head came exactly to Brad's eyebrows.

He raised his lips but did not take his arms from around her. "Almost, but not quite," he said softly.

"What?"

"Almost but not quite a woman," he said. "You kiss like a child."

In the firelight she could see her reflection in his eyes. "How do you do that?" she asked, her breath hurting in her chest.

"What?"

"Kiss like a woman?"

"Open your mouth a little," he said, and kissed her again. . . .

Brad was practiced and polished, an expert who regarded the making of love as a creative art. He had led her well through the preliminaries of sex, undressing her deftly and quickly.

"Don't," he said, when she turned her face away from him and closed her eyes. He put his fingers to her cheek and brought her face back toward his own. "If you are going to feel shame, Allison, it is not going to be any good for you, not tonight or any other night. Tell me what it is that makes you turn away from me, and I'll take care of it or explain it away. But don't begin by closing your eyes so that you don't have to look at me."

"I've never been naked in front of anyone before," she said, against his shoulder.

"Don't use that word 'naked,' " he said. "There is a world of difference in referring to yourself as nude. Nude is a word as smooth as your hips," he said, caressing her, "but naked has the sound of a rock being turned over to expose maggots. Now, what is it about being nude that embarrasses you?"

She hesitated. . . . "I'm afraid that you'll find me ugly," she said at last.

"I am not going to say anything, because no matter what reassurances I made in this moment, every one would sound false to you. Besides, that is not what you are afraid of, you know."

"What is it then?"

"You are afraid that I will think badly of you for allowing me to have you. It is a perfectly normal feminine fear. If I gave you a reason that was convincing enough for why you are doing as you are, this fear would leave you. It is an odd thing, but most

363

women need excuses of one kind or another. It is much easier for men."

"How?" she had smiled at his descriptions of women.

"A man says, 'Ah, here is a gorgeous creature whom I should love to take to bed.' Then he begins to work toward his goal. If he achieves it, he jumps into the nearest bed with her and fornicates for all he is worth, before she can change her mind and demand that he present her with a good reason for what she is doing."

She turned on to her back and put her arms over her head. "Then you think that sex between unmarried persons is excusable."

"I've never thought of it as being either excusable or inexcusable. It is just there, and it can be good if people just won't mess it up with reasons and apologies. Have you understood one word I've said?"

"Yes, I think so."

"May I look at you, then?"

She had clenched her fists, but she did not close her eyes or turn away from him. "Yes," she said.

He did it slowly, following with his eyes the path created by his hands as they traveled over her.

"You are truly beautiful," he said. "You have the long, aristocratic legs and the exquisite breasts of a statue."

She let out her long-held breath with a sigh that made her quiver, and her heart beat hard under her breasts. He placed his lips against the pulsating spot, while he pressed gently at her abdomen with his hand. He continued to kiss her and stroke her until her whole body trembled under his lips and hands. When he kissed the softness of her inner thighs, she began to make moaning, animal sounds, and even then he continued his sensual touching and stroking and waited until she began the undulating movements of intercourse with her hips. She was lying with her arms bent and raised over her head, and he held her pinned to the bed with his hands on her wrists.

"Don't," he commanded, when she tried to twist away from him at the first thrust of pain. "Help me," he said. "Don't pull away."

"I can't," she cried. "I can't."

"Yes, you can. Press your heels against the mattress and raise your hips. Help me. Quickly!"

In the last moment a bright drop of blood appeared on her mouth, where she had bitten into her lip, and then she had cried out the odd, mingled cry of pain and pleasure.

Later, after they had smoked and talked, he turned to her again.

364

"It is never as good as it should be for a woman, the first time," he said. "This one will be for you."

He began to woo her again, with words, and kisses, and touches, and this time she had felt the full, soaring joy of pleasure without pain.

"I thought I was dying," she said to him, afterward. "And it was the loveliest feeling in the world."

By Sunday morning, she had been able to walk nude in front of Brad, and feel his eyes probing her, without feeling either shame or fear. She had arched her back, and lifted her heavy hair off her neck, and pressed her breasts against his face, and gloried in his swift reaction to her.

This is what it is like, she had thought exultantly, to be in love with a man with everything that is within oneself.

Too soon, it was Sunday night, and they made their way back to New York over the Merritt Parkway. Brad held her fingers in his and she giggled.

"It would be terrible if I got pregnant," she had said, thinking that it would not be terrible at all, "because then we'd have to get married and I'd never get any work done. We'd be spending all out time in bed."

Brad withdrew his hand from hers at once.

"But my dear child," he said, "I was extremely conscientious about taking precautions against anything as disastrous as pregnancy. I am already married. I thought you knew."

She had felt nothing but a numbness which seemed to insulate her body with ice.

"No," she said, in a conversational tone, "I didn't know. Do you and your wife have children?"

"Two," said Brad.

She should have felt something, but the nothingness inside her would not dislodge itself.

"I see," she said.

"I'm surprised that you didn't know. Everyone does. David Noyes knows it. He met my wife in the office one day, as a matter of fact."

"He never mentioned it to me," she said as if she were talking about someone who had met a vague acquaintance and had attached no importance to it.

"Well," said Brad, with a little laugh, "Bernice is not the type who impresses a stranger on a first meeting." He pulled up expertly

365

in front of her door. "I'll read the novel tomorrow. Let's hope that it's as good as you make it sound."

"Yes." She got out of the car. "No, don't bother to come up, Brad. I can find my way. Good night. Good night," she had repeated, "and thank you for a lovely time."

Steve Wallace had been entertaining a friend in the apartment when Allison came through the door.

"Beat it," Steve said to her friend, and as soon as the door had closed behind him she turned to Allison. "What?" she demanded. "What is it? What happened?"

Allison put her suitcase down on the floor. "Brad's married," she said, in the same tone she would have used had she told a stranger that Brad had black hair.

Steve went over to the coffee table, took two cigarettes from a box, lit them both and passed one to her. "Well, it's not a tragedy, is it? I mean, it's not as though you were in love with him or anything. Allison?"

"Yes?"

"I said, it's not as though you were in love with him or anything. Is it?"

"I never heard anyone talking about his wife," she said in a puzzled tone. "Isn't that odd? I didn't even know Brad was married until he told me on the way home."

"Allison! Answer me! I said, it's not as though you were in love with him or anything. Is it?"

"I've spent the whole week end in bed with him. I don't believe that a woman could know Brad and not think herself in love with him, or that she could sleep with him and not know that she loved him."

"Oh, my Lord!" said Steve and sat down on the edge of a chair and burst into tears. "Oh, Allison," she wept. "What can you do?"

"Do? Why, I'm going to bed."

When Steve looked into the bedroom to see if Allison was awake the next morning, she found her lying on her back, staring dry eyed at the ceiling.

"Are you all right?" Steve asked anxiously. "I have an appointment at nine, but I'll call up and cancel it if you aren't all right."

"I'm perfectly fine," she had said, feeling as if she were encased in ice.

"Oh, Allison. What are you going to do?"

"Do?" she had asked, in exactly the same tone as the night before. "Why, I think I'll go for a walk. It looks like a lovely warm day."

She swung her legs over the edge of her bed and stood up. "You'd better run if you have a nine o'clock."

"Oh," said Steve, "I forgot to tell you. Your mother called you on Saturday. I told her that you were spending the week end in Brooklyn, with a girl friend. She said it was nothing serious, that she just had a piece of local news that she thought would interest you. I told her that I'd have you call when you got back."

"I'll do that. Thank you."

She had drunk three cups of coffee and smoked four cigarettes, but she did not eat, and she did not call Constance. She left the apartment and began to walk, and she walked all morning. Around noontime, she found herself on Broadway, near Times Square. She was almost fifty feet away from the newsstand before what she had seen there registered on her tired brain. She had seen a folded newspaper, and the bold letters of the headline had nudged something in her. "Peyton Place," were the letters she had seen. She fought her way against the crowd and back to the stand.

"That paper there," she said, pointing.

"Ten cents," the man said.

It was a four-day-old copy of the *Concord Monitor*.

"PATRICIDE IN PEYTON PLACE," she had read. Then she hailed a cab and told the driver to hurry her to her address, that she was ill and had to get home.

When she had reached the apartment Steve had told her that Brad had called three times.

She had walked past Steve and into the bedroom. She took her suitcase from the closet where Steve had put it the night before.

"I'm going home," she had said to Steve.

Allison sat still and listened to the quiet which was part of Peyton Place at night. She had not got away from New York before Brad called, she remembered.

"I've read the book," he had said, as if nothing had happened between them over the week end. "Can you come down to the office?"

"No, I can't, Brad," she had replied, trying to match her tone to his. "I'm going home."

There was a long pause. "Listen, Allison. Don't be silly, please. Come down to the office and we'll talk."

"What did you think of the book, Brad?"

Again there was a pause. "It lacks something," he said at last. "It doesn't seem alive or quite real."

367

"Is it impossible to fix?" she had demanded.

"I didn't say that, Allison. I simply think that you should put it away for a while. You are young. There is no hurry. Write me a few more stories for the magazines, and perhaps you can try on the novel again next year."

"You mean the book is no good, don't you?"

"I didn't say that."

"Can you sell it?"

Brad had allowed another silence to spread from his telephone to hers. "No," he had said finally. "I don't think that I can sell it."

Allison stood up and went to the fire. She poked the dying log apart so that the fire would go out more quickly, then she turned and went upstairs to her room. She was thinking of what David Noyes had said about *Samuel's Castle*. "If you goof—" he had said. Well, she had goofed and the book was no good. She went to the small desk in her bedroom and took out the letters she had been receiving from David all summer. She smiled as she reread them, for each was a miracle of tact and cheerfulness. He must certainly have heard about her novel from Steve Wallace, yet he did not mention it in his letters. He wrote of his daily activities, the work he was doing on his new book, the places he went, the people he met. And in every letter he asked her to hurry back to New York.

"I miss you," he wrote. "Your sharp tongue, or should I say the lack thereof, has left a big hole in my daily existence. No one has called me a 'boy genius' since you left and my ego suffers."

He wrote: "Today I am puking with disgust over the words of various popular songs. 'Take me. Leave me,' say these sickening things. 'Knock me down and kick me in the teeth. Grind your lovely heel into the bridge of my nose. It matters not. I'll understand.' Can you imagine a guy that stupid? I can."

Oh, David, thought Allison wretchedly. I am going to hurt you, but I cannot help myself.

She sat down at her desk and wrote a letter to David. She wrote to him as if she were writing a story, and she described her Connecticut week end in the most minute detail. But it was not until she put down the last sentences that she began to feel comforted.

"The measure of my shame, David, is that I did not love him," she wrote. "This is the worst part of it now. I should have liked to think of myself always as the type of woman who needs sex only to express love of the highest kind. But this was not so with Brad. I used to think that the business of confusing love with sex

368

was childish and stupid, but now I know why so many women do this. It is because it is too painful afterward, if one can remember nothing of love."

She did not hear from David again, nor did she write him again. But his silence created a feeling of apprehension in her and she was almost sorry that she had written to him as she had.

But she could not imagine being careful of what she said in front of David. She decided to return to New York at the end of October and she wrote short notes to Steve Wallace and to Bradley Holmes to tell them. She was able to write Brad's name on the envelope without a trace of feeling, with her hands steady and her heart not pounding.

It is done, she thought, and yet she felt none of the calm satisfaction which she had generally associated with the tying up of loose ends.

One afternoon, late in September, Allison and Tom walked up the hill to Samuel Peyton's castle.

"I've never been there," she said. "Perhaps that's why I couldn't write about it successfully. A long time ago I realized that it was a waste of time to try to write about something one does not know about."

"Are you going to give it another try?" asked Tom. "The novel, I mean."

"Not for a while," said Allison. "I think I'll go back to the short stories for another year or so. Tom—" She paused and bent to pick up a stick which she poked into the ground as she walked. "Tom, I'd like to make peace with my mother."

Tom bent in his turn and picked up a stick. "That sounds like a good idea," he said calmly. "But don't do it on the spur of the moment. Don't do it if you don't mean it because that would only hurt her more, and I would not stand for that."

"I mean it," said Allison. "I understand how it could happen. Mother was just unluckier than most, that's all."

Tom laughed. "I wouldn't say that," he said. "She got you, didn't she? Maybe she was luckier than most."

"I wonder what Peyton Place would say about us if they knew," murmured Allison.

"You wonder too much about Peyton Place," said Tom. "It's just a town, Allison, like any other town. We have our characters, but so does New York and so does every other town and city."

"I know that," said Allison, lowering her head to watch a rabbit skitter off into the woods. "But I can't make myself feel it. It is

369

like a lot of other things with me. I know that something is so. I can even write about it the way I think it, but I don't feel it the same way. Like love. My agent says that I write a very creditable love scene but Tom—" She raised her head to look at him. "Tom, what a difference there is between writing something or reading something, and living it."

"The main difference is that it is easier to read or write than to live," said Tom. "I guess that's the only real difference."

Allison leaned against one of the gray walls which surrounded Samuel Peyton's castle. "To me, the main difference has always been that writing and reading are less painful. In fact, when I first came home, I had almost made up my mind to stick to those two and forgo living."

Tom smiled. "But on the other hand, to coin a phrase, life is too damned short not to be lived every minute."

"And besides, people don't have much choice anyway," added Allison and laughed. It was the first time she had laughed over nothing much all summer. "We'd better start back," she said. "The days are getting shorter and shorter. It'll be dark soon."

Constance and Allison had never been comfortable with the words of sentimentality. So, when Constance noticed after dinner that the silver-framed photograph of Allison MacKenzie which had stood for so many years on the living room mantelpiece was gone, she merely turned a startled, hopeful look at her daughter. Allison smiled, and Constance smiled, and except for Tom nothing would have been said.

"Listen," he remarked, "this is supposed to be a big scene, like Hollywood. Allison, you're supposed to break into the weeps and cry, 'Mother!' And Connie, you're supposed to smile through your tears and say, tremulously, of course, 'Daughter!' Then the two of you are supposed to fall on each other's necks and sob. Soft music and fade-out. God, what a couple of cold fish I got tangled up with!"

Allison and Constance both burst out laughing and Constance said, "Let's open that bottle of cognac I was saving for Christmas."

The autumn rains began that night. It rained almost steadily for two weeks, and then one morning Allison awoke and knew before she got out of bed and went to her window that Indian summer had come.

"Oh!" she cried aloud, a few minutes later, as she leaned as far out the window as she could. "Oh, you came after all!"

She dressed rapidly and hardly paused to eat breakfast, and

370

then she set out to walk to Road's End. She climbed the long sloping hill behind Memorial Park, and when she reached the top it was all there, waiting for her, as she had remembered it. She walked through the woods with her old light-footed grace, and came at last to the open field hidden in the middle of the woods. The goldenrod stood as tall, and straight, and yellow as it always had, and the same maples, loud with the paint of Indian summer, surrounded everything. Allison sat for a long time in her secret place, and reflected that even if this spot were not as secret as she had once believed, the things it said to her were still secret. She felt now the assurance of changelessness that had comforted her as a child and she smiled and touched a goldenrod's yellow head.

I saw the starry tree Eternity, put forth the blossom Time, she thought, and remembered Matthew Swain and the many, many friends who were part of Peyton Place. I lose my sense of proportion too easily, she admitted to herself. I let everything get too big, too important and world shaking. Only here do I realize the littleness of the things that can touch me.

Allison looked up at the sky, blue with the deep blueness peculiar to Indian summer, and thought of it as a cup inverted over her alone. The feeling was soothing, as it had always been, but for a single moment now, Allison felt that she no longer needed to be soothed and comforted as she once had. When she stood up and began to walk again, the sun was high with noontime brightness, and when she came to the sign with the red letters painted on its side, she had to shade her eyes with her hand to look down at the toy village that was Peyton Place.

Oh, I love you, she cried silently. I love every part of you. Your beauty and your cruelty, your kindness and ugliness. But now I know you, and you no longer frighten me. Perhaps you will again, tomorrow or the next day, but right now I love you and I am not afraid of you. Today you are just a place.

As she ran down the hill toward town, Allison fancied that the tree sang to her with the many voices of a symphony.

"Good-by, Allison! Good-by, Allison! Good-by, Allison!"

She was still running with a spate of excess energy when she reached Elm Street. Her mother called to her from the front door of the Thrifty Corner.

"Allison! I've been looking all over town for you! You have company at home. A young man all the way from New York. He says his name is David Noyes."

371

"Thank you!" cried Allison and waved her hand.

She hurried, and when she reached Beech Street she ran all the way up the block to her house.

RETURN TO
PEYTON PLACE

FOR JACQUES CHAMBRUN—
Who talked me into this book in the first place.

BOOK ONE

1

SOMETIMES, WINTER COMES GRADUALLY TO NORTHERN NEW ENGLAND so that there is an element of order and sequence to time and season. When the first snow comes it is not surprising because it has been expected for quite a while. When winter comes that way, it usually begins to snow big, fat flakes at mid-morning and by noon there is a thick edge of white on everything. The skies clear after lunch and the sun comes out and by the time school is out in the afternoon all the eaves on all the houses in town are dripping melting snow.

Then the old-timers say, " 'Twon't stay. Not this time. Not yet."

And everyone who is still young enough is disappointed and a little apprehensive because maybe it's really true that old-fashioned winters have left northern New England forever.

Old-fashioned winters usually happen after hot, dry summers. Then the fall rains begin right after Labor Day and they are cold, wind-driven rains that are gray and destructive, and after those rains there is no beautiful autumn, no glory of red and gold leaves. The trees turn quickly from green to withered brown and the rain cuts the leaves from the branches in fast, vicious swipes. After the rains, the ground freezes hard and quickly and one day is like the next, cold and gray and waiting for the snow.

Then it begins. A fine powder that sifts down from the dark sky in a seemingly unending screen and does not accumulate on streets and roads until after the wind has had enough of blowing, and cold, dry piles of white have gathered around the base of every fence post and tree. By suppertime the wind dies down and still it snows, so fine and thin that children are afraid it will take forever for enough of it to fall to cover the palms of their mittened hands.

But those who are older remember other old-fashioned winters. They are the ones who check the gallon gauges on oil-burner fuel tanks, who have long since made sure that their car radiators are full of anti-freeze, and who know that with the coming of tomorrow's dawn, the wind, too, will return.

Fireplaces do not exist in the houses of northern New England purely for their friendly, hospitable hearths. They are there because every once in a while there is an old-fashioned winter and power lines break like dry straws in the face of the wind and snow. Those who remember have small, wood-burning stoves in their cellars to keep water pipes from freezing; every wood box is filled and overflowing with logs and kindling, and the young sit in front of blazing fires and wax their skis and wonder what the accumulation will be at Franconia by morning.

That was the way winter came the second year after Allison MacKenzie returned to Peyton Place. It was four o'clock on a November afternoon, and Allison was standing in front of the window in her bedroom when she saw the first flake of snow.

Perhaps it will be tomorrow, she thought. Maybe tomorrow Brad will call and say, I've sold it, Allison, I've sold it; your novel has been accepted and will be published in the spring.

• **2** •

TUTTLE'S GROCERY STORE WAS LOCATED ON ELM STREET, PEYTON PLACE'S main thoroughfare, at a point halfway between the Citizens' National Bank and Prescott's Pharmacy which stood on the corner of Maple Street. From the front window of Tuttle's, the old men who hung around the store in the winter could look out and see the courthouse and the benches where they loitered when the weather was warm and fair. During the summer, Tuttle's was something of a tourist attraction, for it was one of the few remain-

377

ing stores in northern New England where you could buy Cheddar cheese by the slice or by the pound from Ephraim Tuttle's enormous cheese wheel. Tuttle's still sold rock candy and licorice drops by the pennyworth, and a nickel would buy a fat pickle, sour enough to set your teeth on edge, from a huge barrel that stood in a dark corner at the back of the store.

Right after Memorial Day, every year, Ephraim Tuttle made his yearly concession to what he called the "summer trade." At that time he brought brightly colored bolts of gingham and calico up from his cellar and lined them all in a neat row on the front counter as had his father and grandfather before him in the days before ready-made clothing. Once in a while, someone bought a few yards of material to make curtains for a summer camp, but otherwise the bolts of fabric stood on the counter until after Labor Day, when Ephraim sent them off to Ginny Stearns to be washed and ironed and then rewound to be stored in plastic coverings in Tuttle's cellar for another winter.

"Waste of space," said Clayton Frazier, "settin' all that cloth right up there on the front counter that way. Nobody ever buys nothin' to speak of."

"Lends the place a tone," said Ephraim. "Summer folks like tone. What they call *atmosphere*."

But with the coming of fall, Tuttle's reverted to what it had always been—a rather dusty, very old sort of general store where you could buy almost anything, if you were able to find it. This jungle of merchandise included magazines and cough drops and ear plugs and old sunglasses; tomatoes in a cellophane package and fish by the pound on Fridays only, eggs that you took from a carton yourself and put by the dozen into a paper bag; deerskin work gloves and pipe tobacco, Alka-Seltzer and lollipops and the Sunday papers. In the fall, Ephraim shut off the two circular ceiling fans that had whirred around slowly all summer and set up his potbellied wood and coal stove, but it was not until he took down and put away the awning, which shielded his front window all summer long, and began saving wooden packing crates suitable for sitting purposes, that the old men who occupied the benches in front of the courthouse knew it was time to move across the street to wait for winter.

"Gonna snow," said Clayton Frazier. "Gonna snow sure'n hell."

" 'Bout time," said one of the old men who sat with his feet up on the base of the stove. "November. And we all knew it was gonna come early this year."

"Foolishness," said Clayton, and sat down on the one wooden chair that was reserved for him. "I've seen it cold as this many a time and it never snowed 'til clear into January. But it's gonna snow today. Sure'n hell."

"Don't snow in hell, Clayton," said another man, and waited for a chuckle from his friends.

"How'd'you know, John?" asked Clayton Frazier. "Been there lately?"

And then the men around the stove did laugh, and Clayton leaned back happily and lit his pipe.

The front door of the store opened suddenly, letting in a sweep of cold air that immediately stifled all conversation around the stove. Clayton Frazier looked up at the stranger who had entered, and the only way that anyone could have known that Clayton was upset was that he kept his pipe out of his mouth when everyone around the stove could tell that he hadn't drawn on his pipe anywhere near long enough to be satisfied with its glow.

"Ephraim!" said the stranger.

Ephraim Tuttle looked up slowly. "Ayeh," he said. "What can I do for you?"

"Ephraim," said the stranger and laughed. "For God's sake, don't you remember me?"

Everyone around the stove knew who the stranger was, but not a man moved to make an acknowledging gesture.

"I'm Gerry Gage," said the stranger, still laughing and now clapping Ephraim Tuttle on the shoulder. "S. S. Pierce Co., out of Boston. Don't you remember? It was me that remembered about bringing that Navy fellow back to town, the fellow that was murdered by his own daughter. Remember me now?"

"Stepdaughter," said Clayton Frazier, and put his pipe into his mouth.

"Well, whatever she was," said Gerry Gage. "Anyway, it was me that remembered."

"Ayeh," said Clayton.

There was a silence, and the stranger rubbed one of his gloved hands over the edge of his briefcase.

"Well," he said at last. "What do you need, Ephraim? I've got your usual list here, and I could go by that."

"The usual," said Ephraim.

Gerry Gage was suddenly angry. "Listen here," he said, "I only did what I thought was right. I never meant to do anything in the first place. I just happened to mention something about a fellow I let off here in Peyton Place. A hitchhiker. How did I know I was talking to the sheriff. It was him that started everything. All I did was what I thought was right. That's all."

Sheriff Buck McCracken glanced at Gerry Gage. "Whyn't you do the business you come for," he said, and he did not ask it as a question.

Gerry began to make check marks next to the items listed on a slip of paper in his hand.

"No need for any of you guys to hold a grudge against me," he said. "A man doing what he thought was right."

"Ain't nobody in Peyton Place holdin' a grudge aginst you that I know of, Mr. Gage," said Clayton Frazier. "It's just that some people talk a God-awful lot, and that does get tirin'."

"Believe me," said Gerry Gage, "I know exactly what you mean. Believe me, in my business I meet a lot of talkers. But then, it takes all kinds to make a world," he added, as if he were the first man ever to have noticed this.

"Ayeh," said Clayton.

"By the way," said Gerry. "After all that murder business and all, I asked to be transferred off this route. And I was, too. The company understood. I mean, about all the notoriety and all. I haven't been back this way since the cops dragged me back to answer a lot of questions about Lucas Cross."

Nobody said a word, and, as the seconds passed, Gerry Gage became more and more uncomfortable.

"Well anyway," he said, finally. "What's new in Peyton Place? I haven't heard much about this neck of the woods since all that stuff about the murder quieted down in the papers."

"Nothin'," said Clayton Frazier.

"What?" asked Gerry.

"Nothin'," repeated Clayton. "There's nothin' new in Peyton Place. Seldom is. Nothin's different at all."

And to the uneducated eye of a stranger it would have appeared

380

that Clayton Frazier's words were true. Peyton Place looked as it had always looked—pretty, quiet and untouched by turmoil. In the late winter afternoon the lighted windows of the shops and houses presented friendly, innocent faces to each other and to the rest of the world.

The war was over and the Harrington Mills no longer throbbed in twenty-four-hour shifts straining to fill the demands of Army contracts, but that was true of factories nearly everywhere. Leslie Harrington still lived alone in his big house on Chestnut Street, and while time and the loss of his only son, Rodney, had aged and gentled him a little, he was still Leslie Harrington, a fact of which everyone in town was still very much aware.

Down the street from Leslie, Dr. Matthew Swain still practiced medicine and his friend, Seth Buswell, still wrote editorials for the Peyton Place *Times*. The house of Charles Partridge was as empty as it had ever been, for neither time, nor acquisitions, nor the lawyer's wife, Marion, had been able to fill it with any degree of warmth or love. None of the old families had moved away, and no new people had moved into town, leastways, as Seth Buswell put it, not enough of them to shake things up or to amount to anything.

No, nothing much had changed in Peyton Place. At least, nothing that anyone was willing to pour into the ears of a stranger. And if there had been changes in private situations and in individuals, surely these changes were the concern of those to whom they had happened and, again, nothing for the ears of a stranger.

Nope, thought Gerry Gage, as he left Tuttle's Grocery Store and climbed into his car, nothing new in Peyton Place. Hell, that girl killing her old man was probably the only big thing that ever did or ever will happen here.

Gerry Gage drove his car down Elm Street toward the highway that led to White River and was, as he put it, damned glad to be heading for a town where there was a hotel with a bar, where other salesmen gathered and there was something to talk about, drinks to be bought, and jokes to be told.

In the Thrifty Corner Apparel Shoppe on Elm Street, Selena Cross finished covering a counter top full of blouses that were on sale. Then, looking up, she saw a flake of snow flatten itself and spread against the windowpane. She left the counter and walked toward the front window of the shop to make sure that what she had seen was really a snowflake, and as she looked she noticed a car with Massachusetts license plates heading toward the highway to White River. She wondered briefly, as people will in a town like Peyton Place, just who from out of state was visiting whom, but then Gerry Gage's car was out of sight and Selena thought no more about it.

It really is snowing, she thought. I'll have to hurry home to Joey.

She glanced up again as another snowflake fell against the window and saw two hurrying figures cross her line of vision. For just a second, her heart thumped hard and then she turned quickly away from the window.

Outside, the two figures turned quickly into Maple Street and were out of sight.

"Hurry, darling," said Ted Carter to the girl whose arm he held. "I don't want my wife to freeze to death during her very first winter in Peyton Place."

The girl laughed up at him. "Remind me to buy a pair of flat-heeled shoes tomorrow. I can't keep up with those long legs of yours when I'm wearing high heels. I saw a shop back there—Thrifty something—I'll go there tomorrow."

Ted Carter did not laugh with his wife and his steps grew even more hurried.

"They don't sell shoes at the Thrifty Corner," he said, and, holding tightly onto his wife's arm, he tried desperately not to think of Selena.

• 3 •

SELENA CROSS HAD JUST STARTED TO TURN OFF THE LIGHTS IN THE store when the front door banged open and Michael Rossi came in.

"Hi, Selena," he called. "In the words of us natives, 'It's gonna snow, sure'n hell.'" He brushed at the shoulders of his overcoat where the snow had already left a fine, white dust and he stood there and grinned at her.

"Hi, Mike," said Selena. "How's Connie?"

"Fine," he answered, "and I have strict orders to bring you home with me. Connie always makes hot buttered rum for everyone on the day of the first snow. Come on, get your coat. The car's right outside."

Selena turned her eyes away from his. "I can't," she said. "I've got to get home to Joey. It's snowing."

"Selena," said Mike, and his voice was very gentle as he put his hand on her arm, "come with me. It'll be all right. When I saw that it was going to snow, I told Joey to go right to our house from school. He's there now, with Connie and Allison. Come on, Selena. It'll be all right."

She looked up at him, her eyes darker than ever, dark with remembered fear and horror and pain.

Mike Rossi picked up her coat and helped her into it. There was in his way of doing this something of the bullying gentleness of a nurse with a convalescent patient.

"Come on," he said. "You're staying for dinner, too. I'll drive you home, afterward, if you want to go."

Selena's hands fumbled blindly with the buttons on her coat, and as they left the shop she tried the front door carefully before she followed Mike to the car.

Time had been good to Michael Rossi. His shoulders were still broad and straight under the dark cloth of his coat, and, if there was a slight thickening at his waistline, it was only his wife who knew of it and laughed at him in the privacy of their bedroom.

"Is my Greek god getting a little old and paunchy?" Constance teased, and smiled at him in a way she knew he found challenging.

He took her hands and pressed them against him. "Paunchy, eh?" he said, laughing. He smiled into her eyes, returning her challenge.

"Show-off," she said. "Always strutting around like a bantam rooster."

Constance broke loose from him and made a dash for the bathroom, but she was not fast enough. He grabbed her again and held her tightly while she struggled, laughing, against him.

"I don't strut," he said. "Take it back or you'll rue the day."

"Never, never, never," cried Constance, and squealed and kicked when he began to tickle her, his hands moving all over her body.

Her struggles loosened the belt of her robe, and he stripped the garment from her.

"Stop it!" Constance yelled. "Stop it at once!" She tried to sound severe but did not succeed.

As Mike kissed her his fingers began to unbutton her pajama coat; then he slowly pushed the coat off her shoulders and she let it slide down her arms and fall to the floor. His hand found the tie of her pajama bottoms, he eased them over her hips until they slithered down around her ankles. Then he lifted her up and out of the crushed circle of pink silk and carried her to the bed.

"You are nothing but a big corny Greek, Mike," she said, and was surprised to hear how her voice shook. I sound like a frightened bride, she thought.

His lips brushed against her nipples, his mouth caressed her. "And you," he whispered, "are nothing but a pure and innocent Peyton Place housewife."

"What are you going to do about it, Mike, an old man like you?" she said, her voice slow and teasing.

"I shall corrupt you," he said, and when he bent toward her again her body twisted and she flung her arms over her head.

"Ask me for it," he demanded, his voice harsh.

"Go to hell. I'll never ask you!"

"Yes, you will," he said, "oh yes, you will."

"Make me," she cried. "Make me, darling, make me." And then, quickly, "Now, darling. Now."

"Say it, damn you. Say it to me now!"

Constance arched her body and twisted it in the effort to get even closer to him. Her hands clutched him and she threw her head back.

"Say it," he repeated, his voice low and savage.

The words tore from her throat, anguished, as if they were the last words she would ever utter.

When it was over he held her in the curve of his arm, and she felt protected from the whole world and safe against all its dangers.

"You're never the one to go to sleep first," she murmured drowsily against his shoulder.

"It's ungentlemanly," he replied. He stroked her hair and smiled in the dark. "Besides, only old men go to sleep on their women."

Constance sighed, and just before falling asleep she said, "Everybody knows Greek gods never grow old."

Mike kissed her gently and thought, There is nothing in life that's better than this, lying beside the woman you love, in your own bed, in your own house.

The house was still the same white, green-shuttered house that it had always been, and, in spite of Mike's marriage to Constance, the townspeople still referred to it as "the MacKenzie Place."

"Don't let that bother you, darling," Constance had told Mike. "Long after everyone thought I'd become a MacKenzie, they still called this house 'the Standish Place.' Don't worry. It'll happen. One day, everybody'll say 'Rossi house.'"

"I should live so long," said Mike ruefully.

Mike had gone to Leslie Harrington, who knew more about real estate than anyone in Peyton Place.

"Listen, Leslie," he had asked, "what do you think Connie's house is worth?"

"Connie's house?" asked Harrington. "What the hell are you talking about, Mike? You and Connie and Allison aren't going to leave town, are you?"

"You ought to learn to mind your own business, Leslie," said Mike. "But if it's any satisfaction to you—no, we aren't about to leave town. Now, how much is Connie's house worth?"

"Well," Leslie hedged, "real estate values went up with the war and all. But Connie's house, well taken care of as that's always been—let's see. Hm-m, well, I'd say, offhand, that I'd go eighteen five on it."

"Jumping Jesus!" roared Mike. "Eighteen thousand five hundred dollars! Where the hell do you think you are? Downtown Dallas?"

Leslie Harrington leaned back and smiled. "Nope," he said, "but if I was Connie, I'd never take a nickel less."

Mike had gone back to Constance and said, "Darling, will you please sell me your house for, God help us all, eighteen thousand five hundred dollars?"

"What ever in the world for?" she asked, puzzled.

"Never mind why," he told her. "Just will you?"

"Yes," she said.

Mike took every cent he had managed to save and made a down payment on Constance's house. Then he borrowed the rest

385

and finished paying for it. And when everything was done, he held the new deed, with his name on it, in his hand.

"Leslie," he asked. "Is it my house now?"

Leslie Harrington leaned back and smiled. "Yes, Mike, it is. And Connie got a good price, too, even if I do say it myself."

"Well, if it's really mine, I want to give it away as a gift," said Mike.

The chair in which Leslie Harrington had been leaning back fell forward with a thump.

"What the hell are you talking about?" he asked.

"It's my house," said Mike, "and I want to give it to Connie for her birthday."

"Well, of all the goddamned foolishness I've ever heard of," roared Leslie, "this beats it all. You didn't have to buy the goddamned thing. We could have changed the deed to read so that your name was on it. You didn't have to go through all this nonsense."

"It wouldn't be the same," said Mike.

So it was done, and Mike brought the new deed home to his wife and it read: KNOW ALL MEN BY THESE PRESENTS, That I, Michael Rossi of Peyton Place, State of New Hampshire, for the sum of one dollar and other good and valuable considerations to me in hand paid by Constance Standish MacKenzie Rossi of Peyton Place, State of New Hampshire, do hereby give, grant and convey to her, her heirs, successors and assigns forever, in fee simple, absolute, all that certain tract of land, with the buildings and improvements thereon, situate in Peyton Place, State of New Hampshire.

Constance burst into tears. "You nut," she wept. "You didn't have to go through all that nonsense."

But her tears were tears of pride and happiness, and she held her husband very tightly.

"Thank you, darling. Thank you."

"Well," said Mike and grinned down at her, "it's nothing to cry about. Listen, do you think people will start calling this the Rossi Place now?"

Constance went to the sideboard and fixed a drink for her husband.

"Nope," she said cheerfully, "they won't. Not for a while."

She took a sip from his glass before she handed it to him.

"But I'll know, darling," she said. "I'll call it the Rossi Place for the rest of my life."

And now Mike's car drew up to the house he had bought from his wife and given to his wife. He looked at it with proprietary eyes. It had never seemed to him his own until he had given it to Constance. What made it his was that he had earned the right to give it away.

"Here we are," Mike said, and Selena's head jerked around, her eyes frightened and startled. His voice had brought her back to the reality of Peyton Place. In her thoughts she had been worlds away. Only daydreams now could protect her from the horrors of memory.

She walked up the path in front of the MacKenzie Place and the front door opened quickly, revealing Allison's delighted smile.

"Selena!" cried Allison MacKenzie. "For Heaven's sake, we've been waiting and waiting for you to get here. Hi, Mike." Allison put up her cheek to be kissed. "Did you bring the milk?"

"Yes, my darling daughter," said Mike and slapped Allison on the behind. "Now everybody inside. It's cold and it's gonna snow, sure'n hell."

"Hello, darling," said Constance, and came to put her arms around her husband and then Selena. "Come on in. Shut the door. Listen, I've got the most divine brew brewing. If you have just one cup of it, you can't possibly catch cold. It's my own secret potion, handed down to me from my great-great-grandmother, who was a witch. Guaranteed protection against head colds and malignant spirits." She put her hand on Selena's arm.

Selena Cross looked across the room to where her brother, Joey, sat waiting for her. The living room was bright and warm. The blaze from the fireplace cast warm dancing shadows on everything.

"Come and sit down, Selena," said Constance.

Selena stood in the doorway of the living room, and Joey stood up.

"Hi, Joey," she said.

"Hi, S'lena," said Joey. "It's snowing."

"Yes, Joey," said Selena. "It's snowing."

There was a little pause, and neither Mike, Constance nor Allison then could find anything to say. Selena's presence had, for a moment, brought the darkness of unhappiness into that light, gay room. They shared her pain, they stood around her like body-guards fearful of assassins. They could think of nothing to say that would release Selena from the strain of memory and the pain of loss. Finally, Mike broke the tension.

"Good weather for a hot buttered rum," he said. "And, as for you, Joey, I've got a dozen Cokes with your name written all over them."

Selena held Allison's hand, and finally she sat heavily and gratefully on a chair by the fire.

Thank you, she cried inside herself. Thank you. Thank you. Thank you. Thank you for still loving me. You are the only people who care.

It was not the kind of love she wanted most, but it was better than nothing.

• 4 •

IT WAS A LITTLE AFTER ELEVEN O'CLOCK THAT SAME NIGHT WHEN Mike Rossi stopped his car in front of the Cross house, and Selena and Joey got out.

"I'll come in with you, Selena," said Mike. "I'll help Joey to get a fire going."

Selena stopped him with a gesture of her hand. "No, thanks, Mike," she said. "We'll manage. Thanks anyway."

Mike did not insist. "All right, then."

"Run up ahead and turn on some lights, Joey," said Selena, and when her brother had gone she turned back to Mike. "Good night," she said. "And thank Connie for me again. It was kind of her to have us. Tell her it'll be my turn next time."

"Anytime, Selena," said Mike. "You know that. Good night."

Selena waited until he had turned his car around and headed for his own house before she walked up the path to her front door.

"I started a fire," said Joey.

"We'll have some hot chocolate," said Selena.

"And a game of checkers, Selena."

"It's too late, Joey. School tomorrow."

"Not if the snow keeps up all night."

"All right," Selena said, relenting, and went toward the kitchen. "I'll be right with you."

Would it be better if we talked about it? Selena wondered as she heated milk. But what words did one say to alleviate a horror-filled memory?

The first time it had snowed after Lucas Cross's death, Selena had not realized, at first, what was happening to her. It had been late afternoon, she remembered, when it started. It had begun as it did today, with the first snowflake flattening itself against the front window of the store. Selena had watched it and suddenly she had been filled with an unreasoning, all-consuming panic. She had run to the telephone and called Constance Rossi.

"I'm closing the store early," she told Constance, unable to keep her voice from trembling.

"Selena! What is it? Are you ill? I'll be right there."

"No. No, please, Mrs. MacKenzie," cried Selena. "It's just that it's snowing and I have to get home to Joey."

"Quick, Mike," Constance said to her husband. "Get the car. We've got to go to Selena."

"What's happened?" asked Mike.

"I don't know," said Constance. "But Selena sounded hysterical, and she called me Mrs. MacKenzie. She said she had to hurry home to Joey because it's snowing."

But when Constance and Mike Rossi arrived at the Thrifty Corner, the shop was in darkness.

"Oh, darling," cried Constance. "Please hurry."

The car skidded on the new-fallen snow as Mike wrenched the wheel and headed for Selena Cross's house.

They saw her running down the dirt road that led to the Cross house, her feet sliding from under her as she ran, her unbuttoned coat flying behind her.

"Wait!" shouted Mike. "Wait, Selena!"

But she did not hear him. They saw her fall and pick herself up, and she was already through the front door of her house before Mike and Constance could jump out of the car and follow her.

Joey Cross was on his knees on the hearth, building a fire as he did every evening during the winter so that his sister would always find the living room bright and cheerful when she came in out of the cold. But now his thin body was rigid and his eyes were glazed. Selena flung herself at her brother so that both of them were kneeling on the hearth. They held onto one another as if they were drowning, and Joey cried, "S'lena, S'lena, S'lena," over and over.

Her trembling fingers tried to cover his lips and she sobbed, "Oh, Joey. Oh, Joey."

"He'll come back," Joey whispered, his voice faint with fear. "He'll come back, Selena."

"No, Joey. No, Joey. He can't come back ever again."

But her whole body shook and she glanced fearfully over her shoulder. Constance had come forward into the room, but Mike had gone back to close the door so that all Selena saw was the dark outline of his body against the light and she began to scream. She pushed Joey away from her and in one motion she was on her feet, her fingers tight around the top of the fire tongs.

"Selena!" shouted Mike and came toward her. "Stop it!"

He grabbed her wrist and twisted, and the fire tongs fell to the floor and still Selena screamed.

"Let go of me, Lucas! Let go!"

Mike Rossi slapped her hard across the face, and his arms were waiting to catch her as she fell forward in a faint.

Joey Cross stood up, still dazed. "Go home," he said to Mike. "I can take care of my sister."

"You sit down and shut up," said Mike and carried Selena to the couch. "Constance, get a blanket. They're coming home with us."

Always, after that, when it began to snow and the wind swept and shrieked behind it late in a winter afternoon, Mike Rossi always went to where Selena and Joey Cross were and brought them home with him. But Selena and Joey Cross would not spend the night with Mike and Constance and Allison. When it was late, and the wind had died down, Selena always stood up and said, "Come on, Joey. It's time to go home."

Selena carried the cups of hot chocolate into the living room.

"I'll beat the pants off you," she said, as she sat down at the checker board opposite Joey.

"Go ahead and try, big stuff," said her brother.

The wind was a whisper around the corners of the house, and Selena and Joey pretended not to hear when a board creaked or a log snapped.

"I saw Ted Carter today," said Selena.

"Him," replied Joey.

"He had his wife with him."

"They make a good pair," said Joey. "Why don't they go back to Boston where they belong?"

"Ted doesn't belong in Boston," said Selena. "He belongs in Peyton Place. At least, that's what he always said."

"Ted Carter always said a lot of things he didn't mean," said Joey.

"Never mind," said Selena. "I don't like to hear you talk like that, Joey."

"He's a rat," said Joey. "A two-faced rat."

"Stop it at once."

"How can you stick up for that guy after the way he treated you?" demanded Joey.

"Ted did what he thought was right and that's the end of it," said Selena.

The end of it, thought Selena; life has so many endings. Maybe Ted did what he thought was right, but it stung all the same.

Selena mechanically moved a checker toward the center of the board, remembering the last time she had talked to Ted. It had been just after the war had ended and Ted had been at the Harvard Law School less than six months. In Peyton Place to see his parents, he had telephoned Selena and asked to see her.

"Sure, Ted," Selena said. "Come over about eight o'clock."

"Ted Carter wants to talk to me," she told Joey. She had no secrets from Joey. They had shared too much ever to keep anything from each other. "How'd you like to go to the movies or something?"

"Him?" Joey said, too contemptuous even to mention his name. "You're going to let him come to the house after the way he acted when you were—"

"When I was waiting to go on trial?" finished Selena. "Joey, you don't have to be afraid to mention that. It's not good to think about something a lot and never talk about it."

"What if he wants you to go back with him?" asked Joey angrily. "What're you going to say?"

Selena turned away and fussed with a bowl of flowers on an end table.

"I don't know," she said. "But I think I'll say yes."

"You're nuts," said Joey disgustedly. "You're worth a dozen Ted Carters."

Selena rubbed her knuckles gently over his head. "You're prejudiced." She smiled.

Joey went off to the movies, as joylessly as to a chore. And Selena waited for Ted, hardly able to breathe at the thought of seeing him again. She knew it was a terrible mistake, but she permitted herself to hope. More than anything in the world, she wanted to be with Ted again. Terrified by life, she had in desperation come to think that only with Ted could she ever be safe.

"It's been a long time, Selena," he said. He stood with his back to the door, nervously turning his hat in his hand.

Selena motioned him to a chair, and thought, How reluctantly he has entered my house. It was obvious to her at a glance that he had come not out of love, or even desire, but only because his New England conscience had nagged him into it.

"I didn't know that you and I had to bother with social niceties," Selena said, a tight smile on her face. "But if that's the way you want it, all right." Then, in a false "social" voice, like a little girl playing grownup, she said, "Yes, Ted, it has been a long time. Would you care for a drink?"

"I don't drink," said Ted. "And I shouldn't think you would, either."

His tone was almost sanctimonious, and it annoyed Selena.

"Why?" she demanded. "Because Lucas was a drunkard? Is that what you meant?"

"Selena, for Heaven's sake, I didn't mean anything of the kind."

"Then what did you mean?"

"I don't know," said Ted uncomfortably. Selena's tight control made him nervous. He wanted to get on his knees, declare his guilt, beg forgiveness, but, instead, he only said, "This cocktail business has always seemed sort of citified to me."

"I wasn't going to offer you a cocktail, Ted. It's eight o'clock in the evening and I thought you might like a brandy to settle the excellent dinner your mother must have fed you before she let you out."

"No, thank you," said Ted, rather stiffly. He sat in an armchair, his hands on his knees; he leaned toward her yet was remote, isolated by his feelings of guilt and the anguish that seeing Selena caused him.

Selena poured brandy into a large snifter. "Well, Happy Days," she toasted, hoping the irony of it would not be lost on him. "I don't suppose you smoke, either?"

"No."

"Well, I do," she said defiantly, and lit a cigarette. "What did you want to talk to me about?" she asked.

Ted stood up and walked to one of the front windows. He put his hands in his pockets and tipped his head back as if to ease tightened muscles in his neck.

"I'm thinking of getting married," he said. "To a girl I met in Boston."

Selena did not make a sound. She put her glass down silently and put her cigarette into an ashtray.

"I see," she said at last, and her voice had not changed.

Ted turned around slowly and extended his hands as if asking for help.

"I haven't told anyone else yet," he said. "I wanted to tell you first."

"Why did you bother?" Selena asked, and this time the bitterness showed. "Why?"

"Peyton Place is a small town. People are going to talk, and I just didn't want you to hear it from someone else."

"That was damned white of you, Ted," she said.

"Selena, for God's sake, don't make it any harder than it is."

"Oh, is it hard, Ted?" she asked. "Why should it be? I knew back before the trial that the great Ted Carter wasn't going to be able to afford a murderess for a wife. So why should it be so hard for you to tell me about your new girl?"

"You know damned well how I feel about you, Selena," said Ted in a tight voice. "That's never going to change. We had a lot together, you and I, but we wouldn't have a thing together in the future."

"Don't you dare come in here and tell me how much you think of me," shouted Selena, jumping to her feet, her fists clenched.

"Everyone in town knows how you feel about me, so don't stand there and make pretty speeches. You're a little late."

"Selena, will you sit down for a minute and hear me out? I want to try to explain this to you as best I can."

"There's nothing to explain, Ted," she said wearily. "Why don't you just leave?"

He put his hands on her elbows. "Please," he said. "Sit down."

Selena shrugged and sat down and swirled brandy around in her glass.

"Selena, you know that I've always wanted to be a lawyer," began Ted. "Not just an ordinary lawyer like old Charlie Partridge, but a first-class lawyer."

"There was a time when you didn't think Charlie was so bad," interrupted Selena. "Of course, that was back when you didn't know whether or not you'd ever get to Harvard and Charlie was still in a position to help you."

Ted ignored her barbed remark because there was no answer for it. It was true. He knew better than anyone else how true it was.

"Harvard alone isn't going to make me into a big success," he continued. "Being a successful lawyer takes backing. You've got to have someone big behind you to give you a push."

"I begin to see the light," said Selena, pouring herself more brandy. "This girl in Boston, could her father perhaps be a big-time lawyer?"

Ted looked at the floor. All the reasons that had made so much sense to him as he had walked toward Selena's house now seemed utterly shameful. Face to face with the reality of Selena, the machinations of making a career were both sordid and childish. But he had already committed himself to it; there was no turning back. In his heart he knew that salvation for him lay with Selena, but it could not be. It could not be. He soothed himself with this thought. It could not be! It was Fate at fault, not Ted Carter. It is by such means that weak men salvage their pride.

"Her name is Jennifer Burbank. Her father is John Burbank of Burbank, Burrell and Archibald, one of the biggest law firms in Boston."

Selena threw back her head and began to laugh. "No, stop," she gasped. "Honestly, it's too much! Jennifer Burbank! The biggest law firm in Boston!" She tried to stop laughing but was almost afraid to, for if she did not laugh she knew she would cry.

"Selena, please," begged Ted.

And Selena stopped laughing. She twitched her head, and her long, dark hair flew away from her shoulder and rested on her back. Now there was no possibility of tears. Her purple eyes were almost black, and the soft, red mouth that Ted had kissed so often was set in a tight little smile.

Dear God, thought Ted, looking at her, I can see now how she must have looked when she murdered Lucas. I never thought she could look like that.

"Tell me about her, Ted," Selena was saying in a soft voice. "What does she look like? Small, blond, with a pink and white skin and breasts like lemons?"

"Selena!"

"Oh, but be careful of that kind, Ted," Selena continued, her voice too controlled, too soft. "Some of those rich-bitch Boston families are terribly inbred, you know. She's bound to be a delicate type. Peyton Place would kill her. That thin blue blood can't stand up to our winters."

"We won't be living in Peyton Place," said Ted quietly. "When I finish at Harvard, her father is going to take me into his firm."

"And tell me, Attorney Carter, do the too-blue Burbanks know about us? You and me, I mean, and about Lucas? Or did they stop reading newspapers when Henry Adams died?"

"They know that you and I were at school together."

"My, my," said Selena, in mock surprise. "Listen to little Ted Carter. 'At school.' Did you ever notice that it's only people with a private school education who talk about having been 'at school'? Have you noticed that, Ted? The rest of us poor slobs who went to public schools always say 'in school.' I'm so happy to see you're learning the language of your new family, Ted. I'd hate it if your inlaws had to think of you as a *meat-ball*."

"Selena, will you please not talk this way? Can't we talk to each other like old friends? This isn't *you* talking, Selena."

"Maybe it isn't the old Selena, Ted. Maybe you're right, maybe it isn't *me*. But it's *going* to be me, Ted. I don't want to be good old sweet little innocent Selena, everybody's friend. And most of all, Ted, I don't want to be *your* friend." Her voice was no longer soft; it tore from her throat, tortured and coarsened.

"Get your coat and get out of here," she cried.

Ted stood up and watched Selena pour herself another drink. He put on his coat and stood helplessly in front of her.

"Will you kiss me good-by?" he asked.

"Get out of here!" Selena screamed. "I never want to see you again. You make me sick, do you understand? I'd as soon kiss dirt as kiss you. Now get out!"

When he had gone, she sat for a long time, holding the brandy snifter in both hands. Then she stood up slowly and walked into the kitchen and poured the drink down the sink, as if Ted's presence had tainted it.

She was sitting in an armchair, knitting, when Joey came in. "What happened?" he asked at once.

"He's going to be married," answered Selena calmly. "To a girl named Jennifer Burbank from Boston, Massachusetts."

Joey looked at his sister and began to unbutton his coat.

"Does it hurt, Selena?" he asked at last.

She rolled up her knitting and put it away in a box.

"Yes," she said, and went into the kitchen to make coffee.

Joey's black king went click-click-click across the checker board and he removed three of Selena's red men.

"That's eight games for me," he said. "Who was going to beat the pants off who?"

"Whom," corrected Selena.

The clock on the mantelpiece struck twice. "It's two o'clock in the morning," said Selena. "To bed."

Joey stood up and stretched. "I think I'll just get a blanket and curl up here on the sofa," he said casually. "I want to watch the fire."

"All right, Joey," said Selena. She kissed his cheek. "Good night."

The wind had died down to almost nothing now, but, beyond the black squares of the front windows, Joey could see the endless flakes that would fall all night. He tried the lock on the front door again and put another log on the fire.

Selena lay facing the window, watching for first light, praying for day and an end to night's menace. I wish I were a child, she thought. I wish I still believed that ghosts were real and houses truly haunted; it's my own memories that haunt this house. She cried noiselessly into her pillow. She thought of Ted, but it was not for him she cried. He was merely the symbol of all she had lost. All I have now, she said to herself, all I have now is loneliness. That's the prize I've won from life.

It was daylight and the wind had started up again before Selena and Joey slept.

· 5 ·

MAYBE IT WILL HAPPEN TODAY, THOUGHT ALLISON MACKENZIE AS she awoke. It had been her waking thought every morning for two months.

She jumped up and ran to close her bedroom window against the early morning cold and stood shivering with her hands against the sash, breathless at the beauty she saw outside. For a moment, she pressed her forehead against the cold windowpane, as if to shock herself awake and scatter the night dreams, to make way for those of the day. So much of her days were spent in reverie, dreaming of the phone call from her agent, Brad Holmes, that never came: dreaming of her novel, printed, bound, published, and of the fame and success that would follow.

It was still snowing and the wind picked up huge handfuls of it and hurled them everywhere in gigantic plumes. Everything Allison saw was white and clean and soft looking, so that it appeared the whole world was new and pure and it was as if nothing bad or evil could ever have happened there.

Allison went softly, on bare feet, to open her bedroom door and, as soon as she had done so, she felt the little tendrils of warmth from downstairs creep around her ankles. She jumped back into her bed and snuggled down under the blankets to wait for the room to warm up.

The whole world is still asleep, she thought, remembering a childhood fancy, and I am the only one awake.

At once, she felt warm and safe and sure of herself, much as she had felt when she had been a little girl and had gone to her secret place in the woods at Road's End. Except that it was better now, for she had learned not to be afraid when it was time to go back to the world of reality. Living in New York, she thought, has at least done that much for me. Her experience with Brad, that brief, intense interlude, made her feel old and wise. She knew she was neither of those things, but she wanted very much to think so. When you've given so much of yourself, she thought, it's necessary to salvage something from the ruins, no matter how small it is. Even a lie.

It's going to snow all day, she thought. And I shall get up and eat an enormous breakfast and help my mother with the housework after my father has gone off to school. I'm not a famous author, I'm just my mother's daughter.

She never called Michael Rossi "father." Sometimes, jokingly, she said "Daddy-O," and hoped he understood that she meant more than she could yet bring herself to say; but most often she called him Mike. It was just to herself that she said, "My father." At first, she had done so as an experiment, to see if she would be overcome with guilt at her disloyalty to Allison MacKenzie, her own father who was dead, but she had felt nothing. It was as if Allison MacKenzie had never really been her father at all, but just a man with whom her mother had had a rather unfortunate love affair a long, long time ago.

"I've never been sorry," her mother had said. "I loved him and he was good to me. And I got you. That's a lot more than most women ever have."

At first, when Allison's bitterness against her mother had been at its peak, she had repeated the ugly word over and over to herself.

Bastard.

And she had thought that she would die of shame and horror. She guarded her secret as well as her mother had ever done. She hugged it tightly to her, carried it with her, waking and sleeping. *Illegitimate, out of wedlock*—words like these leaped off the pages of books she read; they seemed to be printed in a heavier type.

More than that, at her most sensitive period she had the feeling they had been used only to wound and hurt and insult her.

She had never told anyone the facts of her birth, not even Stephanie Wallace, who had been her roommate in New York, nor Bradley Holmes, who had been her lover.

During the weeks and months of self-pity and self-laceration that had followed when Allison first returned to Peyton Place, she had wondered often and bitterly about Bradley Holmes. She did not even know how to place him, how to identify him in the scheme of her life. Could he be called her lover, she wondered. But that implied love, and on his side there had been none. No, he was simply her first man, the one who had introduced her to sex, who had taken something from her. And given her something, too. For this reason he was important to her. A man she would never forget. For all the sophistication of her writing, Allison could not yet rid herself of the belief that you had to marry the man with whom you had made love.

She had wasted a lot of time hating Brad, but in the end it was due to him that she had begun to understand her mother and to love her again. Knowing herself now to be human and capable of weakness, she no longer expected others to be supermen, not even her mother.

Allison heard a stirring downstairs, and in a few minutes her mother's laugh drifted up the stairwell to Allison's room. Her mother and Mike never got up separately, just as they never did anything apart one from the other. If she had ever needed anything to convince her that what she and Brad had was not love, she had only to look at Mike and Constance. Allison had heard them giggling together like school children more than once as they made coffee.

"It's indecent," Allison had laughed, for her mother always bathed while Mike was shaving.

"I can't help it," Mike said. "Your mother always has aroused the most shocking feelings in me. And, I suspect, she always will."

"Shocking my arse," said Constance inelegantly. "The day that you're shocked by anything will be occasion for the declaration of a national holiday. School children will celebrate it with fireworks, parades, and essays."

When Allison went downstairs it was to the smell of coffee and bacon, and the first thing she saw was her mother, in a pale blue robe, her golden head outlined against a snow-covered window-pane. Allison's eyes stung with tears as they always did when she saw something beautiful.

"Good morning, darling," said Constance, and kissed Allison's cheek. "Isn't this a morning!"

"This morning I am masquerading as a short-order cook," said Mike, as Allison put her cheek up. "One egg or two?"

"Two!" cried Allison, suddenly overwhelmed with love and a wonderful certainty that today was going to be a marvelous day.

"It's going to happen today!" she cried, and almost danced over to the stove to pour herself a cup of coffee.

"Oh, darling, I hope so," said Constance. "Did you dream that it would?"

"No, but I know it just the same," said Allison, and sat down at the kitchen table. "Today Bradley Holmes is going to call me from New York. 'Hello, Allison,' he will say. And I'll say, 'Hello, Brad.' And then he'll say, 'I have wonderful news for you. I've sold your book.' Then if I don't faint I'll start to cry, and he'll tell me to whom he's sold it and you, Mother, will have to call Mike because I'll never be able to do it, and when Mike comes home he'll break down and get two bottles of that champagne he's been saving and we'll all celebrate."

Mike assumed a pose with his coffee cup raised and said, "And I'll stand like this and say, 'Here's to Allison MacKenzie and her best seller *Samuel's Castle.*' And then, ladies, we shall all proceed to tie one on."

"And then," said Constance, "I'll have to get busy and call up everyone we know and say, 'Please come over to our house be-cause we are having a party for the celebrated authoress Allison MacKenzie,' and then Mike will have to start serving beer be-cause we don't have that much champagne in the cellar."

"Damn it," cried Mike, "now the eggs are burning!" And all three of them laughed.

Allison sighed. "Brought back to earth by burning eggs. How prosaic." But she preferred the dream, and said, "Wouldn't it be wonderful if Brad *did* sell it?"

"Yes it would, darling," said Constance. "It would make us all so happy, and you especially. You deserve it, darling. Not just

400

because you have a wonderful talent, but because you've worked so hard."

"It'll happen," said Mike. "One day soon, mark my words. Now come on, let's eat. I'll be late for school."

Worked so hard, Allison thought. It was an accurate description, yet it did not begin to express all that she had put into her novel. The years of writing and the drudgery of rewriting. What made it so hard was not, after all, the book itself, but *doubt*. Doubt haunted her, plucked at her nerves, kept her from sleep and rest. Would it be any good? Would it find a publisher? She could never trust her own judgment. The chapter that read so well at midnight would appear in the light of day as fit only for the wastebasket. It was a book she had cried over—as much, she sometimes thought, as any mother ever cried over an ungrateful child.

Samuel's Castle was the culmination of over two years of work for Allison. When she had first returned home at the time of Selena Cross's trial, she had come in defeat as a writer; for, although she had managed to support herself with what she earned as a short story writer for the magazines, her novel had been a failure. Bradley Holmes had told her flatly that he could not sell her book, and that, even if he could, he would not do so. The publication of an inferior work would do her more harm than good in the long run, he had told her.

"Try the novel again," Brad said. "Wait until you're older, more experienced."

Well, Allison had thought ruefully when she got home, she was certainly more experienced if not much older.

David Noyes, whom she had met in New York, was the only person to whom she had ever told the whole story of her brief affair with Bradley Holmes, and it was David who came to Peyton Place to help and comfort her.

"I won't say it didn't hurt like hell, Allison," David had said to her. "No man likes to hear from the woman he loves about her sex experiences with another man. Women think we do, but we don't. The single standard is something that women have accepted much more readily than men. I think they invented it." He laughed, was silent for a moment, then said, "It's ended, Allison—you and Brad, that's all over and done with. And now is going to be the roughest time of all for you because you have to pick up the pieces of your life and try to assemble them into a pattern."

"Oh, David. How? It's always easy to give advice like that, high-sounding and vague. I want you to help me. Be specific. I don't want advice. I guess what I want is a prescription."

"Get to work," David had told her. "It may sound trite but it's true. Work your damned head off. Work. To work at one's chosen task is one of the truly great satisfactions that life offers. It's a better healer than time."

In the end, Allison had said that she would try.

"And about us, Allison?" he asked then, his eyes sad and imploring.

"Nothing about us, David. Not now. Not yet. Maybe not ever. Perhaps when you think about it, you won't be so sure that you want secondhand goods." She turned her head away from him; her lips tight, trying to hold back the tears. She did not know whether it was the memory of Brad or David's question that had caused something in her breast to break.

"Shut up," said David harshly. "I've never been a holdout for virginity."

"I'll write to you, David. Maybe when I've gone back to work it'll be different. Maybe it's true. Perhaps time and work will accomplish what I haven't been able to."

So David Noyes had gone back to New York, and Allison had unpacked her manuscript and gone to work.

Samuel's Castle was the story of Samuel Peyton, a rich Negro, who had married a white girl and had escaped from the ostracism of the world by building himself a castle on the hills outside of Peyton Place. This was the background, the counterpoint to the story of a town very much like Peyton Place and of the people who lived there. When Allison had finally finished writing the sixth draft and had sent it off to Brad, he called her the day after he had received it. It was not usual for an agent to give all his attention, and so quickly, to the work of a new, young, virtually unknown writer, Allison knew.

"Allison, it's great!" Brad had said joyfully. "I'll sell it! I'm certain of that."

"At last," said Allison laconically, too tired and sick of the manuscript now to care what happened to it. She had done her best for it; now it was in the hands of others. It did not seem to belong to her any more.

"Listen, is Peyton Place at all like the town in the book?"

"Yes. Why?"

"Oh, nothing. Except that it must be one hell of a snake pit."

"Peyton Place is no different from any other small town, Brad, and neither is the town in the book. They're all alike."

"Keep your fingers crossed, baby," said Brad. "You'll be hearing from me!"

And every day since, Allison had awakened with the same first thought: *Maybe it will happen today.*

"I've got to get at that living room today," said Constance when she and Allison had finished the breakfast dishes. "It looks like a pigpen."

The living room did not look like a pigpen, but Constance was a meticulous housekeeper and the least sign of dust was enough to send her scurrying for the vacuum cleaner.

"You just went over that room with a fine-toothed comb the day before yesterday," said Allison.

"Nevertheless," said Constance, "I can't go around giving champagne parties for authoresses in dirty rooms."

"I'm going out to shovel the front walk," said Allison, "and get the cobwebs off my brain. It must be cobwebs that make me have such impossible ideas the first thing in the morning."

She bent to the task. Holding the shovel with its familiar, worn handle in her mittened hands, she hoped that work as mechanical as removing snow would deaden her too active mind, would stop the endless brooding on the novel and its fate. Allison had finally to admit to herself that the novel was more than a book, more than a job of work—her whole life depended on it. She could imagine herself only as the author of *Samuel's Castle*. If she was not that, she was not anything.

It was eleven-thirty in the morning when Allison came in from outside. She was stamping snow from her boots when she heard the phone ring, and picked up the extension in the kitchen.

"Hello, Allison?" It was Bradley Holmes.

It can't be. It can't be, Allison said over and over in her head. Wishes don't come true just like this. "Yes, Brad," she said into the receiver, trying not to reveal her intense excitement.

403

"Sit down, darling," he said. "I've got wonderful news for you!"

It can't be. It can't be. Please, God, let it be.

"Allison? Allison, can you hear me?"

"Yes, Brad, I can hear you. Don't shout."

"I've sold your book!" he shouted.

Constance was making Allison's bed when she heard her daughter shout.

"Mother! Come quick!"

Dear God, thought Constance and ran for the stairs. She's hurt herself.

Allison was crying into the telephone. "Yes," she was sobbing, "I can hear you, Brad. I can hear you."

"It can't be," cried Constance, and grabbed for the phone.

"This is Constance Rossi," she said. "What happened?"

"I sold Allison's book to Jackman," said Brad. "She'll have to come to New York on Monday."

"Jackman," repeated Constance stupidly. "Monday."

"Tell her to call me and let me know what train or plane she's coming on. I'll meet her. And tell her I'll make reservations for her at the Plaza. Jackman, I think, is going to put everything behind this book. I have the feeling Allison will soon be able to afford the best hotels and she ought to start getting used to them."

"Yes, Mr. Holmes. Good-by, Mr. Holmes," said Constance.

◆ 6 ◆

CHESTNUT STREET WAS A WIDE, TREE-SHADED AVENUE WHICH RAN parallel to Elm Street, one block south of the main thoroughfare. Chestnut Street had always been, and still was, considered to be the "best" street in Peyton Place. Every town has its Chestnut Street. On the hottest summer day, the Chestnut Streets are cooler than all the others. The houses that line these streets always indicate, unmistakably, that they were built at a time when servants were cheap and plentiful, and that the owners could afford them. To the people who live on the other streets, these houses are always mysterious. One thinks of secret rooms and hidden staircases.

There had never been any danger that anyone undesirable would find his way to Chestnut Street, for each great house was surrounded on all sides by the land of the individual owner. The land was "Old Land," acres of ground that had belonged to the families who had come to live in the shadow of Samuel Peyton's castle when the castle was new.

The men who lived on Chestnut Street were the life's blood of Peyton Place. They were the men with money and position and, therefore, the men who were in control.

"Takes more than money to run a town," said Dr. Matthew Swain to his friend Seth Buswell. "Folks'll take just so much of cottoning down to money and then they say to hell with it."

"Then the ungrateful bastards unionize," said Leslie Harrington before Seth could answer. "I can't open."

The men of Chestnut Street were gathered at the home of Matthew Swain for one of their Friday night poker games. These games had become legend in Peyton Place.

"Age cannot wither him, nor custom stay his lousy, two-edged tongue," said Seth, looking at Harrington.

"I can open," said Charles Partridge. "And I will."

Charles Partridge still jumped into a conversation, as he had always done, when words between people threatened to become unfriendly; but he needn't have bothered to play the role of pacifist between Leslie and Seth, for those two hurled insults at each other only from habit now. The animosity that had motivated them in earlier years had been forgotten at last.

After the death of Rodney Harrington, Leslie's only son, his friends on Chestnut Street had been worried about the wealthy millowner. Overnight, Leslie Harrington had changed from the hard, pushing businessman he had always been to a blurred imitation of himself. Even those who had always hated Leslie began to feel sorry for him.

"He got his comeuppance at last," said a great many people in Peyton Place. Some said it with complacent pride, as if Leslie Harrington's comeuppance had been the result of their efforts.

"Yep. But it don't seem's though he should have got it so hard, all at once like that," said others.

If Leslie Harrington could have heard the voices, he would have felt that fate was words, that his life was nothing except as it was described by others. Gossip brought back to Peyton Place the dead and the missing. Rodney's and Betty's names were spoken more often now than when they had lived in Peyton Place. The rusty voices of old men and women were like a litany.

"Mebbe. But I'll wager there's some that ain't as sorry as others that Leslie Harrington got his at last."

"Oh, yeah? Like who?"

"Like John and Berit Anderson over on Ash Street."

"Yep. Run that girl of theirs right out of town, Leslie did. Can't blame the Andersons if they ain't sorry for Leslie now."

"Wonder what happened to Betty Anderson. John never says a word about her. Like she was dead."

"Well, I guess when she went and got herself knocked up by Rodney Harrington it was the same to John as if she *was* dead."

"Yep. Them Swedes got their pride just like anybody else."

"Mebbe she's livin' over to Rutland. Didn't she have an aunt over there?"

"Nah. Jared Clarke's been over to Rutland a million times, and you can trust Jared to know if Betty was living there and to tell everyone here about it."

There had been plenty of speculation in Peyton Place about what had happened to Betty Anderson, just as there always was about a girl who left town the way Betty had. But what no one in town knew, not even the men on Chestnut Street who usually knew everything that happened in Peyton Place, was that Leslie Harrington had made a quiet search of his own for the girl he had tried to destroy. He had not gone to Buck McCracken because Peyton Place's sheriff was a notoriously slow mover and, besides, he had a big mouth. If he contacted a nearby branch of the Missing Persons Bureau they would send people to town to ask questions, and this, above all, Leslie did not want. There were no private detectives in Peyton Place, nor in the whole state, for that matter, and they would have been impossible anyway. They, too, asked questions.

And so it appeared that Leslie Harrington had failed, but failure was a luxury that Leslie had never permitted himself and he did not intend to start now. He'd find a way, he was sure. It might take time, but he'd find a way.

"I raised, Leslie," said Matthew Swain. "Are you playing cards or daydreaming about chorus girls?"

"I'll see you, Matt," said Leslie, and shoved coins into the middle of the table. "Straight as a string with a black queen high, Matt. Beat me."

"Can't," said Matthew Swain disgustedly. "You always did have the goddamnedest luck, Leslie."

Not always, thought Leslie. Not quite always.

"Saw Ted Carter today," said Charles Partridge. "Had his wife with him. Nice-looking girl."

"Humph," said the doctor.

"Now hold on, Matt," said Leslie. "You can't hold it against Carter forever just because he didn't stick by Selena Cross. After all."

"After all, my ass," said Dr. Swain. "None of my business anyhow. Come on, deal."

"A young feller like that, trying to make something of himself and get ahead in the world. You can't blame him," continued Leslie, as if Matt had not spoken. "It'd be all right if he was going to stay right here in Peyton Place, but it wouldn't do for him to have a wife like that anywhere else. People got long memories, most of 'em."

"Yes, they do," said Seth Buswell. "And not only about murder. There's other things folks remember."

"What the hell are you trying to say, Seth?" demanded Leslie. "Come on, spit it out. Better to say it than sit there thinking it all evening."

Seth threw his cards down on the table. "About Betty Anderson and her kid, for one thing," he said angrily.

Leslie looked as if Seth had slapped him across the mouth.

"Now, now," said Charles Partridge. "All that's over and done with. Water over the dam. Doesn't do any good at all to keep bringing it up. Let's play cards."

"Who brought anything up?" demanded Seth. "Did I start anything? It just seems to me that before Leslie starts in talking about anybody else in town, he ought to look after his own fences."

Leslie put his cards down very quietly and looked at Seth straight in the eye.

"I've been trying to find that girl for two years," he said quietly.

His three friends stared at him in disbelief, but there was no mistaking the truth etched in the suddenly obvious lines in Leslie's face.

"Why?" asked Matthew Swain gently.

"Goddamn it," cried Leslie, "because of my grandson. That's why. He's the last of the Harringtons, and I don't know where he is."

"Why didn't you let us help you, Leslie?" asked Charles. "We didn't know."

"Well, I'd never lift a goddamned finger to help you, Leslie," said Seth angrily. "What're you trying to pull anyway? You want to find a girl so that you can get her baby away from her, is that it?"

"Seth," said Matt Swain. "Be quiet a minute."

"I never said I wanted to take the boy away from his mother," said Leslie defensively. "If I found them, naturally I'd take them both in. If she wanted to come, I mean."

"Yeah, and you'd make damn sure she didn't want to, wouldn't you?" said Seth bitterly. "Christ, but you are a son-of-a-bitch, Harrington. You always were, but I was dumb enough to think you'd changed with age."

"Seth!" shouted Dr. Swain. "Shut up!" He turned back to Leslie Harrington.

"Would you, Leslie?" he asked. "Take them both in, I mean?"

Leslie looked at his hands. "Yes," he said at last. "I would. I want to. But I've done everything I know how, and I still can't find her."

"What have you tried, Leslie?" asked Charles.

"Christ, I even went to that goddamned family of hers. If they knew anything, they weren't telling, and, as for the girl, she never did have an aunt over to Rutland."

"Anything else?" asked Seth, still not convinced of Leslie's motives.

"Well, what the hell else could I do?" demanded Leslie. "Listen, Seth. I know how it sounds. But, Jesus, I couldn't go to Buck McCracken. And as for that Missing Persons outfit, they'd have had cops all over town asking questions. I even thought of hiring a private detective, but they'd have been the same way. I tell you, I was afraid."

It was a word that Seth had never thought he'd hear from Leslie Harrington. Afraid. And he began to understand, a little, the emptiness that filled Leslie's life.

"We could help you," said Seth finally.

"How? What can we do?" asked Leslie.

"We can put advertisements in the personal columns of the newspapers," said Seth.

"Ah-h," said Leslie disgustedly. "That was one of the first things I tried. I had ads in every paper in towns from the Canadian border clear down to Boston."

Seth leaned back in his chair. "Leslie," he said, "go into any house on Ash Street, or into the home of any of your mill hands, for that matter, and look at the newspapers they read. They don't buy the Boston *Herald* or the Concord *Monitor*. They buy tabloids. Either the Boston *Record* or the New York *Daily News* or other newspapers like them. Those are the papers with all the stories about knife killings in Harlem and rapes in the Back Bay, the gossip columns about people in New York and Hollywood. I'll bet anything that wherever Betty Anderson is, if she buys a newspaper at all, she buys one of those."

"What if she doesn't read the personal columns?" said Dr. Swain. "I imagine that there are lots of folks who don't."

"Maybe not," said Seth. "But she reads Winchell, I'm sure of it. Leslie, you could buy an inch of space on the same page as Winchell's column in every newspaper in the country that publishes him."

"That'll cost you something, Leslie," said Charles Partridge, who, some said, took better care of other people's money than he did of his own.

"Can you fix it up, Seth?" asked Leslie.

"Yes," said Seth. "Not from here. I've got to go down to Manchester, day after tomorrow. I'll do it from there."

"Now we'll see," said Leslie, and smiled at his friends. "Now we'll see."

When Leslie and Charles had left, Matthew Swain helped himself to another drink and then extended the bottle to Seth.

409

"What do you think about Leslie, Seth?" he asked. "Do you think he means what he says?"

Seth gazed at his friend. "Well, for Christ's sake, Matt, it was you telling me to shut up in the beginning when I didn't believe him. Now that he's got me convinced, you turn around and ask if I think he means what he says."

Dr. Swain smiled. "I guess what I really was wondering was whether I believe him."

"What is it, Matt?"

Matt made a gesture of self-annoyance with his hand. "Oh, hell," he said. "I guess I've known Leslie Harrington for too many years and I'm cursed with one of those long memories I'm always yapping at other people about. Don't pay any attention to me, Seth."

"No, you don't," cried Seth. "Don't pull that on me, you old bastard. Now what the hell are you driving at?"

Matt Swain looked down into his drink. "I keep remembering," he said. "I keep remembering how Leslie never could stand to be beaten at anything. Not even when he was a kid."

"But he did get beaten," Seth said. "The worst beating a man could take, just about. He lost his son, Matt. His only son. It changed him, you know that. He's never been the same."

"Like I said, Seth. Don't pay any attention to me. It's been a big day and I'm tired to the point of imagining things."

But when Matthew Swain went to bed, he was wondering. Does the leopard change his spots, or does he merely camouflage himself by hiding behind something? Behind something that would fool even the most observant eye. Matt groaned aloud. Like Leslie, he was alone. Whether he groaned or roared with laughter, no one would be disturbed. Matt was haunted by nothing but loneliness, and he had decided he was too old to take the cure.

◆ 7 ◆

ROBERTA CARTER SAT UP IN HER BED SO SILENTLY THAT THE TOP sheet barely rustled against her nightgown. She looked across

410

the narrow aisle that separated her bed from Harmon's and saw that he was well covered and sleeping soundly. In the dark, she stood up and fixed her pillows under her blankets so that if Harmon awoke and looked across to her bed it would appear that she was there, asleep. She left her slippers on the rug, just as they had been when she had taken them off, and she was very careful not to disturb the folds of her robe at the foot of the bed. Then she tiptoed across the room and out the door. The rest of her plans had been carefully made earlier in the evening and she had smiled to herself as she carried them out right under the very noses of the people concerned. .

It had been a very good dinner that evening, she congratulated herself. Heavy enough to make Harmon feel full and rather logy afterward, but not heavy enough to make Ted and Jennifer feel anything but contented and well fed. Then there had been the sedative in Harmon's coffee, not enough to hurt him, of course, but just enough to make him say that he couldn't keep his eyes open a minute longer by nine o'clock.

"Well, now, dear," Roberta had told him. "You just sit still one more minute and I'll go up and turn down the beds."

"Oh, please let me help you, Mother," said Jennifer, jumping up.

Roberta put a restraining hand on her shoulder. "Now, you just sit down and finish your coffee, dear," she said. "I won't be a minute."

"But I'd like to help you," protested Jennifer.

Roberta was hard put to keep annoyance from showing on her face and in her voice. That was just one more thing about Jennifer, she thought. Always arguing over the simplest things. Ted had never been like that. The only time her boy had ever been pigheaded about anything was when he was younger and had a crush on Selena Cross. But he'd got over that and he'd never dug his heels in about anything since. Now it appeared that Jennifer, who had seemed so sweet and tractable when Ted had been courting her, had a little stubborn streak that could prove to be very annoying if it weren't curbed. But right now was not the time to be annoyed.

"All right, then." Roberta smiled. "Why don't you and Ted go into the kitchen and make a pot of coffee? I'd love a fresh cup when I come down."

Roberta went upstairs, humming to herself, and turned down the beds in her room. Then she went down the long hall to the room that had always been Ted's and which he now shared with Jennifer whenever the two of them came to Peyton Place for the weekend. That had been another of Jennifer's ideas. Roberta had wanted "the children," as she called Ted and Jennifer, to use the large guest room next to her room, but Jennifer had turned stubborn again.

"But, dear," Roberta had said, "that old room of Ted's is way down at the other end of the hall, and the bathroom is at this end. It just won't do, dear. You'll be much more comfortable right here next to me."

"That's sweet of you, Mother," said Jennifer, "but really, we'd rather use Ted's old room. Wouldn't we, Ted?"

"Doesn't matter to me," said Ted.

He did not see the sudden glare that his wife gave him, but Roberta did.

"Well, it matters to me," said Jennifer with a pretty pout. "I like your old room. It has so much of you in it, and I like to think of you as a little boy, sleeping there."

Ted put an arm around her. "Anything you say, darling." He smiled.

Roberta had made up the bed in Ted's old room, but right then she had begun to wonder just what it was that Jennifer had to hide that she wanted to be stuck off in a corner somewhere in a house with her own inlaws.

She's talking about me! The thought had come to Roberta in a flash, like a divine sign from Heaven. She's talking about me! Trying to turn my boy against me!

Well, as Roberta put it to herself, she'd never been one to let herself be undermined without fighting back. But she couldn't begin to fight until she knew what she was up against. And it did not take her long to find a way.

Roberta smiled to herself as she turned back the blankets on the big double bed in Ted's old room. She spread an extra quilt across the foot of the bed, and then she went very quietly to the room next door. It was a small room, containing a bed, dresser and one chair, and had originally been used as a maid's room when old Dr. Quimby, Roberta's first husband, had been alive.

412

In later years, Roberta had used it as a place to store extra blankets and dishes and other odds and ends which a family accumulates over the years.

Harmon Carter and Ted would have been surprised indeed to see the narrow bed freshly made up and to find the hot-air grate open. It was a good-sized grate, fully twelve inches square, and Roberta had examined it carefully from both rooms. When it was dark in the storage room, no one could possibly tell, without getting down on all fours under Ted's bed, that the lever had been moved and that the squares in the grate were now open. Roberta had occupied the bed in the storage room every time Jennifer and Ted came to Peyton Place to visit. In six months she had heard many things. She knew that Ted had had nothing to say about the apartment that he and Jennifer rented in Cambridge. It was a lovely apartment, large and sunny. Roberta had seen it herself, but Ted was not comfortable there because Jennifer's father paid the rent.

"Damn it, it makes me feel kept," said Ted.

"What would you have us do?" demanded Jennifer. "Would you move me into some furnished room and support me on what you could earn as a part-time soda jerk or gas station attendant?"

"Lots of guys work their way through," said Ted. "A little work never killed anybody. I've always worked."

"What if you fell down on your grades?" asked Jennifer. "Daddy's firm doesn't take in people who got bad grades at law school. Not that they object to a nice, gentlemanly 'C' once in a while, but they don't like men who make a habit of getting marks like that. Oh, darling," she said, her voice dreamy and gentle now, "someday it's going to be Burbank, Burrell, Archibald and Carter. Won't that be wonderful? Won't it make a little pride swallowing now worth while?"

"Burbank, Burrell, Archibald and Carter," said Ted. "Yes, darling. It'll make everything worth while."

Roberta was pleased when she heard that from her side of the grate. Her Ted had never been a small thinker and he wasn't going to become one now. And it wasn't as if the Burbanks did everything for the children. She and Harmon sent them a nice check every week. There had been a few bad moments, too, during Roberta's eavesdropping. Once, Jennifer had questioned Ted about Selena Cross.

"Were you in love with her?" asked Jennifer.

Roberta held her breath as Ted hesitated. "No," he said at last, and Roberta let out a silent sigh. "We went around together a few times, but that's all."

"Is she pretty?"

"She's all right."

"Is she prettier than I?"

"Sweetheart, no one in the world is prettier than you."

Roberta had listened shamelessly as her son made love to his wife and once she had almost felt sorry for him. Jennifer seemed to be awfully wishy-washy about sex, and sometimes she had sounded frightened and it had taken Ted hours to calm her and then arouse her gently so that she let him take her. It hadn't been that way with Harmon and her, Roberta remembered, smiling in the dark. But then, too much sex wasn't good for a man who had to keep his mind on his books. Luckily, Harmon had never been a student. In six months, Roberta had heard the children making love only three times, and after each time, Ted had been pale and shaky the next day. Yes, thought Roberta, it was a good thing that Jennifer was a little frigid.

Never once, in all the time that Roberta Carter had spied on her son and his wife, did she feel shame or remorse. Ted was her son, her only son, and she had a right to see that everything went well for him. If he were disturbed about anything, she wanted to know. And if his wife should try to turn him away from his mother, she had a right to know that, too. It did not matter to Roberta that in six months' time she had never heard Jennifer make a single derogatory remark about her. The girl might, in the future. Just because she hadn't until now was no reason to suppose that she never would.

"My!" exclaimed Roberta, coming into the living room and giving an exaggerated shiver, "it's going to be another cold night. Still snowing, too. Our windows won't be open much tonight, I can tell you that."

"Ours will," said Jennifer and laughed. "I'm married to the biggest fresh-air enthusiast in captivity."

Harmon yawned. "Warm or cold," he said, "bed's going to feel good to me."

Roberta put up her cheek to be kissed. "I'll be up shortly, dear," she said.

When she did go upstairs it was ten o'clock and Ted and Jennifer were playing backgammon in front of the fire, and at ten-thirty, when she crept down the hall toward the storage room, she could hear their voices coming faintly up the stairwell. Roberta Carter locked the storage room door behind her and got silently under the warm blankets in the narrow bed. It was quarter to twelve when she heard Ted snap on the lights in the room next door.

Jennifer Burbank Carter was twenty-two years old and never once, in the six months of her marriage, had she undressed in front of her husband.

"It's not nice," she had told him with finality.

Jennifer had always lived in an environment where everything was Nice. There had been Burbanks in Boston for almost as long as there had been Cabots and Lowells, and the standards of behavior in Jennifer's family had not changed in over two hundred years. A lady did not make an exhibition of herself, ever.

Once, when Jennifer was twelve, she had gone shopping with her mother and in one of the stores they had seen a girl with bright, blond hair and a swollen-looking, red mouth. The girl was chewing gum and looking at costume jewelry and she had a pair of enormous, hard-looking breasts under a very tight sweater. Jennifer had stopped and stared at the girl until her mother noticed. Mrs. Burbank's face got very red and she almost shook Jennifer when she took her arm.

"I've never seen such a display of vulgarity in my life!" said Mrs. Burbank. "Remember, Jennifer. Women who have to use their bodies to create an impression are vulgarians of the cheapest, crudest sort."

"But, Mother—"

"Don't argue, Jennifer. You know I'm right. As you grow older, you'll realize it even more."

For a long time after that, Jennifer thought of her body only as something to be kept clean, covered and hidden. As she grew older she was measured by her mother's dressmaker and in due time she found a dozen satin and lace brassières in a box on the foot of her bed. Later, there had been wispy panty girdles to be worn on dress-up occasions, but there had never been any discussion of any sort on the subject of underwear between Jennifer and her mother.

When Jennifer was sixteen years old and in her last year at a very fine girls' school just outside of Boston, she roomed with a girl named Anne Harvey. Anne was a year older than Jennifer, and her father was head of the largest brokerage house in the state of Massachusetts. Anne was a big, muscular girl but so full of good humor that the other girls at school never teased her about her looks. They admired her and made her captain of the volley-ball team and president of the student council, and every one of them wanted to be "Anne's best friend." But Anne chose Jennifer Burbank.

The two of them were inseparable. They went everywhere together and were thought of as a team, but Jennifer never could manage to feel secure in her relationship with Anne. There was too much competition, she thought, and was very, very careful never to offend Anne because Anne had a hundred little ways of letting her know that the school was full of girls who'd give their eye teeth to be in Jennifer's place.

One spring afternoon, Jennifer was alone in the room she shared with Anne. She was changing her clothes, getting ready for a trip into town, when Anne came in quietly. Jennifer whirled around quickly and grabbed for her robe.

"I didn't expect you," she said, almost stammering with embarrassment.

"Don't let me bother you," said Anne. "I just came up for a book."

"If I'd known you were coming, I'd have used the bathroom but I—"

"For Heaven's sake, Jennifer," said Anne in good-natured exasperation, "it's not the end of the world. We're both girls, you know."

Jennifer turned away in confusion and as she did so she tripped over the edge of her robe, almost falling, and dropping the robe altogether.

"Be careful!" cried Anne, running to her. Anne's hands were on Jennifer's waist. "Did you hurt yourself?"

Jennifer could not move. "No," she said. "I'm all right."

Anne did not take her hands away. "You scared me," she said softly.

Still Jennifer did not move, but kept her back turned as Anne's hands caressed her soft skin.

"Such beautiful, lovely skin," whispered Anne into Jennifer's ear. Suddenly her hands tightened hard enough to make Jennifer gasp.

"Stop it," said Jennifer. "You mustn't."

Anne's hands were gentle again, the fingers trailing softly. She heard Anne's breathing go ragged and felt Anne begin to tremble. But Jennifer stood as still as stone and without knowing how she knew, she knew that Anne was making a terrible, terrible effort to keep her hands light and soft.

"You're so beautiful," said Anne, and began to sob. "So lithe and perfectly made and beautiful."

And then Jennifer turned around. She moved away slowly from Anne's hands and went to lie down on her bed.

"Am I, Anne?" she said softly and her eyes glittered. "Am I?"

Anne went on her knees next to the bed, her face wet with tears. "Oh, yes, my darling," she said. "Yes, you are."

She kissed Jennifer on the mouth, a long kiss, and when she raised her head, Jennifer was looking straight into her eyes.

"For Heaven's sake, Anne," she said coldly. "Don't be so sloppy."

Anne rocked away from her as if she had been struck and Jennifer stood up slowly. She walked over and picked up her robe, but she did not put it on. She stood in front of Anne, nude.

"Now, I'll have to bathe again," she said and walked into the bathroom, her robe trailing from her hand.

All the while she was in the tub, she could hear Anne crying. She walked back into the bedroom, still drying herself, and watched Anne looking at her. She dressed slowly and carefully.

"I'll be gone for a while," she said when she was clothed. "Wait right here. Don't go down to dinner without me."

Anne waited. Not only that day, but every day after that whenever Jennifer felt like telling her to wait. She waited for the rare occasions when Jennifer allowed herself to be touched and she

417

let her wretchedness show whenever Jennifer sat naked in front of the dressing table and said, "Brush my hair, will you, Anne?" She lavished gifts on Jennifer and dropped all her other friends, and whenever Jennifer snapped her fingers, there was Anne, waiting to do as she was told. Once in a great while, Anne rebelled.

"I don't need you!" she shouted. "There are plenty of others who'd love to be in your place."

"Really?" asked Jennifer, raising her eyebrows. "Others? Right here at school?"

"Right here at school," said Anne.

"Hm-m. I wonder if Miss Fenwick knows about that. Do you imagine so, Anne?"

"Don't threaten me," said Anne angrily. "You wouldn't dare go to her with anything like that."

"Maybe," said Jennifer. "Maybe I would and maybe I wouldn't. I'm not like you and you know it. Go ahead and get yourself someone else. Boston is full of young men who, I'm sure, will find me just as attractive as you ever did."

Anne snorted. "I know your kind," she said. "You'd never have anything to do with a man now. You put too high a value on your virginity to give it away for less than a wedding band."

"Darling, don't be naïve," said Jennifer with a little laugh. "I've been doing a lot of reading since I found out about you. All kinds of reading. A man is the easiest creature in the world to fool. I'm not worried about my virginity or the lack of it."

"What do you mean, 'lack of it'?" demanded Anne furiously. "Have you already been with a man?" She grabbed Jennifer's shoulder and shook her. "Have you?"

"Take your hands off me, Anne," said Jennifer coldly. "You have no need to be concerned about my affairs. You said yourself that you could find plenty of others to take my place. Well, go ahead."

"Oh, God," cried Anne, "I didn't mean it, darling. Please forgive me. I didn't mean it. Tell me it isn't true about your being with men."

Jennifer pushed Anne's arms away.

"Not yet, it isn't true. Not yet. But don't annoy me, Anne, or I might just have to go out to discover if I've been missing anything."

Anne Harvey and Jennifer Burbank were "best friends" all the rest of the school year and during the next summer. Jennifer dated frequently, but she had answers for every one of Anne's miserable questions.

"I have to," she told Anne. "What would my parents think if I never went out with men?"

"I can't stand it!"

"Oh, don't be so sloppy," said Jennifer impatiently. "You bore me when you go all weepy like this. I go out with men because I have to. I'm afraid you'll just have to take my word for it, Anne."

When Jennifer denied intimate knowledge of men, Anne found it easy to believe. Not only because she wanted to, but because Jennifer's very appearance lent truth to her words. Anyone would have believed her. There was nothing of the voluptuary in Jennifer's appearance, none of those obvious points that men look for. She did not have the big breasts, the swinging hips, or the rich mouth that most men think adds up to a "good piece."

Like most frigid women, Jennifer needed men. It was not, on her part, lust but hatred that motivated her actions. To her, the sex act was not an act of shared communion; she shared nothing and only used men. When they were finished, she pushed them off with disgust. Not disgust with herself, but with them. She had her first man the summer she was seventeen. He was a Portuguese fisherman nearly forty years old with hard hands and a dark, sharp face. She met him on the beach every night for a week.

After that there was a long series of college boys in the back seats of cars or at a motel. She never went with the same one twice, and after she had had a man she never spoke to him again. He ceased to exist.

Even the college boys who had stroked her breasts and thighs, even they sometimes doubted, seeing her, that they had really succeeded. It was not that her manner was shy and virginal, she had too much style for that; it was that she looked unapproachable, like a girl one would hesitate even to kiss. She held her head high, her features were fine and revealed not a hint of coarseness; she had small breasts and hips. The boys who had known her in the back seats of their cars had a difficult time believing this was the same girl. This was Jennifer Burbank. The other was a brazen, shameless, coarse creature. The young men could see no connection between these two people, so utterly different one from the other.

It was Jennifer's father who introduced her to Ted Carter. He had singled Ted out at the law school, he spotted him as one of the promising young men. Ted came to tea and Jennifer watched him, clinically observant. She saw how respectful he was to her parents, but she saw even more than that. Watching him, she became aware that Ted was the kind of man who would grovel and toady to gain the success he wanted. Jennifer smiled behind her teacup and said to herself, Well, Ted-boy, if that's what you want, that's what you are going to get. The thought of how much Ted would have to pay for his success gave her infinitely more satisfaction than any man ever had or ever would.

Their wedding was announced a few weeks later. And on the first night of their honeymoon she tried out on Ted all the sadistic tricks she had used on Anne. She teased, she withheld herself from him, and only after she had exhausted him and reduced him to begging did she yield; and then it was as if she were conferring on him a priceless gift. Ted never doubted that she was a virgin. Nor did he suspect that within a few days after the return from a honeymoon in the West Indies she began to be unfaithful to him. It was impossible for Ted to be suspicious of the daughter of Mr. Burbank. Jennifer had correctly judged him; he had married a law firm, she was only a means. He would take anything, would permit nothing to stop him short of his goal.

"Let me get into bed before you open the windows, darling," said Jennifer. "These Peyton Place winters are colder than anyone would ever believe."

"I'm not going to open them yet," said Ted Carter. "I don't want you to catch cold."

"But it's late, darling. And you said you wanted to go skiing tomorrow."

Ted got into bed next to her. "Tomorrow I want to go skiing. Not tonight," he said.

"Sometimes I think that you're insatiable," said Jennifer, laughing at him.

"Open your mouth a little," he said.

"No."

"I'll make you."

"I don't like to be kissed wet."

"You'll learn."

"You'll have to teach me."

Every time Ted made love to his wife, he had to seduce her first, and while this excited him at times beyond endurance so that he climaxed before he could enter her, he often wondered, the next day, if Jennifer would ever welcome him freely so that he could feel as if she wanted his body as badly as he wanted hers. Sometimes, when he was not with Jennifer, he remembered the way Selena Cross had opened her arms to him and the way her mouth had been as eager as his.

But when he was with Jennifer, he could think of no one but her. A few times, he had taken her by force, tearing her clothes off, slapping her until she lay still on the bed, naked and helpless under his eyes and hands. Afterward, he was overcome with shame and wept as he begged her forgiveness. But in some dark corner of his mind, he realized that the times when Jennifer goaded him into violence were the times she enjoyed the most. It was a silent, unspoken contest between them, with Ted determined to win her with gentleness and Jennifer equally as determined to turn him into a savage animal. She never hated him so much as when he begged forgiveness.

She came to his bed in nightgowns that covered her completely, and it took his most gentle efforts before she let him undress her. She seemed to be terrified of showing herself and sometimes her body quivered like a frightened bird when he uncovered her breasts to caress her.

"No!" she cried, as he opened the buttons on her gown. "Oh, no, don't. Turn off the light, darling. Don't."

"Yes, I will," he said against her throat.

"Teach me," said Jennifer. "Make me open my mouth, if you can. Maybe I won't let you."

"Come here."

She moved away from him and began to redo the buttons on her nightgown.

"No," she said. "I'm not going to let you."

He pulled her to him roughly.

"Be sweet," he pleaded. "Please, be sweet."

She laughed up into his face and taunted him. "Listen to my

421

big, brave man begging for favors. Sit up, Fido, Mamma give you liver."

Ted jumped out of bed and yanked the blankets off her.

"You little bitch," he said harshly, his hands trembling. "You little bitch."

He grabbed her nightgown at the neckline and tore it from her body and his hands left angry, red marks against her white skin.

"You love it," he said into her mouth, bruising her lips as he bit into them. "You love it and you know it."

And then it was Jennifer who was insatiable. Her body heaved and her eyes glittered.

"Hit me," she cried. "Hit me."

"You're goddamned right I'll hit you," said Ted. "I'd like to kill you."

He used his belt on her until her back and buttocks and thighs were covered with welts and when he finally took her, her lips were red with blood from his shoulder and she fainted.

"Dear God, what have I done," cried Ted.

He began to weep. "I'll never do it again, darling. Never. My God, I'm no better than an animal. I'll never do it again. Please. Please forgive me."

Ted slept at last, the sleep of exhaustion, and for a long time Jennifer lay awake in the dark, smiling. She touched the welts on her thighs, running her fingers over them hard so that the pain burned all through her and her teeth gleamed white in the dark room. She moved so that her back scraped against the sheet, hurting her, and her nipples grew rigid and she felt the tightening of excitement between her legs.

"Again," she whispered into Ted's ear. "Again."

But Ted did not awaken. He stirred in his sleep and his hand found her breast and covered it gently. And finally, Jennifer, too, slept.

In the narrow bed in the storage room, Roberta bit her lips to try to stop her trembling. She was stiff with horror and with the effort she was making to keep herself silent.

I knew it, she thought. I knew something was wrong with that girl. She's crazy, that's what she is, making Ted do a thing like that. Ted was never that kind of boy. He was good and clean. Oh, dear God, what am I to do?

She waited another half hour and then she let herself out of the storage room and crept back to her own bed, but it did not comfort her. She could not stop trembling.

She's crazy. Jennifer is crazy. She's making Ted crazy. Oh, dear God, help me. I've got to do something.

But when the sun rose on another gray, threatening day, she had had no answer to her prayer.

◆ 8 ◆

I'M GOING TO REMEMBER EVERY SINGLE THING THAT HAPPENS, thought Allison MacKenzie, as the train pulled away from the Peyton Place railroad station. Everything has to stay very sharp and clear this time, so that when I'm old I'll be able to remember every little detail. Too many things happen, and when they do people always say, "I'll never forget," but they do, and then the image blurs with time and finally they don't remember very much about anything. I suppose that's why some people keep journals and diaries. They do it so they can never forget what happened to them. But I'll remember everything without writing it down. When I'm very old, I'll remember how it was the day I left Peyton Place to go to New York to sign a contract for my first book.

Allison had gone to bed late the night before her trip, and even then she had been unable to sleep, and she had awakened early. When she had gone to her bedroom window the tops of the snow-covered trees outside were just turning pink.

In the east, the sky was the color of a pale, pale winter rose. She breathed deep the cold snow smell, almost sweet; she thought she could taste it on the back of her tongue.

Allison wet her fingers and then brushed them across the thick slab of snow on the outside window ledge. The snow stuck to her hand and she put her fingers quickly into her mouth.

It's going to be sunny but cold, she thought, and nothing will melt away or change while I'm gone. It will all be the same when I come back.

She ran downstairs to the kitchen to start the coffee and she paused as she was setting the pot on the stove.

Except me, she thought suddenly. I'll be changed. I won't be the same.

Suddenly, it was terribly important that she look at everything, and that she remember everything she saw. She sat down abruptly at the kitchen table. Her mother almost always kept a yellow cloth on that table, and a low copper bowl filled with yellow flowers.

She does it so that even on cloudy days we eat breakfast at a table full of sunshine, thought Allison in amazement. I never realized that before. And in the living room the colors are subdued and relaxed so that you want to lean back and put your feet up, but in the bedrooms they are very soft so that when you lie down nothing glares on your eye. And all the curtains are really picture frames. I've got to remember everything just the way it looks this morning.

The gas burner on the stove made a hissing sound as the coffee boiled over.

"Damn it!" cried Allison, jumping up.

"And what cloud were you on?" said Constance, coming into the kitchen. "I could smell coffee all over the house."

"I was thinking that I'd better hurry and get dressed," said Allison.

"Sit down and have some coffee," said Constance, laughing. "It's more than two hours until your train leaves."

"Good morning, Famous Author," said Mike Rossi, coming into the kitchen. "Good morning, Famous Author's mother."

Constance kissed him. "Good morning, Maker of Bad Jokes Early in the Morning and of Which There Is No More Revolting Creature."

"That talkative so early?" asked Mike. "This *is* going to be a day!"

"Yes, it is," said Allison, "and I've got to dress."

"You've got to eat something first," said Constance.

"I can't," objected Allison. "I'll throw up on the train if I do. Hurry up, Mother. You have to dress, too."

424

Mike and Constance drove her to the station, and all of them went inside while Mike bought Allison's ticket.

"Clear through to New York, eh?" asked Mr. Rhodes. "Round trip?"

"Nope," said Mike. "One way."

"Save money, buyin' the round trip," said Mr. Rhodes. "How long she gonna be gone?"

"Who?" asked Mike.

"Why, Allison, of course," said Mr. Rhodes. "She's the one goin', ain't she?"

"Yep."

"Goin' down to get that book of hers sold, ain't she?"

"Yep."

"Well, it don't take forever to sell somethin' like that. Saves to buy the round trip."

"But she may decide to fly back, or drive, or walk, for that matter."

"Don't make no difference. She can cash in the ticket, if she don't use it."

"All right," said Mike, resignedly. "One round-trip ticket for New York."

"That man had me running around in circles when I first came here," said Mike when they were outside, "and I've never managed to get the best of him yet. And how the hell does he know why Allison is going to New York?"

"Everybody in town knows," said Constance. "Does that surprise you?"

"No," Mike admitted. "But I've never been able to figure out how it happens. If somebody farts on Chestnut Street, the guy in the stockroom at the Mills knows about it in a matter of seconds."

"You're vulgar," said Constance.

"I know it," said Mike.

Allison stood still and from far away she heard the whistle of the train.

It's coming across the river, she thought. And the arch of the trestle is black and sharp against the sky. By now a passenger must have looked out the window to see Samuel's castle far above him.

"What's that big place up there?" the passenger asked.

"Why, that's the Peyton Place," replied the conductor. "Got a whole town named for the feller built that castle, just down the line."

Allison stood very still in the cold, watching and listening, and at last the faraway sounds were a roar and the train rounded a curve in the track and came straight toward her through the towering banks of snow.

A conductor was on the platform between two cars, leaning out, one gloved hand clinging to a rail on the side of the car, and one foot a step lower than the other. His high-crowned cap had a brass plate on the front that read "Boston and Maine R. R."

"Peyton Place," called the conductor, "Peyton Place."

His voice seemed to echo down the long tunnel of snow and to rise over and around Allison so that the sound came back to her filled with an ineffable sadness, and she felt the old, familiar sting behind her eyelids.

"Good-by, darling," said Constance. "Be careful, now, and call me as soon as you get there."

Allison turned to her almost with a start.

"Good-by, Mother," she said, and put her arms around Constance. "Yes, I'll call you." She turned to Mike.

"'By, Poppa."

Mike bent and kissed her. "So long, Gertie. Good luck."

Her bags were already on the platform and the conductor was holding her elbow to help her up the steps.

"Don't forget to go to Saks for my shirts," Constance called. "I wrote down the size and colors for you."

"—'BO'O-AARD!"

Go back! Allison thought in sudden panic. Go back to what you have and hold onto it tight! Nothing is going to be the same when you get back. Run! She was on the platform and the train was moving. Her mother was waving, the winter sun on her golden hair. Jump, Allison! Run! Mike had one arm raised, waving, the other around Constance's shoulder. Get off, Allison!

"Seats in the forward car, Miss," said the conductor, and held the door open for her.

And then it was too late. Allison found a seat next to a window and turned her head quickly to wave to Mike and her mother.

"Don't forget to call me," Constance was shouting. "Good-by, darling."

426

But Allison could not hear the words. She only saw that her mother's lips were moving and that her hand was still raised; then she was gone and the train was moving very fast.

Not enough sleep and too much coffee, thought Allison as she tried to relax. But it was not until the train had stopped at Boston and she had transferred to the New York train at South Station that her stomach stopped quivering. Of all the ridiculous things! she scolded herself. Anybody would think I was going to be away from home for ten years instead of five days. Even the snow won't be any different when I get back, let alone anything else. Of all the foolishness!

She ate lunch in the dining car and returned to her seat; the train moved with a soothing motion, lulling her anxieties and fears.

I'm going to New York! she thought. I'm an author. Not just a writer for the magazines, but An Author! I made it!

Her nervousness was gone now; she relaxed and watched the frozen landscape slide past her window, and recalled her meeting with Norman Page the day before.

They had bumped into each other outside Seth Buswell's office. "I'm supposed to be back at work," said Norman, "but this calls for a celebration. Come on over to Hyde's and I'll buy you a cup of coffee. It's wonderful news about your book being published, Allison. Wonderful. I'm so very glad for you."

Behind the plate-glass window of his office, Seth Buswell looked at his watch and made a threatening come-in-here gesture at Norman, but Allison stuck her tongue out at him and Seth laughed, and Allison and Norman crossed the street to the diner.

Norman Page no longer used his crutches when he walked, and Peyton Place marveled at his recovery.

"Got guts, that boy," they said.

"Yep. Nobody'd ever think he'd been hit during the war at all."

"It certainly was a terrible thing, his getting all shot up like that."

"Ayeh. But he come through it good. Walks just like everybody else now."

When Peyton Place discussed Norman Page, Matthew Swain and Seth Buswell did not take part in the conversations, nor did they look at one another lest a glance betray the terrible secret they shared with Norman and his mother, Evelyn.

"Except nobody has to worry about Evelyn giving anything away," said Seth Buswell. "She's told herself that lie so long and so often that now she really believes that Norman was wounded in the war."

"Less said about the whole thing the better," said Matt Swain gruffly.

Norman Page had not received a leg wound in battle. He had been discharged as a psychoneurotic, and Evelyn had made the trip, alone, to bring her son home. She had taken him directly from the Army hospital to a large, midtown hotel in New York City and there she had begun to school him in the things he must say and do at home. Norman had been wounded in battle. His right leg had been practically shot out from under him. He must practice with the crutches she had bought for him and never, never let anyone know that he had been discharged from the Army for any other reason than his leg. When Norman had protested she had screamed at him.

"Do you want everyone in Peyton Place to think you're crazy? Think of me, Norman. At least, spare me this!"

And Norman, weaker than he had ever been, sick and tired and beaten, had come home to a hero's welcome.

It was Matthew Swain who realized almost at once that there was nothing the matter with Norman's leg. He had confided in Seth, and the two of them had contacted an old friend of Matt's who was a doctor in the Army. They had learned the truth, then, and had done all they could to protect Norman. No photographs of Peyton Place's hero appeared in Seth's newspaper, lest some other paper pick up the story and reprint it for its human interest.

"If that happens, someone who was in the service with him might recognize him," said Matthew Swain.

So the legend that Norman Page was a war hero persisted in Peyton Place. Eventually, Norman discarded his crutches for a cane and at last he used nothing at all for support and walked upright by himself. But Evelyn Page had so thoroughly convinced herself of the truth of her own lies that often, when it was cloudy and looked like rain, she would ask her son, "How does your leg feel?" Norman always said, "Fine."

"Tell me all about it, Allison," said Norman, as Corey Hyde put coffee cups down in front of them.

"There's nothing much to tell, really," said Allison. "I started reworking a book I had written in New York right after I came home, and now my agent has managed to sell it. It sounds so simple when I say it that way."

"Who?" asked Norman. "I mean, who bought it?"

"A house called Lewis Jackman and Company. In New York."

"I never heard of them," said Norman. "But then, that doesn't mean anything. About the only publishers I ever heard of are Lippincott in Philadelphia and Little, Brown, in Boston."

"Jackman is a very small house," said Allison. "Brad—that's my agent, Bradley Holmes—says I'll be much better off with a small house because they'll have more time to spend on my book."

"What's your book about?"

"It's always hard to describe what a book is about. It's just about a town and the people in it and what they do and think and feel. Just an ordinary small town in northern New England."

"Like Peyton Place?" asked Norman.

"If you want to think of it that way," said Allison defensively. "But as far as I'm concerned, the town in *Samuel's Castle* is just like any small town anywhere."

"How do you know so much about small towns anywhere?" demanded Norman. "The only one you ever lived in is Peyton Place."

"Don't be so silly, Norman," said Allison crossly. "Small towns are small towns everywhere."

Suddenly, it was as if they were very young again, the way they had been in high school, when they had sat on the banks of the Connecticut River and had argued about books and people and words.

"Remember, Norman?" asked Allison, her voice gentle. "Remember how I took you to my secret place once, up behind Road's End?"

Norman's voice was low. "Yes," he said, "I remember."

"You kissed me," said Allison.

"Yes."

"It seems so long ago."

"Yes."

Allison made herself brighten and gave a little laugh. "Well,

429

what are we so down in the mouth about?" she asked. "It *was* a long time ago."

"You wore your hair in a pony tail and the buttercups made little, yellow shadows on your skin," said Norman, as if she had not spoken.

"I've got to go," said Allison. "I'm leaving for New York tomorrow, and I've a million things to do."

"Yes," said Norman. "Of course." His eyes glistened with unshed tears. "Good luck, Allison. Don't forget to come back to us."

Allison leaned across the table and touched the back of his hand.

"I won't forget, Norman," she said gently. "I'll be back."

Walking home from Corey Hyde's diner, she wondered if success had already begun to change her. Road's End, buttercups, the day she kissed Norman—all that seemed so remote now. It was another world; and she was a wholly different person, not young Allison grown up but, simply, Allison. Allison sometimes felt that she had created herself, just as surely as she had created the characters in *Samuel's Castle*.

The train lurched and Allison's forehead bumped hard against the windowpane.

"NEW HAVEN!" called the conductor. "NEW HAVEN, NEW HAVEN."

Oh dear, thought Allison, sitting up and rubbing her forehead. There's still such a long way to go. Does Providence come after New Haven? No, it can't possibly. Damn it, I never can remember.

She smoothed her skirt and lit a cigarette to try to get the train-sleep taste out of her mouth.

I hate the snow when it looks stepped on and has black specks all over it, she thought crossly as the train picked up speed. Damn it, my head aches.

She went to the ladies' room and swallowed two aspirin and some water, and when she got back to her seat she flipped disinterestedly through the pages of a magazine. There was one of her stories. "Marianne Said Maybe." Complete with four-color illustration. She read it through, and then flung the magazine down on the seat.

What inexcusable tripe! she thought viciously. But then her eyes cleared. No more. Not now. Now I'm an author of books. It'll be different now. Now when anyone in Peyton Place wonders what I do for a living and I say that I write, they'll know what I'm talking about.

The news of the sale of Allison's novel had traveled quickly through Peyton Place, and as she leaned her head against the back of the train seat, she smiled a little and imagined the comments and conversations she had evoked all over town.

"Allison MacKenzie went and wrote a book."

"Some feller down to New York sold it for her, I heard."

"Who's he? The New York feller, I mean?"

"Dunno. Some feller down there makes his livin' sellin' books."

"What's it about?"

"Dunno. Calls it *Samuel's Castle,* so I reckon it's somethin' to do with the castle up on the hill."

"It'd seem that way."

"Don't see how anybody could set and write a whole book about some nigger marryin' up with a white girl."

"Don't seem as though anybody could."

"Well, Allison MacKenzie was always one for makin' things up in her head."

"Ayeh. Well, there's some calls it makin' up and there's others call it lyin'. Take your pick."

"When you put it in a book and get paid for it, it ain't lyin'. It's makin' up."

"Same thing, if you ask me."

"Nope, it ain't. Writin' is one of them what'cha call creative arts."

"Well, listen to him! Where'd you get fancy words like that?"

"Elsie Thorton, the schoolteacher, told 'em to me. Says writin' is like paintin' pitchers and all like that."

"Lyin'! Allison MacKenzie was always a little liar."

"Don't seem to me," said Clayton Frazier, putting an end to the conversation, "that any of us got any business discussin' books. Ain't one of us read one in thirty years."

"Well, I'm sure gonna read Allison's."

"Me, too."

"Talk, talk, talk," said Clayton.

Allison was smiling to herself and a young man in the seat across the aisle from her leaned forward and smiled back.

431

"Cigarette?" he asked.

Allison shook herself. "Oh," she said. "No. No thank you."

"GRAND CENTRAL STATION, NEXT!" shouted the conductor. "GRAND CENTRAL."

Allison jumped up and adjusted the jacket of her suit and straightened her hat. When the train came to a halt, she was one of the first ones off and she carried her two bags herself rather than stop one of the hurrying redcaps who passed her as if she were invisible. Her arms were aching as she came into the main lobby of the station, and she stopped still as she saw Bradley Holmes coming toward her.

I thought I'd forgotten what he looked like, she thought in sudden panic. I hadn't forgotten at all. I have to get away. He mustn't see me.

She turned, her eyes seeking the stairs that would take her to the street. But she was too late. Brad had seen her.

"My dear," he cried, and put his arms around her. "I thought you'd never get here!"

"Hello, Brad," said Allison, and her throat began to ache. "Here I am."

◆ 9 ◆

LEWIS JACKMAN WAS A TALL THIN MAN OF FORTY-FIVE YEARS; HE had a cavernous, carved-looking face and smooth, dark hair. His voice was very deep and soft. Allison thought he looked like young Abe Lincoln. There was something dark and brooding, almost melancholic, in his face.

He looked at her with dark, searching eyes. "You know, Miss MacKenzie, after twenty years of reading manuscripts and meeting authors I have come to be pretty good at guessing what a writer will look like from reading what he's written." He smiled, but his smile did not relieve the brooding sadness of his eyes. "I must confess that this time I was completely at a loss. I didn't

432

know what to expect. There's youthful energy and curiosity in your novel, but there is also a long lifetime of lived experience. Now that I see you, all I can say is that I'm amazed. And, of course, very proud to be the publisher of your remarkable novel."

"Thank you, Mr. Jackman," she said.

"I want to go over it with you," he said, "page by page. I'd like it to be as nearly perfect as we can make it." He began to turn the pages of the manuscript, those familiar typed pages that she had given her life to. "There are a few changes—minor ones— that I think will help to give the novel greater unity and more impact."

"Changes?" Allison turned to Brad. "You didn't tell me there had to be changes," she said.

"It's not unusual for a publisher to request changes, Allison," said Brad. "Mr. Jackman has had a great deal of experience with books."

"What changes?" demanded Allison, turning back to Jackman.

He fingered pages of her manuscript and Allison wanted to slap him. She felt as if she had had a child and that Lewis Jackman was now fondling that child in a depraved, obscene fashion.

"There are places, Miss MacKenzie, where your manuscript is a little too much, if you get my meaning."

"No, I don't, Mr. Jackman," said Allison. "I don't get your meaning at all."

Jackman put on a pair of heavy, dark-rimmed glasses. "For instance, here," he said. "In chapter fourteen you have a poor, demented woman committing suicide by hanging. Now, that's all very well, but I think that we could all do with fewer gory details. I don't believe that it is necessary to describe the body swinging on the end of the rope, for one thing, nor to go to such great lengths in the descriptions of the bulging tongue and eyes and the color of the face. In the first place, it's been done many, many times before; and in the second place, it's not very good taste."

Allison jumped to her feet. "I don't give a damn if it's been done in every book that's ever been published and I also don't give a damn about what you consider good taste. What I've written happens to be true, good taste or not."

"Miss MacKenzie," said Jackman, "believe me, I know how you

433

feel. All authors of all first novels feel the same way. You have the feeling that I am defiling a child of yours, isn't that right?"

Allison sat down. "How did you know?" she asked.

"I've published a great many first novels," said Jackman, smiling. "Now listen to me, Allison. May I call you Allison?" She nodded. "Allison, I am not going to ask you, as I have never asked any author, to make changes with which you are not in agreement. However, I do think that if we talk a few things over we can wind up with not only a good book, but a fine book. Shall we try?"

Allison nodded, ashamed of her outburst. "All right," she said, "let's try."

They spent the rest of the afternoon in discussion. On a great many points Allison refused to budge, and Jackman gave in to her. A few times Allison yielded to Jackman, and once or twice Bradley Holmes had his say. Once Allison strode to the window and whirled on both men, crying, "Whose book is it, anyway? If you can both do so much better, why don't you write your own book?" Except for that single outburst the afternoon went pretty well. She and Jackman signed the contract at four-forty-five, and as soon as she and Brad were out of the office he said, "I need a drink."

"I'll treat," said Allison.

"No, you won't," said Brad and took her arm. "Don't let that fifteen-hundred-dollar advance go to your head. It'll be a long time before there's more where that came from."

"Why?" asked Allison, as they stepped out into New York's exciting twilight. "How long do you think it'll be before they publish?"

"Late spring, probably. That'll give you the rest of the winter to make the changes we agreed to make. Perhaps in April."

"So long?" asked Allison. "I thought it would be sooner than that. It won't take me long to make the changes. It involves just patching, really. There won't be any major rewriting."

"Count on April," said Brad. "Then you'll be surprised and happy if it's sooner."

"Where are we going?"

"To the Oak Bar at the Plaza," said Brad. "It's right over there. Allison, I'll never understand why you didn't want to stay at the hotel. You can't spend the rest of your life staying with people in grubby little flats in the Village."

"To me, Brad, it is not a grubby little flat," said Allison. "I was very happy there once. And I like Steve Wallace."

"Steve," said Brad. "What a ridiculous name for a girl. Really, you'd be much better off here at the Plaza."

"It's short for Stephanie," said Allison and laughed at him. "Besides, I don't like to stay in hotels by myself."

They sat side by side on a leather-covered seat in the dark, paneled room. When their cocktails came Brad raised his glass to her.

"To your success, darling," he said. "I wish everything wonderful for you."

"Thank you," said Allison and drank. She put down her glass and looked around. "This is a nice room."

"Yes," said Brad. "We should be drinking champagne, but I'm saving that for later, at dinner. I'll take you to '21.' "

Allison did not answer.

He has no nerves at all, that man, she thought. He acts as if I were merely an old friend, as if there had never been anything more than that between us. She could feel her cheeks begin to redden as she remembered the way they had been together. Her hand trembled when she picked up the glass.

Brad telling her she kissed like a child and teaching her to kiss like a woman. Brad undressing her, looking at her, making her want him to look at her. Brad with the words of seduction so ready on his lips and the technique of love-making so practiced and perfected as to be almost a perversion at his fingertips. And her shamelessness after the first time of pain and fear, wanting him again and again, thrusting herself at him, caressing him with her hands, as he had taught her to do, until he was erect and stimulated and ready to take her once more. And the words of love that had poured from her until Brad put a stop to them and brought to an end all her dreams.

"But I'm married," he had said. "Didn't you know?"

Allison's glass was empty, and Brad signaled the waiter.

"You will dine with me, won't you?" he asked.

"No," she said quickly. "I can't. I have another engagement. In fact, I'm late now."

435

"I've ordered another drink for you, so you'll have to stay a minute anyway," said Brad. "With whom are you dining?"

She was suddenly angry at this cold, nerveless man. "With David Noyes," she said.

"Ah, yes, David," said Brad and smiled. "You know, after you left New York the last time, David came to call on me. He seemed highly disturbed that you had left and wanted to know if I knew the reason for it."

"And what did you tell him?" asked Allison, her eyes dangerously hot.

"David Noyes," said Brad, as if she had not spoken. "A fine talent, that boy. Pity his stuff doesn't sell better. But he gets marvelous reviews and one can't have everything."

"What did you tell him?" asked Allison again.

"Tell him?" asked Brad. "What should I have to tell David? I told him that you'd decided you'd had enough of New York and wanted to go home for a while."

Allison was furious. "Thank you very much, Brad," she said. "But you needn't have been so careful of my honor, you know. I told David all about us. I wrote him a letter and told him everything."

"Oh?" said Brad, sipping his drink. "And what did our Angry Young Man have to say about that?"

"How can you act like this?" she demanded, her voice low and trembling. "As if nothing at all had happened."

"And what did happen? What happened, Allison, so dreadful that you sound like this now? That your face flushes and you tremble with anger?" asked Brad, and he was not suave and smiling now. He was almost as angry as she. "I'll tell you what happened. You lost your virginity and became an adult. You lost your pretty illusions about sex and became a writer. You stopped thinking of love twenty-four hours a day and began to dwell on reality. What the hell are you complaining about? I think you gained far more than you lost."

"I hate you," said Allison in a harsh whisper. "I hate you."

"No, you don't," said Brad and put his hand on her arm to prevent her from leaving. "You're insulted because I haven't regarded your maidenhead as a pearl beyond price, but you don't hate me. You don't hate me at all, Allison. You're still a little bit in love with me, and I with you, and that's the way it will always be between us. We each have our own reasons for feeling as we do, but the feeling is there and we are stuck with it."

"I have to go," gasped Allison. "I have to leave right now. Don't get up. I'll find a taxi."

"Of course I'll get up," said Brad, and did so. "I never permit a lady to whistle for her own cab."

Walking through the lobby of the Plaza, Allison looked at the expensively groomed, beautifully dressed women who sat chatting or strolling about. They were at their ease, in their element; places like this were a customary part of their daily lives. For them, there was nothing dreamlike or exotic about stopping at the Plaza for cocktails. Will it ever be like that for me? Allison wondered.

As they walked down the steps to the sidewalk, a doorman opened the door of a Rolls. A woman stepped out, a gloved hand holding her fur coat closed. She was the most beautiful woman Allison had ever seen. She walked past Allison with unseeing eyes. If Allison had not smelled the odor of her scent, she might have believed the woman to be a ghost.

Brad touched Allison's arm. "Rita Moore," he whispered. "The actress." He smiled, watching Allison turn to catch a last glimpse of the famous actress. "It won't be long now, Allison. I have the feeling that within a few months you'll be getting very friendly with people like Rita. And a few months after that you'll be saying that celebrities bore you."

No chance of that, Allison thought, getting into the taxi. The Rita Moores are too many worlds away from me. I am snowbound in my obscurity.

· 10 ·

LATER THAT SAME EVENING, ALLISON SAT WITH DAVID NOYES IN A dark corner of a little restaurant in Greenwich Village. She was wearing slacks and a pullover sweater and David had on an open-necked sport shirt. They had come to this place because Allison had been much too tired to dress and face the chic of an uptown restaurant after her afternoon with Bradley Holmes and Lewis Jackman.

"Let's see it," David had said, as soon as she stepped through the front door of Steve Wallace's apartment, holding out his hand for the manila envelope that Allison carried.

Allison tossed it to him. The manila envelope contained her copy of the contract she had signed that afternoon.

"Sweetie!" exclaimed Steve. "You're beat. Come on, I'll run a hot tub for you. Let this monster stew in his own juices. Contracts, indeed."

Allison had sunk gratefully into the hot, pine-scented water, and felt the tight nerves at the base of her neck begin to loosen. She thought about Lewis Jackman's dark, unhappy face; and Brad's harsh, wounding words. Could life really be reduced to Brad's simple equation? She thought not. One plus one makes two —at least, it ought to make two. By Brad's reckoning it added up to one and one, each as separate as before.

"Allison!" shouted David from the other side of the bathroom door. "This is marvelous! Say what you will about Brad Holmes, there's no one like him when it comes to getting a contract for one of his authors. Come on out of there, I want to talk to you."

"Well, I don't want to talk to you," said Allison. "I want to go somewhere for dinner, somewhere small and French where I don't have to get all dressed up, and I want to drink a whole bottle of wine. Then, maybe I'll talk to you. Can Steve join us?"

"No," said David. "She's entertaining one of her buyer friends from out of town."

"You go to hell," yelled Steve, and threw a magazine at David.

Allison came out of the bathroom, wrapped in Steve's terry-cloth robe, a towel around her head.

"Can't you come with us?" she asked Steve.

"No, sweetie. I've got a date. And not with a buyer, either," said Steve. "This one tells me he's going to make me the biggest star in television. Naturally, I don't believe a word of it, but he has a charge account at El Morocco, so who am I to say no?"

Allison finished picking at the last shred of chicken on her plate and then leaned back against the leather seat. The candle on the table flickered smokily; the muted voices of the other diners swirled around her. Nothing can touch me now, she thought. Her joy in her success was so intense that she felt isolated and unreachable.

"I didn't realize I was so hungry," she said, smiling at David.

David poured wine into her glass. "It's wonderful, isn't it?" he said. "There's no other feeling like it, except for holding your first printed book in your hand. But signing a contract is something you never get used to." He smiled and picked up his glass. "I've done it four times, and it still makes me feel special."

"It made me feel neat," said Allison, trying to find the perfect word, the word that would describe it most exactly. "It was as if all the loose ends of my life were nicely tied up in a bundle and then I didn't even have to worry about the bundle."

"What about changes?"

"Nothing that really amounts to anything. Brad says he thinks Jackman will publish in the spring."

"Rewriting is the lousiest job of all," said David. "It makes you feel as if you're being forced to travel back through a place you never wanted to visit to begin with, where everything is shabby and frayed at the edges and the ground is littered with torn newspapers."

"Not I," said Allison, laughing. "It makes you feel like that because you're a genius. I'm not. I'm a hack and very pleased with myself."

"Stop belittling yourself," said David. "You're no hack, and if you were, you'd never have to say it yourself. The critics would say it."

Allison put down her glass and stared at the candle's wavering orange flame. The high elation had begun to leave her, but she had known it could not last. As her happiness dissipated itself—it was as if it were seeping out of her pores, she thought—doubts began to enter.

"Sometimes I get scared, David."

"We all do."

"What if nobody buys my book? What if nobody likes it if they do buy it?"

"Then there is nothing to do but try again." He poured more wine. "Come on. Drink up and stop worrying. This is supposed to be a celebration. Do you want to go to a movie or something?"

"No," said Allison. "Let's just sit here and talk."

"I'm an obliging soul. What do you want to talk about?"

"I don't care," said Allison. "Anything. Everything."

"Are you over Bradley Holmes?" asked David.

Allison picked up a cigarette. "I guess there was never really anything to get over," she said. "I didn't love him to begin with." But she could tell by the way her heart raced that she wasn't over him yet. The memory of herself and Brad still had the power to move her.

"Is that what *he* told you?"

"No. He said that I did love him, a little, and that he loved me a little, too."

"Crap," said David. "That guy may be good at contracts but he's the biggest crap artist in New York."

"Because he said what he did about love?"

"Love, my can," said David. "Maybe he wants to sleep with you again, but that's the extent of his love."

"Stop it," said Allison, snapping the cigarette between her fingers. "I don't want to talk about it."

"Why?" demanded David. "Does it still scare you? Shame you? Make you want to run?"

"No," cried Allison. "Now, stop it, David."

"I can't stop it," said David with quiet desperation. "I have to know about *me*, you see." He moved the ashtray and then stared into it, as if he might find the answer there. "I've been waiting a long time, Allison. I have to know."

"Not now, David. Let's go." I'm not ready yet, Allison thought. Brad's like a poison in my system. I have to get rid of him completely, before I can be good for anyone else.

"No," said David. "Let's get it over with."

"Get what over with?"

"Us. You and me."

"David, for Heaven's sake, can't we leave things the way they are? Can't we be friends without this everlasting talk of turning it into something else?"

"I told you before, Allison. I told you two years ago and it's

440

still true. I don't want to be your goddamned friend. I want you, and I want you any way I can get you. I'd like to marry you, but if you don't want that, I want to be your lover. I want to live with you if I can, but if I can't, I want you anyway."

"Oh, David," she sighed. "I'm so tired I can't think now. Let's go home."

They sat close together on the sofa in Steve's apartment. Allison's head rested on David's shoulder and he stroked her hair.

"David?"

"Yes?"

"Kiss me."

He turned her face toward his and kissed her gently, as if he were afraid to hurt or startle her, and Allison put her arms around him. He began to seek her tongue with his and his hand rested gently on the underslope of her breast, and very quickly Allison began to kiss him harder. Her mouth opened and she moved against him and he pressed her back gently, so that she was lying down. His hand touched the skin under her sweater and he stroked her.

"But not here, darling," he said against her cheek. "And not today. Not until you're sure."

"I'm sure," Allison lied. She wanted him to take her; she wanted David to drive Brad out and claim her for himself.

"You're sorry for me," David said. "I don't want that."

She sat up and tugged at the bottom of her sweater.

"Damn it," she cried. "Don't always be telling me what I am and what I'm not!"

"I'm playing for big stakes, Allison," said David. "I want all of you, or I don't want you at all. I want you whole and unafraid and I don't want you haunted by the ghost of Bradley Holmes."

Allison burst into tears. "Please, David," she sobbed. "Please wait. Just a little longer."

"I'll wait," said David. "It's a habit I seem to have acquired." He put his arms around her. "Come on, darling. Stop crying. Everything's going to be all right. I'm here."

Allison fell asleep with her head in his lap. Steve Wallace found him holding her when she came home at one o'clock in the morning.

441

• 11 •

THE WINTER PASSED WITH AGONIZING SLOWNESS. IT SEEMED TO
Allison as if not only every stream and inch of ground, but time
itself was frozen by winter's iron, unyielding grip.

Allison MacKenzie had finished the revisions on her manuscript
before Christmas and had mailed them to Lewis Jackman. She had
worked with a craftsman's skill, with the coolness of a surgeon.
She got a two-word telegram in return.

"Well done."

In January, Bradley Holmes telephoned and told her that
Jackman was ready to publish and that he planned to release the
book on April tenth.

"Did you have a good Christmas?" asked Brad.

"Very nice," said Allison. "Steve Wallace and David Noyes
came up for the holidays."

"David again?" asked Brad. "Everytime I see or talk to you, I
seem to trip over David Noyes."

"Does that annoy you, Brad?" asked Allison stiffly.

"Not particularly."

"Well, it doesn't annoy me, either. I enjoy having David around."

"Why not get a French poodle?" asked Brad. "At least you
wouldn't have to listen to him chatter."

Allison slammed down the receiver.

David's and Stephanie's visit had been a joyful interlude for
Allison, breaking the monotonous ritual of her days. She took
long walks with David and talked to him about her work. They
held hands as they walked, they drew closer together; but it was,
Allison felt, the closeness of friendship, nothing more.

She invited Seth Buswell and Matt Swain to come on Christmas Day. Allison wanted these old friends to meet the two people
who meant so much to her now. It was her attempt to tie together

442

her old life and the new. It bothered her that there should be such a high wall separating the two parts of her life. She wanted it not to be so, she wanted to be able to move easily from Peyton Place to New York City without being assailed by a sense of strangeness.

The old friends and the new took to each other well. Seth talked literature to David for hours, talked as if he might never have the chance again. To Allison's amazed delight, Matt Swain sat on the sofa beside Stephanie and listened for hours to her stories of life among the TV actors. He never took his eyes from Stephanie's bright young face.

When they had gone back to New York, Allison met Matt Swain on Elm Street coming out of the pharmacy.

"Allison," he said, "I liked those friends of yours."

"Especially Stephanie," said Allison, smiling at him.

Doc Swain looked over Allison's head to the bleak, wintry hills that ringed the town. "There's something about her face, Allison —I don't know what it is—there's something about her face that breaks my heart. When I look at her I feel young again—and, at the same time, I feel very old. I guess she makes me remember youth, and that gives me a greater awareness of my age." He smiled at Allison, almost apologetically.

"You're not old, Doc."

"I wish I thought so," he said. "Dear God, how I wish I thought so."

Now, having just hung up on Brad, Allison pushed the phone away from her and turned unseeing eyes toward the window. She knew without really looking that gray, gaunt winter stood just outside the window.

By now, everyone was tired of the winter; it had lost the charm of newness. But everyone continued to talk about the weather, because there was very little else to talk about that winter in Peyton Place.

"Got us a real, old-fashioned winter this time."

"Ayeh. Ain't been this much snow in fifty years."

"That's what everybody says every winter," said Clayton Frazier. "Every damned year it's the most snow in fifty years."

"Well, it's true this year. Them fellers up to Mount Washington got it all figured out. When the thaw comes there's gonna be two hundred and sixty inches of snow that's gotta melt. Gonna be floods all over the place."

"There won't be no flood," said Clayton.

"The hell there won't. With all that snow meltin', the river'll go over its banks sure."

"The Connecticut ain't a floodin' river," said Clayton Frazier. "And that's the end of it."

"You'll see, you pigheaded old bastard. You'll see."

But Clayton Frazier was right. There was no flood. An early thaw set in at the end of January, and the snow began to melt gradually. In February nearly all the snow was gone, and by the end of the month the ice in the river had begun to loosen around the edges. When March was half gone, people began to look around and think that spring would come again after all. But this time it would come gently, like a well-mannered maiden, and not like a roaring, screaming harlot barging her way into northern New England.

On the twenty-fifth of March, Allison received the six advance copies of her novel, and immediately burst into tears.

Now she knew what David had meant when he spoke of the thrill that came with holding one's first book. She stroked the paper jacket and studied the photograph of herself on the back. Then she removed the jacket and looked at the smooth, black binding.

Samuel's Castle she read, and under the title on the spine, *MacKenzie.* She gazed at it with eyes that slowly filled with tears. Here was the end result of years of work, this compact thing she could hold in her hands.

"It's the most beautiful thing I've ever seen," said Constance, and she, too, began to cry.

"Here we go again," said Mike. "This is costing me a fortune in handkerchiefs."

"But it is," wept Constance. "I never saw a more beautiful book in my life."

"Neither have I," agreed Mike, putting his arm around her.

"And it's mine," cried Allison. "*Mine.* There's no one between these two covers but me. Nobody did it for me, nobody told me what to say. I did it myself."

"If this keeps up," said Mike, "we're going to go broke buying champagne."

Allison did not pay much attention to the note Lewis Jackman had sent her along with the books.

"I have taken the liberty," he wrote, "of sending individual copies of *Samuel's Castle* to various people in Peyton Place. I think their reactions to the novel may be of some publicity value to us in our advertising."

Who cares about advertising? thought Allison. Let Lewis Jackman sell books. All I ever want to do is write them.

She began to inscribe the six copies she had received. For David, with all my love, Allison. For my Mother and Mike, with love and gratitude. For Selena Cross, with love, Allison. For Dr. Matthew Swain, who remembers poems about Eternity, with love from Allison. For Seth Buswell, who paid me the first money I ever earned for writing, with best wishes, Allison MacKenzie. And the sixth copy she kept for herself. She propped it up on her dresser so that she could see it when she first awoke in the morning.

At eleven o'clock that night, Seth Buswell called Matthew Swain.

"Have you read it?" he demanded, his voice harsh with excitement.

"Read what, for God's sake?" asked Matt.

"Allison's book!"

"No, I haven't," said Matt patiently. "I work for a living, remember? I've got more to do than sit around reading books all day."

"Matt, all hell is going to break loose."

"What are you talking about?"

"She's got everybody in town in it!"

"What the hell do you mean?"

"I mean thinly disguised portraits of every single person in Peyton Place," said Seth.

"Oh, stop it," said Matt. "Allison wouldn't do a thing like that."

"I don't say it was intentional," said Seth, "but by God, Matt, people are going to take it that way. She's got rape, incest, murder, suicide, and a dozen different kinds of screwing around in that book!"

445

"So? Sin isn't at home only in Peyton Place, you know. It dwells in other places, too."

"Matt, don't argue. Sit down and read it. That's all I can tell you. Oh, yes. Marion Partridge got a copy from the publishers. They want her to sit down and list her reactions to the book and let them know. She called me an hour ago, sore as a boil, and she wants Allison MacKenzie run out of town on a rail."

"Marion's always been a troublemaker," said Matthew Swain. "Born that way, Marion was. Well, I'll get busy and start reading right now."

"Matt?"

"What?"

"Call me back when you finish. No matter what time it is. I want to hear what you have to say."

Matthew Swain built a fire in the fireplace of his living room. He made himself a tall drink, and when he had changed to his robe and slippers, he sat down and began to read.

"There is a little town in northern New England," he read, "and all year long the hills that roll gently away from it are green, for they are topped with pine. On the highest hill of all, like a jewel in the center of a crown, sits Samuel's castle."

Matthew Swain read until three-fifteen in the morning, and when he had finished Allison's novel, he picked up the telephone and called Seth Buswell.

"I still say it could have happened anywhere," he said. "It doesn't have to be here."

"Matt, you've lived in this part of the country all your life. Do you know of any other New England town with a castle right in its own back yard?"

"Well, no," said Matt. "But it could happen. There's no law says that castles are limited to Peyton Place."

"Tell that to Marion Partridge and every other woman in town like her," said Seth. "Wait and see, Matt. Just wait and see."

"I know," said Matthew Swain. "I know. I guess I was just trying to convince myself that nothing is going to come of this."

"Stargazer," said Seth.

"I'm afraid so, Seth," said the doctor. "I'm afraid so. There's no doubt of it, Seth. All hell's going to break loose here when that book is published."

BOOK TWO

• 1 •

ALLISON WAITED. NOW THAT HER NOVEL WAS SCHEDULED FOR PUB-
lication, there was nothing to do but wait. She could not work.
She had planned on beginning her second novel, but soon gave up
all thought of it. She found it impossible to plunge into something
new before knowing how the critics and public would accept her
first effort. She did not worry, but waited with a quiet resignation
that only occasionally broke down. At those times, impatience and
a terrible sense of urgency assailed her and she wanted to strike
the walls of her room with her fists, as if the walls themselves
were a barrier to immediate publication.

While she was writing her novel, it had seemed an endless
task; she could not imagine that a day would come when the
pile of manuscript on her desk would be gone. She felt like a
convalescent, at ease with herself, quietly grateful that she had
come through. She sat at the window and gazed out at Peyton
Place, the part of the world she knew best. She felt that for two
years she had, in a sense, been cut off from life; she had not
participated in it actively, with her whole being, but only as an
observer, clinically detached. Sometimes she was afraid that this
had become too much a way of life for her, and she wondered
if her rejection of David had not been motivated by a fear of
entering passionately into life again.

Every day she picked up her copy of *Samuel's Castle* and wondered what its fate was to be. Obscurity, she thought. That was
the fate of most first novels. She did not know that in New York
certain wheels had been set in motion and that the novel was no
longer altogether hers, or that its fate was not to be left to chance.
Fate had an accomplice, a man she had never heard of, named
Paul Morris.

Paul Morris was a small, compact man with a crew haircut, soft brown eyes and a smile which, people said, would charm the pants off a nun. He was thirty years old and for the last ten of those years had worked in New York at the nebulous trade known as public relations.

At the age of eighteen, Paul had managed to get himself hired by a small advertising agency by tacking five years on his age and claiming that he was a graduate of Columbia University. As he said later, the closest he had ever come to Columbia was riding down Morningside Drive on a bus, for his formal education had ended after two years at a high school in the Bronx.

By the time he was twenty, Paul felt that he had learned everything about the advertising business that could be useful to him later and he went, with excellent references, to a job in the publicity department of one of the largest radio stations in New York. It was there, he said later, that he really found himself. He rose quickly in his chosen field. Within three years he was head of his department, married a girl singer who gave up her budding career for him and moved into an apartment at a good address in the East Sixties.

Two years later he opened an office of his own, and many of the big names with whom he had worked in radio and who were to become the pioneer stars of television followed him. The printing on his door read, "Paul Morris, Publicity and Public Relations," and, as Paul said, he could always tell a square the minute he spoke to one, because the square always asked, "Just what is it that you do, Mr. Morris?"

For his clients, Paul Morris did everything, and he did it better than anyone else. One of his most important clients was a man named Jerry Baldwin who had a coast-to-coast television program called "Fun with Uncle Jerry." Baldwin was an alcoholic who could enjoy sex only with girls under fifteen. It was Paul Morris' job to see to it that none of Baldwin's escapades became open scandal. Paul had often arrived on the scene of a barroom brawl, minutes ahead of the police, to drag Baldwin, fighting and screaming obscenities, into a waiting automobile, and he had been called upon frequently to soothe, with cash, the outraged parents of teen-age girls.

"You'd better knock it off, Jer," he told Baldwin. "You're going broke. Pay-offs aren't deductible, you know."

Another of Paul's prize customers was an ex-gangster named Manny Kubelsky, who had turned respectable in his old age and wanted the whole world to know it. Paul saw to it that Manny made the gossip columns every time the ex-hood gave to charity or opened another store in his chain of sporting goods shops. Paul found a teacher who erased the lower East Side from Manny's speech, and a good tailor who succeeded in making the little mobster look like a Madison Avenue executive. Paul traded Manny's long, black Cadillac for a medium-sized, gray Buick and he had Manny's apartment redecorated to look like the home of a moderately successful businessman.

"You can't afford ostentation, Manny," said Paul.

"Ostentation, my ass!" cried Manny, sulking over the loss of his velvet drapes and white fur rugs. "I don't want to live like no bum, neither."

"*Any* bum," corrected Paul patiently.

Very often, a man grows to hate a person who knows his innermost secrets and hidden vices, but this was not the case with Paul Morris and his clients. He was everything to them from nurse to father confessor and they worshiped him. He procured jobs for them, got their names and photographs into newspapers and magazines, bought them front-row seats for opening nights and patched up lovers' quarrels.

"Just what do I do?" Paul Morris often said. "Why, everything or nothing, depending on your point of view. But if you want me to do it for you, it'll cost you, and cost you plenty."

When Lewis Jackman began to realize that in Allison MacKenzie's novel he had a book which, with good advertising and clever publicity, could be turned into a runaway best seller, he sent at once for Paul Morris. The realization of what he had had not been long in coming to Jackman. As soon as the comment cards which he had sent out with each advance copy of the book began coming back to him, Jackman knew.

"Makes Caldwell sound like a choirboy," read one card.

"Tobacco Road with a Yankee accent."

"Earthy. Real. Truthful."

"Wowie!"

These were the remarks of the booksellers. From the people to whom Jackman had sent books in Peyton Place, there was an ominous silence.

Paul Morris read all the comments and studied a photograph of Allison MacKenzie.

"She's just a kid," he said to Lewis Jackman.

"Exactly," replied Jackman.

"But I've read the book. No kid ever wrote that!"

"She did, though. Makes rather a nice gimmick, doesn't it?"

"I'll say," said Paul. "The face of a schoolgirl and the mind and vocabulary of a longshoreman. We just might have something here."

"That's what I think, Paul. Do you think you can do anything with what we have?"

Paul Morris sat quietly and tapped a pencil against his front teeth.

"Can you get her to come down here?" he asked at last.

"Yes, I'm sure of it. The thing that may make it easier all around is that she wants this book to be a big seller almost as badly as I do."

"Call her up right now," said Paul. "I'll wait. Tell her you need her the day after tomorrow for four or five days."

Jackman picked up the telephone and called Allison Mac-Kenzie. After a few minutes of conversation, he winked at Paul Morris and formed the words "She'll come" silently with his lips. He spoke into the telephone a moment longer, and when he hung up he was grinning.

"Not only is she coming," he said, "but she's very excited about the whole thing."

"Good," said Paul. "I'll start setting up appointments as soon as I get back to my office."

"Just a hint for what it's worth, Paul," said Jackman. "Allison is sweet, tractable and co-operative, for the most part, but when she turns stubborn she's pure, shell-backed Yankee and next to impossible to deal with."

Paul laughed. "You're paying me to cope with little problems like that," he said. "Don't worry about a thing."

"I won't worry," said Jackman, and although he smiled there

was a little edge of warning to his voice. "I know you won't botch this one, Paul."

You're damned right, I won't, thought Paul as he left Jackman's office, for although he had plenty of clients as it was, the job he was going to do for Jackman now was the first one he had attempted for a book publisher. Jackman had opened a whole new untapped field for him, and he was determined to do the best job of his career on Allison MacKenzie and *Samuel's Castle*.

"Hundreds of books are published every year," Paul told his wife. "If I do a spectacular job this time, there'll be other jobs. It's a potential gold mine."

Allison had taken Lewis Jackman's telephone call in the kitchen, where she, Mike and Constance had been drinking coffee. Watching her on the phone, Constance realized how lacking in animation Allison had been these past weeks. Just talking to someone in New York, Constance thought, brings her back to life again. With a pang, she wondered whether Allison would ever be content with Peyton Place again.

"Mr. Jackman wants me to go down to New York," Allison said, when she had hung up the phone. "I'm going to be interviewed by some newspaper and television people. He says that they are all very interested in the book and want to talk to me."

"Why, that's wonderful!" said Constance. "When do you have to go?"

"The day after tomorrow."

"Good Heavens!" Constance exclaimed. "What are we doing just standing here! We've got to find you something to wear."

Michael Rossi did not say anything, but his eyes narrowed a little as Allison and Constance left the room. He could hear them upstairs, laughing and chattering, as they looked over Allison's wardrobe.

I don't like this, he thought. I don't like it at all.

He felt there was a reckless fervor in Allison's manner, an eagerness to throw herself into life. He did not want her to be hurt. He had read her novel and, unlike Constance, he had not been blinded by a mother's love; he knew its publication would not pass quietly in a town like Peyton Place, that those who were offended by it would strike back. Sometimes he found himself hoping that the book would not be a success; he was afraid that

Allison was all too ignorant of what success can do, how destructive it can be.

But he said nothing to Allison and Constance, for he would have had no answers for the questions they would have asked. He didn't know precisely why he felt as he did, he only knew that he had a feeling of apprehension and that he wished that Allison were not going to New York. Later, he was to wish desperately that he had voiced an opinion, no matter how vague, for his anxiety had been more well founded than he knew.

• 2 •

WHEN SHE GOT OFF THE TRAIN AT GRAND CENTRAL, ALLISON SPOTTED Lewis Jackman immediately. His height would have made him recognizable even if she had forgotten his face. She had seen him only once before, but he had a darkly handsome face that was hard to forget. Jackman was so touched by her youth that he held her hand a moment longer than was necessary. Allison saw revealed in his eyes a naked longing that caused her heart to lurch.

"I've reserved a room for you at the Algonquin," he said. "At our expense, of course. It's close to everything and still has a certain literary flair about it that I think you'll enjoy." His voice was warm, resonant, but his words impersonal; he acted like a man determined to let nothing interfere with business.

"I've read about the Algonquin," said Allison. "Do famous people still gather there to insult the world and each other?"

"Not any more," laughed Jackman. "But their ghosts survive. The place is full of them. I asked the manager to be sure to give you one of the haunted rooms."

They were sitting on one of the sofas in the hotel lobby having a cocktail when Paul Morris joined them.

"Hello, Allison," said Paul, and smiled his famous smile. "I read your book and I think it's terrific. I enjoyed it tremendously."

"Thank you very much," said Allison, thrilling to the words of praise she knew she would never tire of hearing.

How nice he is, she thought. Not at all what I expected. Well, what *did* I expect? she asked herself, and smiled inwardly at her own answer.

She had only just heard of him from Jackman and had expected a caricature of a motion picture publicity man. Someone with dark-rimmed glasses and hair that was a shade too long and who smelled of constant hurry and tension.

Paul Morris began to talk about New England, the towns he had visited and the summer camps he had attended as a child, and within fifteen minutes Allison felt as if he were an old friend she had known all her life. This was the measure of one of Paul's greatest talents because, in reality, the only time he had ever set foot in New England had been to cart one of his clients, an actress with a penchant for the bottle, to a theater in Boston. He had been forced to spend the weekend there, stuck in a small hotel room near the North Station, and when he had finally been able to leave he had sworn to God that it would be a long, cold day in hell before he ever left New York again.

"We're having lunch with Jim Brody tomorrow," said Paul. "Ever hear of him?"

"I think so," said Allison. "Doesn't he write some sort of news-paper column?"

"I'll say he does," said Paul. "A column that's syndicated in over six hundred papers all over the country. He wants to interview you."

Allison's hands began to tremble. "I'll never be able to think of anything to say."

"Yes, you will," said Paul. "All you have to do is be yourself. Now, listen. This is going to be a very important interview. Not only because Brody is big, but because it's your first time out. What are you going to wear?"

"I have some new dresses," she said, "and my mother let me borrow her mink stole."

"No," said Paul, "I don't want you to look dressed up. I want

455

you to look very young, innocent and little-girlish. Come on. Let's go upstairs and take a look."

The three of them went up to Allison's room, and Paul examined every garment in her clothes closet. Allison felt that she should be embarrassed and she knew that with anyone else in the world but Paul she would have been. But he handled her clothes so impersonally that she could not mind. Besides, she was beginning to have the feeling that none of this had anything to do with her. Finally he selected a gray wool with a round, white collar.

"This one," he said.

"But that's not new," Allison argued. "I've had it two years and the only reason I brought it along on this trip was to wear it home on the train because it doesn't wrinkle easily."

"This one," said Paul again, more definitely. "And no fur stole. The coat you had on downstairs is fine."

Before Allison knew what was happening, he had picked up her hairbrush and was working on her hair.

"No fancy hair-do, either," he said. "Get a rubber band and tie it all up in a pony tail."

"But I haven't worn my hair like that since I was fourteen," she objected.

"Exactly," said Paul with a smile. "And no make-up except for a tiny bit of lipstick. Do you have a pink one?"

"No."

"I'll bring one when I come to pick you up," said Paul. "I'll be here at twelve-thirty."

"But I don't want to go dressed like a child," Allison almost wailed. "I want to look nice."

Paul put a friendly arm around her shoulder. "Sweetie," he said, "you'll be a smash. The United States has glamorous lady authors, and old lady authors, and housewifely lady authors and school-teacherish lady authors. We do not have a scrubbed, clean-looking, young girl author, and you are going to fill this big gap. Trust me, will you?"

Allison looked into the soft, dark eyes that smiled into hers.

"All right," she said at last. "I'll be ready at twelve-thirty."

"And go to bed early tonight," said Paul as he went out the door. "I want you to look as if you'd had twelve hours' sleep tomorrow."

When he had gone, Allison turned to Lewis Jackman.

"Do you think I'll be all right?" she asked nervously.

"My dear," said Jackman, "don't give it another thought. Just leave everything to Paul."

But now that Paul Morris was gone, all of Allison's doubts began to return.

"Is all this necessary?" she asked Jackman. "I mean, this masquerading as something I'm not in order to impress someone?"

"Publicity is a delicate business, Allison. We are paying Paul Morris quite a lot of money to handle it well for us. He is an expert in his field, and the best thing for both of us to do is to put ourselves entirely in his hands. You do want to sell books, don't you?"

"Of course I do," said Allison.

"Then just do as Paul says," said Jackman. "I repeat, he's an expert."

Allison walked to the window of her room and looked down on New York spread out and waiting. As if it wants to be conquered, she thought. She sat down on the edge of the bed and lit a cigarette, then piled the pillows against the headboard and, for the first time since she had arrived, relaxed and began to feel herself. Until this moment, she thought, I've been playing a role, the role of the young novelist coming to New York to see her publisher. It was too unreal.

"I never expected it to be like this," she said to Jackman.

He smiled and pulled a chair over to the bedside and sat down. Like a doctor, she thought, and smiled at him.

"It never is," he said. "Authors always have a hard time learning the facts of literary life today. It's not that it's so complex, but rather that writers don't want to accept the facts."

"Try me," Allison said.

"It's quite simple, Allison. Publishing is a business—like any other. The motive is profit. Books are something we sell. The only difference between a so-called good publisher and a so-called bad one is that the good ones like to think a profit can be made from publishing good books."

"Which kind are you?" Allison wanted to call him Lewis but could not yet bring herself to do so.

"I have always imagined I am a good one," he said, smiling.

"You know, publishers are very much like authors in a way. After I got into this business it took me quite a few years to accept the reality of it. I suppose that in my youthful fervor I believed that a publishing house was something like a charitable institution for the talented young men and women who submitted their manuscripts. I had to make up my mind to one of the primary facts of business life, which is that the first duty of a business is to stay in business. If my company had gone under, I wouldn't be much good to you now."

"You have a way," Allison said, "of making the most unreasonable things sound like sweet reason herself."

Jackman laughed. Allison looked up at him, startled, not knowing why. Then she realized what it was. "That's the first time I ever heard you laugh, Lewis," she said.

"I suppose I am a little out of the habit of it." He touched her hand with his fingertips. "You must come to New York more often, and stay longer. Apparently, you are good for me."

They were both silent then, looking into each other's eyes. Jackman was the first to turn away. "You touch something in me, Allison. But I have no right to talk like this. I am married. I have a son who is almost as old as you."

Allison turned her hand over; their palms touched. He bent down and kissed her, a kiss that for all its gentleness shook her with its intimation of suppressed passion. "Even your lips are young," he said, his voice soft, hardly more than a whisper. "Even your kisses taste young." He moved toward her again. And Allison thought, I don't care, I don't care, I want this. She opened her arms to him. He was on the bed with her and they were lying side by side.

They spoke not another word to each other, as if both realized that there would be time for speech later. Now they wanted only each other, and with a terrible hunger. He undressed her with hands that trembled like a boy's and, noticing this, she permitted herself to feel a moment of selfish triumph. When their naked bodies touched she gasped; it took her breath away, it was like the shock of diving into a mountain pool.

She was ready for him in an instant and, when he began to stroke her breasts, she cried out and opened herself to him. He took her with a harsh intensity that left her spent and breathless and dazed. She felt Lewis' lips kissing her eyelids. She felt release flowing through her, she cried soundlessly. Lewis held her close and said, "Oh, my dear, my dear," over and over again, and caressed her gently and with love.

Later he took her to dinner and gazed at her across the table. He made Allison feel she was the rarest being in the world.

"You are so beautiful," he said, so softly that the words barely reached her ears, as if he had spoken across vast distances.

"Only moonstruck boys have ever told me that, Lewis," she said.

"Then I am a moonstruck boy, my darling." His face became sad again, the word "boy" had reminded him of his age and of the great difference between his age and Allison's. Allison was aware of what he must be thinking and reached out and took his hand.

"You are young, Lewis," she said. "You are young when you are with me because you have love to give. A man is old only when he's exhausted his store of love."

"I wish that was true, Allison. How I wish that was true! It would make us contemporaries. I've spent as little love in my nearly fifty years of life as you have in half that time. I want to tell you about this, Allison, not only because you have a right to know but because I *want* to tell you."

He told Allison of his loveless marriage to a neurotic wife. "I married young," he said, "young and full of hope. Because I loved her I hoped she would change. But she never has. We should have got a divorce twenty years ago, but then my son was born and for a long time that was enough for me." Lewis was so unused to revealing himself that it embarrassed him; he paused often and shifted the silverware beside his plate. "I gave up all thought of personal happiness. We drifted along. My son's at college now. And my wife . . . she is very much an inhabitant of her own world. A world she has created out of her own neuroses. Madness, I should say, but it's not a fashionable word any more, is it? *Nice* women, women of good family, don't go mad; they have neuroses. Only peasants are susceptible to madness these days." He looked down at Allison's hand in his. "You will have gathered by now that I stay with her out of pity. But don't let me give you the impression that it is a noble thing to do," he said, sarcastic at his own expense. "It's not an act of courage or sacrifice, Allison. Believe me. It's an act of weakness, I'm afraid. The courageous thing would be for me to leave her. But

I haven't yet had the strength to do that. Instead, like a weakling, I sit and wait for her to commit suicide or get run over by a car. I have the absurd dream that one day I will be free of her without doing anything myself."

"It may happen yet, darling," Allison said, reassuring him.

"Oh, Allison, don't let me draw you into my silly dreams. Nothing happens but what we make happen."

"I don't care, Lewis. I don't care about any of that. Just love me and everything will be all right."

He smiled his love to her, but behind the sadness of his eyes he thought, Oh God, how young she is. How young she is.

That night Allison slept in his arms and felt safe, protected from a menacing world.

♦ 3 ♦

SHORTLY BEFORE ONE O'CLOCK THE FOLLOWING AFTERNOON, ALLISON sat next to Paul Morris at the bar of a Third Avenue restaurant called Kelly's. It had a floor made of small hexagonal tiles, and the old gas chandeliers, converted to electricity, still were in use.

"Brody's been coming here for twenty years," Paul told Allison. "He made the place fashionable."

"I lived in New York for over a year," said Allison, "and never heard of it. It must be very, very fashionable indeed."

Paul picked up his drink and was silent for a moment. Then he said, "Look, doll, I'm not trying to put words in your mouth or keep them out, for that matter, but don't mention the fact that you once lived in New York to Brody."

"But what if he asks me?" demanded Allison.

"Then hedge," said Paul, and put up a hand to stop the words that came to her lips. "Look, you're a clever kid. You've written a novel that has not only been published but is going to be a best seller. You're smart enough with words when you want to be, and I want you to be extra, super smart with Brody. Don't tell him about living in New York. And another thing. During the war Brody got the Pulitzer for news coverage in Italy. You might remember to mention that. It's his pride and joy and not many people remember it."

"How did you happen to remember?" asked Allison.

"Trade secret," smiled Paul, "but I'll tell you. Ever since I set this interview up, I've been reading stories by and about Jim Brody. I've studied everything about him so carefully that I bet I could tell you what color pajamas he wears to bed."

Jim Brody was a big, hearty-looking man who looked as if he enjoyed good food and good jokes. When he walked into Kelly's, practically everybody there waved and called out a greeting to him. A waiter quickly removed a "Reserved" sign from a back table and another waiter put down a huge glass of beer before Brody had even had time to take his coat off.

"Here we go, honey," whispered Paul Morris. "Smile."

"I can't," Allison whispered back. "I'm too scared."

"Yes, you can and no, you're not," said Paul and led her to Jim Brody's table.

"Hi," said Brody, barely glancing at Allison as Paul introduced her. "Sit down."

Allison sat next to Paul Morris. He fools you, she thought, looking at Brody. He's so big and friendly looking, like a Saint Bernard, except for his eyes. His eyes are cold and they see everything.

"Want a beer?" Brody asked.

"I'll have one," said Paul. "Miss MacKenzie doesn't drink."

How can he lie like that and still smile? wondered Allison, shocked, as she remembered the dry martini she had just had at the bar.

"How old are you?" asked Brody.

Before Allison could answer, Paul took a slip of paper from an inside pocket of his suit coat.

"I wrote down all the biographical stuff, Jim," he said. "Thought it might save time."

Brody took the paper and studied it. "Nineteen, hm-m?" he asked, glancing up at Allison.

For a moment she was speechless. She was twenty-three years old and was just opening her mouth to say so when Brody spoke again.

"You look even younger than that," he said. "Been writing long?"

"Ever since high school," she said.

"Ever sell anything?"

"Just short stories. To the magazines."

"What kind of stories?"

"Oh, you know. Just silly, frothy things for a lot of empty-headed women."

Brody smiled. "Be careful how you talk about American women," he said. "A helluva lot of them read my column."

"Not the same ones who read my stories," said Allison. "You write about real things and real people."

"And your stories weren't real?"

"I suppose they were, to the people who read them, but they never were to me. In my stories, all the heroines were blond and beautiful with green eyes and fabulous figures, and all the men were tall, dark and handsome with square, cleft chins and tweed jackets."

Brody threw back his head and laughed, and under the table Paul Morris gave Allison's hand a gentle squeeze of congratulations.

"Well, you certainly don't have characters like that in your novel," Brody said. "I read it last night. Where'd a kid your age learn so much about smut?"

Allison was suddenly and thoroughly angry. "I'm very sorry that you think my book is smutty, Mr. Brody," she said. "I never intended it to be. All I tried to do was to be truthful and to give an accurate picture of small towns as I know them to be. The things that happen in *Samuel's Castle* happen everywhere, and I should think a man who's smart enough to get the Pulitzer would know that."

"Oh," said Brody, with a smile. "You know about the Pulitzer."

"Yes," Allison lied, praying that she was right. "I remember when you got it. Your picture was in all the papers."

Why, it isn't hard at all, she thought in surprise. I can lie every bit as well as Paul when I put my mind to it.

"You've got a good memory," said Brody. "Most people remember the column I wrote yesterday and that's as far back as they go." A waiter put another glass of beer in front of him and Brody picked it up. "Tell me, Miss MacKenzie," he said, wiping a tiny mustache of foam from his top lip, "what are people in your home town going to say about your book?"

462

"They have already said it," said Allison. "Mr. Jackman, my publisher, sent advance copies to a few people in town and the word circulated very quickly."

"And what have they said?" asked Brody.

Allison's fists clenched and her eyes burned with remembered rage.

"They say that I should be run out of town," she said and her voice quivered. "They say that my mother should sell her house and that my father should lose his job and that we should all leave Peyton Place forever."

"And will you?" Brody asked. "Leave town, I mean."

"Never!" cried Allison. "I was born in Peyton Place and I'm going to live there just as long as it suits me."

Brody looked at her. "I was born in a small town in Indiana," he said. "When people in small towns get riled up they can make things pretty unpleasant for whoever got them mad."

"I know it," said Allison.

Brody drained his glass and another was waiting. "Well, to get back to my first question. I used the wrong word, so I'll rephrase. Where did a girl your age learn so much about sex and sneakiness and perversion?"

"If you come from a small town you don't have to ask me that, Mr. Brody," said Allison. "There are no secrets in a small town."

"Then what you're saying is that Peyton Place taught you everything you know."

"That most certainly is not what I said, Mr. Brody. I merely reminded you what small towns are like."

Brody smiled. "Cagey, aren't you?"

"Not unless you want to think of me that way," said Allison. "I was trying to be truthful."

They ordered lunch then, and Brody asked her casual questions about Peyton Place and the people who lived there.

"Must be quite a town," he said as he stood up to leave. "I'll have to go up there for a visit one of these days."

When he had gone, Paul Morris took Allison's hand and squeezed it hard.

"You did it, sweetheart!" he said.

Allison was tired and angry. "What was the idea of telling him

463

that I'm nineteen years old?" she demanded. "I'm twenty-three, and you know it."

"Honey, that's publicity," said Paul Morris, "and nine-tenths of all publicity is nothing but pretty stories someone made up sitting in an office just like mine. Look. Do you really believe all the crap you read in movie magazines about the stars? Do you really think that our sexy sirens are in their early twenties, that they attend P.T.A. meetings and get up early every morning to make breakfast for their kiddies?"

"I never thought much about it one way or the other," said Allison irritably.

"Well, start thinking, sweetheart," said Paul. "Publicity is used to create an illusion about a place, a thing or a person. An illusion that people will believe because they want to believe it. Publicity is a means of selling merchandise and the merchandise can be a hotel room in Miami, a box of soap powder, or a human being. We're going to sell you, Allison, because if we do it well enough we will, in turn, sell copies of your book."

Allison looked at him in horror. "I'm not something on a bargain counter!" she cried. "I'm a person. Me!"

Paul put a hand on her arm. "Honey, I know that and you know that, and everybody in the world knows that everybody else is a person. But what we are going to do with you is to make you into a very special person. One that millions of people will recognize. They'll know your name, your face and your book. In short, we are going to try to make you into a celebrity."

Allison said, "Now that I'm of age again, I'd like a drink, please."

"You can't have one right now. After today, people here are going to remember that you sat with Jim Brody and that you didn't drink with him. In fact, he'll probably put the fact that you don't drink in his column, so you can't turn around now and do anything to disturb the illusion."

"This is ridiculous," said Allison.

"Is it?" asked Paul. "Listen. We're going to sell you as a genius type. A sweet, untouched, young girl from the country who lived for years with a situation until she could not stand the sham and hypocrisy of it any longer and exploded into print with the truth. Now the public already has the idea that sweet, untouched girl

464

geniuses don't drink, so whenever you are in a place where people might remember, you don't drink. It's as simple as that."

"The whole thing is nothing but outrageous lies!" said Allison.

"Not really," said Paul. "Don't things happen in Peyton Place the way they happened in your novel?"

"Of course they do," said Allison. "But I certainly never meant to imply—"

"Look, doll. You want your book to sell, don't you?"

"Yes, but I still don't see—"

Again he cut her off. "Leave it to me," he said. "And talk to everyone I introduce you to just the way you talked to Brody. Do what I tell you and together we'll make *Samuel's Castle* into the biggest thing that ever hit the book business." He glanced at his watch. "Come on," he said. "We're due over at C.B.S. in twenty minutes. You're going to be interviewed by Jane Dodge. Her show is on in the morning but she tapes all her interviews."

"I've heard her," said Allison. "She has the loveliest, deep voice."

"That's right," said Paul. "The voice of an angel and the soul of a true bitch. Come on. I hope we can get a cab."

"With Jane," said Paul, before they went into the studio, "don't belittle women's magazines, women's organizations or women's anything. She's a professional Woman and has made a big, profitable business out of it."

Jane Dodge wore a large hat, long black gloves and used an ebony cigarette holder. She was so sleek and had been made up with such precision that she looked to Allison like a manufactured article.

"For Christ's sake, Jake," Jane was yelling, as Paul led Allison over to her, "are you going to screw around all afternoon or do we get a show taped?"

"Almost ready, Jane," said the man named Jake.

She turned to meet Allison. "Oh, hello, sweetie," she said. "We'll be able to get going if that dumb bastard ever gets things organized."

Her sharp, quick eyes behind green, harlequin glasses scanned the sheet of notes Paul Morris had handed her and she mumbled under her breath.

"Nineteen. Peyton Place. Only child. First book."

Allison stood watching her, her heart thumping.

"Ready, Jane."

465

Jane Dodge watched the nervous man named Jake and at a signal from him she began to speak in the deep, soft voice that Allison remembered.

"And now, ladies," she said into a microphone, "it gives me great pleasure to introduce all of you to a little girl I met several years ago in New England. Her name is Allison MacKenzie and she's only nineteen, but my little friend has managed to fool quite a few of us. She is the author of the sensational new best seller, *Samuel's Castle* and, girls, if you haven't had an opportunity to read this marvelous book yet, let the dishes go and run to your bookstore. Well. Good morning, Allison. How are you, dear?"

When it was over, Allison's knees were trembling and all she wanted to do was to get out of the hot, stuffy studio and into the fresh air.

"Paul, sweetie," Jane Dodge said. "Leave a copy of that book for me, will you?"

Paul took a copy of *Samuel's Castle* from his briefcase and put it on Jane's desk.

"Thanks a lot, Jane," he said. "It was a great interview."

Allison could not take her eyes off the book Paul had put down. "Haven't you read it?" she asked Jane.

Jane looked at her in astonishment and then she began to laugh. "Sweetie," she said, "with the rat race the way it is these days, I don't even have time to read Lenny Lyons any more."

When Allison and Paul were outside, she turned to him.

"I know men who work in the woods who don't have the vocabulary of that woman," she said. "And as for two-faced hypocrisy, Jane Dodge would make the women of Peyton Place look like children."

"Could be," said Paul cheerfully, "but thousands of women listen to her every morning. And when they listen tomorrow morning they'll hear you. And then they'll run out and buy *Samuel's Castle* because Jane told them to. Because anyone who's a friend of dear old Janie's is a friend of theirs."

What a dirty business this is, Allison thought wearily. And I am part of it now. I have given in to it without a struggle. I want my book to be read. I want it to be a best seller. And so I do these awful things. How easy it is to become a liar and a fraud when you are able to tell yourself you're doing it with the best intentions.

Paul hailed a taxi, but Allison said she wanted to walk. Paul's last words as he drove off were, "Allison, we are going to sell one hell of a lot of books."

Walking crosstown to meet David she felt a moment of fierce hatred for Paul. But it's not Paul, she told herself, he's only doing the job he was hired to do. And he's doing it damn well. It's me. I've become a huckster. I'm not doing the job I trained myself to do. I should be home with Mike and Constance writing my new novel.

But now it was not only the excitement of publication that kept her mind from her work, now there was also Lewis Jackman. For the first time since she met Paul at Kelly's did she think of Lewis, so caught up had she been in the hectic business of publicity. Now, walking the busy street in the bright spring weather, she remembered his voice and the touch of his hands. This is the thing that matters, she told herself, not a few lies to people who make a living out of lying. What's growing between Lewis and me, that is what matters.

As she walked toward the café where David waited for her she thought of him with a pang of guilt. But we don't choose an object for our love, she told herself. Love chooses us. Lovers can always find an excuse for the hurt they do to others, she thought. And the excuse is always love itself.

She met David at an Italian coffeehouse in the West Fifties, a dark place with guttering candles on marble-topped tables. The walls were covered with a dark red cloth that absorbed what little light there was. There were mirrors, speckled and yellowed with age, in which she saw her face, wavering and dark, as if seen through smoke. At the back, the only bright object in the place, stood a great, ornate, silver coffee machine. When the operator depressed one of its long handles, steam hissed through tightly locked coffee grounds and a delicious elixir, the very essence of coffee, dripped drop by drop from a silver faucet into a small cup.

David watched Allison as she entered and looked for him and walked toward his table. He thought she moved with a new assurance. He smiled to himself. Our little Allison is growing up, he thought. Allison dropped wearily into the chair across from David, and the waiter brought coffee and Allison recounted her day. She told David about Paul Morris, Brody and Jane Dodge.

David listened quietly, not interrupting once. Allison was too full of herself to notice how angry David had become and was startled

467

when she finished speaking and heard David's voice tremble with anger as he said, "You're not in this business to sell books! You're supposed to be a writer, not some clown on a radio or television program. Not some idiot running off at the mouth to some fifth-rate lush of a reporter."

"You just shut up, David!" cried Allison, doubly angry because his words echoed her own thoughts. "Maybe you don't care what happens to your books, but I care what happens to mine. What's the good of writing anything if nobody reads what you write?"

"People discover good books for themselves," replied David. "And *Samuel's Castle* is a good book. People would have realized that in time without every paper in the country touting it as a work of pornography."

"It isn't pornography," cried Allison.

"*I* know it isn't," said David. "*You* know it. But what about people who read Jim Brody's column? They're not going to see any of the beautiful things in your work. They're going to buy and read it for your graphic sex descriptions."

"Mind your own damned business," said Allison.

David stood up. He took a newspaper clipping from his pocket and threw it on the table. "Get the news while it's still hot, Allison. Your interview with Brody is in the late afternoon edition. He lost no time. And neither have you. You've got what you wanted, Allison—success with a capital S. It will be interesting to see what you do with it, or what *it* does to you." He smiled bitterly. "We don't seem to have much to say to each other any more, do we?" Then he walked out. Allison sat for a moment without moving; then, she read Brody's column.

"If you want your young girl to learn the facts of life the hard way," Brody had written, "make sure that she's brought up in a town like Peyton Place. That's what happened to the young authoress of a sensational new best seller called *Samuel's Castle*. Here is a book that pulls no punches." The column ended with, "And what of Allison MacKenzie, the youngster who kicked over the rock of New England respectability to expose the rot underneath? She says, quite cheerfully, that business at her mother's dress shop has fallen off by 50 per cent and that her father, the principal of the Peyton Place High School, will probably lose his job. But we don't think that Miss

468

MacKenzie has much to worry about. *Samuel's Castle* should make her rich and famous."

For a moment she felt sick and angry, infuriated by Brody's betrayal. Then she slowly crumpled the newspaper clipping and pressed it into a small hard ball. If that's the way the game is played, she thought, then that's the way I'll play it.

4

IN THE FIRST FIVE DAYS OF ALLISON'S STAY IN NEW YORK SHE GAVE nine interviews to members of the press and to people in radio. She was interviewed twice on television. Before it was over she had become a polished performer, had learned to parry and thrust with the best of them, to think twice before she spoke and to phrase her answers with such care that even the most unethical reporter had a hard time misinterpreting her statements.

On what turned out to be her last night in New York, she dined with Lewis Jackman at a fabulous new restaurant that was then all the rage. It was one of the postwar "expense account" restaurants; real money was never spent there, only company money. The menu was so long that only people of leisure had the time to read it all, and only professional gourmets understood what they read. Waiters stood by to translate as well as to serve.

The headwaiter led Allison and Lewis to one of the "good" tables reserved for celebrities. These tables surrounded a white marble fountain where sprays of water bloomed like an exotic tree.

The headwaiter bowed to Allison as he drew out her chair. "We are very happy to have you here, Miss MacKenzie," he said, and Allison gave him the gracious, noncommittal smile that success had taught her to use.

"I'm very proud of you, Allison," Lewis said. "Only a few weeks ago you were a writer, and today you're an author." His loving smile took the sting out of the words, but Allison understood what he meant and smiled ruefully.

Was it only five days ago? she thought, with wonder. She remembered her outraged innocence at discovering that Jane Dodge had not read her novel. Of all those who had interviewed her since, only one reporter claimed to have read it; and there was one who said he had "perused" it. But they all, each and every one, wrote knowledgeably about it.

Her thoughts were interrupted by the presence at the table of a burly businessman who stood beside Allison's chair and asked for her autograph on the menu. He offered her his small gold pencil. "It's for my wife," he said. Men who asked for her autograph always smiled apologetically and said it was for their wives. Allison wrote her name across the wide margin of the menu and returned it to the man with a smile.

How meaningless, she thought, how goddamned silly this all is. And yet, it had a strong appeal. Only a saint or a psychopath, she thought, would willingly withdraw from the world of the celebrated to an ivory tower. It was something Allison had wanted for a long time, had dreamed of since she was a girl and had traded Hollywood fan magazines with Selena. She had made up her mind: if there was a price to be paid for all this, then she would pay it. But she would not take David's way, would not sneak out the back door. She was young, but not so young that she still believed that art could be found only in a cold-water flat.

"Shall I order for you, Allison?" Lewis asked.

"Please," she said.

And while the waiter hovered with pencil poised above the order pad, and the steward came and consulted with Lewis over the wine list, Allison recalled that day when she walked crosstown and met David at the coffeehouse. She had thought about it often. Success, the knowledge that almost everywhere she was stared at, made her suspicious of herself and her every action. Am I doing this because I *want* to? she often asked herself these days, or am I doing it because Success demands it?

She wondered if she had not provoked the argument with David, whether she had not entered the coffeehouse unconsciously wishing to end their relationship. David was a reminder of her old life, of the days before she became an author and was merely a writer, struggling to achieve something. She had outgrown him.

Allison sometimes found herself thinking—in those rare moments when her new life left her any time for thinking—that Success brought with it a fantastically hastened maturation. It reminded her of those flowers whose bloom had been forced to meet the demand of the market. The maturity may have been artificially induced, but it seemed to her, nevertheless, real. It brought with it a heightened sensitivity, a deeper and sharper perception.

This new insight sometimes revealed to her things she would rather not have seen. About David, for example. His anger at the coffeehouse, she realized now, was motivated in part by envy. He was envious of her success, what must have seemed to him an easy success. He had been working for years, had published four novels, and it had brought him none of the material rewards that he now saw pouring into Allison's lap. It had made him bitter and nasty at the moment she most needed his understanding.

To Allison, it was another lesson in the complexity of life. David's sudden realization of his lack of success, a realization forced on him by knowing Allison, had changed him, just as surely as winning success had changed Allison.

There ought to be some way of ordering success, Allison thought as the waiter served her hot cherry consommé from a silver bowl. In just the right amount. In the perfect quantity for each of us, not too much and not too little. But she knew it could not be ordered that way. Life would not be controlled, it could not be molded into the shapes we wanted it to be.

After the third autograph hunter had interrupted her dinner, Allison said to Lewis, "I feel like such a fraud. I know it's only me, little Allison MacKenzie. Why doesn't everyone else see that?"

"They are blinded to that simple fact, darling, by another simple fact: they do not know you. When they look at you they see the public woman, the figure created by Paul Morris and columnists and interviewers."

He took her hand. He did not do it often; in public he was usually circumspect, he kept up the pretense of the publisher-author relationship. "Nothing very bad can happen to you, Allison, as long as *you* don't forget who you really are."

"I'll never forget," Allison answered.

"No, I don't think you will. I think your practical New England common sense will protect you. I'm not worried about you, Allison. And you mustn't be either. Please try to enjoy this while it lasts. You know, one of the facts you haven't yet faced up to is that it may not last forever."

"While it lasts." She repeated the phrase. It had the sound of tumbrils in it. It chastened her. "I love you for many reasons, Lewis," she said, "and not least of all for your wonderful talent to throw a bucket of cold water on me at just the right moment."

"And I love you. And this wine and"—pointing at Allison—"that face makes me want to leave this place. I want to be alone with you."

Allison picked up her purse. "Tell the driver to hurry," she said, smiling at Lewis and not taking her eyes off him.

In a few minutes they were in a taxi and Lewis was saying to the driver, "Hurry, man. We're on our way to visit a sick friend."

"There's a lot of it around, Mac," the driver said. "Spring is the most dangerous time of year. You gotta watch yourself."

Allison had a hard time suppressing her laughter. She buried her face in Lewis' shoulder. He kissed the top of her head and gently stroked her face and throat.

And when they got to Allison's room, though they had been together every night, they faced each other with passionate longing, with a hungry intensity, and only half undressed they began to seek each other.

Afterward, they smoked in the darkness and talked until dawn. Allison told him that she was going to take an apartment in New York. "I want to be near you, Lewis. I want to be there when you need me. Marriage isn't important to me."

Not now it isn't, Lewis thought, but it will be, it will be. He knew the terrible odds against them, but loving her, desiring her, he fell in with her plans and said nothing of his misgivings. It's just that I've lived so long and seen so much more than she has, he told himself.

And Allison lay in the curve of his protecting arm and asked herself, Have I chosen this because marriage now would interfere with my plans? Is it possible that I don't want to share what I've achieved with anyone? And when finally she fell asleep she groaned in anguish, tormented by her dreams.

472

When she woke at noon Lewis was gone. He had left a note on the desk. *Darling, Only you beside me when I woke this morning could have convinced me that all this was not the most beautiful dream of my life.*

Allison smiled and folded the note. She ordered breakfast sent up to her room and had the operator put in a call to Peyton Place. She wanted to tell Mike and Constance that she was going to stay in New York.

She was sipping her orange juice when the phone rang. It was Constance. Allison's voice was jubilant when she said, "Isn't it wonderful, Mother? *Samuel's Castle* has been out just twelve days and it's already on the best-seller list in the *Times* and *Tribune!*"

"I'm so glad for you, darling," Constance said.

"Mother? What is it? There's something wrong, Mother, I can tell by your voice."

"Oh, darling," Constance's voice broke down. "Oh, darling. Mike's contract hasn't been renewed."

"*What?*"

"That's right. Everybody else at the school got a contract for the coming year except Mike. He's through here."

"But why?" demanded Allison. "Did they give him a reason?"

"They just said they thought it would be better all the way around if he got a job someplace else."

"Well, of all the filthy, rotten tricks!" said Allison.

"Never mind, dear," said Constance. "Just come home as soon as you can. We've got to think about moving."

Allison packed her things hurriedly and before she left the hotel she called Paul Morris.

"Do you know what's happened with all your rotten publicity?" she demanded. "My father's lost his job!"

"What?" shouted Paul.

"He's been fired. Canned. Let go. Is that clear enough?"

"Allison, stay right where you are. I'll be right there."

"Don't bother. I'm leaving here this minute to go home."

"Allison, for God's sake, tell me what happened?"

"There's nothing to tell," said Allison and began to cry. "He's just through in Peyton Place, that's all. We'll have to move and my mother will have to sell her house."

"Allison, I'm truly sorry," said Paul. "I guess you'd better go home. I'll call you in a few days."

Then she phoned Lewis at his office, but he was out and she could only leave an impersonal message for him with his secretary.

As Paul Morris said later, Rossi being fired couldn't have happened at a better time. The papers were hard up for news that night and welcomed his story. Before Allison reached home the front pages of the Boston papers were covered with black headlines about her and her family.

PEYTON PLACE HEAD OUSTED the papers shouted, and under the headlines was the story. According to the press, Michael Rossi had been fired because his stepdaughter, Allison MacKenzie, had written a shocking book about a small New England town. Paul Morris had seen to it that the title of the book was prominently displayed. Allison held the newspapers crushed in her lap as the train swayed toward Peyton Place.

Dear God, what have I done, she wept silently.

• 5 •

NOW IT WAS MAY, AND THE PROCESS OF TURNING NORTHERN NEW ENG-land into a vast summer boardinghouse had begun. Along the "Rocky Coast" of Maine, in the "Heart of the Lakes Region" and "High in the White Mountains" of New Hampshire and "Among the Rolling Hills" of Vermont, summer cottages were given thin coats of paint that would begin to peel and blister by the end of July. Hotel owners unnailed boards from windows and wondered if the front-porch chairs could stand one more season of almost uninterrupted rocking.

Every town that boasted an attraction of any sort was flooded with signs that read, "Rooms. Day. Week. Season," while the more exclusive hotels placed discreet advertisements in the New York

Times that said "Reservations Suggested." Golf courses were rolled and mowed, tennis courts repaved, swimming pools cleaned and filled and cretonne slip covers returned to the seats of wicker furniture.

Highway departments hired extra men to pick up the discarded waxed paper and beer bottles of summer picnickers, and merchandise in native-owned stores was marked up 20 per cent. Northern New England was preparing itself to work at the only big industry it had left—the tourist.

In Peyton Place, Ephraim Tuttle made sure that the circular ceiling fans in his store were in working order and he put up the awning that shielded his front window. To the accompaniment of derisive remarks from Clayton Frazier and the other old men who had occupied the packing-crate seats around his stove all winter long, Ephraim removed his bolts of gingham and calico from their plastic coverings and lined them up in a row on the front counter.

"Gives the place a tone," he said defensively as he did every spring. "Summer folks like tone."

"Goddamned foolishness," said Clayton Frazier.

"Ayeh," said Ephraim in agreement.

But, nevertheless, he began to dismantle his wood and coal burning stove that same afternoon, and the old men moved to the benches in front of the courthouse across the street. The "Season" had officially begun in Peyton Place.

Peyton Place was not a tourist town in the true sense of the word, for it had no lake, ocean front or mountain of its own. But summer people driving west to Vermont, east to the White Mountains or north to Canada usually detoured to Peyton Place in what they called a "side trip." The more morbid of the visitors nudged one another and remembered that "this is the town where that girl murdered her father." They drove with maddening slowness past the Cross house and said, "Her stepfather and she buried him in a sheep pen right there behind that house." But this year they came to stand and stare at Samuel Peyton's castle.

"That's the place that girl wrote the book about," they all said.

"Have you read it?"

"Of course. I loved it. So true to life."

"I hear that the natives in Peyton Place are in an uproar over the book."

"I know it. The poor girl's father lost his job over it. Well, it just goes to prove what I've always said. New England is a fine place to visit but I wouldn't want to live here."

"The narrowness is something fantastic, isn't it?"

"If I were Allison MacKenzie, I'd be worried for my life. No kidding. Some of the faces on the natives have an absolute look of stone."

"And she seems to be such a darling. I saw her on television and she's so sweet looking."

"I put a copy of *Samuel's Castle* in the glove compartment when I knew we were coming up this way. I'll bet if we found her house and went there that she'd autograph it for us."

"Let's ask somebody."

"One of those old men sitting over there."

The pale blue convertible drew to a stop at the curb in front of the courthouse and, without seeming to do so, the old men on the benches stared intently at the two women who got out of the car and approached them. The women wore identical white shorts and striped jersey shirts and their toenails were painted with red, chipping polish. Their shoes were sandals made entirely of thin straps with heels that clacked against the pavement and their noses were red with yesterday's sunburn. They wore harlequin-shaped sunglasses in red frames and carried oversized handbags. They stopped in front of Clarence Mitchell, who occupied the end seat on the bench nearest to them.

Through half-closed eyes, Clarence had watched the car with the out-of-state plates draw to a halt. As soon as it had, he had taken a pocket knife and a piece of wood from a trouser pocket and begun to whittle.

"There's a pair of beauties for ya," he said to his neighbor.

"Fifty if they're a day and got themselves rigged up to look sixteen."

"Reckon they're wearin' iron brazeers under them shirts?" asked Clarence speculatively.

"Must be. Their tits'd hang down to their belly button if they didn't."

"Pardon me," said the first woman to Clarence, "my name is Mrs. James Delafield and this is Mrs. William Cameron." She paused, but when Clarence kept right on with his whittling she went on.

476

"We want to find the house where Allison MacKenzie lives. Could you please direct us?"

Clarence glanced up. "Who?" he asked.

"Allison MacKenzie," repeated Mrs. James Delafield.

Clarence assumed a puzzled air. "Never heard of no MacKenzies around here," he said. "You, John?"

John Barton pushed his hat up over his eyes and looked at the woman.

"Nope," he said. "Nobody around here named that, that I know of."

"But you *must* know her," protested Mrs. William Cameron. "She's very famous. She wrote a best seller."

"Best-selling what?" asked Clarence.

"Why, a *book*," said Mrs. James Delafield. "A best-selling book. Everybody's talking about it. *Samuel's Castle*."

"Don't get much time for readin', myself," said Clarence and went back to his whittling.

The women stood by indecisively for another moment, and then Clayton Frazier, who had remained silent until now, spoke up.

"Why don't you try the telephone book," he said. "Seems as though if there's anybody named MacKenzie livin' here they'd be in the telephone book."

The faces of the two women cleared. "Why, yes!" said Mrs. James Delafield. "Now why didn't we think of that, Elaine?"

Mrs. William Cameron smiled at Clayton Frazier. "Why, of course," she said. "Thank you. Thank you very much."

An almost inaudible chuckle traveled the length of the benches as the two women went back to the car. There was no MacKenzie listed in the Peyton Place telephone directory. Disappointed, the two women drove away.

"Well, at least they wasn't from the newspapers," said Clarence. "Always askin' questions and wantin' to take your picture. That's somethin' in their favor."

"Yep. Twice in one lifetime is twice too many for anybody. Or any town, for that matter."

"Yep. They was worse this last time, though, than they was about Lucas Cross."

"Yep. But this time it didn't last so long."

"You got no call to say anythin', Clayton. The way you was so friendly with that newspaper feller from Boston the first time."

"Friendly with him this time, too," said Clayton. "Nice feller, Tom Delaney. Always was."

"You'd fit in good down to New Yawk or someplace like that, Clayton. Always gettin' your picture in the paper."

"That," said Clayton smugly, as he put his hat back down over his eyes, "is because I am a quaint but typical New England type with a face hewn of the granite of my native land. Said so, right in the *Daily Record.*"

The men laughed again and settled back to rest in the sun and watch the traffic on Elm Street.

The tumult and the shouting engendered by the publication of *Samuel's Castle* and the careful fostering of publicity by Paul Morris was short-lived but decisive. Within seven weeks of publication, Allison's novel had reached the number-one spot on best-seller lists all over the country, and at the end of the second week in June, Bradley Holmes telephoned the biggest news of all.

"Allison?"

"Yes, Brad."

"I've sold it to Hollywood!"

Allison sat down abruptly. "Hollywood?" she cried. "But, Brad, that's marvelous! I can't see how they'll ever make a movie from it, but it's still marvelous."

"Aren't you going to ask me what I got for it?" asked Brad.

"Oh," said Allison, with a quick laugh, "I forgot!"

"Two hundred thousand dollars," said Brad with the same reverence he would have used for "In the name of the Father, the Son and the Holy Ghost."

Allison gasped. "Brad, for Heaven's sake. I can't believe it!"

"It's true, though. Jackman gets 10 per cent and I get 10 per cent. That leaves you with one hundred and sixty thousand dollars."

"It's unbelievable. It's almost indecent."

"Never mind, darling," said Brad. "After taxes the only thing that will seem indecent is the government. Can you come down to New York on Friday to sign the movie contract?"

"I suppose so, if I must."

"How are things in Peyton Place?"

"The same. People still aren't speaking to me, for the most part, and Mike hasn't a job."

"Is your family planning to move?"

"No. They feel the same about things as I. Mike is trying to get a job in one of the towns around here but, so far, nobody'll have him."

"Don't be sad, Allison," said Brad. "We *are* selling books."

"I know," said Allison, and knew before she had hung up that if she had asked Brad, At what price? he would have given her the practical answer.

"At three ninety-five a copy," he would have said.

Allison sat down wearily at her desk where a stack of mail waited. In the beginning it had been exciting to receive fan letters. Where one word of praise for *Samuel's Castle* was enough to make her happy, Allison now opened letter after letter containing nothing but admiration for her work. From all over the United States people wrote to praise her talent and the courage she had shown in exposing ingrown small towns for what they are.

But there were unfavorable letters, too, many of them anonymous, telling Allison that her work was trash and filth not even fit for burning. Men wrote her notes filled with obscenities while others proposed marriage and a few offered to come to Peyton Place to "take her away from all that." Allison and Constance separated the letters into what they called "good" and "bad" stacks, and in the evening Mike read all the bad ones aloud, acting out the part of the writer with such hamminess that Allison and Constance were reduced to helpless laughter.

But although Allison laughed, the unfavorable letters were like the cavity in a tooth to which her mind, like a probing tongue, returned again and again. At times, she was depressed to the point of tears and overwhelmed with the idea that the world was made up entirely of women who had read *Samuel's Castle* and hated her. Constance's rage was like that of a tigress whose young was threatened.

"Of all the goddamned nerve!" Constance shouted. "Some rotten-minded bitch whose husband is probably sleeping with the village whore has the nerve to write like this to Allison!"

"Allison," said Mike calmly, "women who write letters like this are sick. Sick with envy and greed and jealousy. Don't cry. It may sound trite, but try to be a little sorry for her."

"But why does she hate me?" wailed Allison, sounding for all the

479

world like a grade-school child who hasn't been invited to a party. "What did I ever do to her?"

"You wrote a good book and got paid for it and became famous," said Mike flatly. "And this is the way the world turns."

Allison had been back in Peyton Place for over a month, sharing with Mike and Constance their involuntary exile. She spent restless nights prowling about the house, unable to sleep, unable to read. Invariably, dawn found her at the kitchen table writing long letters to Lewis. Her body ached for him; in loneliness, her love for him grew. She lived for his letters, and they came nearly every day, full of a gentle, enveloping love.

Both Mike and Constance told her to leave, assured her there was no reason for her to stay. But she could not leave them. She had brought this trouble upon them and she knew that her staying with them was an act of devotion they needed so badly now.

She had not told them about Lewis. That was a secret she shared with no one. She held it close to herself with a superstitious fear, as if she were afraid that spoken aloud it would disappear into thin air.

• 6 •

PEYTON PLACE HAD BECOME A SOLIDLY DIVIDED CAMP. PEOPLE WERE either for or against Allison MacKenzie, and there was no middle ground. The majority was almost frighteningly against her. People who had done things far worse than those described in *Samuel's Castle* were the first ones to stand up and attack Allison.

"How does she know about all them dirty things in the book unless she done them herself?"

"She never saw or heard anything like that in Peyton Place!"

"I always thought that Rossi feller was too good lookin' and slick for his own good."

"You wouldn't think Constance would stand for such goings on."

"Always was uppity, Allison was. And a liar."

"The whole kit and kaboodle of them oughta be made to leave town."

"Well, Rossi won't be teaching here any more, I'll guarantee you that," said Roberta Carter. "Marion Partridge and I took care of him."

And that much was true. Charles Partridge had been elected to the school board when Leslie Harrington had decided not to run again, but when it came to the question of Rossi and his contract to teach for the coming year, old Charlie had been no match for his wife and Roberta.

"He's not going to teach here, Charles," said Marion, "and that's the end of it. Roberta and I are voting against him and there is nothing you can do."

"This has always been a decent town," said Roberta, "with a decent high school. Allison MacKenzie did not learn filthy language at the Peyton Place High School, nor did she gain her knowledge of filth and perversion in this town. Young people learn things like that in the home."

Except Ted, thought Roberta with the sickening coldness in her stomach that was always there whenever she thought of Ted and his wife, Jennifer. He was always a good, decent boy until he married. He never learned anything else but decency and goodness in his home. It was Jennifer that had taught him all those bad things.

"You're absolutely right, Roberta," agreed Marion. "Believe me, I know people and I'm not often wrong. I always told Charles that Constance MacKenzie was no better than she should be. I'll never set foot in that store of hers again, I can tell you. It was bad enough when she hired Selena Cross, a confessed murderess, to work for her, but when she led her own flesh and blood into the paths of wickedness that was the bitter end."

"Oh, for Christ's sake," said Charles Partridge in disgust.

"Charles," said Marion icily, "there is no need to curse. You sound like a character out of that filthy book."

"I've been saying 'Oh, for Christ's sake' ever since I learned to talk," said Charles.

"Well," said Roberta, "I'd certainly never stand for that kind of talk from Harmon."

481

"I'll bet," said Charles in a rare burst of spirit. "You probably had all of that kind of talk you could take from old Doc Quimby."

"Charles!" said Marion in a cold voice, "that's enough!"

"Don't feel badly, Marion," said Roberta. "Charles knows that it's wicked to speak badly of the dead."

"Oh, for Christ's sake," said Charles.

It was at that moment that Doc Swain entered the school board office and said, "As soon as the prayer meeting's over, I'd like to say a few words about the reappointment of Mike Rossi."

"You're too late," said Roberta.

"It's already been put to the vote," Marion told him. "The school board is now on record, as of this date, against the renewal of the contract of Mike Rossi."

Charles Partridge shrugged his shoulders, indicating to Matt that he had tried and failed.

"Now that I'm here," Matt said, "I think I'll say my piece anyway."

"If you have anything to say, you can say it at town meeting, Matt," Roberta told him.

Matt ignored her. "Mr. Chairman," he said, and Charles quickly said, "The chair recognizes Dr. Matt Swain."

Matt stood at the long board table, across from Roberta and Marion. "It seems we aren't content with pillorying Allison MacKenzie because she had the courage to hold up a mirror and make us look at ourselves, we have to attack her through her stepfather and punish an innocent man because *he* has the courage to stand by his child."

Doc Swain put his hands in his pockets, bent his body forward and looked down at the table. "It's a sad day for all of us," he said in a low voice. "We've come a long way from our early days in this land when our grandparents, those misguided fools, thought that courage was a virtue." He raised his voice. "I ask you this, ladies. I ask you this. Will we now reward cowardice? Since courage has become a punishable offense in your eyes, I propose we set up statues to the men who beat their wives and abandon their children."

Roberta stirred restlessly in her chair, her mouth drawn to a tight line. It was as if she thought that by keeping her mouth closed tight she would not be able to hear Matt's words.

482

"Years ago," Matt continued, "years ago I was afraid that Peyton Place was too much isolated from the world. Now I have the opposite fear. I'm afraid we have come all too close to the foolishness —and worse than foolishness—that's raging through our land today. Radio and television is a mixed blessing. It looks to me like we're trying to get into the act—and in the worst possible way."

Roberta cleared her throat, and Marion tried to catch Charles Partridge's eye, but Doc Swain would not wait for them.

"We've joined the rest of the country with a vengeance. We're setting back the clocks and imitating the witch hunters who are a shame on the pages of our history. We who prided ourselves above all else on our individualism are now demanding that everyone conform. Be like us, think like us—or into exile you go."

He turned to Charles and in a tired voice said, "I think that's about it, Charlie. The only hope I have left is that one day—and I trust it will be sooner rather than later—we'll look back on what we have done and have the decency to feel ashamed of ourselves. I thank you, ladies, for your kind indulgence."

And he turned and walked out of the room, leaving Roberta and Marion speechless.

"Do I hear a motion for adjournment?" Charles asked.

Marion and Roberta were not the only women in Peyton Place who stopped shopping at Constance's Thrifty Corner Apparel Shoppe. Dozens of women who had bought exclusively from her now made shopping expeditions to Concord and Manchester and they saw to it that their daughters did the same. Occasionally a husband, with all the furtiveness of an amateur about to hold up a bank, sneaked into the store to buy a pair of socks, but for the most part the men too kept away.

"It'll blow over," said Constance, determined to keep her shop open. "In a little while they'll have something else to stew about and they'll be back. To give me the newest gossip if nothing else."

Matthew Swain roared his outrage to anyone who would listen to him. Those who would not listen voluntarily had an arm gripped in the doctor's firm grasp and were forced to stand still while Matthew talked, and he pulled no punches in his words.

"What the hell are you looking so outraged for?" he demanded of several of his patients. "Maybe you can fool the town, but you can't fool me."

And then the doctor was liable to drag up some bit of scandal or gossip about the patient himself, and when the patient left Matt's office he was apt to keep his mouth shut about *Samuel's Castle* in the future.

Seth Buswell, as had always been his policy in the Peyton Place *Times,* took neither side. But he reprinted only favorable reviews of *Samuel's Castle* and only the favorable letters which came to him for doing so. He kept it up in the face of diminishing advertising and canceled subscriptions, and Allison would never have known of this if Norman Page had not told her.

"Fifteen people canceled yesterday," he told Allison. "I don't know how much longer he'll be able to keep going."

Allison went at once to Seth. "I appreciate everything you've done, Seth," she said, "but please don't hurt yourself like this any more. Print the bad reviews. Heaven knows there are plenty of them. And as for unfavorable letters, I can bring them down to you by the bushel basket."

Seth smiled at her. "Remember, Allison," he said, "what you said to me once, a long time ago, about men standing up to be counted?"

"Yes," she said, "I remember."

"Well, I'm standing up. Count me." He picked up his jacket. "Now that's enough of the long faces and the noble talk. Come on over to Hyde's. I'll buy you a cup of coffee."

"Thank you, Seth," said Allison very humbly.

"Chin up, Allison. Summer's coming. There'll be plenty of things happening then, and plenty for people to talk about."

"I hope so," said Allison, and took Seth's arm as they crossed Elm Street.

And as the weeks went by, flowing as gently as melting butter from spring into summer, Seth's words of prophecy began to turn into words of truth.

· 7 ·

ONE SUNDAY AFTERNOON, WHEN HE WAS SIX YEARS OLD, TIMOTHY Randlett did an impersonation of Al Jolson singing "Mammy." This one performance had been enough to convince not only his mother, Peg Randlett, but also the assorted aunts, uncles and cousins who were relaxing in the Randlett living room, passively digesting a heavy dinner, that Timothy was born to be an actor.

"I always knew he was different," said Peg Randlett to her husband, Sam. "He was born with a gift."

Sam Randlett was one of six brothers and four sisters and he was the first one of his family to "Make Good." Sam was a foreman in a brewery in Newark, New Jersey, and he made what was described, in the idiom of his family, as a Good Week's Pay. But when Peg began to spend money in a fashion referred to by her sisters and brothers-in-law as Hand Over Fist for dancing and elocution lessons for Timothy, Sam rebelled.

"Money don't come that easy, Peg," he said. "I work plenty hard for my week's pay. Too hard for you to be throwing it away on foolishness."

"Sam, I should think you'd be ashamed of yourself. A man in your position denying his son the advantages."

"Suffering God! Is it an advantage to spend money so that you can dress the boy up in a velvet suit and make him show off in front of the family every Sunday? I don't mind telling you my sister Helene thinks there's something the matter with Tim. The way he's always off in a dream world someplace and won't play with his cousins like all the other kids."

"Helene has no soul," said Peg. "She's got those three stupid children of hers and a husband that'll never amount to anything and she's just jealous of you and Tim."

485

"Peg, that's enough!" roared Sam. "She's my sister and she's a good woman."

"Then tell her to keep her nose out of our business," retorted Peg. "If she's so good, she'll do that much."

"I won't stand for any more," said Sam. "You're turning the boy into a sissy and a pantywaist."

"Timmy is going to be a great actor when he grows up," said Peg, "and neither you nor any of your brothers and sisters are going to stand in his way. You wait and see, Sam Randlett. Someday you'll be sorry."

By the time Tim was nine years old, Peg Randlett's plans had been a long time made. One day, after Sam had left for the brewery, she hauled her suitcases and her son into a waiting taxicab, made a stop at the bank where she withdrew all the money from a joint savings account she had shared with Sam, and she and Tim boarded a train for Hollywood, California.

Timmy Randlett had a mop of blue-black curly hair, enormous blue-green eyes and the pallor and mien of a choirboy. Although he was of only average intelligence, he had a remarkable amount of poise for a child his age and he had learned early in life to take orders and direction. Besides, as one Hollywood producer put it, Timmy could cry good. One of the major Hollywood studios cast him in a picture as a woebegone orphan who is taken in, befriended, taught and loved by an aging, crusty sea captain, only to have the welfare society step in and attempt to remove the child from this unconventional, unsanitary environment. But the social worker that the welfare society sends to investigate is young and pretty, and the sailor who helps the old sea captain around the lighthouse is young and handsome, and together the two of them unearth the fact that the sea captain is, in reality, the father of the orphan child's mother who ran away from home at the age of sixteen to marry a carnival barker. The smash ending of the film showed the orphan child sitting in the lap of the man he now knew to be his Grampy, with his little, thin arms encircling the social worker and the sailor, tears of gratitude running down his pale cheeks. The picture was called *The Littlest Sea Captain* and it made Timmy Randlett a star who shone brightly in the Hollywood firmament until he was fifteen years old. Then he was a has-been, with stringy legs, a hollow chest and pimples.

Peg returned to the East with her son. She took an apartment in New York and saw to it that Timmy finished his education. But it wasn't easy. Twenty-room mansions with swimming pools and fifteen servants are expensive in Hollywood, to say nothing of chauffeured limousines and furs and jewelry and handmade suits. By the time Timmy, who was now called Tim, was sixteen years old there was very little money left. Producers and directors who had wooed Peg Randlett with money and attention and offers during Tim's short career now refused even to speak to her on the telephone, and people nagged her about things like the rent, the gas bill and the unpaid balances on her checking accounts. She died when Tim was nineteen, hating her son for giving her everything and then, when she had just begun to get used to it, snatching it all away with his awkwardness and his acne. Peg Randlett should have clung to life with a little more determination, for by the time he was twenty, Tim Randlett had begun the long, laborious trip known as the comeback.

During the next fifteen years, Tim Randlett worked hard at every acting job he could get. He acted in soap operas and played Voo-Doo the Magician in a radio serial. He took small parts in Broadway productions and slightly larger ones with road companies. With the advent of television he found himself almost constantly employed, but he left New York every summer just the same to act with various stock companies. In barns, tents and old theaters made of broken clapboards, in small-town auditoriums and small-city music halls, Tim Randlett was a star.

He was thirty-six years old the summer he signed with the Barrows Company to play stock at the Barn Theater at Silver Lake, eight miles north of Peyton Place. He had been at the lake only three days when Seth Buswell drove up and asked to interview him.

"I'm with the Peyton Place *Times*," Seth said. "We're not much of a paper, by big-city standards, but we get around. It'll be free advertising for your play, if nothing else."

Tim had just finished with a late afternoon swim and was standing on the beach, drying himself with a white towel. He was a shade over six feet tall with a slender, wedge-shaped body that appealed to women and was the envy of older, paunchier men. His blue-black hair was dusted with white at the sides of his head, but his deeply tanned face was youthful and unlined. Seth Buswell patted his wide belly and sighed.

"Sure," Tim was saying. "And I have heard of Peyton Place. I guess everyone has since *Samuel's Castle* came out. Do you know the girl who wrote it?"

"Known her since she was a baby," said Seth.

"Wonderful!" said Tim. "I'd love to meet her. Think you could fix it?"

"Might," said Seth. "Want to take a ride over to Peyton Place? We can talk on the way."

"Give me ten minutes to dress," said Tim.

Seth sat down on a tree stump and watched the actor run swiftly away from him, toward a building at the other end of the beach. Seth glanced at his watch and sighed again.

"Nothing like a man like that to make a man like me feel old, fat and foolish," he thought woefully.

Later, on the same afternoon, Selena Cross locked the front door of the Thrifty Corner behind her and crossed the street to Hyde's Diner for a solitary dinner. On this particular evening, Joey was attending a class party and would not return home until nine-thirty. Selena did not like to eat alone in the Cross house.

"Evenin', Selena," said Corey Hyde, as she sat down in a booth. "Joey out gallivantin'?"

"His class is having a clambake down at Meadow Pond," said Selena.

"Oh. Things pretty slow over at the Thrifty Corner, ain't they?"

"We're getting along," said Selena, a little edge of annoyance to her voice.

It had been a long, hot day, and in almost nine hours Selena had sold only one blouse, two pairs of socks and one pony-tail clip.

"Rotten shame, I say," said Corey. "All that fuss over one little book. Mess of foolishness, I call it."

"What's good for dinner, Mr. Hyde?" said Selena. "I'm starved."

"Pot roast," said Corey, a little put out at Selena's lack of sociability.

"Is that all?"

"Nope. Got some pork chops, if you want, but they're no good. Mostly fat. Summer folks'll eat 'em, though. Got some fish chowder, too, but that's canned."

488

Selena sighed and lifted her heavy, dark hair away from her neck.

"Can you make me a salad?" she asked. "Something cold, with a lot of cucumbers in it."

"Sure," said Corey. "Put some crabmeat in it too, if you want. But that ain't no kind of meal for a girl's been workin' hard all day."

Selena let the remark about working hard pass. "I'll have the salad, Mr. Hyde," she said. "With crabmeat and a tall glass of iced tea." She opened a book and began to read.

"Humph," muttered Corey, heading for the kitchen. "Ain't like Selena to be so touchy."

And it wasn't. But lately, Selena herself had to admit that she was quite often what Corey called "touchy" and what she referred to as "cranky." At times, she was even short with Joey.

"You've got spring fever or something," said Joey.

"Spring fever in summer?" asked Selena.

"Don't split hairs," said Joey. "There's something ailing you, and I'm trying to find a polite term for it."

It took Selena a long time before she admitted to herself that she was bored. Not only with the shop and its slackened business, but with herself and her life. Boredom, with a little thread of fear running through and under it. Occasionally she went out to dinner with one of the salesmen who came to the Thrifty Corner, but the word had circulated quickly through their clubby circle. Selena Cross doesn't sleep around. So it was, for the most part, the older, more settled men who asked her out. She saw more of Peter Drake, the young attorney who had defended her at her trial, than she did of any other man. Peter took her dancing and sometimes to the theater, down in Boston. They ate dinner together frequently, either at restaurants at White River or at Selena's house, and, most important of all to Selena, Peter and Joey got along well together. Every time Peter took her out, he asked her to marry him, and every time her answer was the same.

"I can't, Peter."

"You're not in love with anyone else, are you, Selena?"

"You know better than that."

"You're not still thinking about Ted Carter, are you?"

"I don't think anything about Ted any more. I don't even dislike him."

"Selena, I'm in love with you."

"I know," she said. "I'm sorry, Peter."

"It's not all that business about Lucas, is it? You're not afraid of me because I'm a man or anything like that?"

"Peter, will you please stop with the two-bit, street corner psychiatry? Lucas wasn't a man, he was an animal. I never thought of him as a man and what I remember of him certainly hasn't turned me into a couch case. Now will you please leave me alone?"

"Selena, what are you waiting for? What do you want?"

"I don't know, I tell you. I don't know what ails me."

"I love you, Selena. I'm not asking you to love me back all at once. Marry me. Maybe with time—"

"I can't, Peter. I wish I could, but I can't."

But all the same, there were times when Peter Drake was a comfort. She could rest her head on his shoulder and give him her troubles to carry for her. If I married him, he'd be good to me. And good to Joey. But at other times, when her boredom was like a prickly sweater, making her itch with impatience and annoyance, she thought, Peter is such a bore. All that love is like too much ice cream. He's tiresome and I wish he'd find himself a nice girl and settle down and leave me alone.

I'm a pig, she thought in self-flagellation. Peter is good and kind and I should either marry him or let him go.

But time went by, and Peter still courted her, and Selena kept on saying No.

Sometimes she would wake in the night, covered with perspiration and feeling the hard, hurtful beating of her heart.

"What's happening to me?" she asked silently, in panic. "Where am I going? Is this all there is to life?"

Often, she caught herself in an attitude of waiting, but she could not think of what it was she was waiting for, nor for whom, nor why.

"There you are," said Corey Hyde, putting a plate down in front of her. "Crabmeat salad. That enough mayonnaise for you?"

"That's fine, Mr. Hyde," said Selena. "Thank you."

"Eat it up," said Corey. "Make you feel better."

At the same moment that Selena dipped her fork into her salad, Seth Buswell stopped his car in front of Hyde's Diner.

"Don't know about where you come from," he said to Tim Randlett, "but in Peyton Place it's suppertime. We can't go calling on

490

Allison MacKenzie for another hour or so. Come on. I'll buy you a sandwich."

"Good," said Tim, smiling. "This will be my wild night on the town."

Selena Cross lifted her head when she heard the door to the diner open.

"Well, if this isn't luck!" said Seth. "Now we can eat with you, Selena."

Selena barely saw Seth at all. Her eyes stared into those of the man with him, and she could not look away. Usually, she noticed everything about a person she was seeing for the first time. Her glance took in every detail of coloring, structure and clothing, but with this stranger she saw nothing but eyes. They were a blue-green color, the kind to which Selena had always referred privately as "lucky eyes," for she had noticed the same coloring in photographs of handsome, talented people, the ones upon whom the gods had showered extra gifts, leaving the blue-green eyes behind as the only external sign of their generosity.

"Selena," Seth was saying, "this is Tim Randlett. Tim, Selena Cross."

It was as if Seth had pulled a lever, releasing her, so that she could move again, and speak.

"How do you do, Mr. Randlett?" she said. "Hello, Seth. Please sit down."

"Tim, here, is with the summer theater up at Silver Lake," said Seth. "He's an actor."

"Yes, I know," said Selena. "I've seen you in movies, Mr. Randlett."

Tim laughed. "You must have been a very little girl. That was a long time ago."

"Not so very," said Selena. "My friend, Allison MacKenzie, and I used to go to the movies every Saturday."

"And, speaking of Allison—" began Seth, glancing at his watch, "we'd better eat and—"

"Yes," interrupted Tim Randlett quickly. "If you have to see her, Mr. Buswell, I imagine you'd better run along." He turned to Selena. "May I have dinner with you?" he asked.

Selena closed her book, not remembering to mark her place, and looked up at him.

"Yes," she said. "Yes. I'd like that very much."

As Seth Buswell said to Matthew Swain later that night over a drink, "And that was when I knew that I was *de trop*, as they say."

"As who says?" demanded Matthew, through the beginnings of a small alcoholic glow.

"A bunch of fairies I went to college with," said Seth with Scotch-and-water dignity. "Not that I consorted with them, mind you, but I sometimes overheard their conversations."

"Seth," said Matthew Swain, "you are one of the few remaining members of a species commonly known as bullshit artist. If you ever got anywhere near a fairy, you'd run like hell the other way, worried pissless over your virtue."

"And you, sir, are a vile-tongued old man."

"Maybe vile-tongued and old, but I'd never be so goddamned dumb as to leave Selena with some actor I'd picked up. How do you know what kind of fellow he is?"

Seth swirled ice around in his glass. "Seemed like a decent enough sort," he said.

"What d'you mean by that? Decent enough sort."

"Well, you know. Polite and well spoken."

"On the outside," said Matthew Swain. "How do you know what he's like on the inside?"

"I wasn't with him long enough to know," said Seth, "and even if I had been, and he turned out to be a son-of-a-bitch, there wouldn't have been a thing I could have done. The two of them just looked at each other, and the air between them was enough to give anyone an electric shock."

"You're full of shit and talking like a teen-age poet," roared Matthew. "Things like that don't happen."

Seth Buswell finished his drink and poured himself another.

"Yes, they do, Matt," he said finally. "Yes, they do. I was there, and I saw it happen."

· 8 ·

IN PEYTON PLACE, THE BLACK-TARRED SIDEWALKS SOFTENED IN THE summer sun and were scarred with U-shaped heel marks that would show forever. Green Meadow Pond was filled with screaming, splashing children, and all day long the cicadas hummed in the trees. But it was a good summer, with rain in proportion to sunlight, so that the northern countryside had an almost tropical lushness. There was a heavy, ripe greenness to everything that stunned the granite-spined farmers, who were too used to either drought or the puny growth caused by no sunshine at all.

"There's somethin' almost indecent about it," said Kenny Stearns aloud, snipping still another red rose from one of his heavily laden bushes. He looked at the thick green of his lawn and saw his apple tree with its burden of swelling fruit so heavy that the branches hung almost to the ground. "Yep," he said. "Almost indecent. Like a whore with big breasts and honey between her legs."

It was easy, that year, to blame the unheard-of, green summer for just about everything. At the Harrington Mills, workers shirked their jobs and gazed out the factory windows while Leslie screamed in impotent rage and blamed the weather. Young girls who had clung to their virginity with leechlike tenacity now surrendered, with little squeals of anguished joy, to the erect demands of their teen-aged lovers. They returned home with their behinds covered with poison ivy, their arms dotted with mosquito bites and their hair full of pine needles.

As Matthew Swain said to Seth Buswell, "If all the maidenheads lost in the woods this summer were laid end to end, they'd reach clear from here to the planet Saturn."

Fathers blamed mothers, mothers blamed boys, boys blamed

girls, girls blamed themselves and everybody blamed the weather for everything except the behavior of Selena Cross. For Selena there was no excuse in the eyes of Peyton Place.

"Who is he?"

"Actor feller from over to Silver Lake."

"Come up here from down to New Yawk."

"Usta be in the movin' pitchers."

"Hmph. Think a girl like Selena'd know better. After all, it ain't as if she was born yesterday and didn't know no better."

"Ayeh. There's one girl learned whatcha call the facts of life early. And the hard way."

"Think she'd have a little shame, a girl like that. But no. There she goes, flauntin' herself right in front of the whole town."

For Selena Cross it was a summer of such unbearable sweetness that every moment was almost like pain. There was an ache in not being able to clutch every second that passed, to have to let the hours go, and finally the whole day.

"When I was young," said Selena, "I thought I knew all there was to know about love."

"And what do you know now, my darling?" asked Tim, stroking the soft inside of her arm. "I mean now that you're an old woman of twenty-five."

"I know that I didn't know a thing until now," she said, and turned to rest her forehead gently on his chin.

They were lying side by side on the beach at Silver Lake, talking softly, caressing each other.

"This is agony of the worst sort," said Tim, his lips brushing her ear. "To lie here next to you and be able to touch only small bits and pieces of you. Your ear, your hand, your ankle. It's a form of masochism."

As always, his voice reached deep inside of her, so that her whole body was flushed with excitement.

"Do I turn pink all over when you talk to me like that?" she asked.

"Not really," he teased. "Anyone looking at you would only think that you had a mild case of sunburn."

"I'm not sunburned."

"Selena. If you don't stand up and come with me at once, there's going to be a terrible scene right here on the beach because

I'm going to start taking off your bathing suit in exactly three seconds."

Selena sat up. "Come on," she said and led the way to his car.

From the moment Selena had met Tim in Hyde's Diner, she had known the way it would be between them and she had wondered, too, how it would end, for in the beginning there had been no feeling of permanence for her in their relationship. The emotion between them was too ephemeral to be named, too delicate to be used as a rock on which to build.

"Let's walk," Tim had said to her that first night when they had finished dinner.

And she had gone with him at once. Outside, he had taken her hand in his and they had walked through town to Memorial Park.

"There are nights like this on islands in the South Seas," he said.

"Oh?" asked Selena. "Tell me about an island in the South Seas."

"The night is just like this," said Tim. "All black and heavy with stars. You can smell a hundred different flowers all at once and their perfume fills you with a longing and languor such as you've never known before. You lie on a white beach and the ocean is only a whisper at your feet, soft and tractable and not frightening at all. You could reach up and touch the moon if you wanted to and it would be as soft as yellow cotton in your hand."

"How lovely," said Selena softly. "I wish I could go there one day."

Tim looked down at her. "You're there now," he said. "Can't you smell it and feel it?"

"Is it really like this?"

"I imagine so."

"But don't you know?"

"I've never been there, but I'm sure it's just like this."

Selena sat up straight on the bench they shared.

"You mean you've never been there at all? You just made all that up about the flowers and the moon?"

Tim laughed. "Yes," he said. "I made it up."

Selena smiled at him in the dark. "You're just like Allison MacKenzie," she said. "She used to do the same thing to me when we were in school. She'd make up the most fantastic things and have me believing her, then she'd laugh and tell me she had made everything up."

"Then she is far more honest than I," said Tim. "Sometimes I make things up and they become so real that I believe them myself and I never do confess the truth."

They sat for a long time, hands loosely clasped, Selena's head resting easily on his shoulder. He told her about his work in New York and Hollywood and about the way things had been for him once and the way they would be again.

"There is only one bad thing about fame," he said. "Once you have had it you can never do without it again."

"Is that really the only bad thing about it?" asked Selena.

"You bet it is," said Tim. "And don't believe any of the nonsense you read that tells you differently. Don't take the movie queens seriously when they tell you how rough it is to be rich and well known and in demand. They all whine about lack of privacy, but leave them alone for five minutes and they're on the phone to their agents asking where everyone is."

"You too?" asked Selena.

"No," said Tim. "At least I'm honest about that."

"And is that all you're honest about?"

He turned her hand over in his and kissed her palm.

"No," he said. "I'm going to be honest about you."

It was after midnight when they walked to Selena's house.

"Come in and meet my brother Joey," said Selena.

"I'd love to meet your brother Joey," said Tim. "And your mother and father and anyone else who concerns you."

Selena felt her hand stiffen in his. "My mother and father are dead," she said. "There's only Joey. Just Joey and me."

Tim had felt the change in her. "I'm sorry," he said. "But I'd still like to meet Joey. And I have to call a cab."

"A cab?" asked Selena.

"Yes," said Tim. "I have to get back to Silver Lake somehow."

"But how did you get here?"

"With that newspaperman—what's-his-name?"

"Seth Buswell," said Selena. "And I have sad news for you. There are no taxicabs in Peyton Place. I thought you had your own car with you."

"No problem," said Tim, as they walked into Selena's living room. "I'll stay at a hotel."

"Not in Peyton Place," said Selena. "We don't believe in hotels here. They attract tourists."

"Hello," said Tim.

Joey Cross looked at Tim for a long moment. "Hello," he said at last.

"Joey," said Selena. "This is Tim Randlett."

"I know," said Joey.

"Do you?" asked Tim, laughing. "Has my minuscule fame spread so swiftly in Peyton Place?"

"Nope," replied Joey and found himself laughing along with Tim. "Heard you and Selena had met down to Hyde's at suppertime."

"And that," said Selena, going into the kitchen to make coffee, "is the story of Peyton Place. Joey, get some sheets and a blanket out of the linen closet. Tim is staying here for the night."

"Fine," said Joey. "Tomorrow the town will really have something to talk about."

Later, Selena lay still in bed. The house was so quiet that all she could hear was the sound of her own breathing and the beat of her own heart. She could not relax but lay stiffly, every nerve in her body tensely aware of Tim, asleep on the couch in the living room. A sharp resentment went through her.

How can he sleep? she wondered angrily, as annoyed with herself as she was with him.

But a few minutes later she heard a sound. Tim coughed, and then she heard the scrape of his cigarette lighter.

Selena smiled in the dark, and was at last able to sleep.

Within less than a week, Peyton Place talked of little other than Selena Cross and Tim Randlett. Tim was spending every spare minute away from the theater with her, and every day Connie Rossi went to the Thrifty Corner so that Selena could take time off.

"At least it's good for business," Connie told Mike. "People are coming into the store hoping to gossip about Selena."

"When are we going to meet him?" asked Mike.

"Friday," Connie replied. "They're coming to dinner."

497

"Good," said Allison, coming into the room. "He can tell me all about Hollywood."

"I wonder," said Mike, "which member of our genteel population elected himself to tell Tim Randlett all about Selena Cross."

"I don't know," replied Connie, "but you can bet somebody did."

And, of course, somebody had. It was the policy of the Barn Theater to take in a group of young people every year whom the management called apprentices. For a sizable fee, the apprentices were allowed to paint scenery, act as ushers, look after props and do every other job that was beneath the dignity of actors. One of these was a tall, leggy girl from White River named Helen Dowd, who had sighted Tim Randlett the moment he landed at Silver Lake and had decided to make him her own. When Tim began to make daily trips to Peyton Place, Helen lost no time in telling him, in explicit detail, about Selena.

"Her stepfather," she said. "And she murdered him in cold blood. He was in the Navy and he came home on leave and she killed him with a pair of fire tongs. Then she buried him in a sheep pen."

"Why?" asked Tim, lighting a cigarette and blowing a leisurely smoke ring.

"What do you mean, 'Why'?" demanded Helen, enraged at Tim's lack of reaction.

"I mean, why did Selena kill her stepfather?"

"Oh. Well, it came out at the trial that it was incest. At least that's what they called it. But there are plenty of people around who don't believe it. Maybe Lucas Cross was a drunkard, but lots of people don't believe that he'd do anything like that to Selena."

"Anything like what?" asked Tim.

Helen blushed. "Well, you know. Like what I said. Incest."

"Do you believe it?"

Helen was angry. "I don't see that you've got any call to cross-examine me," she said. "After all, I just told you for your own good."

The next day Tim went to the public library at White River and looked at the back copies of the Boston newspapers that had carried the story of Selena's trial. When he had finished, he sat for a long time, smoking and staring at motes of dust caught in a sunbeam that slashed across the library floor. Without knowing that it was happening, Tim's personality and character were changing to meet the demands of the new situation which faced him now.

Sometimes, the personality of an actor is like a blank slate. When he is confronted with a new role, the slate is written upon and the actor becomes what he reads until the part has been played. Then the slate is wiped clean and is ready for still another role.

When Tim Randlett left the library at White River that afternoon he knew that he must go to Selena. He would not tell her what he knew directly, but he would, nevertheless, let her know that he knew. He would be gentle with her, yet masterful, and he would teach her not to be afraid and to trust in him. He would restore her faith in love and in men. As he drove toward Peyton Place, Tim was filled with an almost saintlike feeling of gentleness spiced with the emotion of a virile young man and topped with an overwhelming sense of outrage at the thought of Lucas Cross.

Selena watched him walk toward her and, without knowing what had happened, she knew that he was somehow subtly different.

"Hi," she said, and was annoyed with herself because her voice almost quivered.

"Hello, darling."

He drove away from Peyton Place without a word, and Selena turned to him.

"Where are we going?" she asked.

"My place," he said.

Immediately, her arms were covered with goose flesh and she quivered in the hot July sun.

Inside, Tim's cottage was cool and dim and quiet. From very far away, on the other side of the lake, came the faint shouts of the summer bathers and there was a smell of sunshine and water and pine. Selena turned from where she had been standing in front of the empty fireplace.

"Why did you bring me here?" she asked.

"Because I've never kissed you," said Tim. "And when I do I didn't want it to be in a parked car or in the back room of the Thrifty Corner or on a bench in the park." He walked toward her and stood in front of her without touching her. "I want it to be here where it's quiet and where no one will come barging in, and I think you do, too."

"I want to go home," said Selena in a frightened whisper.

Very gently, he put his hands on the sides of her face.

"Selena," he said. "Look at me." He looked long and deeply into the eyes she raised to his. "Who am I?" he asked. "What's my name?"

"You're Tim," she said, and the color of his eyes was like the ocean. "You're Tim Randlett."

"Yes," he said. "I'm Tim Randlett. I'm Tim and I love you." He put his arms around her then, but still he looked into her eyes. "I'm Tim," he said again. "I'm not Lucas Cross."

"Don't!" cried Selena, and tried to pull away from him.

But he held her tightly against him, and with one hand he rubbed the small of her back and then the nape of her neck.

"I'm not going to hurt you, darling," he said over and over. "Please don't be afraid of me. I love you, darling."

And at last Selena stopped trembling. "Tim," she said. "Tim."

"Yes, darling," he said softly. "Tim."

He kissed her softly with his lips together in dry, unhurried kisses, and all the while he stroked her as if she were a frightened kitten he was trying to calm. He undressed her slowly, almost lazily, and when he put her on the bed it was as if she were that same kitten, quieted now, but who might, at any moment, jump up and run away in terror. He made her look at him but did not speak as his hands caressed her thighs and pressed gently against her abdomen. He watched her eyes grow dark and heavy and still he continued to stroke her, and when he kissed her the next time it was Selena who opened her lips, who probed against his teeth with her tongue. Only then did his fingertips seek her breasts, caressing and stroking until she responded to him.

"Open your eyes," he said. "Selena, open your eyes."

He loved her slowly and watched, exultant, as the wildness grew in her eyes, as her mouth opened to cry out. It was as if a dam had burst within her, as if she were fighting a tidal wave

500

of feeling. Until, finally, she let go and gave in to the strength that claimed her, that took everything from her in one shuddering, screaming, ecstatic moment.

• 9 •

IT TOOK MIKE ROSSI A WEEK TO DISCOVER THAT HE DID NOT LIKE Tim Randlett.

"I don't know why," he said in answer to Connie's question. "There's just something about him that rubs me the wrong way. He's like a chameleon."

"He's no such thing," said Connie. "He's a very nice boy and I, for one, am very happy for Selena."

"I agree," said Allison, smiling at Mike.

But, as Mike often said, Connie had an overworked sense of curiosity.

"What do you mean 'chameleon'?" she demanded.

"He talks to everyone in a different way," said Mike, wishing he'd never brought up the subject. "His manner changes with everyone he meets just as if he were changing color."

"Mike's just jealous," said Connie to Allison. "He's jealous because Tim is young and handsome and sleeping with Selena."

"Mother!" cried Allison, flabbergasted. "How do you know he's doing any such thing?"

"What?" asked Connie, innocently studying her fingernails.

"You know damned well what," said Allison. "Come on. Tell."

Connie shrugged. "It's just a look a woman gets," she said. "And Selena's got it. That slept-with look."

"Honestly, Mother," said Allison.

"Well, it's true," said Connie defensively. "And not only slept with, but slept with damned well."

"All I care about," said Allison, "is Selena being happy. And if sleeping with Tim Randlett makes her happy, I'm all for it."

Mike stood up. "All this sleep talk has made me warm and uncomfortable," he said. "Anybody for a cold beer?"

"You know, Mike," Allison said, raising her voice so that he could hear her in the kitchen, "Peter Drake doesn't like Tim Randlett, either."

"Well, what would you expect?" asked Connie. "Did you think he'd be overjoyed at the appearance of a rival? Peter's been in love with Selena for years."

"He said that Tim's a big phony and I quote," said Allison.

"Maybe he's right," said Mike, coming back into the living room with three brimming glasses of beer. "Not that I'd go so far as calling Randlett a phony. I don't think he means to be phony, but I do think that he's been insincere for so long that he doesn't even realize he's that way."

"Sour grapes," said Connie, licking a little rim of white foam from her top lip.

"You've been in Peyton Place too long," laughed Allison. "You've become a native and now you distrust Tim because he makes a living at something as unorthodox as acting."

"And not only that," said Connie, "but you've become a gossip."

"Ayeh," said Mike in an exaggerated drawl.

But Mike Rossi was not the only one who was worried about Selena's relationship with Tim Randlett. Dr. Matthew Swain had met Selena on Elm Street and, as he told Seth Buswell later, he almost didn't recognize her. It was as if a light had been turned on inside Selena. She glowed and her smile flashed continually.

"Hello, Matt," she said.

It was the first time in her life that she had called him anything but Doc.

"Well, hello, Selena," said Matt. "My goodness, you look radiant this morning. No need to ask how you are. It's obvious."

"I feel generous, too," Selena laughed. "Come on into Hyde's and I'll treat you to coffee."

Matthew Swain waited until Corey Hyde had served them before he spoke.

"Are you in love with him, Selena?" he asked.

"In love with whom?" she teased.

But Matt did not laugh with her. "With Tim Randlett," he said.

"Yes," she said. "Yes, I am, Matt."

"I thought that summertime actors moved around a lot more than Tim does," said the doctor, lighting his pipe.

"In the first place," said Selena, "Tim is not a 'summertime actor.' He's a full-fledged, year-around actor. And, yes, actors usually do move around in the summer, but the theater at Silver Lake is conducting an experiment this year in repertory theater and Tim is even getting a chance to do some directing."

"I see," said Matt. "What's he going to be doing this fall?"

"Matt, I told you. Acting isn't a part-time thing with Tim. He'll be acting in the fall in New York."

Matthew Swain took a deep breath. "Are you going with him?" he asked.

Selena looked down into her coffee cup. "I don't know," she said. "He hasn't asked me."

"Will you go if he does ask?"

Selena raised her head and looked the doctor straight in the eyes.

"Yes," she said. "And if he doesn't ask me, I'll ask him."

"What about Joey?"

"Joey stays with me, no matter where I go."

"And what does Joey say about all this?"

Selena laughed. "Stop being such a worry wart, Matt," she said. "Joey's crazy about Tim. They get along beautifully together."

"Have you told Peter Drake?" asked Matt.

For a moment, some of the glow left Selena's face.

"No," she said. "But I will."

"He'll take it hard," said Matt.

"Matt, I can't help it," said Selena a little impatiently. "I never meant to hurt Peter, but he's known for a long time that I'm not in love with him and never have been."

"Peter's in love with you," said the doctor.

"Matt, what are you trying to say?" demanded Selena. "For Heaven's sake, spit it out and get it over with."

He looked at her for a long moment. "We've known each other for a long time, Selena," he said at last. "I'm just trying to make sure that you're not going to get hurt. That's all I care about.

After all, none of us knows anything about this Tim Randlett, so bear with an old man's concern for a minute."

Selena was suddenly in a raging anger. "No, you don't know anything about him," she cried. "He's not from Peyton Place so therefore he's suspect. Well, how come no one ever suspected a nice Peyton Place resident like Lucas? Tell me that."

"Selena," said Matt, putting out a restraining hand, "I never meant anything like that, I only wondered—"

"I know goddamn well what you were wondering," said Selena furiously. "You're wondering if I'm sleeping with him, aren't you? You and everybody else in Peyton Place. Well, yes I am, Matt. Every single chance I get and even that isn't often enough!"

"Selena," said the doctor calmly, "we've known each other too long. Don't try to shock me."

Selena wilted. "I'm sorry, Doc," she said, reverting to the name she had always used. "I love him. I can't help myself. If he doesn't ask me to marry him, I think I'll die."

Matthew Swain reached out and patted her arm.

"If he doesn't ask you, you send him along to me. It'll be because he's sick."

At the end of the first week in August so many things happened at once that, as Connie Rossi put it, she was hard put to remember which end was up. Mike was offered and accepted a position to teach history at the high school at White River. Allison was invited to go to Hollywood as a "technical adviser" for the making of the motion picture based on *Samuel's Castle* and Betty Anderson came home. As Selena Cross said to Tim Randlett, "Thank heavens! When they're talking about someone else, they're giving us a rest."

So August passed in a series of heavy, heat-laden days, and the farmers looked with stunned eyes at the earth which seemed ready to explode with its load of fruitfulness. They began to harvest their second crops of hay while in sheds and barns all over northern New England women nailed apple crates together for the outsized crop to come. Potato plants wilted and died as the vegetables below the ground sucked life from them and grew fat with solid, white meat, and everywhere flower gardens struck the eye almost hurtfully with their overloads of bloom and color.

Those grown old resisted hope and promise with a suspicion older than outcroppings of granite.

"'Twon't last," they said. "There'll be the day of reckoning."

But the young stared at the magnificent summer as if each of them had received an overwhelming, unexpected gift. They forgot the summers of drought and the summers of wet cold, and after a while they ridiculously began to assume that all summers to come would be just like this one.

"Well, thank God we won't have to put the house up for sale," said Connie Rossi to her husband. "With White River only nine miles away, you can commute very nicely."

"Before anything," said Mike, "I'd better start reading a few books. It's been a long time since I thought of teaching history to a bunch of kids who don't give a damn about the War of 1812 and are bored glassy-eyed with the Declaration of Independence."

Connie and Allison made several all-day trips to Boston, choosing a new wardrobe for Allison to take to Hollywood, and all of Peyton Place buzzed with the news of Betty Anderson's return and waited to see what Leslie Harrington would do.

No one had the time nor the inclination to think about Selena Cross, and as the end of August drew near no one but Joey and Peter Drake noticed the change in her. The shine of happiness that had marked her and set her apart had faded and her figure grew almost gaunt with an unbecoming thinness. Her eyes were circled with dark shadows and even the electric darkness of her hair seemed faded and lifeless.

"For God's sake, Selena," said Peter Drake. "What's the matter with you? Are you ill?"

"No," she replied shortly. "It's nothing."

And Joey was frightened. He remembered the way Selena had looked all during the months Lucas' body had been decaying under the ground almost at her feet, and she looked the same way now.

"Please," said Joey. "Let's go see Doc Swain."

"It's nothing," Selena insisted. "It's just the heat."

But to Peter Drake, Joey confessed his suspicions.

"It must be Tim Randlett," he said. "He's doing something to her. Something awful, and she won't stop seeing him."

"It can't be Randlett," said Peter. "She claims she loves him."

"I don't care," said Joey, and his voice shook with anger at Tim and worry for Selena. "It must be something he's doing."

"He's asked her to marry him."

"I know it," replied Joey. "And she said yes, but now I don't want her to. In the beginning I thought he was all right. But not now."

Peter Drake closed his eyes for a moment, as if by doing so he could stop the pain that Selena's actions had cost him.

"There's nothing we can do, Joey. There's nothing to do but wait."

· 10 ·

IT WAS RAINING HARD THE WAY IT WILL ONLY IN AUGUST, WITH plump, heavy drops that splattered out on the roads and sidewalks like silver pennies. Betty Anderson held her son, Roddy, tightly by the hand as the train pulled into Peyton Place. The conductor held a black umbrella which he opened when the train stopped and Betty stepped down onto the platform. The conductor reached up one arm to swing Roddy down, but Betty pushed his arm aside.

"I'll do it," she said, and then, as the conductor stepped back, she added more gently, "He doesn't like to be handled by strangers."

"Lots of 'em don't at that age," said the conductor cheerfully. "What is he? About five?"

"He'll be five years old next month," said Betty.

"I'm more than four and a half," said Roddy proudly. "I used to be four and a half, but now I'm more."

The conductor grinned. "Well, then," he said. "You must be strong enough to carry your mother's suitcases."

"No," said Roddy seriously. "I don't have to carry anything but Wendel."

"And is this Wendel?" the conductor asked, extending a hand toward the rather grubby giraffe that the child held.

"Yes," said Roddy. "That's Wendel, and he is very tired from his long trip. When my grandfather gets here, Wendel is going to ride in a car. He likes to ride in cars."

"And do you like to ride in your grandfather's car?" asked the conductor.

"I don't know," said Roddy.

"Come on, darling," said Betty. "It's damp out here. Let's go inside."

"Good-by," said Roddy.

The conductor waved as he boarded the train and Betty and Roddy started toward the station. She did not look back as the train pulled away, but she felt her back stiffen.

I should get right back on, she thought, and keep going, right the hell out of here. I never should have come in the first place. I must have a screw loose or something.

The station hadn't changed any, she noticed. It was still the same shabby structure it had been when she had left Peyton Place five years before.

A little older, she thought, looking at the buildings. A little more weathered and beat up, perhaps, but substantially the same. Like me, I guess.

Roddy was looking up at the high-ceilinged waiting room.

"Is this where my grandfather lives?" he asked.

"No," said Betty. "This is a railroad station where people buy their tickets so that they can ride on the train. Your grandfather lives in a house. A great, big, fine house. The biggest house on Chestnut Street."

"Are we going to sleep there?" asked Roddy, beginning to rub his eyes with the knuckles of one hand. "Wendel is tired."

"I don't know yet," said Betty, and she spoke with an effort, for she had just looked up and saw Leslie Harrington coming toward her. He had Charles Partridge with him.

He must be worried, thought Betty wryly, to bring his lawyer with him. The son-of-a-bitch.

507

It was Charles who said hello and extended his hand to Betty first. Leslie was staring at Roddy.

I knew it, he thought. I knew all along that it was a boy. And the image of his father.

It was true. Roddy had the same dark good looks, the same sturdy body that had been Rodney Harrington's.

"Hello, Betty," said Leslie at last. "Welcome home."

"This isn't home," said Roddy. "This is where we came to visit."

Leslie hesitated, and although he spoke to the child his eyes were on Betty.

"Well, maybe after you visit for a while, you'll like it here so much that you'll want to stay," he said.

Betty looked Leslie straight in the eye.

"Don't count on it, Leslie," she said.

"Are you my grandfather?" asked Roddy.

Leslie felt as if he had been struck a hard blow in the pit of his stomach.

Goddamn old fool, he chided himself. Getting all soggy at the sound of a word.

"Yes," he said, when he could speak. "I am your grandfather."

"Are we going to sleep in your great, big, fine house?" asked Roddy.

Leslie looked at Betty, who stood still and merely looked right back at him.

"Yes," he said. "There is a very special room all ready for you at my house."

"Wendel is tired," said Roddy.

"Wendel is a very fine-looking giraffe," said Leslie. "And you're right. He does look tired." He looked down at his grandson. "Come on," he said, extending his arms, "I'll carry you and Wendel both right out to my car and we'll hurry home and put him to bed."

"Don't," said Betty quickly, putting a hand on one of Leslie's arms. "Roddy doesn't like to be handled by people he doesn't know."

But Roddy went at once to his grandfather. "It's all right," he said. "Wendel wants to be carried."

"Of course he does," said Leslie as he swung the child up into his arms.

508

Betty followed Leslie out of the station, and it was only Charles Partridge who noticed the tightening around Betty's jaw.

Same old Betty, thought Charles; and then as he watched Leslie, he thought, And the same old Leslie. Getting exactly what he wants every time. But he'd better not try to put anything over on this girl. She may have let him get away with it once, but she's older and smarter now, and she's still got that stubborn streak.

"You drive, Charlie," said Leslie, as they got into the car. "I have to sit here and hold Wendel."

He'd better not try any tricks on me this time, thought Betty as she slammed the car door. I was dumb once, but I'm not any more. Five years in the city toughens you up real good.

The past few years had not been easy ones for Betty Anderson, but then, she hadn't expected them to be. In the beginning, when she finally knew that Rodney was not going to marry her and that all the money she was going to get from Leslie was two hundred and fifty dollars, she had been almost desperate. Her own family would not help her, she knew. She was on her own and there was nothing to do but make the best of it.

Thank God, I've never been a weeper, thought Betty as she boarded the train for New York. If I were, I'd sure as hell be bawling all over the place now.

She was grateful, too, that her figure still retained its slimness and that she was not plagued with the morning sickness or fainting spells that would have made working an impossibility.

When she got to New York, she found a job before she found a place to stay; then, with her immediate future momentarily secured, she looked for a room. She found one, and although it was a dark, depressing place she was pleased with the rent and, she told herself cheerfully, it wasn't as if she were going to be stuck there forever. Once she got the foolishness of having the baby out of the way and the business of placing it for adoption, she would be free to look for a better job, to look around for a man with money and, finally, to get married. She had not counted on the fact that she might love her child and that, in fact, she might begin to love him even before he was born.

She was working in a restaurant where the tips were fairly good and the customers easily satisfied.

Which, Betty thought ruefully, was a lucky thing for her because she had never been cut out to be a waitress.

She was constantly forgetting things, a napkin, glasses of water, filled sugar bowls, but Betty had always had a warm smile and the customers were mostly men. Betty smiled and laughed out loud at herself and twitched her hips, and the men laughed along with her and watched her behind appreciatively and tipped generously.

They asked her for dates, too, but Betty always flashed her left hand with its dime-store wedding band and told them that her husband was six feet tall with shoulders like a brick wall and that he'd kill any man who tried to date her up while he was away in the Army. But she smiled when she said it and she spoke in such a way that every man thought that if things had been different, if she were the kind to run around, he would be the one man she would choose.

If I ever get rid of this goddamn bundle, thought Betty savagely, then I'll really cut loose.

But one afternoon, when she was changing from her uniform to her street clothes, she felt a twinge in her belly that left her weak, not with pain but with surprise.

Well, I'll be damned! she thought.

She walked all the way to her room and, as soon as she got there, she undressed and lay down on her bed. She put her hands flat against her abdomen and waited, and then it happened again. She could actually see the movement under her skin.

Well, I'll be damned, she thought again and grinned. Well, I'll be damned. It's alive!

She did not know exactly when the determination to keep her baby had formed in her. Later, when she thought about it, she supposed that it must have been when she felt that first twinge of life within her body. The new thought caused radical changes in her plans and Betty, who had never been one to put things off, sat down at once and began to plan.

Within a week she found an obstetrician who promised to deliver her baby for seventy-five dollars. He reserved a room for her in a hospital and told her exactly what it would cost her to stay there for five days.

"Will you have someone to look after you and the baby when

510

you return home, Mrs. Harrington?" asked the doctor, using the name she had given him.

"Yes," said Betty, hiding the rather wry smile on her lips. "I have a family."

She spent the next months learning everything she could about baby care. She bought diapers and nightgowns and safety pins and decided that she would need neither blankets nor bottles. The baby would sleep in the same bed with her and she would nurse him herself. Now, she gorged herself on the one meal a day she was allowed at the restaurant and she hid cake and bread and cheese in her handbag so that she could eat in her room without using any money.

Instead of taking a drink of water at the restaurant, she drank milk. Water she drank at home. And every cent she could keep from spending went into a bank account to pay for the hospital and to support her during the weeks after the baby was born when she would have to stay with him.

Rodney Harrington, Junior, she thought. That's what I'll name him. He has a right to the name, and he's going to have it. To hell with Peyton Place and everybody in it.

Luckily for her, the owner of the restaurant where she worked was an Italian with six children of his own. His wife had worked right up to the last minute and it hadn't hurt her a bit. So he kept Betty on as she grew larger and larger, cautioning her against lifting heavy trays and to watch out for wet places on the kitchen floor.

"You need something lifted, you call me," he told her. "And don't worry about a thing. It's good for a woman to stay on her feet when she's that way. Makes it easier when her time comes."

The Italian's wife said, "Don't worry about nothin'. Your husband's away, I'll come visit in the hospital. After, I come help you with the baby. Don't worry about nothin'!"

"These days," said the Italian, snapping his fingers, "it's nothin' for a woman to have a baby. Bing, in the hospital. Bing, with the ether. Bing, the baby. All over."

The baby was born at the end of October and things worked out just as Betty had planned. Her delivery was an easy one in spite of Roddy's husky nine and a half pounds, and Betty's breasts overflowed with milk to feed him. From the first, he was

511

a contented baby who never cried except when he was hungry or wet; and, as the weeks went by, he seemed to grow right in front of Betty's eyes. When he was three months old, she knew that it was time for her to go back to work. There were twenty-one dollars and sixty-seven cents left in the bank.

A woman named Agnes Carlisle lived in the room next door to Betty's, and during the time that Betty had lived there, she and Agnes had become good friends. Agnes was a retired school-teacher, who struggled every month to make ends meet on her pension and was only too glad to look after Roddy every evening for the small sum that Betty could pay.

"He's so good, he won't be any trouble," said Agnes cheerfully. "And even if he were, I wouldn't mind. He's such a beautiful baby."

Betty almost laughed out loud at the sight of the gray, stern-looking woman bending over the bed talking baby talk to Roddy.

"He looks just like his father," said Betty.

The years passed quickly. When Roddy was three, the Italians opened a new restaurant in another part of town and Betty was made manager of the old place. She earned a decent wage now and often thought of moving from her dark, dingy room. But Roddy was as fond of Agnes Carlisle as she was of him, and Agnes was teaching Roddy to read and write so that he'd be ahead of the other children when he started school.

"With our school system the way it is today," said Agnes, "the only child who has a chance is the one who gets outside help. I'll see that Roddy gets that."

So Betty stayed where she was. She dated a variety of men but, as she told Agnes, she wasn't about to get married.

"I like my life the way it is," she said. "Uncomplicated. I've got Roddy and my job and no entanglements. I'm going to keep it that way."

Agnes was the only person in New York who knew that Betty had never been married. Betty never discussed the subject with the men who took her out except when they got serious. Then she would tell them that she had been married and didn't want to make the same mistake again.

It was on the Fourth of July that Agnes saw the advertisement in the personal column of a tabloid newspaper. She, Betty and

Roddy had returned from an afternoon in the park and Betty was making iced coffee.

"This is a funny one," said Agnes.

"What?" asked Betty, leaning over Agnes' shoulder.

"This," said Agnes, pointing out the advertisement.

"Read it to me," said Betty. "I forgot to put an ice cube in Roddy's milk and as soon as he realizes it he'll start yelling."

"Betty, where are you?" said Agnes.

"What?" asked Betty, turning around, surprised.

"That's what it says here in the paper," replied Agnes. "Betty, where are you? Please contact me as soon as you see this. Urgent. Leslie Harrington, Box 213, Peyton Place *Times*."

Betty sat down on a hassock at Agnes' feet. "Well, I'll be damned," she said softly.

"It's meant for you, isn't it?" Agnes asked.

"Yes," said Betty.

"Is it—" She hesitated and glanced at Roddy who was looking solemnly from Agnes to his mother. She lowered her voice. "Is it Roddy's g-r-a-n-d-f-a-t-h-e-r?" she asked, spelling out the last word.

"Roddy what?" asked Roddy, and then he glanced down into his glass. "Eye-cube! Eye-cube!" he yelled.

Betty took an ice cube from her glass of iced coffee and put it into his glass.

"Yes," she said to Agnes.

"Are you going to write to him?"

"I don't know."

"Are you out of your mind?" asked Agnes. "You told me that he had plenty of money. It's about time he did something for R-o-d-d-y."

"Roddy!" cried Roddy triumphantly.

Agnes groaned. "Why did I have to teach him to spell," she said.

"I don't know as I want anything from him," said Betty.

"Don't be a fool," said Agnes. "If he wants to do something for the child, let him. Are you going to be stuck in a hovel like this all your life? And Roddy, too? Take what you can get. Don't wind up like me."

Betty looked at Agnes for a long time. She saw herself, grown old, living alone in her dark room. Living on pennies and in fear.

"I'm not going to write," she said. "I'll see how serious he is about wanting to get in touch with me. I'll telephone him. Collect."

She put in the call, smiling gleefully at the thought of Leslie's discomfiture at hearing from her through a nosy, Peyton Place telephone operator.

"What do you want, Leslie?" she asked, as soon as she heard his voice.

Leslie hesitated for only a moment. "I want you to come home," he said.

"Isn't this a little out of character for you, Leslie?"

"I've been trying to find you for years," said Leslie.

"Why?" asked Betty coldly. "There was a time when you couldn't wait to get rid of me."

"Betty," said Leslie, and she was almost shocked at the note of pleading in his voice. "Tell me about the baby."

"Well, he's hardly a baby," replied Betty. "He's going on five."

"A boy," said Leslie, and for a long minute the phone was silent except for his breathing. "A boy. What's his name?"

"Rodney Harrington, Junior," said Betty, and waited for Leslie to protest.

"That's wonderful, Betty," said Leslie, and Betty was so surprised that she took the receiver away from her ear and looked down into the mouthpiece as if she wanted to see Leslie's face. "Please, Betty," he was saying. "Say you'll come."

"I'll have to think it over," said Betty.

"I'll send you a check for the fare," Leslie offered.

"You're damned right you will," said Betty with a humorless little laugh.

"I'll put it in the mail right now," he said. "Just give me your address."

"Nothing doing," said Betty. "The last thing I want is to find you camped on my doorstep. I told you I'd think it over and I will. I'll call you at the end of the week."

"At least give me your telephone number," said Leslie.

"No," said Betty, and hung up abruptly.

The following week was one of hell for Betty. All her life she had hated indecision, and her days were not made any easier by Agnes' almost constant nagging.

"Stop thinking of yourself," said Agnes. "Think of Roddy."

514

And: "Do you want to spend the rest of your life working in a greasy restaurant?"

And: "I'm not going to be around forever, you know. Who'll look after Roddy then?"

And: "Roddy's one of the most intelligent children I've ever known. Are you going to cheat him out of the advantages he should have?"

And: "What if you should get sick? What would happen to Roddy then?"

"For Christ's sake," yelled Betty, "will you kindly shut up for a minute? I can't think!"

"There's nothing to think about," said Agnes decisively. "Call the old man. Pack your things. And go."

In the end, Betty telephoned Leslie Harrington.

"I can take a week off from my job," she said. "We can come for a visit, but only for five days. We'll have to spend the other two traveling."

"Now will you give me your address so that I can mail you a check?" asked Leslie.

"No," said Betty. "I've thought it over, and I don't think I want to be beholden to you for a damned thing. The only reason I'm going to see you at all is that you're Roddy's grandfather. Every child should have a chance to meet his grandfather. And that's the only reason, believe me."

"Wire me what train you're taking," said Leslie.

"Yes, I will."

The car turned into the wide, graveled driveway in front of the Harrington house.

"Here we are," said Leslie. "Roddy's asleep."

Yes, thought Betty. Here we are, indeed.

· 11 ·

AUGUST HAD BEEN MORE THAN HALF GONE WHEN SELENA HAD BECOME aware of an almost imperceptible change in Tim Randlett. He began to question her about her past, and if she didn't answer him he sulked.

"Listen," he said, "I want you to be my wife. Husbands and wives don't have secrets from one another. If they do it's no kind of marriage."

Selena barely heard his last two sentences.

"What did you say?" she asked in almost unbelieving joy.

"I said that I want you to be my wife and—"

She put restraining fingers across his lips.

"Don't say anything else," she said. "Just say that again."

Tim laughed and took her in his arms.

"Darling," he said, "will you please do me the honor of becoming my wife?"

"Yes," said Selena, "yes, yes, yes. When?"

"In the fall," replied Tim. "After I'm finished here. We'll go to New York and find an apartment and then we'll go to Tiffany's and I'll buy you the biggest diamond in the store with a wedding band to match."

"I love you," said Selena softly. "I'll bet that no one else in the world loves anyone the way I love you."

"You'd lose," said Tim. "Because I love you that way."

Selena believed him in spite of the way he could, on occasion, look at her with a coldness that chilled her with fear.

"Tell me about this Ted Carter," he demanded.

"There's nothing to tell," replied Selena. "We were friends all through school and then one day we weren't friends any more. That's all."

516

"You're lying, Selena," he said.

She turned to him in disbelief. "I am not," she cried.

"Did you ever sleep with him?"

"Are you out of your mind?" she demanded angrily.

"Don't raise your voice, Selena. And why are you so angry if your conscience is clear?"

"I'm angry because you've not only doubted my word, but because you could even think such a thing about Ted and me."

"Well," said Tim with a sarcasm that hurt her more than any raised voice could have done, "let's face it, darling. I wasn't the first. Not by a long shot."

"You're behaving like a child," said Selena and turned her back to him.

Tim Randlett often behaved like a child. When he was not acting a part, either on or off stage, he reverted to the actions of the spoiled, petulant darling he had once been in Hollywood, and the worst facet of this was that he didn't believe that he was acting childish at all but that he was asserting himself and standing up for his rights. When the few people who had seen him this way accused him of immaturity, Tim either lost his temper completely or exerted himself to correct what he was convinced was a mistaken impression.

"I'm not being childish, darling," he said to Selena. "It's just that I love you so, and I want to know every single thing about you."

"Then couldn't you wait until I'm ready to tell you?" she asked.

"Of course, darling," said Tim. "There's no hurry. We have the rest of our lives to talk and find out about each other."

After every such argument, things went well between them for a short time, but then, invariably, Tim would begin again, and what hurt Selena most of all was that he usually chose a time immediately after they had finished making love.

"What did you and Carter do during all the years you were such dear, good friends?" he asked.

"Just what most other kids do," she replied, and prayed silently that he would stop the slightly twisted smile from appearing on the mouth she had just kissed.

"We went to school, and to dances and talked about getting married someday. Just kid stuff."

"Didn't you ever neck?"

517

"Yes," said Selena.

"Ah. Now the truth begins to emerge. Was he good at it?"

"Tim," she asked quietly, "what does it do for you to hear about such things? Do you get a big bang out of thinking of me kissing someone else?"

"Just answer my question," he ordered.

"I don't know," she said. "Ted was the only boy I ever kissed while I was growing up so I really have no basis for comparison."

"Do you mean to say that in a town like Peyton Place kids don't play kissing games?" he demanded, his eyebrows raised in disbelief.

"Of course they do," she replied wearily.

"And you, of course, being so pure and virginal, refused to participate in these games. Is that what you're trying to tell me?"

Selena jumped up from the bed and pulled a robe around her.

"For God's sake, Tim," she cried, "will you cut it out. You're just like a goddamned peeping Tom."

"Well, did you or didn't you?"

"Did I or didn't I what?"

"Join in the kissing games."

"Of course I did. Every kid does."

"Then you lied to me about Carter being the only boy you ever kissed."

"For God's sake," Selena shouted, "how can I remember every boy who was at every party I ever went to."

"If you'd lie about kissing, Heaven only knows what else you'd lie about."

"You're sick!" Selena yelled.

"Don't shout, darling," he said with maddening patience. "And I'm not the one who's sick. People who lie to others and to themselves are the sick ones."

"I don't lie," said Selena evenly. "I never have and I'm not about to start now."

She began to dress, keeping her head averted so that he wouldn't see the tears that she couldn't keep from rolling down her cheeks.

"What are you doing?" he demanded.

"I'm getting dressed," she replied. "I'm going home."

He was at her side at once. He turned her around to face him and kissed the tears away from her face.

"Darling," he said contritely, "I am an absolute heel. I didn't mean to make you cry. Please forgive me."

"Forget it," said Selena. "I just want to go home."

His arms went around her, holding her tightly against him.

"Don't say that," he said and his voice was harsh with fear. "Don't ever say that. If I lost you I couldn't bear it."

"I have to go," said Selena wearily. "I can't take any more arguing, or sarcasm, or your terrible accusations. I'm all punched out, Tim. I just can't stand it any more."

"Please," he begged, and now tears rolled down his cheeks. "Please, darling. Forgive me just this once more. I'll never do it again."

And then, unknowing and uncaring, Selena gave him one last hostage. She threw her arms around his neck and sobbed against his cheek.

"You don't even have to ask me," she said. "Of course, I forgive you. I could never leave you and we both know it. The idea of living without you is something I can't even begin to imagine. I'll never, never leave you."

And again it was better for a while, but now Selena found herself waiting for the quarrels to come. She was constantly tense, watching for the signs that would warn her of the approaching storm. At night she often lay awake, wondering why Tim's constant probing and prying affected her as it did, but the only conclusion she could come to was that she had never been a dweller in the past and that not being so was the only way she had managed to survive at all. She knew, too, that there had been times when she could not remain in complete control of her thinking and then she would have terrible nightmares about her mother, Nellie, in which she saw her mother hanging, dead, a corpse with a black face and congested eyes that moved on the end of a silken cord with every breath Selena drew. At other times she dreamed of running while a gigantic all-powerful Lucas chased her and then she would scream in her sleep until Joey came into her room and shook her awake.

"Time," Matthew Swain had said. "It may be a cliché, but it's true that it heals all wounds."

It happened the way the doctor had said it would. As the years passed, Selena's bad dreams recurred less and less frequently until at last they ceased altogether and the only time she gave in to fear

519

was once every year on the day of the first snow. Until she had fallen in love with Tim Randlett. Now the nightmares were back, the fear, the sleepless nights. For Selena knew that soon now, Tim would get around to asking her about Lucas and Nellie and the trial and that she would have to dredge up the buried ugliness and show it to him in detail.

I won't think about it, she told herself as she tossed in her bed. I won't talk about it, and if Tim wants to get ugly about it, I'll leave him.

But she knew she would not leave him, no matter what he asked of her, and the sleepless nights grew longer and Selena gagged at the sight of food, and her brother Joey said, "What's the matter, Selena?" and she had no answer for him.

I'll be calm, she thought. I won't let myself become upset about anything. Tim loves me. He's not cruel.

And that much was true. Tim Randlett did love her, in his fashion, and he was not a cruel man. It was just that now he fancied himself in the role of psychiatrist and had convinced himself that the dark secrets which festered in Selena's mind were like a poison that coursed through her body and that would end up by destroying her and, therefore, him. He saw himself as a great healer and believed that the feeling of accomplishment he got from fitting one small piece of information after another into the puzzle of Selena's background was the joy of a scientist on the brink of discovery, and he never admitted to himself that there was something unlovely and perverse in his excitement.

"I only want what's good for you," he told her.

And Selena believed him because there was nothing else she could do.

They were on the couch in the living room of his cottage one sunny afternoon at the end of August, he was sitting up and Selena lying down with her head in his lap. He stroked her hair gently away from her forehead, and Selena had the wonderful, floating feeling she always had after they had made love and were quiet and close together. She was on the very edge of sleep when he spoke.

"Tell me about Lucas," he said.

For a moment, Selena was absolutely still; calmness filled her the way it sometimes will when someone has been terribly shocked and thinks, Now the worst has happened, whatever comes after this can't help but be better. But then her heart began to pound and she began to tremble.

"Stop it, Tim," she cried. "I don't want to talk about Lucas or anything connected with him."

"You have to, darling," he said gently. "It's the only way you'll ever get rid of it."

She tried to get up, but he had twisted her long hair around his hand and she was held fast.

"Let go of me," she demanded.

"Darling, don't be afraid," he said softly. "Believe me, I only want what's good for you. You have to talk about it, darling. You can't go the rest of your life with all that hatred bottled up inside you."

"I don't hate Lucas any more," she said. "I stopped hating him the second he died."

"That's not true," said Tim.

This time she pulled away from him with such a wrench that he let go of her hair in surprise. She stood up and faced him, her eyes blazing with anger and pain.

"What the hell do you know about it?" she cried. "You with your insulated childhood and your playacting and your games of psychiatrist and patient. You don't know anything about anything real. All right. I'll tell you about Lucas. Maybe that'll shatter your sickening smugness."

"Don't shout, darling," Tim said in the patient, conciliatory tone that maddened her.

"I'll shout all I want," cried Selena. "You want to hear about Lucas. Well, I'll tell you. He was a pig, a drunk and the worst son-of-a-bitch that ever lived. When I was fourteen he knocked me unconscious and tore my clothes off and raped me. And after that, I don't even remember how many times, he'd send my brother Joey out and he'd lock the door and he'd beat me before he got on top of me."

She was standing in front of him, bent forward, with her fists clenched while she screamed. He took her wrists and tried to pull her down next to him on the couch.

"Please, darling," he said, almost frightened at the change in her.

She pulled away from him and kicked his shin when he tried to stand up.

"Sit down," she shouted. "You wanted to hear it and now you'll sit still until I finish. The times when Lucas knocked me out weren't the worst times, you know. It was when I was only stunned and before I could pick myself up off the floor he grabbed me and tied me to the bed and then did it to me. Then I'd be awake and aware of every second and I'd feel him hurting me and smell his sweat and his breath and hear him grunting like a rooting pig. Those were the worst times. What's the matter, Tim? Don't you like the grubby details? My mother knew. I don't know how, but she knew. I'd catch her looking at me and I knew she knew. And Lucas was careful, too. Careful as could be. He'd wait until she was out working before he'd get to me. He was big, Tim. Bigger than you. And most of the time I'd bleed before he got through with me. Lucas didn't bleed though. He got me pregnant and I had an abortion."

Her whole body was shaking now and her breath hurt in her throat.

"I didn't really have to, you know," she said, and her voice was softer now with an almost weird hush. "Have an abortion, I mean. Lucas wasn't my flesh-and-blood father. The baby would probably have been all right. Not an idiot or anything. Lucas used to say that while he was on top of me. That I wasn't his own daughter. It seemed to excite him, as if I were a stranger. No. I didn't really have to have the abortion, but I did. I bled then, too, but not Lucas. Lucas never bled at all until I killed him. And then he bled. Oh, how he bled. Blood gushed from him like a fountain, and I kept on hitting him."

Selena's eyes gleamed and her mouth was like a cut in her white face.

"I killed him," she whispered. "I hit him over the head, and I hit him and hit him and hit him until he was dead, and I enjoyed every minute of it. When I was finished his head was like an egg that had been shattered and I was happy for the first time in years. Lucas was dead, like my mother. Like my baby."

She stopped and stood still, her arms hanging limply at her sides, her dark hair falling over the side of her face.

"Is that what you wanted to hear?" she asked at last, not looking at him.

Tim came to her and she could hear the heavy sound of his breath. He was almost panting and when she did look up she could hardly believe what she saw. His eyes were gleaming and his hands trembled as he reached for her.

"Darling," he whispered hoarsely.

And when he pulled her close to him she could feel his excitement. Too late, she tried to turn and run from him but he held her tightly.

"So you do remember," he said. "You remember how big and strong he was, like a bull. You've never forgotten him."

Selena beat against his chest and tried to bring her knee up, but she could not move.

"A girl always remembers her first lover," he said softly. "Especially if she's been raped."

His hands were hard on her, hurting her through the thin material of her summer dress, and when he kissed her his mouth was heavy and wet and merciless. She twisted and pushed against him and panic was a sickness that threatened to engulf her.

"That's what you've wanted all along," Tim said. "To be raped, the way Lucas raped you. Every time I took you in my stupid, gentle way, you were remembering him and how big and brutal he was. Well, I can be that way too. Like this."

But when he tried to push her down on the floor she managed to break away from him. She ran around the table in front of the fireplace and her hands found the fire tongs as if they had been waiting for her.

"I'll kill you!" she screamed as he started for her. "Don't move, or I'll kill you!"

But Tim was beyond listening or caring. He crept closer to her, and when he was close enough she swung the tongs in a great arc and struck him. If he had not moved at the last second, the tongs would have struck him on the side of the head. But he did move, so that only his shoulder was hit, and he staggered backward and fell over the table and landed against the stone floor in front of the fireplace.

For a moment he was still, and in those few seconds Selena looked down at her hand and saw it clutched around the tongs.

She watched in horror as her arm started to raise itself to strike again, and just then Tim groaned and sat up. Selena stared at him and then back at the weapon in her hand.

Almost! screamed a voice inside her head. Almost! I almost killed him!

And she turned and ran out of the cottage. She ran through the woods, dappled green and yellow in the summer sun, and she ran to the highway that led to Peyton Place.

Almost! the voice screamed, and Selena ran until the world blurred in front of her eyes and the sandy shoulder of the road came up to strike her face.

BOOK THREE

1

IN SEPTEMBER, ALLISON LEFT PEYTON PLACE FOR A WEEK IN NEW York before going on to Hollywood. It meant arriving at the studio two days later than they expected her, but she decided it was more important to have a week with Lewis, an uninterrupted week of being with him and loving him.

Distance does not lend enchantment, she thought, thinking of the weeks of separation, the two months when all she had of Lewis was his letters. Absence had not diminished her love for him, but, sometimes, she was not able to capture the image of his face. She knew that in the first few minutes of meeting him again there would be constraint and hesitation; it would be like meeting a stranger.

She looked out the train window at the familiar landscape. Summer had lingered into September; the blaze of autumn had not yet consumed or even touched the greenness. What a summer it had been! Allison thought. What had begun in beauty and fruitfulness had ended with Selena found wandering, dazed, lost and helpless, by the side of a road. Mike had been fired. And Seth Buswell and Matt Swain had made enemies trying to help her.

Peyton Place had been a battlefield. Allison wondered whether she was fleeing in defeat or departing victorious. A little of both, she thought. Mike had got a job and she, at least, had not surrendered to the pressures. Her career was in full flower, her success had gone far beyond even her wildest dream.

Allison had never thought of success in terms of money. To her, it had always been a vague, amorphous dream with success consisting, in equal parts, of fame and freedom. Money was the least important part of it. Often she said to herself, I am a rich woman. It was an attempt at convincing herself of this fact, but it was an attempt that always failed. She never believed it, she could not think of herself that way.

Only *old* women are rich, she told herself, trying to push away the thought of herself, Allison MacKenzie, as a rich woman. It was an image she was not willing to face and thought the reason for it was that it interfered with an image she preferred: herself as a writer; as Allison MacKenzie, Author.

She did not want to be a corporate entity, endlessly involved with the investment counselors and tax accountants that Brad had been recommending to her. One of the things she had to do while in New York was to see these people. She had decided that the only way to handle this was to find people she could trust, and turn it all over to them. She did not want to be bothered with it. To think of money matters took one's mind from the writing of books, and that was her real work.

Perhaps David was right. He may have been motivated by all the wrong reasons, but perhaps what he said was correct. The writer's only function is to write. From now on, she determined, that's the way it's going to be. No more interviews, no more salesmanship.

The conductor punched her ticket and made a few remarks about the kind of summer it had been. I've practically become a commuter, Allison thought, between Peyton Place and New York. She looked around her at the faded green plush seats, most of them empty. She felt almost proprietary about this train.

She had an imaginary conversation with Lewis in which she said, "We should all take more train rides, Lewis. It's one of the few places left where we can commune with ourselves and ask the deep questions and make judgments of ourselves and others. It's too dangerous to think of anything but the traffic when you're in a car; and planes are too fast."

Allison put her head back on the seat and closed her eyes, gave herself up to delicious thoughts of her reunion with Lewis. Love's hungers, she thought, are as real as any other kind.

She smiled, thinking what Constance would say if she knew that Allison had become involved with a married man. Constance, remembering her own past history, would think it was a family curse, a seed she had transmitted to Allison, and she would feel guilty and responsible.

That is the difference between our generations, Allison thought. Her mother had felt guilty, had felt a sense of sin at being the mistress of a married man. Allison did not. She accepted it; it was an arrangement; it was the best thing that life had thus far offered her.

Allison sat up, startled by her thoughts. *Thus far?* Was she admitting to herself that what she had with Lewis was just a temporary thing, to be superseded by something better, more permanent? She pushed the thought aside, denied the possibility of it. I am not a gypsy, she told herself, not a wanderer. I have found what I want, Lewis is what I want, and I'm going to hold onto it.

At Boston she changed trains. Walking through the station, she smiled to herself. The world-weary traveler, that's what I am. Such a short time ago, this trip from Peyton Place to New York had been an exciting, new experience, a dream come true. But already it was something she could do with her eyes closed. Is that the way it's going to be with everything? she wondered. Is that what life is?

From Grand Central Station she went directly to the residential hotel where she had reserved an apartment. Driving up Park Avenue, her luggage all around her, she tried to keep from her face the smug smile that tugged at her lips. Oh, give in to it, she told herself. Relax that tight New England conscience of yours. After all, no one gave you this, it wasn't handed to you on a silver platter. You earned it with your own two hands. Now enjoy it.

Her apartment was on the twentieth floor. Following the boy who carried the luggage, bowed in by the manager, she entered a grand living room all white and gold. The manager bustled after her, opened the long windows that led to the terrace, showed her the bedroom which was only a little smaller than the living room, and led her to the butler's pantry where she could, if she wished, do her own cooking.

When she was alone, she looked at herself in the long mirror, as if to assure herself that it was really she, Allison MacKenzie, in this place. Then she went to the phone and called Lewis.

"I am here," she said. "Come to dinner."

"Must I wait till then?" he asked. "I could sneak out the back door. I think it still opens, though I haven't used it since 1936 when the bill collectors used to sit and wait for me in the reception room."

"Oh, how I wish I had been around then, darling."

"I wish it too. You would have charmed them right out of the place, the bills forgotten in their hands. Listen, darling, I know I'm being terribly undisciplined and all my authors are going to start writing me angry letters, but I'm leaving right now and I'll be there in fifteen minutes."

"Oh yes, darling, come at once," she said. And hung up before she could add, "We have no time to waste." The thought had come unbidden, from nowhere.

She undressed quickly. She wanted to shower and dress and be ready for him. She planned on ordering dinner and having it served on the terrace, with candles on the table and a bucket of champagne, able to see all of New York yet remaining unseen. That their life together was secret made it all the more delicious, she thought.

But when he knocked on the door she was not ready and had to pull on a terrycloth robe, the ends of her hair still wet, her face washed clean of make-up.

"Don't look at me, Lewis. I'm not ready to be seen."

He laughed. "That's like telling a thirsty man to stay away from the water."

He put his hand on her arm and drew her toward him. When they kissed, Allison went limp in his arms and cried, "Oh, Lewis, how I've missed you!"

"If it was anything like the way I missed you, then I understand full well what you've gone through."

Allison drew away from him and said, "Oh, Lewis, I wanted to be dressed when you arrived, and made up, and looking my best. And now look at me."

"I am," Lewis said.

"I wanted to order dinner and have the table on the terrace, with crystal and candles and champagne."

"We'll have it later," Lewis said, smiling his quiet smile.

When he kissed her again, his hand was inside her robe, cupping her breast; and then, arms around each other, hurrying, they moved toward the bedroom. Allison's knees felt weak and her thighs trembled.

"Oh, hold me, darling," she cried. "Don't ever let me go."

"Never," he said, and the word echoed in his head.

Never, she thought, repeating the word to herself. Lovers are mad, they use crazy, impossible words. What's worse, they believe them.

She buried her face in Lewis' breast in order to shut out the sight of him, of his gray hairs that were the sign of age. She could feel his heart beating against her mouth. *Never* will last only as long as that, she thought, and began to cry.

"What is it, love? What is it?" Lewis asked. "Why are you crying?" He stroked her hair and her back, calming her as a father does a child.

"It's nothing, Lewis. It's nothing." And she took his head between her hands and consumed him with kisses, as if she wanted to make up for all the years that she had not known him, all the years she had not even been born, by the intensity of her love.

Allison was assailed by the thought that there was no time to lose; and that because of the disparity in ages, she must cram into a short space all the love and experience that the years had denied them. She caressed him with her hands and her mouth, and under her hands felt the quiver of his pleasure. She assaulted him with love, with a passionate fury; and when he was ready for her, he turned on her savagely and threw her down, covered her with his hard body, and held her arms pinned to the bed so that she could not move. Like a sea's retaining wall she lay and allowed herself to be buffeted, and felt the tidal pull that, at the end, seemed to draw her soul out of her body. Only then did he let go of her and she drew his throbbing body down to hers.

This is the only truth there is, she thought, this expression of love. The rest is acting out a part.

Her body ached with the knowledge of him. They lay side by side, resting, and Allison watched day slowly dimming and the room receding into darkness. The days were shorter now. Summer was ending graciously, with days of sweet, soft winds, but winter's advance was making itself tentatively felt. Remembering that soon she would leave for California, Allison thought, I am going to follow summer west; I'll have a few extra weeks of it.

At the thought of leaving, she turned to Lewis and kissed him.

"How are you feeling, darling?" she asked.

"There's a possibility I may recover," he said. "I believe there are some grounds for hope. If I take good care of myself, I might be able to walk out of here under my own power—sometime around ten-thirty tomorrow morning."

Allison laughed. "You'd better summon up all your strength right now, Lewis, because I suspect my reputation will suffer if the waiter walks in and finds you like this."

Lewis sat up. "What waiter?"

"The waiter who is going to bring our dinner." She reached for the phone. "I am about to order dinner, Lewis. Have you any special requests?"

"Yes, I have," Lewis said, jumping out of bed and running to the bathroom. "Wait till I'm dressed."

An hour later, when the manager, headwaiter and waiter arrived—the waiter pushing a cart containing their dinner under covered dishes—Allison and Lewis were sitting, all prim and proper, on the terrace's white wrought-iron chairs.

The headwaiter opened the champagne, the waiter served their food without rattling a single dish and the manager stood anxiously by; he was the kind of man, Allison thought, who seemed always to be fearing the worst. After the waiter had placed before them the bowls of cold vichyssoise, set in larger crystal bowls filled with cracked ice, Allison said, "I will serve the rest myself."

The waiter and the headwaiter bowed themselves off the terrace; the manager took one last worried look, as if he half expected the terrace to fall off the side of the building. Assuring himself it would last a few days more, he wished them *bon appetit* and followed his waiters from the room.

Allison said, "He gives me the feeling that he's terribly sorry New England doesn't have a king and a flag. I think he'd like to fly the flag to announce that I am here."

Lewis was still smiling at the sight of the three men backing out of the room. "New York is full of apparitions," he said. "It's become the final resting place of the ghosts of half of Europe. Those three men, for example, died in Budapest in 1935. New York is the Paradise their souls migrated to."

"The chef's ghost has done well by us tonight," Allison said.

After the cold soup, there was filet mignon with sauce Béarnaise, artichokes vinaigrette and a small salad pungent with herbs. They finished the champagne with tiny wild strawberries that tasted of sun and summer fields.

Standing at the parapet with their coffee cups, they looked at New York, winking and flashing around them. That is what it's all for, Allison thought, not knowing quite what the words meant. Moments like this make the agony of success worth while. But immediately she asked herself, Is it true? Does this make up for the lies and the estrangement of friends?

She thought of David. It pained her to think of him, in his lonely room, only a few minutes away, bent over his work. Perhaps she had misjudged him. Perhaps his integrity was real and his anger with her was genuine, not envy of her success but outrage that success was what she wanted. He believed in her talent. She decided she would phone him, invite him and Stephanie to dinner the next night.

Below, Central Park looked wilted and tired after its three months' struggle for survival against the city summer.

Lewis said, "We should ask the Parks Commissioner to send Central Park away for the summer. It's too old and careworn to spend any more summers in the city."

"I'll draw up a petition in the morning," Allison said. "We'll call it the Fund for Sending Central Park to the Catskills. School children will send in nickels and dimes. Our slogan will be: Central Park Needs Fresh Air."

Lewis put his coffee cup on the top of the parapet and, leaning forward, kissed her mouth gently.

"And I need you," he said. "It's as simple as that. You're my sun and air."

Lewis stayed till after midnight. They talked of their love and, like newlyweds, came back again and again to their plans for being together, to Allison's taking an apartment in New York when she got back from Hollywood. She would be back in October, go to Peyton Place to see Mike and Constance, and then come to New York and they would take up their life together.

"It's pretty rare, you know," Lewis said. "I mean, an arrangement like ours. It's pretty rare when it works. Very few of them last, I'm afraid."

"Why do you tell me that?" Allison asked.

"Because we have to face up to all the dangers, all the pitfalls of our situation if we are to succeed."

"I know what you are thinking, Lewis—that I will become dissatisfied, that I will want more. That I will begin to nag you and demand you get a divorce so we can get married. Darling, don't you think I've thought of all that? I've considered everything. *You* are what I want. *This* is what I want."

"I pray it will always be like this, Allison. And I hope I will never become selfish. I have thought about it a great deal, too, while you were in Peyton Place. I hope I will never make demands on you. . . ."

"And I hope you will, darling."

"—I don't mean lover's demands. I'm talking about the demands of—well, of a selfish partner, demands that have nothing to do with love but only with self."

Lewis swirled the brandy around in his glass; for a moment, it caught the light and glowed with a deep flame, then died and subsided.

"I guess that what I mean, Allison, is this: when my age becomes burdensome to you, don't keep me around out of pity. Not even if I beg you to."

"Oh, darling, darling," Allison cried, and clasped Lewis in her arms. "Don't think of such things. Don't. You are not old. You aren't."

Lewis smiled for a moment. "I'm not now. In fact, I haven't felt this young for twenty years. I suppose I am like most people—fearful of old age. I'd only admit it to you, darling. I have the crazy notion that someday I'll wake up and see my face in the mirror and have to tell myself, You are old, Lewis, you are old. Men are vain and they can fool themselves for a long time; but I imagine the day comes when even the vainest man has to give in to the truth because his bones will no longer permit him to lie."

"I don't want to talk about it, Lewis. Please don't let's talk about it. We're living in the present, here and now. Let's leave the future to the ladies who write the horoscope columns. I'll just take life day by day; and that means you'll have to take it that way, too, because you are going to be with me. Every day."

Lewis left after midnight, and Allison, tired from the day that had begun early in Peyton Place and ended late in New York, went to bed. She opened the windows wide to the cool night air; the traffic noises were diminished by distance, a stillness seemed to rise from the quiet, deserted park. It enveloped her, she drifted, she slept.

In the morning she had breakfast brought to her on the terrace. It was only eight o'clock. Country girl, she said to herself, making fun of herself for not having fallen into the New York way of sleeping late and then breakfasting on black coffee. She ate a country girl's breakfast of fried eggs, bacon, fruit and coffee with cream.

She was glad she had wakened early. Allison hated to hurry the first meal of the day, loved to linger over the breakfast cigarettes that tasted better than any other. She watched the city wake up. Standing at the parapet, she saw the water truck's white spray; it left the surface of the street a little darker, if not much cleaner.

Beginning at eight-thirty, more and more men and women left apartment buildings and were swallowed up by the omnivorous subway entrance at the corner. Allison smiled, amused to observe that as the hour approached closer to nine, the men and women walked ever more quickly.

At ten, dressed in a tweed suit with a jacket cut like an elegant cardigan, Allison stepped into a waiting taxi, the door closed behind by the hotel doorman.

The driver said, "You know something, lady? Doormen at good hotels are the only people who know how to close taxi doors. They don't slam 'em but they always get it closed on the first try. My taxis would last a lot longer if people knew how to close the doors."

Allison spent the morning in paneled offices, putting into the hands of lawyers and investment men her now considerable earnings. She nodded as they explained things to her; but, no matter how closely she tried to listen, her mind drifted on to other things. But she knew they were honest and capable men; it did not matter that she didn't understand. Perhaps it was better, she thought; at least, I won't be an interfering amateur. Things like this are better left to the pros.

She went shopping in the afternoon and bought the kind of

535

clothes and lingerie she had only looked at before. She ordered suits and dresses that bore the labels that meant money. The floor managers invariably recognized her; charge accounts were immediately arranged.

"I can give you a check," Allison offered.

She laughed to herself at the thought that, now that she had money, she didn't need it.

She had only to give her address and it was sent; her name was the only currency she needed.

When she got back to her apartment, the boxes were unpacked and the contents hung in the closets by the maid. Allison kicked off her shoes and dropped down on the sofa. I'll never get used to this, she thought.

The phone rang. It was Stephanie. A television producer had just called. "It's a small part, Allison, but I have to take it. And rehearsals start tonight, I'm afraid. It's seven hours in a drafty theater for me. I'd much rather be having dinner with you."

Stephanie was in a hurry. She'd call tomorrow, she said, and they'd make a date for lunch.

I adore Stephanie, Allison thought. She's practically the only one to whom my success hasn't made a bit of difference. Some people seemed to feel that there was just so much success around and that if their friends won any part of it, that left less for them. It was an attitude Allison could not understand.

I could understand it, she thought, if I had just picked a winning number in the sweepstakes, or a rich uncle in Australia had died and left me everything he owned which included half of Australia. But I *worked* for everything I have. Nobody gave it to me. She remembered the bitter, vicious letters she had received, hundreds of them, from people who thought that her success made their success less possible of achieving.

She sighed, stirred herself to a sitting position and phoned Lewis. She told him about her day and that only David would be coming to dinner because Stephanie had got a part. "Won't you change your mind and come, darling?"

"I'll phone you at midnight. Perhaps if you're not too tired then, I'll come over. Have a pleasant evening with David, darling. He can give you a lot of information about Hollywood, you know. He was there for a while. I don't know how helpful it'll be, though. He has a pretty jaundiced view of it. But we'll talk about that later."

After she had spoken to Lewis, she called Room Service and ordered dinner for two, to be served at eight o'clock.

Before David arrived, she drew a bath and sprinkled it with lavender scent. In the bottle, the drops were amber, but in the bath water they turned to a smoky purple. She was enclosed by the fragrance.

When David came, he found her wearing a simple black dress, its severity relieved only by the rich velvet piping around the cuffs. Her hair was pulled back.

She looked older, he thought, and more beautiful than ever before.

"I was surprised when you called this morning, Allison. And terribly pleased, of course. I want to thank you for ending this ridiculous situation. It was all my fault. That day we met in the coffeehouse—well, to put it bluntly, Allison—I was jealous. I gave myself all sorts of others reasons for what I was feeling, but it was plain, old-fashioned jealousy and nothing else. Forgive me, Allison."

"There's nothing to forgive, David. Let's have a drink and a long evening of talk. We'll drown it all in talk."

After dinner, over coffee on the terrace, the talk turned to Allison's coming trip to Hollywood. By that time, all constraint between them had been dissipated by the good food and the wine that had been chilled to just the right temperature. The hovering Hungarian ghosts had done their job well; and, at ten o'clock, they evaporated, taking their food cart with them, leaving David and Allison with their coffee and brandy.

"You'll hate it out there," David said. "Hollywood is filled with haberdashers who made good, and men who call themselves writers though they've never had an original thought in their lives."

"Nevertheless, I'm going," said Allison. "Brad has already told them so."

"Just what are you supposed to be going there for?" asked David.

"I'm to be technical adviser for the film. I'm going to give the script writer a few pointers and talk with the costume and set designers. Things like that."

537

"Allison," said David earnestly, "they're making a fool out of you. They don't need you to tell them anything. All they want is to make use of you, to exploit your publicity value for their own ends. They'll make you feel important, invite you to a few parties, flatter the hell out of you so that you can come back East and tell everyone who'll listen what a swell bunch of people they are out on the coast."

Allison laughed. "Well, if that's all they want, they're certainly willing to pay a good price for it. Twenty-five hundred a week plus all my expenses."

David shrugged. "You won't like it, Allison. I'm sure you won't."

"Maybe not, David, but I've got to find out for myself. I want every experience that's offered me—or just about."

"I'm only thinking of you," David said. "Wait until they start ripping your book to pieces. You'll feel differently then. You won't be able to stand it. Nobody could."

"I don't have your sensitive, artistic soul," said Allison. "As far as I'm concerned, all I want for *Samuel's Castle* is another forty weeks on the lists. And after what they paid me for the picture rights, they can do anything they damn well please with it."

"I just don't want you to be hurt," said David quietly, and Allison was suddenly ashamed.

"I know it, David," she said contritely. "But I have to find out for myself."

"Let me hear from you," said David.

"Yes," said Allison. "I'll phone you. With the studio paying my hotel bills, I'll be able to do it with a clear conscience."

David smiled. "You've changed a lot, Allison. But basically you're still the little girl from Peyton Place, still keeping your conscience clear. I don't think you could change that part of you if you submitted to surgery."

· 2 ·

THE HOTEL WAS A HUGE, TEN-TIERED SEMICIRCLE MADE OF WHITE stone and glass and it sat in the middle of vast, manicured lawns that were dotted with symmetrical, evenly spaced flower beds.

Allison stood on the terrace outside her ninth-floor suite and thought, I wonder if anything ever gets dirty in Beverly Hills. It was ten o'clock in the morning and everything below, beyond and behind her sparkled as if the world had just been removed from a tissue-filled gift box.

In the room behind her, the telephone rang, and she stepped through the floor-to-ceiling glass doors and went to answer it. The room itself was like a theatrical set, all modern furniture, white rugs and abstract paintings. The furniture was upholstered in a deep royal purple and the linen drapes over the sliding glass doors matched exactly.

"Hello," said Allison into the white telephone receiver.

"Are you ready?" asked Bradley Holmes.

"As much as I'll ever be," said Allison. "I've been standing here admiring my surroundings and I can't quite figure out whether I'm living inside a frosted wedding cake or a purple Easter basket."

Brad laughed. "Wait until you see the studio," he said. "That'll really give you something to think about."

"I can't wait," said Allison. "Are you on your way down?"

"Right there," replied Brad and hung up.

A few minutes later there was a knock at her door and he came into her room.

"This is indeed very plush," said Brad, looking around. "The denizens of Glitterville have done right well by you. Naturally, my

539

room is not anywhere near this fancy, but then, I'm paying for mine."

Allison put on her hat and a fresh pair of white gloves.

"You don't like Hollywood much, do you?" she asked.

"Nobody from New York likes Hollywood," replied Brad, as they walked down the hall toward the elevators. "Of course, half the time it's a pose. New Yorkers who'd give their eyes to be called to Hollywood are the ones who scream the loudest about prostitution and lack of artistry in the films. No, I don't like Hollywood, but I keep my mouth shut about it. They keep a great deal of money out here and I enjoy getting my share of it."

"David hated it out here," said Allison.

"Yes, he did," replied Brad. "But, on the other hand, David is never going to get rich. It all comes down to what a person wants from life."

A Cadillac limousine pulled up in front of the main entrance of the hotel and a uniformed chauffeur got out to hold the back door of the car open for Allison and Brad.

"You see," said Brad, "the little niceties, such as being driven about in a car like this, cost money. If one wants things like this, one must sacrifice something. David was never willing to give an inch. I was out here with him a few years ago. He was impossible. Miracle Pictures had paid him a very decent price for his third book in spite of the fact that the hard-cover edition never went over three thousand copies. They wanted David to help on the script. Well, we came out here, David and I, and, let me tell you, I never want to spend another such two weeks. David was unbending, unyielding and absolutely deaf to all suggestions made by the producer, the director and the other writers. We were supposed to be here for eight weeks, but at the end of two David went out and got drunk and took a plane to New York. Believe me, it wasn't easy explaining that to the studio. But in the end, they decided that they were better off without him."

"He thought I shouldn't come out here," said Allison.

"I can imagine," said Brad. "Listen, darling, I don't know why you bother with people like David. You're a success now. You don't need these somber, social worker types."

"But David is a great writer," said Allison. "Not just good, not just successful, but *great*. And you know it."

"I know it," admitted Brad, "but I also know that if David relaxed a little and listened to me a little more, his books would do a lot better on the market."

"David hasn't a commercially minded cell in his body," said Allison.

"One of the privileges of the chosen few," said Brad as they rode past the gates.

Allison sat up and smoothed her gloves nervously. As always, when facing a new situation, she was wishing fervently that she had stayed safely at home. The car pulled up in front of a white stone house that looked as if it might belong in a New York suburb. On the front lawn there was a black lettered sign in a wrought-iron frame that read ARTHUR TISHMAN.

"For Heaven's sake," said Allison, "is this Mr. Tishman's office?"

"Yes," said Brad. "Fancy, isn't it?"

"A man with a wife and three children could move in here and live very comfortably," said Allison.

In what would have been the foyer of the bungalow, had it been used as a home, were a desk and two filing cabinets, but these had been so artfully arranged and camouflaged that they did not seem at all out of place amidst the brocaded sofas and oil paintings. Behind the desk sat one of the most beautiful women Allison had ever seen. She was small but with an exquisitely molded figure and her hair was like a gold cap. She wore a severe black dress and silver bracelets on both arms, and her shoes were tiny scraps of black leather.

"I'm so glad, Miss MacKenzie," she said, rising to greet Allison. "My name is Gloria Muir and I'm Mr. Tishman's secretary."

"How do you do?" said Allison.

Miss Muir had an English accent, thought Allison, that would have made Laurence Olivier proud of her.

"And how are you, Mr. Holmes?" said Miss Muir. "It's so nice to see you again."

"It's wonderful to be in California again," said Brad.

You liar, thought Allison.

"Mr. Tishman is expecting you," said Miss Muir. "Please come with me."

Mr. Tishman was tall and heavy and looked rather like a young

541

Sidney Greenstreet. He wore dark trousers and one of the most brazen sport shirts Allison had ever seen.

"Brad!" he exclaimed, coming around the vast desk in front of him. "How nice to see you again. It's been much too long."

The two men shook hands and before Brad could introduce Allison, Tishman turned to her.

"And this is the little lady who has caused all the commotion," he said, smiling and extending his hand. "Miss MacKenzie, I can't tell you what an honor this is."

"How do you do, Mr. Tishman. It's very nice to be here," said Allison, feeling a little as if she were at the Mad Hatter's tea party.

Mr. Tishman took her arm. "And this is Conrad Blanding, our director," he said, "and Joel Parkingson, our script writer."

Conrad Blanding wore dark-rimmed glasses and smiled with all his teeth, but Joel Parkingson did not smile at all. He bowed stiffly and sat down, his eyes fixed broodingly on the sheaf of yellow paper in his hand.

"Would you like a drink?" asked Arthur Tishman. "Coffee?"

"Coffee, please," said Allison and sat down on a leather-upholstered chair.

The walls of Mr. Tishman's office were paneled in walnut and across one wall there was a colorful poster in a frame.

"It's one of Lautrec's best, don't you think, Miss MacKenzie?" asked Mr. Blanding.

Allison started. "Oh," she said. "Yes. Yes, indeed."

In a few minutes, Miss Muir came in carrying a silver tray on which rested a complete silver service.

"Shall I pour?" she asked.

"Yes, if you please, Miss Muir," said Mr. Tishman.

A quiet little ceremony followed during which all the men stood silently while Miss Muir filled cups from the silver pot.

"Now, then, Miss MacKenzie," said Mr. Tishman, leaning back comfortably in his chair. "By the way, may I call you Allison?"

"Please do," Allison replied.

"Good. Puts things on a friendly, warm basis. I'm Arthur, and," he waved a vague hand in the direction of the writer and director, "they're Joel and Conrad. Well, Allison, we've all been very busy on your book and already have a script of sorts."

542

Allison glanced at Joel Parkingson, but the writer did not look up. He just sat and looked sadder than ever.

"I'd like to see the script," said Allison.

"Certainly," said Arthur Tishman. "We want you to take a copy along with you when you leave. Read it tonight and tomorrow we'll get together again and discuss things. But please don't think that what we have now is what I call a good, working script. It isn't. Joel here has just been putting down ideas. We've got a long way to go yet, but I do think, and Conrad agrees, that Joel has given us a good base to start working on. Our final script will follow the same lines as the one we have now, but I'm sure that, as a writer yourself, you understand the long, slow process of finishing and polishing."

At first, Arthur Tishman gave the impression of a man who is accustomed to command, and Allison was a little frightened of him. But she soon realized that her presence, meeting her, had made him nervous. As a result, he did not converse but made speeches; it was as if he had it all written down, and then read the lines badly, like an amateur actor.

Allison was familiar with the Tishman legend. He had come up the hard way; everything he had he had made himself. She felt a feeling of kinship with him.

"Now, that's enough business for today," said Arthur Tishman. "We have a busy week plotted for you, my dear. Later today, you have a meeting with Harold Jenks, our publicity man. The papers have been on his neck ever since they heard you were coming. Then, tomorrow morning, we've made a date for you with one of our best photographers, and tomorrow afternoon we want you to go on a tour of the studio. Sort of to get the feeling of the way we work here. Then tomorrow night, there is to be a dinner party for you at my home. Everyone connected with the picture will be there, and a lot of other important people, too. We're all looking forward to it."

"But I had planned—" began Allison.

Brad stood up. "Wonderful, Arthur," he said. "As usual, you've done everything that has to be done very efficiently."

"It's the way we have to work," Arthur said. "Efficiency prevents ulcers. That's my own secret success formula, which I reveal to everyone."

Allison was back in the car sitting next to Brad before it occurred to her that neither Conrad Blanding nor Joel Parkingson had spoken one word to her, once the producer had begun to speak about the script.

"There," said Brad, as the car pulled away. "Painless, wasn't it?"

"Yes," agreed Allison, "but we didn't accomplish much."

"Wait," said Brad. "You'll have plenty to do when things get rolling."

The car stopped in front of a stone building that looked like a post office in a medium-sized city. Brad helped Allison out and led the way to Harold Jenks's office.

Harold Jenks was short and potbellied with dark curly hair and a beaked nose that would have gladdened the heart of a Nazi cartoonist.

"Howarya?" he asked, not rising from behind his desk as Brad introduced Allison.

"Fine, thank you," said Allison.

"Sit down, sit down," said Jenks, indicating a chair. "Just get in?"

"No," said Allison. "We arrived last night."

"Met Tishman?"

"Yes. Earlier this afternoon. Before we came here."

"You're cute," said Jenks. "Clean-cut and all that. Should be able to do something with that." He looked Allison over thoroughly, then he pressed a key on the box that sat on his desk. "Send Joe Borden in here," he said. A man came into the room, but Jenks did not introduce him to Allison. He merely waved in her direction. "Allison MacKenzie," he said, as if she were merchandise on a store counter. "Writes books. We've got to get something ready for the papers. Take her out and show her around a little. Get a line on her and give me something before she leaves."

Allison felt now, not only like merchandise on a counter, but merchandise that had been rejected by a prospective customer.

"Better get a few pictures," said Jenks, glancing at his watch. "Can't have the papers doing it on their own. Go over to Photography with her now."

"But Mr. Tishman said that I'm supposed to do that tomorrow morning," said Allison. "I can't be photographed today. My hair's a mess and I'm all wrinkled and my gloves are soiled."

Jenks laughed. "We've got people who get paid to worry about

544

details like that," he said. "Go on. Go with Borden. He'll take care of everything."

"But I don't like to have my picture taken," said Allison. "It's bad enough in the morning, but—"

Jenks put his hands, palms down, on his desk with a gesture of infinite patience.

"Look," he said, "sitting in the same chair you're sitting in now I've had all the big names in the business. Monroe, Turner, Hayworth. All of 'em. I know what I'm doing. Just don't give me a hard time and I'll do a good job for you."

And he will too, Allison thought, finally impressed with Jenks's professionalism. He was the kind of man, met all too rarely, who knew his job, every part of it, better than anyone else. Like Tishman, Jenks was quite clearly not a man who held his job because he was somebody's brother-in-law. In Hollywood, the day of the brother-in-law ended with the birth of television. They're probably all working at the TV studios now, Allison thought.

Allison was combed, made up and photographed. Then she was recombed and rephotographed. The photographer looked at her as if she were something under a microscope and mumbled things to himself, and by the time it was over Allison was almost in tears.

"I wish I'd never come!" she cried as the car drove back toward the hotel. "David was right."

"There, there," Brad consoled. "You're just tired, Allison. You'll feel better after a drink and a good dinner."

At nine-thirty that evening, Allison finished the last of her dessert and looked gratefully at Brad.

"You were right," she said. "I have been acting like a child. Just pet me and feed me and I'm all smiles again. Disgusting, isn't it?"

Brad laughed. "You're wonderful," he said. "With just the right amount of temperament to make you exciting."

"The only thing that excites me now is the thought of a good, hot bath and a nice, soft bed," said Allison.

"Are you going to read the script?" asked Brad.

"While I'm soaking in the tub," replied Allison.

"I'll call you at nine-thirty in the morning," said Brad as they left the dining room. "We'll have breakfast together."

Ten minutes later, Allison drew a tub of very hot water, perfumed it lavishly with bath oil and prepared to soak, relax and read. An hour later, when she had finished the script, she was far from relaxed. Joel Parkingson had left out of his script what Allison considered some of the best parts of her novel; instead, there were pages and pages of inane dialogue and hollow characterization.

I mustn't care, thought Allison, tears streaming down her face. I *won't* care. They bought it and now it's theirs to do with as they see fit. I'm not entitled to care.

But she did care, and with the caring went the only defense that she had been able to build against a world suddenly too much aware of her. She had constructed her wall of indifference carefully, in the very beginning, for she had known that she would need something to hide behind.

"In a little while," Lewis had warned her, "say when *Samuel's Castle* gets close to the hundred thousand mark, it is going to become fashionable to pan the hell out of it."

"But I don't understand," Allison replied. "The first reviews were good. Not raves, exactly, but good."

"That was in the beginning," said Lewis. "But there are a lot of phony people in the world. They are the ones who 'discover' people, places and things and can't bear to keep their mouths shut about how clever they've been. But the minute that the great unwashed public begins to share their enthusiasm, whatever has been discovered is no longer palatable to the discoverers. Then they backtrack." Lewis imitated the voice of one of them. They always sounded like victims of some terrible fatigue. "Capri used to be *the* place to go, my dear. But lately it's simply too full of the most undesirable types."

Allison laughed. "And is that what they will say about *Samuel's Castle?*" she asked. "That it used to be a good book but now it's become so dreadfully common?"

Lewis' face wrinkled in disgust. "I've listened to them at a thousand cocktail parties," he said. "And believe me you can't fight them. They are the opinion makers and they have got themselves into positions of power."

"I'm not their sort," Allison had said. "They won't waste their valuable time on me."

"They may," Lewis said. "And if they do, it can hurt."

"Don't worry about it, Lewis," said Allison.

But it began to happen as he had said it would. The first indication that Allison had of it was when a reviewer who had written a favorable review of her book wrote an article in the same magazine when the movie rights were sold.

"Century Films have bought the rights to the sexy silly, *Samuel's Castle*. All we can say is that Hollywood must be more hard up for material than usual."

Allison was stunned. She began to overhear conversations at parties and in theater lobbies.

"No, I haven't read *Samuel's Castle*," she heard one woman, who had referred to the book on her television program as "exciting," telling her companion. "I glanced through it, but, my dear, what a bore!"

The head of a television network, who had tried to buy the rights to the book for a ninety-minute spectacular and had been turned down by Bradley Holmes, gave an interview to a national magazine in which he said, "I dread to think what a number of good books have been ignored while *Samuel's Castle* has clung to the top of the best-seller list."

It was only with Lewis that Allison could let down the barriers a little, and even with him she was careful not to reveal how much she was hurt. For the most part, she did her weeping alone.

"The public loves to create a hero," Lewis had said. "Sometimes I think they do it for the sheer joy of knocking him down from the highest peak. Like a child who builds a house of blocks and then destroys it with one vicious kick."

"I don't care," Allison had cried with forced gaiety. "It's wonderful to be famous while it lasts. And I don't really care that much what anyone says about the book. I don't really care at all."

Allison wept without sound into the pillow on her bed.

I don't care, she cried. Century bought it. I took their money. It's theirs, and I don't care what they do with it.

• **3** •

AT NINE-THIRTY THE NEXT MORNING, WHEN BRADLEY HOLMES JOINED her for breakfast, Allison MacKenzie looked as if she had never shed a tear in her life.

"Did you read the script?" asked Brad, sipping his coffee.

"Yes."

"How did it strike you?"

"As the biggest piece of foolishness one man could possibly get down on paper," said Allison. "If he worked really hard at it, that is."

"Well, it's not the end of the world," said Brad. "Arthur told you that it was only their first effort."

"He also said that the basis they have now will remain the same," said Allison angrily. "If that's so, they're going to be laughed out of every theater in America."

"Come now," said Brad. "It can't be that bad."

Allison shrugged. "See for yourself," she said.

"No time," said Brad, glancing at his watch. "We have to get started for the studio."

"I'd just as soon get started for the airport, if you don't mind," said Allison. "The sooner we leave here the better."

"You sound like David Noyes," said Brad. "Come on, Allison, cheer up."

She found it impossible to do so. All the way out to the studio, she sat in the back of the limousine in a little world of her own. It was a world of rancor. She hated Hollywood, Tishman, the writer, the director. All she could think of was that Tishman had bought her book because he admired it and thought it would make a great film; but he had bought it only to change it. She

548

thought of the flat, platitudinous lines of dialogue and shuddered. The film would be called *Samuel's Castle,* her name would be listed on the credits; but it had nothing to do with her.

And yet, it would. She knew that in Tishman's Hollywood world, as in the Broadway world, no matter how remote was your connection with a flop—even if you were only the author of the book and had nothing to do with the adaptation—you were still considered to be partly responsible for it.

Having read Tishman's script, she had no doubt that the film would be a flop, that it would be laughed off the screen, that audiences would be so bored by it they'd leave their popcorn behind and flee the theater.

When she and Brad entered Tishman's studio, he was at his desk going through a loose-leaf folder containing the costume designer's preliminary sketches. On the margins of each sheet he wrote comments in red ink. Allison noted that he had the calligraphic handwriting that always reminded her of monastic orders, of dedicated men working alone. So much for handwriting analysis, she thought; Tishman was no monk, and Hollywood was a million miles from the nearest monastery.

Arthur Tishman looked closely at Allison from under his heavy, hooded eyelids. He swung his chair around and, in a sudden movement, stood up.

"Brad," he said, "why don't you go over to Publicity and look over what Jenks has prepared. I'd like to take Allison and show her around the lot."

"Of course, Arthur," Brad said. "That's a very good idea."

Allison looked at Brad and thought, You've missed your calling; you'd have made a perfect Yes man.

When Brad had gone, Arthur turned to Allison. He moved toward the door and she found herself following him.

"Do you mind walking?" he said.

"I like walking," Allison told him.

"I like it, too. But it takes too long," he said.

Then he was silent. Allison walked along beside him, thinking, What kind of man is this? He has the handwriting of a monk, dresses like a man from Mars—today he wore a sport shirt on which palm trees swayed across his chest, casting their shadows on beautiful Waikiki Beach which stretched across his stomach—

549

believes walking is too slow, and thinks he can make a great movie out of this incredibly dull and unimaginative script.

After five minutes of walking, the ordinary world of ordinary buildings was behind them. Allison felt like Alice; the world had gone topsy-turvy. Next door to a crumbling southern mansion was the façade of the palace at Versailles; and when they left those behind, they walked down the main street of a small town that Hollywood, by using it so often, had made the American people (and half the world) believe to be typical. Six cowboys wearing green eye shadow, their lips rouged, loped past them, their horses' hoofs clattering on the asphalt road.

When they left the typical small town Allison saw, on her right, an artificial lake. A rowboat with three wet actors was being tossed about by high waves. From a tower, a voice called, "Okay. Turn off the storm." The wind machines stopped; the storm ended; the actors stepped out of the boat into the knee-deep water and waded ashore.

"When you see that on the screen," Arthur said, "you will be certain it was filmed on the open seas. And if the director is good and the producer is imaginative and the actors right, you will believe in the plight of that shipwrecked trio."

They came to a western town. There was the dusty main street, the sheriff's office, the saloon, the general store, the wood sidewalks. Allison expected at any moment to see Gary Cooper, tall and lean, cautiously move out of the sheriff's office.

Arthur pushed open the swinging doors of the saloon and they went inside. Sunlight filtered through cracks in the roof; the long mirror behind the bar returned their images. Seeing herself, Allison had the feeling she was out of place and out of time, an interloper in the American past.

She sat down at one of the tables. Arthur leaned against the bar.

"You've seen this saloon in a hundred movies. Each time it looked a little different. A few minor changes, a change of lighting, a change of faces, and it becomes a new place. All you need are creative film makers with a new way of looking at things, and the most familiar object or place can be made to look strange to you."

He crossed the room and sat down next to her.

"I want to tell you, Allison, that I know how you feel about

550

the script. You think we've ruined your book. And you say to yourself, I don't care that they've ruined my book but they haven't even made a good script out of the ruins. It's all dull, flat and unimaginative."

Allison opened her mouth to speak, but Arthur went on.

"A lot of skills go into the making of a film, Allison. But after twenty years in this place I've come to the conclusion that the most valuable skill of all is the ability to read a script. To read it, see it and hear it. All at once. And then to be able to judge; will this script make a good movie, or just another mediocre movie."

He stood up and began to pace restlessly around the tables, then stopped with his back to the swinging doors.

"It's difficult to explain all this, Allison. You read our script like a novelist. You can't. You've got to read it like a sound camera. A sound camera with an imaginative human brain. Listen, Allison. You've heard the expression, 'the magic of the theater'?"

Allison nodded.

"When idiots use that expression, they mean the 'glamour' of the theater, its aura, its spectacular appeal. But when theater workers talk about 'magic,' they mean something altogether different. To them, 'magic' is the odd, mysterious, inexplicable thing that happens between a director and his actors. The magical thing is that those lines you consider to be dull and innocuous suddenly become meaningful, and reveal qualities you never suspected were there. You make a great mistake to expect that a film script must be literary. In a sense, it must *never* be literary. It has got to have *extra*-literary qualities."

He came and sat down across the table from her.

"What you are looking for is a script that reads like a novel. What I am looking for, always, is a script that reads like a movie. Allison, I'm an old pro. I know what I'm talking about. If I didn't, I'd have been thrown off this lot years ago. Are you going to take my word for it?"

Allison did not answer. All she could think of was her mutilated novel. She walked to the window and looked out. She saw, walking down the dusty street, a group of white-robed, barefooted men. One of them was leading a white donkey. They were on their way to the lot where a Biblical movie was being made.

It was one of the strangest sights she had ever seen, these early

551

Christians walking through a town of the American West. It was all wrong, yet out here it made sense. She realized suddenly that these people could do anything, that on the outskirts of Los Angeles they could, if they wanted to, create New York or a planetary city of the future. They had worked their magic on her since she was a little girl. Why did she suddenly begin to doubt them now?

She turned and smiled at Arthur. "I think I've been suffering from Novelist's Disease. It's what other people call arrogance. We work alone so much that we begin to think we are the only creative people in the world. And, what's worse, that we don't need anyone else."

"Only hacks don't take pride in their work," Arthur said.

He took her arm and they began to walk back toward the administration buildings. At the open door of a sound stage, two ladies in waiting at the court of the Empress Eugénie, wearing ball gowns and powdered wigs, were talking about their favorite rock-and-roll singer. For the first time, Allison began to feel the excitement of Hollywood's creativity and, listening to Arthur, began to have some understanding of the technical aspect of film work.

"We expect to wind up with a great film, Allison," Arthur told her as he helped her into the car. "Not just a good film, but a great one. Tomorrow we'll have an office ready for you. I want to hear all the ideas you've got."

The driver picked up Brad outside Jenks's office. Brad got into the car and handed Allison a large manila envelope. "Your photos," he said, smiling.

She opened the envelope and took them out. She hardly recognized herself. It was her own face, but somehow it had been invested with mystery, with glamour and with a kind of beauty she had never seen in any mirror. She smiled to herself and thought, The magic is even working on me.

She said to Brad, "That lens looked at me with a lover's eyes."

She quickly stuffed the photographs back into the envelope. For some reason, it embarrassed her to look at them; it was as if she had been caught in a fraudulent act.

By her second week in Hollywood, Allison had had to throw out the window every preconception she had brought along with her. It was true that there were more swimming pools in Beverly

Hills than in any other town in the world, the houses and grounds were the most fanciful copies of Spanish castles and English manor houses, and without doubt Hollywood attracted to itself the most beautiful women—and even beautiful men—from every part of the world.

But the overriding fact about Hollywood, what made the trappings unimportant, was the work of making movies. She never anywhere saw people work with such energy, with such furious drive. It carried over into their private lives; there was the same kind of driving energy in their love affairs and their marriages and in the way they relaxed.

Making movies was for Hollywood what making automobiles was to Detroit. From the window of her office she could see a large area of the studio lot, the trucks and motorized freight wagons that plied endlessly up and down the studio streets, carrying scenery and costumes. Hundreds of men moved about, each performing an assigned task, hundred of extras and a handful of highly paid actors and directors committed themselves and their reputations to film.

Allison sat at her desk and spent the first week reading the script. She read it now with new eyes, eyes that had been opened and made more knowledgeable because Tishman had shared with her some of the knowledge that only years of working in films can give.

Parts of the script that, on first reading, had seemed to her arbitrary and capricious, she now saw as reasonable changes.

They had changed the time scheme of her novel. She had thought them stupid for doing so. But now, she understood the reason for making a scene she had set in summer take place in winter. The coldness, the bleak landscape, the white and black of snow and bare trees, all this would heighten the mood and give the sequence precisely the emotional overtones it needed.

She met with the set designer and the costume department and gave her opinions on their work. She found only minor errors, the kind of thing no one would notice except the experts who looked for such mistakes.

She left the studio at five every day and returned to her hotel. It was not the studio but the hotel that was the Hollywood of every small-town girl's imagining. In the lobby and around the pool sat the beautiful girls who were not waiting to be discovered but working very hard at it. And there were the rich widows, elderly women who spent hours each day in beauty salons, and who were always accompanied by handsome young men.

Allison was soon able to spot an agent by the way he walked, and could tell at a glance whether a man was an unemployed writer or a director waiting for an assignment. In a very short time she had learned all the gossip and knew, as the waitresses in the dining room knew, why the famous star was *really* getting her divorce, and who the other man *really* was.

Lewis called Allison every evening. They spoke for five or ten minutes and hurried to say all they wanted to say to each other, spoke of their love and their plans and what each had done that day. Until the day finally came when Allison was able to say, "Oh, Lewis, tomorrow is the last day and I can come back to you!" She had her reservation for six o'clock the next evening, she would be in New York, with Lewis, in the morning.

The night before she left, Arthur Tishman gave a party for her. He wanted her to meet Rita Moore, especially, knowing she was a favorite of Allison's.

Brad had returned to New York at the end of the first week. Allison rode alone in the back seat of the studio limousine, her elbow on the arm rest, smoking a cigarette. She smiled. I'm acting as calmly, she thought, as if I've done this sort of thing all my life.

She wore a simple, sheathlike black gown; her hair was drawn back; a small diamond clip was her only ornament. It was the only jewelry she had bought herself, thus far, with her new money. She always referred to it, to herself, as new money. She had seen the clip one day in the window of a Beverly Hills jeweler's and walked in and bought it. She knew that whatever might come in the future, this clip would always be her favorite, because it was the first and because it had been bought with money made from her first success. As the car drove up the graveled drive to Arthur Tishman's house, she touched the clip; it gave her assurance.

Tishman's house was one of the great old houses. It was not California modern; it looked like one of the houses in an old Long Island suburb. It was an extravagant relic, a dinosaur from the ice age of Doug and Mary; it was a proud reminder of Hollywood's regal past.

Architecturally, it was part Spanish, part Tudor; yet this did not, somehow, result in a hodgepodge. As is so often the case with early twentieth-century American houses, the architect's vulgarity had, over the years, become charming. It was a place, Allison decided, that she would enjoy living in. It had not the look of the postwar houses; she thought them mean and inhospitable with their functional little rooms and uncomfortably low ceilings.

The car came to a stop at a graceful flight of stone steps with low risers and a carved balustrade. Arthur came down the steps and helped her out of the car.

In five minutes she had had two drinks, was holding her third and had been introduced to twenty people. She remembered the names of none except those actors she recognized. There was one she had had a crush on when she was fourteen. He had sallow skin, thinning hair and an obscene little belly. On the screen he still looked as handsome as ever.

She had quickly gulped down her first two drinks in an attempt to get over the nervousness she felt at being with these people. But all she succeeded in doing was to make herself a little light-headed. She looked around for Rita Moore but did not see her. She's probably the fat, ugly woman in the corner, Allison thought; I only know her screen image. She owns a loving camera lens that makes her slender and ravishingly beautiful.

Conversations swirled around her. She put down her drink and stepped out the open doors to the terrace. She took a deep breath of air. I must clear my head, she thought. She walked to the end of the terrace, her heels making a satisfying noise on the terra-cotta tiles. The brightly lighted living room gave way to a dark wing of the house.

In one room an amber light glowed and Allison, peering through the french doors, saw it was the library. She tried the door. It opened, and she entered. It was a high-ceilinged room, vaulted, with a deep stone fireplace. The walls were lined with books, beautifully bound.

They even look as if they've been read, Allison thought.

She took a step toward the books when a head popped up, peered for an instant over the top of the leather sofa and disappeared. But that moment was enough for Allison to recognize Rita Moore's famous face.

"Are you real or are you the ghost of Norma Talmadge?" Rita Moore asked from behind the sofa.

"I'm real enough," Allison said. She walked around the sofa and looked down at Rita Moore. She smiled at Rita and said, "I'm glad to see you have a body and aren't just a voice."

"I *used* to have a body," Rita said, looking down at it. "Christ, did I have a body! When I see myself in old movies on the telly, it breaks my ever-beating heart."

"You're still the greatest, Miss Moore."

Rita's mouth curved in a mirthless smile. "Thanks a whole lot. You could have it for one small farthing if I could have your youth."

She reached for the cut-glass brandy decanter on the small table, but could not quite reach it. Allison picked it up and tilted some of the liquid into Rita's glass.

She drank it down like medicine, like something she had to take because it was good for her. She grimaced and said, "Christ, I'm tired! I'm just plain body tired, and I'm most of all tired of parties like this. When I come to a place like this, the first thing I do is look for the exits. After twenty years in this town I've learned the library is the best place to be alone in. Most of us out here are afraid of books. Reading a book is a sign that we've been alone for a few hours. And out here, to be alone is a phrase that strikes a fear unknown since the black plague swept across Europe."

She filled her brandy glass again. Her soft, silver-blond hair caught the light and shimmered like a jewel. She had high cheekbones that made a diagonal of shadow in her cheeks, like smudges made by her thumbs. Her eyes were sea green and her dress was a deep green embroidered in gold. It clung to her body like a second skin, and where her breasts swelled out of the top her flesh was like heavy cream.

"You must be Allison MacKenzie," she said. "You must be, because I've never seen you before and because you are the only one here who looks bright enough to have written a novel. Especially a novel as good as *Samuel's Castle*."

"Thank you," Allison said.

"Please don't say thank you, dear. It reminds me of my second husband. My second husband was the kind of man who was always saying thank you. He was humble—in an arrogant sort of way."

Allison smiled, but not because she felt like smiling; she smiled because she had the feeling she was expected to.

"My second husband seduced me with Brahms and Scotch," said Rita at last. "The poor bastard."

"Why do you say that?" asked Allison.

"Because that was all he knew how to do," replied Rita. "Seduce women to a sad violin and the tinkle of ice cubes. He was good at it though, I'll say that for him."

"How many husbands have you had?" asked Allison.

Rita laughed. "Don't you ever read the fan magazines?" she asked.

Allison smiled and shook her head. "Not any more," she said. "But I used to. When we were in high school, Selena Cross and I used to buy every issue of *Photoplay* and *Silver Screen*. Then we'd cut out the pictures and make scrapbooks. I wonder if kids still do that."

"In Hollywood, we hope so," said Rita. "Anyway, it's four."

"Four what?"

"Husbands," said Rita. "Isn't that what you asked me?"

"Four!" said Allison. "Good Lord!"

"Well, at least I married the men I fell in love with," said Rita with a little pout. "I know plenty of women who will jump into bed with just anybody. At least I always kept it legal."

"I don't think that I'll ever get married," said Allison.

Rita poured more liquor into her glass. "Why not?" she asked. "What have you got against marriage?"

"I want everything to stay just the way it is right now," said Allison, an unaccustomed toughness in her voice.

Rita glanced at her sharply, then said, "Well, aren't you a smug little punk kid."

Allison's head snapped up in surprise. "What do you mean by that?" she asked.

"Just what I said," replied Rita belligerently. "You think you know it all, don't you?"

"For Heaven's sake," objected Allison. "What in the world did I say?"

"You love having things the way they are now," said Rita. "You love being a success, being way up on top where very few people ever get. You love all that lovely money that rolls in day after day, and you love the idea that it's yours, all yours."

"And what's wrong with that?" demanded Allison. "You're in the same position yourself. Don't tell me that you hate being successful."

Rita looked down into her glass and thought for a moment.

"I don't know," she said. "I don't know whether I hate it or love it or just don't care any more."

Allison laughed. "I know a fellow in New York. His name is Paul Morris and he's quite well known in his field so you've probably heard of him."

"I've heard of him," said Rita.

"Well, Paul told me once that successful people who complain about being successful are nothing more than lousy poseurs. If they didn't glory in it, they'd run and bury themselves where no one had ever heard of them."

Rita gave a short, humorless laugh as she poured herself another drink.

"I'll tell you about success," she said. "And, believe me, I can tell you a helluva lot more about it than your friend Paul Morris. He never made it except as somebody else's shadow." She leaned back and sipped at her drink. "I think that you have to decide when you're very young that you want success more than anything else in the world," she said.

"Well, I certainly didn't," said Allison angrily.

Rita looked at her. "Don't kid me, love," she said. "I know enough about you, Allison. I've heard enough. I can figure you out like you were my twin sister. When you were a kid you didn't think you were good looking. You were the odd one who couldn't fit into the group, and you resented everyone who did belong. Without even knowing it you began to think in terms of 'I'll show them all,' and you did."

"All you need is a framed diploma and a couch and you could go into business," said Allison, and she poured a glass of brandy for herself.

"Don't get wise with me, sweetie," said Rita. "I've been there, and I know. Where the hell do you think I sprung from? Well, I'll tell you. From a lousy shack in the backwoods of Georgia. My old man was a sharecropper and my mother was worn out and tired before she even married him. Her father had been a sharecropper, too, and all she ever knew was work, work and more work. And kids and filth and no money and a constant hole in your belly from being hungry. I never had a pair of shoes on my feet until I was fourteen, and even then they were discards, but my mother sent me to school anyway."

She paused and drank deeply and refilled the glass. "I don't know what sets anybody else off," she said. "But I know what it was with me. We had a teacher at school who was a real old bag. She didn't have any more business teaching than I'd have, but with her shape and face I guess she couldn't do anything else. She reminded me of a wrinkled-up old prune, but she taught us geography. One day she was telling us about Paris, and she got a kind of look on her face that made her almost good looking for a minute. She showed us pictures, too. The most beautiful pictures I'd ever seen in my life, and she told us about the trip in a ship that got you there."

She leaned her head back and looked up at the ceiling, as if to look back into the past more comfortably. "Right then and there I made up my mind that I was going to Paris, but I was still a kid and too dumb to keep my mouth shut about it. I told her and she laughed at me. She told me that sharecroppers' kids never got out of Georgia, let alone make trips to Europe. But I knew better. I was going to Paris. And I did, too. Five years ago. With four trunks and sixteen suitcases and two maids and a poodle. I stood under the Arc de Triomphe and thought of that old bitch back in Georgia and thumbed my nose at her. I'd made it and I'd come first class all the way. I was with my third husband then. Jay Keating. You've heard of him, I suppose."

"Yes," said Allison. "I've heard of him. He's an English actor."

"English my foot," said Rita. "He was born in South Dakota. He was a pansy on top of everything else."

"A what?" said Allison.

"Pansy," said Rita. "A real fruit. I caught him in my stateroom with the ship's purser on the trip home. But you never would have read that in any fan magazine. We called it incompatibility and I went to Reno for a divorce. Heigh-ho, and so much for number three." She raised her glass. "Here's to success. It's what you tell yourself you have when it dawns on you that you haven't got anything else."

"It doesn't have to be like that," said Allison. "I've heard of plenty of people who are successful and happily married besides."

"Maybe," said Rita. "If the man is as successful as the woman. It doesn't work if the woman is the big name. Not once in a million times! It didn't work with me, and I guess I knew it wouldn't right from the beginning. I was married when I first began to be somebody. My first husband. Alan. A real, sweet kid. He worked for the Los Angeles Telephone Company and I married him because I kidded myself into believing I really loved him. What I was was hungry. And lonely. So Alan fed me and kept me company. When I was around. But I was going to make it and make it big and I didn't want a husband around who was going to make the road up any rockier than it was to begin with. I had a shape back then, too, and I wasn't particular who I showed it to as long as there was something in it for me. Alan didn't like the pictures he saw of me wearing a little more than a G-string and two sequins, but not much more. He crabbed when I went out with my agent and he couldn't understand that I had to be seen in the right places. He wanted me home and I wanted out. So that was the end of that."

Rita smiled her mirthless smile. "I felt rotten that time. I cried for almost the whole six weeks I had to stay in Nevada, but my agent, Charlie Bloom, told me what the score was. Charlie said that I could either have a diamond necklace around my neck or a husband. Naturally, I chose the diamonds. Do you know Charlie?"

"No," said Allison.

"He's the biggest agent in Hollywood," said Rita. "Charlie has all the big names in his stable now, but when he started out with me he was nobody. Just a smart, sharp little guy who knew all the answers and had more nerve than a brass monkey. Charlie dressed me in a tight sweater and an even tighter skirt and he taught me how to walk with a sexy jounce and how to pinch my nipples so that they'd show under the sweater. He changed my name, too. From Alice Johnson to Rita Moore. And there was a time when a man could get fired at Century if he slipped and called me Alice. Alice Johnson was a name without class. It took

Hollywood ten years to find out that I could do more than stick my chest out and wiggle my backside. That's when I became An Actress. Anyway, three years ago I married John Gresham. John was a real smoothie. He played the piano and told me I had eyes that he could drown in and that my body was like a flame. So what the hell. I married him."

"Just because he was a good talker?" asked Allison.

Rita shrugged. "No. He pressured me into it."

"Oh, come now," Allison objected. "Women don't allow themselves to be pressured into a marriage they don't want."

"What the hell do you know about it?" demanded Rita. "John was an artist, let me tell you. He knew what he was doing. The son-of-a-bitch used to make love to me for hours before we were married. He'd stroke and kiss and handle me until I thought I'd go out of my mind, but he never finished anything. He'd tell me he wanted to wait until after we were married because I was so pure and he didn't want to dishonor me by taking me without a ceremony. So I married him."

She stopped to light a cigarette. Allison could not take her eyes from her. "He was good in bed, I'll say that for him. And for a while it was great. We'd spend all day in bed. John was an expert. He knew every trick in the book and when I thought I couldn't do anything else, he'd come up with something new. But there came a day when I had to go back to work and that left John without a job. Still, he was nice to come home to. I'd walk in the door and he'd undress me and make me a drink and play with me while I drank it, and it was fun. I guess he got bored after a while, though, because last year he stopped playing with me and began to play with my money. He got away with over fifty thousand before I put a stop to it. As usual, I put the stop to it all by going to Nevada."

She turned her green eyes, searching and sad, to Allison. "So now you can go back to New York and tell your friend Paul what success is really like. You go along for years kidding yourself that if you're successful you can have everything you want, but all the time you know that the only way you can make it is alone."

Rita fixed herself another drink, and when she had done so she held the glass up to the light and squinted through the dark fluid.

"Alone," she said. "I guess that's the saddest word in the world.

You stay at a hotel and order your own coffee in the morning and you hire a masseuse to rub your back and at night your bed is as big a. Texas and as cold as Alaska. But you're successful." She swallowed her drink and looked at Allison. "Don't forget that, Allison. You're a success! You're a goddamned big success! And just see what it'll get you. Just you bloody well see!"

When Allison entered her hotel room, much later that night, its expensive splendor suddenly seemed tasteless and repellent. She threw her purse across the room. It struck the wall above her dressing table and fell with a crash among the bottles of perfume and jars of cream. Allison wanted to break every window and rip to shreds the royal purple curtains. She wanted to do something so wild and destructive that it would shake her back into sanity, into a realization of her true self which she now felt was lost.

She had success, more than she had ever dreamed of. But never in her life had she been so fearful of the future, so frightened of the present, as she was now.

She sank down into a chair and cried bitterly. What is to become of me? she asked herself. Will I, ten years from now, be another Rita Moore, working on my fourth divorce or my fifth husband? Oh, Lewis, Lewis, take care of me. Never let me go.

BOOK FOUR

♦ 1 ♦

ALLISON RETURNED TO PEYTON PLACE IN LATE OCTOBER, HAVING SPENT a week in New York with Lewis. She had had to tell Constance that the stopover in New York was necessary for business reasons. As the train pulled into Peyton Place, she thought, Lewis has become a guilty secret. She did not want to have secrets from her mother, but she knew that Constance would be worried and terribly upset to learn that she was involved with a married man. She wanted desperately to be able to sit down with Constance and discuss it with her, but knew that for Constance's sake she could not.

Peyton Place lay sheltered under the dome of October's bright blue sky. The tattered brown leaves that hung on the bare branches of trees were winter's flags, Allison thought, the sign of his coming. The air was not cold, but there was a wintry feel to it. On Armistice Day the first snow would fall, and by Thanksgiving the town would be in winter's grip.

She was hardly off the train before Mike and Constance threw their arms around her, welcoming her home. Tears sprang to her eyes; she felt guilty, felt she had betrayed them by staying with Lewis for a week. Constance carried her off to the waiting car while Mike followed, carrying her suitcases.

Constance and Allison sat in the back seat, and Constance held her hand and looked into her face as if to see if those weeks in Hollywood had changed or altered her in some way. Mike took a look at them in the rear-view mirror and laughed.

"Be careful, Allison," he said, "any minute now she's going to whip out a microscope and put you under it."

"You go to hell, Mike," said Constance, and smiled at him in the mirror.

Mike went on, "She was certain you had 'gone Hollywood' and that you'd come back with platinum-blond hair and at least three Mexican divorces."

Allison turned to Constance. "I was working too hard to become tainted," Allison said.

"Tell me all about Rita Moore," Mike demanded.

"That's all *he's* interested in," Constance said. "That old man of mine has hot pants for Rita Moore. Every time I open the bedroom door I expect to find that he's got pin-ups of her over our bed."

"I may be old but I'm not a fool," Mike said. "I know what side my bread is buttered on."

"Mike!" Allison said. "Honestly, I never heard people talk like you two, not even in Hollywood."

Mike and Constance roared with laughter. Constance squeezed Allison's hand. "I'm so glad to have you home, baby," she said.

The car drew up to the house. Allison looked at it with loving eyes. If only Lewis could see it, she thought, if only he were here with me now.

They went into the kitchen. It was, Allison thought, the warmest, kindest room she had ever seen anywhere.

"I'll unpack later," she said. "Right now I want a cup of Mother's coffee."

Mike said, "I'll carry your luggage upstairs, and then I've got to drive downtown and pick up some things for your mother." He bent down and kissed the top of her head. "Welcome home, Allison," he said.

Why is it always such a relief to me when I come back? wondered Allison. Peyton Place is small-town America at its worst. Narrow, provincial, gossipy. Yet, I never feel really safe anywhere else, nor contented. And why is it that I love the winter best? Is it because I can stay safe and warm in my mother's house while the storm rages outside?

Allison yawned and stretched and turned away from the bleak, wintry view outside the kitchen window.

"Tired, darling?" asked Constance, setting down a coffeepot and two cups on the table.

"No," said Allison. "Just lazy. I was wondering why I always feel better when I'm in Peyton Place than when I'm anywhere else." She shrugged. "I guess it must be immaturity. But I love to snuggle down into the cocoon of this house while life raises hell outside my protective shell. How's that? Deep and psychological, huh?"

Connie laughed. "I don't know much about psychology. I only know that I'm happy when you are, and wretched when you're not. Maybe I have an apron string complex or something."

Allison squeezed her mother's shoulder and picked up a coffee cup.

Constance said, "I didn't think you'd want to see anybody today, so I invited Selena and Joey and Peter Drake for dinner tomorrow night."

"Oh? I didn't know that Peter was still on the scene."

"Very much so," said Connie. "Selena never told me what happened between her and Tim Randlett, but when it was over, there was Peter, ready and willing to pick up the pieces."

"I wish Selena would get married," remarked Allison. "Either that or leave town. She's in a dreadful rut here. What is there in Peyton Place for a girl with her looks and intelligence? Nothing."

Connie smiled. "Maybe she feels the same way about Peyton Place as you do," she said. "Perhaps there is a degree of security here for her that she's afraid would be missing everywhere else."

"What security?" asked Allison. "She not only has to look after herself, but Joey, too. And all she has to depend on is her job at the store."

"And Peter Drake," Connie added.

"Perhaps it's just as well that it ended with Tim the way it did. I guess Mike was right about him all along."

Connie shrugged. "I don't know. I always liked Tim well enough. At any rate, he was Selena's last chance to get out of her rut. I don't imagine that she'll be too eager to fall in love with another stranger." Connie paused and looked searchingly at Allison. "And, speaking of love," she said at last, "what about David Noyes?"

Allison looked down into her empty coffee cup. "I don't know," she said.

She longed to tell Constance it was not David she cared about but Lewis Jackman. David, however, provided a perfect smoke screen, so she went on discussing him with Constance.

"He's in love with you, you know."

"It's not David that I don't know about," said Allison. "I'm not sure of myself."

Connie sighed. "I guess every mother wants to see her daughter safely and happily married," she said. "And I'm no different."

"David has been everywhere and has done just about everything," said Allison. "He's been on a safari in Africa and skiing in Switzerland and he's even had himself put in prison so that he could write a book about it. I've never been anywhere or done anything. David would be perfectly willing to get married, buy a house right here in Peyton Place and settle down to writing his books."

"But you've just been telling me that you're never happier than when you're right here," objected Connie.

"I am," agreed Allison. "But it's a selfish sort of thing. I want to be able to come home anytime I want to. But I want to be able to leave, too. At any time for any place. I wouldn't be able to do that if I were married to David. He has this thing where he always wants to shield me from everything."

"What's wrong with that?" asked Connie. "You'd be much worse off if you got stuck with a man who didn't give a damn what happened to you."

Allison sighed. "I know it," she said. "But I can't live through David's experience, either." She stopped and grinned at her mother. "You know what's the matter with me?" she asked. "I want everything. Every experience, every sight and smell and taste and feeling. But I don't want anything to hurt me." She stood up and went to the window. "So you see how impossible it is," she said. "Nobody can have both, can they?"

Connie refilled the cups. She thought, Allison has grown a lot in the past year, but in many ways she's still a romantic little girl. "I can see why you want to wait," she said. "But I do wish that David were coming for the holiday."

"He's working on a book," said Allison. "And when David is working, all the furies of hell couldn't tear him away from his typewriter. Perhaps he'll be up for Christmas. Stevie is coming for Thanksgiving, though. And if it's all right with you, Mother, I'd like to ask my publisher to come too," she added hurriedly.

Constance turned and looked at Allison. "You mean Lewis Jackman?"

"Yes," said Allison. "I'd like him to see Peyton Place."

"Well, of course, dear. You know you can invite anyone you like." Constance paused to light a cigarette and glanced at Allison over the wavering flame of the match. "He's married, isn't he?"

"Lewis Jackman? Yes, he is. And he's in his forties, too."

"Well," Constance said, "that doesn't matter. Some men are younger at that age than others are when they're twenty."

Allison laughed. "Where did you learn all that, Mother?"

Constance said, "Darling, there are some things you learn just by living and keeping your eyes open. You don't have to personally experience all sorts of men to know that there are some who are born old and there are others who are still young when they're sixty."

"Well," Allison said, "all this has got nothing to do with Lewis Jackman. He's just my publisher and a very charming man. It doesn't matter to me whether he's eighty, married, or unmarried."

Constance said, "What about his wife? Will she be coming, too?"

"I don't think so," Allison said, looking down into her cup. "From what I hear, she's quite sick. She doesn't see anyone but her psychiatrist."

"Oh, I see," Constance said. "Too bad."

Surreptitiously she watched Allison's face. She wondered why talking about Lewis Jackman had made her so nervous, and why Allison did not look at her when she spoke of Jackman's wife. There were a hundred questions Constance wanted to ask her daughter, and it was only with a conscious effort that she kept her mouth shut. You must not pry, she warned herself. When Allison is ready to tell you about this, she will tell you.

Constance was certain something was going on. A young girl's infatuation with an older man, she thought, can sometimes be a very strong thing. She wondered if the fact that Allison had never known her own father might not have something to do with it. Perhaps Lewis Jackman was providing Allison with the father image she had always lacked.

Mike returned. He burst into the kitchen carrying two large bags of groceries. Then he sat down at the table with them, held up the empty cup and said to Constance, "Reward me. I have been a good boy."

Constance filled his cup. "There," she said. "Is that reward enough for you?"

"Ask me later," Mike told her in a stage whisper.

Allison laughed. "Sometimes I feel like you two are my children," she said.

She asked Mike how he was enjoying his teaching job in White River.

He made a face. "If my wife could support me in the manner

to which I've grown accustomed, I'd give up that job with just one minute's notice."

Connie put her arm around his shoulders. "You should have swallowed your pride and your honor when the school board here told you they were sorry and wanted you back," she said.

"What's this?" Allison cried.

"It happened just after you left," Constance explained. "Mike's being fired became such a scandal in educational circles that even Roberta got scared. Also, the new principal turned out to be an absolute dud."

"They came to me, Roberta and poor old Charlie, with their hats in their hands—and, let me tell you, Roberta looks better with it in her hands than on her head—and offered me my old job," Mike said.

"Mike told them he wouldn't take the job back until they agreed to a few demands he had to make."

"It'll do them good to stew in their own juice for a year," said Mike. "Besides, they'll need that long to make up their minds to give me everything I asked for."

"Everything like what?" asked Allison.

"Like tenure and a thousand dollar a year raise every year for the next five years," replied Mike.

"Charlie Partridge is all for it," said Connie. "But he can't convince Marion. Roberta is on the fence."

"We'll see," Mike said.

"Yes, but when?" asked Allison.

"In March," replied Mike. "When the new contracts come out."

"Thank God it'll be in March," said Allison. "In April the group from Hollywood will be here, and I don't imagine that they'll do anything to improve our public relations with Peyton Place."

"They're really coming then?" asked Connie.

"Yes," replied Allison. "God help us all."

"I heard that it was quite a session when their advance guard met with the selectmen," said Mike. "Tishman's representative was a man named Blanding . . ."

"Conrad Blanding," said Allison. "He's the director."

"Well, Blanding told old Tom Perkins that all the studio wanted to do was use the town for a few weeks, and in return they'd leave approximately a hundred thousand dollars of their money behind. But old Tom wasn't impressed."

"He wouldn't be," Connie said. "He's New England through and through. What's good enough for his grandfather is good enough for his grandchildren. I wish some of these people would get over the idea that progress is sinful. I'm surprised Tom Perkins hasn't organized hatchet parties to smash up every TV set in Peyton Place."

"Stop interrupting with your seditious talk," Mike said. "If you're not careful, I'll have you run out of town on a rail." He turned to Allison and continued his account.

"Perkins told Blanding that Peyton Place had managed to get along very well without outside money for a good many years and that as far as he was concerned we could all stagger along for another century or two without any help from Hollywood."

"I warned Arthur Tishman," said Allison. "But he took one look at photographs of the castle and made up his mind. And when Arthur makes up his mind, *nothing* can shake it."

"Well, it'll give the town something new to talk about," Mike said. "Maybe they'll give Marion Partridge a job as an extra—"

"She could play one of the witches," Connie said. "She wouldn't even need make-up."

"—and she'll forget about me and my job," Mike finished, a look of exaggerated patience on his face while he waited through Constance's interruption.

"Nitwit," she said. "You can help me with dinner while Allison goes up and unpacks. And there's time for a nap, darling, if you're feeling tired," she said to Allison.

"Perhaps I will lie down for an hour," Allison said, and went up to her room.

Her room was the same, exactly as she had remembered it, exactly as she had imagined it during those lonely nights in the expensive hotels in New York and California. It was a simple room, still full of reminders of her girlhood.

Her luggage, which Mike had stacked neatly at the foot of her bed, seemed a violation of the simple spirit of the room. The luggage was new, it was full of new things. It had nothing to do with the Allison MacKenzie whose room this was, with the Allison Mac-

571

Kenzie who had gone to movies with Selena, taken walks with Norman and dreamed childhood's peculiar dreams.

The luggage seemed to Allison a dreadful reminder of how much her life had changed. She lay down on her bed and thought, I live in two worlds now, I am a completely divided person. There is the world of Peyton Place, and I will never be so much at home anywhere else. And there is the outside world of New York and Hollywood in which I play a role, as surely as any actress does.

Except with Lewis. That is the one genuine aspect of the other world.

When her plane had landed at La Guardia, Lewis was waiting for her. All the way back to the city they held hands and just stared at each other, as if their eyes could never get enough of the sight of each other.

At the apartment hotel where she had reserved her suite of rooms, the manager awaited her in the lobby and welcomed her back. Bellboys ran to get her luggage from the car. And when they were finally alone, a small bottle of champagne cooling in a silver bucket, she then had to phone Constance.

It was only after this was done that Lewis finally took her in his arms. It was as if they waited till all the petty little details were out of the way, and they would not have to be interrupted by anyone or for anything, that they turned to each other.

"My God, darling!" Lewis said. "How I've missed you!"

"Oh, I know, I know," Allison said.

"I couldn't sleep nights for missing you. Talking to you on the phone, and you so many miles away, was a torture. And yet I had to phone you. It was better than nothing."

"We'll have a week together now, darling, and after Thanksgiving I'll be back for good and all. But I have to spend some time with Constance and Mike. And I want to be with them for a while, Lewis. I need it. These last few weeks have been exhausting."

Lewis opened the bottle of champagne. "We'll start building you up with this," he said. "It's full of vitamins, as you know."

She smiled at him and looked around the high-ceilinged, beautifully proportioned room. It had come to seem almost like her second home, not because of its grandeur but because of the hours she had shared here with Lewis. The terrace doors were closed against the cold; the chairs and table had been taken away from the terrace. It looked bleak and deserted.

She picked up an empty glass and Lewis filled it for her. They toasted each other wordlessly, with their eyes alone. Allison felt the cold liquid explode against the roof of her mouth and send bubbles of warmth coursing through her veins.

When Allison had finished her second glass she broke away from Lewis' arms, and, picking up the champagne bottle, went into the bedroom. Lewis undressed her and when she was standing naked before him he raised his glass to her beauty and drank. In bed together, they finished the bottle, their thighs touching under the blankets and Lewis' arm around her shoulders.

"Shall I order another bottle sent up, darling?" Allison asked.

"Do you think we need it?"

Allison smiled. "I don't think we needed the first one. But it was very nice."

She dropped her empty glass on the rug as Lewis touched her breast and stroked the smooth soft flesh.

"Oh, Lewis, darling, darling," she whispered.

But he paid no attention to her urgency and caressed her with his hands and bit her ear lobes until she cried out. She felt she would suffocate and she threw off the blankets. Words of love came from her mouth in a fierce whisper. She closed her eyes and when he pushed her over she felt the whole world was turning with her. She put her arms around him and drew him to her.

There has never been anything like this, she thought, never, never, never. She rose upward on a curving wave until all thought was driven out of her and only love filled her, tirelessly, until she was replete with love and helpless in his arms and her face glistened with tears of joy.

◆ **2** ◆

ON THE DAY AFTER ALLISON RETURNED TO PEYTON PLACE, PETER DRAKE backed his car out of his garage and drove toward the Cross house to pick up Selena and Joey. Peter rolled up his window against the cold wind that stripped the last leaves from the tortured trees.

Elm Street was deserted. The only moving thing that Peter could see was a torn sheet of newspaper that blew against a curbstone in front of the bank. Peter thought he had never seen a lonelier sight in his life.

Connie's house will be warm and cheerful and good smelling, thought Peter. Maybe Selena will be able to relax today.

He did not give voice, even silently, to his other hope.

Maybe today Selena will be over Tim Randlett for good. Maybe today she'll decide that she wants to marry me after all.

Peter Drake was what Peyton Place described as a "well-set-up" man. He was moderately tall, with good shoulders and square hands. His hair was dark brown and his eyes matched it almost exactly. As an attorney in Peyton Place, Peter was not quite as well set up as he looked. Into his office came the people whom Charles Partridge was too busy to see. The ones with rather insignificant problems and the ones with no money. The only way that Peter managed to make a living was by traveling to the surrounding towns and taking the cases of the people there; but he clung stubbornly to Peyton Place.

Peter had never meant for it to happen that way. When he had undertaken the job of defending Selena Cross at her trial for the murder of Lucas, he had planned to make this his last case in northern New England. But when it was over, he had lingered. The job with a law firm in Connecticut that had been waiting for him was soon filled by someone else, and when, a few weeks later, he was offered another job with a firm in Massachusetts, he turned it down.

I'm out of my mind, he told himself often and angrily during the years that followed.

But he was in love with Selena and believed that, in time, she would come to love him.

In the beginning, he had waited while she recovered from the dreadful experience of Lucas Cross. Then he had waited for her to forget the defection of Ted Carter. Now he was waiting for her to stop remembering Tim Randlett.

"I'm stuck," he had once confessed to Constance Rossi. "I love her and I always will and there's not a damned thing I can do about it. And don't think I haven't tried, because I have. I've *almost* taken jobs away from here. I've *almost* become involved with other girls. I've *almost* convinced myself that I could get over her. Almost. But I've never made it."

"Have you ever told any of this to Selena?" asked Connie.

"Many times," said Peter. "And every time she tells me that I'd be better off without her. That she's no good for me." He shrugged helplessly. "It never does any good," he said. "I still wait and hope."

Peter stopped his car in front of Selena's house and made his way up the walk to the front door.

"Come in, Counselor!" cried Selena, flinging the door open for him. "Welcome!"

She was holding a glass in her hand, and Peter knew it was not her first drink of the day.

"Hail, the conquering hero comes, Joey," called Selena. "Fix him a drink. Well, don't just stand there, Peter. Come in."

Behind her back, Joey looked at Peter and hunched his shoulders as he poured liquor into a glass.

"Here, Joey," said Selena. "Freshen mine, will you? I have to finish dressing."

"You look wonderful, Selena," said Peter.

For a moment, she looked completely sober. "Don't lie, Peter," she said. "I look like a hag and I know it."

She turned and went quickly into her room and closed the door behind her.

"When did it start, Joey?" asked Peter.

Joey handed him a glass. "I guess she never really sobered up from last night," he said. "She didn't eat any supper. I found her sitting there, with the lights out and a glass in her hand."

It had started at the end of August, Peter remembered. And since then, Selena had not once gone to bed sober.

"Don't worry too much about it," Connie had told Peter. "Women have different ways of getting over unfortunate love affairs. Selena is hiding right now. Trying to pretend nothing is wrong. Give her a little time. She's a sensible girl. She'll snap out of it."

But the weeks went by and Selena did not snap out of it. She started drinking in the morning, to clear her head, she told Joey, and Peter had caught her drinking in the back room of the Thrifty Corner.

"For Christ's sake, Selena," he had said. "What do you suppose Connie would say about this?"

Selena whirled on him. "Mind your own damned business," she said. "If Connie Rossi has any objections to the way I run her store, let her tell me herself."

"You're acting like a fool," said Peter angrily.

"Perhaps that's because I am one and always have been," said Selena.

"Drinking never solved anybody's problems," said Peter.

"Maybe not," said Selena, "but it does bring a measure of forgetfulness."

In desperation, Peter had gone to Matthew Swain.

"Believe me, Peter," said the doctor, "if I knew anything, I'd tell you and ethics be damned. But I don't know a bit more than you do. A couple of tourists, folks from Ohio, found her lying on the side of the highway, and since this was the closest town they brought her here to the hospital. She had fainted on the road. Her face was banged up some, where she hit the gravel, and she was suffering from too much sun, but outside of that there wasn't anything the matter with her. The next day I tried to find out what the hell had happened, but she wouldn't say a word. That actor fellow, Randlett, came over to the hospital to see her, but when I told her he was waiting she just turned her face to the wall and told me she didn't want to see him. He didn't believe it at first, but he finally went away. Joey told me that he went to the house after I sent her home, but Selena called Buck McCracken and told him that there was a man ringing her doorbell and that the sheriff should get rid of him. Then I heard that the summer theater was closing up. Right around Labor Day, that was, and I went up to Silver Lake to see this Randlett. He shut up like a clam when I started questioning him. Wouldn't tell me a thing. The next thing I knew, the whole kit and kaboodle of them had gone off to New York. And good riddance, I say. Selena was getting along fine before Randlett hove into view."

"She's drinking," Peter told him. "Too much. Every day and every night."

Matthew Swain sighed. "I'll talk to her," he promised.

But it did no good.

"Doc, don't worry about me," Selena said. "Just go back to Chestnut Street and forget that you ever heard of me."

Matthew felt his stomach tighten. He remembered the night, a long time ago, when he had tried to interfere when Lucas had been drunk and beating his wife. A very young Selena had looked up at him.

"Go on home, Doc," she had said. "Go back to Chestnut Street. Nobody sent for you."

"Selena, I only want to help you," said Matthew.

Selena poured another drink. "Doc, there are some people who are born crippled, aren't there? I mean, with only one leg or one arm or no eyes?"

"Yes," said the doctor.

"Well, then," said Selena, "why is it unreasonable to suppose that other people are born with something wrong and twisted inside?"

"What do you mean?" asked Matthew.

Selena smiled. "I mean something evil, like a desire to commit murder, for instance."

"Selena, all that was a long, long time ago. You only did what you had to do to protect yourself. Anyone would have done the same. Forget all that. Put it behind you."

Selena squinted at the remaining liquor in her glass.

"Go home, Doc," she said wearily. "Go home. Nobody sent for you."

Matthew Swain stood up to leave, but he paused at her front door.

"That stuff never solved anything for anybody," he said.

Selena giggled. "That's what Peter always says," she said. "And I always agree with him. I only point out to him that, while it may not solve anything, it blunts the edges a little. Good-by, Doc."

Selena came out of her room. "I'm ready," she said gaily. "Let's go. Will you get my coat, Joey, while I finish my drink?"

"Sure," said Joey.

"Maybe we'd better bring a bottle of our own in case Mike Rossi has been forgetful," said Selena. "There's nothing worse than a party that runs out of liquor."

"I'm sure that Mike has a well-stocked bar," said Peter.

"Oh dear," said Selena. "Look who's getting all stuffy."

"Selena, I'm not getting stuffy," said Peter.

"Well, I don't care if you are," she said. "Go ahead and get stuffy if you want to. I won't stop you."

The afternoon seemed interminable to Peter. Selena was like a toy that had been wound too tightly and would soon snap and break into a mass of pieces and twisted wire. She pecked at her dinner but her glass was filled to the brim.

In the kitchen, Allison said softly to Connie, "Why didn't you tell me about Selena?"

"I thought it would pass," said Connie.

"How long has she been drinking like this?"

"Ever since Tim Randlett left town."

"Good God."

"Yes," said Connie. "Let's just hope that she gets over it soon."

"Has anyone tried talking to her?"

"We all have. It doesn't help."

"What does Peter say?"

"He's waiting for her to stop, the same as the rest of us. What else can he do?"

"Hey, you two!" said Selena from the kitchen doorway. "What's all the whispering about?"

"You," said Allison and turned to her with a smile. "We were wondering how much longer you're going to keep poor Peter hanging fire."

Selena sat down on a kitchen chair. "Let's have a drink, shall we? Just the three of us."

"Sure," said Connie. "Let me bring the coffee in for the men and I'll be right back. Allison, get some ice, will you, dear? There's a bottle of bourbon in the cabinet behind you."

"Yes," said Selena, when she had the fresh drink in her hand, "poor, poor Peter. He loves me, you know. You know that, Allison, don't you?"

"Yes, I do," said Allison. "He has for a long time."

Selena began to cry. "Poor Peter. Poor, poor Peter."

"Don't cry, darling," said Connie. "Everything's going to be all right."

"Nothing is all right," cried Selena, her voice rising. "Nothing is all right at all, and it's never going to be!"

"Sh-h," warned Connie. "You don't want the men to hear you."

Selena calmed down. "No," she said. "No, I don't want them to hear me."

Then she put her head down on her arms and sobbed as if her

heart would break. Allison went to her at once and put her arm across Selena's bent shoulders. She and Connie looked at each other and both of them knew that there was nothing to be done.

Later that same evening, Joey went to meet some friends with whom he was going to the movies, and Peter Drake drove Selena home. The wind was stronger now; he felt it tugging at the car and tightened his grip on the wheel.

"Make me a fire, Peter," said Selena, when they went into her living room. "A big, beautiful, bright fire to chase the dark out of all the corners." She dropped her coat carelessly over the back of a chair. "I'll make us a drink," she said.

Peter almost said, Don't you think you've had enough? But he stopped himself and began to build the fire.

"No, I haven't had enough," said Selena into the silence. "There isn't enough in the whole, wide world."

Now the fire was burning brightly and Peter sat down. He reached for the glass that Selena extended to him.

"I can't lick you," he told her, "so I might just as well join you."

"Don't you ever stop playing the heavy?" asked Selena. "Anytime you don't feel like joining me you don't have to. Just put on your coat. You know where the door is."

"Don't try to pick a fight with me, Selena," said Peter. "I won't let you."

"Who wants to fight?" asked Selena. "I've had a bellyful of fights. Enough fights to last me a lifetime."

"Do you want to talk?" asked Peter.

Selena smiled humorlessly at him. "You remind me of someone I used to know," she said. "Always prying. Always poking his nose in where it wasn't wanted." She gulped thirstily at her drink. "Tell me about it, Selena," she mimicked. "What's troubling you, Selena? Tell me, Selena. You'll feel better for it." She refilled her glass. "I'm sick of talking," she said.

"I wasn't trying to pry," said Peter.

"Yes, you were!" she said angrily. "Everybody in the world is a goddamned prying busybody. Well, what do you want from me, Peter? Do you want to know if I slept with him? Yes, I did. Are you wondering if I loved him? Yes, I did." Her voice rose until she was almost screaming. "Are you wondering if I've forgotten him? No, I haven't."

Peter watched her, appalled, as the tears streamed down her face and her voice rose higher and higher.

"Are you wondering why I left him?" she cried. "Are you wondering what went sour, and why and how?"

In that moment, the front door blew open. Apparently, Peter had not closed it securely when they had come in, and now the wind took it and sent it smashing back against the wall with a crash.

Selena jumped to her feet, her drink spilling all over the front of her and the glass smashing at her feet.

In one motion, she had turned and her fingers had closed around the fire tongs on the hearth.

"Don't!" she screamed. "Don't come a step nearer! I'll kill you!"

Peter grabbed her from behind, and for a long moment Selena stared at the empty black square at the door, that door which on a night like this had once framed the dark bulk of Lucas Cross.

"There's nobody there, darling," said Peter. "Nobody."

The tongs fell from Selena's nerveless fingers and she began to sob. Peter turned her to him and pressed her face against his shoulder.

"I tried to kill him," she cried. "He was just like Lucas and he came at me and I tried to kill him."

Peter held her very tightly against him while she sobbed.

"He wanted to tear my clothes off," she wept. "He said I wanted to be raped and he was just like Lucas and I picked up the fire tongs and wanted to kill him."

"It's all right, darling," soothed Peter. "Don't cry any more. It's all right."

"What's wrong with me, Peter?" Selena cried. "Why did it happen? What do I do that makes men like that?"

Peter kissed her soft hair. "It's not you, darling. You've just had bad luck, that's all. It's not you."

Selena's whole body trembled. "I drank and drank," she said, gasping for breath, "and it didn't do any good. I couldn't forget that I tried to kill him."

Peter gave her a gentle shake. "But you didn't, darling. It's over now. You didn't."

He led her gently to the sofa and held her cradled in his arms.

"Peter, I'm so scared. There's something wrong with me. I know there's something wrong with me," she sobbed.

"There's nothing wrong with you, darling," said Peter. He began to mop gently at her face with his handkerchief. "There's nothing wrong. Come on, now. Stop crying."

Huge, dry sobs shook her as she put her head against his shoulder.

"You react to violence with violence," said Peter. "Some people do, you know." He tipped her head up and looked down at her. "I'll have to remember that," he smiled, "whenever I get the mistaken idea that I can get rough around you."

"You're so good, Peter," she said, and a sigh went through her whole body as she relaxed against him. "I don't deserve anyone like you."

Peter smiled against her hair. "You deserve the best of every thing," he said. He began to stroke her.

This is what I need, Selena thought, this is what I've always needed, Peter's gentle strength. It will protect me from all harm.

His hand continued to stroke her hair and back. It was as if his fingers were drawing out of her all the pain of the past and the agony of memory.

"When we get married," Peter whispered, "it will be the true beginning of our lives. You'll see, Selena—what's happened up till now has nothing to do with us. We were other people then. And it all took place in another world."

He had a profound understanding of Selena's needs. She wanted to be able to shuck off the past as cleanly as a farmer rips the corn from the stalk. With Peter, she wanted to be newborn and washed clean of the taint of the past. Her arms moved around him and held him tightly. She lifted her head and he bent to kiss her tear-stained face.

This will be the first time, Selena thought, this will be the first time.

She drew Peter down with her until they were lying side by side on the sofa; she moved and adjusted her body to the length of his. Hesitantly, his hand caressed her thigh, moved up until it gently touched her breast. Her lips parted, he kissed her; she moaned softly when he pushed up her sweater. She clasped her hands behind his head and held him.

"Oh, Selena, darling," he whispered, and she heard the breathlessness in his voice.

He began to undress her. Selena felt faint, felt as if the world were slipping away from her. She covered her face with her hands, and in the darkness under her hands the world held still.

"Oh," she said, "oh, I want you." And she raised her hands to him as if imploring him and drew him to her.

• 3 •

WITH THE COMING OF AUTUMN AND ITS ELECTRIC AIR, ROBERTA CARTER always felt brisk. It was as if she were sweeping up the sloth and indecision of the past year along with the dried, fallen leaves of her front yard trees. She rubbed her hands together mentally and thought, Now that all the summer nonsense is over with, let's get down to business. Roberta looked around her now spotless living room and should have felt completely satisfied with her house-wifely accomplishment, but her pleasure was tainted. Even though Ted and Jennifer had returned to Cambridge early in September, Roberta could still feel the presence of that horrible girl in her house.

I've got to get rid of her, thought Roberta, and refused to feel futile.

She had been trying to get rid of Jennifer for over a year now, and nothing had worked. Ted turned a deaf ear to any remarks about his wife, and Harmon, who had been so diabolically clever when Roberta's problem had been old Doc Quimby, was next to useless where Jennifer was concerned.

"She seems to be a nice enough sort," said Harmon.

"So was Dr. Quimby," snapped Roberta, "but you managed to see that he didn't remain on our scene too long."

"That was something else entirely," replied Harmon.

Dr. Quimby, who had been the only physician in Peyton Place until Matthew Swain came home to practice, had been old and rich when Roberta had started to work for him as a combination house-keeper, secretary and companion. Roberta and Harmon, the children of mill hands, were engaged to be married, but, with the money

Harmon earned as one of Leslie Harrington's bookkeepers, marriage was impossible. Until Harmon Carter came up with his plan.

It was a clever, simple plan which, if it worked, would set Roberta and Harmon up for life. Roberta had not needed much persuasion to put Harmon's idea to work. She married Dr. Quimby and he rewrote his will in her favor, and then she and Harmon settled back and waited for the old man to die. They didn't have long to wait. Peyton Place made life intolerable for Dr. Quimby. The town rocked with laughter, and people who had always gone to him with their ailments now assumed that he had turned senile and refused to consult him.

Roberta and Harmon cuckolded him openly, and in the end the old man put his revolver into his mouth and blew his head off. Within a year, Roberta and Harmon were married and had begun the long fight to become accepted by Peyton Place. With time and new-found respectability they had won to a degree. Of course, there were those who remembered and talked, but with every passing year the story grew less and less interesting and there were always new people in new situations to be gossiped about.

It helped a great deal, too, when Roberta and Harmon's son, Ted, turned out to be such a nice guy. So the scandal died and was almost buried, and people forgot. But Roberta Carter did not forget. She remembered very vividly how she had fought to become someone who was looked up to in town as a good wife and mother and an asset to the community. Now there was Jennifer, who threatened to turn Roberta's son from the paths of righteousness with her insane, abnormal sexuality.

I've got to get rid of her, thought Roberta.

But during the past year she had thought up and discarded hundreds of plans. Nothing worked. Ted was as much a prisoner in his marriage to Jennifer as he would have been in a maximum security cell at Alcatraz. Jennifer was crazy and she would make Ted crazy, and in the eyes of most of Peyton Place it was a far greater crime to be insane than it was to be a thief or a rapist.

I've got to get rid of her, thought Roberta.

But it was not until after the end of summer that Roberta decided on a course of action that she had previously discarded as foolhardy and dangerous. Roberta burned leaves and vacuumed her rugs and began to plan her strategy.

Jennifer would be back in Peyton Place for the Thanksgiving holidays. I've got to kill her, she thought, and I have to do it well enough so that no one ever suspects a thing.

Roberta Carter began to read murder mysteries, but she did not borrow these from the Peyton Place public library nor did she buy them at the local bookstore. She traveled eighty miles to a city to shop, and she bought paper-backed novels in a large drugstore where she was not known, and she read secretly, behind the locked door of her bathroom.

During the day, when Harmon was at work, she wrote down the plot of each novel and listed the clues that had finally landed each murderer in the nets of the police. In this way, she discarded murder by shooting, stabbing, strangling and poison; and since Jennifer was not the type to commit suicide, Roberta realized that her daughter-in-law's death would have to be made to look like an accident.

Although Jennifer drove a car, Roberta could never hope to tamper with an automobile to the extent of causing a fatal accident. Household mishaps were out, too, for whenever Jennifer visited in Peyton Place or Roberta went to Cambridge, Harmon was always around, or Ted, or both of them. No. It had to be something that happened when Roberta was not with Jennifer and when Ted, also, was away from his wife so that no breath of suspicion fell on him.

Roberta closed the cover of still another murder mystery and sighed deeply. It wasn't going to be easy, but then, she hadn't expected that it would be. In the meantime, there was plenty to do. She must begin to fabricate a fiction of her relationship with Jennifer. Peyton Place must be impressed with Roberta's magnanimity. When it was over and Jennifer was dead, people had to be able to say, "What a pity. And that this should happen to Roberta Carter, of all people. Why, she is the soul of goodness and she and Jennifer were so close."

Roberta was, as she had always been, clever about sounding out people and when, within two weeks after the reopening of school in September, she discovered that the town was more than displeased with the man who now acted as headmaster of the Peyton Place school, she began to agitate for the return of Mike Rossi to his rightful position. Behind the back of her best friend, Marion Partridge, she let Charles know that when the school board considered the contracts for the next year she, Roberta, would be behind

Charles one thousand per cent in his campaign to rehire Mike.

"The whole thing has given this town a terrible black eye," she confided in Charles. "I mean, firing Mike just because of Allison's book. I was never really for it in the first place."

And Charles Partridge, the town pacifist, forgot that Roberta had been one of Mike's sworn enemies and accepted her new attitude gratefully.

"It'll take a while for people to get over the way we acted about Mike," said Roberta. "We've managed to make ourselves a laughing-stock in educational circles. But it's nothing that can't be patched up."

"And the sooner the better," amended Charles Partridge.

Roberta began to make frequent visits to the Thrifty Corner where she not only made purchases, but became very friendly with Connie and Selena.

"I'm so very glad for you and Peter," said Roberta to Selena. "He's certainly a lucky man."

"I wonder what ails her," said Selena when Roberta had gone. "I've never known her to be so sweet. It's almost sickening."

But Connie, the incurable optimist, said, "Perhaps she's mellowing. After all, Roberta's no teen-ager any more. She's getting on."

"I still don't believe that the leopard changes its spots," said Selena.

But, as the weeks went by, even Selena had to admit that Roberta Carter had changed. In October, Mike Rossi was offered, and accepted, on terms he had made clear to the school board, his old job as principal of the Peyton Place school. The whole town, with a few die-hard exceptions, had been overwhelmingly on Mike's side of the fence. One of the exceptions was Marion Partridge, and in the interests of, as she put it, doing the right thing, Roberta Carter broke with her lifelong friend.

To various women in town Roberta said, "I'm sorry that Marion feels as she does, but I wanted to do what was best for the school."

The women carried the word into their homes and practically everyone agreed that Roberta Carter was the soul of unselfishness. They sympathized with Roberta, too, for Roberta let it be known that what she wanted more than anything was a grandchild, but Jennifer, so far, had not conceived.

"It's a shame," said the women of Peyton Place. "It isn't as if Ted and Jennifer had to worry about money or anything. Heaven knows Roberta and Harmon are more than generous."

Then Roberta let it be known that her son, Ted, wanted to come back to Peyton Place to practice law when he graduated from Harvard, and if there had been any doubt at all in the minds of the town, it was now assuaged. Peyton Place loved a local boy who went away and obtained the best education money could buy and then returned home to put what he had learned to use.

"Ted always had a good head on his shoulders," said the town. "A good boy, Ted. And a smart one."

"Old Charlie Partridge ain't gonna last forever. We'll need somebody like young Carter to take over when Charlie goes."

Roberta counted heavily on the quality in her son that kept him from hurting anyone if he could possibly refrain from doing so. When anyone in Peyton Place mentioned Ted's eventual local practice, rather than answering flatly that he had no intention whatsoever of coming home to set up an office, Ted merely smiled and said modestly, "I've got to get through school first, and that's not going to be easy for a dull fellow like me."

By the end of summer, Roberta knew that the time had come to act. Jennifer's parents had begun to talk of a trip to Europe for "the children," and Ted was obviously enthused at the prospect.

I've got to find a way, Roberta thought, with the beginning of panic.

Day after day she stayed in her house with her murder mysteries and her notebook. October was nearly over before she finally decided on a course of action, and then she spent hours writing in her notebook. She worked out all the drawbacks to her plan, the risks, the clues she must not leave behind; and she planned a meticulous timetable of the day when it would happen. At last, she locked her notebook away in her desk and breathed a sigh of relief.

Now it was over except for the actual act. She had found a way to get rid of Jennifer that was simple, safe and foolproof. She sat at the desk for a moment, her hands clenched into tight, avenging fists, her mouth compressed into a thin determined line. In her head, Jennifer's terrible words still echoed, the horrible things she had told Ted on their last night in Peyton Place.

She had been listening to them through the air vent, lying in her own sweat on the cot in the storage room. She had heard them make love, had heard Jennifer torture Ted and tease him into doing all sorts of perverse and evil things. She had writhed in anguish for poor Ted.

Then she had heard Jennifer's salacious whisper.

Ted said, "You're insatiable, darling."

"More," Jennifer said. "I want more. Oh, goddamn men, anyway!"

Ted laughed. "We're badly designed," he said. "You'll have to wait for next year's models."

Roberta heard the bed creak as Jennifer sat up and rested her back against the headboard.

"I think I'll get myself a seventeen-year-old boy," Jennifer said.

Ted laughed. To him, talk like this was part of Jennifer's smartness and sophistication. In Ted's eyes, being born to money and high social position gave her the right to say things like this.

But Roberta was so shocked that her body went numb. She could not bear the thought that her Ted would be a cuckolded husband, laughed at and pitied by his friends. She thought of Doc Quimby. For a moment, she believed in divine retribution and that her sins were being visited upon Ted.

Jennifer's cool voice went on. "Or maybe I'll get myself two or three young boys. Yes, that would be even better."

"Where do you buy young boys these days?" Ted asked.

"Oh, you can pick them up cheap anywhere," Jennifer told him, a ring of authority in her voice. "There's that sweet curly-haired boy who delivers the groceries. I can tell by the way he looks at me that he wouldn't have to be bought. It's dull being alone in the apartment all day, Ted. Wouldn't it be nice if I whiled away an hour or two with him in the morning?"

Ted did not answer.

"It would be, Ted. It would be very nice. The idea of corrupting an innocent boy is the most exciting thing in the world. And then, in the afternoon, I could have a daily arrangement with that handsome young Italian who runs the elevator. He goes off duty at two o'clock. How would you like to have a man in uniform come every afternoon to service me?"

Ted laughed, but it was a forced, uncomfortable laugh.

"Teen-age boys are so full of energy," she said. "They have to be taught how to use that energy, of course. I read in Kinsey, Ted, that they can do it four or five times in an hour. And some of them can do it more than that. Isn't that marvelous, Ted?"

She did not wait for him to answer. "I don't think I'll wait for the new models, Ted. I think I'll just buy a couple of those untried, young boys. You wouldn't mind, would you, Ted?"

"Oh, go to sleep, Jennifer," Ted said.

"No, Ted, you wouldn't mind at all. Oh, maybe you'd mind because it would hurt your male pride, whatever that is. But you wouldn't do anything about it, would you, Ted? Not you. As long as you can get your name on the door, as long as you can have success, you'll put up with anything. And I mean *anything*, Ted."

"Go to sleep, Jennifer. You're talking like a child," Ted said.

They were silent then. After a while, they fell asleep. Everyone in Peyton Place was asleep except Roberta Carter. She lay on the cot with her hands pressed tight against her mouth, her eyes staring at the dark ceiling.

I must kill her, she thought. I must kill her. She wasn't just talking. She's going to do these things. Maybe she's already started doing them. I must kill her.

• 4 •

THE MEN OF CHESTNUT STREET GATHERED AT THE HOME OF SETH BUS-well for their usual Friday night poker game. Seth put a bottle of liquor on the sideboard and filled four glasses with ice while Leslie Harrington began to shuffle the cards for the first hand.

"Another winter is here," said Matthew Swain as he sat down.

"Yep," said Seth. "Ephraim Tuttle's got his stove set up and his bolts of material put away."

"Where did the year go?" said Charles Partridge. "Seems as though it was only a few weeks ago that we were sitting here talking about Allison MacKenzie's book, and that was last April."

"That's because we're getting old," said Matthew. "Time goes by quick as a wink for us nowadays. But I can remember how it used to drag by when I was a youngster."

"You ain't got that good a memory to remember that far back, Matt," said Leslie Harrington.

"Neither have you, Grandpa," said Matt. "Although I must say, you've looked better this past year than I've ever seen you look."

"I've got to keep healthy to keep up with that grandson of mine," said Leslie. "He's a holy terror."

"How's Betty?" asked Seth.

"Fine," said Leslie. "I think she's finally made up her mind to stay right here in Peyton Place."

"Good," said Matthew and Seth almost simultaneously.

Charles Partridge did not say anything. Except for Leslie himself, Charles was the only man in town who knew what torture Leslie had suffered at the hands of Betty Anderson.

"Five pretty little black spades," said Seth Buswell gleefully and raked up the coins from the center of the table.

Spades, thought Charles Partridge. That's what Betty Anderson paid Leslie back in. In spades.

Rodney Harrington, Junior, had been no problem, Charles remembered. The boy had taken to his grandfather as if he had known him all his life, and Leslie, of course, was overwhelmed with love. Little Roddy was the image of his father, and the lines of age and worry erased themselves from Leslie's face every time he looked at his grandson. His friends were not the only ones in Peyton Place to notice how much better Leslie looked. Betty Anderson noticed it, too, and she smiled a tight little smile at the man who had never been her father-in-law. She had been in Peyton Place for two weeks, just long enough for Leslie to begin to hope that she would stay forever, when she started packing to leave.

"I have a job to get back to," she told Leslie when he protested.

"You don't have to work," said Leslie. "There's more than enough money right here."

Betty turned on him. "Listen, Leslie, I got along fine without your money when I was pregnant, when Roddy was born and ever since. We don't need you."

Leslie humbled himself. "I know," he said. "I need you."

"That's just too bad," said Betty. "You should have needed us when you threw me out of your office with a lousy two hundred and fifty bucks and a load in my belly."

"Betty," pleaded Leslie. "I'll make it up to you. I swear I will."

"We don't need you," said Betty and went on with her packing.

In the end, she promised that she would stay another week and Leslie breathed again. But at the end of the week, she started packing again.

"For Christ's sake, Charlie," said Leslie in desperation. "Do something."

"What do you want me to do?" asked Charles Partridge. "You have no legal claim on that child."

"Goddamn it, he's my grandson!"

"Betty and Rodney were never married," said Charles. "And you can't prove that Betty's been an unfit mother. There's nothing you can do except hope that she'll change her mind and stay on voluntarily."

"Well, talk to her, then," demanded Leslie. "Make her see that it's best for the child if he stays there. I don't give a damn what she does as long as she leaves Roddy with me."

"She'll never leave him," said Charles. "If you want the child, you'd better make up your mind to want the mother, too. But I'll talk to her."

"What's in it for me?" asked Betty Anderson when Charles went to see her.

"You could be very comfortable here," said Charles. "You could live in this house and you wouldn't have to work and you and Roddy could be well taken care of."

"I can take care of myself," said Betty. "I always have. And of Roddy, too. I don't mind working for a living. And as far as this house goes, it gives me the creeps. It's like a goddamned museum."

"I'm sure that Leslie would be willing to let you do the house over," said Charles, worried lest he bite off more than he could chew. "I can't see what objection he'd have to that."

"I don't want to do Leslie's house over," said Betty. "I want a house of my own."

Charles's jaw sagged. "But Leslie wants you to live in the house with him. You and little Roddy."

Betty shrugged. "In the words of little Roddy's father, that's tough titty," she said.

"Will you stay until Christmas?" asked Charles.

"Nope."

"Until the end of the month?"

"Nope."

Charles went to Leslie and told him what Betty wanted if she were to remain in Peyton Place.

"A house!" roared Leslie. "What the hell's the matter with my house? It's big enough for an army!"

Charles spread his hands in a gesture of defeat. "I can't help that, Leslie. That's what she wants."

"She can go right straight to hell," yelled Leslie.

But the next day, Betty began to pack again, and Leslie ran to Charles.

"Get her a house," he said wearily. "Any one she wants."

So Betty Anderson became the owner of a cottage at the end of Laurel Street.

"It'll be a nice place to spend my vacations," she told Charles.

"What do you mean, vacations?" asked Charles. "Don't you plan to live here?"

"On what?" asked Betty. "Does Leslie think I'm as rich as he is and can afford to sit on my backside all day long without working?"

"Leslie is perfectly willing to provide for the boy," Charles objected. "You could find work here to take care of your own needs."

"Where?" jeered Betty. "In the Mills? Like my old man? No thanks."

"But we thought—" began Charles.

"I don't give a damn what you thought," said Betty angrily. "I'm not going to take a two-bit job in the Mills working for Leslie Harrington. If I have to work to support myself, I can do that a lot better in New York. And that's where I'm going just as soon as I can get packed."

In the end, Leslie Harrington settled a sum of twenty-five thousand dollars on Betty Anderson and deposited another ten thousand in an account for his grandson. In addition, he agreed to give Betty a household allowance of one hundred dollars a week and buy her a new car every year.

"In writing," said Betty Anderson.

So Charles Partridge drew up the papers and Leslie Harrington signed them.

"One more thing," said Betty before she signed. "There's a friend of mine in New York who used to look after Roddy for me. I want her to come up here to live with me and help with the house and with Roddy. Leslie'd have to pay her fifty a week."

So Agnes Carlisle came to live in Peyton Place with Betty Anderson, and Leslie Harrington agreed to pay her wages. In return for what he gave, Leslie was to be allowed unlimited visiting privileges and the right to keep his grandson with him for a full day, one day a week. In the event of Betty's marriage, she was to keep all monies settled on her and Roddy, but her weekly allowance was to stop and Leslie was to be allowed the same privileges.

Betty Anderson leaned back comfortably in her new living room and Agnes brought her a drink. The two women took their shoes off and sipped their martinis.

"Now I've got it made," said Betty. "Who wants to get married?"

"Didn't I tell you?" asked Agnes smugly. "I told you to get in touch with him, didn't I?"

"Yes, you did," agreed Betty. "And you never made a wiser suggestion in your life."

"For Christ's sake, Charlie," said Leslie Harrington crossly, "are you playing cards or not? We've been waiting for you to tell us whether you can open or not."

Charles Partridge looked at his cards. "I pass," he said.

"One card," said Leslie to Seth, who was dealing.

Old Leslie, trying to fill an inside straight, thought Charles. He'll probably hit, too. He usually gets what he wants. Even if there's a price on it.

At eleven o'clock, Leslie Harrington and Charles Partridge said good night to Matthew Swain and Seth Buswell.

"Let's walk a little," said Leslie when the two men were outside.

"Where to?" asked Charles. "It's late and I'm tired."

"I just want to walk past Betty's house," said Leslie. "I like to make sure everything's all right before I go to sleep at night."

"Do you go down there every night?" asked Charles.

Leslie nodded. "You never can tell," he said. "I might catch that little bitch in a compromising situation someday."

"Leslie!" cried Charles in horror.

"Oh, cut it out," said Leslie. "You've known me too many years to be shocked at anything I say. Come on."

The two men walked slowly down Chestnut Street and turned into Laurel.

Betty Anderson's house was dark and still. Leslie stopped and looked at it, stared at it as if his eyes could see right through the walls—and right into the bitter, unforgiving heart of Betty Anderson, his grandson's mother. It was not only little Roddy's love that made Leslie appear younger these days; it was also the smell of battle. He was locked with Betty in a clash of wills. Nothing made him feel younger than a good fight.

He looked at the house and thought, You've won the first battle, Betty, but the war isn't over yet. Before I die, little Roddy will be living in the big house with me.

• 5 •

THE TRAIN PLUNGED HEADLONG INTO THE LONG SPACE THAT SEPARATED Lewis Jackman from Allison MacKenzie, and Lewis sat in the club car, impatient with his drink and with the way the hands on his watch moved as slowly as if they had been trapped in molasses. The wheels of the train, too, seemed to move forward in slow motion, and Lewis watched water condense on the outside of his glass and looked again at his watch.

Sitting next to him in the observation car was Stephanie. Allison had introduced them during the week she spent in New York after returning from Hollywood. They left Grand Central together and had been traveling together for eight hours. And that's about as many words as we've exchanged, Stephanie thought, eight. If I didn't know better, I'd have to conclude that Lewis Jackman was a man on his way to a heavy date.

"Hello, there!" said a feminine voice behind him, and, even before he turned, Lewis was resentful at anyone who would break into his thoughts.

"Hi," Stephanie said, disinterestedly.

"I remember you," the girl said. "You're Stephanie, Allison's friend."

"Yes."

The girl would not be put off with coolness. "I'm Jennifer

Carter," she said. "My husband will be here in a minute. May we sit with you?"

Stephanie wanted very badly to say No, but instead, she said, "Of course." She introduced Jennifer to Lewis.

"Here's Ted now!" said Jennifer, and turned to her husband. "Darling, you remember Stephanie, don't you? Allison introduced her to us last Christmas."

"Sure," said Ted and extended his hand. "How are you?"

"Are you going up to Peyton Place to visit Allison, too, Mr. Jackman?" asked Jennifer.

"Yes, I am," replied Lewis.

The girl's eyes were bright with a shrewdness that reminded Lewis of a snake, and although she was very beautiful there was something about her that was too finely drawn. Her cheekbones were too prominent and her chin had an aggressive tilt to it and her eyes darted everywhere so that they not only seemed to miss nothing but to probe beneath the surface of everything they saw.

"Allison must be a very important writer to drag a busy publisher like you so far away from civilization," said Jennifer, and her eyes fastened on his with a demand for an answer.

"She is," said Lewis. And the simple, unemphatic way in which he said it gave his words a great deal of authority.

Jennifer laughed. "It's so hard to think of little Allison MacKenzie of Peyton Place as an important writer, as someone to be taken seriously."

"Jennifer!" said Ted. "Don't say things like that."

"Don't be ridiculous, darling," said Jennifer. "I can't help it if that's what I thought, can I?"

Ted looked away uncomfortably. "Let's order," he said.

"Good idea," replied Jennifer. "I want a Scotch and water, please." She turned again to Lewis. "How long have you had this high opinion of Allison?" she asked, with the same persistence that had characterized her previous questions.

Lewis wanted to stand up and tell her that it was none of her business, but he didn't.

"A long time," he said, and his voice did not encourage further interrogation.

"Since before she got famous and began to make pots of money?" asked Jennifer.

"Yes," said Lewis. "Even before that." He looked at Stephanie and stood up. "I think we ought to be getting back to our seats, Stephanie." He nodded to Jennifer and Ted and said, "If you'll excuse us."

Jennifer laughed as he turned to walk away. "That's what people always say when they don't want to talk to you any more."

"Jennifer!" said Ted.

"Oh, stop saying 'Jennifer' like that," she said crossly. "You sound like a broken record." She sipped at her drink. "Allison isn't getting much of a prize in him," she said. "He's as close-mouthed as you are."

"Perhaps he resented your prying," said Ted with more spirit than he usually showed in front of Jennifer.

"I don't pry," she said. "I'm just interested in people."

"Anyway," Ted said, "he's her publisher, not her lover."

"That's what you think," Jennifer said.

"What makes you think otherwise?" Ted asked.

"Stop cross-examining me, Mr. District Attorney. I just know it in my bones, that's all. Big New York publishers don't come all the way to Peyton Place just to look at a manuscript."

"You're just plain nosy," said Ted and leaned back in his chair. "Plain nosy."

It was true. Jennifer was one of those people who cannot visit anywhere without peeking into the bathroom medicine cabinet and checking the pile of towels in the linen closet. Whenever the opportunity presented itself, she pawed through other people's desks and dresser drawers, and it gave her a deep sense of satisfaction to know that her best unmarried friend kept a supply of preventatives in the drawer of her night table and that another friend received dunning letters from Jordan-Marsh. She knew that her father's dearest friend wore a wide elastic girdle, and every time she saw him she could scarcely keep from laughing right in his face, especially since she also knew that the same man's wife carried on a lively correspondence with a noted French cellist.

Jennifer also knew that her mother-in-law had taken to reading lurid, paper-backed murder mysteries and that her father-in-law collected pornographic picture playing cards. She knew that Roberta and Harmon Carter had seventeen thousand dollars on deposit at the Citizens' National Bank and that they carried fifty thousand dollars' worth of insurance, and she knew that when Roberta wanted to be free in the evening she put a sleeping powder in Harmon's after dinner coffee. But best of all was a knowledge so gratifying that Jennifer was hard put to keep it to herself. Jennifer knew that whenever she went to Peyton Place with Ted, Roberta sneaked into the little room next to Ted's and listened to her son and daughter-in-law at night.

"It must be the air up here," Ted said to his wife. "Whenever we're in Peyton Place, you're as horny as a French whore who enjoys her work."

Jennifer almost laughed in his face. "You make me that way," she told him, and thought up new ways to arouse him and make him do unheard-of things to her. It excited her to distraction to know that Roberta was listening to every word and sound. Jennifer squirmed under Ted's hands and she moaned and cried out.

"You're hurting me. You're hurting me. Don't stop, darling. Deeper. Deeper."

And then her muffled scream, and even as she cried out Jennifer thought that she could hear the sound of panting from the other side of the wall.

"Again, darling," cried Jennifer. "Again."

Ted put his hands on his wife's quivering body and said, "Dear God, what makes you like this?"

And, thinking of Roberta who was listening, Jennifer smiled in the dark.

"I love you," she said. "All you have to do is look at me, and I begin to think of us like this."

It would have been a delicious secret to share, thought Jennifer. But Ted would never understand. He'd turn cold and refuse to touch her in his mother's house.

So she had to be content with watching Roberta's face the next morning.

"What's the matter, Mother?" asked Jennifer with a sly, little smile. "Didn't you sleep well?"

"As a matter of fact, I didn't," replied Roberta. "I guess I shouldn't have had that second cup of coffee."

"Well, I slept like a baby," said Harmon.

I'll bet you did, thought Jennifer, thinking of the sleeping powders that Roberta kept locked in her dressing table.

Roberta kept her secrets locked up, but she wasn't very smart about it. She kept a ring with the keys to everything in the house under her pillow. It hadn't taken Jennifer long to find her hiding places.

As the train hurried toward Peyton Place, Jennifer smiled into her drink and wondered what was new at her inlaws. She hadn't been to the Carters' since August, and there was bound to be a whole new crop of secrets by now.

Jennifer began to complain of a headache right after the train pulled out of Concord, and by the time she and Ted reached the Carter house in Peyton Place she had convinced her husband that all she wanted was to go to bed with some aspirin and a cup of hot tea.

"What a shame," said Roberta sympathetically. "And we were all going to the church supper tonight."

"I won't hear of the rest of you missing it," said Jennifer. "The three of you run along."

"Of course not," said Ted. "I don't want to leave you when you aren't feeling well."

"Don't be silly," replied Jennifer. "And please don't be stubborn, darling. If you don't go along with Mother and Dad, I'll feel like a heel and I'll have to force myself to join you. Please don't make me do that."

At last Ted capitulated and he, Roberta and Harmon left. Jennifer waited until she could no longer hear the sound of the car, then she got quietly out of bed and went to Roberta's room. She picked through Harmon's drawers without discovering anything new and when Roberta's dressing table yielded nothing but a new supply of sleeping powders, Jennifer was petulantly annoyed. Her fingers groped under Roberta's pillow and she straightened up in shocked surprise. The key ring was not there.

Jennifer's annoyance fled on the wings of excitement, and she began to search the room. Jennifer was very good at discovering hiding places, and for that reason she discarded the more obvious nooks and crannies that Roberta might have selected. Her fingers moved expertly through the pockets of all the garments in Roberta's closet, but with no success. She examined the bathroom minutely and when she had finished there she stood for a moment in the upstairs hall, concentrating with all her mind on what Roberta must have been thinking when she hid her keys.

In another moment, Jennifer went directly to the linen closet off the bathroom. Her fingers closed around a box of soap flakes which Roberta kept for washing stockings and nylon underwear, and in another moment her probing hand touched the key ring. She lifted it carefully out of the box of soap flakes, cupping her hand under it so that she would leave no telltale trail of soap on the shelf, and she laughed out loud.

She unlocked the cedar chest in the front hall, but there was nothing there but winter blankets, a bottle of brandy and sixty-eight dollars in two-dollar bills. Jennifer left everything as she had found it and slammed down the cover of the chest. So her mother-in-law nipped at imported brandy on the sly and saved two-dollar bills. How dull, thought Jennifer in disappointment.

She went downstairs and unlocked the desk in the living room. There was the usual collection of bills and canceled checks and unanswered letters. Jennifer examined everything without interest and glanced at her watch. The family would be back in less than half an hour. She unlocked the bottom drawer of the desk, expecting to be disappointed again, but she felt her interest quicken as her eyes fell on a loose-leaf notebook that hadn't been there on her last visit.

She picked it up and began to leaf through it, and her face paled as she read. Roberta had mapped out a plan for murder. A plan so simple and stupid that it might just work for those very reasons. Jennifer's heart pumped hard and fast as she read, and it was not until she heard a car stop outside that she raised her head. They were back.

In a flash, Jennifer locked the desk and ran upstairs. She buried the key ring deep in the box of soap flakes and ran to her room. Before she got back into bed, she looked out the window and was just in time to see Roberta coming up the walk. You sly old bitch, she thought. You jealous old bitch. What a surprise you have in store for you!

Lying in bed, listening to Ted's footsteps coming up the stairs, Jennifer thought, This is going to be a memorable Thanksgiving Day.

Roberta had scheduled her murder for tomorrow.

· 6 ·

ALLISON, MIKE AND CONSTANCE SAT UP LATE WITH THEIR GUESTS on the night before Thanksgiving Day. Stephanie lay sprawled on the rug in front of the fireplace, Lewis sat in the armchair. Allison could tell that Mike liked Lewis very much. They had all begun the evening by talking about politics and literature, but now the night was coming to an end with gossip about Jennifer.

Stephanie described her behavior on the train, and added, "I know the type. New York is full of them. Glossy, teasing little bitches, all golden promise on the outside and empty as a tin cup on the inside."

Lewis smiled, amused by Stephanie's colorful language. He said, "I've known a few Jennifers. And they've all run pretty much to type. They have the feeling that they can say anything or do anything, and Daddy's money will always be there to protect them. I hope you ladies won't jump on me, but I must say that no man I've ever met—and in my business I've met some pretty egocentric ones—has ever been as arrogant as these women are."

"Why is that?" Mike asked, like the good teacher he was.

"I think there's a very simple explanation," Lewis said. "Men are always a bit worried that if they are too arrogant, someone will haul off and punch them in the nose. But women don't have that worry."

"You can say anything you like about Jennifer Carter," Constance said. "I won't jump on you. She's a queer one. I've never seen a girl so drawn and tense. And, at the same time, there's a nerveless quality about her. I have the feeling she could do the most monstrous thing, and not turn a hair."

Mike stood up. "If I refill everybody's glass, will you all promise to change the subject? I don't think Jennifer Carter is the best choice for an end of the night conversation. I think I'd have pleasanter dreams if we told stories about vampire bats."

"I promise," Stephanie said, and held up her glass.

Not long after that they all went upstairs to their rooms. Allison shared her room with Stephanie, and Lewis slept in the guest room next to it. It tormented her, lying in bed with the knowledge that Lewis was just the other side of the thin wall.

As if reading her thoughts, Stephanie murmured, "Your friend Lewis is a beautiful man." She sighed. "I've come to the conclusion that all beautiful men are married."

"You'll find someone someday who is both beautiful and unmarried," Allison told her.

"I suppose," Stephanie said. "But meanwhile, back at the ranch, things are very lonely. I'm a girl who's good and tired of the single state, Allison. If I didn't have an exaggerated sense of my own worth, I'd accept the first producer who asked for my hand. Not that it's my hand they ask for."

Allison laughed. "You needn't worry. Eventually you're going to meet a man who sees right through you, right through your hard beautiful shell to the soft warm heart beneath. And that will be the end of him and the end of you."

"That's the first and probably the last time I'll ever feel complimented at being called a fraud," Stephanie laughed.

"Oh, I didn't mean that you're a fraud, and you know it. But you've built up defenses, we all have. God knows, after my experience since the book's been published, I wouldn't dream of accusing you of being fraudulent. It would be a case of the pot calling the kettle black."

"Why do you say that, Allison?" Stephanie raised herself up on her elbow and looked at her.

Allison replied, "Lewis says nearly all writers feel this way. They feel like confidence men who have pulled off a fast one on the public. When your novel is successful, when a million people are reading it, when everyone is talking about it, you can't believe that all this is the result of your talent. So you begin to think you've tricked them all and that you're a walking fraud."

"Do you still feel that way?"

"I don't know, Stevie. I really don't know. With one or two important exceptions, I feel my whole life is unreal and fraudulent now. I need to get back to work, to start writing my new book."

"Why don't you? This is the most perfect place for work."

"It's not easy. Sometimes I think it's because life is too exciting. I don't want to seal myself up and cut myself off from it. I have the feeling I'll miss something, something important."

She turned to Stephanie. "I've developed such a large appetite for life, Stevie. Success makes living so delicious that you don't want to miss a moment of it. I guess that's why the Hollywood people are so frightened of being alone. Even for an hour. I guess they figure that they've given so much for success that it would be a sin not to enjoy every minute of it to the full."

"Do you know what you want yet, Allison?"

"Yes," Allison said. "Everything."

Stephanie was silent then, and after a little while Allison could hear her regular breathing and knew she was asleep. She thought of Lewis, so near and so unreachable. She wondered if she dared sneak into his room. I can't, she answered herself, not in Constance's house. Finally, she fell asleep, exhausted by her thoughts.

It seemed only minutes later that she opened her eyes to the brightness of day and heard, remotely, as if from miles away, the sounds of Constance in the kitchen preparing the Thanksgiving dinner. She dressed quickly and hurried down to help her mother.

Mike was at the kitchen table with Constance; they were drinking coffee and talking in soft voices. Allison thought she heard Lewis' name mentioned.

Constance saw Allison standing at the door and said, "What are you doing up so early?"

"I wanted to help you with the dinner," Allison said.

Mike said, "We have the perfect job for you. It calls for intelligence and requires that the applicant be a person of responsibility."

"I don't think she's old enough for it yet," Constance said, playing along with Mike.

"I think we ought to give her a chance," Mike said.

He said to Allison, "Have you got grit and determination? Do you want to make something of yourself? If not, do not apply for this job."

Allison smiled at them. "You crazy fools," she said. "All right. I've got grit and determination. I want to get ahead. Now, what's the job?"

Mike pointed to the stove. "You see that little window in the oven?"

Allison nodded.

"Your job," Mike said, "is to draw a chair over to the oven, sit down on that chair and watch the turkey through the little window. We wouldn't want it to get away, would we?"

"I think the job is too big for her," said Connie. "After all, she's had very little experience as a turkey-watcher."

"I could rise to the challenge," Allison told them, speaking with mock fervor. "Please. This job could be the making of me."

"It's a lifetime career," Mike said. "Don't rush your decision. Here." He pulled out a chair. "Sit down, have a cup of coffee and think it over."

"We'll keep the job open while you're making up your mind," Constance said.

"Fools," Allison told them, shaking with laughter.

"Slacker," Mike said. "Coming down when the work's all done and offering your services."

"Why didn't you wake me?" Allison said.

"Because," said Constance, "we are the kind of parents who like to make sacrifices for our children and then tell them about it."

"Yes, we get our kicks that way," said Mike.

Allison got up and kissed them both.

"What was that for?" asked Mike.

"That," said Allison, "was for *not* being that kind of parent."

Thanksgiving Day at the MacKenzie house began with laughter and continued with laughter, through dinner and after it. Allison had never seen Lewis so happy, his face suffused with the joy of living and the happiness of being with people whom he liked. He sat next to Allison at dinner and, in the midst of laughter, squeezed her hand under the table. It was quick and almost painfully hard, and it expressed his joy and his gratitude to her for having brought him this.

He had once told Allison that until he had met her he had given up all hope of happiness. There were times that Thanksgiving Day when the look of love on his face was so naked that Allison thought Constance and everyone else was bound to notice it.

Dinner lasted two hours. It was late afternoon when they finished. Allison had wanted to take Lewis walking. She wanted to show him Road's End and the view of the town, wanted to share all her secrets and memories with him.

"I wanted to take Lewis up to Road's End," she said to Mike and Constance, "but I'm afraid it's going to be dark soon." She turned to Lewis. "We won't have time, I'm afraid."

"Nonsense," Mike said. "Take the car. You can be there in ten minutes and back again before nightfall."

"Wonderful idea," said Allison. And wondered why she hadn't thought of it. The car would give them more privacy, too. It would be the only chance they'd have for being alone together before Lewis left in the morning.

At the door, with the alpaca hood of her old coat over her head, she called back to Constance and Stephanie, "Now wait for me. Don't start on the dishes till I get back."

"Slacker!" Mike called after her.

When Allison and Lewis had left, Mike admitted that he was stuffed to the ears and needed nothing so much as a nap. He got up and walked to the stairs where he turned and smiled at Constance and said, "Now listen, darling. I want you to promise me that you won't start doing the dishes till I get up."

Constance wadded her napkin and threw it at him. From the top of the stairs, he called down, "Missed."

"He's a wonderful man," Stephanie said.

"Yes, he is," said Connie, "but don't tell him I said so."

Constance and Stephanie began to clear the table and carry the dishes into the kitchen. Steve was wearing a pair of tight, leopard-spotted slacks and she looked more like a contented well-fed cat than anything else. As they washed the dishes they began to gossip. Steve began it by asking about Selena.

"She's going to marry Peter Drake," Connie said.

"Really?" asked Steve, delighted.

"Yes," said Connie. "In June, after Joey graduates from high school."

"I'm so glad," said Steve. "She's such a doll and she's had such a helluva time."

"Worse than you think," said Connie. "Did you ever run into an actor in New York named Tim Randlett?"

"Him!" yelled Steve. "Jesus, yes. He's one of the biggest pains I've ever met."

"Well, he was up here this past summer and made a big play for Selena. For a while, she thought that she was in love with him."

"Oh, no," moaned Steve. "Listen, I'll tell you about that guy. He's the biggest phony in the business."

"What do you mean?" asked Connie, remembering Mike's words about Tim Randlett.

"Oh, you know. The big star bit. He never got over the fact that because he could cry convincingly and made a pot of money in Hollywood he was a star. He still thinks he's the greatest. Honest, like he was Olivier or something. I worked with him on a TV program once. Believe me, he's strictly from squaresville. Thinks he's irresistible because of his profile. You know what he does? He *acts* twenty-four hours a day. I'll bet he even poses in the shower. He chose to see me as the small-town girl gone wrong in the big city and gave me a big pitch about how he could save me from all this emptiness and false glitter. You know. A real creep. Selena is well rid of him. I've watched him with girls when he's been acting the father, the priest, the vile seducer, the big brother. The whole bit. Tell me, what did he play for Selena?"

"I don't know," said Connie thoughtfully. "But it must have been something dreadful. I thought she was going to die from it."

"It must have been his season for villains," said Steve. "That phony!"

"Well, it's over with now, thank God. Now that Selena is going to marry Peter Drake, I'll have only you and Allison to worry about."

"I'm waiting for a rich producer," said Steve. "So I'll probably die an old maid. All producers are married. Sometimes I think their mothers marry them off when they're thirteen."

After they had finished the dishes they took the coffeepot and cups into the living room and sat before the fire. They sat quietly, resting, watching the beautiful and strange shapes the fire made, enjoying the peace and silence of the house.

• 7 •

AT ROAD'S END, ALLISON AND LEWIS SAT IN THE FRONT SEAT OF THE car and looked at Peyton Place, diminished and toylike below them. The houses seemed to have absorbed from the wintry sky its dead grayness. They look like tombstones, Allison thought, and shivered.

Lewis drew her closer to him.

"I don't know why," he said, "but it makes me rather sad to look at Peyton Place from here. It seems so forlorn."

"It's that time of year," Allison said. "I feel it too. It's the melancholy of autumn. Even though we know that every season is a new beginning, autumn always seems like an ending. So many things die."

Lewis took her face in his hands and looked at it for a long time; then, very gently, he kissed her eyelids and her lips.

"I love you, Lewis," Allison said.

"I hope it lasts forever, Allison."

"I know that our love will, Lewis. I wish that we could, too."

He laughed. "Autumn doesn't just make you melancholy, Allison. It makes you downright morbid."

"I know. I'm sure that once I get back to work it will be all right again. When I'm working, I forget what day it is, what season it is, what year."

"I hope you won't forget me," Lewis said.

"Not even if I tried, darling," Allison said. She pushed open his overcoat and pressed her body against his.

"Necking in a car," she said. "I feel like a schoolgirl. Not that I ever did this when I *was* a schoolgirl."

She looked around her at the bleakness of Road's End's landscape while Lewis' hands caressed her body. "I don't think I ever had even a crush on a boy," she said, thinking aloud more than talking. "My daydreams kept me so busy, I guess, that I didn't have time for boys. This is where everything began, Lewis, here at Road's End. Sometimes I think there would never have been a *Samuel's Castle* if there hadn't been a Road's End."

She smiled dreamily in the cocoon of warmth they had created in the small enclosed space of Mike's car. Lewis' hands roved freely over her body. She put her mouth against his ear and with her tongue traced its outline. His hands gripped her tightly for a moment; then he relaxed and said, "Tell me more."

"Once a boy named Norman kissed me here," she said.

"I am insanely jealous," Lewis said, and Allison felt his warm breath on her throat as he laughed.

"If it hadn't been for Road's End," she said, "there'd have been no novel, no New York and no Lewis Jackman."

"Impossible," Lewis said, "Unthinkable. I refuse to consider such an impossibility. If you hadn't existed, I would have invented you." He bent and kissed her sweater where the tips of her breasts pressed.

She held his head, rested her own on the top of the seat, her eyes closed. Lewis' hand moved gently and slowly, her head turned, her eyes half opened.

"Talk to me," he said.

She thought, All of Peyton Place can look up here and see this car, but they can't see us.

"Talk to me," Lewis repeated.

"I can't," she whispered. "Oh, Lewis, I can't."

She drew his head to her and kissed him, her tongue seeking his. He bit her and she groaned at the sweetness of the pain. When he had brought her to the very peak of pleasure, she pushed him away.

Her lips were dry and her voice trembled. "I want all of you." She did not hear her own voice crying out or the fierce words of love she uttered. She was enfolded in darkness, and her voice, hoarse and savage, was unrecognizable to her own ears.

When she opened her eyes, she found herself lying in Lewis' arms. Night had fallen and a sparse winter moon gave a watery light. The shadows of the trees were black on the hillside and black on the road.

"My God," Allison said, her voice low and unbelieving. "I thought we had had everything."

Lewis smiled and said nothing.

"I didn't think it could ever be better than what we already had," Allison said. She put her face to Lewis' chest and felt his heart beating against her lips. "Will it keep on like this, Lewis?" she asked, in a small, frightened voice. "Getting better and better, I mean. Will it? I hope it doesn't. I'm afraid I'd die if anything like this happened too often."

Lewis stroked her hair. Smiling, he said, "I don't think there's any cause for alarm, darling. Human beings are so oddly constructed that they get used to pleasure just as quickly as they get used to misery."

"I'm glad I found you, Lewis." She tightened her arms around him. "You'll always take care of me, won't you?"

"Always," Lewis promised.

"And in a few weeks I'll be back in New York, darling," Allison said, "and then I will be there always to take care of you. I'm going to take a year's lease on that gorgeous white and gold room, and I'm going to work all day and make love all night."

She sat up and lit a cigarette.

"Lewis," she said, "do you think that little manager will mind your coming to my apartment every night?"

Lewis laughed. "You are, at one and the same time, the most sophisticated and the most naïve woman I've ever met. The answer is: Yes, the manager will mind; and no, he won't say anything."

"Why won't he say anything?" Allison wanted to know.

"Because you are paying such a high rent that it's profitable for him not to mind. That's why," Lewis said. "As long as we're not noisy and don't disturb the other tenants, you'll never hear a word of complaint from him. The manager of that kind of hotel, the very expensive kind, is a professional not-minder. One of the first lessons he had to learn at school was how to avert his eyes gracefully."

Allison laughed. "He also took a course in How to Walk Backwards. For the final examination, he had to walk backwards through a crowded room, bowing all the way, and never bumping into anything."

"And he did postgraduate work in finger-snapping," Lewis added. "When he snaps his fingers at those Hungarian ghosts, it goes off like a pistol shot."

"If it can't be heard across a hotel lobby, it just isn't good enough," Allison said. "Flabby-fingered managers don't grow up to be Conrad Hilton."

They laughed at themselves; everything seemed delightful. Not even the bleak New England landscape seemed depressing any more, and Peyton Place glowed like a jewel in the valley below. Allison imagined she could tell which house was hers, and imagined Mike and Constance and Steve around the fire. She wondered if they were talking about Lewis and her.

"What are you thinking about?" Lewis asked.

"I was just wondering if they are talking about us."

"If we don't get back soon," Lewis said, "they most certainly will be."

"Oh, I know," Allison said, groaning. "But I hate to leave here. It's so private, darling. It's the last chance to be alone with you until after the New Year." She kissed him lightly. "But I see that now that you've had your way with me all you're interested in doing is getting back to civilization."

"That's the way we men are," Lewis said. "I plan to tire of you in a week or two and cast you aside like a worn-out rag."

Allison started the car. "You'll have to wait for a snowy night," she said. "It wouldn't be fair to turn me out in nice weather."

They began the long, curving descent to Peyton Place. Lewis turned on the radio and was bent forward, looking for music, when Allison became aware that something was wrong. She had tried to slow for the wide curve, but the brakes did not seem to respond; the car only swerved oddly. She made the curve and, taking her foot off the brake, found the car handled better. She sighed with relief.

"There," Lewis said. He sat back to enjoy the symphonic music he had found on a Boston station.

Allison touched the accelerator very softly with her toe; she wanted to increase the speed just a little for the upgrade. The car shot forward at a much greater speed than she had expected. What in the world's going on! she said to herself. Again she applied the brakes, and again the car swerved. She released the brakes and then, by the feel of the car, she knew what had gone wrong. The accelerator had stuck!

They were on the downgrade then and the car was going at sixty miles an hour. Allison tapped the accelerator with her toe; she gave it a sharp rap, thinking that would release it. But it remained stuck, only now it was in farther than it had been before and the speed of the car and her helplessness made her feel sick. She gripped the wheel tightly and watched with agonized eyes as the curve drew closer and closer.

As Lewis said, "Don't you think you'd better—" she slammed her foot on the brake, pushed it down to the floor boards and held it there. She smelled the brake linings beginning to burn.

"What's happening, Lewis?" she screamed, overcome with horror.

She saw his hand moving with terrible slowness toward the steering wheel. And then they went off the road and the car turned over and over.

She closed her eyes. She thought, Oh God, how many more times will it go over before it stops?

She sat in the kitchen with Mike and Constance; they were drinking coffee and laughing at one of Mike's jokes. I will never leave them, she thought, they are so good, so good.

Allison. Allison, Constance said. Allison. Allison. *Allison, darling!*

Allison opened her eyes. Gaunt trees swayed and bent above her, the moon caught in the branches like a bird in a trap. She pulled herself up and looked wildly about her.

The car, she said, the car. I must find Lewis.

She felt the pain stab in her chest; it made her weak and she fell to her knees.

Lewis, she called, Lewis. I'm coming, darling. I'm going to take care of you.

She raised her head and saw the car. She began to crawl toward it.

• 8 •

JENNIFER STARED AT ROBERTA OVER THE BIG THANKSGIVING TURKEY.

That cold-blooded bitch, she thought savagely. Nobody had better ever say anything about my being nosy again. If I weren't, there's a damned good chance that, by tomorrow night at this time, I'd be dead.

Roberta poured coffee and smiled and talked about who had been at the Congregational Church.

"And did you have a good nap, dear?" she asked.

Jennifer, giving a headache for an excuse, had stayed behind to take a nap while the rest of the family went to the Thanksgiving services.

"I couldn't sleep," replied Jennifer. "So I decided to read."

She waited to see if Roberta would react to that, but her mother-in-law remained as calm as ever.

After they were finished with dinner, Harmon and Ted went to the home of one of Harmon's friends, where they played chess and drank beer until nightfall. Roberta and Jennifer were alone in the house.

"I think I'll take a nap," said Jennifer. "Those enormous dinners of yours always make me sleepy."

"Go ahead, dear," said Roberta. "I have some letters to write." I'll bet, thought Jennifer acidly.

She went upstairs and, when Roberta peeked into the room a half hour later, Jennifer seemed to be fast asleep. Roberta closed the door quietly and went to the linen closet in the hall.

Thank God for well-oiled hinges, thought Jennifer as she opened her bedroom door.

Through the narrow opening she watched Roberta pick up the box of soap flakes and dig for her key ring. Then she watched her tiptoe quietly down the carpeted stairs. Jennifer went to her dresser and took out the notebook, and then, just as quietly as Roberta had done, she followed her down the stairs. From the doorway to the living room she watched Roberta unlock her desk and reach into the bottom drawer. She watched her stiffen in surprise and yank the drawer wide open and paw frantically through it. When Roberta turned, Jennifer was standing very still in the doorway with the notebook in her outstretched hand.

"Is this what you were looking for?" she asked sweetly.

Roberta jumped up, her face so white that for a moment Jennifer thought that the older woman would faint.

"How did you get that?" Roberta whispered in horror.

"By unlocking your desk drawer, Mother dear," said Jennifer. "Tell me," she asked, and her lips curved in a contemptuous smile, "did you really think you could get away with it?"

"Give me that notebook!" cried Roberta.

"Not yet, Mother dear," said Jennifer with maddening calm. "You know, I wondered why you'd taken to reading murder mysteries. I'd always thought you were a real, dyed in the wool Book-of-the-Month type. But I really never guessed that you'd think up anything as dumb as this. You don't have to tell me why, either, because I know that, too."

"I don't know what you're talking about," Roberta gasped.

"Oh, yes you do," said Jennifer. She advanced slowly toward Roberta and the little smile never left her face. "You're jealous of me," she said softly. "Every time Ted and I go to bed, you're huddled in the little room next door to us and you listen to your son make love to me and you're so jealous you can't stand it."

Roberta staggered back toward the desk as if she had been struck.

"You're jealous," said Jennifer. "So jealous you can't stand it. You wish it was you in bed with Ted."

"You're crazy!" said Roberta and was sure that she had screamed, but her voice was nothing but a harsh whisper.

Jennifer burst out laughing. "*I'm* crazy!" she said. "Here. Listen to this, and we'll see who's crazy." She flipped the notebook open and began to read. "One-thirty: Jennifer goes upstairs for nap. Two-thirty: I wake her with a cup of coffee in which sleeping powder has been dissolved. Three o'clock: I suggest a visit to the Page girls. Three-thirty: Jennifer and I get into car in garage and I start car while wearing gloves. I tell her I've forgotten my glasses and leave her there while I re-enter house. Car is still running. Four o'clock: Jennifer has fallen asleep and I move her into driver's seat and go back into house. Five-thirty: Ted and Harmon return home to find me sound asleep in bed. They discover Jennifer dead in car." Jennifer closed the book with a snap. "I never would have known what hit me, would I?" she asked.

Roberta had sunk down into the chair in front of the desk.

"You're evil," she was saying, over and over, "you're a bad, evil girl."

"At least I never planned to kill you," retorted Jennifer. "And now, do you know what I'm going to do?"

Roberta looked up at her stupidly.

Jennifer smiled. "I'm going upstairs to get my coat, then I'm going to take this notebook, get into your car and go directly to the sheriff." She started to walk out of the room and Roberta jumped up to follow her, just as Jennifer had known she would.

Jennifer ran upstairs with Roberta behind her, and when she reached the top she waited until her mother-in-law was standing beside her.

"Did you really think you could get away with it?" asked Jennifer tauntingly, holding out the notebook so that Roberta could almost reach it.

Roberta leaned forward to grab the notebook, and in that second, Jennifer dropped the book to the floor, put her hands against Roberta's shoulder and pushed with all her strength. Roberta fell forward with a scream and Jennifer coolly noted that her head hit the wall twice as she fell. It seemed to take her forever to reach the bottom.

Jennifer stood still at the top of the stairs, and the only sound was the echo of Roberta's startled cry and the quiet of Jennifer's breathing. Jennifer went quietly down the stairs and stepped over Roberta's body. She bent and felt for a pulse, but she knew from the angle of Roberta's head that her mother-in-law's neck was broken and that she was dead.

Jennifer went back upstairs and burned the pages of the notebook in the bathroom sink, then she flushed the ashes down the drain. Her heart had never altered its steady beating, for she had known that she could not fail. If Roberta had not been killed by the fall, but only injured, Jennifer would still have been safe because she had the notebook with its terrible story and Roberta would never be able to tell that she had been pushed.

Jennifer smiled as the last of the ashes flowed smoothly down the drain. She went to her bedroom and took off her shoes, stockings and panty girdle, just as she did every Sunday afternoon when she got ready for a nap. The bed was already rumpled from when she had used it while waiting for Roberta to look in on her.

Wearing only her slip, Jennifer walked down the stairs and stepped over Roberta's body without so much as a glance. She went to the telephone and paused a minute before she picked it up. When she did, she had held her breath long enough to make her voice a gasping breath. She gave the number of Harmon's friend and when he answered she was screaming for Ted.

"An accident!" she screamed. "Your mother. Come quickly!"

Roberta Carter was buried three days later, and everyone in Peyton Place sympathized with the bereaved family.

"What a shame," said the town. "She was the soul of goodness, Roberta was."

"And how terrible for Jennifer. She and Roberta were so close. Roberta told me herself how much she thought of Ted's wife."

"I know it. Why, Roberta just lived for the time when Jennifer would have her first baby."

"It's terrible. You don't often see a mother and daughter-in-law as close as Jennifer and Roberta were."

The following Friday, Ted and Jennifer boarded the train for Boston. As Harmon said, Ted couldn't stay forever, he had his career to think of. Jennifer wore a wide-brimmed black hat with a veil that hid her little smile. Ted helped her up the steps and onto the train. Inwardly, he shuddered when he touched her. In his heart he harbored a terrible suspicion. He would spend the rest of his life—the rest of his eminently successful life—in dark wonder.

· 9 ·

ALLISON KNEW THAT LEWIS WAS DEAD. EVEN IN THE DARK DEPTHS OF her drugged sleep she knew it. When they had brought her broken body into the receiving room at the hospital she had been calling for Lewis, and had continued to call for him until Matt Swain arrived and injected a sedative.

Now, a week later, Constance and Mike sat by her bedside. Allison was still under sedation. Constance stared at her bruised face with tears in her eyes. According to Matt Swain's medical report, Allison had four broken ribs and a crushed collarbone and had suffered a fairly severe concussion. But Constance knew that the tortured, anguished look on Allison's face, the sudden starts, the way she turned her head, was not the result of her physical injuries. Allison was the captive of the terrible, haunting dreams of her drugged sleep.

Constance and Mike came and sat at her bedside every afternoon and evening. Matt let them come only during the regular hospital visiting hours. If he had permitted, Constance would have been there twenty-four hours a day.

"She's young. She'll heal quickly enough," Matt told Constance.

"It's not her broken bones I'm thinking about," Constance said.

"And what makes you think *I* am, Connie?" Matt blustered. "How much of a goddamn fool do you take me for?"

"I'm sorry, Matt," Connie said.

"Damn well should be," he said, and stormed off down the hospital corridor, his white coat flying out around him.

Stephanie stayed with them through the first week and then had to go to New York, promising to come back as soon as Constance or Allison needed her. When Constance said good-by to her, they both cried; and Mike stood by, a helpless look on his face, saying,

"Everything's going to be all right, everything's going to be all right."

It was on the second day after the accident that Mike came home with the police report, the results of what had been uncovered by the State Police's examination of the car.

"The accelerator stuck," Mike said. "Allison hasn't had enough experience as a driver to know that you just stick the toe of your shoe under it and push it up. I suspect she stepped down on it, thinking that would release it. But, of course, it didn't."

Constance sat listening quietly, with her hands in her lap.

"Judging by the tire marks on the road," Mike went on, "the police think she then tried to stop the car by applying the brakes. It went out of control. She was probably doing eighty to ninety miles an hour by that time."

"Oh God," said Connie.

"They know where the car went off the road, but they can only guess how many times it rolled over. Four or five times, they think, until the trees stopped it."

The car was completely demolished, unsalvageable; and Lewis' body had been found inside. Allison had been thrown clear, she had fallen on the grassy bank and had slid and rolled to the bottom. A car full of teen-agers had come upon the scene minutes after it happened. They had found Allison trying to pull open the buckled door of the car, trying to get to Lewis.

She knew he was dead. She threw her head from side to side on the pillow, trying to shake the horror of her dreams. Horrible as anything else was the feeling of helplessness that came over her as the car began to careen along the road, its tires screaming. There was nothing she could do, nothing.

"Lewis," she had cried, "Lewis, what is happening?"

She remembered his hand moving slowly toward the steering wheel, to help her control the car. And then they began to turn over. That was all she remembered, but, hour after hour, the dream of those hideous moments pursued her. And deep in her unconscious brain, at the very center of her being, was the knowledge that Lewis was dead.

Early in the morning of her second week in the hospital, that time of day when the nurses begin to turn off lights, Allison woke and found Matt Swain watching her.

"Good morning, Allison," he said. And he spoke to her as gently as he had ever spoken to anyone in his life.

Allison began to cry, weakly; the tears welled up and spilled over and ran down her face. "Tell me, Matt," she said, her voice a cracked whisper. "Tell me."

"You know," he said.

"Tell me!"

"He is dead, Allison," Matt said.

Matt took her hand. She pulled it away. "I don't want to hear any of your consoling words, Doctor," she said. "Words aren't going to help me." Her voice was flat and dead. She closed her eyes.

"Allison," Matt said, "Allison, whether you help me or not, I am going to make you well. Make no mistake about that."

Constance brought books and magazines, and returned the next day to find them untouched. And, in the same way, the food trays brought in by the nurses were returned to the kitchen.

Matt Swain came in and stood by the foot of the bed, stood silently until Allison looked up and met his eyes. Then he said, "If what you're trying to do is commit suicide, Allison, there are simpler and less painful ways of doing it."

He waited for Allison to speak. She closed her eyes and turned her head away.

He made his voice sound rough and brutal; even he was shocked by the sound of it. "In this hospital, I'm the boss. What I say goes. When you get home, when I discharge you from this place, you can do what you like with yourself. It'll be no affair of mine. But you're not leaving here until I say so."

He put his hands behind his back and leaned forward, the stethoscope like a black noose around his neck, his white coat billowing open like a tent.

"You have your choice, Allison. You'll eat what is brought to you, what I have prescribed for you, the nourishment that will bring you back to health; or I will have your hands tied to the bed and stick needles into you and feed you intravenously. It's up to you."

He signaled the nurse who was waiting at the door with a tray of food. She rustled into the room, set down the tray and cranked up the bed. Unwillingly but inexorably, Allison was raised to a sitting position. Matt went to the window and opened the curtains, flooding the room with light. The nurse put the tray on the bed table and pushed it up to Allison.

Allison sat and looked at it, as if it were something dangerous and full of menace.

Matt said to himself, Well, if this doesn't work, I don't know what the hell I'm going to do. Aloud, he said, "This news is going to make your mother very happy, Allison."

Allison did not look at him. She picked up the spoon and slowly began to eat the broth.

Matt Swain walked out of the room. In the corridor he leaned against a wall and wiped his forehead. If you hadn't been a doctor, you'd have made a damn good actor, he said, congratulating himself.

In December, Mike came in the new car the insurance company had bought him and took Allison home. She was shaky on her feet but, with Mike's arm supporting her, she walked to the car. When Mike opened the door she began to cry; she turned her head into Mike's shoulder and sobbed. "Oh, Mike, I can't, I can't!"

Mike spoke soothing, meaningless words into her ear, like a mother crooning to a baby, and gently eased her into the car. He ran around the other side and slid under the wheel. Then, driving very slowly, he took her home.

Constance had made up the sofa in the living room with blankets and pillows; a fire burned cheerily. Allison looked around her, as if she had never seen this house before and was wary of it.

If only she would tell me, Constance thought, looking at her daughter, her heart breaking for Allison. If I only dared to tell her that I know.

And Allison, lying on the sofa, with Constance and Mike fussing around her, was filled with bitter thoughts. She felt that her body had betrayed her by getting well again. And that she was betraying Lewis by being alive when he was dead.

David and Stephanie wrote to her, Brad Holmes and Arthur Tishman sent messages and flowers. But she wrote to no one. She read a great deal. Constance wrote to David and Brad, and they kept a steady stream of all the new novels coming into the house. During the day she prowled around the house, walking from room to room, always returning to the sofa. The sofa had become for her the protected place.

Like Road's End when I was a girl, she thought. Road's End. It had truly been road's end for Lewis.

And sometimes she thought: Now you are free. Now you can

616

have all the experience of life that you wanted. You can go anywhere, see everything, do anything. You are free.

And when this thought came she pushed it quickly away, repelled by it. It is like dancing on Lewis' grave, she thought, and hated herself for having such thoughts.

Two weeks before Christmas, Constance asked Allison if she'd like to have David and Stephanie up for the holidays.

Allison shook her head. "I don't want to see anyone yet," she said.

At night, Constance and Mike lay in their bed and listened to the sounds of Allison, prowling about the house, drinking coffee in the kitchen. When they came down in the morning, every morning, there was a coffee cup in the sink and a pile of books on the table. Allison only slept when she took a sleeping pill.

When Constance went to Matt Swain, all he could say was, "I have faith in Allison. We'll just have to be patient, Connie, and bear up and see her through this bad time."

Connie nodded.

Matt said, "Connie, you can just tell me to mind my own damned business if you want to, but was there something between Allison and Lewis Jackman?"

"Mind your own damned business, Matt," Connie said, and smiled for the first time in weeks.

Looking back on it, Connie thought it was probably Matt who had broken the ice and started things moving again. She walked home with a livelier step, and when she opened the door she was struck by the stagnant odor of the house. It smells like a place where life has come to a standstill, she thought. It's wrong, it's all wrong. I must do something.

As she passed the living room she saw Allison lying on the sofa, staring at the ceiling, her eyes full of nothingness. Connie went into the kitchen and began to heat the coffee.

She went to the living room door and said to Allison, "I'm heating the coffee. Would you like a cup?"

"I don't care."

"Well, have one then, darling. I like company."

She filled the cups and brought them in and set them on the coffee table next to Allison's sofa. Allison sat up and Constance sat down beside her.

"It's cold out," Connie said. "And I think it's going to snow. I'll be glad when this year is over and Mike will be able to stop commuting to White River. It's only nine miles, but when winter comes I begin to worry."

Allison did not say anything.

Connie sipped her coffee. "Mmm, that tastes good. I needed something hot. Would you like some cookies?"

"No, thank you, Mother."

Connie looked up then and saw the first snowflakes flatten themselves against the windowpane. Allison followed her glance, saw the snow and got up. She went to the window and looked out.

Allison had lost weight. Her face had lost the last of its youthful flesh. Looking at her, Connie thought, You're a woman now, Allison. She followed Allison to the window. They stood side by side and looked out at the snow falling from the dense, low, late afternoon sky.

"Why is snow always exciting?" Allison asked, hardly realizing she was speaking aloud.

"Maybe it's because it reminds us of childhood," Connie said, "of the days when the world was our oyster and life was a beautiful dream without end."

"It has ended for me," Allison said, and, throwing her arms around her mother, she began to cry. Constance held her close and stroked her hair.

"Cry, baby," she said, "cry." She held her daughter in her arms and thought, She's crying the last of her youth away. Perhaps after the shock of being born, Constance thought, there comes the shock of realizing one is adult, of accepting age and its responsibilities and surrendering to the idea of death.

"Oh, Mother," Allison sobbed. "I loved him. I loved him."

Then Constance led her to the sofa and held her hand. They looked at the fire, and Allison spoke at last and told Connie all about herself and Lewis.

When she was finished, Constance kissed her and dried her tears. Then she said, "Now you must live for him, Allison. And don't think you're the first woman who ever had to make that decision. You haven't a child to live for, as I had. But you have your talent. You must start working again, darling."

"I'm going to try, Mother. I'm going to try."

And in the days that followed she did try. As the snow fell and drifted around the house, she sat for hours before her typewriter, staring at the blank, white paper. But what little she wrote she scratched out. It's so hard to get back into it, she thought. Usually she ended by drawing pictures on her note pad.

"But at least," Connie said to Mike, "at least she's trying. And she's talking more."

Mike was home all day now, for Christmas vacation had begun; his determinedly cheerful presence was good for Allison. They spent hours sitting at the kitchen table talking about Allison's work, and her inability to get her second novel started.

"Maybe I've got second novel fever," Allison said.

"Could be," Mike granted. "But I think writing is like any other job. When you've been away from it for a long time, it takes a while to get back into the swing of it. You're not so different from the lumberman who has had a three months' layoff. He has to get his muscles toned up again, and you've got to get your mind and temper toned up."

"Sometimes I think I'm written out and don't have anything more to say."

Mike laughed. "If you never moved out of Peyton Place, you'd have enough material to keep you going for two lifetimes."

On Christmas Day, surrounded by the debris and litter of gift wrappings, they were having dinner when there was a sharp rapping on the door.

Mike raised his eyebrows and stood up. Constance said, "Now who can that be?"

"Probably some kids out for tricks or treats," Mike said. Bending down quickly, he kissed Constance and said, "And a Happy Halloween to you, my dear."

"Oh, if I only had something to throw," Connie said, as he walked to the front door. The rapping continued and Mike shouted, "I'm coming, I'm coming."

There was a silence after the door had been opened. Then they heard Mike say, "You are either Rita Moore or the loveliest apparition I've ever seen."

Allison jumped to her feet as she heard Rita's clear, ringing laugh.

"It can't be anyone else," said Allison to her mother's inquiring look.

Rita swept into the room. She was wearing a black greatcoat

lined with fur, its high, wide collar framing her beautiful face that glowed with the cold.

"Well, I'm glad to see you on your feet," she said to Allison. "I heard in New York that you were doing the Elizabeth Barrett Browning bit." And before Allison could answer, Rita turned to Mike and handed him the wicker hamper she was carrying. "Here, Mr. MacKenzie, it's full of champagne and I don't think it will have to be cooled. That taxi I took from White River was refrigerated."

"Taxi!" Allison said. "How did you get anyone to drive you over here on Christmas Day?"

"Not only drive me over, darling. But he's going to wait at some crony's house and then drive me back in time to catch the Boston train. And it cost me only twenty-five dollars, one autograph and my best smile."

Mike stood next to her with the hamper of champagne in his hands. "You should have phoned, Miss Moore. I'd have been glad to come over for you."

"Oh, Mr. MacKenzie," Rita said, "you are nice."

"He's like that all the time. A regular boy scout," Constance said.

"You've gathered, Rita, that these are my parents," Allison said. "Mike and Constance Rossi."

"Rossi," said Rita. She turned to Mike. "And I've been calling you MacKenzie. I am sorry."

"Oh, that's all right," Mike said. "Of course, I'd have killed anyone else." Mike took the hamper into the kitchen.

Rita joined them at the table.

"Now," Allison said, "what in the world are you doing here of all places?"

"Well, I was in New York and I heard about your smashup and I just decided I wanted to have a good old-fashioned white Christmas dinner and so I came. Besides, I've been curious about the background of your story."

"How does it look to you?"

"It looks awfully like New England," said Rita. "Is it supposed to? I mean, when anything is so like I expect it to be, I'm sure it must be a fake."

Mike came in with the champagne and four glasses. "By the time we've finished this bottle, Miss Moore," he said, "I'm going to be able to tell you just how much I adore you. Right here in front of my wife I shall tell you."

620

"That's the best way," Rita said. "It's no good having secrets from your wife."

"That's the way I figure it too," Mike said.

"And after the second bottle," Connie said, "you can take off your shirt and show our guest your tattoo. You know, dear—the one with the beard that says 'Rita and Mike Forever.'"

"You mustn't be edgy, dear," said Mike to Connie. "I plan on going off with Miss Moore for only a year or two. But I am definitely coming back to you."

"That's what I call devotion," Connie said. And she was thinking, I could kiss you, Rita Moore. Because Allison was laughing. She was alive again, and it was because of Rita, walking into the house so unexpectedly, and bringing with her the bracing air of the outside world.

It was the world that Allison had been trying to hide from, that she had been unwilling and afraid to face. It had brought her a success that frightened her, and a love that had ended in tragedy.

When they had finished the second bottle, Connie said to Rita, "I know this will break your heart, but I'm going to take Mike away now. I think you'll want to spend some time alone with Allison."

"I suspect I'm being taken off to the kitchen to be put to work." He headed toward the kitchen door, saying, "The next sound you hear will be the sound of breaking china."

"They're nice," Rita said. "You've had more luck than most of us, Allison."

Allison made a gesture with her hand, as if to say, That's what you think, and she smiled a bitter smile.

"Full of self-pity, aren't you, kid? You smashed up and your man got killed, and now you're hurt because the whole world didn't crumple up and die with you. And if you stay here much longer, it'll go right on without you, for good and all."

"I'm trying to get back to work again, Rita. It just won't come."

Allison's hand was on the table. Rita reached across and tapped it with her long tapering finger. "It will come," she said, emphasizing each word with a finger tap. "It will come because it must. This is the final lesson, Allison. That is what success means for people like us—that when everything else is gone, friends and lovers and husbands, we have got our work. It's the only constant thing in our lives. And when we betray our talent, then we might as well give up and return to the original chaos."

She emptied the champagne bottle into their two glasses.

"I've got to get back to White River. My lovesick taximan is probably frozen to death by now. And besides, my husband is waiting for me at the White River Hotel."

"Are you married again, Rita?"

"I've been married for two weeks, child. If you weren't snowbound in the Rockies, you'd have heard about it."

"Are you happy?"

"Well," Rita said. "I don't know what's happy any more. I tell you, love, we're cozy together. We understand each other. And it's a nice change. I mean, Jim isn't a fairy and he isn't a gigolo. He's really the first husband I've had in years who works for a living. Some mornings I'm almost tempted to get up and pack his little lunch pail for him."

"I'm glad you came, Rita. You've helped me a lot," Allison said.

"Now how did I do that?" Rita asked.

"By reminding me," Allison said, "that the world isn't full of monsters waiting to cut me down. And by showing me that work will exorcise all the ghosts that haunt me."

"Here's to Love and Work," Rita said, raising her glass.

"I'll drink to that," Allison said.

The taxi horn sounded, a loud blast that shattered the silence of the snow. Mike and Constance came out of the kitchen. Mike helped Rita into her coat. She kissed Allison good-by. "There are a lot of people working for you, love. Don't ever forget that."

Allison went to the window and watched Rita walk down the snow-filled walk to the waiting taxi. She felt the cold through the glass and leaned her head against it.

I won't forget, Allison said. And I won't disappoint you.

She stood at the window and watched till Rita's taxi was out of sight, then she went to the kitchen door and looked in on Mike and her mother.

"I'll be up in my room, working, if you want me for anything," Allison said.

Constance smiled. "I think we'll manage, dear."

They watched her walk up the stairs to her room. Constance sighed her relief, and as Mike took her in his arms, she said, "Happy New Year, darling. I have the feeling it's going to be a great year."